W9-CNL-742

THE AUTHOR

MARGARET LAURENCE was born in Neepawa, Manitoba, in 1926. Upon graduation from Winnipeg's United College in 1947, she took a job as a reporter for the *Winnipeg Citizen*.

From 1950 until 1957 Laurence lived in Africa, the first two years in Somalia, the next five in Ghana, where her husband, a civil engineer, was working. She translated Somali poetry and prose during this time, and began her career as a fiction writer with stories set in Africa.

When Laurence returned to Canada in 1957, she settled in Vancouver, where she devoted herself to fiction with a Ghanaian setting: in her first novel, *This Side Jordan*, and in her first collection of short fiction, *The Tomorrow-Tamer*. Her two years in Somalia were the subject of her memoir, *The Prophet's Camel Bell*.

Separating from her husband in 1962, Laurence moved to England, which became her home for a decade, the time she devoted to the creation of five books about the fictional town of Manawaka, patterned after her birthplace, and its people: *The Stone Angel*, *A Jest of God*, *The Fire-Dwellers*, *A Bird in the House*, and *The Diviners*.

Laurence settled in Lakefield, Ontario, in 1974. She complemented her fiction with essays, book reviews, and four children's books. Her many honours include two Governor General's Awards for Fiction and more than a dozen honorary degrees.

Margaret Laurence died in Lakefield, Ontario, in 1987.

THE DIVINERS

MARGARET LAURENCE

AFTERWORD BY
TIMOTHY FINDLEY

First published in 1974 by McClelland & Stewart.
First New Canadian Library edition 1988.
This New Canadian Library edition 2007.

Library and Archives Canada Cataloguing in Publication

Laurence, Margaret, 1926-1987
    The diviners / Margaret Laurence ; with an afterword by Timothy
Findley.

(New Canadian library)
Originally published: 1974.
ISBN 978-0-7710-3490-9

    I. Title. II. Series.
PS8523.A86D5 2007   C813'.54   C2007-903188-9

We acknowledge the financial support of the Government of Canada
through the Book Publishing Industry Development Program and
that of the Government of Ontario through the Ontario Media
Development Corporation's Ontario Book Initiative. We further
acknowledge the support of the Canada Council for the Arts and the
Ontario Arts Council for our publishing program.

 ANCIENT FOREST
FRIENDLY

Typeset in Garamond by M&S, Toronto
Printed and bound in Canada

McClelland & Stewart Ltd.
75 Sherbourne Street
Toronto, Ontario
M5A 2P9
www.mcclelland.com/NCL

2 3 4 5   13 12 11 10

For
the Elmcot people
past   present   and   future
and for the house itself
with love and gratitude.

CONTENTS

ACKNOWLEDGMENTS

My deepest thanks to the following:

— Ian Cameron, who wrote the music for "Lazarus," "Song for Piquette," and "Pique's Song," and who did musical arrangements for all the songs, and tape-recorded them for me so I could hear them sung;

— Sandy Cameron, who set down the musical notations;

— Prue and John Bawden, who transcribed the songs;

— Jocelyn Laurence, who typed the manuscript for me;

— Bob Berry, Paula Berry, David Laurence, Peter MacLachlan, Joan Minkoff, John Valentine, who helped with either the singing or the playing of the songs, or with the obtaining of copies of the musical scores and Xerox copies of the manuscript.

I should like also to thank the Canada Council for the Senoir Arts Award which assisted me during the writing of this novel.

(Music © 1973 Heorte Music)

but they had their being once
and left a place to stand on

Al Purdy
– Roblin Mills Circa 1842

PART ONE

RIVER OF NOW AND THEN

ONE

The river flowed both ways. The current moved from north to south, but the wind usually came from the south, rippling the bronze-green water in the opposite direction. This apparently impossible contradiction, made apparent and possible, still fascinated Morag, even after the years of river-watching.

The dawn mist had lifted, and the morning air was filled with swallows, darting so low over the river that their wings sometimes brushed the water, then spiralling and pirouetting upward again. Morag watched, trying to avoid thought, but this ploy was not successful.

Pique had gone away. She must have left during the night. She had left a note on the kitchen table, which also served as Morag's desk, and had stuck the sheet of paper into the typewriter, where Morag would be certain to find it.

Now please do not get all uptight, Ma. I can look after myself. Am going west. Alone, at least for now. If Gord phones, tell him I've drowned and gone floating

down the river, crowned with algae and dead minnows,
like Ophelia.

Well, you had to give the girl some marks for style of
writing. Slightly derivative, perhaps, but let it pass. Oh jesus,
it was not funny. Pique was eighteen. Only. Not dry behind
the ears. Yes, she was, though. If only there hadn't been that
other time when Pique took off, that really bad time. That
wouldn't happen again, not like before. Morag was pretty sure
it wouldn't. Not sure enough, probably.

I've got too damn much work in hand to fret over Pique.
Lucky me. I've got my work to take my mind off my life. At
forty-seven that's not such a terrible state of affairs. If I hadn't
been a writer, I might've been a first-rate mess at this point.
Don't knock the trade.

Morag read Pique's letter again, made coffee and sat looking out at the river, which was moving quietly, its surface
wrinkled by the breeze, each crease of water outlined by the sun.
Naturally, the river wasn't wrinkled or creased at all – wrong
words, implying something unfluid like skin, something unen-
during, prey to age. Left to itself, the river would probably go
on like this, flowing deep, for another million or so years. That
would not be allowed to happen. In bygone days, Morag had
once believed that nothing could be worse than killing a person.
Now she perceived river-slaying as something worse. No
wonder the kids felt themselves to be children of the apocalypse.

No boats today. Yes, one. Royland was out, fishing for
muskie. Seventy-four years old this year, Royland. Eyesight
terrible, but he was too stubborn to wear glasses. A marvel that
he could go on working. Of course, his work did not depend
upon eyesight. Some other kind of sight. A water diviner.
Morag always felt she was about to learn something of great

significance from him, something which would explain everything. But things remained mysterious, his work, her own, the
generations, the river.

Across the river, the clumps of willow bent silver-green
down to the water, and behind them the great maples and
oaks stirred a little, their giant dark green tranquility disturbed only slightly by the wind. There were more dead elms
this year, dry bones, the grey skeletons of trees. Soon there
would be no elms left.

The swallows dipped and spun over the water, a streak-
ing of blue-black wings and bright breastfeathers. How could
that colour be caught in words? A sort of rosy peach colour,
but that sounded corny and was also inaccurate.

*I used to think words could do anything. Magic. Sorcery.
Even miracle. But no, only occasionally.*

The house seemed too quiet. Dank. The kitchen had
that sour milk and stale bread smell that Morag remembered
from her childhood, and which she loathed. There was,
however, no sour milk or stale bread here – it must be all in
the head, emanating from the emptiness of the place. Until
recently the house was full, not only Pique but A-Okay Smith
and Maudie and their shifting but ever-large tribe. Morag, for
the year when the Smiths lived here, had gone around torn
between affection and rage – how could anyone be expected
to work in such a madhouse, and here she was feeding them
all, more or less, and no goddamn money would be coming in
if she didn't get back to the typewriter. Now, of course, she
wished some of them were here again. True, they only lived
across the river, now that they had their own place, and visited
often, so perhaps that was enough.

Something about Pique's going, apart from the actual
departure itself, was unresolved in Morag's mind. The fact that

Pique was going west? Yes. Morag was both glad and uncertain. What would Pique's father think, if he knew? Well, he wouldn't know and didn't have all that much right to judge anyway. Would Pique go to Manawaka? If she did, would she find anything there which would have meaning for her? Morag rose, searched the house, finally found what she was looking for.

These photographs from the past never agreed to get lost. Odd, because she had tried hard enough, over the years, to lose them, or thought she had. She had treated them carelessly, shoved them away in seldom-opened suitcases or in dresser drawers filled with discarded underwear, scorning to put them into anything as neat as an album. They were jammed any-old-how into an ancient tattered manilla envelope that Christie had given her once when she was a kid, and which said *McVitie & Pearl, Barristers & Solicitors, Manawaka, Manitoba.* Christie must have found it at the dump – the Nuisance Grounds, as they were known; what an incredible name, when you thought of the implications. The thick brown paper stank a bit when Christie had handed it to her, faintly shitlike, faintly the sweetish ether smell of spoiled fruit. He said Morag could have it to keep her pictures in, and she had taken it, although despising it, because she did not have any other sturdy envelope for the few and valued snapshots she owned then. Not realizing that if she had chucked them out, then and there, her skull would prove an envelope quite sturdy enough to retain them.

I've kept them, of course, because something in me doesn't want to lose them, or perhaps doesn't dare. Perhaps they're my totems, or contain a portion of my spirit. Yeh, and perhaps they are exactly what they seem to be – a jumbled mess of old snapshots which I'll still be lugging along with me when I'm an old lady, clutching them as I enter or am shoved into the Salvation Army Old People's home or wherever it is that I'll find my death.

Morag put the pictures into chronological order. As though there were really any chronological order, or any order at all, if it came to that. She was not certain whether the people in the snapshots were legends she had once dreamed only, or were as real as anyone she now knew.

I keep the snapshots not for what they show but for what is hidden in them.

Snapshot:

The man and woman are standing stiffly on the other side of the gate. It is a farm gate, very wide, dark metal, and old – as is shown by its sagging. The man is not touching the woman, but they stand close. She is young, clad in a cotton print dress (the pattern cannot be discerned) which appears too large for her thin frame. Looking more closely, one can observe that her slight and almost scrawny body thickens at the belly. Her hair is short and fluffy, possibly blonde. The man's head is bent a little, and he is grinning with obvious embarrassment at the image-recorder who stands unseen and unrecorded on the near side of the gate. The man appears to be in his early thirties. He is tall and probably strong, narrowly but muscularly built. His hair is dark and somewhat unruly, as though he had combed it back with his fingers an instant before. In the far background, at the end of the road, can be seen the dim outlines of a house, two-storey, a square box of a house, its gracelessness atoned for, to some extent, by a veranda and steps at the front. Spruce trees, high and black, stand beside the house. In the further background there is a shadow-structure which could be the barn. Colin Gunn and his wife, Louisa, stand here always, in the middle 1920s, smiling their tight smiles, holding their now-faded sepia selves straight, hopeful, their sepia house and sepia farm firmly behind them, looking forward to what will happen, not knowing the future weather of sky or spirit.

Morag Gunn is in this picture, concealed behind the ugliness of Louisa's cheap housedress, concealed in her mother's flesh, invisible. Morag is still buried alive, the first burial, still a little fish, connected unthinkingly with life, held to existence by a single thread.

Snapshot:

The child sits on the front steps of the house. She has lost the infant plumpness which presumably she once had, but she is built stockily, at age about two. Her hair is straight and dark, like her father's. She looks grave, although not unhappy. Thoughtful, perhaps. She wears a plain cotton dress with puffed sleeves and a sash, and she or someone has tucked it modestly around her knees. Beside her sits a grinning mongrel dog, tongue lolling out.

The dog, as one would not guess from the picture, is called Snap, short for Snapdragon. He always follows Morag around the yard, keeping an eye on her. He is a mild-natured dog, easygoing, and he never once snaps at anyone, despite his name. He would snap at thieves or robbers if there were any, but there aren't, ever. Morag's mother lets Snap sleep in Morag's bedroom, to keep her company. Some people wouldn't have allowed a dog to sleep at the foot of a bed, but Morag's mother doesn't mind, because she knows Morag wants Snap to be there so as she will feel safe. Morag's mother is not the sort of mother who yells at kids. She does not whine either. She is not like Prin.

All this is crazy, of course, and quite untrue. Or maybe true and maybe not. I am remembering myself composing this interpretation, in Christie and Prin's house.

Snapshot:

The child, three years old, is standing behind the heavy-wire-netted farm gate, peering out. The person with the camera is standing unseen on the other side. The child is laughing, acting up, play-acting goofily, playing to an audience of one, the picture-taker.

What is not recorded in the picture is that after Morag's father has taken this picture, he asks her if she'd like to have him help her climb the gate. Her father never minds helping her. He always has time. Her father is beside her, then, and lifts her up and sets her on the very top of the gate, holding her so she will not fall. She hangs onto his shoulder and puts her face beside his neck. He smells warm and good. Clean. Smells of soap and greengrass. Not manure. He never stinks of horseshit, even though he is a farmer. Morag's father lifts her down from the gate, and they go into their house. The house is very huge, full of strange corners and places to explore. It even has a diningroom, with good furniture, a sideboard and a big round table. The Gunns eat in their diningroom every single Sunday without fail. There is a cupboard under the front stairs, into which Morag crawls when she wishes to find hidden treasure. It goes a long way back and is just high enough for her to stand up. Inside, there are stacks of books that once belonged to Alisdair Gunn, Morag's grandfather, who came here a long long time ago and built the house and started the farm when probably nothing was here except buffalo grass and Indians. The books have leather bindings, and smell like harness, only nicer, and the names are marked in gold. Also in this cupboard are vases and plates, painted with orange chrysanthemums and purple pansies, and old dresses, long, with lace on the sleeves, blue velvet and plum-coloured silk, fragile and rustling. A few spiders and ants live in that cupboard, but Morag is not afraid of them, or of anything in that house. It is a safe place. Nothing terrible can happen there.

I don't recall when I invented that one. I can remember it, though, very clearly. Looking at the picture and knowing what was hidden in it. I must've made it up much later on, long long after something terrible had happened.

Snapshot:

The child is leaning out the window, an upstairs window. She is smiling down at the person with the camera. Her face is calm, serene. Her straight black hair, neatly trimmed, comes just to the level of her earlobes.

What the picture does not tell is that Morag is leaning out the window of her own bedroom, a room not too small and yet not too large. It has a white dresser with a pale leaf-green ruffled curtain around the bottom, and underneath there is a white (cleaned every day) chamber pot for her to use during the night if she has to go. This is nice, because it means she never has to go outside to the backhouse in the winter nights. There is also a white-painted bed, with a lovely quilt, flowers in green and pink on a white background, very daintily stitched, maybe by a grandmother.

I recall looking at the pictures, these pictures, over and over again, each time imagining I remembered a little more. The farm couldn't have been worth a plugged nickel at that point. The drought had begun, and the Depression. Why in these pictures am I smiling so seldom? A passing mood? Or inherited? In my invented memories I always think of my father smiling, possibly because he really seldom did. He is smiling in the only picture I have of him, but that was for the camera. Colin Gunn, whose people came to this country so long ago, from Sutherland, during the Highland Clearances, maybe, and who had in them a sadness and a stern quality. Can it ever be eradicated?

Snapshot:

The child's black straight hair is now shoulder-length, and she is four years old. She is sitting primly on a piano stool in front of an old-fashioned high-backed upright piano. She is peering fixedly at the sheet music in front of her, which, from the dimly seen word "Roses" may be guessed to be "Roses of Picardy." Morag wears a pullover which appears to be decorated with wool embroidery, possibly flowers, and an obviously tartan skirt. Her hands rest lightly on the keys and her feet do not reach the pedals.

My concentration appears to indicate interest and even enthusiasm. I did not yet know that I was severely myopic and had to peer closely to see anything at all.

Let the snapshot tell what is behind it. Morag's mother, before she married, was a piano teacher in Manawaka. She is now trying to teach Morag how to play, and Morag really loves the lessons and is very good and quick at picking up how to do it. The livingroom is not used for everyday, but Morag and her mother go into it quite a lot in the afternoons. The carpet is royal blue, patterned with birds whose wings are amber, dove-grey, scarlet. On the piano is a red glass filled with cornflowers, and a very miniature tree made out of brass, with small bells attached to it. If you put the piano stool up as high as it will go, and start off quickly enough, it twirls all the way down again with you twirling on it. Morag's mother plays, not the plonk-plonk-plinkety-plonk of Sunday school music, but very light, very light.

And that is the end of the totally invented memories. I can't remember myself actually being aware of inventing them, but it must have happened so. How much later? At Christie's, of course, putting myself to sleep. I cannot really remember my parents' faces at all. When I look now at that one snapshot of them, they aren't faces I can relate to anyone I ever knew. It didn't bother me for years and years. Why should it grieve me now? Why do I want them back? What could my mother and I say to one another? I'm more than ten years older now than she was when she died – and she would seem so young to me, so inexperienced.

Snapshot:

The child is standing among the spruce trees at the side of the house. She wears overalls, and her long hair is untidy. She is now five, or thereabouts. She squints a little, against the painful sun, trying to keep her eyes open so the picture of her will be nice, but she finds it difficult. Her head is bent slightly, and she grins not in happiness but in embarrassment, like Colin Gunn in the first picture. Only the lower boughs of the spruce trees can be seen, clearly, darkly.

Now, those spruce trees, there, they were really and actually as tall as angels, dark angels perhaps, their boughs and sharp hard needles nearly black except in the spring when the new needles sprouted soft and mid-green. The grass, there, didn't grow right underneath the trees, but Morag used to go to the edge of the road and pull up couchgrass as high as herself, carrying it back in armloads and spreading it, already drying in the heat, under the spruces. The walls of her dwelling, her playhouse, were single lines of stones she had found on the dusty rutted road. The fallen spruce cones and the dandelions and wild honeysuckle and purple vetch and pink wild asters were the furnishings – chairs, tables, dishes. All for the invisible creatures who inhabited the place with her. Peony. Rosa Picardy. Cowboy Joke. Blue-Sky Mother. Barnstable Father. Old Forty-Nine. Some of the names came from songs she must have heard, "Cowboy Jack" and "The Wreck of the Old Forty-Nine." The latter was especially fine, inaccurate as the words might have become in her head throughout the years.

> T'was a cold winter's night,
> Not a soul was in sight,
> And the north wind came howling down the line;
> Stood a brave engineer,
> With his sweetheart so dear,
> He had orders to take the Forty-Nine.
> She kissed him goodbye
> With a tear in her eye,
> Saying, "Come back quite soon, oh sweetheart mine."
> But it would have made her cry
> If she'd known that he would die
> In the wreck of the Old Forty-Nine.

And so on. I recall that song from later on, but it must've been sung to me young. Who would have? Maybe we had a radio. Where the other names came from, I wouldn't guess. I played alone, mostly, as it was too far to go to seek out other kids. I don't think I minded. I preferred my spruce-house family, all of whom I knew as totally individuated persons (as the pretentious phrase has it, when describing okay fiction). Strange and marvellous things used to happen to them. Once Cowboy Joke's pinto threw him over a ravine, as in "Little Joe the Wrangler He Will Never Wrangle More," and he would've been a goner except that Rosa

Picardy and myself, with great intuition, had happened to build a couch of moss in that precise place.

Another time, Peony and I, although warned not to by Blue-Sky Mother, went into a deserted grain elevator, hundreds of miles high and lived in only by bats, dragons and polar bears, on different levels, bats highest, and succeeded after many perils in discovering a buried treasure of diamonds and rubies (known to be red, although I had never seen one) and emeralds (which I thought must be the same brave pale mauve as the prairie crocuses we found in spring even before the last snow went).

I remember those imaginary characters better than I do my parents. What kind of a character am I? Old Forty-Nine smoked a pipe and sometimes spat a giant globule into the local spittoon (a word I loved, although I'd never seen one, and visualized as resembling a chamber pot, only more dignified and decorated). Peony, not unnaturally, had curly blonde hair, the opposite of mine, and sweet little rosebud lips like those on the unreachable dolls in Eaton's catalogue. Rosa Picardy, my alter ego, I suppose, was somewhat sturdier. She did brave deeds, slew dragons and/or polar bears, and was Cowboy Joke's mate. Unlike the lady in the song, Rosa Picardy could never have expired gently while sighing –

> Your sweetheart waits for you, Jack,
> Your sweetheart waits for you,
> Out on the lonely prairie,
> Where skies are always blue.

No. Rosa Picardy had her head fastened on right. Not for her the martyr's death, the grave where only the coyote's (pronounced kiy-oot's) wailing voice paid sad tribute. Rosa was right in there, pitching.

Does that say anything about my parents, or only that I was born bloody-minded? I WAS born bloody-minded. It's cost me. I've paid through the nose. As they say. Also, one might add, through the head, heart and cunt.

The spruce-house family must have appeared around the time my mother took sick. The whole thing was so quiet. No outer drama. That was the way, there. But I remember it, everything. Somewhat ironically, it is the first memory of actual people that I can trust, although I can't trust it completely, either, partly because I recognize anomalies in it, ways of expressing the remembering, ways which aren't those of a five-year-old, as though I were older in that memory (and the words bigger) than in some subsequent ones when I was six or seven, and partly because it was only what was happening to Me. What was happening to everyone else? What really happened in the upstairs bedroom? No – the two bedrooms. He was moved into the spare room. People couldn't be that sick together in the same bed, I guess.

Memorybank Movie: Once Upon a Time There Was
Mrs. Pearl from the next farm has come to Morag's house. She is an old woman, really old old, short and with puckered-up skin on her face, but not stooped a bit. Her face is tanned, though, which makes her look clean. She makes dinner and swishes around the kitchen. The stove is great big black and giant – oh, but good and warm. Summer now, though, and it is too *hot*. Morag has to wash her hands. The pump brings the water to the sink, but you have to chonk-chonk-chonk it, and she is not big enough to get it going. Mrs. Pearl chonks the pump, and the water splurts out. Morag takes the sliver of Fels-Naptha and washes her hands. For dinner. That is what you have to do.

"How come you're here, Mrs. Pearl?"

"Your mum and now your dad is kinda sick, honey," Mrs. Pearl says matter-of-factly, "and I just come to help out. You and me's going to have our supper in a minute, so you run along and play now, and I'll call you when it's ready. I'll bet a purty you're hungry, eh?"

Morag does not reply. She tries to reach the pump handle so she can rinse her hands, but although five years old is big, it is not big enough. Mrs. Pearl obliges.

"I think," Morag says, "I'll just go upstairs for a minute and see my mother and father."

Something is happening. Morag senses it but cannot figure it out. Mrs. Pearl is trying to be kind. Morag is scared, and her stomach aches. If she eats anything, she will throw up.

"No, honey," Mrs. Pearl says. "You're not to go upstairs. There's a good girl. Doctor MacLeod will be along in a little while, and he wouldn't want you to go bothering your folks when they're feeling kind of poorly, now, would he?"

"I want to see my mother," Morag says. "I am going up to see her right now. I won't stay long, Mrs. Pearl. I promise."

But the Big Person grabs Morag's wrist before Morag can slither away. Mrs. Pearl's hands are very strong, a trap like for mice or gophers or that, crunching down.

"No, you don't," Mrs. Pearl says sharply. "They're too sick to see you, just now, Morag. They don't want to see you."

"How do you know?" Morag cries. "You don't know anything about it! They do *so!* Let go of me!"

Mrs. Pearl does not let go. Then Dr. MacLeod's car comes whamming into the yard. He is a tall man with brown hair and a smile. Morag now does not trust anyone who smiles.

"Hello, Morag."

She will not speak to him, or smile. She is not letting on that anything is happening.

"It's all right," the doctor says. "It's going to be okay. Don't you worry, now."

When he comes downstairs, he and Mrs. Pearl go into the livingroom (where no one ever lives; it is for Best), and close the door. Morag hears their voices but not their words. Then Dr. MacLeod leaves. Nothing else happens that day or night.

The days snail along, and Mrs. Pearl is still there. Every morning and evening she sprays Morag's throat with a sticky yellow stuff, saying it is good medicine which Dr. MacLeod has given. Morag sleeps in the kitchen now, while Mrs. Pearl takes Morag's upstairs room.

Mrs. Pearl's husband Henry comes over every evening and eats with Mrs. Pearl and Morag. He is old. He milks the cows. Once he asks if Morag would like to go with him to the barn, to see him milking the cows.

"No," she says.

Not *No Thanks*. And feels bad for having been rude. But she hates Mr. and Mrs. Pearl, for being here.

During the nights, there have been no sounds from upstairs, at least none that Morag has been able to hear, for the stairs go up from the livingroom, and the kitchen door is closed and locked at night so that Morag will not wander upstairs. Then one night Mrs. Pearl forgets to lock this door.

Dr. MacLeod had been that evening, and Morag had been sent out to play long after supper, when it was nearly dark. Mrs. Pearl's face looked scary when she put Morag to bed, but she said not a word.

Morag is alone in the dark. The stove hisses a little, and sighs, as the fire dies down. Morag gets up and tries the door and it opens into the livingroom. She stands barefoot, the linoleum cool on her skin, and listens.

From upstairs, there is a sound. Crying. Crying? Yes, crying. Not like people, though. Like something else. She does not know what. Kiy-oots. She knows only that it is her father's voice. There is no sound of her mother's voice, no sound at all.

Morag, terrified, scuttles back to the kitchen like a cockroach – she *is* a cockroach; she feels like one, running, scuttling.

Next morning, Mrs. Pearl does not have a talk with Morag. Not that day. Or the next. But finally. When?

"Morag, honey, they have passed on," Mrs. Pearl says, blushing, as though caught in a lie, "to a happier land, we know."

Morag does not imagine that they have gone to some real good place. She knows they are dead. She knows what dead means. She has seen dead gophers, run over by cars or shot, their guts redly squashed out on the road.

"I want to see them! I have to!"

"Better not," Mrs. Pearl says firmly. "There, there, honey. You just cry."

And so of course Morag does not know how much of their guts lie coiled like scarlet snakes across the sheets. She does not cry, not then. Mrs. Pearl's leather arms and flat breast stifle and sicken her, and she pushes the well-meaningness away. She stares unblinking, like fledgling birds when they fall out of their nests and just stare.

"You *are* the brave girl," Mrs. Pearl says. "Yes, that you surely are."

There is silence all around, and then Mrs. Pearl says something else.

"It was the infantile, dear. The infantile paralysis."

Morag has never heard either word before. She asks, and Mrs. Pearl tells her that it is a sickness which usually happens to children.

The lowest and largest boughs of the spruce reach down and touch the earth, making a cave, a small shelter into which no one can see. She is not doing anything. Cowboy Joke and Rosa Picardy and the others are not here now. They have gone away. For good. Once and for all.

Morag is talking in her head. To God. Telling Him it was all His fault and this is why she is so mad at Him. Because He is no good, is why.

If it was the infantile, though, why them and not her? She is the kid around here.

Next day, Morag goes upstairs and looks in all the bedrooms, carefully, but everybody has gone. Vanished. She has not seen them being taken away.

"Honey, come here a second," Mrs. Pearl says.

Morag comes to her, reluctantly.

"Listen, Morag," Mrs. Pearl says, clicking her false teeth and then putting a hand over her mouth, "you're gonna be living with Mr. and Mrs. Logan, dear, in Manawaka. Christie Logan, that is. He was in the Army with your dad, honey, and he and Prin have offered to take you, seeing as there ain't none of your own relatives hereabouts. They're not what you'd call a well-off couple, but they're kind, and they got no children of their own. I'm sure you'll get on dandy with them, once you're used to it. It was real kind of them to offer."

Morag says nothing. She has learned you can't argue when you are a kid. You can only wait not to be a kid any more.

Mr. and Mrs. Pearl have a broken-down old car, black and rattling, like a hearse for clowns.

They drive off, and Mr. Pearl stops the car on the road just outside the fence and goes back.

"Won't be but a minute."

Morag does not look back, but she hears the metallic clank of the farm gate being shut. Closed.

Now I am crying, for God's sake, and I don't even know how much of that memory really happened and how much of it I embroidered later on. I seem to remember it just like that, and yet, each time I think of it, are there new or different details? I recall it with embellishments which don't seem likely for a five-year-old.

Infantile paralysis – that was what they called polio, then.

The land, house and furniture had to be sold to pay the mortgage, Christie told me years later, but Henry Pearl managed to winkle the piano and a few other things out and over to his place, and quietly sold them when he could, and no one who knew about it in South Wachakwa or Manawaka ever told on him. He put the money into a bank account for me to have at age eighteen. He died of pneumonia about five years later. So I never had the chance to say anything to him about it, when I was old enough.

That's all there was to them, my parents. Christie toted me along once to see their gravestone in the Manawaka cemetery when I was about eight or ten. I didn't want to go, and hardly looked at the stone, and wouldn't place on its grey granite the bunch of peach-coloured gladioli (naturally, half-wilted, one of Christie's salvage operations). Christie scowled but didn't say a word. I was raging because he'd made me go. And now I no longer know whether I was furious at Christie, or at them for having gone away, or whether I was only afraid and didn't know that I was. Now I would like to see that grave, only once, although I know quite well it couldn't tell me anything.

Were they angry at me often, or only sometimes? Did my father feel he'd done well with his life, or that he was a total loss, or did he feel anything? Did my mother feel pleased when she saw him come in from the barn, or did she think to herself – or aloud – that she'd married beneath her? Did she welcome him in bed, or did she make a habit of turning away and muttering she had a headache? Did he think she was the best lay he'd ever had, or did he grind his teeth in hardly suppressed resentment at her coldness? No way of knowing. Why should it matter now, anyway?

They remain shadows. Two sepia shadows on an old snapshot, two barely moving shadows in my head, shadows whose few remaining words and acts I have invented. Perhaps I only want their forgiveness for having forgotten them.

I remember their deaths, but not their lives. Yet they're inside me, flowing unknown in my blood and moving unrecognized in my skull.

PART TWO

THE NUISANCE GROUNDS

TWO

Seven-thirty A.M. and the phone rang. Morag, never an early or easy wakener, surfaced groggily from the submerged caves in which she had been happily floating for some nine hours.

Two rings. Her call. She wondered sourly how many people on her party line would be up and about to listen in. Who on earth could be calling at such an hour?

Pique. Of course. Naturally. It could only be her. Mother, I'm coming home, okay? I've made it up with Gord and he's gonna meet me at McConnell's Landing.

Or no. Not Pique. A welfare officer in Toronto. You the girl's mother? She's unconscious at the moment, under heavy sedation. A bad trip. Naturally, LSD – what did you think I meant, CPR? She was found wandering –

Morag shot down the stairs, tripping on the piece of loose stair carpet which she always forgot to tack down, losing her balance, grabbing simultaneously for her glasses and the stair railing. She had instinctively clapped on her glasses, she realized, not so much because she needed them to find her way downstairs as because she felt totally inept without them. Probably she thought she needed them in order to hear.

"Hello?" Her voice anxious, tense.

"Hello? Is that Mrs. – um – Miss Gunn?"

A woman's voice. Drawling a little. The welfare officer.

"Yes. Speaking."

"Oh, well then. You wouldn't remember me Miss – er – Missus Gunn, but I was in Dragett's Bookshop that day last October when you were there autographing your books, you know, and actually I bought *Stick of Innocence*."

"*Spear of Innocence*," Morag interjected irritably. What a rotten title. How had she ever dreamed that one up? But let's at least get it right, lady. *Stick*, ye gods. Freudian error. Same could be said of *Spear*, probably.

"Yes, that's the one," the voice went on. "Well, I do a lot of writing myself, Miss – uh – Miss Gunn, so I just thought I'll phone you up, like, and I'd be grateful if you would just tell me how you got started. I mean, I know once you're accepted, you don't need to worry. Anything you write *now*, I mean, will automatically get published –"

Oh, sure. Just bash out any old crap and rake in the millions. I get my plots from the telephone directory.

"But, well, I mean, like," the voice persisted, "did you know some person in the publishing field? How could I get to know someone?"

"I didn't know a soul," Morag said heavily, trying to force politeness and consideration into her voice. "I just kept sending stories out, that's all. When I wrote a novel, I submitted it. The second publisher took it. I was lucky."

"Yes. But how did you actually get a *start*? What did you *do*?"

"I worked like hell, if you really want to know. I've told

you. There's no secret. Look, it's awfully early. I'm sorry. I'm afraid I really can't help you."

"Oh, is it early to you? I always rise at six, so as to work at my writing before I prepare the breakfast for my husband, but I guess a successful writer like you wouldn't have to worry about domestic chores —"

Certainly not. I have a butler, a cook and a houseparlour-maid. Black. From Jamaica. Underpaid. Loyal slaves.

"Look, I'm awfully sorry, but —"

"Oh well, in that case, I shouldn't have troubled you, I'm sure." Voice filled with rancour.

Slam!

Morag held the receiver in her hand for a moment, looking at it. Then replaced it. Had she been too abrupt? The woman only wanted to find out. Desperate, likely. Wanting the golden key from someone who had had five books published and who frequently wondered how to keep the mini-fortress here going and what would happen to her when she could no longer write. Golden key indeed.

Morag started to kindle a fire in the woodstove, then changed her mind. The day would warm up quickly enough. Mid-June, and, although it was cool at daybreak, by noon it would be hot. Strange to think she had once cooked on that woodstove, when she first moved in here, not then being able to afford an electric stove. She was fond of the old stove now, black and huge as it was, but in the first days it had been a disaster, smoking like a train and the food either raw or scorched.

The river was the colour of liquid bronze this morning, the sun catching it. Could that be right? No. Who had ever seen liquid bronze? Not Morag, certainly. Probably no one could catch the river's colour even with paints, much less words. A daft profession. Wordsmith. Liar, more likely. Weaving fabrications.

Yet, with typical ambiguity, convinced that fiction was more true than fact. Or that fact was in fact fiction.

Royland came to the door, looking old as Jehovah. Wearing his plaid wool bush jacket and heavy denims – a wonder he didn't melt. Greybeard loon. Royland had a beard for the only sensible reason for having one, because he couldn't be bothered shaving. Large and bulky as a polar bear, he filled the doorway.

"Morning, Morag."

"Hi. Come on in. Want some coffee?"

"I don't mind if I do. I brought you a pickerel. Went out earlier this morning. It's straight from the river."

Ancient myopic eyes mocking her, albeit gently. He knew she had not yet been able to bring herself to clean a fish. He was working on her, though.

"Oh, thanks, Royland. That's – wonderful."

Her face, no doubt, looked gloomy as purgatory. He laughed and produced the fish. Cleaned and filleted.

"Heavens, Royland," Morag said, ashamed, "you shouldn't have given into my squeamishness."

"Well, the last time I tried you with the whole fish, you threw it back into the river."

"How did you know?"

"The Smiths' kid told me. Young Tom, he seen you. It just slipped out, kind of. He never meant to tell on you. . . . Oh, I was about to mention – I'm divining this week."

"Where?"

"A-Okay Smith's. Want to come over?"

"Yes. Please."

"Fine. It'll be Friday. I'll pick you up in the boat. Seven. Morning, that is."

"I'll be ready."

Royland's faded amber eyes grew clearer and sharper, examining her face.

"Why're you so interested in divining, Morag?"

She hesitated.

"I don't know. I wonder why, myself. I guess with one part of my mind I find it hard to believe in, but with another part I believe in it totally."

"It works," Royland said.

"I know. That's the only proof needed. I always think, though, what if one day it doesn't work? And *why* does it work?"

"I don't reckon I really need to understand it," Royland said. "I just gotta do it."

Oh Lord. Of course. Which she had known all along, but still perpetually questioned. Why not take it on faith, for herself, as he did? Sometimes she could. But not always.

"You're alone too much," Royland said, unexpectedly.

"What about you?"

"Oh sure. But I'm getting on in age. And I don't sit around knocking my brains out, like you do."

"I'm a professional worrier, that's all," Morag said. "Did you know Pique's gone again?"

"You worry too damn much about that girl, Morag. She's a grown woman."

"Hell, don't I know it. That's why I worry about her."

"You used to be her age, once. You made out."

"In a manner of speaking. Anyway, when I was her age, beer was thought to be a major danger. Beer! Because it might lead to getting pregnant. Good God, Royland. Babes in the woods. Innocents. The tartiest tarts in Manawaka were as Easter lilies. The world seems full of more hazards now. Doom all around. In various shapes and forms. I used to be very liberated in my attitude towards drugs, incidentally, until Pique got to be about fourteen. Okay, pot. That I can accept. Although nervously. But all the other stuff. I worry. I worry, but can do absolutely sweet bugger-all."

"You brought her up. You should have more faith."

"Yeh," Morag said, lighting her tenth cigarette of the day. "Great example I am."

"Why don't you quit, then?"

"Too late. For her. Anyway, I began when the disastrous effects of the weed were not yet known, and am now addicted."

Excuses, excuses.

"Also," Morag added, "another thing about myself when young was that I got married when only one year older than Pique is now, and Brooke kept me on the straight and narrow for a long time."

"That must've been fun," Royland said dryly.

Dirty old man. Shut up. Shut up.

"It wasn't so bad," Morag replied stiffly.

"Oh-oh. Sorry, lady."

"Think nothing of it."

They both laughed, not uncomfortably.

When Royland had gone, Morag wrapped the fish in aluminum foil (good God, why not fresh leaves or something?) and put it in the refrigerator (natural living – it should be an earth cellar or roothouse). Then, willing herself not to do so, she got out the snapshots again, and began looking at the ones taken after she had gone to the Logans', right up through the years.

She put the pictures away, finally, and walked over to the

oval walnut-framed mirror which hung precariously from a nail above the sideboard.

A tall woman, although not bizarrely so. Heavier than once, but not what you would call fat. Tanned, slightly leathery face. Admittedly strong and rather sharp features. Eyebrows which met in the middle and which she had ceased to pluck, thinking what the hell. Dark brown eyes, somewhat concealed (*good*) by heavy-framed glasses. Long, dead-straight hair, once black as tar, now quite evenly grey.

The films were beginning again. Sneakily unfolding inside her head. She could not even be sure of their veracity, nor guess how many times they had been refilmed, a scene deleted here, another added there. But they were on again, a new season of the old films.

I can smell the goddamn prairie dust on Hill Street, outside Christie's palatial mansion.

Hill Street, so named because it was on one part of the town hill which led down into the valley where the Wachakwa River ran, glossy brown, shallow, narrow, more a creek than a river. They said "crick," there. Down in the valley the scrub oak and spindly pale-leafed poplars grew, alongside the clumps of chokecherry bushes and wolf willow. The grass there was high and thick, undulating greenly like wheat, and interspersed with sweet yellow clover. But on Hill Street there were only one or two sickly Manitoba maples and practically no grass at all. Hill Street was the Scots-English equivalent of The Other Side of the Tracks, the shacks and shanties at the north end of Manawaka, where the Ukrainian section-hands on the CPR lived. Hill Street was below the town; it was inhabited by those who had not and never would make good. Remittance men and their draggled families. Drunks. People perpetually on relief. Occasional labourers, men whose tired women supported the family by going out to clean the big brick houses on top of the hill on the streets shaded by sturdy maples, elms, lombardy poplars. Hill Street – dedicated to flops, washouts and general nogoods, at least in the view of the town's better-off.

Christie Logan's house was halfway up the hill, and looked much the same as the other dwellings there. A square two-storey wooden box, once painted brown but when I knew it, no distinguishable colour, the paint having yielded long ago to the weather, blistering summers and bone-chilling blizzard-howling winters. Front porch floored with splintered unsteady boards. The yard a junk heap, where a few carrots and petunias fought a losing battle against chickweed, lamb's quarters, creeping charlie, dandelions, couchgrass, old car axles, a decrepit black buggy with one wheel missing, pieces of iron and battered saucepans which might come in useful someday but never did, a broken babycarriage and two ruined armchairs with the springs hanging out and the upholstery torn and mildewed.

I didn't see it in that detail at first. I guess I must have seen it as a blur. How did it feel?

Memorybank Movie: What Means "In Town"?
Smelly. The house is smelly. It smells like pee or something, but not like a barn. Worse. Morag sits still on the kitchen chair. The two people are looking at her. Let them look. She will not let on. She will not say anything.

"You'll like living In Town, once you're used to it," the Big Fat Woman says.

In Town? This does not seem like Town. Town is where the stores are, and you go in for ice cream sometimes, like with Mr. and Mrs. Pearl yesterday or when.

The Big Fat Woman sighs. She is so fat – can she be a

person? Can *people* look like that? The Skinny Man looks funny, too. Sort of crooked in his arms or legs, or like that. He has a funny lump in his throat and it wobbles up and down when he talks.

"You'll call me Christie, Morag girl," he says. "And this here is Prin. You hungry, lass?"

Morag does not let on.

"She'll be all right, Christie," the Big Fat Woman says. "She gotta get used to us. Leave her be, now."

"I was only trying, for God's sake, woman." Sounding mad.

"You want to see your room, Morag?" the woman says.

She nods. They mount the stairs, the woman going very slow because fat. The room is hers, this one? A thin bed, a green dresser, a window with a (oh – ripped, shame on them) lace curtain. A little room. You might be safe in a place like that, if it was really yours. If they meant it.

"I want to go to sleep," Morag says.

And does that. They let her.

And after that, for one entire year, my memories do not exist at all. A blank. Nothing of what happened then remains accessible. Not until I was six.

Memorybank Movie: The Law Means School

The long long long long street, and Morag walking, slowly. Her hand, sweaty, in Christie's hand. His hand is like when you feel the bark of a tree, rough rough. Not far now. She wishes it was about another million miles.

All kids have to go to school when they are six. It is LAW. What means *Law*?

Big brick building, with a high wire fence around the big yard, and the yard all gravel. If you fell on that gravel you would skin your knees, all right. Must never trip. What if they push you, though?

So many kids, there. All yelling. Some very big kids. Some about Morag's size. Morag knows for sure only Eva Winkler, who lives next door on Hill Street.

"Do I have to, Christie?"

"Aye. Just give them hell, Morag, and you'll be fine. Just don't you take any smart-aleck stuff from any of that lot, there. They're only muck the same as any of us. Skin and bone and the odd bit of guts."

"Yeh." But not knowing what he means.

She and Christie walk up the cement steps. Forty miles. LAUGHTER? Why? She turns. Many laughers. All around. On the steps and on the gravel. Large and small kids. Some looking away. Some going ho ho har har.

"Lookut her dress – it's down to her ankles!"

"Oh, it isn't, Helen! It's sure away below her knees, though."

Her dress? What's wrong? Prin sewed it. Out of a wrap-around which Prin is now too stout to wear.

Girls here. Some bigger, some smaller than Morag. Skipping with skipping ropes. Singing.

Jamie Halpern, so they say,
Goes a'courting night and day,
Sword an' pistol by his side,
Takes Junie Foster for his bride.

And   oh
Their dresses are very short, away above their knees. Some very bright blue yellow green and new cloth, new right

out of the store. You can see the pattern very clear, polka dots flowers and that.

Well   oh

Eva Winkler's dress same as Morag's.

"Hello, Eva. Hello there, Eva!" Morag's voice loud.

But Eva is bawling her eyes out. By herself.

In the front hall, dark dark floor stinking of oil bad-smelling oil. Boys' voices. Mean.

"Hey, you know who *that* is?"

"Sure, old man Logan. He's the –"

"Sh! Al Cates, you shut your face." Girlvoice.

"Oh shut up, Mavis. He's the – SCAVENGER!"

What means *Scavenger*? Morag cannot ask. Christie's face is stone.

"Phew! Can't you smell him from here?"

"Gabby little turds," Christie mutters.

The room. Grade One. Christie gone. Morag alone with all the other kids. Having taken a seat at one of the desks in the back row. Holding hard onto her wooden pencil-case. Never mind. They are only gabby turds, these kids. And when she goes home today she will know how to read.

The teacher is a lady. Tall, giant, like a big tree walking and waving its arms. A tree wearing spectacles. Morag giggles, but inside.

Then the worst thought. What if she has to pee or shit? Is there a backhouse in this place?

The teacher says a whole lot of stuff welcome boys and girls I know we're going to get along just beautifully and I know you're going to work hard and not make any trouble and I may as well say right now that troublemakers will find *themselves* in trouble and it is the ruler across the hands for them and the really bad behavers get the strap from the Principal.

What means *Principal*? What is *Strap*?

"Stand up and say your names, please. You, the girl at the back in this row, you begin."

Who? Her. Morag. She knows she won't be able to say. Or will wet her pants. She struggles up, stooping a bit so as to hide her tallness. She is taller than any of the other girls, what a disgrace.

Mumble.

"Speak up, dear, we can't hear you."

"Morag Gunn."

"Thank you, Morag. You may sit down. Next, now."

All the names. Stacey Cameron. Mavis Duncan. Julie Kazlik. Ross McVitie. Mike Lobodiak. Al Cates. Steve Kowalski. Vanessa MacLeod. Jamie Halpern. Eva Winkler. And so on and so on.

Teacher's name – Miss Crawford.

"Miss Crawfish," Jamie Halpern whispers.

Eva Winkler's tears go drip-drip-drip-splot onto her scribbler. Morag wants to cry, too. But doesn't. Miss Crawfish is gabbing again. All sorts of stuff now boys and girls if you want to leave the room you must hold up your hand for permission either one finger or two you take my meaning of course.

What means *Leave the Room*? Morag does not think it really means you can go home if you want to. One finger? Two fingers? What for?

"Number One and Number Two," somebody whispers. "If you gotta do Number Two, she lets you go out right away. My brother told me."

Morag now sees that she cannot see what is written on the blackboard. Her ears, though, are of the best. Maybe this will make up for not having a brother who tells you things.

Eva Winkler's brothers are all younger. None yet at school.

A horrible smell everywhere. Who? Eva Winkler bawls out loud now. All eyes on her. Morag clenches her own stomach, holding on. She mustn't. She can't hold up her hand. Not in front of everybody. Especially now.

"Eva – have you had an accident?" Miss Crawfish asks.

Eva cries and cries. Some kids laugh.

"That's *enough*, class. Eva, why didn't you ask permission? To leave the room."

"I never knew –"

"But I told you, Eva. Stand up beside your desk."

"I *can't*. It'll go on the floor, the poop will."

"*Please*. Never use such an expression in this room again. Very well, you had better go to the washroom, Eva, and then go home. You can come back this afternoon when you've got cleaned up. Now, don't worry. It's all right. Just don't let it happen again."

Eva scuffs out. Plop-plop-plop behind her as she begins to run, and the floor has stuff on it yellow-brownish and smelly.

"Jamie Halpern," Teacher says. "Go and find the janitor. In the basement."

A man comes into the room after a while. Hairy and dark, grinning at the kids. Friendly? Mr. Doherty. Winks once or twice when Teacher not looking. Carries a bag, a broom, a dustpan. Empties bag, with greenish powder, onto Eva's shame shame. Morag knows what the powder is. Paris Green. What a music name for that poison stuff. He sweeps up everything and goes.

Recess. *Recess* means you go out onto the gravel. Morag listens, hanging around the edges of bunches of kids who are friends. No talk about Scavenger now. All about Eva. Eva

Weakguts, pale pale face and pale yellow hair. Kids are saying lots of things   scared to ask permission doing it on the floor wow wait'll we see her face this afternoon bet you she'll be blushing like a rose   yeh but not smelling like one   oh Ross think you're so smart dontcha   well aren't I and what about you stuckup Stacey   and lots of other things.

Morag's head is thinking thinking figuring out.

At four o'clock they can go home. She still does not know how to read. Some school this turned out to be. But has learned one thing for sure.

Hang onto your shit and never let them know you are ascared.

Memorybank Movie: Morag, Much Older

Seven is much older than six. A person knows a hell of a sight more. And can read. Some kids still can't read yet. But they are dumb, dumb-bells, dumb bunnies. Morag can read like sixty. Sometimes she doesn't let on in school, though. Just depends on how she feels. So there.

Prin is sitting in the kitchen when Morag gets home from school. Prin is getting fatter all the time, and she looks like a great big huge pear. She buys jelly doughnuts at Parsons' Bakery and sometimes she gives one to Morag. Mostly the bagful has gone by the time Morag gets home. Prin doesn't mean to be mean. She sits all the afternoon in the squashy leather-seated easy chair in the kitchen, chewing, and then she looks and lo and behold no doughnuts are left.

Prin's family was English. She has told Morag about it. Prin's father was a remittance man. That meant his family in The Old Country didn't like him so good, and were pretty mean and all, even though he was a gentleman, a real one, and so they made him come to this country where he didn't want to come to, and for a while, there, they sent him some money, but then they didn't. He wasn't much of a farmer, but he meant well, Prin said. She was the only child and wasn't none too bright (you were supposed to say wasn't *any* too bright but Prin didn't know that) and couldn't be too much help, but then her dad died anyway. Her mother had died Before. When would that be? Long ago in olden times. Prin married Christie when he came back from the Great War. The town said good job too; a pity to spoil two families. Which was mean. But funny, too.

Prin's real Christian name is Princess. Morag thinks this is the funniest thing she has ever heard. But once when she said so to Christie, he told her to shut her trap.

"Hi," Morag says. "Can I have something to eat?"

"Sure. You want some bread and sugar?"

Morag nods and goes to fetch it. Soft brown sugar spread on white storeboughten bread. Her favourite. Prin used to make her own bread, but gave it up. Too hot to bake in summer and too hard in winter to find a place neither too warm nor too cold for the dough to rise proper. Morag is glad. The soft fluffy bread from Parsons' is better. More delicate. Morag is very delicate-minded. She prides herself on it, although she never lets on, of course. Vanessa and Mavis and like them have storeboughten bread in their houses all the time. Or so she guesses, never having been into their houses. Never so much as a bite of anything else, heaven forbid. Storeboughten cookies are another thing. She is sure *their* mothers make cookies because when the class had a valentine's party, they and some others brought heart-shaped cookies with pink icing. Storeboughten cookies are looked down on.

The hell with them. Screw them all. They are stupid buggers.

Morag loves to swear, but doesn't do it at school because you get the strap or else have to stand out in the hall by yourself where the coats are hung.

"Christie has to go out with the wagon again, now. I'm sure I don't know why. I'll bet a nickel to a doughnut hole they won't pay him extra."

Prin's voice is kind of small and high, like a little kid's. Prin really likes Christie. But she is a born whiner.

Christie comes in from the stable at the back where Ginger and the wagon are kept. He wipes some sweat from around his eyes and grins at Morag.

"Hello, lass. Did they *learn* you much today, then?"

He knows better. He says it like that on purpose. A joke. Prin would say it not on purpose.

"No." Morag turns away from him.

Christie is short, skinny, but actually quite strong. He looks *peculiar*. His head sort of comes forward when he walks, like he is in a hurry, but he isn't ever in a hurry. His hair, what's left of it, is sandy. Blue eyes, but all cloudy and with little red lines on the white part. Wires (hair, actually) grow out of his chin – he doesn't shave every day. The lump in his throat is called his Adam's apple, what a name. His teeth are bad and one is missing at the front but he never tries to hide it by putting his hand over or smiling with his mouth closed, oh no, not him. He always wears a blue heavy shirt, and overalls too big so they fall around him and make him look silly.

That is the worst. How silly he looks. No. The worst is that he smells. He does wash. But he never gets rid of the smell. How much do other people notice? Plenty. You bet. Horseshit and garbage, putrid stuff, vegetables and that, rotten eggs and mouldy old clothes.

"Gotta pick up a load of scrap from the blacksmith's," Christie says. "Want to come along, Morag?"

Morag hesitates. She has never gone with Christie in the wagon. Just for once she would like to go, to see the Nuisance Grounds. She nods.

"C'mon, then," he says. "Haven't got all night."

Ginger is a rusty colour. A gelding. Morag knows what *that* means, too, ha ha. Ginger is thin, and his hipbones stick out under the leather skin. Morag climbs up onto the wagon beside Christie.

Why is Christie called Scavenger? Morag does not yet know this and will not ask. She knows what he *does*, collecting the town garbage and taking it to dump in the Nuisance Grounds. But what, really, means *Scavenger*? She is afraid to ask. And why *Nuisance Grounds*? Because all that awful old stuff and rotten stuff is a nuisance and nice people don't want to have anything to do with it?

Clank-clonk. The wooden cart crawls up Hill Street, turning north on the main drag. All the stores are up the other end of Main. Here there is only the Granite Works, which makes gravestones in two colours, red or black, speckled stone, some plain and some fancy with flowers and scrolls and that. Then Christie turns in at a sign above a dark dark brick cave. *W. Saunders, Blacksmith.* Morag isn't going to go down there. She stays on the wagon, looking into the blackness. At the very end of the gloomy dark there is a fire, glowing red but not seeming to light up the place at all. Smells: heat, horses, sweat. An old man is sitting on an overturned nail barrel outside, and inside a younger man suddenly swings a big hammer onto the iron slab and for a second the whole place is full of stars. Christie loads the wagon with scrap iron, old horseshoes,

crooked pieces of rusty oily metal, and they are off again.
Morag thinks of the sparks, the stars, and sees them again
inside her head. Stars! Fire-stars! How does it happen? She
wants to ask, but won't. Christie would think she was dumb.
She isn't the dumb one. Christie is.

Now they are going along the streets where some of the
big houses are, big yellow brick houses or wooden houses
painted really nice. Lawns all neat and cut, and sprinklers sprinkling, swirling around and making water rainbows. Flower
gardens with pink and purple petunias, and red snapdragons
like velvet, really *rich* velvet, and orange lilies with freckles on
the throats. The blinds are pulled down over the front windows
of the houses, to keep out the heat. Cream-coloured blinds, all
fringed with lace and tassels. The windows are the eyes, closed,
and the blinds are the eyelids, all creamy, fringed with lacy
lashes. Blinds make the houses to be blind. Ha ha.

Morag is enjoying this ride more than she thought she
would. Then it happens. A gang of kids. Some from her class
in school. Voices. Yelling. Whistling.

"Hey – there goes Old Man Logan on his chariot!"

"Giddup! Hey, giddup there, ya old swayback!"

"Hey, get a load of who's with him, eh? Got a little
helper, Mr. Logan? Hey, Christie, got a new hand, there?"

Mostly it is the boys who are yelling. Ross McVitie. Al
Cates. Jamie Halpern. The girls are looking away, pretending
not to notice. But snickering a bit. Trying to get in good with
the boys. Mavis Duncan. Vanessa MacLeod. Stacey Cameron.

"Hey, listen – how about this, eh?"

Then, like a song, like a verse, but mean.

Christie Logan's the Scavenger Man –
Gets his food from the garbage can!

Laugh laugh laugh. Har har ho ho. One of the girls, though (which one?), says for them to cut it out. But no. They don't.

"I got a better one. Hey, wait, listen! Listen, Ross!"

Mo-rag! Mo-rag!
Gets her clothes from an ol' flour bag!

Morag is not breathing. She can't feel herself breathing. She isn't hearing, either. She won't hear. She sits still, not looking at Christie. Then she realizes he has stopped the wagon and she glances at him.

Oh. Christie is grinning. He is twisting his face, like different crazy masks. His tongue droops out like a dog's tongue. He crosses his eyes, and his mouth is dribbling with spit. Then he laughs. Oh. He laughs in a kind of cackle, like a loony.

Silence. The kids aren't saying anything. Now Christie's face goes back to its own self.

"Seen enough, then?" he says. "Next time I'll pass the hat."

Then he reaches, very slowly, for the whip which he never uses on Ginger. He lifts it high in his hand.

Give it to them, Christie! Hurt them. But she isn't saying the words out loud.

The kids run, scattering all over the place. Christie puts the whip back, and laughs. Laughs like himself. Morag is crying, but with her head down, so as not to be seen. Christie puts a hand on her shoulder, but she shoves it away.

"Why did you have to act so silly, Christie? Why did you have to?"

Christie hawks and spits into the road.

"Och aye. Only showing them what they thought they would be expecting to see, then, do you see?"

She does not see.

"Look at it this way," Christie says. "All these houses along here, Morag. I don't say this is so of all of them, now, but with the most of them, you can see from what their kids say, what they're saying. Some of them, because I take off their muck for them, they think I'm muck. Well, I *am* muck, but so are they. Not a father's son, not a man born of woman who is not muck in some part of his immortal soul, girl. That's what they don't know, the poor sods. When I carry away their refuse, I'm carrying off part of them, do you see?"

No. She does not see. She sees one thing, though. Christie is working himself into a spiel. He usually gets into a spiel when the whiskey is in him. Prin says so. And Morag has seen it. But there is no whiskey in him now.

Christie's face looks funny, sort of squashed-in. His skin is all sunburnt, and now it's covered with dusty sweat, all that red skin face. Christie is a redskin. Ha ha. But she isn't laughing. She hates the kids for talking like they did, to her but also to Christie. Now she hates Christie for talking the way he is, crazy.

"By their garbage shall ye know them," Christie yells, like a preacher, a downy preacher. "I swear, by the ridge of tears and by the valour of my ancestors, I say unto you, Morag Gunn, lass, that by their bloody goddamn fucking garbage shall ye christly well know them. The ones who eat only out of tins. The ones who have to wrap the rye bottles in old news-papers to try to hide the fact that there are so goddamn many of them. The ones who have fourteen thousand pill bottles the week, now. The ones who will be chucking out the family albums the moment the grandmother goes to her ancestors. The ones who're afraid to flush the safes down the john, them with flush johns, in case it plugs the plumbing and Melrose Maclaren has to come and get it unstuck and might see, as if Mel would give the hundredth part of a damn. I tell you, girl, they're close as clams and twice as brainless. I see what they throw out, and I don't care a shit, but they think I do, so that's why they cannot look at me. They think muck's dirty. It's no more dirty than what's in their heads. Or mine. It's christly clean compared to some things. All right. I'll please them. I'll wade in it up to my ass. I could wade in shit, if I had to, without it hurting me. I'd like to tell the buggers that."

Christie wipes his face with the back of his hand.

"Now then, Morag," he says in his real voice, "what a bloody fool, talking to you like that. I want my head looking at, that's God's truth. But I took this job, you know, because I fancied it. I could've worked for the CPR. Nothing elevated, I not having had the full High School for various reasons. It was after I came back from the war. Lot of muck lying about there, in France, I can tell you, most of it being –"

He stops speaking. Morag's hair is hot around her neck, and the sweat is trickling down between her shoulder blades.

Christie took the job because he fancied it.

"Christie, I think I'll get off and go on home now."

"Are you not all right, then, Morag?"

"It's so hot," she says. "I feel kinda sick to my stomach."

"Suit yourself, then."

So Morag does not see the Nuisance Grounds this day, either. Christie goes on his own way alone.

Memorybank Movie: Parsons' Bakery
is the Worst Place in Town

August. No school for another month yet. The heat is awful. Prin minds the heat, but Morag doesn't. In the house, the flies are in their millions, but slow and stupid with the heat. They get in through the rip in the screen door. Christie always forgets to fix this hole. The flies are *bluebottles* – how

come they got this nice name given to them? They're ugly.
Some of them are all swollen with eggs inside of them, and
they go crawling over the peanut butter pail on the table, or
just burrow and nuzzle their way inside the loaf of bread.
Morag sits with her elbows on the kitchen table, watching
the flies.

When she peers close, she can see that their wings are
shining, both blue and green. Can they be beautiful and filthy?
Should she shoo them away? More would only come.

The oilcloth on the table is dirty. Sometimes Morag
wipes it off, but more often she leaves it. It will only get dirty
again. Neither Christie nor Prin ever notice, or, if they do, they
don't let on. Prin is not really dirty. She just doesn't notice
so much any more. She sits and sits in her chair, Prin does.
Is she dreaming, with her eyes wide open? You can do this.
It's easy. Morag knows. Maybe Prin is dreaming of being
young and pretty. And rich. Prin rich! Pretty! She can't be
dreaming *that*.

Morag likes the kitchen best. The oak bench, with the
coat racks on each side of it, looks like a big moose with
antlers, like in the school Reader. Christie's winter jacket, and
all the scarves and mitts are still there, full of moths. The
bench part is piled with old newspapers and also Morag's
lunch pail for school. Christie's chair is the same as Prin's, armchair, old leather with horsehair (horsehair? Christie says so)
inside. The seats of the chairs go *scree-ee – squ-uff* when
someone sits down, and Morag loves this sound because it's
funny. The kitchen smells, but some of the smells are okay:
melted butter; heat; dust; Fels-Naptha soap. Sour milk and
feet do not smell okay.

Morag likes the sittingroom, too, but nobody ever sits in
it. It is not too good for everyday, like some people's, but it is

full of stuff Christie has brought home from the Nuisance Grounds. Such as:

a black old stove, quite small and round and fat

a blue chesterfield but you can't see the pattern anymore too torn

a lamp with no shade, but it is *bronze* and has a bronze lady with a bronze lily

a real carved wooden chess set, but no bishops (what are bishops?)

a family album, covered in red velvet (mouldy) and no name attached, no *family* name, but the pictures have things written in white ink on the black pages – *Agnes as Fairy Queen in School Play; Mother & Marigold 1901*

a blue *plush* (pl-uush – rich-sounding, but it is really like velvet only cheaper and not so smoo-ooth on the fingers) cushion, with a painted-on picture of King Edward the Seventh

a very *good* china saucer, very good because thin and you can nearly see through it (Prin's father had the *very same kind*; maybe it was his?); tiny *mauve* violets on it, but no cup

books, old old old books, and one has real leather for the cover, and the letters are in real *gold* or used to be but now you can hardly see them, and you can't read the book because it is in *another language*, but Christie says it is the Holy Bible in Gaelic. Throwing out a Holy Bible! Oh. But would God mind so much, seeing as it was in Gaelic? (*What means Gaelic?*)

Christie keeps bringing stuff home. He never does anything with it. But it is there. He calls it *good rubbish*. He says Bad Riddance to Good Rubbish. But you're supposed to say it the other way around. Morag knows.

Prin is puffing and wheezing. Her shoes are off.

"Golly, it's hot enough to fry an egg on the sidewalk, ain't it, Morag?"

Morag does not reply. She is watching two flies fucking, buzzing while they do it.

"Morag, would you run to the store for me, like a good girl?"

"Do I have to?"

"Well, I'd go myself," Prin says, sighing, "but it's these gosh-darned veins of mine. I hope and pray *you* never know what it feels like to have varicose veins, Morag. Sometimes they just burn and sting like I got a whole nest of wasps right there in the veins themselves. Standing on my feet these hot days is murder."

So Morag goes. Up the hill and onto Main. To Parsons' Bakery.

The bread is kept on open shelves, but not the cakes and pastries. They are kept in a glass case. Morag looks at the iced fancies, little tiny cakes covered with pink or green or white icing, and with an almond or a cherry on top.

"Four jelly doughnuts, please."

"Right away," Mr. Parsons says.

At the other side of the store are Mrs. McVitie and

Mrs. Cameron. Morag spotted them when she first came in. Sometimes she has to look hard to be sure who people are, because the faces don't come clear until they're really close up, but she always tries to see who is around. You have to. In case. Ross's mother and Stacey's mother are looking at the walnut slices and the shortbread. Nope. Now they are looking at her. Maybe they don't know she can hear what they're saying?

"It's a wonder some people can afford jelly doughnuts." Mrs. McVitie.

"Haven't you ever noticed, though, that it's *those* who spend their money as though it was water?" Mrs. Cameron.

"Poor child, don't they ever have her hair cut?" Mrs. McVitie.

"And those gangling dresses, always away below the knee." Mrs. Cameron.

Morag takes the bag, pays, and turns. Her hair feels dirty. But it isn't dirty – Prin washed it only a day ago. The two ladies are wearing flowery *chiffon* dresses. Hats, with real artificial flowers.

Morag sticks out her tongue at the both of them. And runs. Home.

"I'm not going there again, Prin. I hate that dumb place."

Why doesn't Prin go and get her own goddamn blistering bloody shitty jelly doughnuts?

Prin gets up out of her chair. Holding on to the chair-arm to heft up.

"Honey, what's the matter, now? Tell me, eh?"

Okay. If she wants to be told, Morag will tell her, all right all right. Morag has got a good memory. She repeats every word the two of them said, there.

Prin looks funny. Her face goes crinkled.

"You think it's my legs, honey?" Prin says. "It's that, but I *could* drag them up the hill. I just don't want to be seen, *like this*. But better they'd said it to me than you."

"What? What, Prin?"

"I never used to look this way," Prin says. "Yeh, well, I know I let myself go. I know. Oh, I know that all right. I don't know. Just didn't seem that much use, bothering. We never seemed to get anywheres, anyhow. He's smarter than what I am, and I only got the Grade Five. I was lucky he married me. I never could fathom why he did. But I never could fathom *him*, neither. He never cared about getting anywheres. It ain't his fault, I guess. But now – I don't kind of know how to be any different, like. That's why I don't, you know, look after you better, sort of. I'm that sorry, Morag."

Morag is crying. Holding onto Prin's awful fat belly wrapped around in the brown wraparound, Prin's good good good.

"Prin – I never meant! I never!"

Prin wipes Morag's eyes with fat warm hands.

"The Lord knows I care about you. I lost my only one."

"What? *What?*"

"Strangled on the cord. A boy. Dead when born."

What? What cord? What means *Cord*? Dead when born? Oh. How could you be born and dead at the same time? Oh –

"I shouldn't have said," Prin says. "Never you mind."

Morag doesn't say. Doesn't say. Doesn't say. Doesn't say.

Evening, and the three are sitting on the front porch. Christie and Prin are on straight chairs from the kitchen. Morag is on the top step. All along Hill Street, summer noises. Gangs of kids playing Kick the Can and Run Sheep Run and Andy Andy Eye Over. Dogs fucking in ditches, or fighting, yelping when somebody kicks them apart. Lots of women leaning on their fences and yakking.

Next door, at the Winklers', old Gus starts to shout. Trouble. Vernon runs outside and onto the road. Vernon is younger than Morag. He is a drip. Also, his nose drips drips drips all the time. He is skinny, and his hair (pale pale like Eva's) looks funny because his mother cuts it by putting a bowl on his head and snipping all around. But he is just a little kid, and it isn't his fault he's a drip. What is Vernon's dad going to *do*?

Gus Winkler has caught Vernon by the arm. Gus has a stick in his hand and he is hitting Vernon with it. On the legs, on the bum, oh on the face. Vern screams and screams. Like a dog when somebody has hurt it real bad.

Morag stares. Blood on Vernon's *face*. He has a nose-bleed. She looks up at Christie.

Christie is sitting very still. His hands are around his knees. He looks away from Morag. She might have known he wouldn't do anything. Scaredy-cat Christie.

Gus pushes Vernon back inside the Winklers' shack. All of a sudden everything on Hill Street seems quiet. Then the ordinary noises begin again, as though nothing has happened. Nothing at all. Christie does not move. Then he speaks, but it doesn't sound like Christie.

"I didn't go over. I didn't go over, did I? Not me. Gus Winkler's too brawny. May God –"

He stops. Prin makes little clucking-hen noises.

"It wasn't none of your business, Christie."

Christie gets up and walks inside the house.

"He's gonna have one of his spells," Prin says. "He ain't had one for a long time."

When they go into the house, Christie is sitting on the oak bench. His blue blue eyes look like they are *blind*. He is shaking all over. He keeps on like this a long time. Then he stops shaking but doesn't move. When Morag goes to bed, he is still sitting there, not moving.

"What *is* it, Prin?"

"Shh," Prin says. "It's nothing. It'll go away by itself. Doc MacLeod says he don't think nothing can be done for it. It's the shell shock, like."

"*What?*"

"In the war," Prin explains. "He was shook up very bad. In his nerves, like. Sometimes it takes him, even now. He never said, but I always had a hunch that was why he couldn't get no other job except Scavenger. He never knows when it might take him, see."

"But – he told me he fancied the job."

"He would," Prin says, crossly.

"Why would Gus Winkler do that to Vern?"

Prin shakes her head.

"Only the Lord can tell. He's got a devil in him, that man."

Morag lies in bed, thinking. Christie would never beat her. He's stinky and he looks so dumb. But he's never beaten her. He wouldn't do that, anyway. But he didn't go over to Winklers'. He was scared of Gus.

Christie, sitting there in the kitchen. Christie, shaking all over.

Morag cries.

Memorybank Movie: Christie with Spirits

Morag is nine, and it is winter. The snow is a good four feet thick outside and you have to walk to school on the road, where the snowplough has been. The windows are covered with frost-feathers and frost-ferns, and it doesn't matter that you can't see out because the patterns are so good to look at. In the kitchen, the stove keeps them warm, although Christie has a job scrounging enough wood. Lots of people on Relief are going to the Nuisance Grounds looking for old wooden boxes, not being able to afford cordwood, but Christie has first pick. Christie is not on Relief. *Relief* means you have no job on account of the Depression, and the government feeds you slop. Ugh. The *Depression* means there aren't any jobs, or hardly any, or like that.

Christie is drinking red biddy he got from somebody across the tracks, and he is explaining about the wood and other things to Morag. Prin is cross about the red biddy, so she has turned her chair away from him.

"I leave some, do you see, then, Morag," Christie says. "It's only right. Garbage belongs to all. Communal property, as you might say. One man's muck is everyman's muck. The socialism of the junk heap. All the same, though, with every profession do you see, there must be some advantages, some little thing or other that you get which others don't. And this here is mine. The Nuisance Grounds keeps us warm. Out of the garbage dump and into the fire. Och aye, that was the grand load of boxes I brought back today. Old butter crates from the Creamery."

He swallows some more red biddy, coughs, then gets into the subject he always talks about when the spirits are in him.

"Let the Connors and the McVities and the Camerons and Simon Pearl and all them in their houses up there – let them look down on the likes of Christie Logan. Let them. I say unto you, Morag, girl, I open my shirt to the cold winds of their voices, yea, and to the ice of their everlasting eyes. They don't touch me, Morag. For my kin and clan are as good as theirs any day of the week, any week of the month, any month of the year, any year of the century, and any century of all time."

Gulp. Swallow. The spirits are really in him. His eyes are shining. His right hand comes up, clenched. He is pretending he is holding a claymore. Morag knows, because once afterwards he said so, laughing. But you aren't supposed to laugh now.

"Was I not born a Highlander, in Easter Ross, one of the North Logans? An ancient clan, an ancient people. Is our motto not a fine, proud set of words, then? *This Is the Valour of My Ancestors.* The motto of the Logans, Morag, and our war cry is *The Ridge of Tears*. The ridge of tears! *Druim-nan deur*, although I'm not so sure how to pronounce it, not having the Gaelic. A sad cry, it is, for the sadness of my people. A cry heard at Culloden, in the black days of the battle, when the clans stood together for the last time, and the clans were broken by the Sassenach cannons and the damned bloody rifles of the redcoat swine. They mowed the clans down in cold blood, my dear, and it must have been enough to tear the heart and unhinge the mind of the strongest coldest man alive, for our folk were poor bloody crofters, and were not wanting to fight the wars of the chieftains, at all. But they thought their chieftains had the power from heaven, Morag. They believed their chiefs were kings from God. And them who didn't believe was raised anyway, with fire and with sword, until they went off to fight Charlie's battle for him, and him a green boy from France who neither knew nor cared for his people but only for the crown gleaming there in the eye of his own mind."

Christie stumbles to the sideboard and opens a drawer. He brings out the book, *The Clans and Tartans of Scotland*, and looks up Logan.

"See there," he bellows. "The crest badge of the Logans. And what is the crest, Morag? What is the way, then, you would describe, in the right words, what is there on that badge?"

She knows it off by heart.

"A passion nail piercing a human heart, proper."

Christie's fist comes down on the table.

"Right! An ancient family, the North Logans, by the Almighty God."

Then the spirits start to get gloomy in him.

"Och, what the hell does it matter? It's here we live, not there, and the glory has passed away, and likely never was in the first place."

"Christie, tell me about Piper Gunn."

Christie sighs, and pours another drink. He sits there, thinking. Soon he will begin. Morag knows what it says in the book under the name Gunn. It isn't fair, but it must be true because it is right there in the book.

> The chieftainship of Clan Gunn is undetermined at the
> present time, and no arms have been matriculated.

When she first looked it up, she showed it to Christie, and he read it and then he laughed and asked her if she had not been told the tales about the most famous Gunn of all, and so he told her. He tells them to her sometimes when the spirit moves him.

Now he rocks back on the straight chair, for he is sitting at the table with the bottle beside him.

"All right, then, listen and I will tell you the first tale of your ancestor."

CHRISTIE'S FIRST TALE OF PIPER GUNN

It was in the old days, a long time ago, after the clans was broken and scattered at the battle on the moors, and the dead men thrown into the long graves there, and no heather ever grew on those places, never again, for it was dark places they had become and places of mourning. Then, in those days, a darkness fell over all the lands and the crofts of Sutherland. The Bitch-Duchess was living there then, and it was she who cast a darkness over the land, and sowed the darkness and reaped gold, for her heart was dark as the feathers of a raven and her heart was cold as the gold coins, and she loved no creature alive but only the gold. And her tacksmen rode through the countryside, setting fire to the crofts and turning out the people from their homes which they had lived in since the beginning of all time. And it was old men and old women with thin shanks and men in their prime and women with the child inside them and a great scattering of small children like, and all of them was driven away from the lands of their fathers and onto the wild rocks of the shore, then, to fish if they could and pry the shellfish off of the rocks there, for food.

Well, now, the Bitch-Duchess walked her castle, there, walked and walked, and you would think God in His mercy would keep the sleep forever from her eyelids, but she slept sound enough when she had a mind to. She was not the one to feel shame or remorse over the people scrabbling on the rocks there like animals and like the crabs who crawl among the rocks in that place. *All the lands of Sutherland will be raising the sheep*, says the she-devil, *for they'll pay better than folk.*

Among all of them people there on the rocks, see, was a piper, and he was from the Clan Gunn, and it was many of the Gunns who lost their hearths and homes and lived wild on the stormy rocks there. And Piper Gunn, he was a great tall man, a man with the voice of drums and the heart of a child and the gall of a thousand and the strength of conviction. And when he played the pipes on the shore, there, it was the pibrochs he played, out of mourning for the people lost and the people gone and them with no place for to lay their heads except the rocks of the shore. When Piper Gunn played, the very seagulls echoed the chants of mourning, and the people wept. And Piper Gunn, he played there on the shore, all the pibrochs he knew, "Flowers of the Forest" and all them. And it would wrench the heart of any person whose heart was not dead as stone, to hear him.

Then Piper Gunn spoke to the people. *Dolts and draggards and daft loons and gutless as gutted herring you are*, he calls out in his voice like the voice of the wind from the north isles. *Why do you sit on these rocks, weeping?* says he. *For there is a ship coming*, says he, *on the wings of the morning, and I have heard tell of it, and we must gather our pots and kettles and our shawls and our young ones, and go with it into a new world across the waters.*

But the people were afraid, see? They did not dare. Better to die on the known rocks in the land of their ancestors, so some said. Others said the lands across the seas were bad lands, filled with the terrors and the demons and the beasts of the forest and those being the beasts which would devour a man as soon as look at him. *Well*, says Piper Gunn, *God rot your flabby souls then, for my woman and I will go and rear our daughters and our sons in the far land and make it ours, and you can stay here, then, and the Bitch-Duchess can have chessmen carved from your white bones scattered here on the rocks and she shall play her games with you in your death as she has in your life.*

Then Piper Gunn changed his music, and he played the battle music there on the rocks. And he played "All the Blue Bonnets Are Over the Border" and he played "Hey Johnnie

Cope" and he played "The March of the Cameron Men" and he played "The Gunns' Salute" which was the music of his own clan. They say it was like the storm winds out of the north, and like the scree and skirl of all the dead pipers who ever lived, returned then to pipe the clans into battle.

Now Piper Gunn had a woman, and a strapping strong woman she was, with the courage of a falcon and the beauty of a deer and the warmth of a home and the faith of saints, and you may know her name. Her name, it was Morag. That was an old name, and that was the name Piper Gunn's woman went by, and fine long black hair she had, down to her waist, and she stood there beside her man on the rocky coast, and watched that ship come into the harbour in that place. And when the plank was down and the captain hailing the people there, Piper Gunn began to walk towards that ship and his woman Morag with him, and she with child, and he was still playing "The Gunns' Salute."

Then what happened? What happened then, to all of them people there homeless on the rocks? They rose and followed! Yes, they rose, then, and they followed, for Piper Gunn's music could put the heart into them and they would have followed him all the way to hell or to heaven with the sound of the pipes in their ears.

And that was how all of them came to this country, all that bunch, and they ended up at the Red River, and that is another story.

"Best go to bed, Morag," Prin says. "*He'll* be asleep at the table in a coupla minutes."

Morag goes upstairs. Her room is really hers, her place. It has always been hers. She likes that it is small, just enough room for the brass bed and the green dresser. She sits on the bed, shivering. The cold is seeping in through the closed window. She does not undress. Prin finds her there, after a while, and scolds.

"Morag, you are a mooner."

Morag puts on her nightgown then, and climbs into bed. Thinking.

A mooner. That sounds nice. She knows what it means. It isn't meant nice. It means somebody who moons around, dawdling and thinking. But to her it means something else. Some creature from another place, *another planet.* Left here accidentally.

She thinks of the scribbler in her top dresser drawer. She will never show it to anyone, never. It is hers, her own business. She will write some in it tomorrow. She tells it in her head.

Morag's First Tale of Piper Gunn's Woman

Once long ago there was a beautiful woman name of Morag, and she was Piper Gunn's wife, and they went to the new land together and Morag was never afraid of anything in this whole wide world. Never. If they came to a forest, would this Morag there be scared? Not on your christly life. She would only laugh and say, *Forests cannot hurt me because I have the power and the second sight and the good eye and the strength of conviction.*

What means *The Strength of Conviction?*

Morag sleeps.

THREE

Today would be better. Today Pique would phone, or there would be a letter from her, saying she had decided against hitching west or else that she and Gord were back together and were going west for a while but all was well.

Morag went downstairs, made coffee and sat at the table, looking out at the morning river. The sky was growing light. Exact use of words, that. The sky actually was *growing* light, as though the sun, still hidden, were some kind of galactic plant putting forth tendrils.

Idiotic to have got up so early. As you grow older, you require less sleep. Could it be that she would become a consistently early riser? Two hours' work done before breakfast? A likely thought.

The swallows were of course awake and flittering out from the nest under the eaves, just above the window, zinging across the water, swooping and scooping up insects to feed their newly hatched fledglings. For years Morag had hardly noticed birds, being too concerned with various personal events and oddities. In the last few years she had become aware of creatures other than human, whose sphere this was as well, unfortunate them. Even plants were to be pitied, having to share home with the naked apes.

Across the river came a boat, its small outboard motor chuffing fitfully. A-Okay Smith and Co. Maudie and Thomas. At five, apparently, Tom could read, taught by Maudie, so that in Grade One he had been to some extent ostracized by the other kids. Now at eight he was full of exotic knowledge. The Smiths were enlightened almost to a fault. Morag, while exceedingly fond of them, sometimes felt ignorant in their presence, which caused her to react towards them with a degree of resentment and chagrin. Also, they believed, somewhat touchingly, that their enlightenment would mean that Tom would be spared any sense of alienation towards them later on, in his adolescence. Morag had, once upon a time, held that belief herself. One of the disconcerting aspects of middle age was the realization that most of the crises which happened to other people also ultimately happened to you.

The boat came to a jolting standstill alongside Morag's dock, and the Clan Smith clambered out and straggled up to the house. Tom, deceptively cherub-faced, was heard to announce that he was going along the road to Royland's. Praise God. Spared his hideously knowledgeable remarks for perhaps an hour, if lucky. *Those birds are not Blackbirds, Morag – the Rusty Blackbird is like that, only smaller and with shorter talons and tail – those are Grackles, Common Grackles.* Tom could confidently be depended upon to know the nesting, breeding and living habits (many of them disgusting) of the Common Grackle, from conception to death. Probably he wanted to pick Royland's brains on the habits of the muskie, pickerel, rock bass and other fish inhabiting the waters of southern Ontario.

"Hi, Morag."

The Smiths entered without knocking, which Morag did not mind. They had, after all, lived here last year until they got the place across the river. A-Okay and Maude were one thing, but a winter enclosed in the farmhouse with the encyclopaedic Thomas was not to be highly recommended. Odd how much she now missed the kid, however, all things considered.

"I brought you some poems," A-Okay said in his earnestly jokey young voice, attempting nonchalance but totally without success.

"Alf read them to me last night," Maudie added, a testimonial, "and I thought they were Right On."

Right On. Dear little Lord Jesus, what did that mean? Like saying Great, Stupendous. No meaning at all.

I'm just as bad. Even if I think the poems are rubbish, I always say Very Interesting, at least before clobbering him with my real opinion. Please God, let them be better than the last couple of bunches. Well, some of those would've been a-okay if he'd worked on them more.

A-Okay thrust a wodge of papers into Morag's hands. He was a tall gangling man in his late twenties, still having something of an adolescent awkwardness about his limbs. He would frequently crash into tables, although sober, unaware of their presence until overtaken, and as an accidental dish-breaker he was without peer. He was, admittedly, short-sighted, and although he owned a pair of specs, he seldom wore them, believing them to indicate a subconscious desire to distance oneself from others. The result was that he was considerably more distanced from others, and from assorted objects, than he need have been. But let it pass. His was a heart of sterling or oak, stalwart. Morag's unofficial protector,

believing her to be in need of one, which indeed she sometimes was.

"Thanks, A-Okay," Morag said. "I'll read them later. As
you know, I don't think well off the top of my head. I'll be over
at your place soon, anyway. I'm going with Royland, when he
does your well. All right?"

"A-Okay," said A-Okay, this being the reason for his nickname. Maudie always called him Alf. He always called her
Maude, a name Morag found unsuitable. Come into the
garden, Maude. Maudie sounded more appropriate. Maudie
herself was slender and small and would probably look young
at fifty, a plain scrubbed face, blonde hair worn long or in a
plait, her dress nearly always ankle-length, granny-type, in
gingham she sewed determinedly herself on a hand-cranker
sewing machine. A wonder she didn't sew by hand with needle,
thread and tiny silver thimble. At night. By coal-oil lamp.

"Can I make some coffee, Morag?"

"Sure, Maudie. You know where everything is."

"Heard from Pique yet?"

"Not yet."

"Well," Maudie said, her voice clear and musical as a
meadowlark's, "she was right to go. You know that, don't you?"

"Yeh." Yes. Truthfully. No need to hammer the point
home, thanks.

"And she's right not to communicate, too." Maudie, like
Shakespeare, knew everything. "She will, in time, but she's got
to find herself first."

"Oh balls, Maudie," Morag said, ashamed of her annoyance but unable to prevent it. "One postcard wouldn't destroy
her self-discovery, I would've thought."

"Symbolically, it might do just that."

"Yeh. Maybe." Morag's voice lacked conviction.

Maudie with a cool efficiency produced a percolator full of real coffee in less time than Morag would have taken to make Instant.

"I've been thinking about that back vegetable garden of yours, Morag," A-Okay said. "How be if I dig it out for you again? It's kind of gone to seed, since – well, since we left. Now don't take offense – you know I don't mean it that way. I know it's a little late this spring, but at least you could put in lettuce and stuff."

"We've got ours nearly dug," Maudie said, eyes bright as goldfinches' wings. "I put in six packets of seeds yesterday."

Morag felt trapped. For one glorious summer the Smiths had grown vegetables in Morag's garden. At present, nothing was there except weeds.

"A-Okay, my dear, there is no way I'm going to slog around in that huge vegetable garden as long as I can bring in supplies from McConnell's Landing."

Both the Smiths looked away, embarrassed, troubled for her. Traitoress. Lackey to the System.

"By taxi?" A-Okay murmured.

"By packhorse would be better? The taxis are running anyway. This way, I'm not adding to the effluvia in the air."

A small moment of triumph. Then the recognition that the reason she shopped by taxi was quite simply that she was afraid of driving and refused to learn.

"True," A-Okay said. "But I was actually thinking of the cost, right at the moment."

"Look at it this way," Morag continued. "If I spent all my time gardening, how in hell could I get any writing done? No great loss, you may say, but it'd be a loss to *me*, and also I need a minimal income, even here. Whatever Susanna Moodie may have said in *Roughing It in the Bush*, I am not about to make coffee out of roasted dandelion roots."

"An hour a day in the garden," A-Okay said patiently, "would do the job. At least enough to have some results."

True. Undoubtedly true. Morag Gunn, countrywoman, never managing to overcome a quiver of distaste at the sight of an earthworm. Lover of swallows, orioles and red-winged blackbirds. Detester of physical labour. Lover of rivers and tall trees. Hater of axes and shovels. What a farce. You had to give A-Okay full marks for persistence – he never ceased trying to convert her.

"I approve of your efforts, God only knows," Morag said. "I applaud. I think it is great. I cannot help feeling, however, that like it or not the concrete jungle will not be halted by a couple of farms and a vegetable garden."

Silence. What a fatuous thing to say. As if they didn't know. As if they didn't know it all better than she did. They'd been part of it all their lives, from childhood, in a way she never had. She had lived in cities as though passing through briefly. Even when she'd lived in one city or another for years, they'd never taken hold of her consciousness. Her childhood had taken place in another world, a world A-Okay and Maudie had never known and couldn't begin to imagine, a world which in some ways Morag could still hardly believe was over and gone forever. These kids had been born and had grown up in Toronto. They weren't afraid of cities in the way Morag was afraid. They knew how to live there, how to survive. But they hated the city much more than Morag ever could, simply because they knew. A-Okay had once taught computer pro-gramming at a technical college. The decision to leave was, for them, an irrevocable one and hadn't been made lightly. Morag had met them through mutual friends in Toronto at the precise moment when they had decided to leave the city. She had suggested they give it a try at her place, and they had done that, paying their way both financially and in physical work. However they might feel sometimes, now they were living and had to live as though their faith in their decision was not to be broken.

"I'm sorry," Morag said, truthfully. "I didn't mean to say that. I didn't even mean it."

"No," A-Okay said suddenly. "We were talking at you, not with you. Weren't we? I guess we've done a lot of that since we got our own place. We didn't have any right."

"Well, now that you mention it, there may be some small degree of the Bible-puncher in you, A-Okay."

More in Maudie than in him. But she did not say this.

"Your writing is your real work," A-Okay said, with embarrassing loyalty and evident belief. "It's there you have to make your statement."

Or not make it. You can't write a novel that way, in any event. They'd been real to her, the people in the books. Breathing inside her head.

Phone. Her ring. Morag leapt up and shot over to the telephone on the sideboard. Pique. Cool it, Morag.

"Hello?"

"That you, Morag?"

Oh God. Him. Not him surely? Yes. How long since she'd seen him? Three years, only. Before the Smiths moved in. The Smiths had never seen him, and didn't even know anything much about him, as Morag only ever talked about him to Pique, sometimes.

"Yes. Speaking."

A deep gust of hoarse laughter.

"Don't try to make out you don't know who this is, eh?"

"Yeh, I know. I'm surprised you're still alive, is all."

"Yeh? I plan on living forever – didn't you know?"

Yes. You told me once you used to believe that, and didn't now. Are you all right?

"Are you all right? Are you okay?"

"Of course not," he said. "What do you think? I got busted for peddling. The hard stuff, naturally. I'm phoning from Kingston Pen. Got a private phone in the cell."

Well, at least he was okay.

"Oh, sorry to cast doubts on your blameless reputation. Why did you phone?"

And do you remember the last time I saw you, and what happened and didn't happen?

"To ask you, you mad bitch," he said, "what in hell you think you're doing with that girl?"

He had two speaking voices, one like gravel in a cement-mixer, the other exceedingly low-pitched, quiet. He used the second when very angry. As now.

"What do I think *I'm* doing?" Morag shouted. "What do you mean by that? Wait – have you seen her, then?"

"Of course I've seen her. She turned up here."

"Where is here?"

"Toronto. Yesterday. Don't ask me how she found out where I was. Ask her. She's a smart kid, I'll give her that much."

"What – how *is* she?" Morag sat down on the high stool beside the phone.

"She's okay," he said. "She's changed a lot since fifteen, eh?"

"Yeh."

"What's with this guy she had this fight with?"

"Gord? He wanted to get married. She doesn't believe in it."

"God, what an example you've been to her," he said, but laughing, really in approval. "Well, why in hell did you let her leave home? You know where she can end up, don't you? You know what can happen to her, don't you? By Jesus, Morag, if she goes out to Vancouver, I'll strangle you. Why did you let her go?"

"Let her? Let her?" Morag cried furiously. "What do you suggest I should've done, then? Chained her to the stove?"

A second's silence at the other end of the line.

"Yeh," he said finally. "Well, I guess she had to go. She comes by it naturally. I guess it isn't your fault."

"Well, never mind. It's not yours, either."

"No," he said. "It isn't. But I keep thinking of them, back there. You know."

"I know. But don't. Just don't, eh? Has she gone, now, then?"

"Yeh. West. I don't know how far, though. She wanted something. Maybe that's why she looked me up. She wanted the songs."

"Did you give them to her?"

"What do you think? Naturally I did."

"Well. Anyway, she was okay as of yesterday?"

"Yeh. Hey, Morag, do you still say my name wrong?"

"I – haven't tried it recently."

"No. I guess you wouldn't."

When he had rung off, she sat without moving. Afraid she would begin shaking, the way Christie sometimes used to do. The Smiths looked worried, curious, startled.

"My daughter's father," Morag said finally. "As I've told you, never having had an ever-present father myself, I managed to deny her one, too. Although not wittingly. I wasn't very witting in those days, I guess."

Maudie rose and nudged A-Okay.

"I think we should be getting along," A-Okay said. "Are you all right, Morag? Is there anything —?"

"I'm all right. Really."

Alone, Morag sat still for another half-hour before she could bring herself to get out the notebook and begin.

Whatever is happening to Pique is not what I think is happening, whatever that may be. What happened to me wasn't what anyone else thought was happening, and maybe not even what I thought was happening at the time. A popular misconception is that we can't change the past — everyone is constantly changing their own past, recalling it, revising it. What really happened? A meaningless question. But one I keep trying to answer, knowing there is no answer.

*Memorybank Movie: The Thistle Shamrock Rose
Entwine the Maple Leaf Forever*

Morag is twelve, and is she ever tough. She doesn't walk all hunched up any more, like when she was a little kid. Nosiree, not her. She is tall and she doesn't care who knows it. Her tits have swollen out already, and she shows them off by walking straight, swinging her shoulders just a little bit. Most of the girls are still as flat as boards. She has started her monthlies, too, and occasionally lets kids like Mavis or Vanessa, who haven't started, know it by a dropped remark here and there. She is a woman, and a lot of them are just kids.

But she's a tomboy, too. You gotta be. If it comes to a fight, she doesn't need to fight like a girl, scratching with her fingernails. She slugs with her closed fist. Boys or girls, it makes no difference. If a boy ever teases her, she goes for him. The best way is to knee them in the balls. They double over, scream, and chicken out. Hardly any boys ever tease her these days.

Nobody much teases Eva Winkler, any more, either, because Morag gives them the bejesus if they do. Eva is her friend, her one true friend. She loves Eva. She looks down on Eva, too, a bit, because Eva is gutless as a cleaned whitefish. It must be awful to be gutless. Gus Winkler still beats his kids, even Eva. He doesn't even have to be drunk. In fact, he hardly ever drinks and then only beer. He just likes beating his kids, that's all. You couldn't imagine Eva, so pale-haired and always saying *Oh sorry I didn't mean to* even when she's done nothing, you couldn't imagine her deserving it. Maybe Gus beats her because she's gutless, like Mrs. Winkler, like all the kids, there. In some awful spooky way Morag can understand this. If you ask for it, you sure as hell get it. But she sticks up for Eva, because Eva is her friend. She doesn't stick up for Eva with Gus, though. She never goes over there. She and Christie sit on the front porch and hear it happening. When it does, they never look at each other.

Morag is the best girl pitcher on the ballfield, and also a good shortstop. She can even play ball with the boys, and sometimes does. The girls yell things at her, but Morag doesn't care a fuck. They can't hurt her. She'll hurt them first. And when the boys laugh, she grins openmouth clowny, then pitches a twister, hard and fast.

The teachers hate her. Ha ha. She isn't a little flower, is why. That will be the day, when she tries to please a living soul.

Conversation Overheard from the Teachers' Room
All of Them in There Gabbing at Recess
Miss McMurtrie: oh, Skinner's bad enough but at least he's away from school half the time and not much missed by me I can tell you but Morag never misses a day

	sometimes I wonder what on earth I'm going to do with her you find her same Ethel
Miss Plowright:	how do you mean exactly
Miss McMurtrie:	well one day she's boisterous and noisy chewing gum in class whispering drawing dirty pictures *you* know and then heavens the next day she'll be so sullen not speaking to a soul and you can't get a word out of her she won't answer just sits there looking sullen if you take my meaning
Miss Plowright:	oh yes yes oh yes she was just like that in my class I always thought you know maybe she wasn't well maybe not quite *all there*
Miss Crawford:	she was a timid little thing in grade one but she learned to read really quickly well not exactly timid more well just very quiet never spoke to a soul except that poor little Eva Whatsername
Miss McMurtrie:	well she is not timid now I can assure you but bright enough I think you're wrong there Ethel she's bright enough but doesn't seem to give a hoot
Mr. Tate:	the home the home always look to the home old Christie and that half-witted wife of his

Morag doesn't let on. If you let on, ever, you're done for.

"How'd you get on today, Morag?" Christie says. "Let's see what you're copying out, there."

Christie's brown cracked stained teeth. Like an old teapot. Ha ha. You can see them all when he grins while reading.

"What in hell is this crap? *I wandered lonely as a cloud.* This Wordsworth, now, he was a pansy, girl, or no, maybe a daffodil? Clouds don't wander lonely, for the good christ's sake. Any man daft enough to write a line like that, he wanted his head looked at, if you ask me. Look here, I'll show you a poem, now, then."

Two large books she has never seen before, red binding a little bit warped, and really small print.

"In the days long long ago," Christie says sternly, "he lived, this man, and was the greatest song-maker of them all, and all this was set down years later, pieced together from what old men and old women remembered, see, them living on far crofts hither and yon, and they sang and recited these poems as they had been banded down over the generations. And the English claimed as how these were not the real old songs, but only forgeries, do you see, and you can read about it right here in this part which is called Introduction, but the English were bloody liars then as now. And I'll read you what he said, then, a bit of it."

A chariot! the great chariot of war,
Moving over the plain with death!
The shapely swift car of Cuchullin,
True son of Semo of hardy deeds.

Behind it curves downward like a wave,
Or mist enfolding a sharp-peaked hill;
The light of precious stones about it,
Like the sea in wake of boat at night.
Of shining yew is its pole,
Of well-smoothed bone the seat:
It is the dwelling-place of spears,
Of shields, of swords, and heroes.

On the right of the great chariot
Is seen a horse high-mettled, snorting,

High-crested, broad-chested, dark,
High-bounding, strong-bodied son of the Ben,
Springy and sounding his foot;
The spread of his forelock on high
Is like mist on the dwelling of deer.
Shining his coat, and speedy
His pace – Si-fodda his name.

On the other side of the car
Is an arch-necked snorting horse,
Thin-maned, free-striding, deep-hoofed,
Swift-footed, wide nostrilled son of the mountains –
Du-sron-gel the name of the gallant steed.

Full thousand slender thongs
Fasten the chariot on high;
The hard bright bit of the bridle,
In their jaws foam-covered, white,
Shining stones of power
Save aloft with the horses' manes –
Horses, like mist of mountain-side,
Which onward bear the chief to his fame.
Keener their temper than the deer,
Strong as the eagle their strength.
Their noise is like winter fierce
On Gormal smothered in snow.

In the chariot is seen the chief.
True-brave son of the keen brands,
Cuchullin of blue-spotted shields,
Son of Semo, renowned in song.

Ossian. Christie says *Aw-shun*. And shows her the Gaelic words, but cannot say them.

"It must sound like *something* in the old language, Morag. My father knew a few words of it, and I remember a little bit of it from when I was knee-high to a grasshopper and that must've been in Easter Ross before my old man kicked off and my mother came to this country with me, and hired herself out as help in houses in Nova Scotia, there, and kicked the bucket when I was around fifteen or so, and I came west, but the hell with all of that. I never learned the Gaelic, and it's a regret to me."

Together they look at the strange words, unknown now, lost, as it seems, to all men, the words that once told of the great chariot of Cuchullin.

Carbad! carbad garbh a' chómhraig,
'Gluasas thar cómhnaird le bás;
Carbad suimir, luath Chuchullin,
Sár-mhac Sheuma nan cruaidh chás.

"Gee. Think of that, Christie. Think of that, eh? Read some more in *our* words, eh?"

But Prin waddles over to the table and lays it for supper, and they eat boiled cabbage and boiled spuds and baloney. Christie chews with his mouth open so you can see the mushy slop of pink meat and greeny mush cabbage and gummy potatoes in there. Morag wants to hit him so hard his mouth will pour with blood. She stares at him, but he does not notice. Or if he does, he doesn't let on.

The Grade Six room is full of maple desks, each with a metal inkwell. Initials of other kids in other years are carved into the desks, with jackknives or by going over and over with a pencil until the lead eats into the wood. This is the easiest to do, and Morag has put M.G. on hers this way. You always have to look up at the blackboard at the front. Should be called the greyboard, always smudged with chalk. Morag can never see the board properly, and never has been able to, but doesn't let on. If she let on, they'd move her to the front row and she likes the back row better. No one is behind you there, looking at you.

On the walls at the side and back, great big framed pictures. No colours, just very dark brown or black, shadowy. One is of two people, a man and a woman, dressed in olden days poor clothes, kneeling down. *The Angelus*. Which means a bell is *tolling*, telling them it is time to pray. The other picture is worse – a whole lot of soldiers looking terrible, and a drooping Union Jack, and in the middle a man falling or fainting (dying, actually) with his eyeballs rolling upwards. *The Death of General Wolfe.*

"Good morning, Grade Six."

"Good morning, Miss McMurtrie."

"We will now sing 'O, Canada.'"

Grade Six shuffles to its feet.

O Ca-na-DA
Our home an' native lan'
Troo patriot LUV
In all thy sons' comman'. . . .

They are also learning it in French. The school board was a mite dubious at first, Miss McMurtrie says, tee hee, but she won them over.

O Ca-na-DA
Teara da nose ah yoo. . . .

The second line always makes the kids titter. They know it means land of our forefathers, but that isn't what it seems to mean. Morag sings loudly. She loves singing and has a good and carrying voice. She doesn't mind standing up any more, at least not when all the other kids are also standing beside their desks. Her dresses aren't away below her knees now, hell no, because she lops them off with the kitchen scissors herself and sometimes even does a hem, which is boring but doesn't take so long if you take good big stitches. Now her dresses are shorter than anyone else's, because she is going to show them, is why. Prin still makes Morag's dresses out of old stuff, though. Who has the money for new stuff these days, Prin says. (Some have.) Prin isn't so hot at sleeves, so usually leaves them out, and in the cold weather Morag wears a sweater underneath the dress. She wears running shoes in warm weather and galoshes in winter, with only socks inside, not shoes, so has to keep them on all day, and how could anyone not have stinky feet if they had to do that? Who gives a christly damn anyway? She's not the worst dressed. Eva is worse – her dresses are still halfway to her ankles, as she is too ascared of what her dad will say if she cuts them off. Also, one of the Tonnerre girls, halfbreed from the valley, is worse dressed; she's away a lot because of TB in one leg but when she *is* at school she looks the worst because her dresses are long-gawky and dirty, and she has a limpwalk.

They are seated again, and it is Spelling.

"Morag!"

Startled, she looks up. The teacher has been talking to her and she hasn't heard.

"That's quite enough, class," Miss McMurtrie says, because of the giggling all around. "Stand up, Morag."

Draggingly, she stands. Whatever is going to happen, it can only be awful. She straightens her shoulders and holds herself so her tits stick out under her dress.

"Now, Morag, you weren't listening, were you?"

Silence. She cannot speak. Her throat is full of phlegm or something. She stares boldly at Miss McMurtrie, so the teacher will think she is being silent on purpose.

"Are you tongue-tied, Morag?"

Morag is not here. She is in the Wachakwa valley, and the couchgrass is high around her. There is a clump of scrub oak trees, easy to climb, and all around are thick chokecherry bushes. It is warm and shady in the hideout, and you can hear the bees singing their crazy buzzsongs as they tumble among the pink wild asters and cowslip bells colour of oranges or suns. Cowslips are the best. For bees. More honey in them.

"I *said*," Miss McMurtrie's butcherknife voice, "I *said* are you tongue-tied, Morag?"

Morag's anger. Like shame, burning in her throat.

"You know I'm not." Loud.

Miss McMurtrie's face gone reddish, splotched.

"Very well, then, if you're *not* tongue-tied, would you be so kind as to answer the question I asked you about ten minutes ago? You're wasting the class's time, Morag. I suppose I will have to repeat the question. Obviously you were away off in Cloud Cuckoo Land. How do you spell Egypt?"

Egypt. Cleopatra, evil and beautiful, dying of a snake bite. Having put the snake right on herself. Ugh. Miss Plowright, last year, reading them *Tales from Shakespeare*. Was Shakespeare there? Did he see the snake being put on the *bare skin*? Cleopatra, drifting down the Nile River in a boat shaped like a giant bird (coloured picture in the book) while her slaves fanned her with fans made out of pink green blue feathers. Plumes. Think of that. Classy.

"Well, Morag?"

If she could've written it down she could've got it. Always the same. But no writing-down allowed.

"E-y –"

"Wrong. Try again."

"E-y-g-t –"

Miss McMurtrie shakes her starched-looking grey head. More in sorrow than anger, as she is always saying.

"You may sit down, Morag. All right, class, who can spell Egypt? Ross?"

"E-g-y-p-t."

Show-off. Smart-aleck McVitie. Who cares? Morag, sitting down, will not look around. Neither to left nor to right. Finally, she takes a quick glance around to see if anybody is still looking at her. They better not be. She catches the eye of Skinner Tonnerre, who also sits in the back row out of choice.

He grins at her. Well, think of that. The grin means *Screw all of them, eh?* Astounded, Morag grins back.

Boys are generally mean. Those girls who have a hope of pleasing them, try. Those who haven't a hope, either stay out of their way or else act very tough and try to make fun of them first. Skinner is just the same as all the boys, in that way. He is mean. He knows a lot of swear words and isn't afraid to use them to make girls feel silly or cheap. *Hey, Vanessa, want me to fuck your ass? It's better that way.* He has never shouted like this at Morag, because he probably knows she wouldn't take it all meek. Or else doesn't think she's pretty enough to be worth embarrassing. The other boys in the class, even Mike Lobodiak, who is really big, never tangle with Skinner. They're scared of him. Also, they think they're better than he is. Skinner is taller than any of the other boys, and has better muscles. He is about three years older than any of the rest of the class, which is why he and his sister Piquette are in the same class. Both having missed a lot of school. Sometimes Skinner goes off with his dad, old Lazarus Tonnerre, and disappears for weeks, setting traplines way up at Galloping Mountain, some say. The Tonnerres (there are an awful lot of them) are called *those breeds*, meaning halfbreeds. They are part Indian, part French, from away back. They are mysterious. People in Manawaka talk about them but don't talk *to* them. Lazarus makes home-brew down there in the shack in the Wachakwa valley, and is often arrested on Saturday nights. Morag knows. She has heard. They are dirty and unmentionable.

Skinner is thin and he has dark dark slanted eyes. He is always scowling. He wears worn unpatched jeans held up by a leather belt with a big brass buckle. Morag has always reckoned that he hated the other kids so much he never even noticed what they said about him and his gimpylegged sister and all of them (and about their Ma, who took off and went to cook for some crazy old man living alone on a farm oh shame). Maybe Skinner does notice the passed remarks? Maybe he just doesn't let on. Like her.

He is *not* like her. She does not glance in his direction again all day.

At ten minutes to four, Miss McMurtrie leads the class in "The Maple Leaf Forever"

In days of yore	
From Britain's shore	
Wolfe the donkless hero CAME	(titters; but what
And planted firm	means *Donkless?*)

Britannia's flag
On Ca-na-da's fair do-MAIN.
Here may it wave
Our boas' our pride
And join in LUV together
The THISTLE SHAMROCK ROSE entwine
The MAPLE LEAF FOREVER!

Morag loves this song and sings with all her guts. She also knows what the emblems mean. Thistle is Scots, like her and Christie (others, of course, too, including some stuck-up kids, but *her*, definitely, and they better not forget it). Shamrock is Irish like the Connors and Reillys and them. Rose is English, like Prin, once of good family. Suddenly she looks over to see if Skinner Tonnerre is singing. He has the best voice in the class, and he knows lots of cowboy songs, and dirty songs, and he sometimes sings them after school, walking down the street.

He is not singing now.

He comes from nowhere. He isn't anybody. She stops singing, not knowing why. Then she feels silly about stopping, so sings again.

Memorybank Movie: Christie's Gift of the Garbage-telling
Morag goes alone to the Nuisance Grounds. Not with Christie. Not with anyone. Eva wants to come along but Morag says No. Just for once she has to see what the place looks like. By herself.

She knows exactly where the spot is. Everybody knows that. A little above the town, the second hill, the same hill as the Manawaka cemetery. All the dead stuff together there on the same hill. Except that the cemetery is decent and respectable, with big spruce trees, and grass which is kept cut, and lots of the plots have flowers which people plant and tend. *Gunn* is just a small stone with grass around it, no flowers. Morag has only been there the once and doesn't want to go again.

The Nuisance Grounds are on a large flat sort of plain, up there, and no trees grow, although the place is surrounded on all sides by poplars and clumps of chokecherry and pincherry bushes, screening it from sight. Morag approaches it quietly, cannily, looking around. Okay. Nobody here. She can feel the sun hot and dusty on her bare arms and legs, and her hair feels snarled and too long and hot for summer. She is sweating in this hot closed-in place. It isn't really that much closed-in. It just feels so. Should she maybe not have come here?

Oh. The Nuisance Grounds contain a billion trillion heaps of old muck. Such as:

a rusty car with no tires and one door off
mountains of empty tin cans, some with labels still on
Best Pie Pumpkin
moth-eaten sweaters and ragged coats
a whole bunch of bedsprings
green mould like fur on things
rotten fruits oranges bananas gone bad soft black
FLIES on them
a car axle but no car
maple syrup tins with holes in them
saucepans and kettles also with holes
a sewing machine with no wheel or handle
broken bottles (beer milk rye and baby)
more rotten stuff   cabbages   phew
a cracked toilet bowl
wornout shoes some bulging where bunions have been
boxes of not-used rubber frenchies she knows what
they're

for Eva told her (why thrown out? holes in the rubber
is
why; that'd fool somebody ha ha)
a pile of clothes and old newspapers, BURNING
and stench sour sicklysweet rotten many smells
STINKS
and a ZILLION crawling flies

A shadow. Somebody here. Morag whirls. He laughs
(meanly?) showing teeth. He is close enough so she can smell
the sweat and woodsmoke on him. The only good smells here.
But she is scared. In his hands, an iron crowbar, bent, and a
pair of pliers. Skinner Tonnerre.

"Hey, whatsamatter, kid?" he says. "You think I'm
gonna –"

"Shut up," Morag says. "What're *you* doing here?"

"Whatcha doin' here yerself?"

"None of your business."

"Seein' the place where yer ol' man works, eh?"

He says *da* instead of *the*. He talks funny, kind of. He
always has. Why? Then Morag feels really mad, thinking of
what he has just said.

"Christie's not my old man! My dad is dead."

"Sure, I know. So *he's* yer ol' man now, ain't he? What the
diff?"

"Plenty. Plenty difference. So there."

Skinner laughs. Hoarse. Like a crow's voice.

"Okay, okay. *Tabernac!* What's eatin' you?"

"My family is named Gunn, see? And you better not
forget it."

Skinner's eyes grow narrow. Cruel. Mean.

"That so? You t'ink that means yer somebody? You're a little half-cunt, dry one at that I betcha."

"Listen here," Morag spits, "my family's been around here for longer than anybody in this whole goddamn town, see?"

"Not longer than mine," Skinner says, grinning.

"Oh yeh? Well, I'm related to Piper Gunn, *so there.*"

"Who in hell's he?"

"He –" She is afraid to speak it, now, in case Christie has got it wrong after all, but she can't quit. "He came from Scotland, and he led his people onto the ships when they were living on the rocks there in the Old Country and poor because they didn't have their farms because the Bitch-Duchess took them, and all, and they were scared, leaving there, but then Piper Gunn played the pipes and put the heart back into them."

Skinner gapes at her. Then grins again.

"Where'd you get that crap, eh?"

"It's true. It's true!"

He looks at her. Then he sits down on an empty tar barrel, not worrying about getting tar on his jeans. He stretches out his long legs and gets out a packet of cigarettes.

"Want one?"

She shakes her head and he laughs. She would like to snatch the cigarette now and light it, but is too proud.

"You ever seen my place, Morag?"

"Yeh. Sometimes. Passing by."

The Tonnerre place, right beside the Wachakwa River down there, is a square cabin made out of poplar poles chinked with mud. Also some other shanties, sheds and lean-tos, tacked onto the cabin and made out of old boards and pieces of flattened tin cans and tarpaper. Lots of old car parts and chicken wire and wornout car tires lying around, stuff like that.

Morag guesses that is why Skinner is here. Looking. Collecting.

"My grandad," Skinner says, "he built the first of our place, and that was one hell of a long time ago, I'm tellin' you. He come back from The Troubles."

"What's that?"

"Out west, there. *You* wouldn't know. You don' know nothin'. My grandad was lucky he never got killed, there. Lucky they never shot his balls off, my dad says. But they couldn't, because he was a better shot than them soldiers. I can shoot pretty good, too. I got his name, see? That means I got –"

He stops. Suddenly. Shuts up. Looks away.

"You mean his name was Skinner?" Morag asks.

"Don't be dumb. Jules. His name was Jules. Skinner ain't my real name."

"Why'd they call you it, then?"

"Some say it's 'cause I useda be so damn skinny. Some say it's 'cause I am real good at skinning any damn t'ing, rabbit, muskrat, even deer. Want me to catch a gopher and show you?"

Morag shudders. No – please. Not a gopher. He will do it and she will throw up. But he only laughs.

"Scared, eh, Morag?"

"Tell me about your grandad. Aw, come on."

He jumps to his feet and leaps over the tar barrel.

"Shit, I can't remember. It's all crap. Anyhows, I wouldn' tell *you*."

"Why not? Why not?"

"It ain't none of yer business. I tell you one t'ing, though. Long time before my grandad, there's one Tonnerre they call Chevalier, and no man can ride like him and he is one helluva shot. My grandad, he tol' my dad about that guy, there."

"What means *Chevalier*?"

"Rider. It means Rider. Lazarus, he says so. Ah, what's it to *you*?"

Skinner begins to walk away, singing "The Old Strawberry Roan," really really loud and sort of through his nose as well as his throat, like the cowboys singing on the radio.

Rattle-rattle-crunk-crash-gronk. Slow horse steps. Grinding wheels, Christie and his wagon. Morag jumps up and heads for the chokeberry bushes, but he has seen her.

"Jesus in sweet paradise, Morag, girl, what in the christly hell are you doing here? And who the fuck's *that*? Oh – hello, Skinner. Found anything today?"

Skinner scowls but does not reply. The crowbar and pliers still lie beside the tar barrel. The air reeks of smoke and rot. The sweat is snaking down Morag's back and between her legs.

Christie's blue workshirt is rolled up at the sleeves, and the sweat trickles through the sandy hairs on his arms. He starts to unload the wagon, swallowing his spit with the effort of the work, his Adam's apple yo-yoing in his throat. He is shovelling off a whole pile of eggshells, vegetable peelings, orange rinds, bones with shreds of cooked meat still on them. Skinner and Morag stand silent, watching.

"Did I ever tell you," Christie says, "how to tell the garbage, Morag, like telling fortunes?"

"*What?*"

Skinner snorts with laughter. Morag hates Christie. Maybe he will fall down, right now, this second, with a *heart attack*. He doesn't. He is chortling, enjoying himself. He likes the sound of his own voice. With him, it's either yak-yak-yakkity-yak or dead silence. No silence now. No such luck. Would it be worse if someone like Jamie Halpern or Stacey Cameron were here, listening? Yes. Let us be grateful for small mercies, Prin always says.

"You know how some have the gift of the second sight?" Christie goes on. "Well, it's the gift of the garbage-telling which I have myself, now. Watch this."

Christie shovels out the stuff onto a heap on the dump. Bends down to throw some of the bones with his hands.

Morag cannot move. She is held there, not wanting to be there but wanting to listen all the same. Skinner isn't grinning. He is just watching. Watching Christie. And listening.

Christie speaks. Like a spiel. Only different.

"Now you see these bones here, and you know what they mean? They mean Simon Pearl the lawyer's got the money for steak. Yep, not so often, maybe, but one day a week. So although he's letting on he's as hard up as the next – he ain't, no he ain't, though it's troubling to him, too. By their christly bloody garbage shall ye know them in their glory, is what I'm saying to you, every saintly mother's son. And these chicken bones right here, now, they'll be birds which have been given to Doc MacLeod for services he's rendered to some farmer who couldn't pay a bill if his life depended on it so he takes it out in poultry, well it's better than baloney which is what a jesus lot of us gets served up on the table. And the huge amount of apple peels from the Reverend George McKee, now, means he gets a crate of apples from his Okanagan sister so they eat a lot of applesauce each summer at the manse, there, but they don't put in a garden or they'd use the peels for compost, so the preacher really means it when he says the Lord provides. Now the paint tins from the Connors' means the old man's on the rampage and he's painting like a devil all the kitchen chairs and suchlike, showing all of them around him that they're lazy worthless sinners, but he's painting out his anger, for he thinks this life is shit."

Finish.

"Climb on," Christie says. "I'm heading back."

Morag doesn't want to. She would rather walk. But can't say so in front of Skinner. Christie offers Skinner a home-rolled cigarette, and Skinner takes it. Without saying thanks. Christie doesn't notice. He wouldn't.

"You know," Christie says, as they go along past the cemetery, "I once saw a terrible thing. It was the worst thing I ever did see in this country. I am not counting the time in France in the War, do you see, for that was worse. Now, then, what is strange is that some people think I don't see what goes into the bins outside their back gates. They put it in and that's the end of it to them. But I take it out, do you see?"

After the garbage-telling, this. Why can't he shut up? Why can't he just shut up? Crazy Christie. But he can't shut up. He can't, at times, and she knows it. She knows it, all right. What *was* it, that time, here? She won't ask. Not her.

"What *was* it, Christie?" she asks, not wanting to know at all, no not at all.

It wasn't terrible at all. It wouldn't be terrible at all. It would just be Christie, like he sometimes is.

"It was wrapped in a lot of newspapers," Christie says.

He stops and turns to look at both Morag and Skinner, Morag is sitting beside him on the wagon seat. Not saying a word. Skinner is sitting in the back part of the wagon, where all the awful stuff has been, just sitting there as though it didn't matter to him what had been there. And looking at Christie. Listening. Not letting on.

"Well," Christie says, "the Lord only knows I would be better off keeping my trap shut. It was a newborn baby. Wrapped in newspapers, but it fell out. Dead, of course. Hadn't gone its full term. It was that small, like a skinned rabbit."

"What'd you do with it?" Skinner.

"Buried her. It was a girl."

"*Where?*" Morag cries, cries. "Buried her *where?*"

"In the Nuisance Grounds," Christie says, spitting into the dusty road. "That's what it was, wasn't it, a nuisance? Well, the hell with their consecrated ground."

Morag sits quiet. Thinking of what his hands have touched. She won't think of it. Once she used to take Christie's hand, crossing the street. She's too big for that now, but even if she weren't, she wouldn't. Dead. Dead when born? Or what? What is *dead*, really? Do you know when you are?

"Didn't you ever *say*, Christie? I mean – I mean –"

"Why? What good would that've done? I knew where it had come from. The girl, the one whose it was, she'd had enough hard talk, I wouldn't doubt, from her people. She's married now. Happily married. They say."

"*Who?*"

"None of your business, girl."

Memorybank Movie: How Sweet the Name of Jesus Sounds
Morag loves Jesus. And how. He is friendly and not stuck-up, is why. She does not love God. God is the one who decides which people have got to die, and when. Mrs. McKee in Sunday school says God is LOVE, but this is baloney. He is mean and gets mad at people for no reason at all, and Morag wouldn't trust him as far as she can spit. Also, at the same time, she is scared of God. You pray at nights, and say "Dear God –", like a letter but slipping in the Dear bit for other reasons as well. Does He really know what everybody is thinking? If so, it sure isn't fair and is also very spooky.

Jesus is another matter. Whatever anybody says of it, it was really God who decided Jesus had to die like that. Who put it into the head of the soldier, then, to pierce His side?

(*Pierce?* The blood all over the place, like shot gophers and) Who indeed? Three guesses. Jesus had a rough time. But when alive, He was okay to everybody, even sinners and hardup people and like that.

Christie doesn't care whether Morag goes to Sunday school or not. He wouldn't. He never goes to church himself. Although a believer. But not liking the Reverend McKee. Prin goes to church. She wears her coat, whatever the weather, even in summer, because it covers her fat up. She says the singing does her good. Morag goes into the basement, where the Sunday school is held, while Prin goes upstairs to the church service.

Winter, and Morag stamps the snow off her galoshes at the United Church door. She pulls her scarf down from around her nose and mouth, and peels off her mitts, covered with tiny hard red bubbles, wool and ice. Colder than a shit-house in hell. Christie's saying. Mrs. McKee, who takes Morag's Sunday school class, would not think that was funny. Still, Mrs. McKee doesn't bawl people out, nor look at their clothes. Mrs. McKee's clothes are none too hot, if it comes to that, old tweed skirts and kind of shrunken twin-sweater sets. Does Mrs. McKee like being the minister's wife? Morag would hate it. Mrs. McKee, though tired-looking, doesn't seem to mind. Should Morag show Mrs. McKee the poem she's brought to show her? Would Mrs. McKee laugh? No. Mrs. McKee isn't a laugher. Maybe.

In the basement, the chairs are all set out in neat rows. The same old coloured paper pictures on the walls – they never change them. Morag doesn't mind. She likes the same ones being there all the time. *The Mothers of Salem Bringing Their Children to Jesus* – a whole lot of ladies dressed in white sheets, with little kids scampering around, and Jesus (also in a white sheet and with that lovely-looking beard) lifting one hand as he suffers them (*suffers?*) to come unto Him. *The Good Samaritan* – an old guy in a blue and yellow striped dressing gown (sort of), leading a donkey on which is lying, draped across it, a very skinny guy who has closed eyes and terrible wounds *pouring with blood. The Loaves and the Fishes* – a huge big mob of people, men with different coloured beards black or blond, women carrying babies, lots of kids running around all over the place, and the Apostles looking really worried, but Jesus looking not worried at all, not by a long shot. He is standing there cool as a cucumber and raising one hand in the magic way and at his feet are two baskets, one with a few hunks of bread and the other with a few tiny fishes, and in a moment there will be a zillion loaves and a whole seaful of fishes because He can do anything.

Mrs. McKee is talking to the Sunday school principal, at the front of the room. Morag slides in the door and waits. Mrs. McKee turns. Smiles.

"You're early this morning, Morag."

Morag nods.

"Can you c'mere for a second, Mrs. McKee? Please."

"What is it?" Mrs. McKee walks to where Morag is standing.

Morag hands the piece of scribbler paper to her. The poem is copied very neatly in best writing.

The Wise Men.
by Morag Gunn.

VERSE ONE
Despite the cold and wintry blast,
To Bethlehem they came at last.

And there amid the hay and straw,
The baby Jesus was what they saw.

"Why, this is just fine, Morag. I never knew you wrote poetry."
Surprised.

"Sure. I write lots. I've got more at home. And stories.
Would you –"

"The only thing," Mrs. McKee says, "is that it was a Far
Eastern desert country, dear, so they wouldn't have a wintry
blast, would they?"

Morag's face – flames of shame. She snatches the paper
back.

"Wait – I'll fix it."

She goes into the classroom where the tables and chairs
are set out for each class. Sits down. Finds a pencil.

Despite the desert sun's cruel ray
To Bethlehem they came that day.

No good. It was night.

Despite the heat of the desert (what?)
To Bethlehem they came that night.

Bright? White? Light? Might? Bite? Of course. Bright
and light. Never mind the weather.

Guided by the Star's bright light
To Bethlehem they came that night.

Good. Fine. Much better. Morag goes out and hands the
new version to Mrs. McKee. Who looks at it. One quick glance.

"Much better, dear. Now we'd better get ready for the service. Sit with your class, dear."

The others have all come in while Morag was busy. She has not noticed them until this very instant.

"Whatcha' doing, Morag? Writing out *I must not tell a lie* four hundred times for the old bag?" Jamie Halpern, his face giggling behind his glasses.

Morag says nothing. Crumples the page and stuffs it in her pocket.

The singing. Carols. Morag sings loudly, loving the carols.

Good Christian men rejoy-oy-oyce
With heart and soul and voy-oy-oyce —

When they get to the line *Ox and ass before Him bow*, Ross McVitie puts a hand to his bum. Morag glares at him. Ignorant slob.

In class, Mrs. McKee tells them that one member of their class will be chosen to sing A SOLO at the grown-ups' Christmas Eve service, and all of them will be in the choir. They will have to try out, those who want to be considered for the solo. They gather around the piano, the five who want to try, Morag among them. She has a good voice. Clear and can carry a tune perfectly. Also, a carrying voice. Christie says she would've made a good hog-caller, but he is just ignorant. They each sing a verse of "Once in Royal David's."

"I'll let you know next week," Mrs. McKee says, "when I've considered thoroughly."

Morag knows it will be her. Or maybe it will, anyhow. At least, there's a chance. Maybe.

"I want to read you a poem today, children," Mrs. McKee says, when they are all around the table again.

Morag's heart quits beating. Hers? She will faint. A talented poem written by one of our members, class. The others will stare. Who'd have thought it? Old Morag. Gee.

"It is by the English poet, Hilaire Belloc," Mrs. McKee's gooey voice says, and she opens a book.

> When Jesus Christ was four years old,
> The angels brought him toys of gold,
> Which no man ever had bought or sold.
> And yet with these He would not play,
> He made Him small fowl out of clay,
> And blessed them till they flew away. . . .

There is more, and some words in Latin, which Mrs. McKee explains, but Morag isn't listening now. At home, Morag takes off her galoshes and coat. Goes to the stove.

"What's that you're burning, Morag?" Prin asks, alarmed.

"Nothing. Just nothing."

Morag goes to her room. Sits thinking. Wants to cry, but will not, must not. *Blessed them till they flew away.* Oh. How could anybody write anything that good?

She has shown "The Wise Men" to Mrs. McKee, and there is no way she can unshow it.

Next Sunday, the verdict. Vanessa MacLeod will sing the solo.

Vanessa MacLeod! A crow with a sore throat could sing better than what *she* could. An old bullfrog honk-honking out there in the Wachakwa could sing better, even. It isn't fair.

"It's not fair, Christie," Morag rages, at home.

Christie cleans his horrible teeth with a straw out of the broom, a wonder his gums don't rot, dirty old broom like that.

"If you expect things to be fair, you'll be waiting until hell freezes over. Anyways, has she got such a lousy voice, then?"

"Well. I guess not. But mine's just as good."

Would Mrs. McKee think Morag would *look* okay, standing up there alone in the choir loft? Would Mrs. McKee be that way? Sure. You bet. Any of them would. Wouldn't they?

On the night, Morag decides to go and be in the choir after all. Vanessa, all gotten up in a pleated tartan skirt with straps over the shoulders and a white blouse with a frill at the front, rises to sing. Her hands, Morag sees, are trembling. She's nervous. Ha ha. Morag hopes that something really awful will happen to Vanessa. But it doesn't. She sings a crappy song but she never misses a note.

> Christ was once a little baby
> Jus' like you an' me

Boy, whoever wrote that song was sure plenty dumb. Serve Vanessa right, having to sing a dumb song like that.

It is a month later. School. Roll call. Vanessa MacLeod? Absent. Morag listens to the recess-time whispers.

"Her dad's died."

At home, Christie blowing his nose on his fingers, stepping outside to throw the snot on the snow already dirtied with yellow dog-piss, comes back into the kitchen and says it.

"Well, then, Doc MacLeod's gone to his ancestors. Pneumonia. He was quite a man, there. You could of had many a worse."

Morag sits at the table in the warm stove-crackling kitchen. But has to go upstairs to the freezing bedroom.

She never meant   never meant   never meant   and a
long time ago   what was it   when   and Dr. MacLeod was
there and

God knows what you are thinking. *He* knows, all right
all right. But is mean. Doesn't care. Or understand.

Vanessa returns to school. Morag neither looks at her nor
speaks to her. Want to but cannot. Vanessa does not notice.
She has never spoken to Morag much, anyway. Vanessa does
not talk much to anyone, now, for quite a while. Morag
watches. From a long way off.

Memorybank Movie: Christie and Red Biddy
and Piper Gunn and Clowny MacPherson

Christie has a jug of red biddy. Prin has waddled off to bed,
not approving. Morag is doing her homework. The ceiling
bulb isn't very bright and she has to bend close over the geography book to read the print which flickers in front of her eyes.
Christie, across the table, brings down one fist – *clump*. Taking
care with the other hand to hold onto the grey bottle-jug
which once long ago used to hold vinegar.

"Now, then, girl, would you like me to tell you about
what happened to Piper Gunn and them, when that ship
landed up north there?"

Morag closes the geography. Grinning.

"Sure, Christie."

"Well, now, then, I read it all in a book somewheres, so
help me, and it is all there in the books, but you don't want to
believe everything them books say, for the good christ's sake.
We believe what we know."

What's he talking about? But she likes this story. He
pours another glassful.

CHRISTIE'S TALE OF PIPER GUNN AND THE LONG MARCH

Now that bloody ship, there, who would know what its name was, but with all of them from Sutherland on board, and struck with the sickness and the fever and the devil's plague, well, then, that ship with the children dying of the fever, it crossed the ocean, do you see, and it came to the new land, which was HERE, only very far north. But what happened? What almighty catastrophe struck that ship? Well, the first catastrophe was that ship had a bloody idiot as captain, then. And he landed the christly vessel, if you'll believe it, away up north there, *at the wrong place*. The wrong place. Can you feature it? Them people, see, Piper Gunn and his woman Morag and all them, were supposed to be landed at the one place, up there by Hudson Bay (that's the water, the sea, like, not the store). But the silly bugger landed his ship at another place. Oh yes. The bloody captain didn't give a hoot. Get landed and well rid of them – that was his thought. So he landed all of them at the wrong place, now, the name escapes me at this moment, but it was on the Hudson Bay, up there. Cold as all the shithouses of hell.

Well, then, there they were. So Piper Gunn, he takes up his morsels of belongs, his kettle and his plaid and his axe, and he says to his woman Morag, *Here we are and by the holy Jesus here we will remain.* And then didn't his woman strap onto her back the few blankets and suchlike they had, and her thick with their unborn firstborn, and follow. But one thing was missing.

Pipes. The pipes.

If we must live here in this almighty godforsaken land, dreadful with all manner of beasts and ice and the rocks harsher than them we left, says Gunn's woman, *at least let's be piped onto it.*

So Piper Gunn, he got out his bagpipes and he piped the people onto the new land, that terrible bad land, frozen as it sure as hell was, and they built their mud shacks to the music that man played.

Now they lived there and they suffered and then they suffered more, through the long days and longer nights, and it seemed there was no end to their suffering. But they didn't give in. They hunted for meat, to live.

(What did they hunt, Christie?)

Oh, polar bears that looked like great moving snowbanks with jaws and claws, then, and great wild foxes with burning eyes in them, and

(Did they eat *foxes*, Christie?)

Well, maybe not the foxes. They would use *them* for the fur, see? But they ate all manner of strange things, and it was a time of misery, but they stayed because they had the heart in them. And in the spring they walked. Yes, they *walked* to the place where the supplies would be. It was a long long long way. It could've been maybe a thousand or so miles, then.

(They walked? A *thousand* miles? They couldn't, Christie.)

Well, it might not have been quite the thousand, but it was a christly long way. And through the snow and muck and that. And who led them? I ask you, who led them? Who led the men and women and the children on that march? Piper Gunn. Himself. He led them with his pipes blaring, there. He was a man six feet nine inches tall, a mighty man of God. And he played the pipes like an angel right out of heaven and then like a devil right out of hell, and he kept the courage of the people beating like drums, or like the wings of brave wild birds caught in a blizzard, for he had the faith of the saints and the heart of a child and the gall of a thousand and the strength of conviction.

Well, then, I guess they must've walked through all of them frozen lands, and through the muskeg there and through the muck and mud of the melting snows, and through the hard snow itself although it was spring. And it was that hard, walking, even Piper Gunn himself began to have his doubts, as who would blame him? And he says to his woman Morag, *What in the fiery hell are we doing in this terrible place?* So Morag says to him, for she had the wisdom and the good eye and the warmth of a home and the determination of quietness, and she says, *We are going into the new country and your child is going along with us, so play on.* And he did that. Yes, he did that.

So then, they got to the place where all the supplies was. And they got boats, big flat-bottomed boats, more like scows or rafts or like that, and they went down all the way to Red River, which is to say they came to this part of the country, not so very far from where we are at this very instant. And there they stayed.

(What happened then, Christie?)

Och aye, it was hard. It was so hard you could barely feature it. Locusts. Hailstorms. Floods. Blizzards. Indians. Halfbreeds. Hot as the pit of hell in the summer, and the mosquitoes as big as sparrows. Winters so cold it would freeze the breath in your throat and turn your blood to red ice. Weather for giants, in them days. Not that it's that much better now, I'd say.

(Did they fight the halfbreeds and Indians, Christie?)

Did they ever. Slew them in their dozens, girl. In their scores.

(Were they bad, the breeds and them?)

What?

*

The story is over. Christie's blue watery eyes look at her, or try to.

"Bad?" He repeats the word as though he is trying to think what it means.

"No," he says at last. "They weren't bad. They were – just there."

He motions with one hand, tired, for her to go to her room. And she sees him again the way he really looks, the way she sometimes forgets when he is talking. Why can't he look different? But she doesn't say. He is yawning – *gawp* – and nearly asleep across the table, spraddled out with his head going down on his arms.

Morag, upstairs. Writing in her scribbler. This one is nearly full, and what it is full of is a long story about how Piper Gunn's woman, once the child was born, at the Red River, went out into the forest and built a chariot for them all, for Piper Gunn and herself and their girlchild, so they could easily move around in that country there. She cut down the trees and she carved out the chariot. It was not a wagon. It was much fancier, and it had:

> four giant wheels
> a big high back with a seat
> the seat covered in green moss
>   (she said velvet at first but where would they get it?)
> the front shaped like a ship and a bird
> birchbark scrolls around the sides
> carvings of deer and foxes and bears
> carvings of meadowlarks
> carvings of tall grasses
> carvings of spruce trees and spruce cones

polished stones for jewels, on the sides and axles
a brass hook for Piper Gunn's pipes

Morag is working on another story as well. In another scribbler. She does not know where it came from. It comes into your head, and when you write it down, it surprises you, because you never knew what was going to happen until you put it down.

She writes in bed, with the eiderdown around her, up to her neck nearly.

The new story is about a guy who was one of Piper Gunn's men. A little scrawny guy. Actually, though, he was very tough. His name was – no, not Cluny, something like that. Macphersons are nicknamed Cluny a lot of the time – why? His name was Clowny Macpherson, because people always laughed at him on account of he looked silly. But Piper Gunn, he knew one thing about Clowny, for sure, and that was he was a great woodcutter and

More tomorrow.

Memorybank Movie: Christie's Presence and Presents
Christie is looking for misplaced longjohns in the kitchen dresser. He and Prin do not have a dresser in their bedroom. For some unknown reason, there is a large phonograph there instead, the kind you wind up, and it has a pile of old records in the cabinet, but is never played.

"Damn things must be lost, stolen or strayed," Christie mutters. "Where the hell'd you put 'em, woman?"

Prin becomes flustered and cannot remember.

"I seem to mind I put 'em in the top drawer. Or was it –"

"Never mind, never mind!" Christie shouts. "I could find something easier at the Nuisance Grounds than here.

You wouldn't know neatness if it was your middle name."

"You're a fine one to talk," Prin whines, her breath coming difficult, in gasps.

Christie stops flinging clothes around and looks at her. His face is strange.

"Ah, Lord, don't I know it. You'd have done better to marry anybody else, Prin. That is the declared truth."

"What chance did I have?" Prin says, very low, but he can hear.

This is mean, Morag considers. She changes in her head, for the moment, to Christie's side. Christie's face frowns.

"Goddammit, you make your own chances in this world!" he roars. "Or else you don't make them. Like me. You have to work bloody hard at it, believe me, to be such a bloody flop as I stand here before you. In my one suit of underwear."

His voice drops then.

"Although that's not the truth of it, neither. It's all true and not true. Isn't that a bugger, now?"

"I don't understand you, Christie Logan," Prin says. "I never have done."

"You're not the only one. I don't understand myself. *Oh what a piece of work is man.* Who said that? Some brain."

He goes on riffling through the drawer, humming to himself.

"Oh what a piece of work is man oh what a bloody awful piece of work is man   enough to scare the pants off you when you come to think of it   the opposite is also true   hm   hm."

He stops.

"Here, what's this?" he says suddenly.

A book. He looks through it, then brings it over to Morag. A purple cover, faded to a sickly mauve at the edges, and dim gold letters.

The 60th Canadian Field Artillery
Battery Book

"It's the regiment book from the War," Christie says. "It's the regiment I and your dad was in from 1916 until we got back in 1919."

He opens it.

CONTENTS

Very blurred photographs here and there throughout the book.

Vis-en-Artois (brick buildings all fallen down into a heap)

Battery Entering Valenciennes (a street, building in pieces, men running)

Protection of Horses (deep ditch; two men and some horses standing in mud)

The Battery (lots of rows, men but looking more like High School boys)

"Christie! Is my father in that picture?"

"Yep. We're all there."

"Which one is he? Which *one*?"

Christie and Morag both peer at the picture. Row after row, faraway faces. They are very very small in the photo. And they all look the same, because no face is clear.

"Lemme see," Christie says. "This one? No. Maybe not. Maybe this one? Which is myself? Lord, Morag, I can't even find my own self."

Morag looks at the long-ago picture. One of these men is Colin Gunn, her father. But it could be any one of them. She says nothing.

"Your dad saved my life that one time, then," Christie says.

"He did? When? How?"

"Bourlon Wood."

He looks up. They read what the book says.

On the night of September 26th the guns were moved into position. Zero hour was 5 A.M. on the 27th September, and, promptly to the second, the guns opened fire, continuing in action until 12:10 P.M.

Notwithstanding the secrecy with which the operations had been performed by the Battery, their position must have been spotted, for no sooner had the barrage started than the enemy shelled the guns with whiz-bangs; if it had not been for the fact that the guns were below the level of the ground, the casualties might have been heavy. As it was, the men escaped by a very narrow margin. Time and again a perfect ring of ground bursts encircled the guns, within a very few yards radius, and as the smoke slowly rose and thinned out, it was with a hopeless sort of hope that their comrades glanced around to assure themselves of the safety of the various crews. This phase of the attack included the capture of Bourlon Wood.

"Oh Jesus," Christie says, "don't they make it sound like a Sunday school picnic?"

"What happened, Christie?"

Christie sits down and rolls a cigarette.

CHRISTIE'S TALE OF THE BATTLE OF BOURLON WOOD

Well, d'you see, it was like the book says, but it wasn't like that, also. That is the strangeness.

Holy God, with all of them guns pounding away that morning, the sky was like fire, *Like* fire, did I say? It *was* fire. We was firing from the trenches. Them trenches, now. You never heard of "trench foot"? The feet would rot. They'd rot, I tell you, because they'd be wet with the mud and slime and shit and horsepiss all the time. You'd be trying to line up them devils of guns, the eighteen-pounders, and you'd be up to your bloody navel in muck, nearly.

It was terrible for the horses. I've seen horses sinking in mud, where there was a crater, do you see, a shell crater and it would be filled with that damned mire. Once I seen a horse going under, and its mouth foaming with the fear, and its eyes wild as a lunatic's eyes, and its voice screaming. Not neighing or like that. Screaming. Drowning in mud. Jesus, it's the mud you recall more than anything, nearly.

(What happened that day, Christie? Go on.)

Your dad and me was both gunners. He was my mate, do you see. We worked the big gun together.

(Gunner Gunn. That's funny, eh?)

Not so funny you'd hardly have noticed it at the time. I was older than Colin, and not so quick, I would say. There we are, getting ready to fire old Brimstone, and a shell explodes so christly close to me I think I'm a goner. The noise. Jesus. And then the air all around me is filled with

(With what, Christie? Why are you stopping?)

Well, then, with bleeding bits of a man. Blown to smithereens. A leg. A hand. Guts, which was that red and wet you would not credit it at all.

(Oh.)

I thought – God, it's Colin. Then the noise or some damn thing got me. I started to shake and I couldn't move my feet from the spot I was standing on. Then – I don't remember. I must've passed out. When I came to, it was away past midnight and it was that quiet you could hear the heart beating in you. The stars was out, and I recall they scared me at first. I thought they'd be more shells, you see. But they didn't move or come closer. Then your dad gave me some water. He must've dragged me into the dugouts where we bunked, out of the fire. The water spilled. A goddamn waste. I couldn't drink it. I was still shaking like a fool.

(What then, Christie?)

But the story is over. Christie gets up. He is, Morag sees, shaking.

"I wish I had not found that christly book at all," he says. And goes to bed.

"Can I have the book, Prin?" Morag says. "If he doesn't want it, then can I have it?"

"Sh," Prin whispers. "I don't think he would want to part with it. Don't ask him, will you, now?"

Christie has heard, though. He doesn't come back into the kitchen that night, but the next morning he opens his hands to Morag.

"Not the book," he says. "And I don't have anything that was your father's. But you can have this if you want it."

It is a knife. About eight inches long including the handle, which is dark-brown and leathery. The blade is wide and comes to a very sharp point at the end. A hunting knife. Morag takes it. Examines it. On the handle, burned into it, it seems is a sign: ◄

"What's that sign, Christie?"

"I dunno. A knife's not much of a thing to give a girl, I guess. I found it in the same drawer as the book. Haven't seen it for years. Some young twerp of a kid offered to trade me it for a package of cigarettes, so I done it. It's never been any good to me, though. He talked me into it. Great talker, he was, as a boy, though not as a man. Killed a year or so ago, when his truck smacked into an oncoming freight, reckless young devil, poor sod, drunk at the time no doubt. Well, I guess it's not much of a Christmas present."

"If you hadn't had that bottle of hooch, you could of bought candies," Prin says.

"Jesus, woman, don't you think I know it?"

"I like this," Morag says. "I like it fine, Christie. Honest."

Christie has never given her a present before, except sometimes candies. But never a lasting present. Ashamed of this one, and of herself, she shoves it away to the back of her dresser drawer.

FOUR

The starlings and grackles began their dawn perform-
ance, a chorus of iron-throated squawks accompanied
by a heavy-footed ballet on the roof. Morag sighed.
Birds should be light in the step. These sounded like carthorses,
tramp tramp tramp. Birds transformed into tiny moose for an
hour at sunup. Never any swallows walking on the roof, you
could be certain. They would no doubt at least have pranced
prettily, but sensibly preferred to fly.

If the farmhouse had had upstairs ceilings, the birdfeet
would not be quite so thundering. But there was only the
rafters. Morag liked it this way because it showed the way
the house had been built, nearly a hundred years ago by a home-
steader called Cooper. Whose sons and grandsons had farmed
the beautifully treed but rocky land until finally giving up,
selling out and moving to some town or other. The house was
log, still as sound as the year it was built. The door frames and
window sills were handhewn timber, although the floorboards
and doors had come from a sawmill. The rooms were small.
Morag had obtained the furniture – old-fashioned straight-
backed chair, pine dressers, the long table in the kitchen – at

secondhand furniture stores in McConnell's Landing. The oldness of the farmhouse, the roughness, were qualities Morag would have loathed as a kid. Now she valued them.

Morag gave up the battle to block her ears against the birds, and got up. The kitchen was cool and would remain so. The thick walls kept out the heat. She put her head outside the door. The river was still. No breeze. The trees across the river were reflected in the water so sharply you could imagine it was another world there, a treeworld in the water, willows and oak and maples, all growing there, climbed upon by river-children, and slithered finnily through by muskie and yellow perch. The day, she predicted, was going to be a scorcher.

Royland would be here in about an hour. Today was the day.

You wondered about people like the Cooper family, all those years ago. Trekking in here to take up their homestead. No roads. Bush. Hacking their way. Wagons and horses? Probably coming much of the way by river. Barges teetering and overloaded. Then the people clearing the first growth of timber. Shifting the rocks from fields, making stone walls to outline the land to be cultivated. The sheer unthinkable back-and-heart-breaking slog. Women working like horses. Also, probably pregnant most of the time. Baking bread in brick ovens, with a loaf in their own ovens. Looking after broods of chickens and kids. Terrible. Appalling.

Healthy life, though. No one died of lung cancer. Strong and fit, they were, tanned and competent. Pioneers oh pioneers.

But what about a burst appendix? Desperately ill kids? Fever? Women having breech births or other disorders of childbearing? The tiny cemetery on the hill contained, among other stones, the one to Simon Cooper's first wife.

In Memory of Sarah Cooper
Who Died in Childbirth
June 20, 1880, Age 24.

She Rests In The Lord.

Probably glad to rest anywhere, poor lady, even In The Lord. How many women went mad? Loneliness, isolation, strain, despair, overwork, fear. Out there, the bush. In here, a silent worried work-sodden man, squalling brats, an open fireplace, and would the shack catch fire this week or next? In winter, snow up to your thighs. Outdoor privy. People flopping through drifts to the barn to milk the cow. What fun. Healthy life indeed. A wonder they weren't all raving lunatics. Probably many were. It's the full of the moon, George – Mrs. Cooper always howls like this at such a time – nothing to worry about – she'll be right as rain come the morning – c'mon there, Sarah, quit crouching in the corner and stop baring your fangs like that – George and me's hungry and would appreciate a spot of grub. *Onward, Christian Soldiers. Thy Way Not Mine O Lord However Dark It Be.*

The fact remained that they *had* hacked out a living here. They had survived. Like so-called Piper Gunn and the Sutherlanders further west. Was it better or worse now? Both. Both. At least *their* children did not wander to God knows where. Unknown destinies, far and probably lethal places. If any *did*, though, there were no telephones and the mail services could hardly have been very snappy. Well, then, *they* did not have to wrench up their guts and hearts etcetera and set these carefully down on paper, in order to live. Clever of them, one might say. Anyway, some of them did. Including women.

Catharine Parr Trail, mid-1800s, botanist, drawing and naming wildflowers, writing a guide for settlers with one hand, whilst rearing a brace of young and working like a galley slave with the other.

From the Birch, A Thousand Useful Utensils Can Be Made.
A Few Hints On Gardening (including how to start an orchard, how to *start* it!)

How To Make:	Cheap Family Cake
	Hot Tea-Cakes
	Indian-Meal Yorkshire Pudding
	Maple Vinegar
	Potted Fish
	Potash Soap
	Rag Carpets
	Candles
	A Good Household Cheese
	Cures For Ague and Dysentery

And so on. It did not bear thinking about. Morag, running her log house with admirable efficiency and a little help from the electric fridge, kettle, toaster, stove, iron, baseboard heaters, furnace, lights, not to mention the local supermarket and Ron Jewitt's friendly neighbourhood taxi. Great God Almighty.

The song sparrow was tuning up in the small elm outside the window. Its song was unambiguous.

Pres-pres-pres-pres-Presbyterian!

Mrs. Eula McCann from several miles away had dropped in with welcome raisin buns when Morag and Pique originally moved in, and had asked Morag if she had heard the bird which said that word. Morag, until that moment, had only heard it as a pleasant trill. Since that day, however, its message came across loud and clear.

Catharine Parr Traill, one could be quite certain, would not have been found of an early morning sitting over a fourth cup of coffee, mulling, approaching the day in gingerly fashion, trying to size it up. No. No such sloth for Catharine P.T.

Scene at the Traill Homestead, Circa 1840
C.P.T. out of bed, fully awake, bare feet on the sliver-hazardous floorboards – no, take that one again. Feet on the homemade hooked rug. Breakfast cooked for the multitude. Out to feed the chickens, stopping briefly on the way back to pull fourteen armloads of weeds out of the vegetable garden and perhaps prune the odd apple tree in passing. The children's education hour, the umpteen little mites lisping enthusiastically over this enlightenment. Cleaning the house, baking two hundred loaves of delicious bread, preserving half a ton of plums, pears, cherries, etcetera. All before lunch.

Catharine Parr Trail, where are you now that we need you? Speak, oh lady of blessed memory.

Where the hell was Pique and why didn't she phone or write? If Pique were not carrying any form of identification (as was likely), how would anyone know who she was and be able to get in touch with Morag if anything happened? Should Morag try to trace her? Pique had been okay not too long ago. The phone message from Pique's father had established that. But where was she now and why didn't she simply *say?* Was this over-concern on Morag's part? No doubt. But still. How could you stop yourself from worrying? The kid was eighteen. Only. What had Catharine said, somewhere, about emergencies?

Morag loped over to the bookshelves which lined two walls of the seldom-used livingroom. Found the pertinent text.

In cases of emergency, it is folly to fold one's hands and sit down to bewail in abject terror. It is better to be up and doing.

(*The Canadian Settlers' Guide*, 1855)

Morag:	Thank you, Mrs. Traill.
Catharine Parr Traill:	That, my dear, was when we were at one time surrounded by forest fires which threatened the crops, fences, stock, stable, cabin, furniture and, of course, children. Your situation, if I may say so, can scarcely be termed comparable.
Morag:	Well uh no, I guess not. Hold on, though. *You* try having your only child disappear you know where, Mrs. Traill. Also, with no strong or even feeble shoulder upon which to lean, on occasion. Okay, don't say it, lady. You'd go out and plant turnips, so at least you wouldn't starve during the winter. You'd pick blueberries or something. Start a jam factory. Make pemmican out of the swayback which dropped dead of exhaustion on the Back Forty. Don't tell me. I know.

The knocking (only now noticed by Morag) at the kitchen door had ceased and Royland had stepped inside. She knew from his step, slow but not heavy, that it was him.

"First sign of going off your rocker, Morag, so they say."

Embarrassed, she returned the book to its place and went back to the kitchen.

"Don't you ever talk out loud to yourself, Royland?"

"Oh sure. It's when I start answering myself I get worried."

Ha ha. The ancient joke.

"I was not answering myself," Morag said. "I was holding a polite if somewhat controversial conversation with a lady of my acquaintance, who happens not to inhabit this vale of tears any more."

"You and Joan of Arc, the pair of you," Royland said, cough-laughing into the grey shagginess of his chin foliage.

"The lady of *her* acquaintance held – um – a slightly more distinguished position than this lady of mine. Want some coffee?"

"Don't mind if I do. You working yet, Morag?"

He got the word right now. Once he used to ask her if she was doing any writing these days. Until he learned that the only meaning the word *work* had for her was writing, which was peculiar, considering that it was more of a free gift than work, when it was going well, and the only kind of work she enjoyed doing.

"I don't know. I mean, about the thing I seem to want to do, or have to. It seems like an awfully dubious idea, in a lot of ways, but I guess I'll have to go on with it. Maybe it's begun. I don't know very much about it yet."

"Heard from Pique?"

"No." Turning away so the old man would not see her request for reassurance.

"I thought not. You have got to quit fretting over that girl. As I keep saying."

Morag turned suddenly and faced him.

"Don't mistake me, Royland. I don't want her living here any more. She can't. She mustn't. She's got to be on her own. Anything else is no good for her and no good for me. It's just that I'd like to hear from time to time that she's okay, is all."

"You think she isn't?"

"Remember that time a year ago, when she left school and took off?"

"Yeh. She came back, though. And is now a whole year older."

"She was in a mental hospital in Toronto for a month. A bad trip, as they somewhat euphemistically say. She hasn't had a very easy life, Royland. I clobbered her with a hell of a situation to live in, although I never meant to. Okay, maybe everything else clobbered her, too, and I'm not God and I'm not responsible for everything. But I chose to have her, in the first place, and maybe I should've seen it would be too difficult for her. You don't think of that, at the time, or I didn't, anyway."

Pique, her long black hair spread over the hospital pillow, her face turned away from Morag, her voice low and fierce. *Can't you see I despise you? Can't you see I want you to go away? You aren't my mother. I haven't got a mother.* The nurse, candy-voiced, telling Morag it would be best for her to leave and in a week or so we would see, Morag, walking on streets, not knowing where, stumbling into people, seeing only small hard-bright replayed movies inside. Pique at five saying *Tell me the story about the robin in our own dogwood tree please Mum.* Pique on the first plane flight saying *Is it safe Mum?* and Morag saying *Yes*, hoping this was true. Pique in England saying *We're going home?* and not knowing where that place could be. Pique saying *Are we really going to live on a farm and can I have a dog?* Pique, when her father visited both those times, ten years apart, and then when he had to go away again, Pique saying nothing. Nothing. Pique's face turned away, her hair spread across the white freeze-drift of hospital linen, saying *I despise you.*

"You know something, Royland?" Morag said. "I guess I feel that sometimes she despises me. And there are moments when I can see her point, there."

"I knew about Pique in Toronto," Royland said. "She told me."

"She did?"

"Sure. She said she couldn't be certain she wouldn't do it again, but she hoped she wouldn't, on account of she wanted to get her head together – that was how she put it – by herself. Also, she doesn't despise you. She has mixed feelings, is all. Haven't you ever had?"

Christie. Prin. Brooke. Pique's father. Dan McRaith. Pique.

"Yes. Of course. Naturally."

"You should try to rest your soul," Royland said. "You ready to go now, Morag?"

A strong south wind had risen, and the river was darker now, the water undulating under the boat.

"What if it rains?" Morag asked.

"Makes no difference. Water's still there underground."

At the Smiths' dock, grey weathered timbers and drift-wood logs, built by A-Okay, Royland drew the boat in, tied it, and they walked up the slope to the house.

The Smiths' house was brick, dark red, with a gabled roof on which A-Okay had already restored the wooden lace, now painted white by Maudie, suffering vertigo on the ladder but never once saying *Die* or even *Down.* They had rented the farm, with an option to buy, always supposing A-Okay could whomp up the necessary money from the pop science articles he wrote. The rent was small, because the land was neglected and overgrown and the house, while pleasing on the outside, had been virtually only a shell. The floors were sound, but that was about all you could say for it. The rest was a shambles. But being restored.

"Hi," A-Okay said at the door. "Maudie's got the coffee on. We'll do it right after, if that's a-okay with you. Any special time of day for this, Royland?"

"Nope. I don't usually do it at night, is all."

"Why not? I mean, is there a —"

A-Okay, ex-science man, groping, wondering about all this procedure.

"Might trip over a tree root," Royland said.

A-Okay laughed, but self-consciously. Royland's cracker-barrel humour embarrassed him. He thought it had been pinched from B-grade movies, as perhaps it had. Royland sometimes took pleasure in his Old Man of the River persona, but was no hick in fact. He had begun life on a homestead — that was all Morag really knew. He knew cities; he knew lots of areas. Probably. But never talked of his past. Morag Gunn, inveterate winkler-out of people's life stories, had never winkled out Royland's. He knew a hell of a lot more about her than she did about him. He, obviously, preferred it this way. Perhaps she did, too.

"Did you read Alf's poems, Morag?" Maudie asked, coming out of the kitchen looking like a very fragile wood nymph, her long pale hair all around her, a wood nymph in dirty beige corduroy jeans and tomato-stained blouse, today. Maudie could not weigh more than a hundred pounds, at most, Morag estimated. That such apparent frailty could conceal such muscularity, physical and spiritual, was a marvel.

The poems.

"I read them, yes."

"And what did you think?"

"Let her get in the door, first, eh, Maudie?" A-Okay said with suppressed irritation, blushing.

"I thought the river ones were good," Morag said truthfully, "but I thought the land ones were kind of abstract. I thought maybe they might need more work, more specific detail. I know what you were aiming at – at least, I think I do, but they seemed too exclusively philosophical. A little more flesh and blood detail might get them across better. You didn't seem – well, to *know* enough about the land. Not that *I* know. I don't know all that much about poetry, either. I really don't like saying."

"Yeh. Well. Thanks." A-Okay's tall frame seemed sunken in despondency, and he blinked slightly, short-sightedly connecting with a footstool and knocking it over. "I guess I might do some more work on them."

Maudie looked dubious. His one-woman cheering section. Well, good for her. But all the same.

"As I've said before, Morag," Maudie said, "if Alf messes them around too much, where does that leave the spontaneity? Maybe they're more for real if he leaves them just as they are."

"Yeh. Maybe."

They went outside. Royland had a Y-shaped piece of willow, one hand on each branch of the fork. He held his hands clenched, palms upwards, clutching the greenwood tightly. The tail of the Y was held well up. They watched.

At the back of the house, Royland began walking slowly. Up and down the yard. Like the slow pace of a piper playing a pibroch. Only this was for a reverse purpose. Not the walk over the dead. The opposite.

Nothing happened.

"Does it ever – well, you know – not work, Royland?" A-Okay asked.

"Alf, sh!" Maudie hissed the sounds, as though A-Okay had interrupted during a symphony or a seance.

"Doesn't fail if the water's there, or at least not so far," Royland said. "You don't have to sh-sh. I don't need quiet."

But all the same, none of them talked after that. Tom stood with his hand in his father's hand. The whiz kid, now subdued.

Morag had once tried divining with the willow wand. Nothing at all had happened. Royland had said she didn't have the gift. She wasn't surprised. Her area was elsewhere. He was divining for water. What in hell was she divining for? You couldn't doubt the value of water.

"Hey – look!" Thomas.

The tip of the willow wand was moving. In Royland's bony grip, the wood was turning, moving downwards very slowly, very surely. Towards the earth.

Magic, four yards north of the Smiths' clothesline.

"How about that?" A-Okay said. "Well, I guess we'll see when the driller comes in, eh?"

Wanting faith, taking it on faith, but not yet convinced. Would the driller strike water?

Tom, encyclopaedic mind suddenly pierced by mysteries, could only stare.

"Will they find water there, Dad?"

A-Okay, naturally, unnaturally, could neither say Yes or No. He grinned, in embarrassment, hoping.

"Morag –" Maudie.

"Yes?"

"What if the driller doesn't –?"

Maudie, feeling intimations and premonitions of mortality. Morag wanted to put her arms around Tom's mother. But could not.

"I know."

Royland marked the spot by sticking the willow bough into it. The driller's truck clanked into the yard.

"'Lo, Bob." Royland. Casual.

"'Lo, Royland. This it?"

"Yep. Should be."

The drilling rig was set up and began chewing the ground. Clay and earth spat out in a steady stream. Maudie shivered and rose from the front steps.

"It's crazy," she said, "but I just can't take this, Morag. I mean, how'll Royland feel if it doesn't, you know?"

"I know. Me, too. Let's go in and make coffee."

The drill hit water at forty feet.

"Lucky there isn't so much rock on your place, A-Okay," Royland said, sucking at his coffee. "Knew one place they had to go down damn near a hundred feet through sheer rock. Had to blast. Cost them enough, I can tell you. Well, you got enough water for a good-size town, here."

"I just don't see, though," A-Okay said, grateful but confused, "how it's done."

"I don't know no more than you," Royland said. "All I know is, it happens."

The river had quieted when Royland and Morag went back across. Royland in his old blue-and-grey plaid windbreaker sat hunched over the motor, his eyes half closed.

"You tired, Royland?"

"Not exactly. I just sometimes get kind of keyed-up. You know? And you get this feeling, sometimes, I guess."

"What kind of feeling?"

"That this time it might not work," Royland said.

Yeh. That.

"What would you have been like, as a young man, Royland?"

"Maverick," Royland said. "Maybe I'll tell you some-time. Or maybe not. Look – carp jumping, see it?"

A golden and fanged crescent, breaking the river's surface. Then gone.

Maverick?

Night. A piercing noise.

Morag shot from her chair and answered the phone.

"Collect call from Winnipeg." Operator's voice. "Will you accept the charges?"

"Yes. Yes."

"Go ahead, please," said the antiseptic voice.

"Hello. Ma?"

"Pique. Are you okay? I mean, how *are* you?"

"I'm fine." Voice sounding strong and maybe okay. "You weren't worried?"

"No. I knew I'd hear from you."

"Liar."

They both laughed. Morag, with relief.

"So how are *you*?" Pique asked. "Are you working?"

"I've begun, yes," Morag said, hands shaking as she lit a cigarette, holding the telephone receiver between her chin and shoulder. "I'm okay. I went over to the Smiths' today. Royland divined their well. Incidentally, Pique, Gord didn't phone."

"It's all right. He's here now. Not with me this minute. I mean, but here."

"Thank God."

"Oh *Mother*. For Christ's sake. All is now fine because I've got a big strong husky dog to fend for me?"

"Don't be ridiculous, Pique. You know I don't mean that."

"You *do*, though."

True, as Morag realized upon a moment's reflection.

"Well, it's just that you alone, honey – look, I'm sorry. I'll get used to it. I'm learning, but I'm not learning fast enough. The usual human condition, if I may say so."

"Philosophical to the last ditch, that's you," Pique said cheerily. "Well, Gord's okay. I mean, he's a real good person and that. I'm just not all that convinced he's my actual destiny. We may as well travel together for a while. I don't guess he knows, really, what I'm looking for."

Gord, however, was six-feet-two, gentle as a lamb flock except when roused to the protection of Pique. This much, in the opinion of some, was decidedly in his favour.

"I won't demean myself by asking if you're eating properly. But *are* you, Pique?"

"Oh sure. No sweat on that scene." Impatience in her voice, then suppressed excitement. "Say, I went out to your old hometown."

"You *did*?"

Manawaka. Pique sauntering along Main Street in her jeans, her guitar on her back, a stranger in a place strange to her. What had she seen or found? Who?

"Yeh." A laugh, not very amused. "I looked it over. I stayed a coupla days. I'll tell you about it sometime. It was a real gas."

"I'll bet. Was there – did you go –"

"I said, I'll tell you sometime. It wasn't quite what I expected."

"I have no trouble in believing that."

"Yeh, but you don't *know* what I expected, and you don't know what I found, do you?"

"Okay, you've got me there. What else?"

"I nearly had the guitar hurt," Pique said. "Luckily, that turned out okay. It was the day I nearly got busted."

"You did? What for? I mean, what did they *say* it was for?"

Morag had to remind herself once again that her instinctive image of the police was one from the distant past – old Rufus Nolan puffing beer-bellied up Main Street. Mooseheaded but harmless. The local constable. When anything serious occurred in town, the mounties zinged in, summoned from somewhere, taut and sinister in breeks with the bright yellow stripe like a stinging wasp, and jackboots, but not living locally so only a sometime and not-quite-real threat, even to Hill Street.

A silence.

"Pique, what happened? Nobody hurt you? Did anyone –"

And if they had, what could Morag do?

"Cool it, eh?" Pique's uncool voice. "It was outside of some little nothing-type town just inside Manitoba. I can't even remember the name. Maybe I blotted it out. Or maybe it actually didn't *have* a name, you know? I'm walking along hoping for a lift but not actually trying that hard because it's a nice evening, see, just after dusk and I'm wondering when I'm gonna start hearing those fabulous prairie meadowlarks you always used to tell me about, remember? Listen, this call is costing you a fortune, Ma."

"Never mind. What *happened*?"

"Well, a car went by, and it was this bunch of, like, you know, kind of middle-aged guys, pretty jowly and obviously the local businessmen or something. So they see me, yes? I take one look and think *uh-uh*. So you know what they do then?"

"I can't imagine."

She could, though, and none of it was human.

"Well, they start pelting empty beer bottles at me. Outa the windows. They're drunk, I need not add. Some charity supper or something they've been to, no doubt. One of the bottles hits the guitar, and the case is only a plastic one as you know, but luckily no real damage, although there's a mark. The car was creeping along slow, there, and I wasn't feeling too happy just about then. Well, one of the guys took this bottle and cracked it hard on the door frame of the car. The bottle broke, of course, and then he heaved it at me, meantime yelling all kinds of shit. Well, the glass got me on the arm, and I guess the blood kind of scared them. They took off."

My world in those days was a residual bad dream, with some goodness and some chance of climbing out. Hers is an accomplished nightmare, with nowhere to go, and the only peace is in the eye of the hurricane. My God. My God.

"Pique – is your arm okay now? What happened then?"

Her arm. What about the other dimension?

"Yeh, it's okay. Oh, I walked into town. I dunno – just thinking of those guys kind of bugged me. Maybe what they really would've liked was to lay me and then slit my throat. I had that feeling. Anyway, I stopped at a house and asked if I could please wash, as I'd had a slight accident, and they called the cops."

She tries to speak my idiom, to me. She never says Pigs, cognizant of my rural background.

"What for? To report on the men?"

"You've got to be joking, Ma. No. To report on me. They took me to the police station. I was let off with a warning."

"*You* were let off with a warning? What about the –"

"I guess it was just I was walking through their town, by myself, like, and how I got the bleeding arm would've been too uncomfortable for them to know, probably. I tried to tell them, naturally, not because I thought it'd do that much good, but I mean, for God's sake, if you're a doormat somebody will be bound to walk all over you, right? But they didn't want to know. So I kept on moving."

If you want to make yourself into a doormat, Morag girl, I declare unto you that there's a christly host of them that'll be only too willing to tread all over you. – Proverbs of C. Logan, circa 1936.

"Pique – honey –"

"Oh shit. Now I've gone and told it like a hardluck story. Appealing to your sympathy. I didn't mean it like that."

"It didn't come across like that."

"It *did*, though. Anyway, I'm going on to the coast. I'll write you. Listen, I'm sorry, this call really is costing you the earth –"

I'm not quite broke yet. It's only money. Don't ring off. Not quite yet.

"Yeh, it is," Morag said. "Well – write when you can, eh? And take care."

"I will. You too."

SILENCE.

The silence boomed resoundingly from wall to wall, The house was filled with it. Only after half an hour did Morag realize that Pique had not mentioned seeing her father, and Morag had not mentioned that he had phoned.

The night river was dark and shining, and the moon traced a wavering path across it. Morag sat cross-legged on the dock, listening to the hoarse prehistoric voices of the bullfrogs. Somewhere far-off, thunder.

Incredibly, unreasonably, a lightening of the heart.

Memorybank Movie: Whose Side Is God On?

Morag stands beside Prin, the back row of the church, hating her own embarrassment but hugging it around her. She is much taller than Prin now, and even though she has finally got Prin a new coat, grey with silverish buttons, at Simlow's spring sale, Prin still looks like a barrel of lard with legs. She has tried to do Prin's long grey hair up in a bun (which is in classy circles called a *chignon*, she now knows), but the hairpins are falling out, and Prin doesn't even realize or try to poke them back in again, so a funny-looking twist of hair is now halfway down her neck. Prin's hat never stays on at the right angle – it sits there all cockeyed, the navy straw brim drooping over Prin's forehead, the pink velvet geranium looking as though it may come unhitched at any moment. It is, as well, a hat which Christie found at the Nuisance Grounds and Morag is in agony, wondering if it once belonged to Mrs. Cameron or Mrs. Simon Pearl or somebody who's here today and will recognize it and laugh and tell everybody. Prin sings loudly, a deep contralto, but is quite frequently off-key, and when she hits a sour note Morag squirms.

She loves Prin, but can no longer bear to be seen with her in public. Prin maybe knows this, and is grateful when Morag goes to church with her, which makes Morag feel bad, that is, feel *badly*.

Morag is dressed nicely. Nobody could deny it. She spends on clothes everything she earns Saturdays working at Simlow's Ladies' Wear. Her hair is done in very neat braids, twisted around her head, and her hat is that very pale natural straw, with just a band of turquoise ribbon around it, in good taste. Her coat, also turquoise, matches the ribbon exactly and is princess-style, fitted, and flaring at the bottom. It shows off her figure, which is a goddamn good one – that is, a very nice one. But all this makes no difference. When church is over, and they're all filing out, chattering, the Camerons and MacLeods and Duncans and Cateses and McVities and Halperns and them, no one will say *Good Morning* to Morag and Prin. Not on your life. Might soil their precious mouths. Maybe they're just embarrassed, like, and don't know what to say? Not a chance. They're a bunch of – well, a bunch of so-and-so's. Morag does not swear. If you swear at fourteen it only makes you look cheap, and she is not cheap, goddamn it. Gol-darn it.

In Christ there is no East or West,
In Him no North or South –

Oh yeh? Like fun there isn't.

"Let us pray," Reverend McKee says.

And prays for all the Manawaka boys who have gone to the WAR.

Morag, head bent, tries to imagine the War. You imagine lots of things about it, but is that the way it really is? Is it like that poem they took this year in English?

The sand of the desert is sodden red.
Red with the wreck of a square that broke.
The gatling's jammed and the colonel dead,
And the regiment blind with dust and smoke –

The rest of the poem is crap, but those lines are really something. Sodden red. Blind with dust and smoke. Is it like that? They don't use gatlings now, though. Much worse stuff. Also, bombing places like London (and in that giant city, *no lights on* at night, how creepy and awful) and even little kids lying there, dead. What does God care? What would it be like, actually to *feel* a bullet going into you, let's say into your stomach or your lungs, and knowing there was no way out, no hospital or cure? *Knowing* you *have* to die, right now, this minute. Was it like Christie described that other war? Gunner Gunn. Age eighteen. Only four years older than she is now. God couldn't have cared less, whoever died *there*. If the War lasts until she is eighteen, she won't join the Women's Army. They'll have to come and drag her away, if they want her. It would be a way of getting out of town, though.

"Amen," Reverend McKee says.

At home, Morag faces Prin, now rocking comfortably in the rocker that was part of Christie's recent loot from the Nuisance Grounds.

"Prin –"

"Yeh?"

"I'm not going to church anymore. I don't like it. It's – it's –"

Christie is watching her. Half-smiling.

"I don't want to go, that's all," she says. "I don't like it anymore."

"Well, you suit yourself," Prin says. Resigned.

Not in judgement. Just – you suit yourself.

"Christie –"

He gathers the phlegm in his throat. Goes to the front door, opens it, and spits outside into the weeds.

"You heard her, Morag. It's like she says. You suit yourself."

It would have been better, almost, if they'd argued with her. Now she feels she's done something awful. But will not change her mind.

Memorybank Movie: Saturday Night in the Old Hometown
Simlow's Ladies' Wear is a lovely place. There are carpets, even,
sort of wine-coloured with black circle patterns, and there are
long counters and you stand behind one and say, *Can I help
you?* It's nice to work here on Saturdays, and you get paid for
it as well.

The racks of dresses are at the back. Morag has looked
through them when the store isn't busy. Right now they have:

> printed silk two-piece dresses for the fuller figure
> a whole load of cotton housedresses blue green yellow
>> etcetera
> silk or rayon afternoon dresses some with velvet bow at
>> the shoulder
> little girls' party dresses very cute with full skirts and
>> embroidery
> dirndl skirts with bright orange and blue flowers
>> printed blouses with lace ruffles at the neck
>> AND
>>> oh
> the most adorable red dressmaker suit size 14

Morag cannot afford the suit but is saving for it. Will it
be bought first by somebody else? She keeps her fingers
crossed. When anyone looks at it, she fixes them with the evil
eye. When anyone tries it on, she holds her breath.

Morag isn't allowed to work in Dresses, not yet. That is
Millie Christopherson's territory. She needs a helper, and
maybe soon it will be Morag. Millie is old (well, *older*, anyway,
as you might say) and she is tiny and light like a dandelion
seed, very skinny legs (*silk* stockings, always, never lisle). She
also looks kind of like a dandelion in full bloom, on account

of her hair which is puffy and permed and a dandelion-yellow. She *dyes* it; imagine having the nerve. But it is a gorgeous colour, and does not make Millie look cheap at all. Millie has very Good Taste.

"Good Taste is learnt," she says to Morag. "No soul in this here world is born with it, Morag. It is learnt, honey, and I am going to learn a teeny bit of it to *you.*"

Morag is proud to have been chosen, and listens carefully.

"It is the colour *harmony* which is all-important, honey," Millie says, the store being unbusy as yet in the early evening. "Pink and purple, now, would you put the two of them together?"

"No, I guess not."

"Don't you guess, honey. You better *know.* Pink and purple, now, they clash. Also blue and green. Clash. Clash. Ugh."

What about sky and grass, Morag wants to know, but doesn't ask.

"Accessories, too," Millie goes on, darting over to the glove counter. "They are also all-important. Take this little dress now – a teal-blue, wouldn't you say? Lightened with the beige flower pattern. Now, would you wear these black kid gloves with it, or these others here?"

"The – beige ones?"

"Right, honey! Very good. The beige carries out the tone of the flowers, doesn't it? You catch on quick, dear. It's a pleasure to tell you things."

Morag has never felt such a warmth before. She loves Millie with all her heart and soul.

Morag is in Lingerie. At first it seemed funny, that people would go to all that expense and bother to wear really nifty underwear when who would see it, unless you were married, but now it seems as though it would be lovely if you could afford it. Mostly the demand is for rayon pants and cotton brassieres, the cheaper lines, but sometimes people will buy one of the beauty garments. Morag sorts and folds them, constantly rearranging. They are nice to touch, cool, slippery. Especially:

the blue satin nightie with a deep band of lace at the neck
the pale peach slip with tiny appliquéd flowers at the neck
the pastel pink panties very short not at all like bloomers

Business is warming up. Between eight and when the store closes, at ten, is the best time. Lots of people just look, of course. Morag stands up straight, behind the slips and nighties, feeling like she owns them, in a way. She *knows* them, is why. And can show them off to anyone interested. She knows the prices of every item by heart. Millie says a good salesgirl always knows the prices without looking, but if you forget, try to sneak a glance at the tag without the customer noticing. It makes a good impression, Millie says.

Quite a few people now, Mrs. McVitie in a new hat, dark purple straw just dripping with mauve and yellow velvet violets, what awful Taste. Young Mrs. Pearl the lawyer's wife, not really young at all but this is so's she won't get confused with her mother-in-law, old Henry's widow, who is hardly ever in town anyhow. A lot of farm women whom Morag doesn't know except by sight, the same ones who flock into Simlow's every Saturday night just to look and finger the stuff, because no money.

Eva Winkler.

"Hi, Morag, how ya doing?"

"Oh, just great, Eva. How's things?"

"Okay, I guess. Dad's in one of his bad spells again. Me and Vern is going to spend the night at Auntie Clara's. I'm a bit worried about Ma, though. She says she can look after herself and keep out of his way when he gets that mad at everybody, but she can't look out for me and Vern as well. Still and all —"

Eva has got Vern with her. Oh horrors. Vern is still awfully small for his age, and his pale hair looks nearly white. His nose is runny, as usual. He is in overalls only, no shirt, and is in his *bare feet*. On Simlow's carpet. Then Morag notices his eyes, scared and sly at the same time. What a life.

"Gee — I'm sorry, Eva."

Sorry, but wanting Eva to go. Right this minute. Not to be seen talking to her.

Eva's hair, the same whitish yellow as it always was, could be really nice but still straggles all over the place. And not always clean, either. Eva's dresses are still the same old cotton things like potato sacks. Eva hasn't smartened up any. She is no longer in Morag's grade at school. She has failed twice and is only in Grade Seven, in the Public School, not the Collegiate. Morag is ashamed to be so glad that they are in different schools. They sometimes walk up Hill Street together in the mornings and then turn different ways.

Eva seems like she is beaten by life already. Morag is not — repeat *not* — going to be beaten by life. But cannot bear to look at Eva very often.

"Gee, I'm sorry, Eva," she repeats. "I gotta go now. Millie doesn't like us to gab to friends when we're supposed to be working."

Eva brightens for a second at *friends*. Then gets the real message.

"Sure, Morag. It's okay. I understand."

And trails off, clumpingly, with Vernon. How can anyone who weighs so little as Eva walk so heavy? Morag wants to call Eva back. But doesn't.

Mrs. Cameron comes in, fluttery as a dusty-miller moth, twittery as a flock of sparrows. In a silk-rayon suit, navy, which looks familiar – aha, it is the old rose one she's worn to church for ages, dyed to look different. She carries white gloves and purse. With her, Stacey, so neat and short and pretty in a cherry-coloured dress, polka-dotted with white, her hair long and in a perfect pageboy at the back and done up in the front in those great big soft rolls like Betty Grable's, and how in the dickens does she get it to stay *up* because even ninety million bobby-pins won't do the trick on Morag's hair, so heavy and thick. Stacey looks uncomfortable. Embarrassed by her mum, no doubt, and no wonder. Mrs. Cameron puts her hand to her heart every third step, and stops, really *breathing*, so you know she's trying hard at it. She always makes out like she's at death's door.

Tough as old boots, that woman, for all her performances (Christie says). *She'll outlive Niall, I'll bet a nickel to a dough-nut hole. Hey, Morag, here's a riddle for you – who buries the undertaker? Give up? Whoever'll undertake it.*

Then it happens. Mrs. Cameron is looking at the Red Dressmaker Suit. If Stacey gets it, Morag will will will well will do nothing, obviously. It's too long and big for Stacey. It's Morag's exact right size and length.

Twenty hours, it seems, in the trying-on cubicles, and then

Heavens.

It is Mrs. Cameron who emerges wearing the suit. To see herself in the better light and the longer mirrors.

"What do *you* think, Stacey?" she chirps.

Mumble mumble. Stacey isn't letting on. Why doesn't she just say *Mother it looks like hell on you it is twenty-five years too young for you?* Not a word. Stacey is studying the little kids' party dresses as though her life depended on it.

"What do *you* think, Millie?"

"Mm – mm –" Millie says noncommittally, torn between truth and sale. "Did you try the chocolate-brown or the grey yet, Mrs. Cameron, dear? They might be more *you*. I'm not saying that's not a lovely little suit, mind –"

"It's cheerful," Mrs. Cameron carols, laughing her nervous laugh. "I'm just going to be a wee bit reckless, Millie. I'm going to take it."

"It'll need some altering," Millie says.

"Oh, that'll be simple enough. I can do it myself. No need to pay anything extra to have it done."

Fuck. Shit. Bloody bloody christly hell. And the hell with not swearing, too.

"Can I help you?" Morag says politely, to a woman pawing around through the garter-belts.

On the way out, Mrs. Cameron stops at Lingerie. Stacey grins weakly at Morag.

"Hi, Morag."

"Hi, Stacey."

When have they ever said much more than this to one another? But now, surprisingly, Stacey gives Morag a look, meaning *I know she looks like mutton dressed as lamb in that suit, but what can I do about it?* Morag permits herself a small return smile. It is all she can do. People with real parents sometimes have a lousy time, too. She has known this all along, of course, but not really.

Mrs. Cameron smiles, friendly, at Morag.

"I just wanted to say to you, dear," she says, "I think you've done really quite well since you started working here. You've smartened yourself up a whole lot."

"*Mother!*" Stacey's agonized cry.

Stacey rushes out of the store. Morag stares. Unblinking. Stare. Stare. A hex. Mrs. Cameron, bewildered, fusses with her gloves and then laughs a tiny girlish laugh.

"Well, I just wanted to –"

And leaves, at last. Morag stands very quietly. In her head:

blue satin nightie with deep band of lace at top
pale peach slip with appliquéd flowers
pastel pink panties
and every goddamn silk stocking in the place
thrown around like confetti
while people shrink and shriek

"Could you keep an eye on my counter for a sec, Janis?" she says to the girl in Kiddies'.

And goes to the john. She sits on the toilet, tearing up little shreds of toilet paper in her fingers. It strikes her then that she will be able to face Stacey next week in school, but Stacey probably won't be able to face her. This is a peculiar thought. After a while she can come out again, and after two thousand hours more, it becomes ten o'clock.

Parthenon Café. Morag sits at the U-shaped counter, not a booth, because she is by herself.

"Hi, Morag. What'll it be?"

"Hi, Julie. Just a coffee, please."

Julie Kazlik works here on Saturdays. Longer hours than Simlow's, and she says Miklos is a rough guy to work for – if you stand still an instant, he's yelling at you. But Julie likes the sociability of the job. She looks good in the waitress uniform. The light applegreen smock-dress goes really well with her blonde hair which she wears in a smooth French-roll when at work although long or in braids at school.

"Hey, Morag. Mike's dad says we can sit in the car, after. Wanna come? I'm off in fifteen minutes."

Mike Lobodiak is Julie's boyfriend. What is it like, to have a boyfriend? Well, who gives a damn anyway?

"Well, sure, Julie, but are you sure you want me to come along?"

"Oh sure. It's a public gathering. Some of the kids will be there. The private stuff comes later. Here's Mike. Hi, glamour-boy. Want a coffee? I can't leave until eleven *on the dot*, or Miklos will scream his lungs out."

Mike sits down beside Morag, smiling. He is tall, kind of rawboned, which means the bones of his face, high cheekbones, can be seen under his skin, but he looks good that way. Morag catches a whiff of the mansmell about him, and for a second is paralyzed because she wants to touch him. His redbrown neck, his arms with the light brown hairs on them, his hand. His mouth. Julie's boyfriend.

Morag envies Julie's breeziness. Ever since she herself decided to drop her tough act, she has been not too certain what to aim for. To act really ladylike would be too old for her, and also kind of phoney. She has therefore gone back to not speaking much, like when she was quite a little kid and scared. She's scared again, now, but she doesn't know what she's scared of.

The Lobodiaks' car. An old Nash, pretty beat-up but comfortable. Steve Kowalski, black-haired and nice, but kind of on the short side, is also there, and he and Morag sit in the back seat. He doesn't try anything, though. She is half-relieved and half-disappointed.

"Ringside seat," Mike says. "I got my dad to park right in the middle of the main drag so we can see both ways."

Morag doesn't often get to sit in a parked car and look, like some of the kids do every single Saturday night, so she really feels good tonight. You can watch everybody going by.

Farmers mostly not in overalls but their good serge or tweed suits if they have them, coming out of the beer parlour and walking along the street yelling to people they know. Their women, sometimes with the men, sometimes in their own groups, as dolled up as possible, some in high heels and wearing makeup, laughing, excited, middle-aged and young, stout and skinny, hauling along their little kids by the arms. Kids all ages and shapes, eating ice cream cones, shouting, snivelling, shrieking, half-asleep, dancing with the circus feeling, some of them complaining, joking, humming to themselves. The town whores looking for a pickup oh the eye-shadow wow and the sticking-out busts in laced-up French brassieres under pink green mauve angora tight tight sweaters. Some girls hooked onto the arms of soldiers. Noise   hooting yelling   *DIN*   wow. Smells, dust from the streets, grittily blown by the wind – French fries from the Regal Café   dusky musky smell of perfume Lily-of-the-Valley Sweet Pea cheap Bad Taste and   also   Tweed   Evening-in-Paris   expensive Good Taste   and finally the smells all mashed into one smell inside your nostrils.

Oh.

Christie Logan, walking, sauntering, dressed as usual in his old overalls and rolled-up sleeves blue plaid shirt sweat-wet under the arms, not drunk but slouching happily along, gawking into the drugstore window at the boxes of chocolates and the hot-water bottles.

Simon Pearl and Archie McVitie, lawyers, coming out of their offices, locking carefully after late work on somebody's farm mortgage or somebody's will, dressed in of course business suits grey pin-striped, Mr. Pearl tall tall like Morag remembers his father old Henry but of course much smarter in the head and the looks than the old guy, and Mr. McVitie much shorter but gold-rimmed specs.

The two meet Christie on the sidewalk just in front of where the Lobodiaks' car is parked with its open windows so you can hear everything oh hell hell.

"Well, well, hello there, Christie," Archie McVitie.

Simon Pearl says nothing. A nod of the head, only. Brisk.

"H'lo there, Mr. McVitie," Christie says. "Fine evening."

Christie. But *Mr. McVitie.* Who decides?

"Hear you're keeping off Relief so far, Christie," Mr. McVitie says.

"Some are still on," Christie says sullenly, "despite this life-giving War."

Then   oh please   NO

Yep. Christie goes into his doormat act. Bone-grin, full of brown teeth.

"Och aye, an honest job is all I ask in this very world, Mr. McVitie, and I tell you, sir, that's God's truth. An honest wage for an honest day's work, as you might phrase it."

Mr. McVitie frowns, suspecting dirty work at the crossroads somewhere here but can't put his finger on it. Morag stifles a laugh. But wants to cry. Wants to go out and be there with Christie. Also, wants Christie not to be there, just not to be there at all, and if she had a loaded gun in her hands this very second, would take careful aim and shoot him in the throat. Failing a gun, a stone. Or maybe would shoot McVitie & Pearl, Barristers and Solicitors.

She does not move.

"That's more or less what I told the Town Council at the last meeting," Mr. McVitie says. "They want to get a truck, you know, for the um ah refuse collection. Younger man, and that. I said we'll only have one more on Relief if we do that. They claim the War's made a difference. Not enough yet, I said. If it lasts another couple of years, yes, we'll be out of the doldrums."

Christie is looking hard at the two men. Deciding. Finally he speaks.

"God will no doubt hear you," Christie says.

And strolls on.

Inside the car, silence.

"Hey!" Morag cries suddenly and loudly. "Get a load of that, eh? Ina Spettigue's got *three* soldiers tonight. Lotsa guys on leave this weekend."

Laughter.

"Boy, I bet she'd be okay." Mike. Teasing Julie.

"Oh *Mike*. She's fat."

"A good armful, is all."

And then Mike's older brother arrives.

"Okay, you guys, everybody out. I need the car."

"Aw, *John*."

"Out, I said. I'm taking Marge home."

"What about me?" Mike complains. "How'm I supposed to take Julie home?"

"I'll drop you off."

"Oh, thanks a *million*. How'm I supposed to get home myself, then?"

John Lobodiak laughs.

"Walk, kid. It's only three miles. True love will find a way."

"Jeez, you make me want to puke," Mike says furiously.

"Puke away," John says cheerfully.

So then they all go home.

Memorybank Movie: Leaves on Trees Can Be Seen By Some
At the Manawaka Collegiate, all the girls wear the same clothes, at least on top. The boys can wear anything they like, but the girls have to wear navy pleated tunics and white blouses. Some of the girls don't go for this idea, but for Morag it is godsend. Also, she gets ten percent off the tunic and blouses at Simlow's.

Grade Nine is lots harder than Grade Eight, but then it is High School. Morag's new policy – work like hell, that is, like the dickens. Although not letting on to the other kids. If you answered questions in class too much, the others would be dead set against you. Morag does not care about most of the kids, but she does not want Julie to be against her. She is not Julie's *best* friend, but she is a friend of Julie's all the same, and has been out twice to the Kazliks' place for supper, and it is a lovely place, the dairy farm, there, a big house with real lace curtains and piles of delicious food, and Mr. Kazlik roaring at them all but not meaning it, and Julie's younger brothers, the twins, laughing and making fun of everything, and Mrs. Kazlik very short and stoutish and very motherly, which Julie resents but Morag likes. Mrs. Kazlik made a blouse for Morag this spring, very full long sleeves and all embroidered at the top with tiny cross-stitch birds and flowers in all colours, and this is a really fantastic thing, and Julie isn't very interested in school so Morag has to watch it and never show off.

But if you work, really really work, and get educated, something will come of it, maybe. Like being able to get out of Manawaka and never come back. Morag listens at nights to the long wailing of the trains crossing the prairies, their voices like the spooky voices of giant owls. She always feels warm and good at the sound, because she knows something which nobody else in this world knows. Which is, one day she will be on one of those trains, going to the city and maybe even further than the city. Going to the whole world.

She sits in the back row in class as usual. Skinner Tonnerre sits opposite, also in the back row as usual. She has never spoken to him since that day at the Nuisance Grounds, but sometimes they give each other a half-grin, if nobody else is looking, like when old Craigson gets off track in History and starts spouting about Planting Gardens for Victory and All of Us Doing Our Bit for the War Effort, and sometimes gets so worked up that the tears come to his eyes and he looks really dumb and embarrassing. Skinner comes to school pretty regularly these days, although his sister who used to be in the same class has quit for good. Maybe Skinner is working on the sly, too, although you'd never know. He slouches in his seat, same as always, and his eyes are usually half-closed.

Miss Melrose is talking. Her voice is gruff and abrupt. Some of the kids don't like her because she doesn't stand for any nonsense. Morag worships her. Because of what she says about the compositions. Sometimes after class as well. No one ever before has talked to Morag about what was good and bad in writing, and shown her why. It is amazing. And when you look at the composition again, you can *see* why. Some things work and other things don't work. Like the Pathetic Fallacy. You can't say *The clouds swooped teasingly over the town, promising rain*, on account of clouds don't feel – they just *Are*. Wordsworth used the Pathetic Fallacy, of course, but Miss Melrose is not a great fan of Wordsworth's. She prefers Browning, who could get inside a person's very soul.

"After last week's free choice of composition topic," Miss Melrose says, "I am forced to the reluctant conclusion that many of you need a lot of exercise – not on the baseball field but in the field of the imagination. Can't you think of anything to write about except *My Holiday* or *The Story of a Cent*? We had that same cent going through almost exactly the same series of adventures at least a dozen times. What did you do? Get together and work out one plot?"

Titters. Denials. Admissions.

"Well, it may be labour-saving," Miss Melrose says, "but it's awfully boring to read. I'm not going to spoon-feed you. Choose your own topics again this week, and for mercy's sake try not to be so dull."

Bell rings for recess.

"Morag, could you wait a moment, please?" Miss Melrose says.

Morag stands by the teacher's desk, her face (is it really or does it only feel that way?) a dark peony-red.

"Yours was one of the very few that showed any originality, Morag. Why don't you submit it to the school paper?"

Published. Fame. Notoriety.

"I don't know," Morag says. "I don't think it's good enough."

"It's good enough," Miss Melrose says, kind of grimly. "The literary standards of the school paper cannot exactly be termed highbrow. The story is a little sentimental in places, it seemed to me, but you haven't opted for an easy ending, at least."

"Well –"

Julie. Scorn, or what? The other kids.

"I can't," Morag says. "I just can't. Not right now."

"Well, then, you must take your own time," Miss Melrose says. "You will."

Morag goes out of the room but not outside. Down to the girls' john. Locks herself in a cubicle. What a terrible world it would be without lockable johns. The thought is funny, which is just as well, because she is crying her eyes out. For what? She is not sad. She has known for some time what she has to do, but never given the knowledge to any other person or thought that any person might suspect. Now it is as though a strong hand has been laid on her shoulders. Strong and friendly. But merciless.

Someone is walking over her grave.

When she goes back upstairs, she meets Miss Melrose in the hall.

"Oh, by the way, Morag, I meant to mention. Can you actually see the blackboard from where you're sitting?"

"Well –"

Glasses are awful. No boy would ever look at you. Never.

"Have you ever had your eyes tested?" Miss Melrose persists.

"Well, no. I – I don't want to wear glasses."

"Why not, for pity's sake?" Miss Melrose, who is undoubtedly Past All That, sounds impatient and kind of cross.

"I look bad enough as it is," Morag says.

When in doubt tell the truth, if you happen to think you know it. (Christie.)

Miss Melrose gives her a really strange look. Then sighs.

"Someday you may find out differently, Morag. Or maybe you won't. Some never do, until it's irrelevant. Look at it this way, then. You need your eyes. In the last analysis, they're all you have."

At the doctor's office, after the drops are put in Morag's eyes, the entire world swims and flounders in front of her. She gets only as far as the second line of letters on the chart. After that, blur all the way.

The new glasses are hideous. Round. Metal-framed. Morag now looks like a tall skinny owl whose only redeeming feature is a thirty-six-inch bust. She begins to wear her hair long again. If she puts it up, she looks like a Sunday-school teacher. In front of the mirror she rages and curses. Life is over. Having never begun.

"They look kind of distinguished," Christie says.

"Shut up! Shut up! They look awful."

"Oh, beggin' your ladyship's pardon. Shall I kill myself now or later?"

"Christie, leave the girl alone," Prin says. "You should know better."

"Why should I know better, then? I'm only the Scavenger."

"That's exactly *all* you are," Morag says coldly.

Has she said it? How could she? How could she? How to make the words unspoken?

"Shut up, girl, or I'll give you the back of my hand," Christie shouts.

"I'd like to see you try," Morag yells.

Christie looks at her a moment, then turns away.

"You know damn well I wouldn't, Morag. It's only my way of talking."

"Christie –"

But he had walked out of the house, out to the stable, and hasn't heard. She wants to go after him. But doesn't.

Morag goes upstairs to her room. She looks out the window at the maple tree. Forgets about Christie. LEAVES! She can see the leaves. Individually, one at a time, clearly. She has not known before this that you are supposed to be able to see the leaves on a tree, not just green fuzz.

Excited, she looks for a long time. Then thinks for a while about the story that will never see the light of day. "Wild Roses."

Hm. Sentimental in places? The young teacher not marrying the guy because she couldn't bear to live on a farm — would that really happen? Maybe all that about the wild roses is overdone? Could it be changed?

Innerfilm

Morag living in her own apartment in the city   a small apartment but lovely   deep-pile rug (blue) and a beige chesterfield suite the thick-upholstered kind   a large radio in a walnut cabinet   lots of bookshelves   a fireplace that really works

She has just had a story called "Wild Roses" published in the *Free Press Prairie Farmer* and is giving a party to celebrate with all her many friends

Shit. Who is she trying to kid? Worse than the story. Nothing will happen. Ever.

Innerfilm

Quiet funeral   privately held in Cameron's Funeral Home a whole lot of flowers snapdragons larkspur peonies florist roses   Eva has brought wild roses and they are wilted and in a quart sealer   Eva crying   has been a real true friend and now it is too late for Morag to tell her so

Morag lying in a white satin-lined coffin   eyes closed
face awfully pale and she is wearing a yellow silk dancing-dress
she has never danced in it and now never will   coffin is closed
and hearse goes to the graveyard Christie is absent   overcome
with sorrow   Stacey Mavis Vanessa   Julie   Ross   Jamie
etcetera   crying   in   sadness   wishing they had recognized
the qualities Morag had before too late

Some time later it is found that among the things in her
dresser drawer is a novel one of the finest ever written in a long
time anywhere it is published   Christie buys two bottles of
rye on the proceeds (*he better not!*)

Morag never knows novel has been published (unless
watching from somewhere, maybe?)

How corny can you get?

Memorybank Movie: Down in the Valley the Valley So Low
Morag is moving slowly along the edge of the Wachakwa
River. Bushes are everywhere – silvergreen wolf willow,
chokecherry, pincherry, and a jungle of unnamed unknown
bushes. If you don't watch your step, here, you will slip and
end up in the brown water. The river rattles over the stones,
but the water is clear. How come the water is both brown and
clear? *Brown* sounds murky. But this is as clear as brown glass,
like in a beer bottle, or no, not that, not like that at all. What
like? Like only itself, maybe, the Wachakwa River, in places
only a creek. *Crick*. Some people say it like that. Different
people say things differently. Eva says *crick*. Gus Winkler
doesn't know how to pronounce things right. Does Christie?
Sometimes, sometimes not.

Another few steps and then the RAVINE. Why come here,
when it is really spooky? Eerie. *Eerie*. What a word. Ee-ee-rie.

She comes here often. *Why* doesn't matter, here. The river is now flowing very far down there, and on the banks the grass doesn't grow – just the bushes, bending over the ravine as though beckoned by the river below, as though wanting to go down there. (Pathetic Fallacy.) If you come here in spring, the marsh marigolds are out in masses down there on the water, and you can look at their juicy gold and green, little gold flowers connected to a whole web of green stalks and floating leaves.

Soon the swinging bridge. Yes, now. Who made it? How long ago? Ropes across the ravine, fraying ropes but still strong, and the pieces of split poplar to walk across, each joined to each by the old old ropes, and if you really *did* walk across, the bridge would sway and shake and maybe you would plunge down into the shallow water and the stones. Morag has never crossed this bridge. She wants to make herself do it. She could do it if she had to. She puts a hand on the poplar pole at the edge of the bridge. She will definitely do it this time. If she can do this, she can do anything. A sign. An omen. She has to make it come true.

She puts one foot on the bridge. It lurches. She leaps back onto safe ground.

She is suddenly convinced that the bridge is trying to send her plunging down into the ravine. She holds onto a willow branch, and it supports her. Pathetic Fallacy? What if Miss Melrose is wrong, though, just in that one way? Not that clouds or that would have *human* feelings, but that the trees and river and even this bridge might have their own spirits? Why shouldn't they? The wolf willow and the chokecherry bushes and the tall couchgrass growing away from the ravine, and the river itself – no threat. Just the bridge. Who built it? Why does it still stay here, rickety, swaying? How old is it? Does someone sometimes patch it up, keep it going? Whose is it? Not hers, that is for sure. Something doesn't want her to be here at all.

Then she hears someone. On the other side of the bridge. He comes out of the bushes and steps onto the bridge. Beat-up blue jeans, brass-buckled belt, rolled-up shirtsleeves, brown hawkish face, dark slitted eyes. His straight black hair cut shorter these days than it used to be. Skinner Tonnerre.

He begins rocking the bridge, which swings like a dangerous hammock. Morag moves further back from it.

"Hey, look out, Skinner, eh?"

"Hi, Morag – I didn't see you, there," he grins, lying. "Whatsa matter? You scared? The bridge is okay."

"I'm not scared," Morag says angrily. "It's just that –"

"It's just that you're scared shitless," Skinner says flatly.

He gives out with the Tarzan yell like Johnny Weissmuller in the movies.

"TAR-MAN-GAN-EE!"

And walks across the bridge, swinging it violently. Morag looks away, expecting to hear his dying body go *splat* on the rocks below. But no.

"Want a cigarette?" he says, beside her.

"Sure."

Morag has not smoked before, so does not inhale. He laughs at her, and shows her how. At first the smoke pinches her lungs, but she soon gets the hang of it.

"How're you liking it at the Pearls' place, then?" she asks.

It seems now to be quite natural sitting on the riverbank and talking to him, even though they don't talk to each other in school. Skinner has been staying with Simon Pearl and his wife this year while going to High School. The Pearls have no kids and have offered to have Skinner board with them because the local welfare officer has said Skinner will never keep on going to school if he stays down in the valley with Lazarus and all, and that he is bright enough to keep on. Everybody in Manawaka knows about this, and many say it is foolhardy of the Pearls, who need not expect any gratitude from a halfbreed.

"It's okay, I guess," Skinner replies, but cautiously. "Mr. Pearl, he's doing his good deed for the year, I guess. I don't give a damn. The Welfare pays my board. Let 'em. My old man and my sisters, they think I'm nuts. The little kids, my brothers, they don't think *anything*, but they say when am I coming back. I don't give a fuck what any of them think."

"You come down this way often?"

"Yeh. On Sundays. The Pearls go to church. I won't go. *Okay*, Mr. Pearl says. No, he don't. He says, *Very well, then, Jules, go to the Catholic Church.* But I won't do that, neither."

"Who – who made the rope-bridge, there, Skinner?"

"How should I know?" he says. But knows.

"You ever go back and see your folks, then? Now that you're at the Pearls'?"

Skinner spits down into the ravine and half-closes his eyes.

"Naw. The hell with them. My old man's always drunk, anyways, and the girls, they're about the same. The little kids are just dumb brats. The old lady my Ma, she ain't coming back, and good riddance to bad rubbish. Me and my old man, there, we don't get on now. He thinks I'm a kid, but he doesn't know what he's talking about. We had a fight, there, and I knocked four of his teeth out. It really surprised him. Val reported me, the crumby little bitch. That's why the Welfare said I had to move out. I would've moved out, anyways. Hey, Morag, want to hear a *real poem*?"

"What?"

He chants it.

"When apples are ripe they should be plucked,
When a girl is sixteen she should be fucked."

Morag wants to touch him, to touch the black fine hairs
on his arms, the bones of his shoulders, his skin smelling good,
of fresh sweat. She edges away. Scared. What if it hurts? What
if he *makes* her do it, and she decides at the last minute she
doesn't want to? What if what if what if.

"I'm not sixteen," she blurts, and then would give anything to reswallow the words, make them unsaid, because
what a dumb dumb *dumb* thing to say.

Skinner is laughing.

"Well, do tell! Guess you're safe for a while, then, eh?"

She gets to her feet. Hovers. Undecided. Skinner remains
sprawled on the grass. Looking at her.

"C'mon, Morag. It feels good. I bet you never done it,
eh? I can do it with Ina Spettigue any time I like. She never
even charges me. She likes what I got. Wanna see?"

He reaches for his fly buttons.

Morag runs. He does not follow.

When she is back home, she goes to her room and locks
the door. Hating herself for having been scared. Slips one
hand between her legs and brings herself, with her eyes closed,
imagining his hard flesh   bones skin   on hers, pressing into
her, feeling her tits, putting his cock there there there.

Next day at school, and forever after, she will not look at
him, she promises to herself, never, not ever.

That evening, Morag starts talking to Christie, who is par-
ing his fingernails really disgustingly with his jackknife. She
does not talk to him much these days, and so he is surprised now.

"Christie – remember those stories you used to tell me
when I was a kid?"

"Sure. How could I forget? Why?"

"Tell me them now, some."

"Great jumping jesus, Morag, I thought you would've been past all of that."

"Yeh. Well."

Why does she want to hear? She doesn't know. But the times when she was a kid and Christie would tell those stories, everything used to seem all right then.

"Okay, Morag, if you want. Let's see."

CHRISTIE'S TALE OF PIPER GUNN AND THE REBELS

Now Piper Gunn lived there along the Red River on his farm for more years than you could shake a stick at. And him and his woman had a fine family, too, five sons and five daughters, the boys all strapping and husky, and the girls all tall and as beautiful as tiger lilies. And Piper Gunn and his wife grew old, in time, and yet both together, for as is well-known, when the Angel of Death spread his wings out for them, they kicked the bucket the selfsame day, for neither could live without the other, so the story goes.

(You're romantic, Christie.)

Hush, girl, I'm about as romantic as a pig in a trough and that's the bloody christly truth of the matter, but can I help it if that's how Death finally took up old Piper and his lady?

Now, then, when Piper was a real old man, and not working the land that much any more but leaving it all to his five sons, it happened that the halfbreeds around the settlement got very worked up. They decided they was going to take over the government of the place. So they got themselves a rebel chief. Short little man he was, with burning eyes. His name was Reel.

(Louis Riel, Christie. We took it in school. He was hanged.)

That's the very man. Well, but he wasn't hanged for a hell of a long time after the time I'm telling you. So this Reel or Riel, however you want to call him, him and his men took over the Fort there, and set themselves up as the government.

Now, all the Sutherlanders, over the long years, had kind of forgotten how to fight, eh? Peaceful farmers, they were, and their sons reared to that way. Not a mother's son of them remembered the old days in the old country, except for Piper Gunn and a few oldtimers. They were not what you'd call a spineless lot, oh no. But they'd grown up here, farming. So when Reel took over, with his gang of halfbreeds, they didn't know what to do. There was a lot of chewing the fat, but nobody moved. Reel and his men started doing a little shooting, do you see, and killed one or two Englishmen. But the Sutherlanders didn't trust the goddamn English, them bloody Sassenachs from Down East, no more than what they trusted the halfbreeds. They kept themselves to themselves. So they sat on their butts and did nothing.

(The government Down East sent out the Army from Ontario and like that, and Riel fled, Christie. He came back, to Saskatchewan, in 1885.)

Well, some say that. Others say different. Of course I *know* the Army and that came out, like, but the truth of the matter is that them Sutherlanders had *taken back the Fort* before even a smell of an army got there.

(Oh Christie! They didn't. We took it in History.)

I'm telling you. What happened was this. Piper Gunn says to his five sons, he says, *What in the fiery freezing hell do all of you think you're doing, not even making a stab at getting back the bloody Fort?* So his five sons, they said, *We're ready to try if you can think up a way of raising all of them Macphersons and Macdonalds and Camerons and MacGregors and all them.* Piper Gunn rises to his feet, and him taller than his five sons even though pressing eighty, and not stooped one inch, no sir, straight as an iron crowbar.

I've played the pipes in sorrow, says he, *and I've played them in joy and I've played them in bad times and in good, and I've played them to put the heart into the souls of men, and now I'll play them for the last bloody time.*

Will we come with you, then? asks his five sons. *I'll go alone*, says Piper Gunn, for that was his way. So walk he did, along every farm on the river front, there, and he played the entire time. He began with the pibrochs, which was for mourning. To tell the people they'd fallen low and wasn't the men their ancestors had been. Then he went on to the battle music. And the one he played over and over was "The Gunns' Salute." A reproach, it was.

The Sutherlanders listened, and they knew what he was saying. They gathered together and Piper's five sons with them, and they took the Fort at the rising of the day the very next morning. The army from Down East got the credit, of course, but the Sutherlanders were a proud lot and didn't give a christly damn. They let it be.

And Piper Gunn went home and hung up his bagpipes and they have been silent from that day to this, for he died soon after, and no one ever dared play them, for no one could ever play the pipes like Piper Gunn himself could play them.

(I like him, though. Riel, I mean.)

That so? Well, he had his points, no doubt.

(The book in History said he was nuts, but he didn't seem so nuts to me. The Métis *were* losing the land – it was taken from them. All he wanted was for them to have their rights. The government hanged him for that.)

Métis? Huh?

(Halfbreeds.)

Well, well, hm. Maybe the story didn't go quite like I said. Let's see.

(No. That's cheating, Christie. Thanks for telling the story, I liked it fine. Really.)

You're welcome. I'll send you the bill at the end of the month.

Memorybank Movie: Down in the Valley, Act II

Early spring, and the air still has a bite in it despite the sun. The snow, so clean before, is melting dirtily, honeycombed with black patches, leaving the winter's hidden accumulation of dogshit and tossed-away empty cigarette packets soggily soiling the streets. Slush everywhere. Maples and elms have not yet begun to bud, but out beyond town, in the valley, the pussywillows are making grey-furred beginnings.

It is also Grade Eleven, and there are a few boys in the class, but in the Grade Twelve class there are none. All in either the Army or the Airforce. One or two have recklessly joined the Navy, but the sea does not have much appeal for the prairie boys, being too distant an element.

Morag is walking home, carrying an armload of books.

"Hi, Morag."

He has, it is clear, been waiting at the corner of Hill Street. Slouched against a telephone pole. Looking heavier than before, in his thick rough-textured khaki uniform with the badge of the Queen's Own Cameron Highlanders on the sleeve. Rank – Private.

"Skinner! How come you're here?"

"Everybody is. Overseas leave. Wanna come for some coffee?"

She has scarcely spoken to him for two years, since that day in the valley. He quit school a year ago and moved back to the Tonnerre shack. Then he joined the Army and left town. Morag is surprised at how glad she is to see him.

"Sure. But can I drop off these books first?"

"Okay by me."

They go into the Logan house. Prin, rocking with sleep-glazed eyes, all at once looks up with what for her, these days, is enormous alertness. Which is to say, she opens her eyes, half rises, thinks better of it, and lowers her heavy obesity, her soft barrel bulk, wrap-around clad, back into the safeness of the rocking chair. She hardly ever moves these days, except from rocker to table to bed. Morag gets the meals. Prin hardly ever talks any more, either. But will not see a doctor. Even Christie, who worries seldom, worries now.

"Prin – this is Skinner, I mean Jules Tonnerre. I went to school with him. He's in the Army. You know?"

Morag feels embarrassed, adding this bit about the Army. But she is not certain Prin will notice or recognize the uniform.

"Pleased to make yer acquaintance, Mister," Prin says, in an oddly girlish voice, formally, as though with reference to some long-forgotten formula learned in a distant past.

"Hi." Skinner looks away.

Morag goes upstairs to change out of her school tunic, which would look dumb and kid-like beside an Army uniform. When she comes down, Christie has come in and is talking to Skinner. Christie, of late years, has taken to chewing tobacco. The spittoon of his choice, culled from his own private happy hunting grounds, is a large china chamber pot with mauve violets on it. He hawks massively into it now. Morag glowers, then thinks that whatever Christie Logan is like, he's probably not a patch on Lazarus Tonnerre.

"Whatcha doing with yourself these days, Skinner?" Christie says.

"Fighting for King and Country. Can't you see, Christie?"

"Yep. Well, then, boy, stay alive if you can. That's all that matters, though why it should the Lord only knows."

Skinner's eyes narrow.

"I joined for the pay, Christie. I don't aim to get hurt if I can help it."

"That's the spirit, boy. It's never the generals who die, you know. Don't let the buggers on either side get you."

As they walk up along Main Street, towards the Parthenon Café, Skinner says something that astounds Morag.

"He's quite a guy, that Christie."

"I'm glad *you* think so."

"Don't you?"

"He's never tried to do anything," Morag says. "He thinks it's just great now because the Town Council have bought him a beat-up old truck for work. He thinks he's pulled a fast one on them because no one ever suspected he could drive. He learned on a Model-T years ago and he drives that truck as though it were a horse. Everybody laughs at him."

Skinner is laughing too.

"Well, let them. You don't like him being the Scavenger, do you? What if nobody would do it, eh? He's worth a damn sight more than a lawyer – all those guys do is screw things up."

At the Parthenon they sit in a booth and drink coffee. Now they are both suspicious of each other again. Skinner is looking hard at her, studying her face as though trying to read what lies behind her eyes, inside her skull. Is she trying to do the same with him? If so, neither of them seems to be getting very far. For a while they don't speak. Is there too little to say or too much?

"Why'd you leave the Pearls' place and go back to the valley?" Morag asks finally.

He reaches out and puts one of his long thin hands on hers. Only for a second. Then he takes it away.

"Really want to know? I guess Simon Pearl didn't spread it around, then, eh?"

"No."

"Well, it was this way. I got some fancy notion I'd like to be a lawyer, see, on account of if you've always been screwed by people it seemed a good idea to do some of the damage yourself for a change. Right? So I asked old Simon how a guy would get to be a lawyer. He didn't actually laugh out loud, but he kinda covered his mouth with his hand to hide the smile. Then he tells me it's a fine thing to get an education, but a person like me might do well to set their sights a bit lower, and he will ask Macpherson at the BA Garage to take me on as an apprentice mechanic after Grade Eleven. So I walked out. I thought of breaking his jaw, but then I thought it'd only land me in the clink and it wasn't worth it. So I went back to the valley. My old man never batted an eye. Just said, *You're back, eh? Well, give us a hand with this barrel – it's about ready to be put in the jugs.* We had a hell of a party, just him and me. Sat around with me singing and him playing out of tune on the mouth organ till near morning. He's not such a bad guy. He didn't give a fuck when I joined the Army, but he'd never turn me out. He'd never turn any of us out. He don't care if we leave, but we can stay if we want to."

"I'm sorry," Morag says. "I mean about Simon –"

"There's no call to be. I don't give a damn. I never have and I never will."

"Where's your sister these days?"

"You mean Piquette? She took off as soon as her leg was okay. She had TB of the bone as a kid – maybe you remember. She's married to a guy in Winnipeg. Al Cummings. I think she's got herself a first-rate no-good, but that's her business. He'll leave her one day. I hope to christ she leaves him first."

"How do you know? You can't tell."

"I can tell. He'll never look you in the eye. Also, he's always telling Piquette what a lousy housekeeper she is. It's quite true, she *is*. But he's a dirty bugger himself. It don't help much."

The Parthenon begins to fill up with the saddle-shoe gang, girls in long loose sloppy-joe sweaters and plaid skirts, boys in grey flannels and smart tweed jackets. All the kids. The jukebox.

"C'mon," Skinner says brusquely. "Let's go."

No one says anything as they walk out. Miklos thought-fully holds the door open, relieved to see them go. To Miklos, the word Tonnerre spells only one thing, Trouble. There will, of course, be plenty of comments after they've left. They both know this, and walk stiffly, not speaking.

"Jesus, I hate this town," Skinner says finally.

"Me too."

"Hey, Morag, come down to my place and meet my old man?"

She glances at him. They both know. She feels nauseated with indecision. Then doesn't care.

"Sure," she says. "Why not?"

The valley road is like a miniature river, the deep ruts in it running with brown muddy water. The snow still lies in the bushes on either side of the road. Morag has her overshoes on, and Skinner's Army boots are impervious to the wet. They splash along, and he takes her arm so she won't slip. Suddenly she feels good, and laughs.

"What's the joke?" he says.

"Nothing. I just feel okay again, that's all."

"Hey, that's good."

He stops and breaks off a couple of twigs of pussy-willows. Hands them to her.

"Orchids," he says.

"My, that is the first time anybody ever gave me orchids. Thanks."

"Well, there's a first time for everything," Skinner says.

He hasn't meant to say that, probably. Then, of course, they both fall silent again.

The Tonnerre shack is really a collection of shacks. The original one has now decayed and is used as a chicken house. The main shack has been put together with old planks, tar-paper, the lids of wooden crates, some shingles and flattened pieces of tin. Around it lie old tires, a roll of chickenwire, the chassis of a rusted car, and an assortment of discarded farm machinery. The backhouse stands at a slight distance. There is also a small shack, built in the same manner as the main one, but newer. Skinner steers her towards this one.

"Mine," he says. "I built it when I came back down here."

Inside it is warm because there is still a fire going in the stove which has been made out of an old oil-drum, bricked around at the bottom. Wooden boxes are the chairs. There is a bucket of water and a dipper, an enamel basin and a slop bucket. A coal-oil lamp hangs from a nail. There is a wooden chest, with a padlock. And Skinner's books from school. On the walls, pin-ups of movie stars, women with big breasts and carmine mouths. Also the pelt of a skunk, black and white.

"Make yourself at home," Skinner says.

By this time they really do both know.

"You remember that time at the bridge, Morag?"

"Yes."

"I scared you, I guess. I was sorry, but I couldn't say, after."

"It's okay."

"And all that I told you, about Ina Spettigue, was a pack of lies," Skinner says. "She wouldn't have given me the time of day, then. She would now, but the hell with her. Anyway, I just wanted to clear that up. Could you do without those glasses, there?"

Then they kiss for a long time, his tongue delicately exploring the inside of her mouth. His hands stroking her breasts. She has wanted this, it seems, now, for a long time. He is lying on top of her, and through all their clumsy layers of clothing she can feel his cock, long and hard.

"C'mon," he says. "We can't leave all these clothes on, eh?"

She hesitates, although only momentarily.

"Skinner – what if somebody, you know, barges in?"

"They won't," he says grimly. "They know better."

She believes him. She is astonished to find she is not scared. What if it hurts? Well, so what? And anyway it won't. She takes her clothes off quickly, expertly, as though she has been accustomed for years to doing so in front of a man. She feels no shyness at all. Only the need to feel him all over her, to feel all of his skin. Her own body, her breasts and long legs and flat stomach, all these seem suddenly in her own eyes beautiful to her, and she wants him to see her.

Then she looks up at him, above her on the bed. She never knew before that a man would look so beautiful, his shoulder bones showing under the skin, his narrow hips, the big ribcage, the warm smooth brown skin, the black hair between his legs, the long tense hard muscles along his legs and his arms, his long hardsoft cock nuzzling her. She thrusts up at him, locks her legs around his. As though she has always known what to do.

"Easy, easy," he says. "Oh God – not so quick, Morag. I can't –"

And goes off on her belly before he can get inside her.

"Oh hell," he says, after a moment, still not breathing steady. "I'm sorry."

But she clings to him. Still moving towards him, holding his shoulders desperately in her arms.

"Please. Don't go away."

Then he realizes, and helps her.

"Hey, that's fine. You're gonna come all over me."

And she does. The pulsing between her legs spreads and suffuses all of her. The throbbing goes on and on, and she does not realize her voice has spoken until it stops, and then she does not know if she has spoken words or only cried out somewhere in someplace beyond language.

Silence. He is very lightly stroking her shoulders, her face, her closed eyelids. She opens her eyes. They smile, then, at each other. Like strangers who have now met. Like conspirators.

"That wasn't so bad for you, after all," he says.

"It was – oh Skinner –"

"Hey, could you call me by my real name, eh?"

As though now it were necessary to do this. By right. Does she understand what he means? Is this what he means? What is he really thinking, in there? But you have to take it on faith, she now sees. You can't ever be sure. She nods.

"Okay. I will. Jules."

He laughs.

"You say it kind of funny. *Jewels*."

"How, then?"

"Jules."

"Jewels."

"You better learn French, kid."

"Do you know it?"

"No. Not that much, any more. Not that much, ever. Just a bit, mostly swear words. I guess we used to know a few things when we were kids, but it's mostly gone now. My old man grew up speaking quite a bit of French-Cree, but he's lost most of it now. You got nice legs, even if you do say my name wrong."

This is true. Morag has got nice legs, and has always wondered if anyone else would ever think so.

The fire has died, and the shack is cold. They dress. He does up her dress for her, and she helps him on with his Army jacket. They laugh a lot, now, over nothing, over everything. Nothing bad will ever happen again, not ever again. Nothing can ever touch them. This is their house. They are safe, here.

Then she remembers.

"When're you going, Jules? How long a leave you got?"

He lies back on the bed, alone, smoking.

"I gotta go back to camp tonight."

"*Tonight?*"

"Yeh. We're coming back to town tomorrow. Dress parade. Wait'll you see me in a kilt, kid. A Tonnerre in a kilt is some sight, I can tell you. In the First War they used to call the Scots regiments the Ladies from Hell. I feel like a twerp in that getup, to tell you the truth. Thank christ we don't have to put it on that often."

"Why're they doing that? Tomorrow?"

"Because the Cameron Highlanders got so many Manawaka boys, is why."

"I see."

"C'mon, let's go over to my old man's. He'll have some home-brew or at least some tea."

The main shack has a bigger stove but with shakier looking stovepipes. Val, Jules' younger sister, isn't home. The two younger boys, Paul and Jacques, are hopping around like sparrows, but when they see Morag they grow quiet and watchful, and take up silent positions in corners. There are some bunk beds, a mattress on the floor, cooking pots and pans on wooden boxes, a table containing half a loaf of bread and a quart pail of peanut butter. On one wall there is a calendar from two years back, with a colour picture of spruce trees at Galloping Mountain, black against a setting sun, and on another wall Jesus with a Bleeding Heart, his chest open and displaying a valentine-shaped heart pierced with a spiky thorn and dripping blood in neat little drops.

Lazarus is sitting in the room's one easy chair which looks like it has been garnered from the Nuisance Grounds, springs protruding at the bottom of the seat. Morag has not seen Lazarus for a long time, and then only on Main Street on a Saturday night. Once he must have been a very large man, taller than Jules, and broader, but now he looks a bit shrunken, his belly fat and loose, but his ribs bending in upon themselves. He has the vestige of a handsome face, bonily handsome in the way Jules' face is now. The same lanky black hair as Jules.

Now everything is changed. Morag feels uncertain again. Scared. What is she doing here? Do they feel she is intruding? She looks at Jules and sees that things are now changed for him, too.

"Who the hell are you?" Lazarus says.

Morag is unable to say anything. Jules scowls at his father.

"She's Morag Gunn," he says. "You know. From over at Christie Logan's place."

"Oh. Yeh. I know now."

Lazarus begins coughing and keeps on until it seems he will retch. There is a glass full of brown sour-smelling liquid, with bits of white floating scum on it, on the floor beside her chair. He reaches for it. Stops coughing at last. Then he rises and stretches. Pulls in his belly. Looks Morag up and down. The same look on his face as on Skinner's, before. Morag is shocked. Lazarus – an old man. How revolting. Yet she feels his man-energy burning out towards her, all the same, so strongly that for a second it almost draws her in.

Jules knows, too, and puts his arm around her shoulders. Definitely. And, towards Lazarus, menacingly. Lazarus laughs, showing several upper front teeth missing. Refills his glass from a bottle, and holds up the bottle.

"My woman," he grunts. "This here is my woman, now."

"I'll be going now, Dad," Jules growls.

For an instant Lazarus looks – how? Stricken.

"You gotta go now, Skinner?"

"Yeh. There's an Army truck waiting at the bus station to pick us all up."

Lazarus makes as though to move towards his son. Then changes his mind.

"Well, you look out, eh?" he says. "You just look out, there, eh?"

"Yeh. Don't worry. I will."

Jules says goodbye to his young brothers, and then he and Morag leave. He does not look back.

Walking up the hill and through the back streets of the town, now nearly dark, they are both silent. Then Jules begins talking.

"How old you think my old man is, Morag?"

"I dunno. How old?"

"Thirty-nine. He looks twice that, eh? I was born when he was the same age I am now. Nineteen. One thing is for sure. I'm never gonna get like him. But he's not always like today. He don't like me bringing girls home. He gets wild for a woman sometimes. Then he gets drunk and gets into a brawl. I guess he was pretty tough on my mother. She was Métis, too, from up Galloping Mountain way. She thought Manawaka was gonna be the big city, and I guess she thought she was getting a king, there, when she got him. Some king. King Lazarus. Laugh now. No wonder she took off. But Jesus, he can't help himself sometimes. I've seen him get so mad, not at anybody, just at everything, that he'll hit his fist against the wall, just hit it, there, until the knuckles bleed."

"Why? Why?"

"I dunno. Things get him down, I guess. He takes off sometimes and goes up to Galloping Mountain or to the city, and he always comes back. God knows why. This town never done anything for him or any of us. He says it's the same everywhere, christawful jobs and treated like shit. He only got to Grade Three or like that. The best job he's ever held was sectionhand on the CPR, but that quit in the Depression. Sometimes he'd feed us by snaring or shooting jackrabbits. He taught us all how to shoot for meat, even if it was only rabbit."

"He's not done too badly, when you think of it. You never starved."

"Sometimes damn near. But yeh. He hasn't done so terrible. But try to tell him that. Jesus, he was some fighter in his day, though. He's had his nose broken four times. I've seen him take a hundred-and-eighty-pound man and lift him and throw him about twenty feet. I guess the time I hit him he could've killed me, even then, if he'd put his mind to it. Now I think back on it, he didn't do a damn thing. Maybe he was surprised. Or maybe not. When I joined the Army and had a bit of money, I told him I'd pay for him to get the dentist to put in some teeth for him, there, in place of them I knocked out that time. But he said no, he was getting along okay without them."

"Did he really used to tell you those stories when you were a kid, Jules?"

"Yeh. Sometimes even now, when he's drunk, but he don't remember them so hot any more."

"Tell me them," Morag says.

"You wanna hear? Why?"

"I don't know. I guess I like stories, is all."

"You're a funny girl, Morag."

But he puts an arm around her, and they walk the chill mudcarpeted streets beside the empty trees and the quiet half-dark houses, and he tells her. Stories for children. As they walk together with their arms around one another, like children away from home with the night coming on.

Then they are at Logans' on Hill Street. They kiss, and want one another but cannot because there is no time left and no place to go.

"So long," Jules says. "I'll be seeing you."

And goes.

The next day, Morag stands at the corner where Hill Street touches Main. The Queen's Own Cameron Highlanders march through the main street of Manawaka. It is very excit-ing. People wave and shout. The soldiers grin a little but do not look around. Eyes front. They are in dress uniform, khaki jackets and tartan kilts, the Cameron plaid. The pipers walk ahead, leading. They are playing "The March of the Cameron

Men." It has a splendour in it. You could follow that music to the ends of the world.

It is in fact to the end of their world that most of these men are following the music.

The news of Dieppe changes the town of Manawaka. It will never be the same again. Not until this moment has the War been a reality here. Now it is a reality. There are many dead who will not be buried in the Manawaka cemetery up on the hill where the tall spruces stand like dark angels. There are a great many families who now have fewer sons, or none.

Morag reads the casualty lists. Column after column, covering page after page, it seems, in the *Winnipeg Free Press*. Among the men from Manawaka, she looks for those she knows.

Chorniuk, S. (That would be Stan Chorniuk, from the BA Garage.)

Duncan, G. (That would be Mavis' cousin George.)

Gunn, F.L. (From Freehold, but no relation to Morag.)

Halpern, C. (Jamie's brother.)

Kamchuk, N. (Nick, who quit school after Grade Ten.)

Kowalski, J. (Steve's brother.)

Lobodiak, J. (Mike's brother John, the handsome one.)

Macalister, P. (The banker's son.)

Macdonald, G. (Gerald, who used to work in the butcher's.)

MacLachlan, D. (Lachlan's son Dave, who would've taken over the *Manawaka Banner*.)

MacIntosh, C.M. (Chris, son of the High School janitor.)

McVitie, J.L. (The lawyer's son, Ross' brother.)

And on. And on.

She has looked first to see, and there is no Tonnerre listed. Did he get away? It is somehow difficult to believe that anyone could have got away.

The newspapers for days are full of stories of bravery, courage, camaraderie, initiative, heroism, gallantry, and deter- mination in the face of heavy enemy fire. Are any of the stories true? Probably it does not matter. They may console some.

What is a true story? Is there any such thing?

The only truth at the moment seems to be in the long long lists of the dead. The only certainty is that they are dead. Forever and ever and ever.

Morag lies awake, thinking of the last time she saw Jules. Wondering if she ever will see him again. If he will survive.

SKINNER'S TALE OF LAZARUS' TALE OF RIDER TONNERRE

Well, my old man, he told me this about Rider Tonnerre, away back there, so long ago no one knows when, and Lazarus Tonnerre sure isn't the man to tell the same story twice, or maybe he just couldn't remember, because each time he told it, it would be kind of different.

Anyway, there is this guy, away back then, and they call him *Chevalier* – Rider – because he handles a horse so good and because his own horse is a white stallion name of *Roi du Lac*, King of the Lake, and how Rider got that horse is – he got it in a kind of spooky way, because once in a dream he saw it and it spoke to him and told him to spend one whole night beside this certain lake, see, which everybody believed was haunted or like that, and Rider *did* that, even though anybody else would've been scared to, see, and just about dawn, this huge white stallion came up out of the lake and stayed with Rider ever after. Of course it could've swum from the other side, or something, but the way Lazarus told it, that horse had special powers. I dunno if it ever talked except that once in a dream, though. And that Rider, there, he could also ride a bull moose, and sometimes he used to do that, just for a joke, and to scare the hell out of guys who bragged how strong and great *they* were.

Another thing is that Rider was also called Prince of the Braves. He wasn't all Indian, though. He was Métis, only back there, then, our people called themselves *Bois-Brûlés*. Burnt wood. I dunno know why. Maybe the fires they made to smoke the buffalo meat. Maybe their own skins, the way they looked.

Okay, so this Rider, eh, he is so goddamn good on a horse he can outride any man on the prairies. They have races, see, and he always wins, him and King of the Lake. And Rider's rifle, now, it's called *La Petite*, and he's so good that he can be going full gallop on that stallion, and he never misses a buffalo at one thousand yards or like that. He's about seven-feet-tall, and he wears a big black beard.

Now, one time there was a bunch of Englishmen – goddamn *Anglais*, as they used to be called – and they came in to take away the Métis land and to stop the people from hunting buffalo. And these guys had a bunch of Arkanys with them.

(*Arkanys?*)

That is how my dad called the Scotchmen. Men from Orkney, I guess. So a bunch of the Métis, there, they said *Shit on this idea: they're not coming here to take over our land and stop us from hunting.* But they sat on their asses all the same and didn't move. So that Rider Tonnerre, he says *We're gonna hunt these Anglais and Arkanys like we hunt the buffalo, so c'mon there, boys*. It was some place around Red River, there, and they see all these Englishmen and their hired guns the Arkanys.

(Hired guns? I bet they weren't!)

Sure, they were. Anyway it's just a story. So Rider Tonnerre and the others, they make an ambush, see, and the other guys fall for it and ride straight in. So Rider, he starts picking them off with his rifle, *La Petite*, and the other Métis do the same. The English and the Arkanys try to shoot back, but they're not doing so hot, and in the end every single one of them got killed. And one of Rider's men made up a song about it, only my old man, he don't remember it. But he said his father, Old Jules, used to sing it sometimes.

(Hey – I know. That would be "Falcon's Song," and the battle would be Seven Oaks, where they killed the Governor.)

That so? I never connected it with that, because my dad's version was a whole lot different.

SKINNER'S TALE OF RIDER TONNERRE AND THE PROPHET

Another time, a long time later, I guess, because Rider Tonnerre was an old old man, anyway, another time, there, the government men from Down East, they're really getting mean and they plan on getting the Métis land, all of it. They are one hell of a mean outfit, and at least I'm damn sure that much of the story is really true. They send in men to take all the measurement of the land, so's they'll know how much they got when they get it. So Rider Tonnerre, he says to himself *The hell with this*. He is an old man, so he knows he can't be leader, see? But he knows somebody who can. Somebody who is just waiting the chance. Now this guy is – I guess you'd call him Prophet. He is like a prophet, see? And he has the power.

(The power?)

He can stop bullets – well, I guess he couldn't, but lots of people, there, they believed he could. And he has the sight, too. That means he can see through walls and he can see inside a man's head and see what people are thinking in there. He's Métis, but very educated. How the hell he ever got to get that way, I wouldn't know.

(You're talking about Riel.)

Sure. But the books, they lie about him. I don't say Lazarus told the story the way it happened, but neither did the books and they're one hell of a sight worse because they made out that the guy was nuts.

(I know.)

Well, the Prophet, then, he's a very tall guy, taller even than Rider Tonnerre.

(I thought he was supposed to be a very short guy.)

No. Very tall. And he carries a big cross with him all the time – this protects him, like. He's a very religious guy, see? Well, so here is our guys, not knowing what the hell to do, and the Prophet is trying to tell them, but all they're actually doing at the moment is hunting, drinking and screwing. So then, Rider Tonnerre, there, he goes to all the families of our people and he tells them a gutted jackfish would have more guts than what they've got, and this really shamed them. They really only needed somebody to tell them to get up off their asses and oil their rifles for a different kind of hunt. So they went along with the Prophet, and they took the Fort, there.

(They lost it again, though.)

Yeh, the government from Down East sent in about ten thousand soldiers, with cannon and like that. But that wasn't the end of it, by God.

SKINNER'S TALE OF OLD JULES AND THE WAR OUT WEST

It would be some time later, out west, near Qu'Appelle or around there in Saskatchewan, and my grandad old Jules who was just a young guy then, he was out there. He was a good hand with a rifle, and he went out to fight with the Prophet's men, because the Métis were putting on a war, there, for their land, see? Having lost it all around here, around Red River. So they got the Indians to join them, the Crees and Stonies and like that.

(Big Bear. Poundmaker.)

Yeh, those chiefs. And more. Lots more. I don't know their names. They weren't as good with a rifle as our people, but they were pretty damn good and they had a lot of men. Anyway, the way my grandad told it – at least, the way Lazarus says he told it – is that when Jules got there, things were going good. The Prophet and his guys and the Indians and their guys, they'd just beat the shit out of the Mounties at someplace, and everybody was feeling pretty fine. But what happens then? What happens is that the government from Down East sends in this fucking huge army, see? Not just with rifles, hell no. They've got the works. Cannon, even machine guns probably, if they were invented in those days. So the Métis are trying the old ambush, like a buffalo hunt. Well, Jules is dug in really fine, there, covered up in a pit with poplar branches and that. And he's sniping and picking off soldiers, and he gets him maybe a dozen or so. The guy they call Dumont, the lieutenant, like, he wants to attack in real full strength, but the Prophet, he's walking around with his big cross, waiting for the sign. From God, I guess. And Dumont's losing his mind because he wants to attack so bad he can taste it, but the Prophet keeps stalling. And Jules and them, they're still picking off as many soldiers as they can. Well, the Prophet waits for the sign a bit too long, because by that time the big guns begin. Jules stays right there in his cover, eh? All that yelling and firing and the big guns – he figures he's a dead duck if he breaks his cover. Guys dropping all around. Dead horses. Jesus, I always thought too bad about the horses, eh? They never done a thing to deserve it. But got shot just the same. Anyway, Jules picks off fifteen or so of the Eastern men before he gets a bullet in the thigh. Then he passes out.

When he wakes up, he's all covered in stiff blood, and he can hardly move, and he's still buried in poplar branches, and the whole goddamn thing's all over and everybody else is gone. He doesn't move for one whole day. He can't, on account of his bullet wound. So then he crawls out and makes it to a farm somewhere, our people, and lives there for a while. Then he gets the hell out, and winds up here, finally, having brought a Saskatchewan Métis girl back with him. Oh yeh – and the name of that place, the last battle, it was Batoche.

(They hanged Riel, the government did.)

Yeh. They hanged him. Dumont got away, though, just like my grandad.

SKINNER'S TALE OF DIEPPE
?

Memorybank Movie: The Flamingo

The RCAF has a training base at South Wachakwa, and this is a boon for many of the Manawaka girls. Not especially, however, for Morag. Sometimes she goes to the Saturday night dances at The Flamingo, with Julie or with Eva, who has become pretty in her pale and gutless way and who dances every dance because it isn't only gentlemen who prefer blondes, it is every goddamn smart-aleck in the whole Airforce. Morag is too tall for many of them, not actually taller than they are, but five-eight and they prefer tiny frail creatures like Eva, who they can look down on and who will say *Gee! Really?* to everything they say. Morag has tried but is not the type. Sooner or later she either finds herself talking, which does nothing for her popularity, or else sinks into a semi-hostile silence, hating their assumed slickerdom, the way they are contemptuous of the girls they are trying to make. Not as though it might be something both might want to do, but only as though the girl were a mare to be mounted by a studhorse.

The hell with them. They never talk to you as though you are actually *there*, but only put a knee between your legs and get a hard-on against you while pretending to dance.

She hankers after them, their tallness, the sexy sweat smell of them. She wants them. She wants them to want her.

When asked to dance, Morag does not know how to flirt. How do girls learn? Does she really want to join the circus, be a performing filly going through her prancing paces? Pride says *Hell, no.* Longing, on the other hand, says *Try anything.* She tries. What are the words? *I'll bet you say that to all the girls.* Not much of an opener if they haven't actually said anything. *Gee, you're some dancer.*

The words won't come up into her mouth. How corny could you get, to talk words like that? The boy with whom she is dancing clamps a damp hand on her breasts and shuffles along, veering her backwards to "Tommy Dorsey Boogie."

"Not very talkative, are you?" he says.

Morag swallows her nonexistent saliva. What is it makes your mouth so dry here?

"Where – where are you going, once you're finished training, I mean?"

The airman shifts his gum to the other side of his mouth, just outside her radio-receiving-station ear.

"How should I know?" he says.

"What do you think of Manawaka?" Desperation. What would Betty Grable say, under similar circumstances? With a bust like hers, what would she need to say? Well, Morag's isn't so bad, either. But B. Grable isn't about nine feet tall.

"This town? It's a dump," the boy is saying. "I come from Calgary. Now *there's* some place."

"Yeh. I guess so. I've never been –"

Anywhere. Except Manawaka. This will change, though. By God and the Apostles and all the Saints, it will.

"I don't aim to stay here," Morag finds herself blurting. "I'm gonna get to college when I've got enough money. I'm through High School now, I've just got a job. I'm working on the *Manawaka Banner*."

Silence from him. Busy with the gum. Spearmint.

"That's the town newspaper," she adds.

"Oh?" the airman says. "Well, thanks for the dance."

The dances are played in sets of three. You are supposed to keep the same partner for three tunes. This is the end of the second one.

Morag bolts like a shot elk to the Ladies' Powder Room, upstairs. Locks herself in the john. Her refuge, as of old.

john of Ages
locked for me
let me hide
myself in thee.

She laughs, but quietly and to herself. Not that even a laugh aloud would be heard over the birdflock voices of the girls who are gathered around the mirrors, putting on lipstick for the millionth time. Some girls hide in the Ladies' all evening.

Well, tonight wasn't as bad as the time she had been emboldened by a boy's friendly half-shy smile and had asked him if he liked poetry. Hell no, he had said, he was raised on a chicken farm and hated the buggers. Thinking she had said *poultry*.

Morag walks out of the cubicle. There is Eva. Looking soft and fragile as a yellow rose. In a blue and yellow dirndl skirt, new. With huge scared eyes, looking at Morag.

"What *is* it, Eva? What's the matter? Are you okay?"

"No," Eva says. Not crying, not sniffling as of yore. Just staring with unblinking eyes like a baby bird does when it falls out of the nest and is too petrified to move away from any kind of danger. "I didn't mean to tell you. I ain't your worry. But – oh Morag. I'm two months gone."

"Oh my God, Eva."

"What'll I do?" Eva's anguished whisper. "I'm ascared to tell my dad. He'll whip the piss outa me. I know he will. You know him."

"Yeh. Well, look, Eva, there must be something. Is the guy – I mean –"

"He says he'd really love to marry me," Eva breathes, a little more softly now, almost smiling. "He bought me this here skirt and blouse. He really thinks a lot of me. He said so. I'm not kidding you."

"Well, then –"

"He's got a wife in Moose Jaw," Eva says.

Happy endings all the way for Eva Winkler, born to grief as the sparks fly upward.

Downstairs, music.

"Eva – I just don't know. I don't know at all what you should do."

Christie, years ago. The parcel in the garbage tin. *I buried it in the Nuisance Grounds – that's what it was, wasn't it? A nuisance.*

A kid. Shakespeare. Milton. Not very likely, with Eva Winkler, admittedly, but you never could tell. Well, even an ordinary kid. A real kid, who would grow up.

"You could – I mean, people *do* have them adopted."

"It ain't that part of it worries me," Eva says. "I'm ascared of my dad. He'd never forgive me for getting in trouble."

Morag and Eva walk home together. Eva shivers, cries a little but not much.

And aborts herself that night with a partly straightened-out wire clotheshanger. As Mrs. Winkler whispers in horror, then goes back to sit with Eva, too frightened to do anything. But later on, doing something becomes necessary.

"My goddamn girl's plenty sick with her monthlies," Gus Winkler bellows at the Logans' midnight door. "She been bleedin' like a stuck pig, there, my woman says. What I do, Christie, eh? Goddamn women."

Christie drives Eva to the hospital in the Scavenger truck. Morag sits up until he returns.

Gutless. Eva? Now really so, but not in the other way. What could Morag have done? Was there anything? Maybe not, but it will stay with her forever. She will never be rid of it. How will Eva feel? If she lives.

"She'll live," Christie says, returning. "Dr. Cates says she'll live. Suppose that's a good thing, although I wouldn't bank on it. She won't be able to have any kids. Maybe that's lucky, too. Och aye, Morag. What a christly bloody life."

"What did Dr. Cates tell Gus?"

"That the girl was anaemic and she haemorrhaged."

"Did Gus –?"

"Yeh. He believed it. Old Gus has never been none too bright. Jesus, he's a stupid man, thank God."

"What happened to the –"

Christie's watery and increasingly red-rimmed blue eyes harden.

"I seen Eva's mother while Gus was yelling at the boy when we come back. Never you mind, Morag. It'll be seen to."

Another candidate for the town's unofficial cemetery.

Eva, when she returns finally, walks a little stooped. Goes out to work as a hired girl. Some not-too-fussy guy will marry her someday, maybe. Or maybe not.

Morag recalls herself two years ago, and the chance she took, was willing to take, and what might have happened if the event had worked out differently. It never occurred to her, then. Now it does. Now she knows one thing for sure. Nothing – *nothing* – is going to endanger her chances of getting out of Manawaka. And on her own terms, not the town's.

But it's not fair. It's not fair. It's the man who has to take the precautions, and if he doesn't, forget it, sister. There are other ways. But how would you find out, or get whatever it is, if not married? Maybe you might in a city, just maybe, but not here.

Jules?

She remembers how it was, and the feeling of his skin all over hers. Wants him again, as she often often does. Well, too bad. Nothing can be done about it. No answers. Is he alive, even? No reports. No news. She reads the casualty lists, always.

When she was a young child, she used to believe that everything would be all right once she was grown-up and nobody could tell her what to do. Now she wishes someone *could* tell her what to do.

Memorybank Movie: The Banner

Lachlan MacLachlan, editor and owner of the *Manawaka Banner*, is not a difficult boss, although sometimes unpredictable. A bulky, thickset man, bald except for a fringe of grey around the back of his skull. Wearing heavy hairy tweed suits even in summer. Suffering often from hangovers, at which times he closes the door into his office and sips Alka-Seltzer or Cokes, answering only to urgent questions, of which there are few. Apart from the three printers, Morag comprises Lachlan's entire staff. He has until recently done it all himself, but his son's death has depleted him. At first, Morag was shy and a little frightened, for Lachlan never ever smiles, much less laughs. But now they get on. She fetches the Alka-Seltzer on the bad days, and calls him Lachlan, like everybody else in town does.

Morag has her own desk. A roll-top oak desk with drawers. A typewriter. Just like a real reporter. She has learned typing at High School. Jock MacRae, one of the printers, has taught her how to read proof. If Lachlan doesn't feel up to doing the layouts, Jock does them and is teaching Morag. Morag writes or rewrites:

> Obituaries
> Town Council meetings
> Courthouse cases (if any)
> Rotary Club dinners
> IODE meetings (the Daughters of Empire in fruit-salad-
>   like hats)
> School Board meetings

News (e.g. Accidents, Broken Legs, Lightning Striking
Barns, etc.)
Local Reports from South Wachakwa, Freehold and
so on.

Many of these items are written down by people who
were there, and given to her. She then rewrites them in newspaper style, as Lachlan has taught her. She is not permitted to
rewrite the Local Reports from South Wachakwa and
Freehold.

Mrs. H. Pearl, widow of late Henry respected farmer
spend the weekend visiting with her son Simon and
wife in Manwaka and a good time had by all at a tea
given in her hounor by Mrs. Cates wife of Doct Cates
son of late Alvin Cates of South Wachakwa Mrs.
Cates had red roses on a silver baskt and four kinds cake
served. Glad you had a good visit Mrs. Pearl and
welcom back!

Morag thinks this is hilarious.
"Lachlan – can't I rewrite it? I *mean*."
It is one of Lachlan's poorer mornings, but he struggles
bravely against headache, nausea, and cramps in various parts
of himself.
"They don't want it rewritten, Morag. They want it as it
is. You can clean up the punctuation, grammar and spelling.
That is all. As I have said before, if my imperfect memory
serves, God help me, I have all the symptoms of a pregnant
woman this morning – except I suppose they don't normally
twitch or imagine their eyeballs are falling out. *Mea culpa.*
Now stop fussing about those reports, girl."

"But –"

"But *what*?" Lachlan's voice is low but slightly menacing.

"They make the *Banner* look like – well, like a small-town paper."

"They do, eh? Well, that is precisely what it is, Morag. And if you think your prose style is so much better than theirs, girl, remember one thing. Those people know things it will take you the better part of your lifetime to learn, if ever. They are not very verbal people, but if you ever in your life presume to look down on them because you have the knack of words and they do not, then you do so at your eternal risk and peril. Do you understand what I am saying?"

Morag gazes at him, embarrassed and angry and partly comprehending.

"Yeh. I guess so. A lot of people here look down on me. I don't think of myself as looking down on anybody, Lachlan."

"No? Well, maybe you better have another think about that one, then, to make quite sure. And for God's sake quit feeling set upon. You're not trapped. The doors are open. You couldn't say the same for some. I know whereof I speak. Go on, get out. Tell Jock he's to handle the layout for Simlow's sale handbills. Green newsprint, tell him. Not that puke-coloured yellow. *Green*."

"Do you want some coffee, Lachlan?"

"Get *out*," Lachlan says heavily. "And bring me four aspirin and a cold Coca-Cola. Make that two Cokes. Tell Miklos to charge it against what he owes me, the chiseller."

The Junior League, young women from the city, bring out an exhibition of prints of paintings to Manawaka, for the enlightenment of the local populace, and Morag wanders around the United Church basement where she used to go to Sunday school, looking. A thirtyish woman in sleek grey skirt and blue twin-sweater set with pearls (real?) at her neck sits smiling graciously at the three people who have thus far turned up. It is all very embarrassing.

And then

The picture is of the head of a girl, features so finely cut, so entirely beautiful that you know all at once this would be how an angel or the Mother of Christ would have looked if ever such had existed. The eyes meet yours, look into yours, without flinching or avoiding. Her hair you could call *tresses*, as it says in very ancient tales and the bardic songs, hair in long twisting tendrils of light brown coppergold filled with the sun and coming from the sun. Like a queen in the old old poems, like Cuchulain's young queen, the woman beloved by all men.

Morag stands for a long time, looking.

"Lovely, isn't it, dear?" the twin-set and pearls lady says.

Lovely. What a word. Like using a marshmallow to picture God. But *beautiful* is nearly as bad. How could you say? How can there be words for that face, for what lies behind those eyes? There have to be words. Maybe there are not. This thought is obscurely frightening. Like knowing that God does not actually see the little sparrow fall.

Morag goes back to the *Banner* office and writes the report four times. Shows it to Lachlan. He reads it carefully. Then looks up.

"It's a pretty good report," he says. "But – this picture wasn't painted recently by someone in Winnipeg, Morag. It's part of a larger painting. *Venus Rising from the Waves.* It was painted by a man called Botticelli. A long time ago. In Italy. I'll bring you a book that tells about it."

Morag takes the sheets of newsprint and crumples them small into her hands.

"You would only have to alter it a little," Lachlan says, not looking at her.

"No."

"You learn hard, with that stiff neck of yours," Lachlan says. "There's no shame in not knowing something. You're not alone."

"That's where you're wrong," Morag says.

The report is never printed. But when Lachlan brings the book, she spends a long time looking at it.

Memorybank Movie: Down in the Valley, Act III

Winter, and the snow squeaks and scrunches dryly underfoot, even on Main Street where the *Banner* office is. Morag has new fleece-lined leather boots and a grey tweed coat with a real beaver-lamb collar, but there is no way of keeping warm in thirty-below weather.

Lachlan is already at the office. He summons her.

"There's been a fire down in the valley, at the old Tonnerre shack, Morag. The older girl – what's her name? – and her two kids were caught in it. You better go down and see what's happened. Rufus Nolan's called in the Mounties, but he'll be there as well – he'll tell you."

For an instant Morag fails to understand what *caught in it* means. Then realizes.

"Lachlan – Piquette and her kids – are they –"

"Dead. Yes, I believe so."

"I can't go. Lachlan."

"What do you mean, you can't go? Of course you can go. Rufus or somebody'll give you a lift back, likely. It's not that far."

"I – don't want to go, Lachlan."

"Oh christ. Of *course* you don't want to go. Who would? But you're the one who thinks the *Banner* shouldn't act like such a small-town paper. Here is a genuine news story. Now go."

The wind worsens at the rim of the town, knifes at her as she flounders through the snow on the valley road. The bare black branches have been enfolded and cloaked with last night's snowfall, and would delight her with their radiance under other circumstances.

Morag has met Piquette on the streets occasionally, since Piquette returned to Manawaka. They have not spoken, except to say *Hi* to one another. Piquette, once slender, has gown flabbily fat and walks with the lurch of the habitual drunk. She has been arrested several times, like her father before her, for outrageously shrieking her pain aloud in public places, usually in the form of obscene insults to whoever happens to be handiest. Her husband took off and left her, just as Skinner said he would, and the two children, two small boys with large solemn dark eyes, appear to be about one and two years old. What went wrong? Or did it go wrong so long ago that there is now no single cause or root to be found?

Morag could at least have talked to her. But Piquette wouldn't have wanted to. How can Morag be sure of that? She is, though.

At the Tonnerre place, there is not a lot of noise going on. Valentine left home after Piquette returned, so the two younger brothers are by themselves, and are now walking towards Jules' shack, which still stands. No one is crying. There is a stillness in the frozen air.

The Tonnerre place, both the original shack and Lazarus' later addition, has been burned to the ground and is now only a mass of tangled still-smoking charred timbers and twisted shapeless blackened metal. Rufus Nolan stands bulky and bewildered in his navy blue greatcoat and absurd policeman's cap. The town fire truck is leaving. There is nothing for them to do now. The Mounties have evidently been and gone.

"What happened, Mr. Nolan?"

"Them stovepipes must've been old as the everlasting hills," Rufus says. "Lazarus and the boys were away. The girl was probably drunk. The place must've gone up like tinder."

Lazarus stands alone, his face absolutely blank, portraying nothing. He looks at Morag but does not see her.

Dr. Cates stands talking to Niall Cameron, the undertaker. There is no town ambulance. Niall has brought his old black hearse instead.

"Well, there's no point even examining them," Dr. Cates is saying. "You can tell even from this distance, all right."

The smell of smoke hangs thickly in the frosty air. And something else, a sweetish nauseating odour.

"Somebody will have to help me go in there and get them," Niall Cameron says in a hard low voice.

He stands there, bareheaded and tall, running one woollen-gloved hand nervously over his light brown hair and looking towards the ruins of the shack, the pile of blackened debris where three generations of Tonnerres have lived. Morag looks, too, and then realizes what is still in there. She can see only smokened metal and burnt wood, but there is something else in there as well.

Burnt wood. *Bois-Brûlés.*

Lazarus shambles over to the two men.

"I'm going in," he says. "They're mine, there, them."

Dere mine dere, dem.

Niall Cameron's face twists momentarily as though in some inexpressible pain. Then he shakes his head.

"It will take the two of us," he says. "Hold that end of

the stretcher, Lazarus, will you? Where's the goddamn draw-sheet? Oh, here."

Morag turns away. Vomits terribly into the snow. When she is able to look again, the job is done and the back doors of the hearse are closed. Niall Cameron walks over to her and puts one arm around her shoulders, pulling her upright again, forcing her upright.

"For God's sake, Morag Gunn, what are you doing here?"

"Lachlan – but he didn't know it would be –"

"Lachlan's out of his head," Niall Cameron says furiously, "and you can tell him so from me. Do you want a lift? No, I guess not – I'm sorry, Morag. That was stupid of me. I'd forgotten the fire truck had gone."

The only vehicle here now is the hearse. Dr. Cates has come down with Niall Cameron. Rufus Nolan has come down with the now-departed Mounties and is at this moment climbing into the hearse.

"It's okay, Mr. Cameron. I know you didn't – well, it's okay. I can walk back."

He turns to Paul Cates.

"All right, Paul. Let's go."

Dr. Cates looks very white and sick.

"You know, Niall, I'm almost glad Ewen isn't here. He fixed the girl's legs, years ago."

That would be Dr. MacLeod, who died some years back. He was the one who had overcome the TB in the bone, who had made it possible for Piquette to walk properly. And dance, briefly. And attract Al Cummings.

"He was probably the only one in town who ever did anything for her, then," Niall Cameron says in his harsh bitter voice.

"Should I say anything to Lazarus?" Dr. Cates asks, as though asking himself.

"What is there to say?" Niall replies. "There's nothing can be said now. Get in, Paul."

The hearse pulls away. Morag begins to walk. Looking back, she sees Lazarus.

He is still standing alone there in the snow.

At the office, Lachlan pours Morag a rye and hands it to her without a word.

"Niall phoned and gave me hell," he says finally. "I'm sorry, Morag. I didn't realize –"

"I know."

"Wasn't there another girl? A younger one?"

"Val. She went away a while ago. I don't know where she is."

"Where's the older brother?" Lachlan asks. "Do you know?"

"He was at Dieppe," Morag says. "But I don't think he got killed."

She recalls then that Lachlan's son did.

Without warning, taking herself by surprise, she puts her head down on the desk and cries in a way she does not remember ever having done before, as though pain were the only condition of human life.

In her report, Morag mentions that Piquette's grandfather fought with Riel in Saskatchewan in 1885, in the last uprising of the Métis. Lachlan deletes it, saying that many people hereabouts would still consider that Old Jules back then had fought on the wrong side.

Memorybank Movie: Beginning and Ending, or Vice-Versa
The War is over. The boys who survived are being sent home.
Morag is leaving Manawaka in the fall, to go to college, having
been adding as much as possible to the bank account which
Henry Pearl started for her, when her parents died, on the proceeds of Louisa Gunn's piano and anything else he could
manage to get out of the Gunn farmhouse before the mortgage company moved in.

Leaving Manawaka. At last. At last. Jubilation. Also, guilt.

Prin scarcely moves at all now, just sits in her chair,
growing heavier and more silent all the time, living only inside
her head, if anywhere. Morag has quit trying to talk to her. Dr.
Cates says it is premature senility and he doesn't know what to
do. Prin can still look after herself, or usually, the toilet and
that, but needs help going upstairs. Who will get the meals
when Morag goes? Christie will have to.

Christie is in none too good shape himself. He drinks very
little any more, but his attacks of strangeness have increased all
the same. Impatiently, Morag sometimes feels he brings them
on purposely. It used to take the bottle. Now he can do it
unaided. First stage, the ranting. The music of the pipes is sometimes described as *ranting*, and that describes Christie. Human
Bagpipes Logan. Blaring up and down, sometimes pacing the
kitchen as he does so, here a pibroch, there a battle march,
etcetera. Fraud. Fraud. Who does he think he's kidding?

Christie has grown even scrawnier with time, and his
Adam's apple is even more frenetic in his throat than it used to
be. He dresses in the same old beat-up overalls, rarely bothering
to change them even when they stink of the Nuisance Grounds.

"Mine was a great family, then," he declares. "The
Logans of Easter Ross, by christ, they used to be a great bloody
family. *This Is the Valour of My Ancestors.* That is a fine motto."

"Oh Christie."

"*The Ridge of Tears*," Christie roars. "That was the war cry. Oh Jesus. Think of it. The Ridge of Tears. And the crest, then. A passion nail piercing a human heart, proper. I always wondered what the hell *proper* meant, and now I'll never know, for who is there to tell me?"

"What does it matter, Christie? It was all so long ago."

The Gunns have no crest, no motto, no war cry, at least according to what it says in the old book Christie still hauls out from time to time. Just as well. It's all a load of old manure.

"It matters to me," Christie rants. "By heaven and all the stars of midnight and by my own right hand and by the holy cross its own self, I say unto you it bloody damn well matters to me, then. What have I done with my life, Morag? Sweet bugger-all. I used to think what was there worth doing? Maybe I was wrong. Oh jesus, I *was* wrong. A disgrace to my ancestors. You get the hell out of here, Morag, you hear, and make something out of yourself. I used to think the only clean job in the world was collecting muck. I chose to be the one who'd collect it. But now I see we're all of us rotting in it all the same, myself as well. It was the pride in me done it. I see it now."

Pride? In being the Scavenger, Keeper of the Nuisance Grounds? He is really wild tonight.

"May I be forgiven," Christie mourns at the top of his voice. "May I be forgiven, but I'm damned if I know who to ask for that. There *is* no forgiveness in the bloody world. None."

"Christie. Sh-sh. It's all right. Sh."

"Them tales I used to tell you. You never knew why I done it."

Oh God. Not this again.

"Hush, Christie."

"I meant well, Morag. That's a christly awful thing to be carved on a man's tombstone. *Here Lies Christie Logan – He Meant Well.* And how can a man even be sure of that?"

Ramble, ramble. And then he would sit in silence, for hours, sometimes shaking all over until the spell passed.

Morag goes out into the soft summer evening. Going into the Regal Café for cigarettes, she meets a man coming out. She stops, does a doubletake. Skinner Tonnerre.

"Jules? Jules!"

He is in civilian clothes, grey flannels, grey sports jacket, snappy grey fedora at an angle on his head. The same angular brown face and slanted eyes. But older. Different. He grins. Neither of them makes any move towards the other. "Yeh, it's me. Got back the other day. How're you doing, Morag? You look different."

"How do you mean?"

"I dunno. Older. I don't mean it bad. You look great."

"Are you – are you staying, Jules?"

"Who, me? You gotta be kidding. I just came back to see – well, how things are. I'm getting out as soon as I can."

"How's – your dad?"

Jules' eyes avoid hers.

"Not so hot. It was a bad thing happened, there."

"Yes. I – I'm sorry."

"I heard you went – well, Val sent me the clipping from the *Banner*."

"Yes."

"Did you –" he searches her face shrewdly, almost angrily. "Did you see *them?* Lazarus won't talk of it. Did you see her, Morag?"

For a moment Morag contemplates saying *Yes*, telling him Piquette suffocated quickly, wasn't touched by the flames. But cannot. He wouldn't believe her, anyway.

"No. Only Niall Cameron and your dad. They went in, and – you know."

Jules nods.

"Was it bad – the place?"

"Yes." It is all she can say.

She gets her cigarettes and walks along Main Street with him. He does not take her arm or touch her.

"I looked in the paper, after Dieppe," she says. "To see if you –"

"Yeh. Well. It wasn't quite the way the papers told it, I guess. All any guy thinks of is staying alive. Some guys were scared so shitless they couldn't even think of that. Yeh, and I guess some guys do think about what's happening to some real close pal."

"Not you?"

"I never had any close pal," Jules says lightly. "Lone wolf, that's me."

Cliché. But true. It *is* him. He is distant, distant from the town, from Morag, from everything, perhaps even from himself.

"Did it – last long?"

"*Yeh.* One million years. Coupla hours, actually. I can't really say. I don't know. Didn't seem very real at the time. Guess you go kind of crazy, like. You just think *Well well that's John Lobodiak dead.* It doesn't mean much at the time."

"You saw John?"

"Yeh. He was right next to me when he got it. He was shot in the guts. He kept trying to hold them in – they were spilling out, there. Ever seen a shot gopher?"

Yes yes when cannot remember the squirming entrails sheets what was it a dream

"Skinner – please. Don't."

For the first time, then, he touches her. Puts an arm around her. She wants to hold him close. But makes no move. Cannot. Why not?

"That's how he was. Like a shot gopher. His guts. Not his eyes, though."

"How –"

"Like a horse's eyes in a barn fire," Jules says flatly.

Always the horses. For the prairie men, always the horses. The comparison. The god, living, dying.

John Lobodiak, handsomer than his younger brother, kicking them all out of the car that Saturday night, so he could take his girl home.

"Well, skip it," Jules says. "How about you?"

"Going to Winnipeg this fall. To college. And I'm never coming back."

"Hey, that's something, eh?" He drops his arm from around her. "Go to college and marry a rich professor, how about that?"

"Yeh, I can see it all now. I *don't* think. What're you going to do?"

Jules shrugs.

"How should I know? I don't much care. Maybe something will turn up. I don't have to *do* anything all that much. I'm not like you."

True. He isn't. She stiffens.

"You're just like Christie." Disapproval in her voice? Disappointment?

"I'm not," Jules says. "I'm just like – never mind. Well, you'll do okay."

.y that?"

. so bad I can just about smell it on you.

rag."

it?"

Jules stops walking. They have reached Hill Street. He is not going to walk home with her. He grins, but not in the old way, not conspiratorially. Not quite hostile, but nearly. To him, she is now on the other side of the fence. They inhabit the same world no longer.

"I wouldn't know," he says. "But I guess you do. Well, so long. See you around, eh?"

And walks away. As before, not looking back.

Morag does not think about him for very long. She will not. Will not. She has to think about getting ready to leave. Soon. Very soon now.

In the night, the train whistle says *Out There Out There Out There*.

PART THREE

HALLS OF SION

FIVE

Morag sat at the table in the kitchen, with a note-book in front of her and a ballpoint pen in her hand. Not writing. Looking at the river. Getting started each morning was monstrous, an almost impossible exercise of will, in which finally the will was never enough, and it had to be begun on faith.

Last night, sleepless until three A.M., long and stupen-dously vivid scenes unfolded. Too tired to get up and write them down, she still couldn't shut the projector off for the night. Got up and jotted down key words, to remind her. Staring at these key words now, she wondered what in heaven's name they had been meant to unlock.

Jerusalem. Jerusalem? Why? Gone. What had she meant by it?

The postcard from Pique yesterday. No address. Mustn't think of it. Morag didn't want to put the hooks onto Pique, nor to have Pique at this point put the hooks onto her. But a some-what more newsy letter would be appreciated. Idiotic. How many newsy letters had Morag written to Prin and Christie, after she left Manawaka? That was different. Oh, really?

infrequently mown grass down to the
ne window, still alive although for how
he small cedars, spearing lightly feath-
fenced-off patch, where once Sarah
vegetable garden all those years ago. Now
d high seed-headed grasses, what a variety,
And purple thistles, regal, giant. And those
le yellow snapdragons, called Butter-and-Eggs.
summer, the goldenrod. And those little pink
ames and those bright orange and brown softly bris-
wers called – ha! – Devil's Paintbrush. The birds liked
place, especially the goldfinches – it was their restaurant,
those seeds. Morag regarded it as a garden of amazing
splendours, in which God did all the work. Catharine Parr
Traill would have profoundly disagreed, likely.

Morag: Now listen here, Catharine, don't bug me
today, eh? All right, I know. You knew more
about wildflowers than I'll ever know. But you
would have said that there were plenty of
wildflowers in the woods etcetera, without
taking up half the yard with them. You would
diligently have grown turnips, carrots, peas,
scarlet runner beans and other nourishing
plants, as Maudie Smith does. I am caught
between the old pioneers and the new pioneers.
At least Maudie can't give names to the
wildflowers, as you did. Imagine naming
flowers which have never been named before.
Like the Garden of Eden. Power! Ecstasy! I
christen thee Butter-and-Eggs!

Catharine P. Traill: You are exaggerating, as usual, my dear Morag. I, as you know, managed both to write books, with some modest degree of success, while at the same time cultivating my plot of land and rearing my dear children, of whom I bore nine, seven of whom lived. No doubt, my dear, were you to plant an orchard, you would also soon find your writing flowing with grace, not unlike the river yonder.

Morag: You are right, Mrs. Traill. You are correct. Except I don't have your faith. In the Book of Job it says *One generation passeth and another generation cometh, but the earth endureth forever.* That does not any longer strike me as self-evident. I am deficient in faith, although let's face it, Catharine, if I didn't have *some* I would not write at all or even speak to any other person; I would be silent forevermore, and I don't mean G.M. Hopkins' *Elected Silence, sing to me* or any of that – I mean the other kind. The evidence of my eyes, however, does little to reassure me. I suspect you didn't have that problem, just as I suspect you had problems you never let on about. The evidence of your eyes showed you Jerusalem the Golden with Milk and Honey Blest, at least if a person was willing to expend enough elbow grease. No plastic milk jugs bobbing in the river. No excessive algae, fish-strangling. The silver shiver of the carp crescenting. My grand-children will say *What means Fish?* Peering through the goggle-eyes of their gasmasks. Who will tell old tales to children then? Pique used to say *What is a Buffalo?* How many words and lives will be gone when they say *What means Leaf?* Saint Catharine! Where are you now that we need you?

C.P.T.:   I am waiting.

The screen door slammed as someone entered. Not C.P.T. reborn.

"You talking to that same lady, Morag?" Royland enquired.

She looked at his bulky hunched greyness. Wearing, of course, his plaid flannel shirt in this Pit-of-Hell weather. His neat greybeard blown very slightly in the humid blast-furnace breeze.

"Yeh. You never fail to catch me at it, do you?"

"You're alone too much, Morag. As I may have mentioned."

"Even if surrounded by a multitude with banners, Royland, I would still talk to ghosts. I got a postcard from Pique yesterday. Want to see it?"

"Sure. Of course."

Postcard: View of Vancouver harbour, taken from west side of city. Many boats, ships, varicoloured vessels of one kind and another. Buildings tall in background. Excessively blue water.

On the back, with no address, these words:

This city the end. They like to classify people here. Matthew Arnold clash by night right on with this place.

Gord and I do not relate so why fight it? Am okay, so
no dramatics. Tell Tom seagulls fabulous.

Love, Pique.

"Hope this finds you well as it leaves me," Morag said.
"Sometimes I think I know what she's about, and other times
I don't. I know it's inevitable, but it hurts all the same. You
know something, Royland? We think there is *one* planet called
Earth, but there are thousands, even *millions*, like a snake
shedding its skin every so often, but with all the old skins still
bunched around it. You live inside the creature for quite a
while, so it comes as a shock to find you're living now in one
of the husked-off skins, and sometimes you can touch and
know about the creature as it is now and sometimes you can't."

"Pique'll be back soon," Royland said, "before she goes
away for good. It'll be nice to see her again. I'm going into
town. You need anything from the store?"

"No – but thanks. And for the reassurance, too. I mean it."

When Royland had gone, Morag got out yesterday's
newspaper and looked it up again.

There was the picture of Brooke. Telling about his new
appointment. Not just Head of an English Department, not
now. President of a university. Well, well.

My God, what a handsome man he still is.

Another shed skin of another life. And it began happening again, again, as it had been doing for years, and perhaps
the film would never end until she did.

Memorybank Movie: Farewell and Hallelujah
Morag says goodbye hurriedly to Prin, who, obese and silent
and almost motionless now except for the awful *crik-crik-crik*

of the rocking chair, hardly seems to know that Morag is leaving once and for all. Like a tub with eyes. The vague eyes, though, are suddenly wet with uncontrolled unwiped tears. What has been going on, all these months and years, in Prin's skull? Morag, and probably Christie also, has tried to assume that nothing was. Now she is not sure. How much has she treated Prin as a dumb beast, these past years?

"I'll write, Prin. Honestly I will."

The hulk of anonymous oxflesh which was once Prin Logan (christened Princess in another world) now speaks, the hoarse guttural tones of someone who has almost forgotten human speech.

"You be – good girl, now. Dear."

Dear. Morag, as a very young child, eating jelly doughnuts with Prin, being protected from Christie's sometimes-stinging tongue, his oddness.

Morag bends and kisses the pasty pouched face, over-whelmed with past love and present repulsion. She straightens and sees the look on Christie's face – stricken.

He drives her to the CPR station in the old garbage truck. She thanks God it is night. Prays *prays* no one she knows will be taking this train. She has chosen to go by train because most of the kids going to the city for university will be taking the bus.

"Goodbye, Christie. I'll – write."

"Yeh. You do that, Morag." No conviction in his voice. "Well, so long."

She resolves to prove him wrong by writing back regularly. Once a week. At least. Knowing she won't. She dreads Christie standing on the platform, looking at her until the train actually pulls away. But he doesn't. He doesn't even wave to her once she's inside the coach. Just turns and walks back to the garbage truck.

The train clonks slowly into motion, and soon the wheels are spinning their steelsong *clickety-click-clickety-click*, and the town is receding. There go the rusty-red grain elevators, the tallest structures around here. There goes the cemetery. There go the Nuisance Grounds, forever and ever.

Morag settles herself. Exultant. On her way. She is alone in this coach, the plum plush seats puffing out ancient dust with every clank and sway of the train. No other passengers, it seems, on the night train to Everywhere. Only Morag Gunn, swifting into life.

Then – panic.

Alone in the coach, Morag Gunn, erstwhile of Manawaka, prudently goes into the john before she will allow herself to cry. The conductor might happen along. She can bear anything, she knows, really, but not for the people to see.

Memorybank Movie: Higher Learning – The Lowdown
A year older than almost everyone in her class – this does make a difference. There are four men who are even older, returned veterans, but they are all married. Or does the difference reside more in the fact that so many of these kids went to High School together in the city? Or is Morag's own goddamn fault, being both proud and humiliatingly shy? Thinking she looks gawky, not knowing half the time whether other people are kidding or not.

The others flow in and out of classrooms and cafeteria, and she does, too. Usually by herself. So what? This is what she's wanted, to be here, and now she's here.

The late September dust fills the city streets, and the prairie maples are yellow, leaves blowing against her face as she walks to the streetcar stop. Manawaka has sidewalks, too, but the cement there isn't as hard on your feet there as it is here, perhaps because there you sometimes walk on the roadsides, through the grass.

She sees the night city rarely, with neon signs of crimson, yellow, blue, shrieking cigarettes or hotels or brands of cars. Lights should be blazing, impressive. Perhaps if you couldn't read these would be. By dark she's usually in her room, in the place where she boards, studying.

Her boardinghouse is away to hell and gone, North Winnipeg, half a mile beyond the end of the Selkirk Avenue streetcar line. No wonder Mrs. Crawley was so delighted when Morag turned up. She'd probably had a hundred others turn down the room. Morag had thought it might not be possible to find another room. Idiotic. The Crawleys rent only the one room. It is a small house and Morag's room is about the size of the one she had at Christie's. The size of a large cupboard. She doesn't care. She's used to it. The room will be freezing in winter, she foresees. It has a bed, a dresser and a chair. She uses the dresser top as a desk.

Mrs. Crawley is a Catholic, although not all that devout. Above Morag's bed, when she moved in, there hung The Bleeding Heart of Jesus. It looked familiar, and then she remembered – the Tonnerres' place. Even without this, the picture would be hard enough to endure, Jesus with a soft, yielding, nothing-type face and a straggling wispy beard, His expression that of a dog who knows it is about to be shot. As usual in these pictures, the Heart Itself is shown in violent purplish red, His chest having apparently been sawn open to reveal It, oozing with neatly symmetrical drops of lifeblood, *drip-drip-drip*. All tear-shaped.

"Why did you take Our Lord down, Morag?" Mrs. Crawley enquires.

Not sternly, just sort of wearily. Mrs. Crawley is still

quite a young woman, in her late twenties, fluffy short beige hair the colour of a camel-hair coat, and meek blue eyes which only rarely spark with the momentary insistence that she, too, may possibly be real. She and Mr. Crawley have four young kids. Mrs. Crawley sighs a lot.

"I'm – I'm sorry." Morag struggles. "It's hard to explain. I was brought up –"

What a great lie she is about to perpetrate. As if it would make any difference what church had been her spiritual home, so-called, in her tender years. She would still have wanted to throw up every time she looked at the Heart. Mrs. Crawley, however, is sympathetic.

"It's okay, Morag, you never mind, then. I understand you've been raised a Protestant. I'll take it for the girls' room."

Lucky girls, now two and four. But Mrs. Crawley is no bigot. Rather, she is wistful and sometimes defiant.

"I'd never go against my Faith, Morag," she declares, "but all the same, I sometimes think – well, you know – if I'd known before I was married what I know now, I'd have had some fun, eh? Not that *we* do anything to prevent God's Will, of course. We're expecting again, did I mention, and soon I'll be bloated up like a stout old lady with the wind. I wasn't a bad-looking girl."

"You're still good-looking," Morag cries, torn with the necessity of saying two things at once, "and anyway, you should've seen the snobbishness that went on in the church where I went as a kid. The United, it was."

Mrs. Crawley nods, but isn't really concerned with Comparative Religion.

"Well, it's nice of you to *say* I'm still not too bad-looking," she says. "I got such awful stretch marks on my stomach and thighs after Marnie. Still, who sees them but Jim?"

Sad. Sad. Morag vows to have umpteen lovers but no husband. No kids. No stretch marks (what are *they?*). Mr. Crawley is balding although only thirty-two, and is skinnily pale. He comes home very tired from the Meat Packers where he works, which is no wonder when you consider he has to heave around sides of beef and he looks as though he'd have trouble hoisting a five-pound bag of flour. He is not, Morag has gathered, of a very romantic temperament. *Romantic* is Mrs. Crawley's word. It means he believes in making love once a fortnight, at most. Mrs. Crawley is perpetually riven, wanting love and not wanting any more kids. It is a trying situation.

Mrs. Crawley cooks mainly boiled cabbage and wieners, or boiled turnips and (very small) portions of bacon. With gobs of watery mashed potatoes. It isn't very different from Christie and Prin's house. Which is disappointing. Morag considers seeking another room. But how can she, after Mrs. Crawley has confided all that about her sex life, and so on? Also, they need the money. A dilemma. Morag knows she will dislike living here more and more as the winter clenches in, and will be unable to move.

If Mrs. Crawley were tough, hard-spoken and angry, it would be easy. It is her flaccid lack of fight which makes it impossible. As with Eva Winkler, whom in some ways she resembles. Morag gags inwardly at the weak, against whom she has few defences. But she resents and fears them.

All the same, Morag talks more with Mrs. Crawley than with any of the golden-appearing college kids. She knows they are not all golden, not all happy, not all inheritors of some as-yet-unspoiled Garden. She isn't that stupid. She has seen the worse-off ones walking alone and quietly, or else trying to ingratiate themselves, clownlike, into the brazen multitude.

These walking wounded she avoids like the plague. It might be catching.

One day, walking the narrow cracked sidewalks from the end of the streetcar line to the Crawleys' house, the bare lean board houses reminding her of Hill Street and the leaves still splendid with the last of the upblazing autumn, she hears the geese.

The Canada geese are flying very high up in their wide V-formation, the few leaders out in front, the flock sounding their far clear cold cry that signals the approaching frost. Going somewhere. Able to go, at will. Last year she saw them and thought *This time next year I'll be away too.* Now she is away. Away is here. Not far enough away.

Morag watches, angrily grieving and loving, until the geese have passed over.

Winter, and snow of many textures. Hard-packed snow on Portage Avenue and the downtown streets, dirty from the trampling boots. Deep, dry snow, creaking underfoot on the ten-million-mile trek from streetcar to house. And on lawns and little-used roadsides, the drifts are three feet high, crusted and white like royal icing, and when you break through the crust, the snow underneath is light and powdery as icing sugar. Snow everywhere. Black bare tree boughs are transformed overnight into white glittering traceries, candelabra, chandeliers of trees, the sun lighting them as though from within. In the mornings, frost patterns on the bedroom window, painted by windbrushes. Beautiful, but bloody cold. The breath seems to freeze in your throat, and your lungs feel full of ice.

Morag's room is so cold in the mornings she can hardly bear to snake slowly out of bed. The Crawleys' furnace is not efficient and Mr. Crawley does not stoke it sufficiently in the evenings, as Mrs. Crawley fears fire during the night. Morag would rather take the chance, and go out of life, if necessary, in a blazing splendour, gloriously warm. It is, however, not up to her. Taking a bath is a torture. Only those truly devoted to cleanliness would ever venture into the Crawleys' tepid bath-water and steel-cold tub in midwinter. Morag is one of these (*what if I smell?*). The Crawley kids are not. Twice a week they scream and shriek as their mother exhaustedly forces them into the bath. The window is right beside the tub, and the storm-window does not fit properly. December seeps in.

Morag studies in bed, the dirty wine satin eiderdown drawn around her. Feels ill. Writes home (home?) to Christie, saying she has flu and will not be back in Manawaka for Christmas. Flu or cowardice?

Christie sends her a money order for five dollars. She cries, under the wine eiderdown, bitterly repentant. But does not change her mind. Reads *Paradise Lost*, sneezing.

Memorybank Movie: Ella

Morag is daring the world of the elect, those who run the college newspaper and who in the literary section print mainly selections from their own prose and poetry. Her story is concealed inside the first volume of Taine's *History of English Literature* which she holds nonchalantly under her arm. In the *Veritas* office, she finds herself standing awkwardly beside a short rather stocky girl with auburn hair. The girl, who is Ella Gerson, is in Morag's year but they have not spoken before. Ella is holding a copy of *Das Kapital* nonchalantly under her arm.

"I'll bet," Morag says, grinning, "you've got a poem or something stashed away inside *that*."

Ella looks, at first, amazed. Then strikes a hand across

her forehead in what later comes to be known as the Sarah Bernhardt gesture.

"Good God!" she cries, although not so loudly that anyone else can hear. "My guilty secret has been discovered. How'd you know?"

Morag holds up Taine.

"Short story."

"Oh. Well, hell, and I thought I was being so original."

"I wouldn't have thought of *Marx*," Morag says admiringly.

"If you'd been me, with *my* mother, you would've," Ella says.

They wait some more. Hoping to catch the eye or polite enquiry of one of the in-group. No dice. Cacophony surrounds them. Slender blonde girls with breasts bouncing under Shetland wool sweaters dash past bearing copy. There are cries of *Who's gonna make up Page Five?* and other technical terms, which fail to impress Morag, as she understands their meaning. Should she offer her services? They'd laugh, probably, to hear about the *Manawaka Banner*. She thinks of Lachlan with a fondness she never felt for him when she was there. The *Veritas* editor, Mark Trilling, strolls past, pipe clenched in teeth, frowning in leonine fashion, as befits one in this high calling.

"Ah, the heck with it," Ella says, snapping her fingers. "I'm gonna mail it in."

"Yeh, me too, I guess," Morag says. "I don't trust the mail, though."

They go to the coffee shop and brood over cups which neither inebriate nor cheer.

"You gotta begin somewhere," Ella says.

"That's just it."

"Even if it's only that crumby excuse for a paper."

"Exactly. Well, they don't know what they've just passed up."

They both despise *Veritas* now, and will continue to do so until something of theirs is printed therein.

They show each other their work. Ella's is a poem, part of a long narrative poem about the Jews in Europe during the war. Auschwitz. Buchenwald. It is written with such an openness of love and bitterness that Morag for a while can't make it jibe with Ella's flippancy in speech, which, she now sees, is as determined a cover as her own.

"Did you have relatives –"

"Yes," Ella says. "But it would've been the same if I hadn't."

Ella does not live very far from Morag's place, as it turns out.

"Want to come over sometime, Morag? Your boarding-house sounds like a whole load of shit."

"I'd really love to come over. But my place – it isn't so terrible. Mrs. Crawley's okay, but just kind of defeated, you know."

"Yeh. I know all right. Lumpen proletariat."

When explained, the term seems unfair, in Morag's view. She says so.

"Whatever gave you the idea I was fair, for God's sake?" Ella shouts.

Then they both laugh. Morag tells – can she? she does, though – about Christie and Prin, and about the town. Some, anyway. It is a world which to Ella seems about as warm and inviting as living six feet deep in a snowdrift.

"How could you *take* it?" Ella asks.

"Tell me how I could do anything else."

This is a point of view which Ella instantly recognizes.

"Yeh. That's so. Let me read your story, now?"

Morag hands it over. As it is longer than a poem, the waiting period is prolonged. Morag smokes five cigarettes. In comparison with the reach of Ella's poem, the story is pure unadulterated crap. She longs to snatch it back. But longs even more to know what Ella thinks of it. It concerns a young farmer during the drought, who nearly gives way to despair, but who finally determines to stay alive and to stay with the land.

"I think it's good," Ella says.

"No kidding?" Morag says hungrily. Then reality sets in once more. "The trouble is, I can see that the ending is kind of implausible, the way I've set it up, but I don't know what to do about it. Not yet, anyway."

"Implausible, nuts," Ella says. "Lots of people did stay, didn't they?"

"Oh sure, but –"

"The barns weren't overcrowded with hanged farmers, were they?"

"Well, no, but –"

"It would have been more implausible," Ella declares, "if you'd had him going through with the rope on the rafter bit."

A friend for life, Ella. Even though Morag knows the story is badly flawed and suspects that Ella knows, too.

"You really think so?"

"Sure. Did you – I mean, did you ever know anyone like that, Morag?"

"No. It's not based on anyone real."

And yet, in a way, it is. She sees the distortion and sees why the story had to end this way. The child, in some way, although without realizing it, saving the father's life. The father going on living. Could it have ended any other way, the story? No. Anyway, the child isn't her. She realizes almost with surprise that this is true. The child *isn't* her. Can the story child really exist separately? Can it be both her and not her?

Ella is looking at her oddly.

"What's the matter, Morag?"

"I – don't know. Sometimes I get – well, scared. I don't feel all that normal."

Ella shrugs.

"So – who wants to be normal, anyhow?"

"I do," Morag says with passionate conviction. "Oh Ella, *I* do. I want to be able to talk to boys the way they want to be talked to. Only I can't seem to get the trick of it."

"Boys like that are schmucks," Ella says furiously. "But yeh, I know what you mean."

"You too?"

"Yeh. I went out with this guy a coupla weeks ago, and I thought *Now this is It. Here is your opportunity, oh Ella bella.* So what did Ella the schlemiel do? Did she tell him how masterful and handsome he was? Not she. Oh no. She began talking in her winsome way about Marx's theory of polarity. Why? Why? I'll never see *him* again."

"Well, then, why?" Morag is laughing, but not in mockery.

"I don't know," Ella says gloomily. "It just seemed so phoney, somehow, all that whole mutual flattery bit. And why should I pretend to be brainless? I'm not brainless."

"I know," Morag says. "And yet I envy girls like Susie Trevor so much that I damn near hate them. I want to be glamorous and adored and get married and have kids. I still try to kid myself that I don't want that. But I do. I want all that. *As well.* All I want is everything."

Ella strikes a theatrical wrist to her forehead. "Engrave it on my tombstone."

Morag goes often to the Gersons' house after this occasion. A small white-painted house, always full of people. Ella's father died several years ago, and Mrs. Gerson now keeps on the bakery, working there during shop hours and coming back at nights to make dinner for her three daughters.

Mrs. Gerson is a tall strapping woman whose voice is brisk and bossy but also loving. She does not complain about the large amount of work she has to do. It never occurs to her that it *is* large. Her daughters are her life. She considers herself blessed.

"A nice house like this," she confides to Morag, "I never thought I would have. You should only have seen the place where me and my husband lived when we first married, in Poland, that was. A hovel. I could tell you things."

She stomps out, evenings, to left-wing meetings. If she can bring up her daughters to be socialists, she will not have lived in vain.

"Ella, she's okay in that way," Mrs. Gerson says, "but Janine and Bernice I sometimes doubt."

The girls shout with laughter.

"Mumma, you wait until I marry a rich insurance man or like that," Janine says, "and you won't turn down a little luxury. A mink coat, maybe?"

"A mink coat, who needs it? I'd die of shame to be seen in such a thing."

Ella is the middle daughter. Janine is at High School. Bernice is a hairdresser. Both Janine and Bernice, like their mother, have dark hair.

"Ella, can I ask you something?" Morag says.

"Ask. I'm inscrutable, but ask."

"How come your hair is auburn? Did your father —"
Laughter from the Gersons.

"Poppa would love that," Ella says. "No. Bernice did it.
It was supposed to turn out blonde. That was part of the
Glamour Campaign, see? This new advanced technologically
perfect method."

"Such nonsense," Mrs. Gerson sniffs. "I told her, you
don't like the colour God gave you? You think you can
improve on it?"

Mrs. Gerson believes in God and Marx simultaneously,
and is not dismayed by her daughters' suggestion of disparity
in such a dual faith.

"You don't *dye* the hair," Ella goes on. "You sort of bleach
it. Only when Bernice got mine down to its basic element,
here I was this colour."

"I thought it was really lucky," Bernice says. "Blonde
would've only made you look cheap, anyway."

"And who says I am so expensive?"

"Brat."

But Bernice, queenly and twenty-three, is their oracle in
the area of beauty. Bernice knows which shade of nail polish to
wear with which colour of dress. Bernice knows perfumes and
lipsticks and shampoos like she knows her own name. This is
great, from Morag's point of view, but she soon realizes that it
has given Ella the feeling of being a hopeless incompetent. As
Bernice prattles on about egg-and-lemon shampoos, the new
Tropicoral lipstick and nail-polish set, and the best way of
removing facial hair, Morag and Ella give each other the Sarah
Bernhardt gesture, meaning in this instance, woe. They will
not, they feel, ever attain the status of high priestesses at

Beauty's Altar. They will, indeed, be lucky if they get even one foot inside the temple door.

"You're crazy, both of you," Bernice says disgustedly. "I don't know what you're complaining about. You could both be *gorgeous* if only you'd put your minds to it."

"Our minds are on higher things," Morag suggests.

"Listen, higher than a man's belt buckle Ella's mind never yet got," Bernice declares, "and I bet you're not any different, either, Morag. Want me to do your hair? Look — it's lovely, that real shiny black, but the way you wear it — those braids over your head make you look like an old-maid schoolteacher. No kidding."

"Now, Bernice, you leave the girl alone," Mrs. Gerson says severely from the kitchen, where she is ironing. "She's right — her mind *is* on higher things. She studies. Reads. Not like some people, you know what I'm talking, who quit after Grade Twelve and turn themselves into such a *lady* they can't even hang up their own nightgown, what a lovely way to be, such encouragement to give a young girl, who needs it?"

"That is Mumma's Bernice Speech Number One," Janine murmurs. "Next comes a brief rundown of the entire Russian revolution."

"Such disrespect."

Mrs. Gerson slaps the iron down on the ruffled blouse and irons furiously. She in fact adores Bernice and stands in admiring awe of her daughter's prowess in the beauty game. She complains proudly about the house being cluttered up with Bernice's boyfriends. She feeds them egg-bread and bagels and strudel and coffee in huge quantities until Bernice, embarrassed, tells her to lay off — it looks like she's feeding them up for the slaughter. She then goes to the other extreme and starts chatting to them about the iniquities of the City Council – all quite true, but it does not make a hit with Bernice.

Bernice does Morag's hair – a home permanent, because Morag cannot afford to go to Miss Bonnie, where Bernice ministers to the better-off. When the apparently endless process is finally over, Morag looks at herself in the long mirror in the Gersons' bathroom. Her hair is still quite long, and falls darkly shining into a pageboy style, very little curl, just enough to make the hair curve under. She feels peculiar. Not like herself. Yet better. Hopeful?

"Hey, it's terrific," Ella cries. "It looks like a million bucks."

Janine and Mrs. Gerson add their fulsome praise. Bernice, looking proud, says that she knew all along it would turn out lovely.

Morag has never known anything like this kind of house before. Its warmth is sometimes very much harder to take than any harshness could be, because it breaks her up and she considers it a disgrace to cry in front of anybody. When she finally admits this, out of necessity, the girls leave her tactfully alone. Not so Mrs. Gerson.

"Mumma, come *here*," Ella hisses.

"I know what I'm doing," Mrs. Gerson says adamantly.

She marches into the bathroom, where Morag has not thought of locking the door.

"So, what's the disgrace, Morag? Look at me – didn't I spend maybe half my life crying? It never meant any disgrace. It never meant I couldn't mop up, after, and blow my nose a little, and get back to work. So cry, child."

Morag Gunn, nearly twenty, five-feet-eight, grown-up, puts her head down on the shoulder of Ella's mother and cries as if the process had just recently been invented. What the hell is she crying about? Because of the unreal stab of hope she felt when she looked in the mirror? Because she fears she can't carry through with the New Her, and because in some ways she doesn't even want to? Because it shouldn't all be necessary but it is? Because she never knew until now that she has missed her mother as much as her father, for most of her life? Because she thinks of Prin and feels ashamed at not wanting to see her? Because she wants her own child and doesn't believe she will ever have one? Because she wants to write a masterpiece and doesn't believe she will ever write anything which will even see the light of day?

Because life is bloody terrifying, is why.

And under the tears, much deeper, Morag sees now why she feels close to Ella's mother. It is not only Mrs. Gerson's ability to reach out her arms and hold people, both literally and figuratively. It is also her strength. Morag doesn't know yet if she herself has the former ability. If she doesn't, it will go badly for her. Because she knows she has the latter. How is it she can feel totally inadequate and yet frightened of a strength she knows she possesses?

Flash – flash – all these thoughts like neons flickering on and off in her head while she sobs ludicrously on Mrs. Gerson's shoulder. Finally straightens up and blows her nose.

"Now, you'll have a nice little bit of dinner with us," Mrs. Gerson reassures, "and then you go home and you don't study tonight, eh? You relax a little, you read a book for pleasure, you don't have to think of an essay on it."

This magic combination is Mrs. Gerson's remedy for most of the psychic ills to which the human skull is prey. After the gefilte fish, Dostoevsky's *The Idiot*. What could cheer you up more?

Ella's ma has adopted Morag in some way or other, and is going to give her the same benefits as her own daughters receive. Cannily, she leaves the HCPSU (History of the Communist Party in the Soviet Union) until later on. For now, Dostoevsky, Tolstoy, Chekhov, Turgenev.

"Take, take, we're not in a hurry to have them back."

Thus it is that Morag Gunn sets a tentative and cramped toe inside the Temple of Beauty at the same moment as she first truly realizes that English is not the only literature.

Memorybank Movie: Brooke

The New Image, courtesy of Bernice, does not actually alter Morag's social life out of all recognition. Still, she is asked out several times, albeit by boys in whom she is not interested. She feigns interest, though. Aims to please. She would go out with Dracula if he asked her, probably. This a despicable attitude to have. She has it. It is not the loneliness of not going out which she cannot bear. She is in fact rarely lonely when alone. It is the sense of being downgraded, devalued, undesirable. She knows men feel pain, too. But does not yet wholly believe it, having never really seen it, except in Christie. Or Lazarus. Or Lachlan. Or, in some way she doesn't understand, Niall Cameron. But like Christie, their pain seems in another dimension, pain perceived frighteningly by her, scarcely to be looked at. Also, not immediately relevant to her situation. They are old and she is not.

What about Jules? Yes. Sometimes she thinks of him, and remembers how it was, and wonders where he is and how he is getting on. But will not will not think of it much. Refuses to think of it.

She discovers, not greatly to her surprise, that the location of her boardinghouse does little to enhance her popularity. Once a boy finds out that she lives half-a-mile from the end of the streetcar line and he has to flounder back out again after taking her home and wait for the next streetcar in the midst of a semi-blizzard or the icy stillness that sometimes puts frost straight into the bloodstream – he usually never asks her out again. Then, too, the Crawleys' arctic front porch cannot be called the ideal place for necking. Morag feels herself burning up with a sweetly uncomplicated lust the moment she is touched by a man. She is not modest or shy about having her breasts or inner thighs felt up, nor is she unwilling to press herself against him and feel the hardness of his cock inside his grey flannels. This she knows is called *leading him on,* which is not honourable on her part, as she is too scared ever to allow him inside her. Scared not of sex but of getting pregnant. She suffers the lack of real sex as much as he does – at least, if he suffers more, he must really suffer *plenty.* Both, no doubt, have the same solitary solution. If he, however, knew this about her, he would scorn her forever. Unfair, but factual. Passion, however, is curbed to some degree by the Crawleys' porch in mid-February. She cannot ask the boy into the livingroom. What if one of the Crawleys woke and came downstairs? There appears no solution except to move. This she is now afraid to do in case it should turn out to be: (a) no better; (b) worse; (c) not the porch but herself, insufficiently alluring.

"I make boxes for myself," she tells Ella, "and then I get furious when I find I'm inside one. Do you think it'll be a life-long pattern?"

"I don't know," Ella says honestly, although obviously she would have preferred to be reassuring.

Ella's poem comes out in *Veritas* and Morag is nearly as glad as if it had been her own. Also, unbearably depressed.

"Did you mail them your story?" Ella asks.

"Yeh. But I don't imagine they'd bother returning it. I mean, think of the postage."

Why did she submit it under her own name? Imagine writing *Morag Gunn* in cold blue ink.

"At this moment," Morag says, "my life seems odious. Apart from your poem getting in, I mean."

"Well, even with that," Ella says, "mine is not exactly one huge barrelful of chuckles."

They stamp snowbooted tweedcoated down the street to Ella's, singing, not caring who hears.

There'll be a change in the weather
And a change in the sea,
And most of all there'll be a change in me,
'Cause nobody wants you when you're old and grey –
There'll be some changes made Today
There'll be some chay-ay-anges made.

They cannot imagine ever becoming old and grey. Simultaneously, they live every day with the certainty of this fact, and with the fact of their own deaths. They seldom discuss this strange presence. There is no need. They know it from one another's writing. It is the unspoken but real face under the jester's mask. They do not pry, nor do they invade each other's areas of privacy. They simply recognize the existence of these.

Morag goes alone into the cafeteria after a late class. Very few people there, she is glad to see.

"Hello, Morag Gunn. Come here."

She looks, and it is Dr. Skelton, who teaches the Seventeenth-Century Poetry course and the Milton course.

He is English (from England, that is) and has an impressive accent. He is also about ten feet tall – well, six-four anyway, and with a fine-boned handsomeness that gives him an aristocratic look, or what Morag imagines must be aristocratic. He wears dark framed glasses, which suit him. He's not terrifically old – in his thirties. His hair is prematurely grey and there is something nice about that, with the youngness of his face. He is, of course, swooned over by various birdbrained females in the class who couldn't care less about John Donne but just go to twitter over Brooke Skelton. Morag, who secretly thinks he is a prince among men, scorns such obvious ploys, although when she can think of some reasonably intelligent comment or question, she speaks it. She has never spoken to him out of class. In the cafeteria, he is always surrounded by his clutch of disciples, who hardly allow the poor guy a second's peace over a cup of coffee. Morag has sometimes wanted to join them, but pride forbids.

"Hello, Dr. Skelton."

He motions to a chair, and she sets her coffee on the table beside his. In his hand is a copy of *Veritas*. Today's. She hasn't seen it.

"I've just read your story," he says, smiling.

Morag snatches the paper from him, now unaware of his presence. There it is. *Fields of Green and Gold* by Morag Gunn. They've certainly set it up rotten – about a million typographical errors, and why did they have to use that airy-fairy type for the title? The story itself. Hm. The ending is rubbish. How could she?

She becomes aware again of Dr. Skelton. What must he be thinking. Amused?

"I quite liked it," Dr. Skelton says. "In fact, I thought it extremely promising."

"*Really?*"

"Yes. Really. Are you so surprised?"

"I'm astounded," she says, truthfully.

"The ending is sentimental, I think," he says, "but –"

"I know. I know it is. The story needs to be rewritten."

"Well, if you'd like me to take a look at any more of your stories, I'd be happy to do so. I might be able to point out a few things which would be helpful."

"Thanks. Oh – thank you."

She must not gush. She clamps her mouth shut. Dr. Skelton smiles, easily, as though if she has been awkward, he hasn't noticed.

"I'm generally free on a Thursday, after four. You can come up to my office then, if you like."

Morag phones Ella in the evening. They talk for one hour, approximately, about this strange happening. Mr. Crawley, timid though he usually is, comes and stands beside the phone, finally, making gestures at his watch, so Morag has to hang up. She goes to her room. Stays up until three in the morning, writing another story. This story is totally unsentimental. Also, totally worthless. She perceives that not even for Dr. Skelton can she write a story which wasn't there to be written. A humbling thought, but not daunting.

Nothing will ever daunt her again.

Our eye-beams twisted, and did thread
Our eyes, upon one double string.

Dr. Skelton glances up at the class.

"What would you say that Donne meant by this metaphysical image? Miss Gunn?"

The only thing that daunts Morag is her sudden realization

that she wants greatly to make the right comment so as to impress Dr. Skelton. Is there such a thing as *the* right comment? Watch it, girl. But when she begins talking, Donne's lines take hold of her, and she forgets about everything else, even the curious eyes of classmates, who always gawk at anyone who opens their mouth in class.

"I thought it was pretty difficult at first," she says, "and maybe I don't really get it, but it seems to me if you can get inside the image, sort of, then it's amazing that anyone could catch in words that kind of closeness — I mean, two people who love each other are separate individuals, but they're both seeing everything, including themselves, through the other person's eyes. At least, I think that's what it means, partly."

"Good," Dr. Skelton says.

But before he can go on to make his own and more complex comment, Morag rushes in once more.

"What I can't understand about Donne, though, is how he can write lines like that, really terrific, and like in some of the Holy Sonnets — 'Death, be not proud,' for instance, and — well, I think he's the greatest poet I've ever read, just about, but how is it he can know so much about people's feelings and then write so many cruel lines?"

"Which cruel lines did you have in mind?" Dr. Skelton enquires, looking surprised.

The class is beginning to enjoy this. Morag is beginning not to enjoy it. But will not stop now — pride forbids it.

"Well, like 'For God's sake hold your tongue and let me love.' That's a very cruel line. Supposing the lady had been able to write poetry — I mean, you wonder what she might have said to *him*."

"You would not take it kindly, Miss Gunn, to be asked to hold your tongue?"

Laughter from the class. Morag's face feels unpleasantly warm – does it show?

"No. No, I would not."

"Well, quite right, too," Dr. Skelton says, seriously, frowning a little at the class's general levity. "But Donne, surely, must be seen as a man of his historical time."

"Oh, of course. I understand that. But you can accept it with Milton, better, somehow, despite all those really awful things he says – 'He for God only; she for God in him.' You think, well, he was all bound up with so many things that were going on in England at the time, and where people's feelings were concerned, except his own, maybe he just didn't know any better. But – well, you wouldn't have expected it of Donne, so much."

"You admire his poetry to a large enough extent that you would like to admire all his concepts as well?"

"I guess so. Yes."

"But concepts were different then."

"Yes. I – guess so."

"I'm not sure that particular theme is really integral to an understanding of Donne's poetry," Dr. Skelton says. "But on the other hand, it can only be a good thing to care enough about a poet's works to want to go back in time and discuss the matter with him. Which is what you almost seem to want to do, Miss Gunn."

Morag considers. Then smiles.

"That's right."

The class convulses. Laughter is rampant. Which does not matter at all, because Morag is well beyond the reach of it.

Morag is sitting in Dr. Skelton's office. He is leaning back a little in his swivel chair behind his desk. He has just finished reading one of Morag's stories, and is thinking what to say about it. The story is about an Austrian nobleman who comes to this country complete with the peasants from his family's lost estate and who tries to create a replica of that feudal system here. Needless to say, he does not succeed, and his end is both nasty and mysterious.

"Quite frankly, it seems a little implausible to me, Morag," says Dr. Skelton, who has taken to calling her by her first name out of class.

"Yes, I guess so. That's my fault for not being able to do it properly. Because it's based on something that really happened."

"Good Lord – where?"

"Up Galloping Mountain way."

"I like your idiomatic expressions," Dr. Skelton says, smiling.

Morag draws herself away from the desk. Country girl. Up Galloping Mountain way indeed. Illiterate.

He sees her face.

"Did you think I meant that sarcastically, Morag? I didn't. Your speech has a directness which one often does not encounter in academic circumstances. Where do you come from?"

She does not say.

"Oh – nowhere, really. A small town."

"Your family lives there?"

"I don't have any family, actually. I was brought up by –"

By no one. She cannot speak Christie's name, Prin's name.

"I was brought up by some friends, well, acquaintances of my parents," she finishes. "They're no relation to me. My parents died when I was very young."

"You seem very calm about it," he says, looking at her as though from a great distance, behind his glasses. Then his face relents and she sees that what she has taken for disapproval is in fact a kind of admiration.

"It happened when I was really very young," Morag says. "I don't remember it. Or at least hardly at all. I guess I was too young to be affected much."

Untrue. But she does not want to pose as brave, which would be even more untrue.

"And these – acquaintances who brought you up?"

"We were never – close."

"Have you had a lonely sort of life, Morag?" His voice is not prying; he needs to know, though, for some reason.

"In a way, I guess. Perhaps no more than most."

Dr. Skelton smiles, as though touching her, not in either amusement or pity.

"You're proud, I would guess. Am I right?"

"I can't bear pity," Morag says.

Dr. Skelton's face is no longer smiling.

"You needn't worry," he says. "You'll not get that from me, ever."

Ever? That is a long time. She does not feel able to interpret him.

"I had a relatively solitary life myself, as a boy," he says. "I was born in India. My father was Headmaster of a boys' school not far from Calcutta. Church of England school. I was pretty much alone as a youngster."

"But if it were a boys' school –"

"No. I didn't go to school there. I was sent to England to boardingschool when I was six."

"That's – awful. Like that kid in that Kipling story, 'Ba Ba Black Sheep.'"

"Not quite like that," Dr. Skelton says. "I wasn't so easily browbeaten. Nor quite so shortsighted, either. I liked the school once I got used to it. Still, in retrospect, I don't remember childhood as a golden era."

"It must be interesting to have a past like that, though," Morag says, regretting the naive words as soon as they are uttered. "I mean, India and like that."

"Fascinating." Dr. Skelton grins. "Exotic as all hell. Don't hunch up your shoulders, Morag. I didn't mean that as any slur against your response. It *was* interesting. I loved India as a child. I used to go back on holidays. I still miss it. What sort of a past do you feel yours was, then? Or perhaps you're still too young to have considered it very much."

"I'm twenty," Morag says. "Or nearly. I don't feel – I don't know, I just feel as though I don't have a past. As though it was more or less blank."

She will not – she will *not* – tell him about the town, and Christie, and all. Scavenger Logan. No. Not ever.

"That's a strange thing to say, Morag. Almost more interesting than having a past."

"You mean – *An aura of mystery surrounded her?*"

They laugh. Morag feels she has never felt so close to anyone before, except of course Ella, which is different.

"Come on, mysterious one," Dr. Skelton says. "I'll drive you home."

"You can't. I live away to hell and – I mean, my boarding-house is away out in the North End."

"No matter."

The car finally skids and slithers successfully through the snow, and they reach the Crawleys' house.

"You were right," Dr. Skelton says. "It *is* away to hell and gone. Why do you live here?"

"It was the first place I looked at, and I thought I wouldn't find another. Now I don't like to move. They're nice people."

"I like you, Morag." He reaches up and removes her glasses, simultaneously removing his own. "Life has many hazards for the not-fully-sighted – have you noticed?"

He then kisses her. It is not a friendly or teacherly salute. It is knowledgeably hard, his tongue exploring her mouth, not coolly or hesitantly but with insistence. Morag responds, as usual, instantly, but more so than ever before. If he should ask her to strip in the exposed and icy car and make love with him here and now, no holds barred, she would do so.

Dr. Skelton breaks away. Heavy breathing from them both.

"I've wanted to do that for quite a while," he says. "Here – have a cigarette."

Cigarettes for safety. Morag, shaking, takes one.

"Dr. Skelton –"

She stops. You cannot call a man Dr. Skelton when he has just kissed you with his entire body.

"Brooke," Brooke says. "At least, out of class."

He sounds miserable, and she enquires with her eyes.

"Oh, nothing," he says. "It's just – well, goddamn, I'm thirty-four and you are a child."

"No," Morag says clearly. "I am far from a child, Brooke – you know that."

"Do I? When you're fifty, I'll be sixty-four. You wouldn't be happy."

"I would. I would. I've never before –"

"You seem very sure."

"I am," Morag says. "I always am, over things that matter. I always know. But what – what do you *like* about me?"

He kisses her some more before replying.

"What do I like about you? I don't even think I can say. You're not exactly beautiful, but you will be. I don't know. You've got a kind of presence."

He laughs, as though being serious is a treat at the moment.

"Perhaps it's your mysterious nonexistent past," he says. "I like that. It's as though you are starting life now, newly."

Morag's feelings exactly. Now, however, now that it matters, she would like to tell Brooke everything, to make sure. Clowny Macpherson. Piper Gunn and the Bitch Duchess. Gunner Gunn and the War. The snapshots. Christie ranting the Logans' war cry, the pathetic motto and crest. The Nuisance Grounds. Prin, so long ago. The valley – the Tonnerre shack.

No. *No.*

"You'd better go now, Morag," Brooke says gently. "Go now, my dear. If you stay here, I'll turn the car around and drive you back to my flat, and that wouldn't be a good idea."

Why not? But she does as he says. His car chuffs off through the loose whiteness of the road.

If she cannot be with him from now on, and live with him inside her and outside her in every way, she will not be able to bear the pain. She is all at once without shame of any kind, totally unscrupulous in what she would do, totally vulnerable. She will do whatever he wants her to do.

It will never happen. He would never consider marrying anyone like her. If he knew where she had come from. Or if he knew what she was really like, for that matter. Could she be exactly what he wants? What does he want? She will find out. She will conceal everything about herself which he might not like. None of Christie's swearing.

It will be useless, though. It will never happen. He will change his mind. Or believe the age difference matters.

She is numb with too much hope, too little hope.

They are walking down Portage Avenue. Brooke reaches out for her hand. Students may see. This matters less and less.

"You know, love, you have a quality of innocence that's very moving," he says. "I don't mean naïveté. I mean genuine innocence. I'm not like that. I've lived too long for that, and in too many places. But it's a quality I love in you."

She wants to tell him she is not like that, either. She also has lived too long for that. The state of original grace ended a long time ago.

"Brooke – I think I should tell you about my childhood. All about it. I think I should."

He laughs a little.

"All right, if you really want to."

Brooke's apartment is the size of five minutes. A miniature livingroom with hideous pale mauve walls which the previous tenant fancied and which he cannot be bothered to repaint. Bookshelves everywhere. A worn sofa covered with a very large and elegant white Kashmir shawl with intricately embroidered flowers and strange unworldlike birds in coral and black and leafgreen. A leather chair. A table. Prints of Renoir and van Gogh on the walls. Some pieces of Benares brass – a vase, several bowls enamelled in soft turquoise and clear brilliant red, patterns of birds and flowers and leaves, from a world too far from this one. The kitchen is actually more of a large cupboard with sink and two-burner hotplate. The bedroom contains a large and beautiful walnut spool bed, Brooke's desk, an austere dresser. The bathroom is so small you couldn't swing a cat in it (if you should ever desire to engage

in such an activity – where do these phrases come from?).
Morag thinks the apartment (*flat*, to Brooke) is beautiful.

"Shall we have some sherry before you tackle the
eggs and bacon, which is all there is here at the moment for
dinner?"

"Please," Morag says, having recently learned to say,
simply, *Please*, instead of *Oh yes thanks I'd just love some*, or,
worse, *Okay that'd be fine*.

"Now what's all this about your nefarious past?" Brooke
says, smiling.

"Not nefarious. But – well – Christie and Prin Logan,
the people who brought me up –"

"*Prin?*"

"She was christened Princess."

Brooke bursts out laughing.

"No – it wasn't all that funny. She – they – were quite
poor, you see, and –"

She cannot go on. She looks away from Brooke and sees
Hill Street.

Brooke is holding her now. She realizes she is crying.

"Hush," he says. "Hush, love. Listen – *don't* tell me. All
I want to know is this – were they cruel to you? I mean, did
they ever – well, mistreat you? Or did the man – you know –
ever try anything?"

Morag stops crying instantly.

"No. Of course not. It was nothing like that. Nothing
like that at all."

"Well," Brooke says, "it has been known to happen, you
know."

"Yes," Morag says. "I know."

"You know in theory," Brooke says, "but you don't really
know. My dearest love, you're very young."

She knows in more than theory, about some things. Vernon Winkler, as a small boy, being beaten by Gus. Eva crying in the dancehall, and the night that followed, and Christie taking the small unformed corpse (could it be called that? what would it have looked like?) and giving it burial. The valley, the snow and the fire.

"I don't think I ever felt all that really young," Morag says apologetically.

"Nonsense," Brooke says, holding her more tightly. "You were and *are*. That's one thing I love about you. You're serious, but you're happy, too. You've got a talent of laughter that's lovely and heartwarming. It restores me, and I love it."

"Brooke – I *am* happy, with you. And anything else – Manawaka and that – it's over. It doesn't exist. It's unimportant."

"That's right, my love. Don't talk about it – it only upsets you. I only want to know you as you are now, my tall and lovely dark-haired Morag, my love, with your very touching seriousness and your light heart. Never be any different, will you?"

"Never. I promise."

Then they are exploring one another's bodies, and Brooke, lying on her, is hard and demanding, and she rises to him. Now neither of them wants to stop, or can.

"A damn sofa is no place to make love," Brooke says grimly, and despite themselves they both laugh.

The bed, true, is better. Morag feels no hesitance about peeling off her clothes. She is, in fact, undressed first.

"Let me look at you," Brooke says, when they are lying together. "Oh my love, you're so goddamn beautiful."

He, too, is beautiful. His long body is taut, spare, lean. His ribs can faintly be seen under the skin, and the hair on his chest is light browngold, the colour his hair was before it became grey. His cock is proud, long, ready, and she wants to touch it but wonders if he would think this too forward of her, so soon. He sees where her glance is, and smiles.

"Don't be alarmed, love," he says. "Women always wonder, the first time they see a man naked and erect, if there's enough room inside themselves. Well, there *is*."

"Yes."

The first time they see a man naked. Should she tell him? But she cannot. What would he think of her? But is she deceiving him? Perfidious Morag. If she tells him about Jules, he will leave her. She cannot. Would he understand? Would any man? She does not think so, and cannot bear to take the chance.

"Put your hands there, my love. There – that's good. You're not shy – you have no false modesty. I knew you wouldn't."

Then their skins are close and touching all over, arms and legs entwined around one another, close close. And then he breaks away and fishes a small purple envelope from under the pillow, and takes out the safe, and she looks away, all at once embarrassed at this intrusion of some world outside their two selves, a world of drugstore and smirks.

Soon it is all right again, though. But when he tries to go into her, and she wanting him with every blood vessel and muscle in her, it hurts her. She tries not to let on, but her body betrays her and she flinches. Brooke is desperate, hardly able to hold back but unable to go on hurting her. Then he collapses, away from her.

"Oh christ, Morag. I can't hurt you. I can't."

"Brooke – I'm sorry. I'm sorry. I'm sorry."

She has failed him. He strokes her hair, her face, her breasts. Then lights cigarettes for them both.

"Hush, love. It doesn't matter. I shall just have to be – well, as gentle as I can, and patient."

"Brooke, I don't mind if it hurts the first time or so –"

He grins wanly.

"I'm not very experienced with virgins," he says. "Well, at least it's proof positive, isn't it?"

"What if I hadn't been?" she asks.

There is a chill in her voice which her own ears catch, but mercifully he does not seem to notice.

"But you *are*, love, so the question doesn't arise, does it? Idiot child, I wouldn't have thrown you out on the street. I would've been – well, disappointed, I expect."

"Why, Brooke?"

Now she is remembering overhearing a conversation between two boys in the college coffee shop. *I was all set to throw her the ice and it wasn't one of your two-bit rings neither and then she gave in and whaddya know I wasn't the first on that road so I thought the hell with that jazz.*

"I don't know, love," Brooke says. "I suppose I like to feel that it's something you've only experienced with me. It's – well, if I didn't care about you, I wouldn't feel that way, would I? I think most men would feel that way about their woman."

Their woman. Her clenched and doubting guts now dissolve with gratitude and care.

"Am I your woman, then, Brooke? For sure?"

He laughs and draws her close.

"For sure, my darling. For absolute bloody certain."

His wife, then? Morag would be willing to be his mistress, fancy woman, kept woman, moll, or whatever. Just so he doesn't leave her. Just so they can always be together, always and always.

"Brooke – I love you so much."

"And I love you so much, my love. Aren't you going to ask if I intend to make an honest woman of you?"

"Well, you haven't made a dishonest one of me yet. Not that that was your fault."

"Oh, it's like that, is it? You're asking for it, then, love?"

"Yes. Yes."

"Well, this time I'll make a dishonest woman out of you. Oh my love, just relax and try to trust me."

"I do trust you, Brooke. And I'll try –"

It still, however, hurts like hell. She wants only to focus upon him, upon the two of them together. But remembers how, in medieval times or somewhere, if the sheets weren't bloody, the bride was considered a disaster and a jezebel and might be sent packing home to Ma and Pa. Imagine being sent packing to Christie and Prin for that reason. Prin wouldn't understand what was going on. Christie would laugh his fool head off.

For one unbelievable and appalling second, Morag is suddenly homesick for Manawaka. Then the moment of inner-talk passes and she is again with Brooke.

"Brooke –"

"My love – oh God, I can't keep it any longer –"

And he goes off, inside deep deep inside her herownself and she is inhabited by him at last.

Afterwards, when they are their separate selves once more, they are not separate.

"Morag, listen, my love, it'll be better for you soon. It really will. I promise you."

"I know. I do know. And it was fine – it was fine, anyway."

"Morag?"

"Mm?"

"Listen, dear one. I've been offered a post in Toronto, full professor. Would you like Toronto, do you think?"

Would she like Toronto? Would she like Paradise? With Brooke, and away from the prairies entirely.

"Of course I would. Of course. Of course."

But so strongly does she feel about this response that her voice comes out like a croak. She clears her throat.

"Sorry. Frog in my throat. Oh Brooke – Toronto would be great."

Dramatic effect is somewhat marred, second time. Frog in the throat? What a gruesome expression. Who could ever have thought that one up? Ugh. Those clammy clambering teeny saurian legs in your *gullet*, for God's sake? Worse, more hideous than crab-claws but why think of that now for heaven's sake, crabs another word for VD or is it lice? She doesn't know enough. Why think of any of that with the cleanest best man ever to walk God's earth? But why did he say *Women always wonder if there will be enough room in themselves*, etcetera, and then said *Not much experience with virgins*. Well, no one would expect or want him to be a virgin at thirty-four and what a disaster it would've been if he had been. Crab is also Cancer the zodiac sign, Morag's sign, and they always say lucky in career but not so hot luck in love, although oriented towards children and family. What a load of garbage. But to have Brooke's children – that is what she now sees is necessary in the deepest part of her being. What a sign to have, though, Cancer, and why think of that in connection with a frog in your throat? Words words words. Words haunt her, but she will become unhaunted now, forevermore.

Brooke is lighting two more cigarettes and smiling at her.

"That's settled, then, I guess the spring would be a good time to be married, would you have thought, Morag?"

Yes. Yes. Anytime. How about tomorrow?

"Yes. It would be a really good time to be married, Brooke."

Then she thinks of something else.

"Shall I go on in university there, Brooke?"

He considers.

"Quite honestly, love, I don't know what to think about it. If you want to go on, of course you've a perfect right to do so. On the other hand, you might feel a bit awkward about attending classes, with your husband teaching there."

"I – don't know."

"Well, you won't need the degree. My salary won't exactly be princely, but I can afford to keep a wife. Why don't you audit some classes? Or simply read. Education isn't getting a degree, you know. It's learning, and learning to think."

True. Hm. And if she isn't attending classes, she will have time to read and also work at her own writing. And care for the house, naturally.

"Another thing, love," Brooke says. "What about seeing a doctor? I mean, a diaphragm would be better."

"Do you think so?"

"Yes. Definitely. More reliable. We don't want accidents."

Accidents. He means kids.

"All right, then, I will, Brooke. But I want a child of yours, Brooke. You know?"

He laughs, but very gently.

"My true love, lots of time for that. Let's not think of it now, shall we? Get yourself fixed up, won't you?"

"Yes. Of course."

*

The doctor's office is small and very dark. Probably in external fact it is normal-sized and normally lighted. When finally summoned Morag finds an unknown resource within herself and does not whisper, stutter or slump.

She explains that she is about to be married. The doc, oldish, with a thin tired face, fixes her with a beady raven's eye.

"Well, suppose you come back to me when you *are* married, eh?"

What if she'd turned up with a Woolworth's brass ring on her left hand? He would not have turned a hair, likely.

"What if I get pregnant before —"

"Would that be the end of the world?"

No. No. It would be fine. For her. But but but. It has to be two people's decision. It would be difficult, moving to another city and that. Not to mention the money. None of which would bother Morag, but then she is not the one who has to worry about the money and all.

She leaves. She does not see whether the expression on the doctor's face is one of boredom, or resignation, or sympathy, or what.

In the waitingroom, going out, she finds herself powerful with fury. She goes to the reception desk and makes another appointment. For the day after her wedding.

Dear Christie:

I have something to tell you. I am going to get married. His name is Brooke Skelton, and he teaches English here in the university. He is an Englishman (I mean, from England) and is a really fine and wonderful man, and I am very happy. As I am not yet 21, I guess I would have to have your permission, although am I legally adopted by you? But I guess you would be classed as my guardian. I feel sure you will say okay, though.

We are not having a real wedding, just very quiet, so we're not actually having any guests, as it seems a waste of money. I hope you don't mind. I will come to see you beforehand, as we will be moving to Toronto soon afterwards. Brooke would just love to come along, also, but cannot, unfortunately, as he will have examination papers to mark and can't get away, but I will show you a picture of him, and no doubt he will write to you.

I hope this is okay with you, and I hope Prin is reasonably all right.

All the best,
Morag

Dear Morag –

Well you are getting married that is some news all right and I wish well to you and him. You know damn well I would not say no and it is your life and I hope all goes well too bad he is English and not Scots ha ha. Come home when convenient. Prin not good in herself these days.

Yours,
Christie

Memorybank Movie: Hill Street Revisited

The house is just the same, only worse. Perhaps Morag notices it more now. The sour smell is sourer. The exposed light bulb in the kitchen looks bleaker, dimmer, than before, the old sideboard more cluttered with newspapers and unironed clothes, Christie's shaggily upholstered chair more shabbily torn and worn.

"Hello, Christie."

He is fifty-six, only. He looks about seventy, his hair sparser than she recalled, his badly shaven jaw more tweedlike with sprouting hairs, his eyes less blue, more clouded. As expected, he also stinks. But has put on a relatively clean shirt for her visit. The effect is somewhat diminished by the fact that the shirt was made to wear with a detachable collar which has got itself detached permanently and is no doubt among the dustballs under a bed or sofa.

"Hello, girl. By all the saints, then, and by the lord Harry, and by the –"

"Yes. Well. How's Prin?"

"She's – she's took to her bed now, Morag. Doesn't rise, these days. Can't hardly manage to rise. She ain't old, you know."

"No. I know."

The hulk in bed is barely discernible under the thick welter of blankets and eiderdown. Christie pulls away the sheet from the face. Prin's skin is the colour of uncooked pastry, yellowish-white. Christie shouts, as though to penetrate the veil of the years which comes between Prin's mind and now.

"Here's Morag to see you, Prin."

The eyes flutter open, and a smile, small and faint as the ghost of a child, crosses the puffy lips.

"Morag – Morag?"

"Leave me be, with her, for a bit, Christie, will you, then?"

"Sure, girl. Whatever you say."

Morag sits down beside Prin's bed. Prin smiles again, trustingly, like a young girl about to be married.

Morag becomes different, in this house. Older, older. With Brooke she feels young, too young sometimes, ignorant. Here she feels too old, too knowing. She should stay here and look after Prin, look after both of them. But cannot. Will not.

"Prin, I'm going to be married."

The faraway eyes try desperately to focus on Morag's face, to understand.

"Marry? Morag – little girl."

A soft giggle from the mound, as though somewhere inside that skull there is the image of an unchanging little girl. Morag who will never grow up, never go away, never be different, always four or six years old.

No use. No use trying to explain. Morag reaches out and holds one of Prin's swollen hands, the left one on which the wedding ring has long been overwhelmed and lost in the fat flesh.

Then an odd thing happens. What causes this swift and then swiftly vanishing streak of almost pure lucidity? Do the very very old have flashes of pure and painful sight, sweeping senility away for a second's unbearable perception of everything, everything? Prin, the doctor says, is prematurely senile. Her voice, this instant, is as clear and sweet as it might have been when she was a young girl. But what she says is neither sweet nor, at first, clear.

"That Colin," Prin says. "He never done that for my Christie. Saved him, like. Or maybe he done it. I dunno. He was a boy, just a boy, and that scared. Poor lamb. The poor lamb. He would cry, and Christie would hold him. Sh-sh. There, there. It's all right now. He's all right now, that Colin. Ain't he?"

Then the shutters come down over the eyes again, and although Prin's eyes remain open, they are seeing something Morag doesn't see, the fields or faces from a long way back.

"Yes, he's all right now, Prin."

Colin Gunn. Christie's tale of Gunner Gunn and the Great War. How Colin saved Christie, staved off his dying, that time away out there, on that corner of some foreign field that is forever nowhere. It hadn't happened that way, then, or probably not. It had happened the way Prin said. Christie holding Colin in his arms. Colin probably eighteen. Eighteen. Amid the shellfire and the barbwire and the mud, crying.

After a while, Morag goes back to the kitchen. On the table is a pot of tea and two cups. She recalls the half-bottle of whiskey.

"Here – I brought this for you, Christie."

"Well, thanks a million, Morag. That was real kind."

Kind. Half a bottle of whiskey. Not even a whole bottle. They sit and drink in silence. Then Christie, slowly, begins and she is terrified lest he launch into one of the old rants. He does not, however, do so.

"Married, eh? When will it be, then?"

"In about two weeks, Christie. It's not a – I mean, it's just going to be very quiet – no one there, really –"

She has all the subtlety of a two-ton truck. He's not stupid.

"It's okay," Christie says, his voice suddenly cracking like fire. "I wouldn't turn up, Morag. Never fear. I'd have to borrow a suit from Simon Pearl, eh? Think he'd lend it to me?"

"Oh Christie – I'm sorry. I never meant –"

"Sure you meant," Christie says, pouring himself another huge slug of whiskey. "No need to fib to me, Morag. I have known you since you were knee-high to a grasshopper. Listen here, now, don't worry. I can tell you plain, and without fear nor favour, and this is the Almighty God's almighty truth, and I'd swear the same on a stack of Bibles and on the blood and bones of the whole clan of Logans from the time of Adam – look here, it's a bloody good thing you've got away from this dump. So just shut your goddamn trap and thank your lucky stars."

"Do you really think that, Christie?"

"I do," Christie says, knocking back the whiskey. "And also I don't. That's the way it goes. It'll all go along with you, too. That goes without saying."

But it has been said. *The way it goes – it'll all go – that goes.* Does Christie bring in these echoes knowingly, or does it happen naturally with him? She has never known.

"You mean – everything will go along with me?"

"No less than that, ever," Christie says.

"It won't, though," Morag says, and hears the stubbornness in her own voice.

Christie laughs.

"Who says so, Morag?"

"I say so."

In some ways she would welcome one of their old arguments. But it is better to change the subject.

"Christie – how do you manage here?"

"I'm still working, for Christ's sake," he growls.

"I know. I meant – with Prin, and all."

"Oh – that. Eva comes in on Saturday and washes Prin and changes her bed and that. I can make do for the rest. Prin has to use the bedpan now. But hell's bells and buckets of blood, girl, if I can still heave around them trash barrels, I can heave around my own woman when need be."

Coals of fire on the head. He doesn't mean it that way. Or does he? With Christie you never ever really know.

"Eva – Winkler?"

"The same."

"Where – what's she –"

"Married one of the McKendrick boys – he farms out by Freehold. The family was that put out, you would have bust a gut laughing."

"You mean, *his* family?"

"Of course. You wouldn't think old Gus Winkler would object, would you? He was glad to get rid of her."

"Did Gus ever find out? I mean —"

"No," Christie says, frowning. "It ain't ever talked about here, neither."

"You needn't worry. I wouldn't. Has she got a — is she — well, it's only a year."

"No kid yet," Christie says, "nor won't be."

"Who told you?"

"Eva did. They're going to adopt. She works her fool head off, that girl. Thinks she should be grateful to young McKendrick for marrying her. He knows, you see. She told him. She would. The Winklers was never well-known for their brains."

"I see. Oh Christie —"

"Yeh, it's a bugger all right. So you go, Morag, and don't look back, you hear?"

Eva, coming into town on Saturdays, coming here and bathing Prin, hoisting that whalewoman, unwholewoman, unwholesome flesh, wholly alone inside her lost mind.

"I hear, Christie. I'm — I'm sorry."

Christie's eyes take on almost the same blue sharpness they once had.

"Don't ever say that word again," he says. "Not to me nor to anyone, for it's a useless christly awful word."

"I can't help it."

"Nobody can't help nothing, Morag, so best shut up about it, eh?"

The next day she goes away again.

Brooke meets her at the bus depot.

"Was it all right, love?"

"Yes. But I missed you. I'll never go away from you again, Brooke. Never. Not even for a day."

They go to Brooke's apartment, and this time she wants him more than ever, and there is no apprehension in her, only the simple need to be with him and to feel him inside herself. His entry into her is gentle and fierce, and they are close close close.

"Brooke – Brooke –"

"Yes. Yes. My love –"

And then no words no words at all, and after all there are no words, none.

She wants, then, to tell him, to praise him. To let him know. But there isn't any need, because he knows. They lie very still and close together, still joined, not speaking. Both shaken by the mystery they have known.

Memorybank Movie: Leavetaking

Morag and Ella are skimming along the street on the way to Ella's house, and it is real spring at last and the time of the singing birds has come. The sidewalks no longer flow with torrents of muddy water, the ex-snow. Small leaves are beginning to appear on the elms and maples, and the winter-anaemic grass shows signs of recuperating after all. The little stucco or frame houses look barer, greyer, without the whiteness of the snow on and around them. In a few yards, people are painting their front doors or porches.

"Hey, Ella, what means *The voice of the turtle is heard through the land?*"

"Well, you see, turtles have got this very soft croaking – well, more sort of creaking voices, heard only in spring. You have to listen very carefully. It helps to be a member of the Turtle Watchers' Association."

They are running running through the warm cool air, their laughter unabashedly loud, brash, brazen.

"Have you ever heard a turtle dove?" Ella enquires.

"Hell, no," Morag says. "I didn't know that turtles *did* dove."

Suddenly Morag feels bereft, about to journey to a strange land, knowing no one there.

"Ella, I'll sure miss you. I feel – well, you know – at home at your place. We'll write – letters, I mean. We won't ever lose touch, will we?"

"Of course not," Ella says. "Of course not."

Then they look at each other, frightened that this will not prove to be so, that friendship may not be weatherproof. Or frightened that neither of them can know what will happen, or how many years are ahead, or what manner of years they may turn out to be.

"It's terribly good of your mother to have the reception, Ella."

"Her pleasure. As you know."

"Does she cry at weddings, your mother?"

"Like the Assiniboine in flood."

"Do you think it's kind of silly, for me to be married in white?"

"What's so silly? A nice virgin like you, white you deserve."

Laughter. Spring. Like kids. Running. Wisecracking. They are almost twenty, both of them. Will Morag be able to act like this, when she feels like it, after this day?

"Ella, I'm kind of scared."

"Don't be dumb. All right – change your mind, then."

"No. I didn't mean that."

"It happens to everybody, so I'm told. Quit worrying. Brooke's probably nervous too."

"Brooke's never nervous."

Is he?

SIX

The air always cooled off at night here, with the breeze from the river, thank heavens. Morag turned on a small lamp on the sideboard and poured herself a careful scotch. Pure malt whiskey. Royalty cheque on small continuing sale of previous books received yesterday and this was the celebration. Or Thanksgiving libation, as the case might be. The case. Did anybody actually buy scotch by the case? Imagine sauntering into the liquor store and saying casually *I'll take a case of Glenfiddich*.

Morag sat down in the big old armchair beside the kitchen window. The chair she had purchased in McConnell's Landing for two bucks fifty, and Maudie Smith had cleverly and beautifully recovered it in grey felt embroidered with leaves and flowers in brash shades of pink and green. Damn Maudie for being able to turn her hand to anything. Or rather, bless her for being so generous with her time and her work.

On the scotch bottle was the motto of the Grant clan. *Stand fast*. Morag sighed. Didn't any of them ever have mottoes such as, let's say, *Take It Easy* or *Rest Your Soul*? Nope. Stiffen the spine. Prepare to suffer, *but good.* The Logan crest with the pierced heart, ye gods.

She wished all at once that she could talk to Christie. As he had now been dead for some seven years, that was not exactly possible. How great if one could believe in a re-encounter beyond this ridge of tears. When They Call the Roll Up Yonder, I'll Be There. How Christie would laugh at that. Would there be a special corner of heaven, then, for scavengers and diviners? Which was Morag, if either, or were they the same thing?

But the need to talk remained. She had long ago given up feeling guilty about long-distance phone calls. She settled herself on the high stool beside the side-board, and dialled.

"Hello – Mort?"

"Hi, Morag. How *are* you?"

She began coughing. It never failed when she began to speak to Mort, he being a doctor specializing in respiratory ailments and obviously not a champion of nicotine.

"Morag, I hate to mention it –"

"Yeh, I know. Mort, I have been trying to cut down."

"Listen, dear, I don't want to lecture you –"

"Mort, you never stop lecturing me. And you're right. You're right. Only I always cough worse when I begin talking to you. I'm addicted, and have the will-power of a flea."

"Some flea, she writes a shelf of books. Want to talk to Ella?"

Shrieks and snorts of young laughter in the background. Then Ella's voice.

"Morag – hi. How *is* it? How *are* you?"

"Well, not bad. How are you?"

Ella, who was presently raising five-year-old twins, had now four books of poems and was working on a fifth while also doing a certain amount of freelance radio work in her spare time. Good God, what spare time? Her first marriage, undertaken the year after Morag and Brooke married, had foundered. She had waited a long time for Mort. Now they were four people, a family.

"Oh, I'm fine, actually," Ella said. "It's going to be all right, but I get this feeling sometimes of living too many lives simultaneously."

"I know. Jesus, do I ever know."

"So what's with Pique, then?"

"She's coming home," Morag said heavily. "She phoned last night. I'm a bit apprehensive. I mean, I'm glad she's coming back. Naturally. But she's split up with Gordon."

"So?"

"So, did I pass *that* on? I mean – what if she can't have any kind of lasting relationship?"

"It is not passed on with the genes," Ella said sternly. "Anyway, if you would kindly examine your own life, you would see that quite a few people have been lasting in it."

"Yeh. Most of them are dead, however."

"Morag. Listen. Christie is dead. Prin is dead. I am not dead. McRaith is not dead. The Smiths are far from defunct. Pique is with us. I could name you a dozen others, but I trust you get the point. Look, kid, why don't you come and stay with us for a while?"

Kid. The word they called each other, way back when. Meaning friend.

"Jesus, Ella, thanks. But I can't. I'm not alone all that much, and anyway, I've got to try to work."

"So *are* you?"

"I don't even know. Yeh, I guess so. I always thought it would get easier, but it doesn't."

"No. It doesn't." A pause. Then, attempting cheerfulness, "By the way, my mother sends you her love. We had a letter today."

"How is she? I can't imagine her in retirement. Does she find it difficult?"

"You should know her better. Difficult, hell. She's a member of the New Left. Actually, yes, I guess she finds it difficult. But she manages."

"The New Left, for God's sake?"

"Well, it's not a *party*, you know."

"Oh heavens, Ella, I know at least that much."

"More a way of thought. I don't imagine she is about to hoist a rifle and woman the barricades or that. She's learning a lot, though, she says. Bernice is embarrassed. Her husband doesn't approve of that kind of mother-in-law – better Mumma should be hovering over the grandchildren, forcing unwanted food down their gullets. Janine goes along with it, though, so that's a help."

Janine, last seen as a High School kid, how many years ago? Now producing TV plays, and, resolutely, no children. Bernice, ex-priestess of Beauty, a matriarch with six, assorted ages from twelve to twenty, she herself still avidly following the new shades of lipstick. Well, good for her. In a way.

"Give your ma my love when you write, eh? She'll survive until she dies. Well, maybe I will, too. I wish I didn't worry about Pique. It serves no purpose, but it's hard to break the anxiety habit."

"It'll be all right. You'll see. I'll phone you next week. Phone instantly if you – well, if the need arises, eh?"

"I will. Listen, I can hear the twins raising Cain – you'd best go. Thanks, Ella. I feel better."

This was true. Morag poured some more whiskey and sat looking out the window, with only one small lamp on in the kitchen, so she could see the night river with stars floating like watercandles in it. No sounds except the sometime shushing of wind through the light-leafed willows and occasionally the ghostfluttering of the wings of a flicker, hunting the moths that were clustering around the house windows, moths that always insanely wanted in, however dim the light inside.

How would Brooke remember those years? Not the same, obviously. A different set of memories from Morag's.

Memorybank Movie: Raj Mataj

The unfamiliar city frightens Morag. Too many cars. Too much noise. When they go out, she holds tightly to Brooke's arm. He laughs, but is pleased. The apartment is small, but beautiful in Morag's eyes. They have filled it with secondhand furniture which they have painted in startling colours, orange and royal blue, lemon yellow. Brooke's prints are on the walls, and the huge bookcases are filled to overflowing with his books. His desk is in a corner of the livingroom, and if he is working in the evenings, Morag sits quietly, reading, so as not to disturb him.

"Are you finished for the night, then, Brooke?"

"Yes, and about time, too. Twenty blasted essays I've marked tonight. You've a good girl, sweetheart, to sit there so quietly all this time."

"I don't mind. I was reading. Would you like some coffee now?"

"Please."

She is reading her way steadily through the novels on Brooke's shelves. English and American. Translations from French and Russian. Brooke is very good about discussing these with her. She is alone most days, and the apartment is easy to care for, so she has all the time she needs for reading. When they go out in the evenings, or when they have some of Brooke's colleagues in, Morag says very little, mainly listening. Picking people's brains.

Now Brooke sprawls tiredly on the chesterfield, stretching out his long legs onto the Indian rug which they have brought with them and which Brooke has had for a long time, having inherited it from his parents' home in England. Brooke's parents went back to England when they retired from India, and lived there until first Brooke's mother and then his father died, a few years before the war. By that time Brooke was teaching in Canada, so he had the carpet and a few other things sent out to him. He has not been back to India since he last went out on vacation when he was sixteen, just before his parents retired. He tried to get there during the war, but instead had spent the duration, infuriatingly for him, as an officer in an Army training camp in Quebec. He refuses to talk about this period of his life, because he hated every minute of it except when on leave in Montreal, where there were lots of women. He talks about India sometimes, though, and with a kind of muted and concealed homesickness. Morag wants to know everything about him, about his previous life, so that she will know all of him.

"Brooke, tell me more about the kind of place you lived in when you were very young."

He takes his coffee from her, and puts his other arm around her shoulders as she sits down beside him.

"What's this? A bedtime story?"

"That's it." She smiles, then doesn't. "It seems such a strange sort of childhood. Weren't you lonely?"

"Not especially. Not then. I played with the servants' children. I was allowed to, when I was small."

"Not later on?"

"Well, no."

"I think that's horrible," Morag says.

"Unfortunate, yes, probably. Just one of those things. It was the custom in those days."

"What was your house like?"

"I remember it," Brooke says slowly, "as a very large whitewashed establishment with a great many rooms, and garden which was almost a jungle, filled with purple bougainvillaea and –"

The way Brooke tells it, Morag visualizes a huge Victorian structure, white as alabaster with slatted wooden shutters drawn against the sun. There would be a wall, also white, around it, and in the garden a tumultuous variety of strange trees and flowers, greens and purples and scarlets in strange shapes. Bright-plumaged birds, unheard of here, would have strutted and swooped there, their voices raucous or else silver. Would it have been like that? Morag cannot ever know, not being able to see the pictures that must grow inside his head when he talks of it. She is glad, however, that he cannot look inside her head and see Hill Street, about which she does not talk.

"Wasn't it very poor, there? The country, I mean."

"Yes. Yes, it was. We didn't often go to Calcutta, but I remember some of the markets there, where they sold carved ivory and teak and brass and all manner of baubles to Europeans, and the beggars there – most of them crippled, all skin and bones. Sometimes they used to maim children purposely, to use them as beggars."

"That's terrible."

"Yes. It was."

His face is grave, almost apologetic, as though he has seen things he would rather she didn't know about.

"Is it better now, there?"

"Not a damn bit better," Brooke says bitterly. "Worse, if anything, I should think. Whatever anyone may say of it, the passing of the British Raj wasn't the answer."

"But Brooke – surely you can't believe it was right for them, the British, even for you, to have lived there like that, in that way, house and servants, while –"

Brooke puts his cup on the coffee table and strokes her breasts lightly.

"Little one," he says, very gently, "there is no real justice in this world. I don't say it was fair. It was just the best that could be done under the circumstances, that's all."

"But –"

"Hush, love. You don't know. You just don't *know*."

True. She does not know.

"What was your mother like, Brooke?"

He smiles, although not with amusement.

"It's odd," he says. "I remember her always, even when they'd retired to England, as a kind of shadow, a quiet grey shadow of a woman, never daring to raise her voice to him. When I was a youngster she used sometimes to make feeble efforts to intercede on my behalf, but it never worked. Never. Not even once. I suppose I resented that, at the time. It always seemed she ought to have been able to do something. I guess I felt sorry for her as well. He was a difficult man."

"What did he do? To you?"

Brooke shrugs.

"Well, he was a schoolmaster, remember, and very keen on discipline. He used to cane the boys at school – he reserved that pleasure for himself, incidentally, and never let any of the Indian teachers do it. He caned me, too, but he had subtler punishments as well. Caning was simple. Once he made me sit on top of a large steamer trunk, tied to it, actually, just outside the front gate of our compound, where everyone passing by, Europeans, and Hindus from Brahmans to outcasts, could see me. On my chest was a placard which read *I Am Bad*. Rather a gruesome sense of humour."

"Oh Brooke —"

He laughs.

"I was supposed to stay there until I begged for his forgiveness. What I'd done I can't remember now. He also thought he could make me cry — I remember being certain that was what he expected and wanted. I must've been nearly six. I didn't cry, though, and I didn't apologize. My mother wept buckets, as I recall, wringing her hands like someone out of a Victorian ghost story. Not that it did any good. Finally he had to cart me back inside."

"That's appalling, the whole thing."

"He was a charmer, all right," Brooke says, his voice cold. "Well, never mind. At least it taught me to stand up for myself."

"Yes, like dropping a kid in the ocean, half a mile out and saying — learn to swim. He might, but what a way to have to do it."

"It came in handy all the same," Brooke says, "when I went to boardingschool in England. If you weren't reasonably tough-fibred there, you were reduced to a quivering jelly in a very short time."

"You make it sound like prison."

"No, not really. I quite liked it, as a matter of fact, once I got used to it. There were awful things about it, but one learned how to cope with them. It was a military school, mainly for the sons of officers. It was considered a desirable place to attend. The boys there were all given ranks."

"*What?*"

"It's true," Brooke grins. "I was absolutely determined I wasn't going to be pushed around. We used to have kit inspection and drill and things like that. I worked at it like fury. I was a Sergeant at the age of eight. What do you think of that?"

He is laughing, but Morag cannot. She stares at him.

"You can't mean it."

"Come now, love," he says teasingly, "don't take it so seriously. It wasn't so bad. I rather enjoyed it. I didn't mean to turn this into a horror story. It isn't."

"I think it was pretty awful of your parents to ship you off like that."

"They didn't have many alternatives. My mother didn't like it much, I suppose, although she never said so. Anyway, one thing I do know – I shall never be like my father was. Never. How his students must have railed inwardly against him. As I did."

"You couldn't possibly be like that in any way at all. Your students adore you. I did, when I was a student. I still do, although in a slightly different way of course."

"How – different?"

"Sexier."

"Well, that is what I call the beginning of a good bedtime story."

Nowadays, when they make love, they almost always come at the same time, and often sleep the night in each other's arms, still joined. Sometimes in the morning he is still inside her, and they separate slowly, reluctantly, but their inhabitance of one another never really ceases and never will.

"Brooke – couldn't we make love and not mind if we had a child? I mean, just let it happen if it will?"

He outlines her face with his hand, as though his fingers are memorizing it.

"Aren't you happy as we are, Morag?"

"Of course. Of course I am. You know that."

"Well, relax then, my love. Plenty of time."

That night Brooke does not sleep well. He is restless, turning away from her, and finally he begins moaning in his sleep, a weird low anguished voice, totally unlike his waking one. Morag puts a hand on him and finds the hairs on his chest wet with sweat.

"Brooke – wake up."

"What? What's the matter?"

"You were having a nightmare."

"Oh – was I? Thanks, love."

"Brooke – you were talking, sort of. I could only make out one word."

"Oh? What was it?"

"It sounded like *Minoo*. Is that a Hindi word?"

"It's – well, not exactly. It's a name."

"For a man or a woman?" She despises herself for asking this, and not unnaturally Brooke is annoyed.

"Oh for heaven's sake, Morag. It's a woman's name. I can't think what it meant. Now can we get some sleep, please?"

"I'm sorry, Brooke. I didn't mean –"

But he is asleep again. What does it matter? It doesn't. Morag does not own him or what goes on in his head, nor does she imagine he has not been with many women. If age sixteen, he would have been old enough. It would not matter at all, had he not sounded so hurt, in ways he would never admit to, when awake.

She wants to console him, for whatever it was, but how could you do that for hurts which must have gone deeper than he wants to know? He is enormously strong within himself.

But once he wouldn't have been. Once he would have been a six-year-old who had to teach himself never to give in, never to reveal his pain. What was it really like for him, away back then? Why would he not say? If he cannot tell Morag, who can he tell? Perhaps no one.

This is a frightening thought. She pushes it away, but lies unsleeping for a long while, beside him.

Memorybank Movie: The Young

Morag Skelton, age twenty-four, has now lived in Toronto for four years. She is able to go downtown without getting hopelessly lost. She has long since learned the various colleges of the university, which city bookshops are the best, where to buy clothes that Brooke will like on her, and how to do verbal battle with hairdressers in order to achieve (even if only partially) the style she wants, without submitting to the outlandish creations which they always seem to want.

She does not venture downtown very often, because unfortunately the city still scares the bejesus out of her. She does not, however, mention this fact to anyone.

Her long straight black hair has been cut much shorter and permed in the prevailing manner of the day, described by Helen of Miss Helene as *just a few soft curls, Mrs. Skelton, and a little swirl over your brow.* She feels slightly peculiar each time she gets her hair done, but Brooke likes her this way, and she has to admit it does look more feminine.

She watches her diet carefully and is slender. She wears lightly tailored suits in the daytime, with pastel blouses, sometimes frilled. In the heat of the summer, cotton dresses with flared skirts. Her shoes have what is known as Illusion heels, so that she will appear to be wearing high heels without adding too much to her height. In the evenings, meeting academic friends, she goes in heavily for the little black cocktail dress, not necessarily black, of course. She looks smart.

She is a competent cook. Her apricot bread and peanut butter cookies are splendid, and her chocolate cake with fudge icing is beyond compare.

She reads a great deal.

She asks the janitor of the apartment block if people are allowed to keep cats. He says No.

She grows African violets, which are pretty, and potted parsley, which can be used as a garnish on such dishes as tomato jelly.

She writes short stories and tears them up.

One day she throws a Benares brass ashtray through the kitchen window.

Appalled, she flashes down to the back alley and retrieves the brass vessel. It is not dented. They made their brass to last, all right, out there in Benares.

She thumbs rapidly through the Yellow Pages, and phones five firms of repairmen, all of whom say they've got more jobs on their plates than they can handle in three months, lady, and very sorry.

It is February. The kitchen is growing icier by the minute.

The sixth attempt produces a repairman who puts in a new window pane. She pays him in cash and flushes the receipt down the toilet, having first ripped it into tiny shreds. All she needs is a blocked toilet right now.

That evening, she and Brooke have their sherry before dinner.

"Brooke?"

"Yes, love?"

"I don't think I have enough to do. I really think we

should try to have a child, Brooke. Don't you see? I really want a child of yours."

Brooke refills his sherry glass and sits on the arm of the chesterfield, putting a hand on Morag's shoulder.

"I know, love, and I'm glad you do, believe me. But once you have a child, you'll be awfully tied down with it, don't forget. You're still very young for that kind of limited life."

"You, however," Morag says, "are thirty-nine."

Brooke laughs.

"Well, that's not quite senility yet, my love. Look, I appreciate how you feel, Morag. It's just that I don't think you quite realize how tied down we'd be. Also, a flat is hardly the place for a child."

"Why don't we get a house, then? I hate this damn apartment." Morag hears her voice speaking; she sounds like a spoiled child.

"I'm sorry to hear it," Brooke says, withdrawing his hand. "I always thought you liked the place. At least, that's what you said. I never realized it was such an ordeal for you to live here."

"Oh Brooke, I'm sorry. Honestly. I didn't mean it. It's just that –"

"Well, you know, my darling, one doesn't just step out and acquire a house. It requires a certain amount of money. We've saved a fair bit, but not enough for a down payment on a decent house."

"We could wait forever, though, and the circumstances would never be entirely perfect for having a child."

"Personally," Brooke says mildly, "I like it here with just the two of us. There's time enough to think of a child when we're able to get the sort of house we want. For now, isn't this all right? I feel awfully close to you, my love."

"Oh Brooke – I do to you, too. You know that. And I'm sorry when I'm unreasonable. Really I am. Please don't ever leave me, Brooke. I couldn't bear it."

He puts his arm around her.

"How could I ever leave you? You're mine. My woman. I'll be with you and protect you always."

Does she really want to be protected, always? If not, this does not seem to be quite the moment to say so.

"Brooke, do you think it would be a good idea for me to get a job?"

"By all means, if you really want to. What sort of job?"

"Oh, I don't know. A clerk in a store, maybe. A bookshop? Or a job in an office – I can type."

"I wonder if you'd really care for that kind of routine job, Morag? Go ahead and try it, if you think you'd like to, by all means. But typing business letters or doing filing all day wouldn't be my idea of fun."

Nor would it be Morag's as she now swiftly perceives.

"No, I guess I wouldn't care much for it at that."

"What about your writing? Have you given it up?"

"No. But everything I write seems bad."

"Why don't you let me be the judge of that? Have you got any stories?"

"One or two."

"Well, let's see them, then."

Morag reluctantly shows them to him.

"I think these are *quite* good," Brooke says finally. "They certainly need a little polishing, and I'm not sure of the plausibility of either ending, to tell you the truth, but – yes, they're definitely worth working on, I'd say."

She is hungry for approval, but suddenly cannot take what he is saying.

"Brooke," she says in a hard voice, "they aren't any good. They're trivial and superficial."

He looks at her in surprise.

"Well, if you don't like them, love, then of course that's up to you."

He glances at his watch.

"My God, Morag, we'd better hurry with dinner. My Third Year Honours English students are coming around tonight – had you forgotten?"

"Oh Lord. I'm sorry, Brooke. I *had* forgotten."

The students, two girls and six boys, troop in about eight o'clock. They drape themselves around the room, some of them sitting on the floor. Brooke sits in the one armchair. He is warm with them, calm even when they make ridiculous statements, dependably friendly and yet never making the error of trying to be one of them. They are confident and yet a little shy with him, arguing tentatively but willing to be convinced when he points out (always carefully, never stabbing any of them to the heart) the flaws in their judgements. Tonight Gerard Manley Hopkins is the subject of talk. Morag sits on a low stool by the window, occasionally chipping in but mostly listening.

"I can't help feeling," one of the boys says, "that at least some of the obscurity is done for its own sake – you know, really just to baffle the reader. A kind of intellectual game, the purpose of which – subconscious, no doubt – was to prove that Hopkins' intellect was superior to most."

"Well, let's face it, his intellect *was* superior to most," Morag finds herself saying. "But you're right about the spiritual pride, which is what I take it you mean. And also self-pity, in a poem like 'Thou Art Indeed Just, Lord.' The point is, he *knew* it. But you're wrong about the obscurity – almost always, if you can get inside the lines, you find he's saying what he means with absolute precision. 'Sheer plod makes plough down sillion shine' – I'm not sure it really does, but it couldn't be expressed more concisely and accurately. Or where he says 'No worst, there is none.' My God, think of that. There really *is* none –"

She stops. There is silence. Embarrassment.

Then Brooke smoothly leads the discussion into different channels.

When the young have finally departed, Morag turns to Brooke.

"I shouldn't have butted in like that, Brooke. I *am* sorry."

Brooke draws her close to him.

"Hush, child. It's all right. It doesn't matter a damn. Truly. Everybody makes exaggerated statements from time to time."

Morag abruptly pulls away from him.

"Brooke –"

"What's the matter? For heaven's sake, Morag, you're awfully touchy today."

"Brooke, I am not your child. I am your wife."

Brooke laughs, but partly in annoyance.

"Is that it? I've offended your pride? My God, Morag, can't you see I only used the word as an expression of affection? Remember how you and Ella used to call each other *kid*? What's the difference, except that I meant this a little more tenderly and in a different kind of relationship?"

Oh God. Quite true. And she has lashed out at him for it.

"Brooke, I'm sorry. I really must be unbalanced. I'm sorry. I love you, Brooke. I do love you."

"I know, my love. I know."

Memorybank Movie: Spear of Innocence

Morag begins writing the novel almost unexpectedly, although Lilac has been in her mind for some time. She has no idea where the character has come from. She has never in her life known anyone remotely like Lilac Stonehouse, the fluffily pretty girl from a lumber town who lights out for the city. An old story, but in this case (hopefully) somewhat different, because Lilac's staggering naïveté is never presented as anything but harmful and in fact it damages not only herself but others. Innocence may well be the eighth deadly sin.

Morag has no idea how long it will take to complete the novel, nor how much rewriting will have to be done, but once started she writes quickly. She knows more about Lilac than Lilac knows about herself, but how to convey this? It is being written in the third person, but from Lilac's viewpoint, and as this is a limited one, people have to be communicated to the reader solely through their words and acts, which Lilac often does not understand. The difficulties of having a main character who is virtually inchoate. When actually writing, Morag is certain she is getting it across. When not writing, she is certain she isn't. A seesaw existence.

"What is it you're writing?" Brooke asks.

"A novel, I think."

"A novel? Well, may as well aim your sights high, I suppose."

"Do you think – no, honestly, Brooke, tell me – do you think I'm trying to run before I can walk?"

"That remains to be seen, doesn't it? The novel is a complex structure."

"Don't I know it," Morag says glumly.

"Here – no long face, please. Come on, smile, love."

Morag smiles.

"That's better," Brooke says. "How about a movie tonight?"

"Lovely. I'd love to. I'll flash up the dishes and be ready in ten minutes."

In fact, she would like to go back to Chapter Three. Lilac, going to work in the seedy nightclub, Crowe's Cave, for the first time, hasn't been presented properly. Lilac should be more hesitant – a combination of hesitancy and brashness. How to get that across?

Unfair to Brooke. Who is, after all, supporting her while she bashes away at the typewriter. And who loves her. And whom she loves.

Morag thinks of her smile. The eager agreement to go out. How many times has she lied to him before, or is this the first time? No, it is not the first time. She never thought of it that way before. It never seemed like lying. Now it does.

Brooke is depressed tonight, as he frequently is. The movie does not interest him, and they leave in the middle. At home, he pours them both a gin and tonic.

"Brooke – what is it?"

"Oh, I don't know. The First Year class this year is singularly lacking in wits. It's discouraging, I suppose. I sometimes think this is a hell of a way to spend one's life. And if you *do* make contact, ever, more often than not you never know it."

"That's not quite so," Morag points out. "Your Third Year class is full of good kids, and you know perfectly well you make contact with them."

"Yes, I guess so. I sometimes wonder."

"Brooke, there's absolutely no doubt about it."

"You may be somewhat prejudiced, my love."

"Of course I'm prejudiced, damn it. But I'm not blind. I can see how they feel about you."

How is it that she once imagined him to be totally certain of himself? No one is, of course. But with Brooke, you have to get within very close range before you can see it. His vulnerabilities are not on display. He learned his lesson almost too well as a child.

"What would you have preferred to do, then, Brooke, if not this?"

Brooke smiles ironically.

"I don't know – run a tea plantation, perhaps. Somewhere in Assam, somewhere very remote, away from the varied awfulness of this world."

"I know. I think I can understand that."

"There is, however, no place, really, to go or to get away."

"Brooke, why don't you get a job teaching in India?"

He shakes his head.

"No, little one. I couldn't go back. It's all changed too much. I wouldn't know it. I wouldn't feel at home there any longer."

Trapped in a garden of the mind, a place which no longer has a being in external reality. Is everyone? Not Morag. She wouldn't go back to Manawaka for all the tea in China or Assam. And yet the town inhabits her, as once she inhabited it.

"Brooke – that's terribly sad. I'm sorry. I wish there were something I could do."

"It's the human condition," Brooke says abruptly. "There's nothing anyone can do about it."

"I can't accept that, Brooke. I just cannot accept it."

"Well, all right. There *is* something you can do, then. Keep on being happy and cheerful – it's a kind of leaven. It's what I need from you."

I will never let him see the Black Celt in me. Morag, shortly before marriage. It seemed an easy thing to undertake, then.

"Brooke, I will. Be – the way you said. I will."

Will is a strange word. Will she, then, by an act of will? And if this act of willing, however willingly undertaken, is false to her, can it be true to Brooke?

That night Brooke has the same (same? who can tell?) nightmare, the one which recurs every six months or so, and speaks the same name.

Minoo.

She cannot bear the weird monotone of his voice. She shakes his shoulder.

"Brooke – wake up."

"Oh God. Not again? What a bore for you."

"I don't mind. Who *was* she, Brooke?"

He rubs his eyes and sits up in bed.

"Did I say – yes, I suppose I must've. Well, I may as well tell you, not that it's all that important. She was a Hindu woman – really, at this point, I have no memory of whether she was young or old. She seemed old but she may only have been a girl. I was about five or six. She was my *ayah*."

"Your what?"

"*Ayah*. She looked after me. She was very – oh, I don't know – very affectionate and tender, I guess, and there was not much of that kind of feeling around our house. My mother spent nearly all her time lying in a hammock, suffering from migraine. Minoo used to play with me, and build little stone forts for me, and –"

"Go on."

"Well," Brooke says, reaching out for a cigarette and lighting it slowly, "actually, when I couldn't get to sleep she would get into bed beside me, and hold me in her arms and stroke me. I mean, all over. I used to have an orgasm or what-ever is the equivalent in a child, and then I'd go to sleep. It was quite a common practise there, as I later learned. Not, however, among Europeans."

"It may be somewhat different from Dr. Spock's recom-mendations," Morag says, "but I can't see anything so heinous about it."

"No," Brooke says. "There wasn't. But one evening my father came into the bedroom."

"Oh. I see."

"That was, as a matter of fact, the reason why, next day, he beat me and tied me to the steamer trunk outside the gate, with the sign *I Am Bad* on me."

"Brooke, that was terrible."

"Not really," Brooke says. "It's a nuisance that it comes back to me, that's all. But it certainly strengthened my resolve. I hated him forever after, and I suppose as a child I must've wondered if he was right about it, but at least it taught me at an early age that life is tough and one has to be pretty tough, as well, to stand up to it. I learned to run my life my way, to keep a firm control over things so that the external forces would batter at the gates as little as possible."

"And yet, earlier tonight, when you were depressed, you said it was the human condition and nothing could be done about it."

"Oh, that. Well, yes, I guess that's more or less fate, that kind of depression. But one can make oneself less vulnerable to the external blows, at least."

"Too much so, perhaps. Brooke – listen. We hardly know a thing about one another. I mean, not really. Even after nearly five years. It's necessary that we find out. I don't think either of us has ever admitted how we really feel about a lot of things. I'm not the way you think I am. And you're not the way I thought you were, either. I just didn't know. I like you better like this. Maybe I wouldn't have, four years ago, but I do now. We've got to find out a lot more."

"We may do," Brooke says, putting out his cigarette and patting her gently on the rump, "but I also have an eight-thirty class in the morning. Let's get some sleep."

This cannot be said to be an unreasonable viewpoint in any sense. If you have to get up at seven you don't lie awake all night yakking about your childhood and so on.

How much of Lilac's childhood remained with *her*? *All*. It always does.

Morag usually stops writing about four, so she will have time to get outside the novel before Brooke arrives home. She does not always manage. Sometimes she forgets that time, outside, is passing.

This afternoon she has forgotten, because Lilac has aborted herself in a way that Morag recalls from long ago. And yet it is not Eva for whom Morag experiences pain now – it is Lilac only, at this moment. Morag finishes the episode, moves away from the typewriter, walks around the apartment, smoking, trying to shed the tension instantly, which is impossible. It is five minutes to six.

The key in the door, and Brooke comes in.

"Hello, love."

"The dinner isn't ready," Morag blurts. "It isn't even begun."

He stares at her.

"For God's sake, Morag, are you ill? What's the matter, love? You're shaking."

A moment ago she felt aggressively defensive. Now she is ashamed to say.

"It's – no, I'm all right. It's just that I've reached a kind of crucial point. I mean, with the novel."

Brooke laughs, relieved.

"Is *that* it? Heavens, I thought you'd been suddenly stricken with something serious."

I have. I have. But she does not say this. Odd – if you had a friend who had just aborted herself, causing chaos all round and not only to herself, no one would be surprised if you felt upset, anxious, shaken. It is no different with fiction – more so, maybe, because Morag has felt Lilac's feelings. The blood is no less real for being invisible to the external eye. She wants to explain, but feels too tired.

"Well, never mind," Brooke is saying. "It doesn't happen often. We'll go out to eat. You run along now and make yourself look presentable."

She wants only to go to sleep for about fourteen unbroken hours. But goes and puts on a decent dress and does her hair. It is, after all, kind of him. It really is. He might have been angry and has not been.

She takes three aspirins and tries to make herself look especially nice.

SEVEN

Work over for the day, Morag walked. The road past
the house was dirt only, supposed to be main-
tained by the municipality, but no voters worth
mentioning lived along here, so the ruts were deep and old.
Small red-branched dogwood bushes were now in white
cluster-flower. The purple and white wild phlox were so rich
and heavy with their July perfume that they seemed almost out
of keeping here, amongst the plain coarse grass and the dust.

Red-winged blackbird. You would not guess their concealed splendour, seeing them on a branch with their wings
folded. Only when they took off, the outfanning of those
scarlet feathers hidden among the black.

A groundhog fatly scuttled from the path. Morag liked
them – they seemed portly and innocuous, vine-gobblers,
meaning well. But Royland said the groundhogs' holes made
the cattle trip and break legs. Idiotic groundhogs, uncarnivo-
rous, scuttlebustling about on their own tiny business, not one
of your great antagonistic creatures, no dinosaurs or jaguars
they, yet busting the legbone of some dumbly innocent cow
all the same.

Morag always carried a stick when she walked these roads. So as to fend off the following: mad dogs frothing with hydrophobia; killer foxes; coyotes or some few ancient wolves which might have survived here since pioneer times, unknown to anyone, but possibly lurking in the underbrush, panting to pounce; and poisonous snakes, of which the snake book said this area had none.

Morag returned to the house. The swallows were positively dangerous, as always at this time of year, dive-bombing anyone who came within eyeshot of the nest, which was above the kitchen window — a goblet-shaped structure of mud and straw, with its patio on either side. The fledglings were nearly ready to fly, and took up all the space in the nest, so the parent swallows slept on the mud-and-straw patio these nights. Admirable parents. Intelligent. Joyous.

"It's okay," she told them now, as they flew to within an inch of her head. "I'm no threat to your young."

Imagine dying from a fractured skull delivered by a hysterical parent swallow. A novel death. In a novel, who'd believe it? *Novel.* Odd word. Swallows never actually hit, though. They possessed fine radar.

The kitchen door was open. Morag had closed it when she went out.

"Hi," Pique said.

"Pique!"

Morag hugged the girl, and Pique did not seem to mind. Seemed even glad to be here. Looking just the same — tall, slender, almost skinny, long straight black hair loose around her shoulders, dressed in blue jeans and what appeared to be a man's shirt of ancient vintage with sleeves cut off short and unhemmed, wide leather belt with old brass buckle which she hadn't had before but which had an oddly familiar look.

"How *are* you, honey?" Morag asked, holding the girl at arms length as though searching for signs of malnutrition, ill-treatment by world, or sadness of any variety. Shadows under Pique's eyes. Sleepless nights? Worry? Over what?

"You look a bit tired," Morag said.

Pique laughed.

"I'm okay, Ma. I hitched from Toronto, and didn't have such good luck. I *am* a bit tired. That's why I was kind of delayed, the luck. I'm starving. Got any peanut butter? I've just arrived this second. Has Gord phoned? I sure as hell hope not. What hassles. He won't go away. I don't want to damage the guy, but what can I do? Where's your bread – in the fridge? Yeh. You shouldn't eat white bread, Ma, it's very bad for you. How are *you*?"

"Fine. Fine." Morag lit a cigarette, hands unsteady. "It's good to see you. Are you okay, really?"

Pique grinned, dark brown slightly slanted eyes filled with faint golden lights, sparks.

"Relax, Ma. Shall I make us some coffee? Where's the percolator? You shouldn't drink that instant slop. It's plastic. Sure, I'm all right. Really. Can't you see? I had a pretty good time. Some times weren't so good. They hate kids hitching, some places. They'd really like you to be dead. Really *dead*, for real. It's the anger that scares me."

"Yeh. Me, too."

"Because they don't know it's there inside them," Pique said. "They think they're sweet reasonableness, and it's *you* that's in the wrong, just by being, and not being like them, or looking like them, or wanting their kind of life. It's the anger you can feel, even if they don't lay a hand on you. It's, like – well, visible. You can see and taste and smell it. You know?"

"I can guess. I've seen it, under other circumstances, when I was a kid."

"I wondered about that," Pique said, in between mouthfuls of sandwich, "when I went to Manawaka. I guess it's changed a lot, on the surface. Underneath – well, I dunno."

"Did you see –"

"I don't think I can talk about it, just yet," Pique said carefully. "I'll tell you about it later on, maybe, sometime. I don't think Christie's old house is there any more. Lotta new little tacky houses on Hill Street."

"I couldn't bear to see it. Although it could hardly look worse than it did then."

"Prosperous town, I'd say."

"Yes. I suppose so. Did you go down in the valley?"

"I'll tell you *later*, I said."

"Sorry."

"That's okay. Got any oranges or bananas?"

"On the sideboard. Where'd you get the jazzy belt?"

"From my dad. He gave it to me. He had to shorten it a lot. It was his."

"Of course. I knew I'd seen it before."

"I saw him in Toronto, Ma."

"I know. He phoned me."

"He *did*? Why?"

"I don't know," Morag said, feeling slightly annoyed. "To say he'd seen you, and what did I mean, letting you go off like that. He has his reasons for saying that, though."

"That's funny," Pique said. "He didn't take that line with me. He said he knew why I had to go out west and that. He did, too."

"Yeh. Well, maybe he only said that to me because he thought it was what I'd expect to hear. I think he really phoned to tell me he'd seen you and you were okay. He always thought I was kind of –"

"What?"

"Bourgeois. Square."

"*Square.* I love your idiom, Ma. It's like an old dance tune from the forties."

"Brat. You wait. Yours will be passé, too."

"Well, *were* you, like, *square*?"

"It all depends where you stand," Morag said. "To him, I suppose I was, at least in some ways. He thought I wanted things that he didn't care about. I did, too, but then, later, I didn't."

"What things?"

"Oh – respectability, wall-to-wall carpets and that."

"Did you really? Poor Ma."

"Indeed. But it wasn't all that bad. It wasn't like that at all, really. I can't explain."

"My dad gave me some songs," Pique said. "That was the best thing he gave me."

"He told me. That's good. That's fine."

Hypocritical Morag. Jealous of the fact that he had that to give. Like A-Okay's poems. Could you hand over a stack of books to someone? Only to someone who wanted to read, presumably. Maybe Pique would read Morag's out of curiosity when Morag was pushing up daisies. But *songs*. And he had been singing them so long ago, long before everyone in sight began going around singing their own songs. Lucky bugger. God knows he'd had a rocky road, withal, though.

"I never thought he'd actually teach them to me," Pique said. "He'd sung them that one time before, you remember? No, twice – didn't he, when I was a little kid, somewhere, as well?"

"Yes. Yes, he did. Some of them."

"Gord couldn't see how important it was to me. He thought it would be just the same if you listened to a record and picked up anybody else's song that way. I couldn't explain. It was kind of strange to see him again, my dad. Did you love him?"

Morag sat with her hands around the coffee mug. Thinking. How to reply and get across that much complexity in a single well-chosen phrase? Impossible.

"I guess you could say love. I find words more difficult to define than I used to. I guess I felt – feel – that he was related to me in some way. I'd known him an awfully long time, you know. I mean, at the time when you were born, I'd known him an awfully long time *then*, even. I'm not sure *know* is the right word, there."

"Who cares about the right word?" Pique cried. Then, suddenly, the hurt cry which must have been there for years, "Why did you *have* me?"

"I wanted you," Morag said, stunned.

"For your own satisfaction, yes. You never thought of him, or of me."

And to that accusation there was no answer. None. Because it was partly true. To have someone of her own blood. But only partly. She had not conned a kid out of him, after all. Or not quite, anyway. How did he look at it? She didn't know. But he'd given the songs to Pique.

Silence. The afternoon sun pouring through the window as though the daylight would be forever. The young swallows fidgeting and flittering in the nest, wanting to fly.

"Pique –"

Pique, sitting at the end of the long table, put out her hand and touched Morag's hand.

"Yeh. I know. Never mind. It's okay. You know something, Ma?"

"What?"

Pique was about to cry, but refused to do so, was forced to reject tears as an indignity against what she was about to say.

"His voice isn't very good any more," Pique said steadily. "The jobs are getting harder to find. Lots of competition around now, and he's only got one thing to cash in on now, in lots of places."

"Which is?" But she knew.

"You know, he's still kind of an oddity," Pique said, in that same unnervingly calm distant voice. "That's a bad scene, for him. And he's not so young any more."

"Nor am I," Morag said. "Nor can I go on forever, either. Sometimes I'd like to see him."

"Why don't you, then? He's there."

"I don't know if he would like to see me. Probably not."

Pique's voice was not calm and distant any longer.

"You make me sick. You make me bloody sick. You're so goddamn proud and so scared of being rejected. You're so stupid in that way, you really are."

"It's not that simple," Morag said.

But maybe it was. No, it wasn't. Indecision all around. If she went unannounced to see him, he would laugh bitterly in her face. Or would he? She felt extremely tired.

"How would some dinner grab you?"

"Okay," Pique said, without enthusiasm. "Shall I cook, or will you?"

"Me, I guess. You can tomorrow."

Unfortunately, at that moment the door was decisively knocked upon. Morag prayed. Let it be Royland. Or A-Okay and Maudie. But of course, no.

Gord. Who else? His straw hair tangled, his boy's face still not quite set into the firmer outlines it would have in a few years, but showing strength of the bones under the skin. A determined tenacious face, but the blue eyes were bewildered.

"Now, listen, Pique," he began. "Just listen for one minute, will you?"

"I asked you not to come here," Pique said, voice low and helpless. Then, flaring up, "I'm going *out*. And don't follow me, either, *see*?"

Like a kid. But only because she didn't know what to do.

"If you're going out," Morag said, "why don't you take a pan and pick some of the wild strawberries up the meadow?"

"Oh, for God's *sake*!" Pique ran, and the screendoor slammed.

Tactful Morag. It had seemed practical, that's all.

"Want some coffee?" she asked Gord, hoping he would say *No* and leave immediately.

He nodded and sat down.

"Why does she *do* it, Morag?" he asked, begging for revelations. "I mean, what've I ever done to make her be like that? She was okay for a while, there, on the way out west, once I caught up with her. Which wasn't easy, believe me. Finding her. Then she just sort of went away. What's she want me to *do*?"

She wants you to get lost, you poor mug. No, that's too flippant.

"Look, Gord," Morag said, "she cares about you. That is, she cares about you as a person. But I just think she feels she has to be on her own awhile, and find out what she's meant to do. You will just have to let go of her."

Would it be kinder simply to tell him that Pique couldn't get on with him any more, through no fault of his or hers, that she was on some kind of search on her own behalf, that she couldn't care about him as once she had and couldn't pretend to feel what she didn't feel? No, not kinder, probably.

Am I only interpreting her through my own experience? Maybe she doesn't feel that at all. Why all that talk, suddenly, about her dad?

"Yeh, I guess I know." He glared for an instant at Morag.

All Morag's fault, he probably thought. Brought up the girl strangely. What could you expect? Bad scene. Morag could feel Gord's hostility like lye thrown in her face.

"Couldn't you suggest anything?" Gord then said, pleadingly. "I feel it must be my fault, but I don't know how."

Morag perceived that what she had taken to be hostility had been in fact self-reproach on his part.

"I don't know what to say," she said. "I don't think there's anything."

Gord rose.

"Yeh. Well. I thought probably not. Thanks anyway, for the coffee. I'll be going now. Tell Pique if she wants to see me, phone. My aunt'll take the message if I'm not there."

No doubt, at least for the time in which it took him to find another woman, he would rise up at 4:00 A.M. if necessary, summoned from his aunt's farm, and come rocketing out. *Through the swamp and fog (or flame and fire, or ice and snow; can't remember) I gotta go where you are.* "Chloe." Done by Spike Jones, a sendup, clanging with tubas and cowbells, aeons ago. Morag was becoming an antique. Also, mind-wanderer. *Mooner*, Prin had said.

"I'll tell her. Gord, I'm sorry."

She was, too. Also for Pique. The infinite capacity of humans to wound one another without meaning or wanting to.

An hour later, when it was nearly dark, Pique returned, carrying an old coffee tin full of aromatic wild strawberries.

"Ma –"

"Mm? Thanks for the strawberries."

"That's okay. Do you think I'm mean?"

"Not wantonly cruel, no. What's the alternative? To go on with him and feel diminished or destroyed yourself?"

"Well, I wouldn't put it quite that dramatically," Pique said.

Morag had perhaps been talking not about Pique but about herself. She must not do that. No parallels. Dangerous.

"What do you plan on doing, honey?" she asked. "I don't mean with Gord. I mean –"

"Yeh. You mean with my life. Do. Do. Always that. Do I have to *do* anything? Don't worry. I'll get a job. And I won't stay here forever – I'm not the millstone type. Ma – I'm sorry. I didn't mean it to sound like that."

"Christie used to say that *sorry* was a christly bloody awful word, and I should never say it. I never quite managed not to, though."

"Well, he wasn't right about everything, from what you've told me. Sometimes a person feels like saying it. It's when you don't feel like saying it, but say it anyhow, that it seems pointless to me. I wish there was something I wanted to do. I feel there must be, but I haven't discovered it yet. Nothing I value that much. I value the songs – my own as well. But I gotta earn a slight bit of bread as well."

"Well, think of it when you feel stronger," Morag said, having often used this advice (unsuccessfully) on herself.

Pique went up to her old room, where the window overlooked the back meadow. Morag remained downstairs for a long time, with the lights out, looking at the river. What she felt, more than anything, was relief that Pique was home. Alive.

The next morning, Royland came over with a pickerel.

"This here's for Pique's breakfast," Royland said. "Saw her arrive yesterday, but thought I'd wait to come over. She okay?"

"Yeh. More or less. Thanks a lot, Royland. Stay awhile. She'll be up soon."

"I'm divining this afternoon – farm just the other side of the Landing. Think she'd like to come along?"

"I'm sure 'she would. Remember how she used to go along with you when she was a kid? It's always fascinated her."

"Not half as much as it's fascinated you," he said.

True. The mystery which still drew her. What had drawn him to divining? How had he come to try his hand?

"Royland – remember that time you said you'd been – well, a maverick? What did – not that it's any of my business. Don't answer if you –"

Don't indeed, practically twisting his arm.

"I don't mind," he said. "I wasn't a drunk or a brawler, if that's what you thought. More than one way of being a maverick. I was a preacher."

"What? You? And what's so –"

"Hold your horses. Let me finish. A preacher. Not the college kind. One of your real ripsnortin' Bible-punchers."

"It doesn't sound like you."

"I thought," Royland continued, "that I had the Revealed Word. God was talking to me, sure as hell, and probably to no one else. At meetings I used to give 'em real fire-and-brimstone. Strong men wept. I'm not kidding. Must've been a godawful sight, eh? I never saw it. I mean, I never saw it that way. Well, I was married, then. You never knew I'd been married, did you? I'd married young, just before the Call came upon me. Well, for all them years I was death on every such thing as drink, tobacco, dances, cards, lace curtains, any dress that looked like anything but a gunny sack, and so on and so forth. My wife led a life which was filled with nothing pleasant in any way at all. I even quit making love with her. I burned, yeh, but virtuously. I thought it was wasting my powers if I – well, you know. She hated it all, but she never stood up to me. If she tried, I brought her down like a shot sparrow, with my speech and also with the back of my hand. Yep. I thought it was a blow for the Lord."

"I can't credit it. I can't believe it."

"True, though. What happened was, she finally took off and left. I couldn't believe she would. Thought she'd come back. She never, though. Finally I went after her. She had a cousin in Toronto, and I finally traced her through him. Saw her. She was living in a terrible little dirty room, alone. Worked as waitress in a café. I saw, soon as I laid eyes on her, what I'd done. I begged her to come back home, and I'd quit being a circuit rider – that's what us Bible-punchers was known as, then. Said I'd go to work on a farm, or like that. I wasn't sure I meant that part, though. I thought maybe it would be enough just not to yell at her, or not so much, anyway."

"Did she go back?"

"She said," Royland went on slowly, "that she wanted to go and see her cousin and his wife, first, and she promised she'd be right back to pack. Didn't see her again until I set eyes on her in the morgue. Drowned herself. I guess she couldn't put her hand to any easier way, that moment. She was scared of me. Scared to come back. Scared not to come back. Didn't believe I'd change any. And maybe I wouldn't have."

"Royland – oh my God, Royland, I'm sorry I asked."

"It's no matter. I don't generally speak of it. But I've known you a long time now. Well, after that I went north by myself. Stayed about five years in all. Did odd jobs, lumber camps and that. Began to see – not all at once, mind you, but gradually – that I'd been crazy as a coot, before. Reasons for that, but too many to explain now. I was brought up by an aunt who – well, it wasn't really her fault, either. You don't know how it is for other people, or how far back it all goes. Anyway, I found I could divine wells, so I came back and settled here. Seemed better to find water than to –"

"Raise fire."

"That's it. Don't believe in hell now, and haven't for some years. But maybe that's just a way of saying that if I did believe in it, I know one man who'd be bound there for sure."

"I imagine you've had yours."

"Oh yes," Royland said calmly. "There's no getting away from that."

Pique clattered down the stairs. Rushed over to Royland and hugged him.

"The Old Man of the River! Hi, Royland!"

"Good to have you home, Pique. Here's a pickerel for your breakfast."

"You're great, Royland. Really great. Hey, you know something? You made a big mistake in not getting married. You should've had grandchildren. You'd make a fine granddad. You know that?"

Please. Pique – *no*. How many times had Morag, over the years, made similar jocular remarks?

But Royland could take it. He merely smiled. Maybe you did reach a point in life, after all, when such chance references no longer could break you into pieces. Roll on, that day.

"Well, Pique," Royland said, "I always thought I was kind of like that to you."

"You are," Pique said.

Late that afternoon, Morag looked out the window and observed that the first of the swallow children had taken off and was now perched or rather huddled in feather-ruffled and uncertain fashion on a low branch of the elm. She kept on looking. Innumerable swallows (parents, aunts and uncles, cousins) veered in towards the nest and veered off again, squeeping in high-pitched voices, obviously saying *This is how you fly, kids! It's easy! Try it – you'll never be immobile again!* The other four, one by one, were lured out, finally, shakily, and landed beside their courageous sibling on the elm bough. All five sat there, looking dejected. *Hey, Mabel, what happens now?* Tomorrow they would all be flitting back and forth across the river, skilled already.

I look at the world anthropomorphically. Well, so what? And even if I didn't, they do learn quickly. Every year, to see them take off is a marvel.

"Hey, Morag, can we come in?" Tom said.

Three of them – no, there were four people at the door.

"Why ask?" Morag said. "Since when couldn't you come in here when you liked?"

Tom was getting taller. He was up a bit beyond A-Okay's waist. A-Okay opened the door, and Maudie, long clean white-blonde hair loose around her shoulders, glided Thomas in.

A-Okay bumped into the edge of the oak table. He had been looking elsewhere, at Tom, and at the other person, a young man with dark straight hair to the shoulders. He was lean (thin? these kids were all thin these days; it was their diet, or maybe their outlook) and was moustached hugely but not unpleasantly, a rather hesitant look in wary grey eyes.

A-Okay decided he had better don his specs, as always when he'd inadvertently rammed a piece of the furniture.

A-Okay was somewhat like Dan McRaith, whose general clumsiness always had a kind of strange gracefulness about it.

"This is Dan," A-Okay said. "Dan Scranton. He's from Calgary, or thereabouts. He's gonna stay with us awhile."

Dan. Morag felt the blade turning inside the heart. Of course, millions of men in this world must be named Daniel. Still, she did not want this kid's name to be that.

"Hello," she said. "Sit down, won't you? Maudie, Pique's off with Royland – he's doing John Fraser's new well. They should be back soon. Stay for dinner?"

When Pique and Royland returned, Pique greeted the Clan Smith as though they were her own, which they were. After dinner Dan Scranton got out his guitar and sang some of his songs. They were for individuals, people with names, places of belonging. And they were, just as much, for the Alberta hills and plains, which he had left some years ago and to which he was determined not to return, but loved them now with his painful words.

Pique sat very quietly. Then, as though now was the right time, she got out her guitar.

"I've got maybe one or two of my own," she said, "but I don't think I can sing them now. This isn't one of my dad's songs, either. It's the one Louis Riel wrote in prison, before he was hanged."

She sang in a low clear voice, the words in French, then in English. The five verses, and then the last verse.

> Mourir, s'il faut mourir,
> Chacun meurt à son tour;
> J'aim' mieux mourir en brave,
> Faut tous mourir un jour.

Dying, for it is necessary to die,
Everyone dies in his turn.
I long to die bravely
For all must die one day.

"Where did you learn it?" Morag asked. "From a book,"
Pique said coldly. "I learned it from a book. Somebody I know
taught me to say the French. I only know how to make the
sounds. I don't know what they mean."

Dan Scranton went over and sat on the floor beside her,
and took her hand.

When the others had gone, and Pique had gone up to bed,
Morag went to the record player and put on a song, turning
the sound very low. It was in Gaelic and the name of it was
"Morag of Dunvegin." She could not understand the words,
nor even distinguish between them, make any kind of pattern
of them. Just a lot of garbled sounds to her. Yet she played the
record often, as though if she listened to it enough, she would
finally pierce the barrier of that ancient speech and have its
meaning revealed to her. Dan McRaith had laughed at her that
time, when she had said, naïvely, that she wished she knew
Gaelic. He didn't have a word of the Gaelic himself, or perhaps
a few words here and there, but nothing to speak of, nothing
to speak with. Why not take lessons, then, he had said. She
hadn't, of course. Too lazy. She would have liked to gain the
speech by magical means, no doubt. Yet it seemed a bad thing
to have lost a language. Talking to one or two old fishermen
in Crombruach, those years ago, she'd realized that. They
spoke a mellifluous English, carefully, as though translating
into it in their heads, and some of their remarks were obscure
to her, but they would never explain, or could not.

Christie, telling the old tales in his only speech, English, with hardly any trace of a Scots accent, and yet with echoes in his voice that went back and back. Christie, summoning up the ghosts of those who had never been and yet would always be.

The lost languages, forever lurking somewhere inside the ventricles of the hearts of those who had lost them. Jules, with two languages lost, retaining only broken fragments of both French and Cree, and yet speaking English as though forever it must be a foreign tongue to him.

Brooke had spoken Hindi, as a child, but had forgotten most of it. That must be different. It was not the language of his ancestors. He regretted its loss for other reasons.

Memorybank Movie: Frictions
"Have you been a good girl, love?" Brooke asks.

It has become his game, his jest, before going into her, and indeed before permitting his arousal or hers. If she protests the sentence, he will withdraw all of himself except his unspoken anger. She has to play, or be prepared to face that coldness. Either way she feels afraid. Yet he cannot help it, and she knows this. There can be no talk of it, for it is, after all, only a joke.

She smiles, hoping this will be sufficient, without having to use words in this service. And it provides enough. Brooke, poised above her, lowers his long body upon hers. Then she is angry and wants to shove him away, wants no part of him. But her flesh responds to him, and she rises to him, rises to his bait, and then everything is all right.

And yet, afterwards, when Brooke is asleep beside her, she cannot sleep, the body's spasm no longer being enough to shut off the alarm-clock head more than momentarily.

Dr. and Mrs. B. Skelton now have a new and somewhat jazzy apartment, in keeping with Brooke's appointment as Head of Department. It is large, on the top floor of a downtown block, and is furnished with Danish Modern, long teak coffee tables, svelte things to sit on (you could not call them *sofas* or *chesterfields*, both words having unseemly old-fashioned connotations). On the cream-coloured walls hang several fairly expensive contemporary paintings, which Brooke says are good, even excellent.

Days, Morag writes. Then comes the day when, astonishingly, the novel is completed. It has taken over three years, and much rewriting. She feels emptied, deprived of Lilac's company.

"Show it to me, why don't you?" Brooke says. "I might be able to make one or two helpful suggestions."

"I will, Brooke. But there's something I want to discuss with you first. Brooke, we're not broke any more. We've been married eight years. I'm nearly twenty-eight."

"Oh. That again?"

She perceives at once her mistake. He cannot ever say to her, finally, once and for all, that he cannot bear for her to bear a child. He will never say that. But he cannot agree to a child, either. She is, she now sees, forcing him into a corner and has been doing so for some years. A corner out of which the exit will be violence, not physical, but violence all the same, to her and to himself.

Brooke rises and pours the last of the martini from the silver jug.

"Does it seem like the kind of world, to you," he says, "to bring children into?"

To that, there is no answer. None. No, it does not seem like the kind of world, etcetera. But she wants children all the same. Why? Something too primitive to be analyzed? Something which needs to proclaim itself, against all odds? Or only the selfishness of wanting someone born of your flesh, someone related to you?

"I shouldn't have brought up the subject," Morag says. "I guess you're right."

"Look, love, let's just see how things are in a year or so, shall we?"

"Yes."

She knows she will not mention the subject again.

Finally she shows *Spear of Innocence* to Brooke. Reluctantly. He stays up until nearly midnight, reading it.

"Well," he says at last, carefully, "it seems to me that the novel suffers from having a protagonist who is nonverbal, that is, she talks a lot, but she can't communicate very well."

"I know that. I know. That was part of the problem."

"I also wonder," Brooke says, flicking pages, "if the main character – Lilac – expresses anything which we haven't known before?"

No. She doesn't. But *she* says it. That is what is different.

"I see what you mean," Morag says. "I'll think about it."

The next day she parcels up the mass of paper and sends it, submits it, to a publisher. She does not tell Brooke.

Memorybank Movie: Prin

Christie's telegram reads: *Prin very bad could you come yours Christie.*

Morag has always known, of course, that this would happen one day, but the time seemed faroff. Now it is time present.

"Brooke – I don't want to go. That's the awful thing. But I must."

"Hush, little one," he says, holding her tightly. "You'll soon be back."

All the way on the train to Winnipeg, and then on the bus to Manawaka, Morag tries to focus on the novel, but it is finished and away from her, and there is no longer any reason for Lilac Stonehouse to talk inside Morag's head. She does not want to think of Prin, but can think of nothing else.

Christie meets her at the bus station, and they walk back to the house on Hill Street, in the dusk, the streetlights not yet turned on. Early summer, and the air smells of dust and the sweetly overpowering perfume of the lilacs that grow in mauve and purple grapelike bunches on the bushes with their heart-shaped leaves, in the front yards even of the small poor houses this side of town.

"Christie – how is she?"

"Not long for this world, Morag," Christie says abruptly, and the euphemism sounds odd, coming from him.

"Is she at home?" Morag is praying she is not.

"She's been in the hospital this past month," Christie says. "She's been pretty low for some time now. Even before she went in."

Christie, coping with her alone. Has Eva continued coming in on Saturdays? How would Morag know, who writes to Christie perhaps once in three months?

Had it been wrong to want to get away? No, not wrong to want to get away, to make her getaway. It was the other thing that was wrong, the turning away, turning her back on the both of them. *The* both of them. As soon as she got back to Manawaka, she even began thinking in the old phraseology. Extraneous *the*, yet somehow giving more existence, more recognition to them than correct speech could have. Escapist. Wordsmith, forging screens.

"You're looking smart, Morag," Christie says.

She is dressed in a fairly pricey cotton dress and light blue summer coat, her hair short and swept back and upwards. At this moment she hates it all, this external self who is at such variance with whatever or whoever remains inside the glossy painted shell. If anything remains. Her remains.

Christie is looking terrible. He is, she realizes, sixty-four. He has looked old for as long as she can remember. Now he looks as ancient as a fossil or the dried and shrunken skin of some desert lizard. His once-blue eyes seem to have retreated rheumily into their sockets, and the skin of his face is brown-brittle, clinging close to his bones as though no flesh came between, mummified as a pharaoh.

"Well, here we are," Christie says.

The house stinks. No other word for it. It has not been cleaned in some time, obviously. The odours seem to be: human sweat, urine from unemptied chamber pots, clinging smell of boiled cabbage, breadmould, and dirt. How could it be otherwise? Christie has done what he could. The house seems smaller than she has remembered it.

"When can I see her, Christie?"

"In the morning."

Morag goes up to her old room. Cannot sleep. The tiny room is huge with ghosts. Ghosts of people and of tales. Morag, a child, a girl, a young woman. Christie ranting the old ironic battle cry. Clowny Macpherson. Piper Gunn who led his people to bravery. Gunner Gunn, who once, unbelievably, had life as Colin Gunn, her father. Rider Tonnerre, the talesman, the talisman. They are all here tonight. Who has been real and who imagined? All have been both, it seems.

Prin. Prin, long ago combing and plaiting Morag's hair. Prin, sitting at the back of the church, going in just before service began, not to be noticed, once she'd grown so gross.

"Christie – they can't do anything for her, there?" Morag asks next morning.

"No. Not a christly thing."

"Would she rather be home then? Now that I'm here."

"She'd rather it," Christie says in a low voice. "She couldn't say so. But I know. It's not right for you, though, Morag. It's not a pretty sight."

"Oh Christie – I've enough to answer for. Let's just let her come home, then."

The doctor, however, is adamant.

"I can't prevent you from discharging her against my advice, Mrs. Skelton," he says. "But she'd never stand the move."

"She's going to die anyway."

The doctor frowns massively. It is not Dr. Cates. It is a younger man, a stranger, a newcomer. Probably been here for ten years. Newcomer. Good Lord.

"We needn't hasten it," he says ethically.

Why not? Why not? But faced with this medical sanctity, Morag finds she cannot argue. And Christie's fighting days are over.

Morag goes alone to see Prin. A public ward, naturally, but the white cubicle-curtains are drawn around Prin's bed. At the first sight of Prin, Morag feels only relief that the doctor has had his way. Impossible, impossible to have Prin home. And then the reverse reaction. Who wouldn't prefer to die at home?

Prin lies in the hospital bed which is really too narrow. The white bedclothing rises over her, over her flaccid hugeness, her quietness. Her body is mercifully hidden by the pre-shroud around her. Her hair is thinner even than

Christie's now, wisps and straggling feathers of the almost-bald headskin, reminiscent (unbearably) of the dead half-bald baby birds fallen from nests in the spring of the year. Prin's face is as blank as a sheet of white paper upon which nothing will ever now be written. Her eyes are open and unseeing.

"Prin –"

Morag touches the untouchable face, the hands. No response.

"I don't think Mrs. Logan knows you, dear," the entering nurse busily says.

Morag says nothing. She sits for a while, her hand upon Prin's white unmoving lard-carved hand. Then she goes away.

In her sleep, as the saying goes, Prin dies two days later. She has been in her sleep for years now, but whether there were dreams or nightmares in there, no one can know. Now at least there will be darkness. She has died a month before her fifty-ninth birthday.

Morag and Christie hold their wake in the kitchen at home, by the thin light of the one exposed bulb, the bottle of scotch on the table between them.

"She was not what you'd call an old woman, Morag."

"I know that, Christie."

"The strange christly thing about it," Christie says, "is that she always seemed old, from the moment I first laid eyes upon her, and yet she always seemed young. I don't mean *happy* young, you see."

"I know. Yes."

"I mean, more, young like a young child who's yet to learn much speech. I think they had told her – her father, and maybe them teachers in the few years of schooling she'd had – they'd made her believe she was kind of simple in the head. Maybe she was. I never figured it out, quite."

"Maybe she was simple in another way," Morag says. "Another meaning of the word."

Even eight or nine years ago, when she saw him last, Christie would have grasped this simple thought, this thought about simplicity. Not now. He looks at her from shrouded eyes, knowing he has not understood her meaning.

"I wouldn't know about that," he says, pouring more scotch for them both, "but I seen the way she was. It's a bloody christly terrible life sometimes."

Morag prays that he will not now go into the old act. He does not. He sits silent and shrunken, diminished. And then she wishes for the lost wildness, which would not, she sees now, embarrass her any longer.

"I was a hard man for her to live with," Christie says. "I had a darkness in me. She could never see rhyme nor reason for it, as why should she?"

"Her life would've been a lot worse without you, Christie."

"That," Christie says, "we don't know."

"*I* know."

"Do you, then?" A momentary blue light in his eyes. "Well, you're young. You know a whole lot you won't know later on."

Morag laughs. How weird to laugh, here and now. But it seems right. They are both getting fairly drunk.

"Christie – remember those stories you used to tell me when I was a kid?"

Silence.

"I remember the telling of them to you," Christie says at last, very quietly, "but I don't recall no more what it exactly was I was telling, then."

Morag wants now to tell him, to tell him all the tales. But cannot. She can do nothing at all, except to reach her

hand across the table and touch Christie's leathered lizard-
skin hand.

Prin's funeral is a church funeral. Prin went to church for all
those years, and liked the hymns, so it is only right and proper.
Christie and Morag are agreed upon this. Morag tells the minister that they will not be requiring any short inspirational talk
– just the service for the dead, and one hymn.

"Who will attend, and sing?" the young minister
enquires pathetically.

"Could you not get the choir?"

"It's not usually done, Mrs. Skelton, unless –"

He breaks off, unhappily. Unless the deceased is a well-
known citizen.

"If you could just get the organist, then," Morag says,
angrily.

"Yes, I can do that all right. It's my wife."

Oh lucky wife.

In fact, there are eleven people there. Eva Winkler's
mother, and Eva, with her husband and three adopted kids,
Eva looking older and thinner. And several elderly ladies,
whom Morag does not recognize. Professional funeral atten-
ders, perhaps, but at this moment Morag is grateful.

"Hi, Morag." Eva, just before they enter the church.

How to say anything at all to Eva, who speaks softly and
apologetically as always?

"Eva – thanks. For all you did for Prin."

"It wasn't that much," Eva says. "She was always good to
Vern and me."

Sure. Prin gave them the occasional jelly doughnut. She
gave Morag her only home.

"Where's Vern these days, Eva?"

"Oh, he's away out at the Coast now. He's doing real well. We had a card, year ago last Christmas. He's changed his name."

"What?"

Vernon Winkler, smallboned, as a sparrow, in those days, being beaten by his father Gus, bear-man, pig-man, himself probably beaten by some longpast father in Europe.

"He calls himself Thor Thorlakson," Eva says, smiling. "Sounds nice, don't it?"

Eva, having dragged around a small brother for what must have seemed centuries to her, is now able to rejoice that Vern has made it. Vern is another one who has decisively left – more so, perhaps, than Morag, even. A card, a year ago last Christmas.

"Yeh. Very nice."

They part. Eva and Morag, drifting apart into the church. Service for the Burial of the Dead. The old words.

We brought nothing into this world, and it is certain we can carry nothing out. The Lord gave, and the Lord hath taken away; blessed be the name of the Lord.

Hear my prayer, O Lord, and give ear unto my cry; hold not thy peace at my tears.

For I am a stranger with thee, and a sojourner, as all my fathers were.

A sojourner, as all my fathers were. Then the hymn. The hymn Prin used to like the best. They stood, all eleven, in the almost-empty church.

Jerusalem the golden
With milk and honey blest –

The singing is embarrassed, sparse. The organ pumps out the tune, to cover the paucity of voices. Christie stands, but silently. Morag sings, feeling crazily that it is all she can do for Prin now.

> They stand, those halls of Sion,
> All jubilant with song,
> And bright with many an angel,
> And all the martyr throng;
> The Prince is ever in them,
> The daylight is serene,
> The pastures of the blessèd
> Are decked in glorious sheen.

Those halls of Sion. The Prince is ever in them. What had Morag expected, those years ago, marrying Brooke? Those selfsame halls?

And now here, in this place, the woman who brought Morag up is lying dead, and Morag's mind, her attention, has left Prin. *Help me, God; I'm frightened of myself.*

The service over, the coffin is carried into the waiting hearse. Niall Cameron stands beside the newish vehicle, not the same as the one down in the valley, a long time ago.

Niall is a great deal older. The lines on his face have extended like shorthand scribblings, perhaps to be deciphered only by someone who knows that particular shorthand. His hands shake on the hearse doors. His eyes are not evasive, only absent. She wants to ask him if he remembers that day, and the fire. But cannot. She has the feeling that it would be too much, that he could not bear it. Niall Cameron, who undertakes the strange responsibility for the town's dead, seems to bear now the mark of his calling upon him. His calling calls.

He has lived among the dead a long time. Will this make it easier for him, or the reverse, to die among the living?

"Mr. Cameron –"

"Morag Gunn."

"Yes."

"I never knew much about her, you know, Christie's wife."

"Most didn't. It's – it can't be helped."

"Lachlan MacLachlan died a year or so ago," Niall Cameron says. "You used to work for him on the *Banner*."

"I didn't know he'd died."

"He chose it," Niall Cameron says. Then, as though pulling himself together for the sake of someone as young as his own children, "Well, he never did get over the boy's death, I suppose."

Lachlan's son, who died at Dieppe. Jules didn't die. Amazingly.

Christie stands beside Morag.

"If I'd had it up to me –" Christie is trying to say.

"What?"

"I would have buried her my own self." Christie mumbles, but strongly. "In the Nuisance Grounds."

Morag takes the old man's arm as they prepare to go to the graveyard.

Memorybank Movie: The Tower

Now, and somewhat oddly, considering the awfulness of the house on Hill Street, the apartment in Toronto seems more than ever like a desert island, or perhaps a cave, a well-lighted and beautifully appointed cave, but a cave just the same. Could one say *cave* if there were windows? Morag looks out the long high-up windows and sees the cars hurtling along

Avenue Road, all apparently bent on destroying one another, or, more particularly, united in their desire to wipe out that anachronistic species, the pedestrians. From this height they look scarcely less lethal than they do at earthlevel. She hates and fears them, and refuses to learn to drive.

She busies herself with this and that – goes out window-shopping, or to an art gallery or the museum. Seeing nothing. She phones friends, women who also have nothing to do and who are not friends anyway. Her own fault. Brooke says she does not make an effort to make friends, and this is true. She does not. Her lifeline depends on letters from and to Ella in Halifax. Morag has not heard yet from the publishers. The waiting is intolerable. Ella writes reassuring letters, counselling patience and cursing publishers.

Maybe *tower* would be a better word for the apartment. Crestwood Towers is in fact the name it bears on the flossy brass plate outside the thick plateglass doors. Crestwood. Crest of what? And not a wood in sight. Who thinks up these names? A tower it certainly is, though. The lonely tower. Self-dramatization. Rapunzel, Rapunzel, let down your long hair. Your long *straight black* hair, not golden waves. Who the hell could let their hair down here? Even the little worshipful group of Honours English students (Thurs., 8:00 P.M.) argue in well-modulated grammatical voices, devoid of epithets, bland as tapioca pudding. Since Prin's death, and the last sight of Christie, Morag has experienced increasingly the mad and potentially releasing desire to speak sometimes as Christie used to speak, the loony oratory, salt-beefed with oaths, the stringy lean oaths with some protein in them, the Protean oaths upon which she was reared. But of course does no such thing.

Morag stops going to the hairdresser and lets her hair grow. How could you ever let your hair down if there wasn't anything there to let down? This is, she suspects, a bizarre concept.

"We're going to the Morgans' tomorrow," Brooke says. "I expect you'll be getting your hair done."

"No," Morag says carefully. "I thought I'd let it grow out. I can't go to the hairdresser any more, Brooke."

"For God's sake, why not? Are you allergic to whatever it is they put on your hair? Why don't you go to the doctor?"

"Yeh. I'm allergic. But not physically."

"Morag, will you kindly enlighten me? Your hair – not to put too fine a point upon it – looks a mess."

"I'll brush it back and hold it with combs until it's longer, it won't look that bad. I don't like those places, Brooke. I never have. You don't know what it's like – all these mauve-smocked little perfumed dollies floating around, making me feel fantastically inadequate, and yet I don't *agree* with the way they turn me out. I don't want to look like that. I don't know. I can't explain."

But all he really wants is that his wife should look decent, a credit to him. Is this asking too much? Sometimes she thinks Yes, sometimes No.

Brooke rises from the Danish Modern sittingplace, and comes over to where she is standing. Puts an arm around her shoulder, and she turns to him and holds him, holds onto him tightly, in need.

"Now wait a minute," he says gently. "I think you're getting all worked up over nothing, little one."

Morag withdraws. He looks at her in – what? Bewilderment? Annoyance? Surprise?

"For God's sake, what is it *now*?" he asks, or states.

What indeed? Perfidious Morag, acting like a child. She sees this, and is trapped by it.

"Listen, Brooke – please don't misunderstand me. Only – I wish you wouldn't call me that."

"Call you *what*, for heaven's sake? What've I said wrong *now*?"

"*Little one*. Brooke, I am twenty-eight years old, and I am five feet eight inches tall, which has always seemed too bloody christly tall to me but there it is, and by judas priest and all the sodden saints in fucking Beulah Land, I am stuck with it and I do not *mind* like I did once, in fact the goddamn reverse if you really want to know, for I've gone against it long enough, and I'm no actress at heart, then, and that's the everlasting christly truth of it."

"You," Brooke says, "are hysterical. Are you due to menstruate?"

Morag stands absolutely silent. *I do not know the sound of my own voice. Not yet, anyhow.*

"No," Morag says. "That was, of course, an ill-considered outburst, and it owes more to Christie's way of talking than mine, I guess. But it was meant."

She is, she realizes, very very angry, and at the same time doubtful about her right to be angry, at him or at the composition of her own composite self.

"As I see it," Brooke says, "you really are – in some way quite mysterious to me, Morag – rejecting affection. Don't you realize that when I say *little one*, it's the affectionate diminutive? You must see that much."

True. All true. How could anyone reply to that?

"I know," Morag says. "Look, I do know. But it's just that, somehow, with the way I am, with the long past I've had – because I *have* had a long past – for me, the term isn't good. When I was a kid, I was never treated like a kid, and that was both fortunate and unfortunate. I guess my own parents must've treated me like a kid, but I don't recall, except a few fragments and the fantasies I composed about them later on."

"It's too bad you had to go back to the town this last time," Brooke says. "You had effectively forgotten it. Now it's all risen up again, and it's only upsetting you, Morag. Can't you simply put it from mind?"

"I never forgot any of it. It was always there."

"When you first came to me," Brooke says, "you said you had no past. I liked that. It was as though everything was starting for you, right then, that moment. You used to make me laugh – I don't mean *at* you, I mean with you. Don't you remember? I don't, I suppose, laugh easily. You had a lightness of heart that I loved – I really loved."

His terrible need. His terrible need for someone who could bring him light, lightness, release, relief. How could you fight that? How could you withdraw from the terrors of the cave in which he lived almost always alone? But what if remaining there meant to be chained forever to that image of yourself which he must have and which must forever be distorted?

"Brooke – I remember. And I'm sorry. I think I lied to you, without meaning to, right from the first."

"You didn't lie, love. You couldn't. Not you. You were without guile. That was the reason I loved you."

"Brooke, I haven't been without guile since I was four years old. I didn't think you'd care about me if I let you know, that's all. I mean, let you know about my own darkness, that comes on sometimes."

Brooke goes and stands by the windows, looking down at the traffic weaving its metallic violent ballet.

"Don't you think we are making too much of all this, Morag? I think you're exaggerating, if I may say so. Look – we've been married nine years. It's been all right. There were bound to be some difficulties. Don't you think I've felt them, too? Don't you think I've held back, many times, coming home and finding you sitting there at the typewriter as though hypnotized, and no dinner in sight? Well, that's trivial – what I really mean is, no welcome in sight. Don't you think I've ever felt attracted to other women, to women who seemed mainly to care about connecting warmly with a man?"

"Yes. Yes, I know. Sometimes I've wished you had –"

"You don't wish that at all," Brooke says bitterly, his face containing such pain and such ambiguity that she has to look away.

"Brooke – just accept that I'm not the same as I was. Or maybe I'm the same, but it scared me, before. Now I can't –"

"Can't what?"

"Can't bear not be taken seriously," Morag says, the words sounding melodramatic to her ears, although true. "Can't bear to be treated as a child."

Brooke looks at her. His very tall frame is rigid and separate.

"*Do* I? Does the way in which we make love strike you that way? Has that been anything except good?"

"It's been – you know it's been good."

But even there, the game these past years, rewards and punishments. *Have you been a good girl?* She cannot bring it up now. Because their coming together has been fine so many times over the years that if she were never to make it with a man, ever again, she couldn't depart this life complaining.

"Well, then," Brooke is saying, "maybe you're simply worrying needlessly."

"Yes. Maybe. I guess so. I'm sorry, Brooke."

"It's all right, love. Everything's all right. That visit to Manawaka just upset you a bit, that's all. Now, I'm going to make us both a very dry martini, and you'll have your hair done tomorrow, and we will cease worrying about things that don't matter, shall we?"

"All right, Brooke. Yes."

She wonders whether, if Brooke now suggested that she should try to have his child, she would any longer agree.

Spear of Innocence comes back after seven months, with a polite letter of rejection. Morag sends it out again, willing herself not to think.

After three months, the manuscript is returned, with a letter saying *We do want to publish this novel but we do feel that certain parts . . .* etcetera.

Morag has not looked at the manuscript for going on a year. Looks at it now. Bloody hell. Some of the editor's remarks strike home as true; others seem ludicrous. She rages. But goes back inside the novel. Tries this time, more than anything, to bring Lilac's own unstilted speech into more being, into more relevance with the rest of the story. This rewriting is a thousand miles from the first setting down. No half-lunatic sense of possession, of being possessed by the thing. In fact, this is much easier, but without exhilaration.

Morag does not know what to do, faced with acceptance and then with editorial criticism which at first seems like the Revealed Word but shortly thereafter seems like individuals' opinions. She embarks upon a vast number of letters.

In Chapter Four, where you say Lilac talks like a totally uninformed person, unaware of the world, I have to say that she *is* a totally uninformed person, unaware of the world, and that is part of the point about her. I see, however, that in Chapter Nine, I haven't given enough

consideration to Paul's wife's responses — am not sure
what can be done here, but will see —

Morag realizes, with some surprise, that she is able to
defend her own work. Also, it is a relief to be able to discuss
it, no holds barred, with no personal emotional connotations
in the argument. Only when the process is completed does she
see that it has been like exercising muscles never before used,
stiff and painful at first, and then later, filled with the knowledge that this part of herself really is there.

"Brooke —"

"Mm?"

"Walton and Pierce have accepted *Spear of Innocence*."

He stares at her, then smiles warmly.

"Well, that's marvellous, darling. That's absolutely splendid. I didn't even know you'd sent it out."

"Are you glad, Brooke?"

Dumb question. What does she expect him to say?

"Of course I'm glad, idiot child. How could I be otherwise? Do they want any changes made?"

"They suggested some things."

"I'll take a quick run through it, if you like," Brooke says.

"Well, thanks, but that's pretty well settled, the changes."

"I see. My reactions aren't any longer welcome to you."

"It's not that. It's — I know you know a lot about novels.
But I know something, as well. Different from reading or
teaching."

"With that insight, perhaps you'd like to take over my
English 450 course in the Contemporary Novel? I'm sure it
could be arranged."

Morag, standing in the diningroom doorway, feels a
spinning of blood inside her skull. She recalls having been as

angry as this as a child, but seldom since. It acts upon her precipitously, like about six double scotches taken at a gulp. She picks up the peacock-blue Italian glass bowl from the centre of the diningroom table and heaves it against the livingroom fireplace. Naturally, it shatters dramatically.

Total silence. Inside her head and stomach, sickness like a hangover. Brooke stands beside the long windows. Very very tall, absolutely straight, his face like the carved face of the unknown soldier.

"You'd better clear that away," he says finally, in a perfectly controlled voice. "I wouldn't advise you to do that again, Morag. The burden of your complaint, these past months, seems to be that I treat you like a child. Might I suggest you stop acting like one?"

True. All true. How in hell has she done such a thing? She can barely believe it herself, even with the blue-chipped evidence all over the carpet. What can ever make up for this enormity?

"Brooke – I'm sorry. I'm sorry."

"Just clean it up, Morag," he says, tiredly. "I'm going in the study. I've got papers to mark. I won't want any dinner."

She sweeps up the broken glass. The doorbell inconveniently rings. It is a telegram. Morag has written to Ella some days ago about the novel. The telegram reads: MAZELTOV AND TWO MILLION HURRAHS LOVE ELLA.

"What was that?" Brooke says, emerging from study.

"The woman in 70-B wants me to take delivery of a parcel from Eaton's."

"Oh. I thought it was a man's voice."

"Her husband."

That night, in bed, they turn to one another.

"Brooke –"

"Listen, my love, let's not have these upsets. Please."

"I won't. Not any more. I promise."

She strokes the skin of his shoulders and back. Then they make love, and it is fine, except that at one time it seemed an unworded conversation and connection and now it seems something else. An attempt at mutual reassurance, against all odds.

The dust jacket for *Spear of Innocence* shows a spear, proper, piercing a human heart, valentine. Morag is beside herself with embarrassment and fury, combined with the feeling that because they have published the damn thing at all, she ought not to experience quirks nor qualms about such trivia.

The reviews, clipped out and sent to Morag by the publishers, aren't all that bad although by no means over-whelmingly laudatory. Stomach churning, Morag forces herself to read them. Some of them do not appear to refer to the novel Morag wrote at all, and this is true even of some of the favourable ones. So she cannot believe even the few comments she would like to believe. A cross-section shows, if nothing else, a bewildering diversity of views.

> "A first novel of some wit and perception, marred by the author's too-obvious playing upon the fashionable theme of homosexuality."
> "Lilac is a winner."
> "Miss Gunn obviously has it in for the Church."
> "A tale of a primitive lumber town."
> "The final scene in court gives an admirable picture of man's misunderstanding of man."
> "A dreary novel about – yawn – a goodhearted tart."
> "A piquant and exciting novel about abortion."

"Lilac Stonehouse, with her nonchalant vulgarity, will live on in the head for some time."

She has not, unfortunately, told Brooke, until the book appears, that it is being published under the name of Morag Gunn, not Morag Skelton. He looks at the dust jacket, agreeing that it is pretty bad, then looks at her.

"Didn't you want to take the chance, Morag? Of putting your married name on it?"

"Brooke – it wasn't that. It was something quite different. It goes a long way back."

Or is he, perhaps, quite correct?

She knows now that she does not want to stay with Brooke. Leaving him, however, remains unthinkable.

Uncertainty grows to panic proportions. She begins forgetting ordinary things such as turning on the oven so the dinner will be ready at the correct time. She stays out longer in the afternoons, sometimes coming back to awareness in some totally unknown area of the city, to discover that she should have been home an hour ago.

The feeling of being separated from herself increases. She is unable to speak of this feeling to anyone, not even to Ella. Her letters to Ella are cryptic, and, as she sees one day, full of passages which are virtually meaningless to anyone but herself.

How many people has she betrayed so far? *Don't count – you might scare yourself too much.* How many will there be before her life is over? Should you count yourself among those, or only others?

She is walking along a street of flimsy board houses, boardinghouses, *Rooms Weekly or Nightly*, no curtains on windows, a greyness over all. The day also is grey, autumnal grey, or seems so until she comes out of herself to some degree and notices that in fact the air is crisp blue. Clear yellow leaves are being blown from the already-sparse branches of the few thin trees that fringe the street, and the sun has the warmth of Indian summer. One day she will be dead and not able to see all this any more, and now she is wasting whatever there is. How can she write if she goes blind inside?

She is filled with the profound conviction that she will not write anything more, anyway. Big deal. Keel over with sorrow, world. As if it would matter.

A man is walking out of one of the houses, and something in his gait makes Morag slow her pace and look at him. Fairly tall, slightly gone to belly around the middle, dressed in denims and a blue flannel shirt, a wide brass-buckled belt at his waist. Lank black hair, hawkish features, light brown skin. Lazarus Tonnerre. It cannot be, of course, but it seems to be. Then Morag sees that it is not Lazarus.

"Skinner!"

She calls the old nickname without thinking. Jules looks up, startled, frowning. Then he grins.

"Great God, it's Morag! How about that, eh?"

Again, without prior thought, knowing only how glad she is to see him, Morag runs towards him and puts both arms around his shoulders, holding him tightly, holding onto him. He gives a surprised laugh, then hugs her, also. Only for a second. Then they look at each other.

"I never thought to see you in this part of the city," Jules says.

"You knew I lived in Toronto, though?"

"Yeh. Christie told me, last time I was in Manawaka, back last spring."

"When did we last see each other, Jules?"

"Going on ten years, I guess. How you been?"

"Oh, not so bad, I guess. You?"

"Not so bad, neither. You want some coffee?"

They go to a small and shabby café where the walls are papered with old Coca-Cola posters and the coffee is served in thick white cups decorated with a dark green line. Not unlike the Parthenon in Manawaka.

"You've got thinner," Jules observes, lighting cigarettes for them both, and eyeing her carefully.

"You haven't."

"Nope," he says cheerfully. "I'm gettin' a beer belly."

"I thought when I first saw you that it was your dad."

His eyes narrow, and only then does she recall that he always said he would never become like his father. Even after he no longer hated and resented Lazarus.

"Lazarus died this past spring," Jules says.

"I didn't know. I'm sorry. How old –"

"Fifty-one," Jules says angrily. "Only fifty-one."

Not to be talked about, she sees. Or not yet.

"How long you been in Toronto, Jules?"

His face, still wary, relaxes a little.

"You still say *Jewels*. Don't worry. I got damn little French myself. More than I used to, though. I lived in Quebec, there, coupla years. I been here for about five years or like that. I done okay. Wanna know how I make a living these days?"

"Sure. How?"

"Singing. How about that, eh?"

"That's great. You always did have a good voice."

"How would you know?"

"I used to sit at the back of the room, too, in school, and I heard you."

"Some memory you got there, Morag."

"What kind of singing?"

"Oh, country and western, mostly. Lotta them are crap. I sing some I made up, too. Maybe they're crap as well, but at least it's my own crap. None of it pays so good. I do a coupla small clubs and some coffee-houses and that, and travel around some. But it's better than working in a lousy factory."

"Your own songs? What about?"

"What about? What a question. People here and there, mostly, I guess. I'll sing one for you sometime, maybe. What about you?"

"You knew I was married?"

"Yeh. You married a rich prof after all. I told you you would, didn't I? Jesus, you sure wanted to go *somewhere*."

She had got what she wanted. Not, however, what she'd bargained for. *It's your bed, Morag. Lie on it.*

"He's not what you'd call rich," Morag says, looking away from Jules. "Not that I'd want him to be. That doesn't matter a damn."

"Something else does, though, eh?"

She looks again into his face. His dark eyes are looking at the expression in her own. What is he reading there?

"Yeh. Well, never mind that."

"You got kids?"

"No," Morag says. "No kids."

She does not realize, until she has spoken, how resentful her voice is. Jules shrugs and does not pursue the subject.

"Jules – come back for dinner, will you? I gotta go and get it ready now, and we've just begun talking."

He hesitates. Then, perhaps hearing some appeal in her voice, he nods.

"Sure. Okay. Why not?"

At the apartment, he sits at the kitchen table while Morag prepares dinner. She pours a scotch for both of them, and drinks hers while she works. Then she sits down, across the table from him, and refills their glasses.

"You play guitar, Jules?"

"Yeh. I picked it up, here and there, along the way. A pal of mine plays his guitar along with me. Billy Joe, that is. He's Ojibway. Comes from away to hell and gone, northern Ontario. I been up there coupla times with him. I liked it fine. Liked his family. They got nothing, though. Except a lot of sick kids, last time I was there. Some died, since."

He falls into silence, and Morag cannot ask him. Everything he knows, everything he has seen, the films there in his head – all unseen by her. It has not occurred to her before to wonder how scornful he must feel about this apartment, but she wonders now. Then he laughs and comes back.

"I don't dress like this when I'm singing," he says. "I wish to christ I could, but no go. You should see me. One-man circus. Satin shirt with a lotta beadwork, and sometimes a phoney doeskin jacket with fringes and a lotta plastic porcupine quills in patterns. That's what they like."

"That's – bad."

"Oh, it's not so bad. It's a load of shit, but I don't worry much as long as they let me do the singing. It's when they start joining in that makes me want to puke. If they want a community singsong, let 'em have it, but not with me. That's mostly the older people do that. Like to go slumming, I guess. They wouldn't know a good song if they heard one. They just get loaded and start thinking they're Roy Rogers or something – for God's sake, who'd *want* to be? Christie said you were writing a book."

"Yeh. It's published. It's a novel."

"Can I see it?"

"Sure. You can have a copy, if you want one."

"I'd like that," Jules says.

She gives him the book, and he gets her to write her name in it. She writes *Morag Gunn*. It seems strange to write that surname, after so long. But it never occurs to her to add *Skelton*.

Brooke is late. Morag and Jules have another scotch. She reaches her hand across the table and puts it very lightly on his hand. He does not move. He neither withdraws nor responds. She does not know, herself, why she has done this. She is not making a play. She wants only to touch him, someone from a long long way back, someone related to her in ways she cannot define and feels no need of defining.

"I'm glad to see you, Skinner. Sometimes it's – I don't know. I hate this city."

"Yeh. It's not much. You're not very happy, are you, Morag?"

"No. Not very."

"Care to say?"

"Yes. But I don't think I can. Well, never mind that. Prin died last summer. I was back then."

"That must've been only a few months after I was back. I saw Christie, and he said his wife wasn't too good. I only stayed long enough to get Lazarus put under the ground."

"What was – what did he die of?"

Jules doesn't reply for a while. Then he withdraws his hand and picks up his glass, holds it up.

"This, partly, I guess," he says. "The doc said it was pneumonia. My dad was alone down there, the past few years. I don't guess he cared much. It was all the same to him, whether he died or didn't die. He had a lotta troubles in his life."

"Yes. I know."

He places the glass back on the table.

"Jesus, sometimes I don't give very goddamn much about my own life," he says, a low angry voice, "but I sure as hell care more about it because of him. That town never knew one damn thing about him. We never starved, none of us, although we came close to it at times. He'd never turn anybody of his out, whatever they had done. Wild horses wouldn't drag me back to live in that town."

"Me, too." ·

"Yeh, maybe. Well, at least the town gave Christie a pension. The only thing they ever gave Lazarus, apart from a bit of Relief money, was the odd night in the town clink. You know something? Jacques, my youngest brother, he wrote to say he'd heard the old man was sick. We both went back, and by the time we got there Lazarus was dead. I wanted to bury him in the valley, beside the shack, but I couldn't. Not allowed. No, no, they said, you can't just bury bodies anywhere. But they wouldn't let him be buried in the town graveyard, neither."

"Why not? Why *not*?"

"Well, he was supposed to be R.C., eh? So the Protestants wouldn't have him in their section. The Catholics wouldn't have him, neither. He hadn't been to Mass for years, and he died without a priest. No go, they said."

"That's terrible."

"Yeh, well I guess I know why they really wouldn't have him. His halfbreed bones spoiling their cemetery."

The Métis, once lords of the prairies. Now refused burial space in their own land. Morag cannot say anything. She has no right.

"I wasn't thinking so good, right about then," Jules goes on. "I'd been away, you remember, when Piquette – when she died, there. Niall Cameron reminded me where Piquette and her kids were buried."

"Where was that?"

"Métis churchyard, up Galloping Mountain way. I was glad then that they'd refused Lazarus in the town cemetery. I thought he'd be better, among the other ones. So that's what we did. People up there helped us bury him. The priest there wasn't too troubled. No headstones there. Just wooden crosses, plain pine or whatever comes to hand, and the weather greys them. I liked it up there."

The apartment door opens, and Brooke comes in.

"Morag?"

"Here."

Brooke stands in the kitchen doorway, looking at Jules.

"An old friend from Manawaka," Morag explains. "Jules Tonnerre. He's going to stay for dinner."

Brooke nods to Jules but does not shake hands. "I've got a devil of a headache," he says. "Where are the aspirin?"

"In the bathroom cupboard."

A moment later, Brooke calls to her from the bathroom. She goes. He is standing there with the aspirin bottle in his hand and an unfathomable expression on his face.

"Your past certainly *is* catching up with you," Brooke says. "I suppose he tracked you down and is here in the somewhat unlovely role of freeloader."

"Brooke! I met him by accident on the street. I asked him back."

"Well, tonight won't be possible, I'm afraid. Charles and Donna Pettigrew are coming over this evening. Had you forgotten?"

"*Yes*. But so what?"

"It may not matter to you, but it matters to me. He

seems to have gone through a fair proportion of my scotch."

"*Your* scotch!"

"Yes. My scotch. Anyway, I thought it was supposed to be illegal to give liquor to Indians."

Morag stares at him. Then turns and walks out.

Jules is standing in the front hall, his hand on the doorknob. He has, plainly, heard. He grins at her.

"So long, Morag."

The door closes behind him. Morag hesitates in the hallway. Then she grabs her coat and handbag and follows him.

"*Merde!* Morag, what d'you think you're doing? You better go back."

They are walking rapidly down Avenue Road. She has, by running, caught up with him.

"I'm not going back. Skinner, just let me talk to you for a while."

"Hey, listen, never mind what he did, eh? It goes in one ear and out the other, by me. Anyhow, it's my problem, not yours. *He's* your problem. Go on back."

"I have *got* to talk to somebody, and you've known me forever, and I am not about to go to the Salvation Army or somewhere and –"

He stops walking and puts his hands on her shoulders, drawing her to a halt. She is, she discovers with chagrin, crying. And cannot stop, probably will never stop. Jules puts one arm around her, as though assisting along the street someone who is maimed or crippled.

"Okay, okay," he says. "Come to my place and simmer down. Do you think you're a bit drunk?"

"Three scotches," Morag says, "would not normally have that effect. It's okay. I can walk."

Jules laughs.

"Shit, I know you can walk, outside. Can you walk, inside?"

"No. Not right now. Don't take your arm away, then. Please."

"You hate to ask anyone to prop you up sometimes, eh?"

"Yes. Yes, I do. And yet that's what I suppose I was asking of him, at the start."

Jules' room has a sink in one corner, one exposed ceiling bulb, a single and unmade bed, a wooden chair, and a floor covered with brown linoleum on which there are, incongruously, patterns of red oriental poppies. There is also a hotplate. He brews very strong tea and serves it to her with three spoonfuls of brown sugar.

"It'll taste like molasses," he says, "but it's good for what ails you. Drink up."

She drinks the nauseating liquid, and indeed begins to feel somewhat better.

"Jules – I'm sorry. This isn't your trouble. You've got your own. I should've stayed. I've known for a long time something had to give, somewhere, but I was too scared to do anything about it. I still am. But I've got to."

She is sitting on the bed, the tea mug in her hands. Jules is tilting back on the precarious wooden chair.

"Lucky I had no work on tonight," he says. "You want to talk, or what?"

"I guess I understand as much as I ever will," Morag says, "what has happened. It's no one's fault. We needed to play each other's game, and it wasn't all a game – a lot of it was good. But I can't play that game any more, because I'm not the same as I was. He taught me a lot, Jules – that was real enough. But we were living each other's fantasy, somehow, and if that sounds smartass –"

"It sounds crazy," Jules says, "but go on."

"Ever hear that hymn, 'Jerusalem the Golden'?"

"I'm not much of a man for hymns."

"It was Prin's favourite. It was singing it at her funeral
that – well, I guess you sometimes see things suddenly, and
then you know you've known them a long time."

She rises and reaches for her coat.

"You going?" Jules says. "You only just got here."

"I should be getting –"

"*Should*, for God's sake. Forget it. You don't want to go.
You want to go to bed with me."

"Yes. That's true. That once –"

"No need to remind me," Jules says. "But I'm not that
speedy now, you'll be glad to know."

Very slowly. Everything is happening with no sense of
haste. When they are in bed together, Morag is surprised at his
gentleness, his pacing of himself according to her. Unlike
his urgent younger self. His body, too, is different from the
taut boy's body she remembers. He is broader and more thickset now, and yet the hard stomach muscles are still there under
the beginnings of the belly fat which he hates on himself. In
her present state of mind, she doesn't expect to be aroused, and
does not even care if she isn't, as though this joining is being
done for other reasons, some debt or answer to the past, some
severing of inner chains which have kept her bound and separated from part of herself. She is, however, aroused quickly,
surprised at the intensity of her need to have him enter her.
She links her legs around his, and it is as though it is again that
first time. Then they both reach the place they have been travelling towards, and she lies beside him, spent and renewed.

Jules grins at her, and smooths her hair, combing it with
his fingers.

"You're okay," he says.

"You too."

They are quiet for a while.

"Jules," she says finally, "where all have you been, these years?"

"All over the place. All over the country. I've done harvesting, and I've done nothing. Once I punched a time-clock in a factory till I felt punch-drunk and then I saw it was that goddamn clock that was punching me. I've worked in logging camps and like that. Picked a lotta songs on the way."

"You could make a song out of what you've just said."

"Yeh. Tried to, coupla times, but it never came out right. Some guys can make songs like that, out of what's with them, but I can't. Don't know why. I made some for Billy Joe, and even for some women, but not for me. Maybe somebody will do it for me someday."

He laughs, mocking himself, but she senses that he half means what he says.

"Did you ever marry yet, Jules?"

"Sure. Three times."

"That's a lot of divorces."

"Who needs divorces? I never meant *marry* by some crazy kind of law. I meant the women I shacked up with for some time – you know, not a one-night stand."

"You got kids?"

"Not as far as I know. I wouldn't say for sure."

Skinner Tonnerre, moving through the world like a dandelion seed carried by the wind. Not such a bad way to be, when you considered the alternatives.

"I can't stay in one place forever," he says. "I stay for a while, then I want to move on. Women like to stay put. But I can't. I just can't. Lazarus, he was like that, and yet different.

He would take off sometimes. But some crazy thing kept bringing him back to that valley. All of us brought him back, I guess, when we were young. After that, I dunno."

"What I'm going to do," Morag says, "is, I'm taking off."

"Yeh? Think you can?"

"I have to. It's complicated, but I have to."

"So you had to do this first, eh?" He puts a hand between her legs and his fingers explore the triangle of hair there.

"How so?"

"Easy," Jules says. "Magic. You were doing magic, to get away. He was the only man in you before, eh?"

"Yes."

Jules rises and goes to a cupboard.

"Shit. Only one bottle of beer left. I knew it. That goddamn Billy. Want some?"

"You have it. I'm not much on beer."

Jules pries the cap off the bottle on the edge of the table, and drinks. Sitting naked on the tottery wooden chair, looking at her.

"I'm the *shaman*, eh?" he says.

"I don't know," Morag says. "I never thought of it like that. But I know that whatever I'm going to do next, or wherever I go, it'll have to be on my own."

"You're right, there. Morag – there's something you gotta tell me about. You never told me, away back then."

"No. I can't. Jules, I can't."

He walks very quietly over to her and takes her hair in his hands. Morag's now-straight-black hair is not yet long enough to be wrapped around her neck, but this is the gesture.

"You will, though. You wouldn't, then. You will say, if you have to stay here a month to do it. You know what Lazarus told me?"

"Yes. Nothing."

"That's it. Nothing."

He turns away from her.

"I have got to have a drink," he says tiredly. "I'll be right back."

He dresses and goes out. In his absence she puts on her own clothes. It never occurs to her to leave while he is gone. He must have known it wouldn't. He returns in half an hour with two bottles of cheap wine. Pours some into two glasses.

"All right. Tell me now, Morag."

"I don't want to. I can't." But she knows she will have to.

"Just tell me. Tell me how my sister died. I have to know."

Morag gets up from the bed abruptly. Goes to the sink and vomits. Jules, unmoving, waits.

"Lachlan sent me down there," she says finally. "He didn't know what it would be like."

"Go on."

"Well, I went down to the valley, and there weren't many there. Niall Cameron was there. The Mounties had gone. Your two young brothers were standing at the side, sort of huddled together. Piquette had been home alone with her kids when it happened. It was the stove – it must've been a wreck of a stove."

"It was. Lazarus knew. But he was always careful with it, even when he got drunk. Was Piquette –"

"It was said so, afterwards, that she'd been on the home-brew."

Jules laughs bitterly.

"It would be said. Well, I guess it was likely true. She had a lot to want to forget about. Her man, so-called, picked her up when it suited him and threw her away when that suited him. She meant no more to him, that's for sure, than a dog you chloroform if it gets to be a nuisance. What was the shack like?"

"Burned to the ground. Still smoking, parts of it steaming. The fire wagon had been there but it was too late. Lazarus was —"

"Say it."

"He was standing there, by himself, beside the — beside what was left of the shack. I guess I've never seen any person look that much alone. Then he said — he said he was going in alone. He said *They're mine, there, them.*"

Jules puts his head down on his outstretched arms, on the table. He is extremely still.

"He didn't go in by himself, though, Jules. As you know, Niall went in with him. One man couldn't carry out the — even if two of them were children."

Jules raises his head.

"When they came out — did you see —"

She is shaking and cannot stop. It is not her right, but she cannot help it.

"No. They — Niall and your dad — they took a stretcher in, and it was covered when they came out — a blanket or something, covered the —"

"Okay," Jules says steadily. "What else?"

"It was the coldest part of the winter," Morag says, and now her own voice sounds oddly cold and meticulous, as though the memory of that chill had numbed her. "The air smelled of — of burnt wood. I remember thinking — crazy — but I thought Bois-Brûlés."

"Shut up!" Jules cries out in some kind of pain which cannot be touched by her.

Silence.

"Go on," he says finally.

Why does he have to inflict this upon himself? Why can't he let it go? Perhaps he has to know before he can let it go at all.

"I guess I vomited, as they brought the stretcher out. I realized then that the air didn't only smell of smoke and burnt wood. It smelled of – well, like roasted meat, and for a minute I wondered what it was, and then –"

Jules lies across the table once more. Then slowly he raises his head and looks at her.

"By Jesus, I hate you," he says in a low voice like distant thunder. "I hate all of you. Every goddamn one."

Morag gets up and puts on her coat. There is nothing more can be said. He watches her walk towards the door. Then speaks, the cry wrenched up out of him.

"No. Wait awhile, eh?"

They hold to one another again, and make love or whatever it is, throughout the deep and terrifying night.

In the morning, Morag wakens and at first does not know where she is. Then she realizes but can scarcely believe it. How could she stay away all night? Will Brooke have phoned the police? Will he imagine her as dead? How could she have done that to him?

"I should've phoned him, Jules. I should've –"

Jules rolls over in bed and stretches.

"Well, you didn't. So what now?"

"I have to go back and –"

"Stay?"

"No. But –"

"Tidy things up neat, eh?"

"Of course," she says angrily, and he laughs.

"It won't work, Morag. If you're going, go. Don't talk. It won't do a thing."

"Maybe not. But it's –"

"Your way."

"Yes. My way."

"Where'll you go then? Christie's?"

Morag begins trembling again. Dressed now, and standing beside the table, trembling as though with chill.

"Skinner – I can't."

"Where, then?"

"Further west. To the Coast."

"Chrissake, why?"

She doesn't know. Maybe it only ever occurs to prairie people, when they light out, to go yet further west. This is idiotic.

"I can't say. I don't know."

"You got any money?"

"Some. From the novel. Not much, but enough to get there and get started on something. Any kind of job."

Jules rises and gets dressed.

"You can come back for a while, till you get yourself together. If you want to."

"Yes. I will, then. And – thanks. Jules, I won't –"

Hesitates.

"Won't what?" he says. "Wash my underpants? Iron my jazzy satin shirts?"

"No. I mean, yes – I'll do that if you want – it's all the same to me. I meant – I won't stay long."

To let him know she understands the terms on which his offer is being made.

"Yeh, that's okay," he says. "I know."

Once out into the street and on the bus, the day strikes like lightning into Morag's brain, and she no longer understands what has been happening. At the door of the apartment, she stops and steadies herself, leaning against her corridor wall. She does not recall ever feeling this frightened before. She takes out her key and opens the door.

Brooke has not gone to work. He is sitting in his study. His glasses are beside him on the desk, and both hands are upon his eyes. He swings around at her entry, and she sees that he has been crying.

Anything else. Rage. Fury. Contempt. Condemnation. Reproach. She was prepared for any or all. But not for this.

He stiffens, straightens, puts on his glasses.

"So you've come back," Brooke says.

It is an attempt to regain the old manner, but it does not quite come off, because his voice is shaking. Appalled, Morag stands in the doorway.

"Brooke – I'm sorry."

That's a bloody awful christly useless word. Proverbs of C. Logan.

"I should've phoned," she goes on. "I should've –"

"Oh, don't worry," Brooke says, and now he is gaining back the control he needs. "I didn't imagine you had thrown yourself under a bus. I knew where you were. Perhaps not exactly, but at least who you were with."

Morag finds herself unable to explain or say anything. Everything was clear, earlier this morning. Now it is not.

"I suppose you went to bed with him," Brooke says.

"Yes."

Brooke looks at her for what seems hours and is in fact about three seconds. And she is, once again, totally unprepared for the cry which comes from his throat, an anguish she has never heard from him except in his crying of that one name in his sleep.

"Why, Morag? Are you so determined to destroy me?"

This is all the more terrible because she knows the pain is real and yet there is something melodramatic, to her ears, in what he is saying.

"Brooke – listen. I don't want to damage you. I honestly don't think I do, but I can't be sure. I don't suppose you want to damage me, either."

"Have I ever?" he says. "Have I ever wanted to damage you? Never. Never. Never."

Add two more *nevers* and it might be Lear at the death of Cordelia. Bitch, to think this way, now. Yes. But.

"Brooke. I can't explain. I get mixed up when I try, and then I feel I must be entirely in the wrong. But all I know is – I have to go. I can't stay."

"I could understand it better if you could just give me one reason for what you've done."

"What do you mean, exactly, what I've done?"

"How do you think I feel, Morag, knowing you've been with another man?"

She is shocked and awed by his pain. At the same time, she sees for the first time that he has believed he owns her.

"Brooke, I'm sorry. Not for what happened last night. I'm sorry that neither of us were different. But Brooke – you've put yourself inside women other than me."

"Not since we married," Brooke says, "unless you want to drag up that one time when we were in Nova Scotia, that girl on old Kenton's trawler, his niece or something. But once she'd hauled me into her bunk, I couldn't."

Morag stares at him. Then laughs. He looks at her as though she has suddenly become demented.

"I never knew," Morag says. "I didn't go along on that jaunt, as you recall. You mean to say it doesn't count cause you didn't come?"

He takes a step towards her, and for an instant she is afraid again. Then he stops himself.

"You *are* a bitch, aren't you?" he says.

She feels exhaustion as never before. Words have lost meaning.

"Brooke. I'm withdrawing the money I earned from the novel, then you can have the account changed from a joint one to yours. I'm going to Vancouver. I'll do anything you want to do about a divorce, whatever it is that people have to do. And I'm sorry. But I just have to take off by myself."

"I suppose your boyfriend isn't reliable enough to provide a living?"

"He is not my – as you repulsively put it – boyfriend."

"No? What then?"

"It doesn't matter. Brooke – I don't know what to say, except that it was fine with us for quite a while. I owe you a lot, and I know it. And –"

And nothing. Quit talking. Babble babble. He wants to quit talking, too. He looks at her from his solitary confinement, but says nothing. Then he turns away. Sits down at his desk and begins marking essays.

Morag packs one suitcase and goes.

Jules is reclining on the bed with a bottle of beer.

"Hi," he says. "Was it bad?"

"Yes. Pretty bad."

"Want a beer? It's all we have. Nothing stronger, I'm sorry to say."

She takes the bottle he offers her, and sits on the bed beside him, shivering.

"Don't think about it," Jules says. "Look, I didn't say before, but you don't want to get pregnant, do you? Because –"

"Would you mind very much if I didn't do anything to try not to?"

Jules looks at her, then laughs.

"Jesus. You're a crazy woman. Do you have to ask permission? I don't mind, no. Only –"

"It's all right. I wouldn't claim support or anything."

"Well, you probably wouldn't stand much of a chance of getting it, from me," Jules says. "It's all I can do to keep myself going, right now. You still plan on going to Vancouver?"

"Yes. If I can just get myself pulled together first –"

"Stay as long as you need to. But not too long, or it'll turn out bad. As I ought to know. Funny thing, Morag. I was gonna sing some of the songs to you. But I got a feeling I won't, not now. Maybe sometime. But this doesn't feel like the time."

"Why not?" she asks.

"I don't guess you'd hear them, really," Jules says.

Morag stays with him for just over three weeks. They speak little, and make love not at nights when he comes home late, but in the mornings, late mornings, when he wakens. He comes home bleak, usually. He hates most of the places where he sings. Only in one, a small coffeebar which pays hardly anything, does the young audience actually listen. The others are all of the cheap nightclub or roadhouse variety, middle-aged middle-class men out with hired women, painting, as they imagine, the town red, and deaf-drunk. He hates giving his songs there, but it is better than not singing at all. Days, when he and Billy Joe practise and work out new arrangements, they do so in Billy's room, one floor down. Morag hears the faint twanging of the two guitars and Jules' rough-true voice but she cannot make out the words. Sometimes she wants to go down and listen, but she senses that Jules is right. This isn't the time.

She wouldn't really hear. She is overtaken by profound lethargy, some days, and sleeps as much as fourteen hours. Other days, she rushes around the city, making her preparations for departure.

Billy Joe brings Jules home one night, Jules unable to walk, Billy dragging him. Billy Joe is short and gentle-featured, but must be tough-muscled to haul along Jules, who is about twice his size and weight.

"What went wrong?" Morag asks.

"He was singin', there," Billy Joe says, "that one song about his grandfather, old Jules. At first they just didn't listen. Then they laughed, some. Then they started yellin' that they wanted him to sing stuff like 'Roll out the barrel.' So he gets mad and leaves and goes drinkin'. I had to leave the guitars there. Knew he'd end up smashing 'em. I guess maybe I better stay up here tonight, Morag. When he wakes up, he's gonna be crazy. He won't really be awake and he'll still be drunk."

When Jules seemingly wakes, after a few hours of restless imitation sleep, he is a man fighting everything he has ever found necessary to fight. A sleepwalker, a sleep-fighter. He is in the valley again, and Lazarus is there, fighting and not fighting. And the fire. And the long long beaches where the fireshot forever kills the same men, over and over. And the satin shirts of now.

"Take off this shit shirt, willya? Look, lemme tear it off, yeh? Like this this this. Know how she died? She was roasted like beef. She smelled like the roast beef they got there, on the Sundays – Jesus Jesus Jesus –"

"What do we do with him?" Morag says, scared, to Billy Joe, who is at this moment wrestling with Jules, wrestling with steadiness and apparently no fear. Doesn't Billy Joe feel fear? Maybe. Maybe he knows something beyond fear.

"Shut up and stay outa the way," Billy Joe says.

And finally Jules subsides into unconsciousness again.

In the morning, Jules is unspeaking, hungover. Finally, after potions of tea, he clears his throat. Billy has gone back downstairs.

"Hey. Morag. Was I bad?"

"Yeh. Not so good. Billy stayed. He was good with you."

"He's my friend. He should be good with me. He oughta know how, after this time."

"Your friends should have to wrestle with you?"

"Sometimes. You don't think I've ever wrestled with him?"

"I guess so. I'm off today, Jules. Not because of last night. Just because I'm ready to go, now."

"Yeh? God, I feel awful. Want me to come with you to the station?"

"Oh for christ's sake, in the shape you're in? Go back to bed. I can manage. I'm travelling light. I'll write to you."

"Well, I probably won't to you."

"No, you were never much of a letter writer. Jules — thanks."

"For nothing."

"So long, then."

"So long, Morag. Look after yourself."

She has five hundred dollars and a one-way ticket to Vancouver.

Clunk-a-clunk-clunk. Clunk-a-clunk-clunk. The train wheels. Once again, going into the Everywhere, where anything may happen. She no longer believes in the Everything out there. But part of her still believes.

Morag goes into the train john. Vomits. Cleans up tidily after herself. When upset or too tense, her digestion is the first thing to go. Her stomach, obviously, not her heart, is the dwellingplace of her emotions. How humiliating. Unless, of course, she is pregnant, which is hardly likely after a couple of weeks. What if she is, though? How could she have been so unbalanced as actually to try to be? How would she earn a living? She hadn't thought of that at the time, but does so, now. Fear. Panic. Where is Brooke?

Brooke's pain. His damage towards her. Hers towards him. Their voices a million miles apart. Their first coming together, and how good it had been.

The train clonks on and on. Through the prairies. She looks out at the flat lands, which from the train window could not ever tell you anything about what they are. The grain elevators, like stark strange towers. The small bluffs of scrub oak and poplar. In Ontario, *bluff* means something else – a ravine, a small precipice? She's never really understood that other meaning; her own is so clear. A gathering of trees, not the great hardwoods of Down East, or forests of the North, but thin tough-fibred trees that could survive on open grassland, that could live against the wind and the winter here. That was a kind of tree worth having; that was a determined kind of tree, all right.

The crocuses used to grow out of the snow. You would find them in pastures, the black-pitted dying snow still there, and the crocuses already growing, their greengrey featherstems, and the petals a pale greymauve. People who'd never lived hereabouts always imagined it was dull, bleak, hundreds of miles of nothing. They didn't know. They didn't know the renewal that came out of the dead cold.

She could have stopped off to see Christie. But has not done so.

There are many other passengers on this train, and Morag sees none of them. This in itself frightens her, but she cannot lessen it or take any lesson from it right now. What will she do when she gets where she's going?

The train moves west.

PART FOUR

RITES OF PASSAGE

EIGHT

Morag walked through the yellowing August grass and down to the river. On the opposite bank, upriver a little from A-Okay's place, the light-leafed willows and tall solid maples were like ancestors, carrying within themselves the land's past. The wind skimmed northward along the water, and the deep currents drew the river south. This was what Morag looked at every day, the river flowing both ways, and yet it never lost its ancient power for her, and it never ceased to be new.

Pique and Dan were not up yet. These kids reversed the order of life, staying up all night and sleeping most of the day. *Order.* For heaven's sake. It flowed in Morag's veins, despise it though she might. What possible differences did it make if the kids wanted to turn the days around? They had both worked for a month in McConnell's Landing, at nothing-jobs, while Dan was still at A-Okay and Maudie's place. Was it Morag's concern if they decided they had enough financial reserves between them to quit work for a while, until the bread ran out, as they put it, because it was more important to get to know one another? They paid for their board; they shared the work of the house with her – in fact, they did more than their share. Nary a dish had Morag washed since Pique and Dan took up residence in the large front bedroom.

So why complain? They're pulling their weight. You said they could move in here together. They didn't take the place by siege.

It was, of course, perfectly obvious what the problem really was. Not the kids' late rising, as Morag fairly often (and ignominiously) pretended to herself, thus justifying her early morning slamming of doors, loud stomping about in the kitchen, full-blast radio (preferably some loudmouth trumpeting the news), and general clashing of saucepans like clutches of cymbals. Clichés of symbols.

Royland came shuffling and crunching through the sundried grass. Old Man River. The Shaman. Diviner. Morag, always glad to see him, felt doubly glad now. He would, of course, not tell her what to do. Not Royland's way. But after a while she would find she knew. Royland sat down beside her on the dock.

"Morning, Morag."

"Morning, Royland."

For a few minutes they both looked at the river and listened to the slapping of the small waves against the wooden posts of the dock.

"Well, what is it this time?" Royland said finally.

Morag laughed.

"How come you always know? Celtic second sight?"

"You're the Celt, not me, Morag. Well, a person wouldn't have to be very smart to see that you're looking grim as granite. Is it Pique and her man?"

"Yes."

"Well, look here now, Morag. There isn't a reason in the

world why the two of them gotta stay at your place, is there? You have got to consider your own work, and that. If they are interrupting it –"

"Royland, it's not that. Well, it *is* that, too, but the reason for it isn't their fault. It's mine."

"Here we go with the guilt again," Royland said cheerily. "I thought you'd got a bit better about that. What terrible thing have you done now, eh?"

Can you tell him, Morag? I've got to tell someone, and it is inconceivable that I should tell the Smiths, who would be sorry for me.

"I," Morag said flatly, "have been reacting badly. Mostly it's been okay. But then the tension mounts in me, and I flip my lid over something trivial, like they're not up by noon or they're not home for dinner at the dot of six. I don't talk with them about this. Not me. I go around slamming doors. Dishes get smashed. Yesterday, my only Limoges cup and saucer bit the dust, not that I give a damn about that. However, Royland, all this mishmash is only an evasion."

"You don't say," Royland said mildly.

"You mean you knew? It's that obvious? Look, it isn't that I don't want them to live together. I do want them to. It seems right. And God knows it isn't that I care one way or another if they're legally hitched. But the plain fact is that I am forty-seven years old, and it seems fairly likely that I will be alone for the rest of my life, and in most ways this is really okay with me, and yet I am sometimes so goddamn jealous of their youth and happiness and sex that I can't see straight. Horrible, eh?"

"Not so very," Royland said. "In fact, hardly at all, except you feel bad about it, and also I guess they wonder what's going on, all those doors and cups and that."

"Oh damn," Morag said, rising. "I'll have to explain. I hate presenting myself in such an unflattering light. The pride is wounded, and a good thing too, no doubt. But difficult."

She looked up the long slope to the house and saw Pique stretching in the sun, on the doorstep, her long hair loose around her shoulders. Royland said nothing. Morag walked back to the house as slowly as possible, stopping to pick a dandelion seedclock and to blow the seeds into the wind. Nine. And it was actually noon. Inaccurate dandelion. Catharine Parr Traill would not have wasted her time puffing dandelion seedclocks. Nor would she have tried to explain the subtleties of her feelings to one of her daughters, either, probably. Maybe never had this problem, and never felt any such thing. Too busy preserving fruit and sketching flowers and weeding the garden. Too tired. Benefits of physical labour. Cold baths, too, like as not.

When she entered the kitchen, Pique and Dan were having coffee and cereal.

"You should have some crunchy granola, Ma," Pique said.

"No," Morag said, suddenly impatient. "I know it is very healthy. But I gag on it. Leave me my depravities, eh?"

"Oh sorry," Pique said, grinning. "Well at least you don't eat Sugar Puffs. Want we should clear out now? Want to work?"

"Not yet awhile. I have to talk to you first. I'm sorry I slammed the door this morning. I hope it didn't waken you up."

"Well," Pique said, allowing her annoyance to surface, "we could've done without it."

"No doubt. I have, however, my reasons."

When Morag had finished saying approximately what she had said to Royland, she looked gloomily into her coffee mug, wishing it were possible to teleport herself out of the situation, literally, in the flesh. The ascension of the far-from-virgin. Mars or heaven her destination. Greetings and salutations to ancestors or bug-eyed monsters.

Silence. Then astonishment. Pique had taken one of her hands and Dan the other.

"We thought that was what it was," Pique said, "but we couldn't say it unless you said it. And, like, we're aware you're alone, Ma. But in other ways you aren't. You know?"

True. Truer than Morag even yet knew? Perhaps.

"I think it'll be okay, now," Morag said, when able to speak, "for you to stay here. I don't really know why. But I feel it will."

"No, listen," Dan said. "Pique and I have talked this over a lot. We've gotta get jobs of some sort pretty soon, and it would really be better for us to live at the Smiths', as it's on the right side of the river for McConnell's Landing."

"We'll be back and forth a lot," Pique said. "I mean – you'll see enough of us. Too much, probably, even."

"No, it won't be too much," Morag said.

She held onto their hands for another moment. Then Pique and Dan went outside.

Morag got out her typewriter.

LETTER TO D. McRAITH, CROMBRUACH,
ROSS-SHIRE SCOTLAND

Dear McRaith –

As to why I have begun calling you McRaith, Pique's new man is named Dan, and I cannot bear confusion. Outer confusion, that is. The inner is quite enough to be getting on with. I once read a novel in which the protagonist, a young man, falls in love with two women (not simultaneously) both named – I can't remember – let's say Flora. Both kept flitting in and out of the pages, and were sometimes given the distinguishing marks of Flora One and Flora Two. Sometimes the reader just had to guess. I was enraged. How come this guy (the writer) doesn't have more imagination, I wondered. Plenty of good names in the telephone directory. Maybe it was his character's fault . . . the poor twit had a fixation on women called Flora. I don't know why names seem so important to me. Yes, I guess I do know. My own name, and feeling I'd come from nowhere. If I could call Pique's Dan by any other name, I would, but that would take some explaining. I think this with Pique may work out better this time, although who knows. Whatever she feels is right for her is okay with me, but no doubt I will continue sometimes to get annoyed over trivialities, and so will she. Hers, actually, are less trivial than mine, not because of any intrinsic difference in degree of our various dilemmas, but only because I've worked out my major dilemmas as much as I'm likely to do in this life. Now that I read that over, I wonder if it's true. The calm plateau still seems pretty faroff to me. I'm still fighting the same bloody battles as always, inside the skull. Maybe all there is on that calm plateau is a tombstone. No, this isn't Celtic gloom – in fact, I'm feeling good at the moment, which is partly why I'm writing to you now. If this is gaiety, you may well observe, what can depression possibly be like? But not so. Do you remember you once told me – we were walking along the shore at Crombruach, and it was freezing and Easter – that a Presbyterian is someone who always looks cheerful, because whatever happens, they've expected something much worse?

Sorry the work isn't going too well for you at the moment. I will light mental candles for it to begin again. Mine has been pretty much nothing for a month, but I think it'll start again now. If God is good and if I'm lucky and if I damn well pick up the pen and begin. Which I aim to do now.

Love,
Morag

She put the typewriter away and got out the notebook and pen. Sat looking for a while at the pale blue empty lines like shelves on the page, waiting to be stuffed with what?

Would Pique's life be better or worse than Morag's?

Mine hasn't been so bad. Been? Time running out. Is that what is really going on, with me, now, with her? Pique, harbinger of my death, continuer of life.

Memorybank Movie: Bleak House

Some of the mountains beyond the city are called snow mountains because the snow is perpetual upon those faroff peaks. They are impressive, but frightening. Uncaring gods, they stand cold and infinitely lofty, diminishing the city and its inhabitants. Perpetual snow – the very thought of it makes Morag experience that iciness crystallizing her own blood. She stares at the mountains from the boardinghouse window, but can never look for very long. This is not to be her final settling-place, obviously. People of the city, the real inhabitants, born here or having adopted the place, do not feel the same way. They do not feel hemmed in or threatened by these mountains.

Insane to have come here. Would have been better to have gone back to Manawaka. Christie needs her, and she needs a home for herself and her child, when it is born. But there is no way she can return to Manawaka. If she is to have a home, she must create it.

Down at the harbour, where Morag sometimes walks, hoping to understand the place, the vast ships cluster and creak, groaning and shunting, wallowing herds of ungainly sea-monsters. Then, surprisingly, one will glide majestically from the harbour, transformed by movement, as clumsy waddling seals are transformed into eel-like litheness when they swim. The gulls scream imprecations, their tongues hoarse and obscene, but the white flash of their wings is filled with grace abounding.

The boardinghouse is in Kitsilano, the rundown part of the area. A tall narrow frame house, last painted around the turn of the century, no doubt, and now a non-unpleasant uniform grey, not the heavy hard grey of a uniform, but the light sea-bleached grey of driftwood, silver without silver's sheen. Having once hated the unpainted houses along Hill Street, Morag now feels at home with this shade, shade in both senses, or perhaps even three, a colour ghostly-subtle as shadows, welcoming cool. It has no pretensions. Weather has created it. She prefers it to the jazzy split-level houses in the west side of the city, across the Lion's Gate Bridge. She likes the bridge's name, but not the steel-girdered giant itself.

The house in Kitsilano is neighboured by others of the same ilk. Firetraps, lived in by people who can't afford to live anywhere else. Morag's landlady, Mrs. Maggie Tefler, some forty-odd years old, frizzy bottle-blonde hair, is a short woman, short in stature, nearly always short of breath (high blood pressure, stoutness) and decidedly short-tempered. Morag, however, is not in any position to quibble. She came to Maggie Tefler's bleak house because it was cheap and the room looked halfway clean. Her first room was on the second floor, and had a divan bed and an old brown carpet with vague geometrical designs in blue and red. It also had a sink. This room lasted only a month. It was the sink which was Morag's undoing. One early morning, her door alas unlocked, she vomited copiously into the sink. Finally able to look up, eyes and nose streaming, she perceived Mrs. Tefler standing in the doorway, arms akimbo in a kimono of artificial silk, nauseatingly pink-poppy-patterned.

Maggie T.:   I thought I heard you coupla times before, upchucking. In the john. Wasn't sure it was you, Miss Gunn.

Morag: Yeh, it was me.

Maggie: (crudely, but with accuracy) I'd say you got a bun in the oven. Either that or the booze, and you don't have the signs of an alkie, as I should know, being probably the world's top authority on rubbydubs.

Morag: Huh?

Maggie: Winos. I get more than my fair quota here, you can bet your bottom dollar. You preggers, kid?

Morag: Yeh, I think so. It seems unbelievable.

Maggie: C'mon, now, honey, don't give me that line, like he only screwed you once and you never thought it was possible the first time. You're no virginal seventeen, Morag – mind if I call you Morag? I dunno what's with you, but why don't you go on back to yer hubby?

Morag: What? How did you –

Maggie: (smirking) Easy. You still got the mark of a wedding ring on yer finger. It hasn't been off you for that long.

Morag: Okay, Mrs. Tefler. You are right. But I am not going back.

Maggie: Kid not yer hubby's?

Morag:	(with admirable restraint) That is my affair, I believe.
Maggie:	Oh beg yer pardon, yer highness. Yer *affair* is right, kid. Well, what you gonna do?
Morag:	(truthfully and with considerable panic) I don't know. I can keep on working for a while.
Maggie:	You reckon Sanford and Willingham Real Estate is gonna put up much longer with a typist who keeps rushing out to puke?
Morag:	(furiously) I *don't*, goddamn it. It only hits me this time of day.
Maggie:	Well, kid, what about when you get big as the backside of a barn? It's your business, of course. But if you wanna work here – cleaning, cooking, doing the dishes – you can stay. Nice room up there on the top floor. Good view and all. Room and board and a little extra. What could be fairer? I know I'm a sucker, but I never could stand seeing a decent girl in trouble without I have to try to help. *Maggie*, my Wayne used to say, *you got a heart soft as the centre of a toasted marshmallow.* How about it, honey? Well, come on, I haven't got all day.
Morag:	Okay, Mrs. Tefler. And – thanks.
Maggie:	Don't mention it, dear. We were put here on this earth to help one another, is what I always say.

So it is that Morag now resides in a room on the top floor, by which the saintly Mrs. Tefler has really meant, as it turns out, the attic, which has been more or less fixed up as a room. Oddly enough (although she does not tell Mrs. Tefler) Morag becomes fond of this room. It is, in a very real sense, all hers.

You have to be on guard against the bare rafters at the extreme edges of the place, or you will bash your skull, but this slight disadvantage weighs small against the room's many good features. If Maggie Tefler suspected this, she would either try to rent it for a huge sum to someone with Morag's tastes but more money, or else she would quit paying Morag the minuscule sum which she now forks out reluctantly each week in exchange for virtually all the cooking and cleaning. From Morag's viewpoint, the bargain isn't at all a bad one. She dips cautiously into what remains of her five hundred bucks and buys a secondhand oak dresser, a desk, a bookcase, a couple of numdah rugs, a crimson Hudson's Bay point blanket to cover the single brass bed. These, plus a lamp with a bulbous Japanese-lantern shade, and a poster of a large ruffle-feathered brown owl, all make the room hers.

A woman, if she is to write, Virginia Woolf once said (or words to that effect), must have a room of her own. The garret bit never appealed to Morag unduly, but by God, it is at least a room of her own. The only trouble is that she feels too tired and lousy most evenings to do any writing at all.

Memorybank Movie: Portrait of the Artist as a Pregnant Skivvy

Morag, growing already in girth at four months, is washing the breakfast dishes. The water is lukewarm and greasy, but her digestion, fortunately, is steadier than it was, and her energy greater. In fact, she is strong as an ox, the doctor tells her, apparently with disapproval.

Old Mr. Johnson, one of the inmates of Bleak House, is sitting at the kitchen table, shooting the breeze with Morag. He looks about a hundred and ninety, and frail as a feather, but he has a powerful pair of lungs.

"Yes, siree," he bellows, "I mind well that time at Williams Lake, talking to old Peter Paulson – he'd bin a prospector and still thought he was. Nutty as a fruitcake. I was a salesman in them days, d'you see. I was travelling in shoe polish, harness polish and brass polish. *Wellsir*, he says to me, *there's only two mortal things in this life I can't stand, Mr. Johnson, just two mortal things – one is racial prejudice, and th'other is Indians.* How'd you like that?"

The two of them are still laughing when kindly Mrs. Tefler sashays in, bearing a letter.

"This here is for you, I suppose," she says suspiciously.

Morag reaches for it. Luckily she has told Mrs. Tefler that such an epistle might arrive, but Maggie still has her doubts, and doubtless hankers to open and read it, ostensibly to make sure she is handing it over to the right person.

Morag has written, painfully, to Brooke, not able yet to mention her pregnancy, but telling him that she is now using her own name. His letter is addressed: Mrs. Brooke T. Skelton. Morag puts it in her apron pocket. Mrs. Tefler waits in vain for her to open it.

Later, in her room, Morag reads it. It says, in part, that Morag has now surely proved her point and shown she could get along alone and isn't it time she began acting sensibly once more? He will be prepared to try to forget that one occurrence. If she needs the train fare back to Toronto, he is prepared to send it.

Morag sits on the bed, looking at the page. Brooke's words – the closest he will ever be able to come, in expressing his need for her.

I need you, too, Brooke. I care about you. I can't stand this.

There is, however, no way back. Would she have gone back if she hadn't been pregnant? At this moment, she feels she would have. Was it only for that reason, after all, she had wanted to get pregnant, so her leaving of Brooke would be irrevocable? So she would not be able to change her mind? And had chosen Jules only so there wouldn't be the slightest chance of pretending the child was Brooke's? How many people had she betrayed? Has she even betrayed the child itself? This thought paralyzes her. Or is she only interpreting herself, now, in the worst possible ways?

Why had she imagined that she could look after and support a kid, on her own? It had seemed a perfectly natural notion at the time. Now it seems merely lunacy. She will have to go on welfare. *Never.* But of course she will, if necessary. What will happen to her, and to the child?

She recalls Brooke's certainty, his control of situations. Even if that calm was only outer, how reassuring.

Don't deceive yourself Morag. For you, ultimately, far from reassuring. I don't know. I just don't know.

She no longer feels certain of anything. There is no fixed centre. Except, of course, that there *is* a fixed centre, and furthermore it is rapidly expanding inside her own flesh.

She stops crying, puts on her coat and headscarf, and goes out. The hell with Maggie Tefler. The cleaning of the rooms can damn well wait.

Winter. Not snow, here, or not this year, anyway. Rain. The sidewalks are awash with it. Interminable grey rain. Morag feels perversely, almost angrily, akin to it.

Go ahead, God, let it rain, then. Let it rain forever. I won't be drowned.

When she returns, she writes to Brooke, telling him.

She does not hear from him again. She receives, instead, a letter from Brooke's solicitors, asking her to forward a doctor's certificate confirming pregnancy, and will she also please send her own signed and witnessed statement to the effect that the father of the child is not her husband, and will she please, further, forward the name of the father and the dates when adultery took place.

Morag complies with the first two requests and refuses the third.

Dear Morag:
There is no way it can be done painlessly, as I know. It is a thoroughly nasty and barbaric procedure, designed to make everyone suffer as much as possible. All you can do is live through it and survive. And you will. So just hang on, eh? And remember, you didn't do it lightly.

> Love,
> Ella

Is, however, this last statement true? Morag doesn't have a clue, anymore. Perhaps it will all become clear in time.

Christie writes with a spidery hand to say he is sorry Morag has split with her husband, and does she need any money because he's got a few-odd bucks stashed away. She reads the letter numbly, and answers no thanks but thanks a million. She has not yet told Christie about the child. She is not sure how he would take it. Would he merely think she is a faithless bitch? She cannot bear that possibility. Not yet.

Late evening, and the Bleak House doorbell rings. A minute later, Mrs. Tefler, voice rich with reproach, shouts up the stairway.

"It's for you, Morag. A guy."

A *guy*? For an instant Morag imagines it is Jules. Realizes how much she wants and needs to see him. Then recalls that he doesn't have her address. Has he got it through the publishers? Impossible. Jules would never do that.

"Who is it, Mrs. Tefler?"

"How would *I* know?" the saintly Maggie replies, verbally withdrawing the hem of her respectable pink kimono. "He *says* he's from some outfit called Walton and Pierce."

"Send him up!" Morag shouts.

Amazing! Astounding! Wait for the next thrilling instalment! An angel of the Lord, probably St. Michael of the Flaming Sword, disguised as a publisher's rep, has come to explain how paradise can be regained.

Or has he come to say *Spear of Innocence* hasn't yet earned its royalty advance, and they want the rest of the money back?

She should have gone down to greet him. Graciously. Yeh, graciously, all three tons of her. No way she is going up and down those ten zillion stairs again today. She puts on her blue flannel housecoat, which makes her appearance resemble only that of a modified schooner rather than a galleon in full sail.

"Hi, Miss Gunn – shall I call you Morag?"

He is a middle-aged moustached man, a little out of breath after the dizzy ascent of the Tefler Grand Staircase, linoleum-covered.

"I'm Hank Masterson," he goes on. "W and P's local representative. They wrote me you were in the city, and separated, you know, and I thought I'd drop around and see how you were doing. Also, I've got some news. They thought it might be good to deliver it to you personally."

"Bad news?" Why should she respond this way, instantly?

"No. Good."

"Really? My God, I could do with some."

Hank looks at her.

"I can see that," he says pleasantly. "Well, your novel's been accepted by a publisher in England and one in the States."

Morag is silent. Stunned.

"Will that mean some more money?" she says at last.

What a question. Mercenary, he will be muttering to himself. If only she weren't so goddamn near being broke.

"Sure," he is saying. "Not a fortune, but some. Listen, are you strapped for dough?"

"Well, more or less."

She explains her domestic arrangements at Bleak House.

"That's crazy," he says. "You should be writing."

"Yeh. Well. I am, to some extent. Stories, mainly. But not many."

"Send them out, then. I'll get the firm to put you in touch with an agent. Ever tried your hand at articles? I mean, feature articles for newspapers? It's a hell of a thing to suggest you spend your time doing, maybe, when you should be at another novel."

"I would do almost any damn thing at all," Morag says truthfully. "I never thought of articles. What sort?"

"Oh – light and amusing, preferably."

"You mean, like – Sunday School Picnics I Never Attended?"

"That sort of thing. You haven't tried?"

It occurs to her that she has not been very enterprising.

"No," she says. "I've been kind of taken up with other things."

"Things will change," says St. Michael Masterson.

*

Things do change, although scarcely at the speed of light. Morag sends her short stories to Milward Crispin, literary agent, and after innumerable tries on his part, one is accepted. On the strength of this, plus the royalty cheques from England and the States on *Spear of Innocence*, Morag resigns from her role as domestic at Bleak House. She would have had to do so anyway, soon, as her girth prevents light-footed action around the place. She continues to rent the room. Maggie Tefler is suspicious, obviously thinking that such a pregnant lady cannot have suddenly become a hustler, but if not that, what?

"You have come into some money, dear?" she enquires.

Morag explains, but guardedly.

"Think of that," Mrs. Tefler says. "That guy said you were an author, but naturally I never believed him."

"Oh, naturally."

"Well," Maggie says, sighing heftily, "it must be nice to be able to earn a living just sitting there."

"Yeh."

Morag embarks on frenzied attempts to write and sell articles, any kind of articles, to the local press. The Features Editor, perhaps growing tired of being bombarded, finally begins to accept these small gems, which could not be confused with deathless prose, but over which Morag sweats and drudges, wishing she had the gift of churning them out. During the months when she is wrestling with these articles, she writes no fiction, nothing involving. Nothing.

Memorybank Movie: Voices from Past Places
"You mean right up the stairs all the way to the top?" the woman's voice says.

"That's what I said," Maggie replies laconically.

"Heavenly days, where does she live? In the attic?"

"The top floor," Maggie Tefler says icily, "has the best view in the house."

Morag, on the second landing, proceeding back from the bathroom, overhears this exchange. Whose voice? She knows it, but from where?

Click-click-click. Heels on the stairs. Morag waits. Then catches sight of the woman. Still slender – thinner, actually – and still fair-haired although her hair has darkened a little and is now done in an upsweep. Smartly tailored suit, the longish jacket of which only partially hides the fact that her hips have become slightly too bony. Her face more sharp-featured, more drawn than it should be at twenty-eight, the same age as Morag.

"Julie! Julie Kazlik!"

"The same," Julie says, grinning. "Hi, Morag. How you been? My God – when is it due?"

"In the spring. End of May. For heaven's sake, come on up."

Julie settles herself on the brass bed, taking off her spike-heeled pointed-toe shoes and tucking her feet underneath her. They look at one another carefully, amazed, glad, hesitant, each sizing up the marks the years have placed upon the other person and by implication upon themselves.

"How on earth did you find me, Julie?"

"God's sake, Morag, I saw your articles in the paper, of course, and phoned and got your address. How you *been*, then? It's been a long time."

"Ten years. I'm pretty okay, actually. I'm happy about the baby, but kind of anxious about how I'm going to look after it and make a living. My husband and I are being divorced. It was my fault. I left him."

"What d'you mean, your fault, you left him," Julie snorts. "It's a two-way street, kid. Don't give me that malarkey. Anyhow, join the club. Buckle and me are getting unhitched, also."

"I didn't even know you were married, although I always thought you'd marry young."

"Well, I didn't marry all that young. But, yeh. Buckle Fennick, truck driver. Does the long hauls, Alaska Highway and that. He's a great driver, matter of fact. I think I married him because he was such a snappy dancer. How dumb can you get?"

"Got any kids?"

"Yeh. One." Julie looks away. "He's a good kid, Steve. He's two years old now, going on three. I don't want him to grow up like his old man."

"You mean – a truck driver? No. You don't mean that."

"No," Julie says, "I don't mean that. I mean, like, crazy. Loco. I grew up on the farm, as you know. You ever seen a loco horse? I guess not. We had one once, like that. A real loner, and crazy. Something in him made him want to knock down everything in sight. He was beautiful – a roan stallion. Great in every way except he was a killer. My dad shot him. I don't mean Buckle's a killer outright – he does it in other ways. Well, never mind all that now. You say you're worried about how to support the kid – won't your husband have to contribute?"

"He hasn't got any obligation. It's not his child, Julie."

Julie looks startled, then laughs.

"Well, you sure as hell don't do things by halves, do you? You'll manage, kid. I know you will. You were always smart, although you always tried not to let on. But I knew. Soon as I'm free, I'm marrying this nice guy who's in the insurance business, and we're going to Montreal. Dennis isn't anybody's idea of a glamour boy, but he is really kind and he cares about me and he's good with Steve."

Julie, landing on her feet. Julie, who always had a string of boyfriends. And yet, the undertone of sadness. *He's kind.* Not *I love him so much I think I'd die without him.* The first hopes shown up as illusions, yet parted with painfully.

"You're lucky," Morag says, despite herself.

Julie gives her a shrewd look.

"I know I am," she says in a low voice. Then, becoming brisk, an individual *Manawaka Banner* reporting, "You know Stacey Cameron's married and living here?"

"Really? My God, how many people from town must be here?"

"Thousands, probably," Julie says in her old slapdash way. "We all head west, kiddo. We think it'll be heaven on earth – no forty below in winter, no blastfurnace in summer, and mountains to look at, not just grain elevators. So we troop out to the Coast, and every time we meet someone from back home we fall on their necks and weep. Stupid, eh?"

Neither of them think it is stupid. You Can't Go Home Again, said Thomas Wolfe. Morag wonders now if it may be the reverse which is true. You have to go home again, in some way or other. This concept cannot yet be looked at.

They discuss people they've known, and whatever happened to them. Then Julie looks at Morag enquiringly.

"You plan on staying in this dump, Morag?"

"It hasn't been so bad. But I can't stay once the baby's here. Can you see me dragging a carriage up these stairs? And can you see Maggie Tefler letting me leave it in the downstairs hall? No. I've been looking for a place, but so far no dice."

"I'm staying in the top floor of a friend's house in North Van," Julie says. "She'll want to rent it when Stevie and I have gone. It all depends on the divorce, just when that'll be. God, I wish it was all over. I hate all this. Buckle's agreed to sue me

– adultery. But he could change his mind at the drop of a handkerchief, and then I'd have to go for the cruelty charge. And I don't want to, Morag. Sometimes I hate him, but I don't want it all brought out in court. It's not the beating-up kind of cruelty – he's never blacked an eye for me, or like that. Better if he had. They could understand that. It's what he says – that I'm out to get his power, things like that. He can't make love any more – he never did, very much, but the last coupla years he couldn't at all. He just jerked himself off in front of me and said these things. Finally I couldn't stand it any longer. But how do I know what's made him that way? I know some, but I'll never understand it all. And even if I did understand, what could I do? And how much of it have I made worse? That bothers me."

"I know," Morag says.

Julie looks up.

"Yeh," she says. "I guess you do. Well, goddamn it, eh? But I am getting out, with my kid. Buckle can live or he can die. Sometimes I don't even care which, anymore. But I'm not dying, not yet, not if I can help it. Well, let's change the subject. I started out to say maybe you'd like my place, if you can hold out until my divorce comes through. Also, if you could get on with Fan –"

"I could get on with the Dragon Lady at this point," Morag says. "Anybody would be better than Maggie Tefler as a landlady."

"Yeh. Well. You haven't met Fan. She's – well, she's fine, but she sort of takes getting used to. So we'll see."

"Don't worry," Morag says. "If that doesn't work out, something else will. I'm not begging."

They look at each other, and laugh.

Memorybank Movie: Through Dooms of Love

Morag is in the hospital. A different zone of human existence, acres of glass and chrome, miles of corridors in which the floor polish seems to have mated with antiseptic, a protected swathed world. Morag has never been in hospital before in her life, so finds it a weirdly isolating experience. At first the contractions are not so severe that she cannot observe what's going on around her, not to her sight, anyway. Everything that is going on is inside herself.

Someone, ghostwhite, formidable, pushes an apparatus into her hand – walkie-talkie? No.

"Breathe in here, Mrs. Gunn, if the pain gets a little too much."

"I'm not Mrs.," Morag says.

"Well, I wouldn't advertise the fact if I was you," the nurse says coldly. "It's nothing to be proud of. You're just lucky they're letting you have the baby here."

"Where do you think I should have it?" Morag says clearly, from somewhere outside her body. "In a ten-acre field?"

Crazy. Crazy. The contractions are coming closer and more severely. Why argue with the nurse now? She needs that nurse.

"I'm sorry," Morag says abjectly, untruthfully. "Please – please don't leave me."

"You're perfectly all right," the nurse says. "I'll be back in a minute."

In a minute, however, Morag has reached the second stage of labour and is trundled hastily into the delivery room.

"Hold back," the doctor's ghostvoice commands from beyond the outer reaches of space. "Don't bear down so hard. It's coming too quickly."

You try holding back. You just try. I can't. I can't.

The child rips its way into its life, tearing its mother's flesh in its hurry, unwilling to wait.

It is over. Relief. Morag, numbed, sleepy and yet totally alert, can feel no pain at all. The nurse places the child on Morag's now-gaunt belly. It is writhing a little, covered with streaks of blood and yellow slime. The cord is not yet cut. Morag cannot see the baby's face. All she can see is its rounded backside. She has imagined her first question will be – what *is* it, boy or girl? Not so.

"Is it *all right*?"

"Certainly," the doctor says in a talcum-powder voice. "She's fine. We just want to get her breathing a bit more deeply, that's all."

She.

The cord is cut, and the placenta comes away without Morag's being aware of it. All she can think of is whether the child is breathing properly or not. Then the girlchild opens her mouth and yells, an amazingly loud sound from so minuscule a creature. The doctor is holding the child, and Morag has still not seen her daughter's face. What if they get her mixed up with all the hundreds of other kids in this baby emporium?

"Let me see her."

"We'll clean her up, and then nurse will bring her to you," the doctor says.

Morag props herself up on an elbow, somewhat hampered by the fact that she is still confined by legstraps.

"Like hell," she says fiercely. "I want to see her right now."

"These conscious births," the doctor sighs, sounding tired.

Morag holds the child, still slippery, very warm. The slightly slanted eyes are tightly closed, and the miniature fists are clenched. The baby's hair, damp, is sparse and straight and black. Her skin is pinkish tan.

"She's – she's great, eh?"

Piquette Tonnerre Gunn has entered her own and unknown life.

*

Morag is back at Bleak House within a week. Julie comes over to help, and seeing the baby for the first time says *My gosh*. Morag bristles.

"It's okay," Julie says quickly. "I was only a little surprised, is all."

"You remember Skinner Tonnerre, Julie?"

"Sure. Well, my goodness. Small world."

They do not discuss it again.

Morag finds she cannot actually call the child by the name of Piquette. She calls her, instead, Pique. When the baby is two months old, Julie takes a whole roll of colour film. Morag sends one to Jules, a picture of the baby alone. She writes a brief letter, and sends it to the place where he was living in Toronto, wondering if he will receive it or if he will have moved by now. She no longer trusts Mrs. Tefler for her own mail, so puts her return address as Fan Brady's house, where Julie lives. After another month she gets a reply.

Dear Morag –
You sure are a crazy woman, but it is up to you, and the baby looks fine. I'm glad you called her what you did. I hope I'll see her one of these days. I moved, awhile back. Still in the same game. Not much news here. Say hello to the kid for me. Good luck.

Jules

The letter is postmarked Trois-Rivières. There is no address.

Morag has to write longhand now, at nights, so as not to waken the child. She can only type when Pique is awake. The room grows smaller every day.

Milward Crispin writes to say that he's sold another two of her stories, but the Piper stories appear to have no appeal to editors, and it could be that editors these days have no damn brains or it could be the stories need reworking, possibly both. The American reviews of *Spear* are pretty good. The English reviews are politely indifferent, some of them damning with faint praise. "A pleasant enough novel from the Canadian backwoods, which attempts with limited success to inject a little sophistication in the form of bizarre if somewhat unlikely shenanigans." Morag, enraged, rips this review into pieces. Then, feeling it unworthy of her to keep only the good reviews, she Scotch tapes it together again.

At nights she communicates glumly with her cheque-book, in the vain but persistent hope that she has miscalculated the total and may in fact have more money in the bank than she thought.

Pique is good-tempered and easy throughout the days, but wakens regularly at two A.M., apparently in the last and vocal throes of angry starvation. Morag weeps with chagrin and tiredness.

Maggie Tefler passes remarks of an unflattering nature about Pique's ancestry.

"Did you get yourself mixed up with a Chinee or a Jap, dear? No? Well, I wasn't going to say halfbreed – I didn't think it *possible*. What's that? *Maytee?* I never heard *that* word.

They're all halfbreeds to me, and I could tell you a thing or two, you betcha."

Morag writes to Christie about the child. He replies that he would like to see her, and he hopes she looks a lot like Morag.

After innumerable letters exchanged with members of the legal profession, Morag's divorce comes through in what her lawyer assures her is record time. She is spared the ignominy of having to appear in court, which is just as well, as she could not afford to go to Toronto. She is now no longer Mrs. Brooke Skelton. She looks at the paper with its unfamiliar terminology. At this moment, she can remember only the good things that happened between herself and Brooke. Appalled, she wonders what has taken place and why she finds herself here, in circumstances which at this moment seem unreal. She half expects to waken and find herself back with Brooke, ten years ago.

Then Pique lifts her voice, and Morag goes to her.

Julie phones to say her own divorce has come through, and she and Dennis are being married and leaving for Montreal.

Memorybank Movie: Begonia Road
"I would have thought," Maggie Tefler says, wounded, "that you would of had the decency to give me a month's notice."

"I pay you by the week," Morag says, "and I'm giving you a week's rent in lieu of notice. That's perfectly fair."

"That it is *not*," Maggie moans sullenly. "*That* it is *not*. You owe me a month's rent if yer just gonna take off like that."

"A month's rent? You're out of your mind."

"*That* is the thanks a person gets," Maggie complains to heaven, "for taking in a girl who's in trouble and letting her stay *even though* it turns out she's got herself mixed up with the Lord only knows who. That is all the thanks a person gets.

She spits on you. I should of known better. But that's me. I feel sorry for people."

"Please, Mrs. Tefler, can't we just stop this?"

"You," Maggie says, "are nothing but a slut, and the sooner you are outa here, the better."

And so, as the sun sinks slowly into the saltchuck, we bid farewell to Maggie Tefler, friend of fallen womanhood.

Fan Brady's house in North Vancouver is at the top of a steeply sloped street, Begonia Road. Looking out the front window of Morag's apartment, you can see the harbour, and beyond that, the tall city, looking cleaner and more stately from this distance than it really is. Looking out from the back balcony, you can see the pine and tamarack marching up the mountainsides. The entire top floor of the two-storey house belongs to Morag. She sleeps in the livingroom where the couch makes up into a bed, and gives the bedroom to Pique. At first, Morag is nervous thinking of the child alone in there – what if the cot blankets slip and she smothers? This is, of course, ridiculous. Pique at four months is active and strong as an eel, a born little scrapper. There is no way that kid would ever lie there passively and let some feeble blanket suffocate her. Her voice, also, has if anything grown in power. Hence another anxiety. Pique may not smother, but will she yell and disturb Fan, who will then order Morag out? Fan, however, works nights, sleeps days and is only in evidence in the late afternoon. Pique, luckily, does most of her lung exercise in the evenings.

Fan Brady does, as Julie said, take some getting used to. It is impossible to tell her age, but she is probably close to thirty. She is tiny, bird-boned, but well-endowed withal, and she cares tenderly for her body, constantly smearing perfumed and pastel-tinted creams and ointments on various parts of herself, whoever happens to be present. False modesty is one thing Fan

hasn't got. She wears her flaming auburn hair in an odd assortment of ringlets, frizz and spitcurls like a calendar girl from
the Mary Pickford era, and yet on Fan this coiffure doesn't
look old-fashioned. Her face isn't beautiful – it isn't even
pretty. In fact, facially, she rather resembles a monkey. She is
well aware of this, and doesn't give a damn. When she has
applied her false eyelashes, green eyeshadow, orange lipstick,
and multitudinous other bits of makeup, she looks weird. But
from a distance, possibly, and under coloured lights, there
would be a certain circus sequinned splendour about her.

"Hi, sweetheart," she says, that first day. "You get settled
in okay? Want a beer?"

"Thanks."

Fan twirls across to the fridge, her apricot nylon house-
coat frothing around her. She is devoid of makeup at the
moment, and her face is drawn tight and hollowed by
whatever it is she has lived through, but she moves with
speed and lightness.

"Now, let's get this straight, sweetheart," she says. "I don't
give a fuck what you do here, just so long as you don't do too
much tramping around when I'm asleep. I gotta get my sleep
or I'm dead. Not that I'm that easily wakened, once I get to
sleep, the amount of Seconal I take. I wish I could sleep
without them, but I can't. You'd think in all this time I'd of
gotten used to sleeping days, but no."

Fan Brady is, in her own terminology, a danseuse, and
she works at a nightclub called, with more publicity than accuracy, The Figleaf.

"Don't get me wrong, sweetheart. I am not yer common-
or-garden stripper. Not by a long shot. I am a dansoose. How
about that, eh? Makes it sound good. The Figleaf is just
another clipjoint, actually, but in a slightly classy way, legal

and not too crude. Spicy but genteel, is the management's slogan, ha ha. Well, never mind, I can laugh, but I tell you, sweetheart, my work is an Art. It is definitely an Art. I am a pro, I will tell you that. Not like some of these kids, all bump and grind – they think if you've got a decent pair of tits, you don't need to learn nothing. I am definitely not like that. I work at it. I exercise daily. I practise. I go on the Swedish milk diet coupla days each month – can't afford a spare tire around my belly. It's my work and I take it serious. Not that all them slobby salesmen appreciate it. I don't do it for them, the cheap bastards. It's my pride. That's what it is."

Morag is fascinated. Does fiction prophesy life? Is she looking at Lilac Stonehouse from *Spear of Innocence*? Fan Brady, though, hasn't got Lilac's naïveté. Fan is tough in the spirit, wiry and wary in the soul. She is not really like Lilac at all, of course. She is almost the opposite. And yet, looking at Fan now is almost like looking at some distorted and older but still recognizable mirror-image of Lilac. There is a sense in which Fan *has* that same terrifying innocence, expressed in different ways.

"That Julie," Fan says. "I'm really fond of her, and I'll miss her, but she was soft in the head, if you ask me."

"How do you mean, Fan?"

"She actually felt bad, leaving Buckle, you know that? Save your tears, sweetheart, I kept on telling her. Don't waste them on that crumb. But oh no. She can't stand the guy, but still she feels bad about it. Can you beat it?"

"It doesn't sound so strange to me," Morag says.

"Like fun it doesn't. That guy is a bastard through and through. An asshole. And she feels sorry for him! She should of fed him arsenic years ago."

"Well, it's not that simple, I guess."

"Yer damn right it's simple," Fan says. "It's plain as day-light."

There is obviously going to be one area which Morag and Fan will not be able to discuss. Something, of course, has made Fan this way. How much is foisted upon a person and how much is self-chosen to mesh gearlike with what is already there? How far back does anything start?

"You want to see Pique?" Morag asks, anxious to avoid argument right now.

"What? Oh, your kid?"

"Yes. She's asleep upstairs."

"Yeh, sure, I guess so. I don't go much on kids, to tell you the truth. I'm not what you'd call the maternal type. I had to look after a whole bunch of young brothers and sisters when I was a kid, and it kind of put me off. How many abortions you think I've had, Morag?"

"My God, I don't know. How many?"

"Five." Fan says coolly. "Five."

"That's – awful. That must have been terrible for you."

"I never batted an eyelid," Fan says.

But why had she got pregnant all those times? As a clue-less sixteen-year-old, perhaps. But after that, what compulsion? Morag does not bring up this question, nor will she, ever.

Pique, sleeping, is as near perfection as it would be pos-sible to get. Faintly smiling, small pinkbrown hands closed but not tightly, the fingers unfolding one by one, like petals.

"Very nice," Fan says stiltedly. "I suppose you're not getting a nickel out of her dad?"

"I never asked him. It was – it wasn't like that. He knows about her. It's all right."

"You should have your head examined, Morag, that's all

I can say. If I was you, I would put the screws on him, but good. It might not get you anywhere. He'd try to weasel out, I'd bet. But at least you could try."

"Look, Fan – just don't tell me what to do for my own good, eh? Not ever. Okay?"

Fan looks up, surprised.

"Hey, take it easy, sweetheart. I only meant –"

"I know. But don't. That's the one thing I can't take."

"Okay, okay. I get the message. C'mon down and have another beer. I wanna ask your advice."

"*My* advice?" This is certainly a quick change.

Fan laughs, a high trilling like a nervous song sparrow.

"Sure. Wait till I show you."

"Show me what?"

"You'll see."

Back downstairs, Fan begins shaving her legs while talking.

"Well, I'm changing my act, see? I figger it's time I got a speciality. I'm not getting any younger. I'll be thirty-four next month, although I never admit to more than twenty-five."

Thirty-four. Ye gods. And what of the future? What of the future for a writer, if it comes to that? But at least Morag isn't dependent upon her shape, which in the course of years can only get worse, in one way or another.

"So what're you going to do, Fan?"

"I'm gonna become a snake dancer."

"A *what*?"

"You heard me. I'm practising right now. I just got it the other day. I met this guy who knew a guy who had an African python for sale, so I bought it."

"Fan," Morag says, in a deadly quiet voice, "*where is it?*"

"In the basement."

"The basement!" Morag yells. "For christ's sake, you're a madwoman! What if it gets loose?"

Pique, strangled not by the coverlets on her cot, but by a python. *A python.* Slithering coils of slippery and probably slimy steel.

"It won't," Fan says, enjoying this. "I give it a quarter-tranquillizer from time to time. The guy I bought it from says it's mostly in a comose state."

"In a what state? Oh, you mean comatose."

"Pretty handy with the big words, aren't you?" Fan says irritably, her drama momentarily dimmed.

"Sorry. But hell, Fan, you can't keep a python in the house. It's – well, it could be lethal."

"It's harmless as a kitten. They don't have no poison, you know, pythons."

"No, they just curl around your windpipe and choke you to death. I warn you – if that thing comes near Pique, I'll kill you with my bare hands. I mean it."

What to do? Move out instantly? To where?

"Worry not, sweetheart," Fan says placatingly, observing that Morag really does mean it. "C'mon – I went and had a look at your pet, so now you come and have a look at mine."

Pet. Child. Oh jesus, deep waters, deep waters. What has Morag got herself into?

The python, looking dead, and less large than Morag has imagined, lies asleep in a cage in the basement. The cage has a handle on top, for easy transportation to the club. It is covered with fine wire mesh, Morag is somewhat reassured to notice. The snake is gaudily patterned in brown and cream, and is really quite beautiful, if you like that sort of thing.

"I call it Tiny," Fan says.

This lady is nutty as crunchy peanut butter. And yet, against all reason, Morag is beginning to like her. Tiny, yet. Merciful heavens, what a choice of name. All the same, Morag vows to keep the upstairs door bolted and locked at all times.

Over another beer, Fan elaborates.

"I gotta get me another name, see, Morag? Something kind of oriental-sounding, know what I mean? So I thought, seeing as how you're a writer, you might dream one up for me. Princess something-or-other, I thought."

"Holy God, Fan, that's some request. I'm not an advertising copywriter."

"For you, it'll be easy," Fan says confidently.

Morag thinks for a while.

"What about Sapphire?"

"No. I don't think so. Not enough zing."

"Hm. Well. Let's see. Zarathustra?"

"Too fancy. Nobody could say it."

Morag thinks again. Then inspiration strikes.

"Eureka – I think I've got it!"

"That's it!" Fan cries, swivelling her hips gleefully on the way to the fridge.

"Huh?" Morag says, momentarily uncomprehending.

"What you just said."

"Eureka? That's just – it's an expression. I think it means 'I've found it,' or something like that. From this ancient Greek philosopher, who – well, never mind. I was going to suggest –"

"Never mind what you were going to suggest. That's my new name. Princess Eureka. Print it down nice and big so I can see how it'll look on the billing."

So Morag prints.

PRINCESS EUREKA

SNAKE DANCER

ORIENTAL DANSEUSE

Dances With Real Live Python!
Thrilling!
Exotic!

"Gee, that's great," Fan says. "Thanks a million, Morag."

"Any time. No charge. I'll be your advertising consultant."

"Times are sure looking up," Fan remarks. "You're not really scared of Tiny, are you?"

"I wouldn't touch that creature with a ten-foot pole," Morag says fervently.

"I'm not ascared of snakes," Fan says modestly. "I got used to them as a kid. I grew up in the Okanagan. My old man had a little fruit ranch, there. He was a worthless hunk of humanity, if ever there was one. My mum and us kids ran the place. We had a lotta snakes around – great big bull snakes, and garter snakes and all kinds. Only dangerous sort was the rattlers. We used to take our two German shepherd dogs along when we went up to the orchards. They were like devils whenever they seen a rattler. They never got bit, ever. Snakes are okay if you know how to handle them. It's very simple with rattlers. You just kill 'em."

"Oh, very simple. Better you than me."

"But Tiny, there, he's friendly. I bet you think a snake feels slimy, eh?"

"Yeh."

"Well, they don't. They're smooth and dry, sort of dusty-feeling. You'll see."

"That'll be the day."

Later, upstairs, Morag thinks about Fan Brady. Lilac Stonehouse begins to look like pretty pale stuff in comparison. Could you get a Fan Brady down on paper? Only an approximation. Even the name of the club, for heaven's sake. "The Figleaf" is much better than "Crowe's Cave." *And you think Fan Brady's crazy?*

Memorybank Movie: Travelling On
Snapshot: Pique, age one, sits on the front steps of the house on Begonia Road. Her sturdy legs are stretched to their small length in front of her, and her feet are encased in new white shoes, high around her ankles so she will learn to walk steadily. She wears a yellow dress, very short, patterned with butterflies green and mauve and blue. Her straight black hair is still not very long and is brushed carefully for the picture. Her round face is unsmiling but not unhappy. Her large dark eyes look openly and with trust at the person behind the camera, namely her mother.

Pique's first birthday is over, and she is asleep. Morag and Fan are having a beer on Morag's balcony. In the garden below, the forsythia is in yellow flower, and the leaves are beginning to come out on the big dogwood tree. The evening air is faintly bright and warm, and there is a smell of salt, the breeze now blowing from the sea. In the distance the white gulls glide, riding the wind.

"You oughta get out more," Fan says disapprovingly. "You go on devoting the whole of your entire life to that kid, and I'm here to tell you what'll happen, sweetheart. She'll grow up and leave without a backward glance."

"Fine," Morag says irritably. "I wouldn't want her to do anything else, when the time comes. And I'm not devoting my entire life to her, Fan. I'm working, and that's what I want to be doing. Anyway, I get out some."

"Should I introduce you to some nice guys?" Fan says, single-mindedly. "Actually the number of *nice* guys I know is precisely none, but they're good for a few laughs."

Fan's continually altering attachments do not appeal much to Morag.

"I'll think about it," she promises.

Fan kicks off her grimy green-feathered slippers and puts her bare feet on the balcony rail. Pedicured toenails with tangerine polish, but her feet, like all the rest of her, are shapely and strong. Beside her, Morag feels too heavy-boned, too tall, despite the fact that her legs are better proportioned than Fan's and she prefers her own long straight black hair to Fan's wildflower arrangement of auburn whorls and curls. Fan is studying her feet and legs with an apparently absorbed and even narcissistic interest. She frequently appears obsessed with her own flesh, although (or so Morag suspects) not so much at home within it.

"It's a problem, eh?" Fan says. "I mean, what to do, you know. You like fucking, Morag?"

"Yeh. Sometimes I wish I didn't."

"Yeh? Well, sometimes I wish I did. Oh sure, okay, I screw like a bitch in heat, but my heart's not in it, know what I mean? I should of been a hustler – I would've been perfect. In, out, pay at the cash desk, buddy. I mighta made a fortune."

Morag ponders the theme of irony. Opportunities for sex are minimal. Has she set it up like this for herself? Her kid, her work. And here is Fan, getting more than she wants. But not really. Fan has set it up for herself as well, in some way or other, unacknowledged.

"Why screw so much if you don't like it?" Morag asks.

Fan shrugs.

"It passes the time. I can't stand being alone. I'm so goddamn jittery when I quit the club, nights, that I can't think straight."

Fan never has breakfast or even lunch with one of her men. She throws them out about 8:00 A.M., when she reckons she may possibly get off to sleep. Morag hears them stumbling solitarily around the kitchen, looking for instant coffee. Morag, her own day having by then begun, walks barefoot and silent around her own kitchen, cursing fate. Unfair, unfair. Oddly, it has not soured her relationship with Fan. Probably it would have, though, if Fan was down there with a man loving every minute of it.

"Didn't you ever love a guy, Fan? Whatever *love* means."

Fan considers.

"Not so's I can remember," she says finally. "I suppose yer gonna expect me to say my dad raped me when I was twelve, or like that, eh? Well, he never. He knocked my mum around some, but she could take care of herself. She wasn't such a big lady, but built like me – wiry. She used to knee him in the groin. It was a laugh. Well, I dunno what it was with me. Sometimes I think about it, but then again, what's the use?"

Look at songs hidden in eggs. Sandburg. Look at laments hidden in eggshell skulls. Gunn.

"Know what I wish?" Fan says suddenly, as though this is costing her something to say.

"No. What?"

"I have sometimes," Fan says carefully, "wished I was lez. Queer. Bent as a forked twig."

"Maybe you are. Would it bother you?"

"It would make life easier," Fan says. "But yeh, it would bother me."

"That's – too bad. That it would bother you, I mean."

"I know," Fan says, and her voice has a sadness in it that Morag has never heard there before. "Yeh, I know."

Then she gets up and patters downstairs, down to the basement to feed the python.

After midnight, Morag finally sleeps. Wakens at three in the morning, a darkness in the room and in her head. She is drenched with sweat. Dreaming? Nightmaring? She has in sleep been back with Brooke, in the Tower. They have been making love, as it used to be, everything drawn into this centre, their bed, their merging selves. Then, just before their moment, she has realized that she had only fantasized the child, her daughter, who is really in the realm and unreality of the unborn. She cannot bear this knowledge. She draws away, tearingly, from him, leaving him bewildered and angry, and herself alone.

Almost awake, Morag pulls herself out of the swamps of sleep, out of the nightmarshes. Rises, groping for lights.

Pique is asleep in her cot, lying on her stomach, her head turned upwards, the small profile visible against the sheet, her hands upcurled into themselves, like new ferns beside her face.

Memorybank Movie: Harold, Lover of My What
"What you need," Fan says, "is a little more makeup, and can't you for heaven's sake leave off your glasses just for the evening?"

"I'm blind as a bat without them," Morag says. "I wouldn't recognize my best friend at three paces."

"Well, take a quick gander at the crowd, when you get there, then take the specs off and stick 'em in your purse."

"I'll try," Morag says halfheartedly.

"That dress looks great on you," Fan says encouragingly, sizing up the new green and blue silk (artificial). "Just slap on a little more warpaint, sweetheart, and go in there pitching."

The party at Hank Masterson's is for a visiting poet whom Morag has not read.

She goes back upstairs and applies more lipstick. She dislikes and feels alienated from herself with a lot of makeup on. She has, however, minimal faith in her own judgement. After all, the women who are successful with men always plaster all this gloop on their faces. Fan's paint job takes her about forty-five minutes. Is it the makeup or Fan's inner assurance that does the trick? Or just the fact that Fan really doesn't give a damn about men, and certainly doesn't need one sexually and is hence in a very good bargaining position? *Bargaining position.* One of the sexual postures not mentioned in the Kama Sutra. *Postures.* The ways in which one lies. Oh, shut up.

"I'm not that fond of games," Morag tells the mirror.

"Well, then, why not stay home with your knitting?" the mirror replies, meanly.

Angrily, Morag slaps on more lipstick. Then, angrily, takes most of it off again.

"Were you speaking to me, Mrs. Gunn?" the teenage babysitter enquires, appearing at the bathroom door.

"No, Carol. Just talking to myself."

"Oh. I see."

Carol, you can bet, does not talk to herself. She talks interminably to Morag, when given the chance, about her boyfriends, of whom there are about three hundred, at a rough estimate.

"Your cab's here," Fan shouts up the stairway.

The Mastersons' house is large and elegant. Hank, out of genuine kindness, tries to steer Morag towards men who are single, divorced or separated. Morag resents this obvious ploy, but is grateful for the motive behind it. After the second scotch, she drinks very slowly. A lady on the make. It doesn't sound too pleasant. On the other hand, why doesn't it?

Morag never gets to meet the visiting celebrity. He is surrounded by a breathless group, all women, who possibly think it would be nifty to be able to say you'd slept with a well-known poet. Morag has observed this phenomenon at Hank's parties before. The woods are perceptibly not full of an equal number of breathless men who have designs upon women writers.

But hist! What have we here?

"Hi. My name's Harold."

About Morag's height. Sandy hair. Glasses. Blond hair on wrists. Blue eyes. Jovial, and slightly drunk.

Harold is a broadcaster. He reads the news. He does not read many books, but of course he would like to, if ever he had the time for it. He has recently split up with his wife, who has their two kids. He misses the kids, and can see them only every other Sunday and even then his wife is always there, so how can he talk to them, with her sitting there vetting his every word?

"Are you married, Morag?"

"Divorced."

The evening grinds on.

"Can I drive you home?" Harold asks, an hour later.

In the car, complex problems go on in Morag's head. Should she ask him up for a drink, or would he interpret that as over-eagerness? Impossible, anyway, as Carol is there. Why worry about Carol? Because Carol will tell her ma, is why, and

Carol's mother will then refuse to allow her innocent (ha ha) daughter to babysit for an immoral lady who brings men home. If Harold makes the suggestion should Morag go to his apartment instead? Nope. Two strikes against that one. Carol has to be home by midnight. Secondly, Morag does not have her diaphragm with her – she will never carry it in her purse, as that seems in some mysterious way unprincipled and also probably a bad omen.

Harold stops the car in front of the house on Begonia Road. He carefully takes off his glasses and places them in the glove compartment. Morag's glasses are in her handbag and she feels as though she is looking at the world through six fathoms of seawater. Then Harold kisses her. Morag struggles with her sex so as not to appear to respond with instant swiftness. The poor guy doesn't want to be raped, after all. But he seems pretty eager, too.

"Can I come up to your place for a while, Morag?"

"Yes," she says, and then, "but do you mind waiting here in the car until the babysitter's gone home?"

"You've got a kid?" Harold enquires, as though appalled. "I didn't know you had a kid."

Is this the exit line?

"Well, I do," Morag says flatly.

"How old?"

"One."

What is he thinking, and why doesn't he say? Why ask how old? Is one year old okay – not talking yet, or not much, and presumably not likely to come pattering in at the wrong moment? What if she'd said *three* or *five*?

"Well, sure, okay," Harold says finally. "I'll wait here."

When Carol has trotted off home, Harold comes upstairs. Morag has checked on Pique. Asleep, thank God.

The appropriate rituals have to be observed. A drink. Lighting cigarettes which are obviously going to burn away in the ashtray. Morag wonders if Harold is only doing it this way because he thinks she expects it. If he thought she didn't expect this small theatrical act before the real act, he'd be out of here like a shot, probably.

Jules never put on that act. But then Jules was never much of a games-player. At this thought, and at her sudden terrible desire to see Jules and hold him, Morag feels she is betraying the man here with her now.

They then are in bed, and this man now and here is inside her, and Morag is present here and now. Her need for him, for the pressure of his sex, is so great that she finds it difficult to hold back enough to accommodate his time. He has drunk a lot more than she has, and is in consequence slower. Then she cannot stop herself, and her consciousness is submerged, drenched in this spasm of gladness.

He laughs a little.

"You wanted that for a long time, didn't you?" he says.

This is true. But she does not like the arrogance in his voice. On the other hand, possibly it is not arrogance at all, but only resentment or even apology for the fact that he has not yet come. Morag wants to reassure him, but does not know what words would be acceptable to him. She tries to bring him, not knowing what acts will be best for him, and not wanting to ask. Finally, his own effort or frenzy succeeds, or appears to. It is so brief and unstrong that Morag is not sure it has really happened at all. Has she ruined it for him by being first? Or was it just the booze? She won't ever know. The casualness of this association now hurts her.

Harold kisses her lightly at the door, and leaves.

"I'll call you," he says.

Morag's own uncertainty tells her she won't hear from him again. But if he did think he hadn't done all that well, he may call again in order to show his prowess.

That is an unworthy thought, Morag.

Harold does phone, for whatever reasons, several days later.

"My, my, living it up, aren't we?" Fan says with approval, as Morag waits for Harold to pick her up.

Restaurant. Dinner. Then back to Harold's apartment, which is glossy and looks unlived-in. Harold drinks very little, and ultimately comes with unquestionable strength. For Morag, it is less good than the first time, although she finds it difficult to understand why. The Black Celt within seems to be threatening her spirit.

"That was great, eh?" Harold says.

"Yes."

She smiles at him, and wonders what they can possibly talk about. Dinner has exhausted the topic of Harold's job at the radio station, his dislike of smartass disc-jockeys who think they own the place, the ways in which a broadcaster has to look after his voice, how to avoid laryngitis, and so on.

They get dressed, and Harold in a remarkably short time goes through half a bottle of rye, probably out of sheer relief.

"My wife," Harold says, "is the bitchiest bitch in this town, you know that? The first year we're married, I go four thousand bucks into debt on account of her. And now she's saying she's going to take me to the cleaner's for alimony. She admits it quite openly. She's out to ruin me. I'm fighting it, though. Just before we split up, she was berserk, I kid you not. Broke dishes, the whole bit. Said I'd been running around. I wasn't running around, Morag. Sure, okay, there'd been a coupla women, but they didn't mean anything."

"Yeh. Well, maybe she was jealous. I mean, of you. If she hadn't been doing the same thing. Maybe she felt she lacked experience, or something."

"Who, her? Not a chance. She was this little girl from Blackfly, B.C., a little mouse. Or so I thought until she blew her stack. She got really impossible, I'm telling you. I couldn't take the dog for a walk but what she'd be quizzing me when I got back. And yell. Could that woman yell. Want another drink?"

"No, thanks. I have to be getting home."

"In a minute. Well, like I was saying –"

Morag is bored and anxious. Her sympathies are increasingly with Harold's wife. This makes her feel apologetic towards Harold. She has been using him. He, however, has also been using her.

"Harold, don't bother driving me home, eh? I'll get a cab."

"Absolutely not. You'll do no such thing. I won't allow it. One more for the road, and then I'll drive you."

Harold handles the car with reckless zeal. Morag curses herself.

Jesus, lover of my soul, get me out of this. Please please please.

"For God's sake, Harold, don't drive so fast."

"I'm okay. I always get there safely. Just relax, relax."

Through some miracle, he does indeed pilot the car to Begonia Road. Then things become all at once strange. He takes Morag's hand and sits quietly for a moment. This gesture surprises her, so she waits, wondering if he is all right. Should she suggest black coffee?

"Know something, Morag?" he says finally.

"What?"

His grip tightens on Morag's hand.

"I really love that woman," he says. "And it was always great, in bed. And then, you know what she said to me when

I moved out? She said it had never been any good for her. Never. Not even once. That's what she told me."

What is there to say? Who hurts whom?

Harold puts his head down on the steering wheel and cries. Morag holds his hand. That is all she can think of, to do. At last he raises his head and takes off his glasses. Dries them with a Kleenex. It is only when she sees his determined hands mopping the surface of his glasses with the flimsy white tissue that Morag wants also to cry.

"Sorry about that," he says brusquely.

"It's all right. Really. It's okay."

"Well – goodnight."

He does not phone her again, of course, but she knows he has got back safely to his apartment because she hears him reading the news the next day.

Even if he had called, she would not really have wanted to see him again. Sadness is everywhere.

Memorybank Movie: Chas

Snapshot: Pique, age three and a half, clad in overalls and a T-shirt, her dark and now-long hair in a ponytail, grins glee-fully as she sits on the new swing in the back yard of the house on Begonia Road. This is all that the picture shows – a small girl, who looks like both her parents and like neither, smiling over a new swing. When Pique grows up, will she have any memory of the other things from this time, the things which the snapshot doesn't show?

"Tell another story, Mum."

"One more, and then you go to sleep, and *no argument*, okay?"

"Okay." Laughter.

"You're a monkey, Pique."

"No, I'm not. I'm full of beans."

"You sure are. All right – settle down."

Pique is still at the small-animal type of story. Once upon a time there was a robin, etcetera. Later on, will Morag tell her the old tales of Piper Gunn who led his people on the long march up north, and Rider Tonnerre the buffalo hunter? Will Pique want to hear the stories, or only be bored?

The story over, Pique still tries.

"I feel sick, Mum.",

"Listen," Morag says with chagrin, "you were fine five minutes ago. Where do you feel sick?"

"Here." Hand on stomach.

The old problem. Is Pique play-acting or not? Is this guile or the beginning of appendicitis? How to tell? Morag goes by the theory that the kid will either get better or will get worse, perceptibly, and if the latter, then it will be time enough to phone the doctor. In practise, however, Morag worries incessantly at such times and often phones the doctor unnecessarily.

"Well, listen, honey, you just try to sleep now and I'll come in after a while and see how you are."

Morag reads in the livingroom for an hour, and then goes into the child's bedroom. Pique is asleep.

The doorbell. Morag flies downstairs to stop whoever it is from ringing again and waking Pique. It is Chas, one of Fan's occasional men. He is never called Charles or Charlie, just Chas. He is bone-thin, with a cadaverous face which is nonetheless handsome, or at least sexy, perhaps owing to the insolence of his eyes, a quality which both repels and attracts Morag.

"Fan's gone to work, Chas."

"I know. I came to see you."

"You might have phoned," Morag says, instantly realizing that this can be taken as a sign of interest on her part.

"I was driving by," Chas says, "so I thought I'd drop in. I saw your light."

Yeh, well it wasn't a red one, buddy.

"Pique's not very well. I don't think I can ask you to stay for a drink."

"We won't disturb her," Chas says. "We can go in Fan's livingroom. She won't mind. I brought a bottle."

You did, eh? Well you can just take it and you know what you can do with it.

This is not what Morag says.

"Well, just one drink, Chas, and then I have to get back to work."

Why does she say this? Which self is talking this time? She's tired. She's exhausted. She's been working every minute possible on the new novel. She's gone for days speaking to no one except Fan, Pique and the milkman – for months, probably. These reasons parade themselves obediently through her head as she pours the drinks in Fan's kitchen.

"You're a good-looking gal, Morag," Chas says cornily, with minimum effort to be subtle. "Some people think you're stand-offish, though."

Stand-offish. Little does he know.

He shortly finds out.

This is insanity. Morag's flesh and her self are two separate entities. She is her own voyeur. She decides that if she is about to go ahead, it will be better to suspend thought for a while. Play now, think later.

"Don't go upstairs to fix yourself," Chas moans, searching for the condom which he has prudently stashed away somewhere. "I can't wait."

"All right."

She wishes he would shut up. She does not want to hear his voice. This is not related to making love with a lover or even a friend. They screw like animals all over Fan's living room, and it is, quite truthfully, fine. When they are both exhausted, Morag pulls away and scrambles back into her clothes. Chas laughs.

"Why the hurry?"

She doesn't know. She usually feels at home with herself and with a man, when naked. Yes, she doesn't know, though. He is getting dressed now, too.

"Chas, you better go now. I have to get back upstairs."

"I'm coming with you. I'll stay the night."

"No, you won't."

Chas's hands are long and slender, and they do not look all that strong, but are. He holds her arm and bends it slowly backward.

"Am I coming upstairs with you, Morag?"

She realizes now that she knows absolutely nothing about him. She does not even know his last name. She is alone in this house with Pique and this lunatic. Maybe he gets his kicks this way. What if he breaks her arm? What if he strangles her? It happens. No one could ever say she hadn't asked for it. Seldom has Morag been as frightened as she is this minute.

What if he goes upstairs and does something to the child?

Morag twists around to lessen the pain. No use appealing to him. Words won't reach him. As soon appeal to a rabid dog. She does not say anything. She is fairly strong, physically, but not nearly as strong as Chas. She is thinking very quickly and she knows that it is better not to do anything precipitous. (Fan's ma used to knee her husband in the groin – ugh.) Unless he heads for that staircase. Morag knows something she did not know before. She is capable of killing, at least under this one circumstance. Fan keeps the butcher knife in the second drawer on the left in the cupboard beside the sink. The fact registers on her mind almost visually.

They struggle without noise or words for another second or two. Then their eyes meet. Chas' pale hazel eyes are alight with a hatred as pure as undiluted hydrochloric acid. And Morag realizes that he may well be seeing the same thing in her own eyes.

He drops her arm.

"Did I scare you, Morag?"

"Get out."

"I just wanted to see how you'd react, that's all. It was just a joke. Can't you take a joke?"

"Get out."

"Okay," he says. "I'll go quietly."

He brings up one hand, and before she can move away, he hits her with full force across the breasts.

He walks out while she is still paralyzed with pain. Morag breathes deeply and forces herself to walk to the hall and lock the front door. She checks the back door. It is locked. She goes back into Fan's kitchen. Chas has left the bottle. She takes it and pours the rest of the rye down the sink. She then goes into Fan's bathroom and throws up.

Only then does she start to shake. She goes upstairs quietly and looks at Pique, almost expecting her not to be there. She is there, and peaceful. Morag takes a scalding bath and after several hours the trembling stops.

He's sick. And I half knew it all the time. Why did I do it? Because I needed a man. It seems a fairly simple thing. Why isn't it? Why the hatred in his eyes? Because he thinks I'm a whore? I don't feel like a whore. Maybe a whore doesn't feel like a whore, either.

Pique continues sleeping. Her forehead is still cool. Her breathing is normal. She is not restless. Is she, perhaps, too quiet?

I know it doesn't work that way, God. I know it but I don't believe it. My head knows perfectly well that retribution is unreal. But my blood somehow retains it from ancient times.

Pique does not become ill. What happens is that Morag is more than a week late with her period that month. She stops work on the novel. She becomes absentminded, except in looking after Pique, which she does with exaggerated care.

"Whatsamatter, sweetheart?" Fan asks. "You're awfully quiet these past few days."

Morag, against her will and judgement, explains. The point has been reached when she has to talk to someone.

"Holy mackerel, *him*," Fan says. "Well, I wish you had of asked me about him first. You needn't apologize to me that it was him. I wouldn't touch him with a barge pole. Don't worry, sweetheart. It's probably just the worry that's delaying you. But if not, I know where you can go."

There would certainly be no alternative. Morag detests the whole idea of having a living creature torn out of her body. But there is no way she is going to bear a child to a man she despises. She imagines it growing in her flesh, totally unknowing, a human which cannot be permitted its life under any circumstances.

Why hadn't she at least put in her diaphragm? The condom was probably faulty. What if Fan's contacts have moved and she cannot find anyone? What about payment? What if she hasn't got enough money? What if she is forced to bear it? It happens all the time. No way out. Trapped irrevocably. No say in the matter. And to look after it until it is an adult? Every day seeing Chas' cat-eyes burning at her? Eighteen years. She would have to try to love it. It would be part hers, and its own person. But could she?

"Come on, Pique – eat your dinner."

"You aren't eating yours," Pique points out.

"I'm just going to." But how?

When she puts Pique to bed, she has to go through the story-telling.

"About the robins, Mum. Tell that one."

"Okay. Well, once upon a time there was this mother robin, see, and she laid four blue eggs in a nest very high up in the dogwood tree in our back yard –"

"That very same tree?"

"Yep. That very same tree."

Morag suddenly bends over the bed and holds Pique, hugging her too tightly, unable to stop crying now that she has unfortunately begun.

"Mum!" Pique is frightened.

Morag puts the child back again and applies Kleenex to her own eyes. This display she must not do. She must *not*. Will Pique retain this memory, years later?

"It's okay, honey. I'm not feeling very well today, that's all."

"Want me to tell *you* a story?"

"Okay. That would be nice."

So Pique tells the robin story, hardly garbling it at all.

Morag wakens next morning with cramps. She has begun to menstruate. Relief. She feels as though she has fought the Crimean War singlehanded, and won. She might not have won, though. It was good luck more than good management.

It may not be fair – in fact, it seems damned unfair to me – but I'll never again have sex with a man whose child I couldn't bear to bear, If the worst came to the absolute worst.

She hopes she means this. It is not morality. Just practicality of spirit and flesh.

The dark bruises on her breasts last only for a couple of weeks.

Dear Ella –

I knew you could do it, and I'm not at all surprised that the collection of poems has been accepted. Well, hallelujah! When does it come out?

The novel progresses, slowly. It's done in semi-allegorical form, and also it has certain parallels with *The Tempest*. Maybe I'm an idiot to try this, but it's the form the thing seems to demand, so I've quit fighting it. I've got the first draft nearly done now, so don't mind saying a bit about it, although it'll take a lot of rewriting. It's called *Prospero's Child*, she being the young woman who marries His Excellency, the Governor of some island in some ocean very far south, and who virtually worships him and then who has to go to the opposite extreme and reject nearly everything about him, at least for a time, in order to become her own person. It's as much the story of H.E. I've always wondered if Prospero really would be able to give up his magical advantages once and for all, as he intends to do at the end of *The Tempest*. That incredibly moving statement – "What strength I have's mine own, Which is most faint –" If only he can hang onto that knowledge, that would be true strength. And the recognition that his real enemy is despair within, and that he stands in need of grace, like everyone else – Shakespeare did know just about everything. I know it's presumptuous of me to try to put this into some different and contemporary framework and relevance, but I can't help it. Well, hell, maybe it's not so presumptuous, at that.

Enough of this. Fan put on a display with Tiny (her python, if you recall) the other day, for Pique and me. I've always refused before. That snake is no friend of mine, although I admit it's never damaged anyone. Pique, however, is totally unafraid. Fan put on her Princess Eureka outfit, which is a few gauzy bits of chiffon (mauve), some gold lace and a sprinkling of sequins. Also some mauve feathers stuck in a small turban-like concoction, which on Fan's flaming hair looks pretty strange. So there she is, winding Tiny around her wrists and neck, and meantime gyrating her hips and belly, all the time complaining we aren't getting the full effect because the oriental music on the record player doesn't give the same atmosphere as the band at The Figleaf. Pique thought it was sublime. It *is* kind of impressive, too. Fan loved having such an appreciative audience. I think she's actually quite fond of Pique now. I worry sometimes about Fan, though. Her nerves are terrible and her age is beginning to show. She says she never gives a thought to the future. I wonder.

Christie's getting so much older all of a sudden, from his letters. I write him oftener than I used to, and send him money when I can, but I don't go back. I sometimes feel I should go and housekeep for him, but Ella, I can't. I don't want Pique to grow up there. And I can't go back to Manawaka for myself, either. I want to find a home, a real one, but I don't know where that would be. I've been feeling lately I'd like to go to England for a while – Britain, rather. Does that sound lunatic? I guess there's something about London, as a kind of centre of writing, or something like that, and maybe it would be a disappointment but I just feel I'd like to go and find out what I can find out there – something I need to know, although I don't know what it might be, yet. Also, and laugh at me if you will (okay, I know you won't), I'd like at some point to go to Scotland, to Sutherland, where my people came from. What do I hope to learn there? Don't ask me. But it haunts me, I guess, and maybe I'll have to go. Not possible yet. Not enough money, and also I don't really want to leave Fan alone just now.

I look at Fan's TV sometimes, and see the terrors of the outside world not diminishing but mounting, and I think – this will be Pique's world, and how much worse will it have become by the time she is 32, as I am now? I recall how it was when I grew up, and I thought *that* was terrifying. This probably sounds pretty gloomy, but in fact I'm mostly fairly okay. Don't worry – I'm a survivor, just as you are. Give my love to your Ma when you write her.

> Love,
> Morag

*

Morag, unsatisfied with *Prospero's Child*, but not knowing what more to do with it, submits it. It is accepted by the three publishers, Canada, America, England, and all three editors have many suggestions, some of which Morag furiously rejects and some of which strike an immediate chord of agreement. She goes back into it and does more work, at first not wanting to do anything, and later not wanting to come out until all the things which obviously need to be done have been done.

The novel is finally published. Hank Masterson throws a party. Morag would rather have had the money it costs to throw a party, but does not say so.

The reviews are mixed, as is their wont. Morag is still vulnerable, but about sixty percent less so than with the first novel. No one is going to please all the people, and who would want to? (*Morag*, actually, but now sees this as a comic-opera desire.) The thicker skin is beginning to grow. She begins to believe the good and the bad reviews about equally.

"A revealing study of the independence complex and its final resolution."

"Yet another updating of *The Tempest*. Boring and contrived."

"The character of Mira shows an interesting development from a child-like state to that of a limited independence and the eventual possibility of spiritual maturity."

"Miss Gunn hitches her tiny wagon to too large a star."

"Sparse, tense writing, effective at nearly every point."

"Grossly over-written."

"The character of H.E. is a perceptive study of authoritarianism, while at the same time retaining his individuality as a human being."

"H.E. (a too-obvious play on 'He') is cardboard through and through."

Memorybank Movie: Princess Eureka
Snapshot: Pique, age four, poses with Fan and Tiny. She looks a little anxious and also proud of herself, her hand gingerly placed

on the python's tail. Fan, looking frail and tired, grimaces humorously for the camera as she holds the snake's head.

*

Tiny's first and last picture. That evening, about the time when Fan is due to take off for the club, Morag hears a scream from downstairs.

"Mum, what is it?" Pique is terrified.

"It's okay, honey. I don't know. You wait here, eh?"

Morag dashes downstairs. No sign of Fan. The screams go on. The basement.

"Fan, what *is* it?"

Fan looks up. She is kneeling beside the snake's cage. She stops screaming and begins to cry, noisily, hiccupping and snuffling. She looks ridiculous, except that it isn't funny.

"He's dead, Morag."

"*What?*"

"Go on up and phone Marilyn at the club, will you? Tell her I'm sick. No – may as well tell her the truth. Say I won't be in tonight, and say why."

Morag does so, and then returns to the basement, pausing only to yell up the stairs to reassure Pique, who is now wailing.

Fan is holding the lifeless reptilian coils on her arms. A live python is bad enough, but the sight of Fan cradling the now-defunct Tiny is enough to make Morag's stomach turn over.

"I thought he was poorly, just lately," Fan says, "and I know I should of taken him to the vet, but that goddamn vet is so *mean*, Morag – always saying snakes aren't his cuppa tea and that. Won't hardly *look* at Tiny. So I never went. And now see what's happened. It's all my fault."

"Fan – it is *not* all your fault. You've had Tiny for more

than four years, and heaven only knows how old he was when you bought him."

"I've had my innings with him," Fan admits, calming somewhat.

Then she puts the limp body back in the cage and looks up, fear in her eyes.

"It was a gimmick, Morag. To stave off what was coming up even then – me getting too old for the dance bit. What'll I do now?"

What indeed? With her hard-masked makeup now runnelled with tears, Fan's face looks like cracked glass. The burning auburn coiffure has come unstuck, and the curls are in messy disarray. Fan's thin hands are shaking, and she looks old. Is it a crime to look old? In Fan's business, yes.

"First thing, come upstairs and I'll fix you a drink, Fan. We'll think later."

Fan permits herself to be led up into the kitchen. Morag shoves a strong rye and water into her hands and then goes upstairs to tell Pique the bad news.

Pique sobs.

Morag has the feeling that everything is both ludicrous and frightening. Pique is finally prevailed upon to be brave, and Morag goes back to Fan's kitchen. Fan has finished the drink and is pouring another. She is now dry-eyed, calm to a chilling degree.

"Well, that's me finished," she says.

"Fan, that's crazy," Morag says, without conviction. "There must be something else –"

"Like, for example, what?"

Morag does not know.

"Well, look, you can't do anything until you go back tomorrow and see what's what."

"I can hardly wait," Fan says.

An hour later, both fairly drunk, they bury the snake in the garden.

"I feel like a murderer concealing the victim," Morag says.

"If I sell this house and somebody digs up *this* when they're planting potatoes, it'll sure give them a turn," Fan says with a small burst of unbalanced laughter.

Next day, Pique and Morag make a headstone, as Pique thinks this would be a suitable thing to do.

Fan dances no more. Neither, fortunately, does she find herself out of work. She tries to talk her way into a cigarette-girl job, but without success. She finally goes to work in the coat-check room, demotion being preferable to starvation. She no longer brings men home. One day Morag, on the balcony, sees Fan in the back garden, burning the Princess Eureka outfit.

As a result of the advance royalties on *Prospero's Child*, Morag's finances improve to some extent, and she begins paying Fan more rent. Fan protests, but only a little. She no longer pretends never to think of the future, now that she no longer has one.

"Someone for you, Morag," Fan calls up the stairs.

Morag goes down and it is, unbelievably, Brooke.

Her first thought is to wonder if he has read *Prospero's Child*. Her next thought is that Pique is crayoning upstairs in her colouring book, and Morag is uncertain whether it would be right for Brooke to see the child. Would it hurt him? Would it make Morag feel a guilt she does not truthfully feel?

"Brooke! Why? And how did you know where I was?"

"From your publishers. How are you, Morag?"

"I'm – fine."

How are you? I am fine. Like a letter a child might write

home. Brooke looks the same. No older, except for some few lines on his forehead and around his eyes. As handsome, as impressive as ever.

"We just happened to be in Vancouver," Brooke says, "so I thought I'd look you up and see how things were with you."

"We?"

"My wife and I," Brooke says carefully. "She's out in the car. May we come in for a minute? We can't stay long."

"Certainly. Of course."

Brooke's wife is younger than Morag, although probably not much so. Her name is Anne, and she is slender and extremely well turned out. Subdued but very smart crimson wool dress, high-heeled shoes, fair hair in a smooth bouffant hairdo, small gold earrings. Morag suddenly realizes that she herself is wearing black slacks which need dry-cleaning, and a white turtleneck sweater which sags all over, having stretched at the last washing. Her hair straight, halfway down her back. Circus freak.

Both Brooke and Anne sit rather uneasily on the edges of their chairs. Now, of course, Morag wants Brooke to see Pique.

"This is my daughter. Pique, this is – an old friend of mine, Brooke Skelton. And – Mrs. Skelton."

Pique says a desultory *Hi* and returns to the pink house with purple chimney which she is creating.

"Do you like it here, Morag? You're getting along all right?"

Brooke is, she sees, genuinely concerned, whatever other motives he may have had.

"Fine," she says quickly. "Fan's not really a landlady. More a friend. She's in kind of bad shape right now. Her snake's just died."

Good heavens – why babble on about that?

"*Snake?*" Anne says.

Morag explains. Brooke smiles, but somewhat forcedly. They stay barely fifteen minutes and refuse a drink. Brooke does not say whether or not he has read the novel. They depart, as politely and mysteriously as they have arrived.

Why? To see if I really was all right? Or only to allow me to see his wife? I could have asked them into Fan's livingroom. I didn't have to take them upstairs. But I had to show off Pique.

They have had to hurt one another, evidently, this one last time.

Brooke, forgive me. May we forgive one another for what neither of us could help.

Memorybank Movie: Songs

Snapshot: After this year, the album will not be so meticulously tended. But now the colour prints are still pasted in, and the place and Pique's age written in white ink on the black page. *Pique, 5. Begonia Road.* Pique is a round-faced sturdy child, her pink apron-dress somewhat incongruously frilled at the shoulders. Pique, like Morag, is scarcely the frilly type, but at this stage she favours frills and Morag is afraid of inflicting psychic damage by discouraging this trait, out of which she will no doubt grow. Morag (age thirty-four, but this is not written down in white ink) sits beside Pique on the front steps, wearing a green summer dress. They are both smiling hesitantly at the person behind the camera, who has just refused to have his own picture taken.

Morag hears the doorbell, and goes out into the upstairs hall to listen.

"Does Morag Gunn still live here?" the man enquires.

"What's it to you?" Fan is growing more suspicious,

paranoid almost, and now opens the front door on the chain, initially, to see.

The man's soft husky voice changes, rasps.

"Listen, lady, I asked you a simple question, there. Is it yes or no?"

"Oh," Fan says suddenly. "You must be —"

"Yeh," Jules says. "I am."

Morag runs down the stairs, and then stops, all at once uncertain. He is standing in the front hall. Fan, eyes watchful, stands in the doorway of her livingroom. All three are held for an instant in suspended animation, waiting.

Jules has aged in five (no, nearly six) years. He must be thirty-seven now. His hair is as black as ever, a little longer than before, and he wears it combed back, like a mane. His body doesn't look any different — still only the beginning of a belly above the wide lowslung leather belt. He wears jeans and a brown shirt open at the neck, the sleeves rolled up. It is his face which looks now more like the face of Lazarus, the narrowed eyes seeming more sunken than before, the bones more obvious, the lines in the skin etched deeper.

What is he thinking of her, of how she looks?

"Aren't you even going to say hello?" he says.

Morag goes to him then, but still with uncertainty, not doing what she wants to do, which is to hold him tightly. What if he does not want her to hold him? When she touches him, however, and catches the warm dust and salt sweat smell of his skin, she forgets to wonder what he is thinking of her. They hold one another with strength, not kissing, just holding together, but Morag can feel his sex stiffening inside his jeans, and her own sex responding.

"I take it," Fan says, disappearing into her livingroom, "that you *do* know this guy, then."

Unclinch, and they both laugh.

"She's upstairs?" Jules asks.

"Pique? Yes."

"That's what you call her?"

"Yes. Skinner, I couldn't call her, every day, by the –"

"Okay, okay," he says quickly. "You don't need to go into it. What'd you say of me, to her?"

What indeed? Many things, beginning when Pique first learned language.

"Oh hell," Morag says, "it'll probably sound like shit to you. I told her you had to be away because you had to sing songs for lots of people – a person has to put things kind of simply for a little kid – and maybe someday you'd sing them for her. I guess I've told her a few lies, like saying you'd written and asked after her. Maybe I'd have done better just to say it was my idea to have her born, mine only –"

Jules reaches out and takes her right wrist in his hand.

"Sure, Morag," he says. "She's yours, all right. But she's mine too, eh?"

They're mine, them, there. Lazarus at the fire. Lazarus, snarling his pain, a stranger in the place where he lived his whole life. Lazarus, dead at fifty-one. Will Morag tell Pique all she knows of Lazarus, or of Christie, for that matter? How will the tales change in the telling?

"Yes. She's yours, too. Come on up."

Pique, Morag now sees, is stationed quietly in the upstairs hall, listening, peering through the stair railing. Pique's eyes are very wide and serious, and it is impossible to tell what she is thinking. She looks straight at Jules.

"I know who you are," she says.

"Sure," Jules says, looking at her carefully, but not approaching too closely. "Of course. Hi."

He walks in and sits down at the table.

"God, I'm beat. Got a drink, Morag?"

"A little rye. Some beer."

"Let's try the rye first, eh?"

He is not ignoring Pique, but neither is he forcing her to recognize him, or to talk.

"I got a picture of you," he says finally to Pique.

"Of me? How come? Where is it? Can I see it?"

"Sure. It's right here."

He pulls out his wallet and shows her the snapshot of herself, aged two months.

"Hey, I know that one," Pique says. "It's in our book."

"It's got your name on it," Jules says, grinning.

He turns it over. On the back he has written *Piquette Gunn Tonnerre*. In that order.

"Are you really – you know?" Pique asks.

"Yeh. Want me to say it for you? Your dad. Yeh, I am."

Pique is silent for a while, but remains beside him.

"How long will you be in Vancouver?" Morag asks.

"Hard to say. Coupla months, maybe."

"Want to stay here?"

"Sure." Then he laughs. "You got room for me?"

"Yes. I've got room for you."

Pique says very little more that evening. This new presence is obviously going to take some getting used to. And what, then, when he goes away, as he will? Time enough to think of that then. When Pique goes to bed, she says goodnight to Jules, but from a distance. She does not call him by any name.

"Why're you here, Jules?" Morag asks.

Jules opens another beer. He does not look at her.

"My sister Val. She's sick."

"I never knew she was living here. What's the matter with her?"

"She's – how the hell should I know what's the matter with her? She's just sick."

"Is she in hospital?"

"Not yet. I'm trying to get her to go."

"Why won't she?"

"Because she's a crazy woman, is why. She don't want no charity, that's what she says. Charity, my asshole. She's crazy. Let's talk about something else, eh?"

"Is there – I mean, could I help in any way?"

Jules puts his hand under her chin and looks at her, only his mouth smiling, his eyes hard.

"No, lady, you could not help in any way."

"You never let me forget it, do you?"

"No. I never let you forget it."

"Where's the rest of your family, now?"

"Jacques moved up to Galloping Mountain awhile back. He's some guy. He's not like me. Nor like Lazarus, neither."

"There were two younger boys."

"Yeh. My youngest brother, Paul, he was drowned. He was working up north as a guide. His canoe overturned at some rapids. At least, that was the story. He just disappeared. Body never found. The tourists, coupla American guys, they got back all right after a few days in the bush, and reported it to the Mounties. Jacques tried to get an enquiry, but he never got to first base with it. They took the tourists' word for it. Paul was the best hand with a carroe I ever saw. They said he'd been out alone in it one evening. We won't ever know."

"What – what do *you* think happened?"

"I don't know," Jules says slowly. "But I'm pretty damn

sure it wasn't what they said happened. So there's only me and Jacques, now. Not many, eh?"

"And Valentine."

"Oh yeh. Her. Sure. For the time being."

"She's really that sick, then?"

"No. Not yet. Let's just say she's not gonna find out how it feels to be an old woman. You know something, Morag? After I wasn't killed there, at Dieppe, I had this crazy idea, see? I thought nothing could kill me. I could do any damn thing, and nothing could kill me. I didn't think I'd live forever, or like that. Just – nothing could kill me before my time."

"It's a nice thought. Maybe it's even true."

"It's a nice thought. But no, it isn't true. I'm not even sure it's that nice a thought. Anyway, about Jacques. He's got a small farm – the land's no hell, but he seems to like it up there. It wouldn't suit me, but it suits him. Maybe he's right. Maybe it's not too late for him and his. He doesn't waste his time in brawls, like Lazarus used to, and I've had my share of that, too, I guess. He never went berserk when Paul got drowned, or whatever happened to him. I never did, neither, although I guess I did, some. Val went nuts. She was the one who looked after Paul the most, when he was a little kid."

"When did it happen, Jules?"

"Two months ago. Know how old Paul was? He was twenty-five."

What to say? There is nothing that can be said. Is this one reason Jules has wanted to see Pique? Morag cannot touch him right now, or say anything that might reach him.

"What do you hear from Christie, Morag?" he asks finally.

"He's – he's seventy now. He still lives in the old house."

"You oughta go back," Jules says offhandedly. "You oughta go back and housekeep for him, there. It's a hell of a town, but this city's no place for the kid, once she's older. It's a killer, and I mean it."

Morag's anger is directed against – whom?

"Listen, Jules, just don't tell me what to do, eh? It's the one thing I can't stand. I can't go back. I cannot go back."

Jules takes her hand.

"Yeh, I guess you can't. Okay. C'mon, Morag. We've finished the beer. Let's go to bed."

We've finished the beer, so we may as well go to bed, seeing as there's nothing better to do – is that what he means? But when they are in bed, his sex rises quickly and the tiredness falls away from him. They make love urgently, both equal to each other's body in this urgent meeting and grappling, this brief death of consciousness, this conscious defiance of death. Only at the final moment does Morag cry out, and he stops her cry with his mouth. They are left drenched with sweat in the summer night, their bodies slippery as spawning fish together.

"Let's sleep now," Jules says, "and after a while we'll wake up and fuck some more, eh?"

In an hour or so, Morag wakens, and puts her head between his legs, sweeping her hair across his thighs. She takes his limp cock very gently in her mouth and caresses it with her tongue, and it lengthens and grows hard before he is even awake. Then he wakens and says *deeper*. After a while, she disentangles and he raises her until she is looking into his face in the grey-light of the room.

"Ride my stallion, Morag."

So she mounts him. He holds her shoulders and her long hair, penetrating up into her until she knows he has reached whatever core of being she has. This time it is he who cries out. Afterwards, they do not speak, but they go to sleep this time in each other's arms and remain so until the morning comes.

Jules goes out most days and stays away until dinnertime. Morag does not ask him where he has been, and he does not say. He tells her one day that Val is in hospital. Two weeks later, he says Val has left hospital. Cured? Discharged herself without cure? He doesn't say. Perhaps he would even in some ways like to talk to Morag about it, if he felt there was a way he could do so without betraying Val, but he clearly does not. Occasionally he comes back shambling drunk, but always very late at night when Pique is asleep, and the next day he sleeps late and is irritable. Usually, however, when the depressions hit him, he merely retreats into silence. Sometimes he sits for an entire evening with Morag, after Pique has gone to bed, and does not speak at all. Sometimes he turns to her in his half-sleep, and holds onto her, shaking in every nerve. But the next morning he does not remember.

He is not morose with Pique, nor does he ever get angry at her, even though (once she grows accustomed to him, which takes a surprisingly short time, at least on the surface) she often pesters him with questions or with her witty converse, hoping to impress him. He permits himself to be impressed, then makes fun of her, but gently, so that she laughs.

"So you're not gonna call me Dad, eh?" he says to her one evening.

"Do you want me to?" she asks.

"Naw – I don't give a shit, really."

"Then I won't."

"What if I'm kidding you, there? What if I want you to?"

"Then I will."

"Okay, so I do, then."

"Okay, I will, then. I guess."

But the word does not come easily to her. After a while she finds she can actually speak it, and then it is easy. So easy and needed that she peppers her talk with it.

"We've got a film in our camera, Dad. Hey, Dad, can you take a picture of me, Dad?"

So he does. A picture of Morag and Pique. He will not let Morag take his picture, not even with Pique.

"Skinner – why not?"

Jules hands the camera back to her, and hitches his belt up around his hips. He tosses back the mane of hair from his forehead and eyes, and laughs a little, warning her.

"Search me. Maybe I'm superstitious. Or maybe it's the same as I can't make up songs about myself. Maybe I don't want to see what I look like. I'm going on okay this way. Let's not get fancy about it."

That evening, Jules gets out his guitar.

"Are you still working with Billy Joe?" Morag asks.

"Yeh. We had a country and western group going for a while, there, but then we split up. So it's just me and Billy again, now. We travel some. More coffee-houses than used to be, but a lotta kids coming up now, singing, too, which is great for them but a bit more difficult for guys like me and Billy Joe. Anyhow, this is the one I did for Old Jules, my grandad. You remember, I told you once?"

"I remember."

Pique sits quietly beside Morag, not asking any questions, waiting. And Skinner sings.

The Métis they met from the whole prairie
To keep their lands, to keep them free,
They gathered there in the valley Qu'Appelle
Alongside their leader, Louis Riel.

They took their rifles into their hands
They fought to keep their fathers' lands,
And one of them who gathered there
Was a Métis boy called Jules Tonnerre.

He is not more than eighteen years;
He will not listen to his fears.
His heart is true, his heart is strong;
He knows the land where his people belong.

Macdonald, he sits in Ottawa,
Drinking down his whiskey raw,
Sends out west ten thousand men,
Swears the Métis will not rise again.

The young *Anglais* from Ontario,
Out to the west they swiftly go;
They don't know what they're fighting for,
But they've got the cannon, so it must be war.

It was near Batoche, in Saskatchewan,
The Métis bullets were nearly gone;
"If I was a wolf, I'd seek my lair,
But a man must try," said Jules Tonnerre.

Riel, he walks with the Cross held high,
To bless his men so they may not die;

"God bless Riel," says Jules Tonnerre,
"But the cannon *Anglais* won't listen to prayer."

Dumont, he rides out to ambush the foe,
To hunt as he's hunted the buffalo;
He's the bravest heart on the whole prairie,
But he cannot save his hunted Métis.

Jules Tonnerre and his brothers, then,
They fought like animals, fought like men.
"Before the earth will take our bones,
We'll load our muskets with nails and stones."

They loaded their muskets with nails and stones,
They fought together and they fought alone;
And Jules, he fell with steel in his thigh,
And he prayed his God that he might not die.

He woke and found no soul around,
The deadmen hanging onto the ground;
The birds sang in the prairie air.
"Now, it's over, then," said Jules Tonnerre.

Riel, he was hanged in Regina one day;
Dumont, he crossed the U.S.A.
"Of sorrow's bread I've eaten my share,
But I won't choke yet," said Jules Tonnerre.

He took his Cross and he took his gun,
Went back to the place where he'd begun.
He lived on drink and he lived on prayer,
But the heart was gone from Jules Tonnerre.

Still, he lived his years and he raised his son,
Shouldered his life till it was done;
His voice is one the wind will tell
In the prairie valley that's called Qu'Appelle.

They say the dead don't always die;
They say the truth outlives the lie –
The night wind calls their voices there,
The Métis men, like Jules Tonnerre.

They are silent for a while. Morag wonders whether he has not, after all, sung it for her as much as for Pique. Pique likes the tune, and the strong simple rhythm, but otherwise it is lost on her. It is not lost on Morag. The echoes, and all the things he could never bring himself to say in ordinary speech, have found their way into the song.

"Hey, you're crying, kind of," Pique says, looking at Morag in curiosity and perhaps embarrassment. "Didn't you like that song? I did."

"I liked it fine," Morag says.

She glances at Jules, who is re-tuning his guitar.

"Yeh. Well. It's good you like it," he says. "It's too long for a lotta people, and they can't listen right through. The older ones, that is. Older, hell – about my age. Or they don't wanna know about it, and start yellin' why don't I sing 'Yellow Rose of Texas' or like that. Jesus."

He turns to Pique.

"Hey, that song's about your great-grandad. How about that?"

But the concept of great-grandfather is too distant for her, even when he explains. She looks bewildered. But wants to please him.

"Sing it again," she says.

"No, I'll sing you some others now. I'll sing you that one again someday."

Someday. He doesn't mean tomorrow or next week. When will someday be? Maybe never. For now, he sings some of the songs he made up for Billy Joe's kids, songs with some quality of laughter in them, some of them based on Ojibway tales and some of them speaking of the kids for whom he wrote them, naming names. Joking. Pique is excited by these songs.

"I want a song for me, Dad. Hey, would you?"

"Maybe someday," Jules says. "Or maybe you'll make up a song for me. How about that, eh?"

"I don't know how," Pique says defensively, sulkily.

"Hell, neither do I," Jules says, "but I do it all the same."

After this, he sings for them often. He says he is working on a song about Lazarus, but he does not sing that one.

"Well, I gotta move," Jules says, one evening. "It's time."

He says this to Morag, not to Pique. He does not say goodbye to Pique. The last night he is there, he and Morag lie together, their arms lightly around one another, their hands sometimes stroking the other's skin, but not speaking and not making love. Morag does not think she will sleep, but she does. In the morning, when she wakens, he is not there. He has stayed two months.

Pique says nothing when Morag tells her that Jules has gone. She does not question why he came here nor why he went away. What may come of this, later on, Morag cannot know.

"I have lost my job," Fan says. "I have been given the axe."

"Oh God, Fan. What're you going to do?"

"I will go back to the Okanagan," Fan says, steadily, her face broken. "My sister's still got the place there, sweetheart.

I will go back and I will cook the jesus meals or feed the chickens or whatever else they ask me to do. And I'll live there until I die, which may not be that long, but probably will be. Fan Brady at age seventy-five or eighty – how does that grab you? Well, I can do it if I put my mind to it. I grew up there."

"Fan –"

"Oh hell, Morag –"

They hold onto one another for a second.

"What'll you do, Morag?"

"I'll go to England. And Scotland, sometime."

"England? Scotland? Why?"

"I've known for a long time I had to go there, Fan. I can't explain it, exactly. I guess I've been waiting for the right moment."

"Hey, did you want to go *before*, Morag? I mean, you haven't stayed here on account of me?"

"Hell, no, Fan. I just needed something like this to get me up off my ass."

"You sure?"

"Sure."

Is this true? It's true in the only way that matters, probably. Fan accepts it.

"We'll keep in touch, eh? We will keep in touch, Morag?"

"Of course."

They both know they won't. But will never forget, either.

NINE

The screen door slammed, and Pique stood there, wearing the usual old shirt and her jeans with Jules' brass-buckled belt. Looking great. How could any woman's belly be that flat and breasts upstanding and unsagging? Morag's once were.

"Hi, Ma. You working?"

Morag was sitting at the oak table, momentarily staring out at the river, the willows and maples on the opposite bank stirring faintly in the merciful breeze, the August heat parching the grass but turning human flesh sweat-dank.

"I'm not sure," Morag said, untruthfully, because she had been.

This had been the pattern of life for how long? Morag at this table, working, and people arriving and saying, in effect, *Please don't let me interrupt you.* But they *did* interrupt her, damn it. The only thing that could be said for it was that if no one ever entered that door, the situation would be infinitely worse.

Pique drew up a chair and peered at Morag's notebook.

"Well, you seem to be putting down words, anyway."

"Yes."

"You sound discouraged," Pique said.

This was a question between Morag and the work. She didn't want to talk about it.

"Oh, kind of, I guess. I don't know if I'll want it published when it's finished. You look different, Pique. It's your hair. Why braids?"

Pique drew one of the long black elastic-held braids over her shoulder and stroked it lightly.

"Cooler. Keeps it away from my face in this weather. Also, I'm part-Indian – it's suitable, isn't it?"

"I don't think I'm hearing you very accurately. What're you trying to say?"

"I don't know," Pique said. "I don't want to be split. I want to be together. But I'm not. I don't know where I belong."

"Does it have to be either/or?"

Pique's eyes became angry.

"I don't guess you would know how it feels. Yes, maybe it does have to be either/or. But I was brought up by you. I never got much of the other side."

Once again, the reproach. Not to Jules; to Morag. When Pique wielded that particular knife, it always found its mark, as she very well knew.

"I told you what I could."

"Sure," Pique said. "But it wasn't much, was it? I never knew what really happened. There was only that one time, when my dad was here – when I was fifteen, eh? And he said a lot of things. And the songs – I've got those. And he said some more, when I saw him in Toronto, this time. But some of those stories you used to tell me when I was a kid – I never knew if they happened like that or not."

"Some did and some didn't, I guess. It doesn't matter a damn. Don't you see?"

"No," Pique said, "I don't see. I want to know what really happened."

Morag laughed. Unkindly, perhaps.

"You do, eh? Well, so do I. But there's no one version. There just isn't."

"Maybe not," Pique said, dispiritedly. "I'm sorry, Ma, going on like this. It's part of things which are worrying me."

"Such as?"

"Dan and A-Okay are going to raise horses. Dan knows about horses – he was raised on a ranch in Alberta. They bred palominos – worth a lot. A-Okay knows nothing about it. But you know him. He's so serious. He'll learn. They're gonna put the land to feed crops. A-Okay will pay for the first coupla nags from the bread he makes out of those articles. Dan's got a few hundred bucks put by, as well. Dan says he can give riding lessons. He learned to ride western as a young kid, but then his dad got these classy ideas and had him taught English style – wanted Dan to be a gent, what a laugh. When they've got all this beautiful bloodstock or whatever you call it, they'll sell selected ones."

"You don't sound exactly ecstatic," Morag said.

"I'm not," Pique said. "Where am I in this whole deal? Listen, Dan and I – we've got on pretty well at A-Okay's and Maudie's place. But Maudie and I, you know, we're kind of different people, and sometimes her – well, I feel awful saying it – her real *goodness* and gentleness, sometimes they bug me. That *is* awful, isn't it?"

"Not so very," Morag said. "It bugs me sometimes, too. She's too good to be true. Like Catharine Parr Traill. But she *isn't*, really, Pique. I mean, it's partly whistling in the dark."

"Oh sure. I know. Well, we do get on, generally, despite her earth-mother bit. But when she says she feels her vegetables out in the garden calling to her so she has to go out and chat them up a little – well, sure it's funny, Ma, but sometimes I feel like saying *Oh come on, Maudie, don't give me that bullshit*. Anyway, this whole deal. Dan's quitting his job in McConnell's Landing, right? A-Okay is bringing in some bread but not enough. Maudie obviously can't. She's got Tom, and she's doing all the cooking and looking after her vegetables and chickens and that. But we need a little something coming in, obviously. So guess who's appointed? And working as a cashier in a supermarket doesn't really grab me that much."

"Have you told Dan?"

"Sure. He says it won't last all that long, and when the horses are bringing in some cash, I can help on the farm. Well, that's okay, if it was outside work. I mean, with Maudie, who could really help with the meals? And would I want to, anyway? I'm not much on cooking. But I'm not sure I want to stay here. Only, Dan doesn't want to move."

"Where do you want to go, Pique?"

"West, I guess. Maybe not this minute. But soon. I guess, like, I have to."

"Wouldn't Dan go as well, for a while?"

"I can't ask him to, unless he really wants to. And he doesn't. He doesn't ever want to go west again, he says. He says he's had it up to here. Trouble is, I really care about him."

"I know."

Silence.

"I gotta get back," Pique said, finally. "Sunday, day of rest, what a laugh, eh?"

"It'll be all right, Pique. It'll work out."

"Yeh. Probably."

Dan came over late that afternoon, by himself, docking the boat a little clumsily, still not totally accustomed to boats, banging it broadside against Morag's dock instead of nosing it in gently as Pique did.

"Can I come in, Morag?"

"Certainly. Of course."

How to write a novel without hardly trying. Morag folded up her notebook, cursing silently:

Lord, I am concerned about them all. But my God, when am I going to get any work done? And yet if they didn't want to talk, I'd be sorry.

Dan Scranton stood awkwardly in the doorway, and finally sat down and accepted a cup of coffee. The ritual – come in, have a cup of coffee. He did not speak for several minutes, but when he did, he came right to the point.

"I get this feeling you don't like me that much, Morag."

Oh jesus. They were so easily offended, so analytical despite their proclaimed lack of faith in words. What was it this time?

"Sure, I like you," Morag said, genuinely surprised. "What would give you the idea I didn't?"

"You hardly ever call me by my name," Dan said contemplatively.

"That hasn't anything to do with you," Morag said reluctantly. "I once knew a man whose name was Dan – I still know him, for that matter, but he lives in another country, and anyway –"

The reaction was instantaneous.

"It's okay," Dan Scranton said quickly, as though picking up the needed message right away but not wanting to know more than the basic relevance to himself. "You don't have to say any more. I'm sorry, Morag."

"I'll try to call you by your name."

"It doesn't matter," Dan said, "now that I know. I'm probably too anxious to have people like me, so then I imagine they don't."

"Pique told me about the horse idea."

"Yeh," Dan said. "And there is a good chance it may work. Only thing, why would Pique want to take off again, just now? I mean, at this point. Or at all."

"Don't ask me. To look for her family, I suppose."

"Has she got any? Back there?"

"Only one uncle, as far as I know," Morag said. "But of course a lot of cousins by now, I expect. Anyway, I'm not sure it's that – I mean, those specific individuals."

"I sort of know," Dan said, "and yet I don't. I won't try to persuade her not to go. If she has to, well, that's that. But I can't go. Not yet, anyway. Maybe never. Maybe I'm afraid to go back, even if it's not to the exact same place. I really hated the prairies when I lit out."

"I know. So did I. I felt that way about the town where I grew up. Then I found the whole town was inside my head, for as long as I live."

"That's terrible," Dan said.

"No. No, it isn't terrible at all."

"For me, it would be. I can't stand the thought. The land, yes – my God, who could help caring about land like that? It's the people I can't stand, some of them, anyway. One in particular, I guess. When I was a kid, you know, I thought my dad was a real hero – I guess it would've been better if I'd never got along with him. But I did. I thought he was great. And maybe in some ways he even *is* great. He comes on very strong. Most people admire him. He still runs the place. He's a very wealthy guy now, although once he wasn't. He belongs to all the right clubs. He even took up golf. He's got this movie image of himself – gentleman-cowboy. Jesus. That's what he wanted me to be, only more so. Just before I lit out, I used to get so I thought either I'd start to yell, really berserk, you know, or else hit him. I guess it might've been better if I had. Hit him, that is."

Dan bent forward, his face hidden, the palms of his hands outstretched onto the table, suddenly clenched into himself.

"You know, Morag," he said, "the trouble isn't that I don't care about them. The trouble is that I *do*. They don't know. They think I don't give a shit about anything. They think I'm some kind of traitor – to them, to everything. But I'm not going back to take over the place from him, not even when he's dead. I don't want his kind of place. Not in any way."

"Yet you're planning to raise horses," Morag ventured.

Morag Gunn, fleeing Manawaka, finally settling near McConnell's Landing, an equally small town with many of the same characteristics.

"That's different," Dan said defensively. "I have to make my own kind of place. I'm not talking about the difference in outside scenery, either."

"I know. Your own place will be different, but it'll be the same, too, in some ways."

"Not if I can help it," Dan said angrily.

"I'm not sure you *can* help it. You can change a whole lot. But you can't throw him away entirely. He and a lot of others are there. Here."

Morag reached out and touched the vein on Dan's wrist.

"Oh jesus," Dan said, anguished, "maybe it's true. I can't take this."

Tactful Morag. What a thing to say. Maybe even untrue. No, not untrue. The remark wouldn't matter in the long run, though, because he wouldn't believe her. Not yet.

"Forget it, Dan. It was a stupid thing for me to say."

"When I met Pique, I thought *This is it. I'm home.* And now – well, I know she's got to go away, Morag. But I've got to stay. I wanted you to know."

"Thanks, Dan. It'll be all right. At least, I hope so."

"Yeh. Well. Maybe."

Across the river, in A-Okay and Maudie's house, was Pique Tonnerre Gunn, or Pique Gunn Tonnerre, who must walk her own roads, wherever those might be. And nothing seemed to be getting much simpler as time went by.

That evening, Morag went out with Royland in his boat, taking the outboard so that he could fish. The river was a thousand percent cooler than the land. The sweat which had been running down Morag's forehead all day, steaming up her glasses, began to evaporate. She might just possibly survive the heat of summer after all. Then, after the marvels and cool warmth of autumn, the battle to survive the godawful winter would begin. What a country, and how strange she cared about it so much.

The willows bowed down on either side of the river, low and globe-shaped trees, their flickering silvergreen leaves now beginning to turn yellow. Behind them, the gigantic maples, an occasional massive oak and the dying elms. They passed areas of cleared land, where the fields came down nearly to the river. The massed clumps of goldenrod proclaimed the fields' extent and ending, the wildflowers as always encroaching, taking over wherever the fields gave an inch. The hay had long since been taken in, and the winter wheat was harvested. The spring crops were ripening now.

"I meant to swim today," Morag said, above the idling motor, "but of course I didn't. I hardly ever do."

"Lotta weed this year," Royland said, having just disentangled his line from a clump of it.

"Yeh. I go out every morning and think – swimming is the best exercise there is, and what is the point in living on a river if you don't swim? Then I see all that benighted weed and I change my mind. If I do go swimming and run into a patch of it, I flail around in a panic, thinking it must be a river-monster, probably prehistoric, which has been hibernating down there in the mud for ten million years and has just wakened. Or Grendel, as in Beowulf, and me without courage or a sword."

Royland laughed.

"Well, you shouldn't swim alone, anyhow."

"I used to be a fair swimmer, believe it or not. A miracle, considering I learned to swim in the Wachakwa River. There were bloodsuckers. You had to make them let go by applying lighted cigarettes."

Morag, terrified of cities, coming out here, making this her place, her island, and still not going swimming because of the monsterweed. But at least she could somehow cope. City friends often asked her if she was not afraid to stay in the house alone, away out here. No, she wasn't. She was not lonely and not afraid, when alone here. She did not think that the loghouse was about to be descended upon by deranged marauders. In New York, Morag's agent and his wife had three locks upon their door.

Maybe I should've brought Pique up entirely in cities, where she'd have known how bad things are all over, where she'd have learned young about survival, about the survival tactics in a world now largely dedicated to Death, Slavery and the Pursuit of Unhappiness. Instead, I've made an island. Are islands real? A-Okay and Maudie, and now Dan, are doing the same. But if they do raise horses, they'll have to sell them to the very people they despise. And, Morag Gunn, who rails against the continuing lies

of the media, does not, it will be noticed, establish her own hand-
set press. Islands are unreal. No place is far enough away. Islands
exist only in the head. And yet I stay. All this, the river and the
willows and the gronk-gronk-gronk of the mini-dinosaur bull-
frogs, it may be a fantasy. But I can bear to live here, until I die,
and I couldn't elsewhere.

"Turn the motor off, quick," Royland said suddenly.

At first, Morag thought he had caught his line in some
weed. Then she saw the huge bird. It stood close to shore, its tall
legs looking fragile although in fact they were very strong, its
long neck and long sharp beak bent towards the water, searching for fish, its feathers a darkbright blue. A Great Blue Heron.
Once populous in this part of the country. Now rarely seen.

Then it spotted the boat, and took to flight. A slow
unhurried takeoff, the vast wings spreading, the slender elon-
gated legs gracefully folding up under the creature's body. Like
a pterodactyl, like an angel, like something out of the world's
dawn. The soaring and measured certainty of its flight.
Ancient-seeming, unaware of the planet's rocketing changes.
The sweeping serene wings of the thing, unknowing that it
was speeding not only towards individual death but probably
towards the death of its kind. The mastery of the heron's wings
could be heard, a rush of wind, the wind of its wings, before
it mounted high and disappeared into the trees above a bywater
of the river.

Royland reeled in his line, and by an unspoken agreement they took the boat home in silence, in awe.

That evening, Morag began to see that here and now
was not, after all, an island. Her quest for islands had ended
some time ago, and her need to make pilgrimages had led her
back here.

Memorybank Movie: Sceptr'd Isle

Morag firmly crashes the door shut on the garden flat. Garden flat – a joke. When she and Pique first came to England, the advertisement in the *Hampstead & Highgate Express*, saying "Garden flat – Hedgerow Walk," sounded reassuringly rustic. In fact it turned out to mean a basement flat, which Morag rented because it was not too costly and was self-contained. Hedgerow Walk does indeed contain hedges, although hardly the tangle of briar roses and blackberries which Morag's imagination suggested. These are closely clipped green-yellow privet hedges which define each narrow yard. The small front gardens have mostly been covered with crazy-pavement, which, as its name implies, is a demented combination of cement and vari-coloured tiles of an unsurpassed ugliness. But easy to look after. The Victorian redbrick houses are tall and semidetached. Also identical, except for the fact that house-holders have all painted their doors a different colour – lilac vies with lemon yellow and deep rose. The individual spirit proclaims itself in paint.

The Yale lock on the door of Morag's flat clicks protectively. No unlocked doors here. And yet, incredibly, London frightens Morag less than any other city she has ever known. She goes out by herself, to friends' houses, at night, and returns alone on the Underground, with less panic than she would have believed possible. Perhaps she still, even after three years, maintains in her mind the myth that the English are an orderly and law-abiding people.

Morag slithers out onto the rain-greased pavement and slops up the hill to Hampstead High Street. At least, praise God, no fog today. This has been the worst winter in living memory here, or so she has been informed by numerous people. She has come to believe that nearly every winter here is the worst in living memory because the season invariably comes as a surprise, no one taking seriously the notion that winter ever comes to England at all, until each year it does so. Although Pique has walked to school alone for several years, this winter in the thick sulphurous fogs Morag accompanied her and went to pick her up in the late afternoons, terrified that the child would get lost if she were on her own. It was all Morag could do, then, to find her way, snailing along block by block, clinging close to the buildings, examining every street name set into the brick walls, to check her position, feeling as though there were no pavement ahead and one might possibly drop off the edge of the world.

It was during the worst of the fog that the greengrocer said to Morag – *Well, what do you think of this royal throne of kings, this sceptr'd isle, NOW?* Perhaps such a literate greengrocer was an exception, but she had replied *It's fine*, and meant it, because of him.

Pique loved the fog, despite the acrid taste that came through the woollen scarf – a primitive gasmask – around her mouth and nose. Pique always feeds on crises because they are exciting.

Morag plods along the High Street in the weak grey-light of the morning, head down against the drizzling rain. She has not put up her umbrella and never does so except in down-pours, as she prefers to get her coat and headscarf damp rather than crash into other umbrella-bearers who walk blindly like a host of mobile mushrooms. She has come to feel in many ways at home here, although she will never feel she belongs. She has, as well, come to value the anonymity of these streets, the fact that people often don't know their neighbours or care about their goings-on of whatever variety. It is, of course, all very well for her, because she made a few friends fairly quickly in the beginning owing to introductions on the part of her English publishers. A person coming to this city totally unknown to anyone could literally die of loneliness, and no doubt many do. Odd, now, though, to recall that she had come here in the first place partly because of a fantasy – Morag getting to know dozens of other writers, with whom she would have everything in common. In fact only a few of her friends are writers, and she has discovered that publishers' parties in London are no more appealing to her and no less parochial than they were in Canada. Useful to know that, probably. At least when she finally does return, she won't ever again feel that she must be missing out on a lot in these ways. Another thing which enabled her if not to overcome her dread of cities then at least to suppress it was the desire to see places she had read about all her life – the Tower of London, Westminster Abbey, Trafalgar Square. For the first year, she and Pique were intrepid tourists, awed by monuments. Now they live here. How long will they remain? She often wonders this, sometimes feeling that she is held here largely by lethargy – the thought of moving again is too much for her at this point; Pique likes her school; they have established a place of their own, some kind of refuge.

Morag turns off the High Street, goes down a small winding street and arrives at the shop where she works mornings.

AGONISTES BOOKSHOP
J. Sampson, Prop.

This play on words is somewhat diminished in effect, for Morag, by the fact that Mr. Sampson spells his name with a "p." He, however, is pleased with it. Morag once asked him if he didn't think the reference was a little unfortunate or inappropriate. No, he said, because after all here he was in a constant state of dreadful labour and mental anguish over trying to keep the business going. Yes, but what about the fall of the temple? Oh that, Mr. Sampson said – well, wasn't he trying his best against the philistines?

"Morning, Mr. Sampson. Chilly day."

"Morning, Morag. The chill shouldn't bother *you*."

Their ritual exchange, nearly every day in winter. He affects to believe that Morag comes from a land of perpetual snow. Mr. Sampson is a slight, thin, rabbity little man in his mid-sixties, whose face is not strengthened by the small wavering moustache he wears. His appearance is not impressive until you notice that his greenish eyes are very clear, intelligent and watchful. He stocks a surprisingly large range of books, considering the smallness of the shop, but his true love is the English contemporary novel, about which he knows everything. This morning he is unpacking new arrivals, slowly, because he has to glance through each one and also examine the jacket design and blurb for saleability.

"Look at this," he cries. "Whom do Lansbury's employ in their Art department, I ask myself. A blind man? Who is going to buy a book with a dust jacket that's all grey, totally, not a glimmer of light in it? Let's hope it gets a few good reviews, to offset this mess. It wouldn't matter so much if it were by a known writer, but it's a first novel. A shame."

When Morag's collection of short stories, *Presences*, came out last year, Mr. Sampson insisted on filling the window with copies, and only Morag's embarrassment prevented him from forcibly thrusting the book onto everyone who entered the shop. When she decided she hated the title, which sounded like one of those small literary magazines which are forever dying quick deaths, he told her sharply that it was unprofessional to think of such things after the book was out.

"Want me to clear some of the last lot from the front counter?" Morag asks, with a pang for the books published a month ago, now to be relegated to shelves.

"I suppose so," Mr. Sampson says regretfully, knowing her feelings. "We need more room, but where could it come from? If I could throw out all those cookery and flower-arranging books and nonsense like that – but I'd starve. So go ahead – clear, clear. We must be ruthless to survive."

Morag grins. He is far from ruthless, as is well-known to impecunious young people who drop in and read books here chapter by chapter.

The phone rings and Mr. Sampson disappears into his tiny crowded office at the back. He emerges in a moment and beckons to Morag.

"It's for you."

"For me?" She is surprised, because people never phone her at the shop.

"It's the school," Mr. Sampson says nervously.

Morag flies to the phone. What has happened to Pique? She sees on her mindscreen a road accident. The terrible vulnerability of children.

"Mrs. Gunn? Miss White here. Pique –"

"Is she all right? What's happened?"

"Don't be upset, Mrs. Gunn. She'll be all right. She just isn't feeling too well, that's all, and I think you should come and collect her."

"I'll be there in a few minutes."

Morag faces Mr. Sampson apologetically.

"I'm really sorry, but I'm going to have to leave for the day. Maybe longer. It's Pique – she's ill."

"Go ahead, go ahead," he says cluckingly, helping her on with her coat. "The lesser matters must give way to the greater."

Morag walks rapidly along the hilly streets to the school. Pique is waiting in Matron's office, her coat on, her face flushed. She did not feel entirely well this morning before going to school, but Morag, after dithering, had decided she was well enough to go. Morag does not like to stay away from work unless absolutely necessary – how far can Mr. Sampson's good nature be presumed upon, and where would she find another job as convenient as this one? Also, she has wanted to work this afternoon on the novel which is taking shape in her head. Now look what she has done.

"Oh honey, I'm so sorry."

Pique looks dejected.

"I threw up," she says in a small shamed voice. "All over the floor beside my desk. Oh Mum, I feel *awful*. I feel sick, and I feel awful about doing that. I couldn't help it."

"That doesn't matter, honey. Honestly. Come on."

Morag thanks Miss White, who twitters in the background, and they leave. The walk home seems interminable and freezing. The rain continues its slow steady *drip-drip-drip*.

Morag puts Pique to bed and takes her temperature. A hundred and four. Morag by now is frantic with worry, and Pique's skin feels as though it were burning. Morag administers aspirin and phones the doctor. After what seems about seven hours, but is in fact two, he arrives and says that Pique has flu and there is a lot of it about.

"There's always a lot of it about, it seems to me," Morag says idiotically, angrily, as though this were in some way the doctor's fault.

"Well, try not to be upset, Mrs. Gunn," he says sternly. "That won't help the child, will it?"

Oh God. True. True. She wants to ask the doctor, young and brisk, to forgive her, to stay for a while, have a cup of tea, reassure her, tell her Pique isn't very ill and will be fine, and that it isn't Morag's fault for having sent her out unwell into the raw morning. There is, however, no external reassurance available, as she learns each time as though for the first time, whenever Pique is sick. The doctor writes a prescription and leaves, nodding brusquely at Morag's profuse and in some ways hypocritical thanks.

"What've I got, Mum?" Pique calls from the bedroom.

"Flu. You'll be fine in a few days."

"I'll miss the Valentine's party," Pique wails.

Now Morag, perversely, feels annoyed at the child. Fancy worrying about a Valentine's party when your health is in jeopardy. How unreasonable. And what is so reasonable about Morag expecting an eight-year-old to be reasonable?

I fluctuate like a pendulum. The terrible vulnerability of parents, though, your life bound up so centrally with this other one.

"Listen, honey, it'll be all right. We'll have our own Valentine party. And I'll get Miss White to send your valentines home, and I'll send yours for the kids. You just lie quietly for a minute, Pique – I've got to whip out and get the medicine for you. Shall I get you some ginger ale?"

"I don't care," Pique says wearily.

If she doesn't want ginger ale, she must really be sick. Morag hurries up to the High Street pharmacy and back again. When she returns, Pique has vomited again. She has not made it to the bathroom and has not even managed the plastic bucket which Morag placed beside the bed. It is all over the sheets and blankets. There could have been very little to throw up except a glass of water and the aspirins, but it seems like gallons. Pique is crying. Her black hair, spread over the pillow, is wet.

Morag cleans up, gives Pique the tablets, praying she will keep them down, sponges the child's face, and sits beside her. After a few hours, Pique's temperature drops a little. Finally she sleeps, although restlessly, and Morag leaves her.

In the small livingroom, which also serves as Morag's bedroom, Morag sits cross-legged on the couch-bed, listening to Pique's hoarse breathing, and the rain, and the wind in the bare branches of the plane trees. It is at times like this that she feels her aloneness. When Pique is well, and Morag is writing, and there are sometimes people to talk to, then the fact that she is alone is bearable. Even the fact that she lives without a man except for occasional casual encounters which leave her emptier than she was before – even that can be survived, although with spates of rage or self-pity. But in the times of the threat of darkness – when Pique is sick, or when Morag herself is sick and wonders what would happen to Pique if anything fatal happened to herself, or when the money is perilously low and Morag, paralyzed with anxiety, cannot write – it is then that she feels the aloneness to be unbearable. Like now.

If only there were someone to talk it over with. Someone to share the pain, I guess. That wouldn't help Pique much. It would help me, though. Or would it? Look at Angie in Flat Two upstairs. When the baby is sick, she says to Dennis that she's worried out of her mind, and he says she always worries unnecessarily and she's inherited it from her neurotic mother and she had better snap out of it. And maybe she is indeed worrying unnecessarily. As probably I am. But you would just like somebody to say – God, love, I KNOW and I'm worried too.

Outside, on Hedgerow Walk, the high-pitched laughter of guests arriving at some party or other. Upstairs in Flat Two, Dennis turns the record player up full volume, and Angie yells at him to turn it down or he'll waken the baby – if one of them doesn't waken the baby, the other certainly will. If they waken Pique, Morag will go up and strangle them both, or at least sit down here and curse them. She takes off the black and scarlet Madras cotton bedspread (meant to make her bed look in daytime as though it were not a bed) and crawls between the sheets. Then crawls out again to look once more at Pique, who is sleeping but whose skin is unnaturally hot. Nothing more can be done at the moment.

Finally Morag sleeps.

Pique's fever continues, up and down, for four days. Then it drops to normal and stays there, but the doctor says she is not to return to school for another week. Morag, on the phone to Mr. Sampson, is assured that she still has a job, but he is beginning to sound irritable. A little more of this, and Morag will not have a job, probably. And she will not really be able to blame Mr. Sampson, who hires an assistant with the reasonable expectation that she will be at work most of the time.

Hell, I'm lucky. I don't know what difficulty means. At least there are some royalties dribbling in from past books, although not much, and I suppose if I were really broke, I could go to the publishers and ask for a small advance on the next book – no, I couldn't do that, though, because then the book wouldn't get written. But Jeremy Sampson is not a mean-minded guy, and I am not a cog in some vast machine, at the bookshop. Suppose I was a waitress in a chain of cheap restaurants? Devil a bit they'd care if my kid was sick and I had to stay home for two weeks. I am lucky. I know it. It's just that I don't feel so very lucky right now.

Morag buys a bottle of Cyprus sherry and drinks it in an evening. That evening she feels better. In the morning, worse.

Pique, recuperating, is beginning to enjoy poor health, a good sign. The two of them have had an impromptu Valentine's day party, Pique opening the valentines from school with varied comments – *Oh gee, I never sent Carla one – hey, it says G. R.; that must be Georgie Rexroth, that twit* – and so on. Pique is getting up now, late mornings, and flitting about in her house-coat. Morag has done no writing for more than a week, and now that Pique is better, chagrin begins to set in.

"Honey, could you leave me be for about a couple of hours, while I try to do a little work?"

"Sure," Pique says with dignity. "Of course."

The arrangement lasts for fifteen minutes, after which Pique tiptoes into the livingroom, where Morag is sitting staring at the blank page.

"Mum?"

"What?" Spoken churlishly.

"I was just thinking – tonight could you tell me some of those stories again?"

"Which stories?" Not wanting to know.

"Oh, *you* know. The ones Christie used to tell you, and that. And about my dad, and all that."

Why this sudden need? Or is it simply that this week the two of them have been together all the time, and Pique has herself been frightened by her sickness, and now is well, and wants this particular closeness to continue for a while longer?

"Okay, honey. After dinner, eh?"

"Sure. Okay."

But now there is no way that Morag can even try to begin to get inside the novel which is beginning. The novel, whose title is *Jonah*, is the story of an old man, a widower, who is fairly disreputable and who owns a gill-netter in Vancouver. He fishes the mouth of the Fraser River and the Strait of

Georgia when the salmon run is on. It is also about his daughter Coral, who resents his not being a reputable character. Jonah inhabits Morag's head, and talks in his own voice. In some ways she knows more about Coral, who is so uncertainly freed by Jonah's ultimate death, but it is Jonah himself who seems more likely to take on his own life in the fiction.

How to get this novel written, in between or as well as everything else?

"Pique –"

"Yeh?"

"C'mon, let's get the dinner now. I'm not going to do any more work today, I guess. And then we'll do the stories."

Whose need is the greater? Morag's, to tell the story of Jonah, or Pique's, to hear the stories of Christie and of Lazarus and all of them, back there?

MORAG'S TALE OF CHRISTIE LOGAN

Well, a long time ago, when I was a kid, Christie used to tell me all sorts of stories. Christie Logan, he was a strange man, I guess. Not a big man – rather slight, really, but tough as tree-bark and wiry as barbwire and proud as the devil. He used to wear the same old overalls, always, and that embarrassed me and I used to think he stank of garbage, but now I'm not sure he did and I wonder why I thought it mattered, anyway. When he told me the tales about Piper Gunn, at first I used to believe every word. Then later I didn't believe a word of them, and thought he'd made them up out of whole cloth.

(What means *Whole cloth*?)

Out of his head – invented them. But later still, I realized they'd been taken from things that happened, and who's to know what really happened? So I started believing in them again, in a different way. Now, when Christie told a tale, then, his voice would become different from the ordinary. It would be like the ranting of the pipe music, wild and stormy, until you could actually feel the things happening that he was telling you about. He had very blue eyes, Christie did, in those days, and when he was telling a tale, his eyes would be like the blue lightning and you would forget his small stature, for at those times he would seem a giant of a man. And I've told you the tale of Piper Gunn — well, now, when Christie told that first tale, about how Piper led his people onto the ship to take them to the new land, he used to describe Piper, and he'd say that Piper Gunn was a great tall man with a voice like the drums, and the heart of a child, and the gall of a thousand, and the strength of conviction. I always liked that — the strength of conviction, even though at the time I didn't really know what it meant.

(What *does* it mean?)

It means that Piper Gunn believed the people could make a new life for themselves. He had faith. And you know, Pique, how Christie used to describe Piper's wife? He used to say *Now Piper Gunn, he had a woman, and she had the courage of a falcon and the beauty of a deer, and the warmth of a home, and the faith of saints.*

(I like that. Would he tell me those stories, if we went to see him?)

Well, maybe. But he's getting pretty old now. He mightn't remember so well.

(He would still remember those stories. He wouldn't forget. Not Christie.)

MORAG'S TALE OF LAZARUS TONNERRE

Well, your grandfather, Lazarus Tonnerre, he brought up his children in the Wachakwa valley, there, just below the town of Manawaka, where I grew up. And there was your dad, and the two girls, Piquette and Valentine, and the two younger boys, Paul and Jacques. And their mother, Lazarus's wife, she – I'm not sure what happened. Maybe she died, or – well, I don't know.

(Why don't you know?)

I just don't. Maybe someday you'll see your dad again and he can tell you. Anyway, Lazarus used to tell stories, too, to his family when the winter evenings were freezing cold and a blizzard wind would be yowling outside and the snow would be blowing across the door in drifts. Sometimes the kids would be hungry, and Lazarus would tell them these stories, all about *his* father, old Jules Tonnerre, who fought in the battle out west, and he really existed, once, and about Rider Tonnerre, a long long way back, who may have existed and maybe not, but it doesn't matter – and he was said to be the best rider among all the Métis and the best buffalo hunter for miles around, in those old days.

(Why would the kids be *hungry*?)

They were very poor. It was during the Depression – that means a whole lot of people were poor, and couldn't get jobs and didn't have enough to eat.

(Oh.)

Anyhow, Lazarus had a lot of troubles, but his family never starved. Sometimes he used to go trapping away up Galloping Mountain way.

(Galloping Mountain? Is that a real mountain?)

Sure. Away north of Manawaka, where lots of very tall

spruce trees grow, and there's a lake there, and a lot of your father's people live thereabouts.

(I'm going there someday.)

Sure, honey. Anyway, Lazarus sometimes went alone on those trips up to the mountain, and sometimes he'd take your dad. Then they'd come back to the shack in the valley.

(And have lots to eat, eh? And tell stories. I wish I'd been there.)

Yeh. Well, there was more to it than that. Lazarus must've felt pretty low in his mind, sometimes, looking after all those kids, there. But he kept on somehow.

(*What* more to it?)

Well, I never knew him that well myself, but I remember the last time I ever saw him. It was at the time of the fire.

(I don't like that part. Don't tell it again.)

Okay. I won't, then.

(He was brave, though, wasn't he?)

Yes. He was that.

A letter arrives from Christie, saying the winter in Manawaka has been colder than all the shithouses in hell, but he is mostly all right, and how are Morag and Pique. He also asks, joking and not joking, when is Morag going to Sutherland, and isn't she ever going to get to see where her people came from?

When, indeed, is she going to go? The pilgrimage. Does that word dramatize it beyond what it is? Probably not. Why, then, has she for so long hesitated?

She is afraid that she will be disappointed, that there will not, after all, be any relations. She is afraid that she will feel nothing and that nothing will be explained to her. Or else she is afraid that she will feel too much, and that too much will be explained in those rocks and ruined crofts, or whatever is there, now, these days.

In those days, a darkness fell over all the lands and crofts of Sutherland. And among all of them people there on the rocks, see, was a piper and he was from the Clan Gunn, and it was many of the Gunns who lost their hearths and homes and lived wild on the stormy rocks there.

Morag writes back to Christie and says *Soon.*

Mr. Sampson has not been so much irritated as alarmed by Morag's absence, it turns out. He has been unable to keep up with the accounts, and is convinced that penury is imminent. Morag agrees to work afternoons as well as mornings for the next fortnight, although grudgingly. She has done no writing at all during Pique's illness and now will do virtually none for the next couple of weeks. A month away from it, and getting back inside will be torture. She thinks of writers with private means (of which she knows none) and puts a mental hex on them.

Had she not been working afternoons, however, she would not have met McRaith, who paints in the mornings and does his wandering around in the afternoons.

He has been standing at one of the counters with a large book in his hands for going on an hour before Morag approaches. She does not want to interrupt his browsing; she wants to speak to him, simply because his sexuality draws her. Why should this be? He is not particularly handsome. A man in his mid-forties, he appears to be, a large-boned large-framed man with a shaggy reddish beard, shaggy eyebrows, a head of thick shaggy hair to match, although his hairline is slightly receding.

"Can I help you?" Morag says, immediately regretting the shopgirl cliché.

He glances up, smiles with embarrassment and closes the book, which she now sees is an expensive edition of Klee reproductions.

"I wish you could." His voice is faintly Scots, but with some kind of difference, a low-spoken and almost formal quality which she has not heard before. "But I can't afford eight quid for a book, and it seems a bit large to steal unobtrusively."

"Would you, if it weren't?"

"I might take it, but the guilt would likely force me to return it. It's in the background."

"Presbyterian, you mean?"

"The same. In my case, considerably lapsed, but we are never totally lapsed."

"I know. It's in my background as well."

His name is Daniel McRaith, and he comes from Crombruach, a village in the part of Ross-shire known as the Black Isle. Hence his accent, which is Highland.

"Strange," Morag says, "that I wouldn't know one Scots accent from another. Most of the Scots families, where I come from, came originally from the Highlands, but they spoke Gaelic when they first arrived, about a hundred and fifty years ago, and they lost that. Even with the ones who came later, though, the Scots accent in English never lasted into the second generation."

"We have lost the Gaelic, too, or most of us."

"And yet – and this was true of Christie, my stepfather, too, at times – there's something in your speech that sounds almost as though it's being translated from another language. Christie never had a word of Gaelic. But there was some echo left."

"That is an appealing thought," Daniel McRaith says, "but possibly not too accurate."

"You mean – sentimental?"

"Perhaps."

"Perhaps," Morag says. "And perhaps not."

McRaith calls himself a painter, not an artist. The word *artist* seems pretentious to him. He makes enough to live on now, although frugally; in the years when he didn't, he had spells of working as a hod-carrier in Glasgow, every minute of which he hated. It was not the physical labour he minded so much; it was the ugliness of the smoke-blackened city.

"I used to find, later, when I had gone back home, that I would be painting some of the children I had seen there, and the way they looked – bitter and old at eight or so – would almost make me angry at my own, for being healthy, which was a terrible way to think, I suppose. God knows Crombruach is poor but it is not that sick poverty."

His own. His own children. Well, so what? Nothing strange about that. She has only just laid eyes on him. Why should it matter that he is married, a natural enough state to be in, for a man of his age.

Mr. Sampson is making angry gestures to Morag. Two customers are hovering vaguely, with books in their hands, looking for someone to take payment, and Mr. Sampson is himself busy with another customer. Morag and Dan McRaith arrange to meet in a nearby pub that evening.

Angie promises to look in on Pique from time to time, and Morag goes out. As usual, with ambiguous feelings. Is she wrong to be leaving Pique alone? What if there were a fire? What if someone broke into the flat? Etcetera. And on the other hand, Pique is no infant, nor is she stupid, and she knows Angie's phone number. Also, why does Pique always always either create a fuss when Morag goes out, or (like tonight) dawdle calculatedly over dinner and preparations for bed, spinning out simple rituals such as brushing the teeth to about twenty minutes? The answer is, of course, obvious. But unpalatable. Morag cannot say to the child *I have to have some life of my own*, because that concept will only be understood by Pique many years later, too late to do Morag any good. Nor can Morag afford (although she sometimes does) to lose her temper with Pique, for this merely brings on a severe attack of her own self-reproach and also gives Pique a legitimate reason for yelling, weeping and generally carrying on, all of which results in further delaying Morag's departure.

The Fox and Grapes is not yet crowded. Dan McRaith is standing at the bar, a pint ale mug held in one blunt-fingered hand. He gets her a drink and they find a table.

"Cheers."

"Cheers."

"After about three of these," he says, "you had best tell me to stop, because after three I forget that my capacity is not limitless, nor is my money."

"Why would I tell you to stop? That's up to you."

McRaith looks at her from amused hazel eyes.

"That's fine," he says, "as long as you are not sitting there thinking that I am drinking too much. Bridie never says anything. She sits there thinking it. She is an expert at the eloquent silence."

"Bridie?" The name seems to have connotations of perpetual bridehood, something childish and affected. "That's an odd name."

"It's a form of Bridget," McRaith says. "She is, of course, my wife."

"Yes."

Morag now prays that he is not about to launch into the boring confessions of one who is misunderstood by his marital partner. He does not do so. Or if he does, it is with some difference.

"There," he says contemplatively. "I have betrayed her, I think. I do that, sometimes. I don't think she ever speaks a word of me to anyone."

"Did you marry young, Dan?"

"Twenty. I'm forty-five now. With seven children. The two eldest are away from home now, thank God."

"*Seven*. Why?"

"Bridie believes in large families, and as having children turned out to be her chief interest in life, it did not seem fair to object to it. She has not objected to my painting, although she has sometimes had cause. You have only the one child, Morag?"

A peculiar way for a relationship to begin, a relationship which is plainly going to be sexual, by talking about one another's offspring. And yet Morag is drawn to him now by both sex and spirit, and senses this is true for him as well. It is as though, both of them, not being young and new and uncommitted, must sound each other out about their areas of commitment. The only alternative is the game, the pretence that nothing matters, the desperation that says moment is all and there does not need to be any other moment to plan for. Morag has played this game, from time to time. But not now. Not any more.

"Only the one, yes," she says. "It must be difficult to have seven. It's difficult to have one, though, in other ways."

"And alone?"

"Yes. That."

She tells him a little about Brooke, about Jules, about

Pique. Even some things about Christie and Manawaka. Is this possible? Is this Morag Gunn, sitting in a pub and talking to someone about these things of which she rarely speaks? Apparently it is.

McRaith tells her that he keeps a room in a friend's house, in one of the grottier parts of Camden Town, and stays there occasionally when the house at Crombruach becomes unbearably small and noisy. Bridie minds, but does not say. He feels guilty at leaving to come here, but does so all the same.

Morag goes back to his room with him, and they make love. The swiftness of this encounter does not seem strange.

McRaith has been in London for going on two months, and Morag has known him for most of that time. His room, as a place of work for him, is no hell, but it does have a skylight and a fairly large east window. It is sparsely furnished – a bed, a dresser, an ancient and threadbare Persian rug. His paints, brushes and paraphernalia are kept in a scrolled and only slightly rainbow-splattered writing desk with a drop-lid top. The place is scrupulously neat, and the paints are always shut away when Morag arrives. He is very protective, almost aggressively so, about his work. His easel, standing in the wide bay window, is always carefully turned around whenever Morag is here, so she cannot see what he is working on. Finished (or at least temporarily laid aside) paintings are stacked against one wall, but facing inward in concealment. On the dresser there is only one thing – a bowl full of oddly shaped and oddly coloured pieces of rock, from Crombruach. Perhaps they are necessary to remind McRaith of those shapes and textures. Or possibly they are his talismans.

She goes there in the afternoons, most days, which is by no means a perfect arrangement. She works mornings in the bookshop. Dan works mornings at his work. She is supposed to be working afternoons at her work. Pique does not get to bed until after nine, so evenings are not much good for Morag's work. The choice for her seems to be not too simple.

How to change our hours to suit? What to do, Lord? How to cope with it all? Maybe I should be able to write evenings, late, so as not to inconvenience anyone? Goddamn, why should I not inconvenience anyone? I couldn't write then, anyway. I am too bloody tired by then.

"Morag?" Dan, on the phone.

"Yes. Oh –"

"What happened to you? I was expecting you after lunch."

"Right," Morag says, furiously. "I'll be right over."

"You don't sound very calm, Morag."

"Really?"

She arrives, walks up the three flights of stairs to Dan's room. He takes her coat, looking bewildered.

"Why are you so strange today?" he asks.

"I was working on *Jonah*. I picked it up as soon as I got back from the bookshop, and I forgot about the time. I should've phoned you, I suppose. But this is going to happen sometimes, Dan, and I just damn well cannot help it. I'm not on call. I am not. If that doesn't suit you, then I'm sorry – but that's the way it is."

Dan laughs, almost with surprise. Puts an arm around her shoulder.

"I'm sorry, Morag – I should've realized. I didn't mean to sound as though I owned you. You know I don't feel like that."

"I hope you don't. Because –"

"It's all right – I do know. My God, you should realize how glad I am that you'll stand up to me. That you'll yell at me if necessary. That's what's so bloody difficult with Bridie – oh Morag, love, I'm sorry, I must not talk about her to you. It is not fair to either of you. But sometimes I want to say to her – sometimes I *do* say – for christ's sake, woman, don't sit there looking injured – if you disagree with me, *say so*. Can't you see that's one thing I value most about you?"

"I know. I do know, Dan."

"Well, you'd better get back to work, then."

"Now that I'm here," Morag says, laughing and yet annoyed at herself, "I don't want to go."

"I'm glad. But I feel as though I've –"

"Conned me? You haven't."

Dan shoulders his way across the room like a sailor in a gale. For him, life is full of pitfalls. He lives dangerously, and imagines minor disasters, which in consequence frequently happen. He is a man who can trip, cold sober, in the middle of an empty room. And yet he does not give the impression of clumsiness. His blundering movements are innerly caused, and have their own peculiar grace. Surrounded by mysteries on all sides, he peers at them with suspicion, awe and gratitude.

"We are, of course, out of whiskey," he says. "But the cupboard contains two small Guinness, if my memory serves me."

His memory does not serve him. The cupboard contains one Guinness. They split it.

"You bought the whiskey only a few days ago," Morag says.

"Are you preaching, Morag Dhu? If so, please do not."

Morag Dhu. Black Morag. Because of her hair, not her temperament, or so she hopes. She has asked him how the Gaelic word is spelled, but he does not know.

"I'm not preaching. You don't drink when you're working. I would've liked the whiskey better than this black molasses, that's all."

"How do you know I don't drink when I'm working? I don't, as a matter of fact, but you've never seen me working. Nor I you, if it comes to that. I don't seem to be doing much here. I never do. I leave Crombruach, to get away from the loony bin up there, and I come here and paint shit."

"Maybe you should go back, Dan."

"Not yet," McRaith says. "Not quite yet."

They make love then, the continuation of their talking, the same thing in a different form. They talk interminably when they are talking; when they are making love, they do not speak. None of the hot violent words are needed. It is different each time. Sometimes so swift they are amazed and amused, taken by surprise, taking one another by surprise. Today, slow and gentle, even their culmination.

"One thing I have always liked about you," McRaith says, as though it had been years, "is that you have not yet asked to see my work. Of course, I have not asked to see yours, either, although I cheated to some extent and got two of your books out of the library."

"Oh?"

"Yes. Strange – that it could be you and not you, at the same time."

"That is just it." She does not want to talk much about this, but is warmed by the knowledge that he has seen it.

"If you want to look at the ones stacked over there, Morag Dhu," McRaith says, with a hesitation that is both protection and pride, "go ahead. I brought those down with me – for the dealers, hopefully."

"It must be hard to part with them, Dan."

"How often do you read your books, once they're published?"

"Never. Yes. Okay, I'll look, but I won't be able to say. I don't know, in that territory."

"For God's sake. Just look at them. Who asked you to say anything?"

Morag looks. Walking naked and therefore less vulnerable than she would have been if clad, among McRaith's paintings.

Dark oils, mostly, but not heavy. The colours black-green, a hundred different greys and browns, but the sun's colours, too, in brief revelations. Some like the rocks of Crombruach, the miniature shore there on the dresser, no recognizable shape nor identifiable form, at least to her eyes. Others bear somewhere within them the forms of fossils and shells, convoluted seashells and rock-fossils of ferns or fish, immeasurably ancient, and behind or through these, the timid angry eyes of humans. Some of the human eyes seem distanced, distorted – no, not distorted; the flesh mirrors the spirit's pain, a greater pain than the flesh even if burned could feel. A grotesquerie of a woman, ragged plaid-shawled, eyes only unbelieving empty sockets, mouth open in a soundless cry that might never end, and in the background, a burning croft.

Morag turns and looks at him, after looking at this last painting.

"The dispossessed."

She puts the canvas carefully back. She straightens, straightens herself, straightens her own back. Then she walks over to where he is lying on his bed. Kneels on the floor and puts her head with its black hair onto his chest with its coarse copper hair, and onto the double bow of his ribcage. McRaith puts his hands on her shoulders and does not move them from there for a while.

What future, Morag does not ask. Bridie remains unreal to her, and Dan's children are fantasy children. Yet Bridie is there, in Crombruach, her veins entangled with Dan's in that real and existing horde of young, her choice, her hold on him. His choice as well. He had not said *No* to them. He had not denied Bridie her children, much as he might and did resent the presences of so many now dependent upon him. However much he needs to get away, will he ever be able to do so except briefly? Bridie certainly will not divorce him. What is Bridie like? Morag does not want to know. Morag does not care about marrying him, nor even about living with him more or less permanently. It will be enough if things can go on as now.

"Will you ever describe me?" Dan says.

"What are you getting at?"

"Will you, though?"

"No. Or – I don't think so."

"You don't think you have a right, do you, Morag Dhu?"

"No. No, I don't think I have a right."

"And if I painted you, or a part of you – would that be different?"

"I don't know. I don't either want you to do it or not want you to do it. I'll give you the right, if you want it."

"I wouldn't do your body. Don't mistake me – it's a good body. But it would just be your face, I think, and your hair. Let me look at you, Morag, so I will remember."

One day he shows her the painting of Morag Dhu, the only painting he has done in London and not destroyed. It is not a large canvas – quite small, in fact. It is not even just her face.

Her features are in shadow. Only her black hair can be seen, and her eyes, clearly and unmistakably the eyes of Morag, angry and frightened, frighteningly strong.

Memorybank Movie: The Black Isle

It was three years since Morag first met Dan McRaith. To her, it seems a much shorter time, because she sees him perhaps twice a year, for a few weeks or occasionally a couple of months at a time. In between, they correspond, he in brief scrawls, Morag in lengthy typewritten letters. Sometimes, after he has once more gone away, she thinks of him in Crombruach, with Bridie, and rages. It is a fine arrangement for him – a woman in two camps. But what about her? At these times, lying sleepless, she feels demeaned, waiting here for him to return, furious at herself but unable to do otherwise. She has written dozens of letters to him, telling him she does not want to go on in this fashion, that she doesn't care a damn about marrying him but she hates feeling like anybody's mistress, that she is nearly forty and is merely marking time with her life, and so on. She always tears these letters up. She knows that Dan does not view it in this way, that he would laugh at the suggestion of Morag's being his *mistress*, that antiquated word. Also, she is in fact not marking time with her life at all. *Jonah* is completed and accepted and will soon be published. Morag works much better when McRaith is not in London, of course, herself and her time not then being divided. If he were here all the time, she suspects that she would become impatient with him, resentful of anyone's constant presence. No doubt under these circumstances, too, she would be expected to make the meals and do the laundry for him as well as for herself and Pique. Dan is accustomed to that pattern, which presumably suits Bridie, but would not suit Morag.

Looked at that way, it's ideal. Why do I keep on feeling badly about it, then? I hate the fact that Dan's never even seen Pique, that there is a whole area in my life that he knows nothing about, and that there is another whole area in my life that Pique knows nothing about. And I'm jealous of his children and of Bridie, having so much of his life. Bridie, apparently cloaked in her disapproving silences. They're not happy together – for God's sake, why don't they part? But I can't say that to him.

Evening, and Pique is reading in bed. The phone rings, and it is Dan. He sounds dreadfully upset. Morag recognizes the symptoms, all too familiar by now.

"Morag, could you come over, right now, do you think? Just for a little while. I really would like to talk to you."

"What is it? You're going home?"

"Morag Dhu, I can't stand this goddamn city a minute longer. Today I nearly walked straight into an oncoming bus. One of these days I will. And I am not working worth a damn. Everything I do here is rubbish. I've got to go back."

"I'll be over in a few minutes."

Aid and comfort. She does not resent it very much, because he also has given her aid and comfort, through the writing of *Jonah*. Not, however, about Pique and all that, but then she has never asked for it, there.

Morag very rarely goes over to Dan's in the evenings, simply because she hates telling lies to Pique, and there is no way she can go to Dan's without telling lies which grow far too elaborate and intricate, and which make her feel as though she is betraying the child, once for leaving Pique in order to go to Dan, and again for not levelling about it.

"Who was that, Mum?" Pique enquires.

Morag goes into Pique's bedroom.

"Just a friend," she says. Then, determinedly, "An artist

called Daniel McRaith – he is going back to his home in Scotland, and he's having a few people in this evening, and they'd like me to go over for just a little while. Okay?"

Only half a lie. Does that make it better?

"I guess so." Pique is more resigned than she used to be, about Morag going out occasionally. But she still does not like it.

"I'll just go up and tell Angie."

"Okay. Mum – don't stay very long, will you?"

"I promise."

Does Pique in some way suspect her relationship with Dan? Why why has Morag been so careful to keep it from the child? If Dan were unattached, then she would not have felt this carefulness to be necessary. But you cannot say to a child *Look, there is this man and he has seven children and a wife in the north of Scotland, and I am in love with him and I go over and make love with him whenever I possibly can, and will continue to do so, however much it might hurt his wife if she knew about it, and I am very much afraid that it would.*

Dan is pacing around the room like a racehorse impatient to be off.

"Morag – I am so damn sorry. But I have to go."

"Yes. I know you do. I don't understand why, but I know you do."

McRaith pours them both a whiskey, and she sees his hands are shaking.

"I wish to God I could explain," he says miserably. "I don't know – more and more I feel like hell about it."

"About what?"

"Why can't I just stay in either one place or another? That's what is bothering me. I go back to Crombruach, and I can work – I never do anything, really, anywhere else.

And then after a while – look, I do not hate my offspring –"

"I never thought you did."

"On the contrary, I am normally fond of them, or so I believe at most times. But –"

"Dan," Morag says, feeling tired. "We have been through all this a hundred times. Go. Just go. But for God's sake stop trying to explain and justify yourself."

"I'm not trying to justify," he says irritably. Then, sitting down at the table, he looks up at her and shrugs. "Yes, probably I am, at that. I wish you would come up to Crombruach, Morag, just once – just to see. Then you'd understand both things – my need of the place, the geographical *place*, the sea and the shore, and also why I have to get away, and did even before I ever met you. Now it's a hundred percent worse, because I want to come down here and see you, and I also feel more guilty about leaving – well, leaving all of them up there."

"How could I go to Crombruach, Dan? Don't be ridiculous."

"You mean – what would Bridie think? Well, the local pub has rooms. You could stay there. You're always talking about going to Sutherland and you never go. It's quite a long way from Crombruach, but I could drive you. It would be a reason for going. Bridie would not think anything if you took Pique along with you. That is how her mind works –"

A woman with a child would be likely to be honourable, in Bridie's book? Bridie herself would, no doubt. Perfidious Morag.

"You've got it all figured out, haven't you, Dan? How would you explain how it was you came to invite me up to Crombruach? Or how you got to know me at all?"

"You're making it too complicated, Morag Dhu. I would tell Bridie I met you a couple of times at parties at Andrew's.

I've quite often asked London friends up there, you know."

"What if she didn't believe you?"

McRaith looks suddenly stricken.

"She would, quite simply, believe me," he says.

"Dan –"

They hold onto one another. But they will not make love this evening.

"I couldn't go," Morag says. "I just couldn't."

"All right. I'll write to you, Morag Dhu."

Early mornings are the worst. Nights, she works late, writing letters, planning a few short stories, drinking wine until she thinks she can sleep. But she wakens with the cold knowledge of Dan's absence, her flesh clamouring for his, her mind reviewing the things she wants to tell him, to share with him, and then realizing he is not any longer just a few blocks away.

After a month, she asks Pique how it would be for the two of them to go to Scotland during the Easter holidays, and stay in a real hotel, and visit these friends, some of whose children are just about Pique's age. Pique is enthusiastic. Morag writes to McRaith, who replies by return post.

The night train to Inverness. Morag lies in the lower bunk of their second-class sleeping compartment, listening to the quake and rattle of the train. Is this going to prove to be a vast error of judgement? And she will not be able to touch Dan, not at all. What in hell has made her do it?

Curiosity. Just that. I've got to see. I've got to know about Crombruach, and Bridie, and why he stays. And if I'm ever to get to Sutherland, it had best be with him.

Early morning, Morag looks out the train window. Small rocky hillsides are sliding past, and fir trees, and white birches.

Brown creeks (here called *burns*?) tumble along over stony riverbeds. A station flashes by. The train does not stop, but Morag reads the sign.

CULLODEN

There is such a place. It really exists, in the external world. Morag feels like crying, but Pique is awake now and the steward is at the door with their morning tea.

Dan meets them at Inverness station. He is wearing his usual brown corduroys and cream-coloured plait-patterned fisherman's sweater. In London, she now realizes, these clothes looked slightly like what a painter might wear who was trying to look like an artist, although it never struck her like that at the time. Here, however, they look like what they really are, the local garb, worn because warm.

"Pique, this is Dan McRaith." This seems very odd.

"Hi. Have you got a farm?"

"Hello, Pique. No, not a farm. Our house used to be a fisherman's cottage."

"Have you got a dog?"

"Yes. A collie."

"I have always wanted a dog," Pique says, giving Morag a reproachful glance.

The drive takes more than an hour, through rolling farm-lands and pastures. Morag barely notices the scenery. In the back seat, Pique is chattering happily. Dan responds with appropriate comments. The small car chuffs on. Morag, sitting beside Dan, is aware only that she wants to touch him, and cannot.

Crombruach village is at the mouth of the firth. The greyish pink stone houses rise in tiers up the hillside. The streets are narrow, cobbled with rough stone. The harbour has a wharf-breakwater and inside this sheltering arm half a dozen boats lie. Fishboats? Not anything like the gillnetters in B.C. These are more like dories, motor-powered but open. Imagine going to sea in those cockleshells.

They go to the local inn and deposit Morag's suitcases. Then on to McRaith's house. They draw up beside a row of stone cottages, not even semidetached. Totally attached, a whole string of them, across the road from the windy harbour.

"Here we are," McRaith says.

The house is low-ceilinged, as he has said, two rooms up and two and a half down. Downstairs, the kitchen which is also the livingroom has as its focus a black iron coalstove. There is also a beat-up table, a variety of chairs in various stages of collapse, two cats, a jumble of anoraks and rubber Wellington boots, books, buckets, cooking pots, rock and shell collections, fishing rods, piles of old newspapers, a sink stacked high with washed but undried dishes, a cardboard box full of broken toys, an aged and yawning collie beside the stove dreaming of sheepherding, a jam jar full of dried grasses and ferns, and another jam jar full of plastic daffodils.

A woman comes down the stairs into the kitchen, accompanied by a couple of copper-haired boys who look about six and nine years old. Bridie. Introductions are made, which Morag scarcely hears, and will later not be able to remember. She is intent upon looking at Bridie. It immediately becomes apparent that Bridie is intent upon looking at Morag.

Like hell she doesn't suspect, kid or no kid. Oh God. Why did I ever come here? I should've known better. Too late now. Have to see it through. With dignity. Come on, Morag. Pull yourself together.

Bridie is only a few years younger than Dan, so she must be about forty-five. She looks older than he does. This seems unfair, for a start. She is a thin slight woman, her hands rough and red from too much hot water and cold weather. Her features are sharp, and indicate that she must once have been if not beautiful then extremely handsome. She wears her brown hair cropped short. Her brown tweed skirt and brown poloneck pullover are clean and sensible, and her shoes, well-polished brogues, suggest that she has to some extent dressed up for this meeting.

Only now does Morag realize what the real mistake has been in coming here. No longer can Bridie be a fantasy woman. She has become, in this instant, real to Morag. Her drawn, tense, determined face will now forevermore come between Morag and McRaith.

Bridie's hands reach down for a second, in an automatic gesture, as though she were about to wipe them on an apron which she now remembers she is not wearing. Morag's heart lurches and she finds herself wanting to say *I didn't mean to hurt you, if I did hurt you; I didn't know you were here.*

"We haven't much to offer Dan's London friends," Bridie says, in the same low almost formal tone as Dan has.

Morag sees suddenly what she has taken for suspicion, before, in Bridie's perusal of herself, has not been that at all. It has merely been shyness, a feeling both of inadequacy and resentment, possibly, in the face of Dan's London friends, people from that glittering world, as she probably imagines it to be, where she herself does not go and does not want to go.

"Would you be ready for your breakfast, then?" Bridie goes on.

"Yes – thanks. But please don't go to any –"

"It's no bother," Bridie says. "I'll see to it now."

But there is a faint undertone now, not of apology but of martyrdom. Dan says nothing, but scowls.

After they have eaten, Pique goes out with the two younger boys and the collie, to see the harbour and the shore. Two more young have clattered into the house – a girl of about twelve, and a boy of fourteen. Mary and Robert.

Bridie clears the table. Morag offers to help. Bridie politely refuses assistance.

"You and Dan go ahead and talk," she says. "I've work to do."

"Couldn't you just sit down for fifteen minutes," Dan says to her, very quietly but angrily, "and have a cup of coffee and talk a bit?"

Bridie looks at him as though puzzled, as though trying to figure out what is expected of her.

"Very well, then," she says.

She sits down on the edge of a chair and sips at her coffee, as though the house were no longer her abode. Morag and McRaith talk – of the proposed trip to Sutherland, which would be shorter by boat but he does not know anyone with a reliable enough vessel here right now. They also find themselves talking about Morag's forthcoming novel, naturally enough, comparing the gillnetters of *Jonah* to the boats in Crombruach harbour. Bridie does not speak. What is she thinking? Morag turns to her.

"Your elder children – where are they?"

"Oh – they're away."

"Sarah left only this year," Dan says, taking over. "She's just eighteen. Taking a business course in Inverness. The two older boys have been away for some time – one's a teacher, and the other is at university in Edinburgh."

"It must be a relief to have grown-up children," Morag ventures once more to Bridie.

"They are doing well," Bridie says. "But they are missed here. When they have been your life, it is hard to see them go."

Well, that remark must make McRaith feel pretty superfluous at this point. Morag's feelings are so ambiguous that she no longer makes any attempt to sort them out at the moment. Bridie is certainly no frail personality – that much is obvious. But her ways of battling are not open ones. On the other hand, they are the only ones she has ever learned, ever been taught, presumably.

Morag and Dan begin to talk again – about London. This is bad, but what else to do? Bridie rises and goes about her work, of which there seems to be an endless amount. She has an old-fashioned washing machine, into which she dumps approximately three tons of clothing, load after load, moving efficiently, unobtrusively, and yet in some subtle way obtrusively.

"Let me show you where I work," Dan says finally.

There is a lean-to at the sea side of the house, which McRaith has built for his studio. The addition is not stone but timber, not well-built but with a good window facing east for the morning light. As in London, the canvases are neatly stacked; the easel is faced away from incoming eyes. There is no jumble of paints; everything is in its place – McRaith's defense, just as it is Morag's, against the chaos of the outer world and the confusions of the inner.

"It's not big enough," he says, "but it's my place. You might not think anyone could work here. How is it I can't work anywhere else? Maybe you'll begin to see, Morag Dhu. When I look out there, I see the firth. It's the place that's important to me. The surrounding circumstances – well, they have happened and they are here."

"You mean your family and all that?"

"Yes, I guess so. But of course it's not quite like that, too."

"I begin to see that it's not."

He puts an arm around her shoulder, gently and in a sense distantly.

"Morag Dhu. I'm sorry."

"Bridie must've been about seventeen when she married you."

"Yes. Exactly that. We were both born in this village. I can't leave, and how could I ever ask her to leave? It's her place, too. If only she could find something else, someone else to draw her away. But she won't. I don't believe she's ever had another man. I wish to God she would."

Morag looks at him, loving and resenting him. He really believes he means it.

"If she went down to London with you, sometime," Morag says, "and went to bed with Andrew, how would you feel about it?"

McRaith considers.

"Andrew wouldn't attract her," he says finally. "He's not her type of person."

Morag laughs, and he looks at her for a moment, bewildered, and then laughs, too. But does he really see what she is laughing at? And is she laughing, or what?

They are eight for dinner that evening. Bridie once again refuses Morag's help. Pique has come in with Ian and Jamie, with a huge number of shells collected on the shore.

"Hey, Mum, you should *see* – you just walk along the beach and there are all these millions of shells – can I take all mine back with me?"

"Sure, honey," Morag says.

She sees McRaith looking at her, seeing her in a different way, the mother of Pique, the child who has been as unreal to him as Bridie and his kids have been to Morag. He smiles, and Morag has difficulty in straightening her spine and talking calmly.

After dinner, the young depart for a time, taking Pique with them. How much has Pique missed being a member of a tribe, a large family? She is taking to this circumstance in a way which makes Morag mourn for all the days Pique has come home alone, after school, to the flat with only the two of them there.

McRaith is battering around the kitchen, looking for something.

"Have you hidden my whiskey, then?" he says at last, to Bridie.

She does not flinch. She is sitting beside the small black coalstove, and for a wonder she is not actually doing anything except stroking the collie's ears.

"You know I have not, Dan."

"Then where the hell is it?" He looks ashamed as he speaks.

"On the lower right-hand shelf of the sideboard, where you left it."

McRaith looks, and of course it is there.

"Sorry, my queen," he says. "I have maligned you once again."

Bridie says nothing. Well, what could you say? These famous silences of hers, Morag now thinks, are caused because he hands her lines to which she cannot respond either angrily or wittily. Her response is silence, possibly because she has not ever figured out any other response. She was seventeen. He has moved on, into other areas. Bridie has not, and knows it well. She runs his house for him; she tends their children and makes the meals. And she has discovered, over the years, maybe with surprise, that her silences are more effective in reproaching him than any words of hers could possibly be. Does it give her any satisfaction to reproach him? Or is she at such times too enclosed in her own pain really to realize his at all?

And yet McRaith does not, at the deepest level, want a woman who will stand up to him. For some of the time, he may indeed want this. But not for most of the time.

McRaith stays, Morag now begins to see, because of the kind of woman that Bridie is. McRaith is not held to Crombruach just because of the place. He is held here by Bridie, whom he has known all his life as she has known him. That is the way it is.

In the afternoons, Morag and McRaith walk, there being little else to do in Crombruach, accompanied always by children. In the hillside fields, the new lambs are everywhere, bravely born into the cold spring. The hillsides are rocky, moss-covered, but in the valleys the earth is black and good. Along the shore, the stones are the colour of jade, rose, amber, seabright at the water's edge, and long shiny strands of yellowbrown kelp float and straggle. At dusk, the tide coming in over the mudflats, the flotillas of wild swans move along the grey waters of the firth, the young cygnets trailing behind, the great cob swans in the lead, their powerful white wings furled.

McRaith points across the firth, to the north.

"Away over there is Sutherland, Morag Dhu, where your people came from. When do you want to drive there?"

Morag considers.

"I thought I would have to go. But I guess I don't, after all."

"Why would that be?"

"I don't know that I can explain. It has to do with Christie. The myths are my reality. Something like that. And also, I don't need to go there because I know now what it was I had to learn here."

"What is that?"

"It's a deep land here, all right," Morag says. "But it's not mine, except a long long way back. I always thought it was the land of my ancestors, but it is not."

"What is, then?"

"Christie's real country. Where I was born."

McRaith holds her hand inside his greatcoat pocket. Around them the children sprint and whirl.

After five days, Morag and Pique leave Crombruach to return to London. McRaith drives them to Inverness station. Pique rushes about, buying sweets. Morag and Dan, conscious of the child, and conscious of an ending which neither of them guessed before, put their arms very lightly around one another.

"Take care, love."

They both say the words, simultaneously.

In Hedgerow Walk, Morag considers going back, taking Pique to see Christie. Moving seems complicated; she makes plans but does not do anything yet. She cannot go back to Manawaka, to stay. She cannot. But must go, even for a time, soon. Christie will be – how? Does she want Pique to see him as he may be now? She is afraid to go back, there.

It is two months after they get back from Crombruach that the cable arrives for Morag, from the doctor she remembers in Manawaka.

CHRISTIE LOGAN VERY ILL STOP CAN YOU COME QUESTION PAUL CATES.

"Pique, we're going back home."

"Home?" (What means *home*?)

"Yes. Home."

Memorybank Movie: The Ridge of Tears

The bus spurts along the highway, and Morag looks out at the green wheat, the summer's beginning, and at the tall couchgrass beside the road, the light yellow sweet clover, the dark yellow sowthistle and the purple wild asters. Bluffs of poplar and scrub oak slip past, the popular leaves as always catching the faintest wind, forever-moving leaves.

Pique has remained in Winnipeg with Ella's mother. It is now too late for Christie to see her. Morag has left it too long. He would not want the child to see him as he looks now. How does he look now?

The Manawaka bus station. No jazzier than of yore. New Coca-Cola posters, that's about all. But of course the young faces of the girls behind the lunch counter are unfamiliar. Perhaps they are the daughters of some of the people Morag once knew. She scans the faces, looking for a meaning which is not there. She phones Dr. Cates.

"I've just got here. How's Christie?"

"Not good, Morag," Paul Cates says, sounding weary and much older than the man she remembers. "He's seventy-six after all. He's not going to live forever."

Isn't he? And does this, obscurely and absurdly, come as a surprise?

"What is it with him, Dr. Cates?"

Dr. Cates coughs, and then, very dimly heard at the other end of the line, sighs.

"His heart's been tricky for some years now, Morag. He doesn't take much care of himself. But this time it's a stroke.

He's only partially paralyzed. He might get over it. But —"

"But *what?*"

"I'm not sure he wants to. Maybe that's nonsense. Hard to tell. But with a heart like his, he could go out any time."

"When can I see him, Dr. Cates?"

"You can go up to the hospital now, if you like, Morag. I'll let them know you're coming."

"I'll just leave my suitcase at the house. Wait – will the house be open, though?"

Dr. Cates' paper-thin laughter.

"You've been away a long time, girl. You won't find many doors locked around here, still. Anyway, what's Christie got that's worth stealing?"

Morag takes her suitcase and walks. Why not get a taxi? Anywhere else in the world, she would have done, but not here. A penance, more than likely, or a leftover from the days when she couldn't have afforded a taxi. The house on Hill Street is different from her last visit only in that it is now frankly and indescribably dirty, stinking and chaotic. No one has cleaned for years. Wrong – someone has evidently made some efforts, just recently, to wallow through the accumulation of grime on the kitchen linoleum and the stacks of old newspapers and spidery floating grey-gauze of dust in every corner. Someone has swabbed discouragedly at the floor. The garbage pail under the sink is empty. Not Christie, surely. Maybe Eva Winkler, coming in from the farm on a Saturday night to visit her mother, looking in at Christie's place.

If I'd stayed or if I'd come back, I'd be dead dead dead. Would I? Who has led a better life, Eva or myself? No doubt I think she has. No doubt she thinks I have.

Morag does not even take her suitcase upstairs to her old room. She leaves it in the kitchen and goes out again.

Everything is very silent. From up the hill and over on Main Street comes the grind and splutter of a motorbike, the whir of cars. But here, along the deserted sidewalks, there is silence, broken only by occasional voices from behind the drawn blinds of the houses. The smell of the grapebunches of mauve lilacs is overpowering.

At the hospital reception desk, she feels alien, apologetic.

"I've come to see Mr. Logan, my – my stepfather. I know it's not regular visiting hours –"

"Oh yes," the girl behind the desk says. "You'll be Miss Gunn, then?"

"That's right."

"I've read your books, Miss Gunn," the girl says shyly, "and I just want to say we're real glad you're from Manawaka. They've got your books in the library."

Coals of fire upon my head. Must I beg this child's forgiveness, as well? She wouldn't know what I meant, if I said it.

"Oh. That's good. Well – thanks. May I go in and see Christie – Mr. Logan – now?"

"Sure. I'll just get ahold of Miss Patterson. She'll show you in."

Christie.

"How is he?" Morag asks the nurse as they patter down the antiseptic-reeking corridors.

"Well, I should warn you, Miss Gunn. He can't speak much at all. And when he does, it's pretty garbled. I'm afraid it makes him angry."

"My God. My God. No wonder. Can he move?"

"He can move his right arm," the nurse says. "At least, some."

Christie lies hunched under the too-white bedlinen. He was never a large man, but now he seems to have shrunk even more. He appears to be composed of bones mainly, and of dried speckled brown skin, stretched barely over the skeleton. He is ludicrously clean-shaven, none of the remembered greyish stubble on his face – they do that kind of thing for people in hospital. His eyes are closed.

"Christie – it's Morag."

He can hear, obviously, and he knows what she is saying. It is just that he cannot reply. His eyes open abruptly, and they are, weirdly, the clear blue of years and years ago. He mumbles, but she cannot make human speech of it. For Christie Logan to be unable to speak – what must that be like? Christie, who told the tales, who divined with the garbage, who ranted in his sorrow like the skirling of the pipes in a pibroch.

"I'm – I'm sorry I didn't come back before, Christie."

He wants to speak desperately, but cannot. His mouth opens, and he strains. No words come. His eyes are filled with such pain and such knowing that Morag can scarcely endure the sight of them. What emerges from his mouth, then, is a squawk, a hoarse unverbal croaking like a bullfrog. He turns away from her, but not before she sees the shame in his eyes, at being thus diminished before her.

Then his right hand, like an eagle claw, reaches out and grasps her hand. They sit there like this for long minutes, both unable to speak, although for different reasons, and Morag can feel the heavy vein pulsing in his wrist.

A tiny blonde nurse scurries in. From her extreme youth and striped blue uniform, she looks to be a student nurse. She carries an object covered with a white linen towel.

"Bedpan time!" she announces ringingly, someone having evidently told her that cheeriness under all circumstances is a nurse's duty.

Christie's one good arm pushes weakly at the girl and the

burden she bears. From his throat comes a sound which Morag has never before heard issuing from a human throat, and hopes never to hear again. A growl – the deep growl of a dog, combined with the wrenched-up sob of a man.

"For God's sake!" Morag cries. "Can't you leave him be, just until I'm gone, then?"

"I was going to draw the curtain around his bed," the girl says, half offended and half scared.

"Get out," Morag says fiercely. "Just get out."

"I'll have to report to the ward nurse –"

"Report, then. Go ahead. Look, I'm sorry. I know it's just part of the routine. But please – not now."

The nurse scampers away. For a second Morag cannot face Christie. When she looks at him, she is astonished. He has regained himself and is peering at her from his shroud of hospital linen, his eyes mocking and shrewd, his mouth in a soundless laugh. Morag laughs too, although it comes out as the travesty of a laugh, but it is their protection, hers and Christie's, as it always has been.

She wants to stay here with him, to keep watch beside him. She also wants to go, not to have to look at him like this. There is something she must say. She wonders if she can discover the words.

"Christie – I used to fight a lot with you, Christie, but you've been my father to me."

His responding words are slurred and whispered, but she hears them.

"Well – I'm blessed," Christie Logan says.

Another way of indicating surprise would have been to say – *Well, I'm damned*. But that is not the phrase he has chosen. She sees from his eyes that the choice has been intentional.

Back at the house on Hill Street, Morag climbs the stairs to her old room. It is overgrown with dust like feathers or grey ferns in the corners and festooned from the ceiling, but it is otherwise unchanged. The one grimy dresser and the single bed covered with a patchwork quilt. She cannot bring herself to look for sheets. She puts on her housecoat and lies down on top of the quilt. This is the first time she has ever stayed alone in this house, and she has dreaded it, but now none of the ghosts seem threatening. Prin is here, and Piper Gunn and Clowny Macpherson and another younger Morag, the felt or imagined presences of real and fictional people, the many versions of herself, combining and communing here, in her head, in this room with its time-stained wallpaper. Outside, a faint rain begins falling, and the open window channels in the smell of wet earth and grass and prairie lilac.

Waking, Morag is at first disoriented.

"Morag!"

The woman's voice, Morag now perceives, is external and not part of a dream or nightmare. She stumbles downstairs, and it is Mrs. Winkler, hideously frail in appearance, although she must in fact be tough as dandelion roots to have survived this long.

"It's the hospital on the phone, Morag. They want you to go there, right away."

"Can I get a taxi, Mrs. Winkler?"

"Well, I wouldn't know about that," Mrs. Winkler says doubtfully. "It ain't but a short walk, there."

By the time Morag reaches the hospital, however, Christie Logan has gone to his ancestors.

*

\When Prin died (a long time ago, it seems), Morag had to make all the funeral arrangements. Christie didn't do a thing. Still, he was there, and they held their wake for Prin, the two of them, sitting at the kitchen table with a bottle of whiskey between them. Now there is no one. Morag takes the necessary steps, robot steps, not thinking, not even thinking of mourning yet.

The sweeping black-branched spruce trees are the same, but the big gloomy frame house looks different. It has, Morag observes, been painted an eye-shattering limegreen. The sign no longer reads "Cameron's Funeral Home." It is now an enormous crimson neon, letters about a million feet high, and it would appear at first glance to apply to some publicity-worshipping evangelical sect.

JAPONICA CHAPEL

Underneath, in more modest lettering, are these words:

Free Parking For Clients

Die now and get free parking forever. Almost worth it. Morag has phoned previously, so is expected. A shortish man, built rather on the lines of an energetic barrel, and wearing light brown slacks and a checked yellow and brown sports shirt, bounces out to meet her.

"Mr. Jonas?" she says uncertainly.

"The same," he carols. "Hector Jonas. At your service, Miss Gunn. Or do you mind if I call you Morag? You being a local girl, and me having read your books, I feel like I know you. We don't stand on ceremony here. At least, *some* do, but I am not of that number, unless, of course, clients prefer the formal approach, in which case I am happy to oblige."

"No – of course I don't mind."

"My name, as I mentioned previously, is Hector. Now come in, come on in."

The office is small but exceedingly tidy. Cherry and blue linoleum tiles on the floor. An impressive desk which takes up most of the floor space. A swivel chair for Hector, and two slender plastic-upholstered armchairs for clients.

"Now, then," Hector proceeds, "I was very sorry to hear about Christie, an old-timer like him. Of course, I never knew him all that well, myself –"

"No one knew him all that well, Hector. He lived nearly all his life in this town, and everyone knew him to see him, and they all called him Christie, but nobody knew him, to speak of, or even to speak to, much, if it comes to that."

Hector stops on his way to the cupboard.

"Why in the world would that be, now, Morag?"

"Oh well, he was the town scavenger in the days when it was still called that, and was looked down on. He was also supposed to be some kind of maverick, as I'm sure you know."

"Well, like I say, I didn't know that much about him," Hector hedges. "Only hearsay, like. Could I offer you a little sherry, Morag? Or a rye? Although I know the ladies usually prefer the sherry, it being sweeter, like."

Morag smiles, unaccountably moved by his flashiness, his public-relations act, and by some kind of genuine solicitude which lurks under the glittery plastic and the veneer of himself.

"Not this lady," she says. "You can pour me a stiff rye. Thanks. That's very kind of you."

"Well, it isn't, really," Hector says, in apparent remorse. "It's really for business. Although I don't usually admit it. But then, most people who come in here are in pretty terrible shape, of course, bereaved and that, kind of knocked-out, you might say, by their dear one's departure from this vale of tears. So they need a little steadying, those of them who aren't teetotallers, and believe you me, we get plenty of *them*. Maybe you think I'm not sounding too serious, but in my business you either have a laugh to yourself sometimes or you'd be climbing the walls, I'm telling you straight. The departed are hard enough to look in the fisheye, to tell you the truth, but the bereaved are usually just that much harder, because they are either all busted-up or else holding themselves together with chewing gum, like, so brittle and held-in that you think they'll crack like a dropped tumbler if you breathe at them. I shouldn't be talking this way, I guess, but you being a writer, it seems natural to talk, although in my profession you learn it's discretion discretion all the way, and in other words you acquire the ability to keep your trap shut. You just seem better in hand of yourself than some, Morag."

This guy will learn to keep his trap shut when he's pushing up daisies. *Who buries the undertaker? Whoever will undertake it.* One of C. Logan's old-time jests. Something good about Hector, though.

"I'm not better in hand of myself," Morag says. "I just show it differently, that's all. Has Niall Cameron been dead long?"

"Some years now," Hector says. "You knew him?"

"Yes. I knew him, and I went to school with one of his daughters. He was a good man."

"Yeh, so I gather," Hector says uneasily, "although he drank himself to death. I mean, like, *sure* he was a good man. But he didn't want to go on living, did he?"

Morag laughs, and the sound is more startling and bitter in these surroundings than she has intended.

"I guess he did and he didn't, both," she says. "It's a common enough trait, hereabouts."

To be or not to be – that sure as death is the question. The two-way battle in the mindfield, the minefield of the mind. Niall. Lachlan. Lazarus. Piquette. Prin. Christie. Jules? Morag?

"Mrs. Cameron and Rachel, they moved out to the Coast a few months back," Hector says. "Mrs. Cameron used to say she'd known you well when you were knee-high to a grasshopper. She never said it when Rachel was around, though, so I kind of wondered. It was after your second book came into the town library."

Parsons' Bakery – Morag going in for jelly doughnuts for Prin. Mrs. Cameron and Mrs. McVitie. Poor little thing – don't they ever cut her hair wash her hair shorten her dress poor poor little thing. Morag behind the counter at Simlow's – the dressmaker suit so suitable for someone about thirty years younger than Mrs. Cameron and Stacey running running from the store in unhealable embarrassment.

"Yeh. Well, you're right. It wasn't quite the way she said. Hector, I suppose they don't call it the Nuisance Grounds any longer, out there?"

Hector, swivelling gently on the large mobile chair behind the desk, gives her an odd glance.

"You mean – the Municipal Disposal Area?"

"Yeh. That's what I mean. The Municipal Disposal Area. Alias the Nuisance Grounds. That's where Christie really should be buried."

"Good Lord," Hector says, "you've got to be joking. You know, don't you, that –"

"Yes. I know. Don't worry. It's all right. I know you can't just bury people anywhere, like that. It's just that – when Prin died, Christie said he'd like to have buried her in the Nuisance

Grounds. He didn't have much use for some things, although it's hard to explain. And he'd buried someone there, once, himself. In the Nuisance Grounds."

"*What?*"

Morag smiles. It is really Christie she wants to talk to, about this. But he has moved not only beyond speech but beyond hearing.

"Don't upset yourself. It was a very long time ago. I don't think he ever meant to tell me – he just found himself telling it. It was, I now see, an aborted child, wrapped up in a newspaper and tied around with a string, and left out with the garbage. Kind of a dumb thing to do, when you think of it, but I suppose the family wasn't thinking too well just then. The string must've come undone. He didn't say what family. He only said the girl had been made to suffer enough. I never knew who she was, or what happened to her. And she never knew that her unfinished child was given a burial."

She does not mention that there was another unfinished child buried there, years later.

Hector is looking at her as though he were trying to see beyond her, as perhaps he is.

"I never knew any of that."

"Nor did anyone, except Christie and myself and – never mind. It doesn't matter any more."

"I thought," Hector says, "that you'd likely want him cremated. I mean, it's kind of the modern way –"

"No," Morag says, carefully and firmly. "I want him to be buried in the Manawaka cemetery, beside his wife. There is a small stone in that place for Prin. I want another one. Grey granite. With both their names. Don't tell *me* it means next to nothing. I know. But that is what will be done."

"All right. Yes, I can sure see to that, all right."

"One more thing, Hector – do you happen to know a piper?"

"Good christ," Hector breathes. "A *what*?"

"A piper. I don't want any service or talk. Just a piper, at the cemetery."

"The things I get myself into," Hector says. "Maybe you should consider a short service here, first? And then just the last few words, *there*."

The Burial of the Dead. *For I am a stranger with thee, and a sojourner, as all my fathers were.*

"All right. Hector. But not here – no offense to you. In the United Church, if the minister will speak the words over Christie, who never went to church in his life."

"Oh, he will." Hector is relieved. "So that settles that, eh?"

"No. I still want the piper."

Hector, thinking she had herself in hand more than most. Now, undoubtedly, thinking he had a madwoman on his hands. He sighs, but rises to the occasion.

"Well, old Scotty Grant usually brings his pipes out in the spring, and walks up and down across his back garden, but I don't know – anyhow, I'll try."

Morag rises.

"Hector, thanks."

"For nothing," Hector says. "Any time."

Then, simultaneously seeing the grotesque quality of this last statement, they both laugh.

*

Morag rummages through the Hill Street house. Finally finds the only things of Christie's which she wants to keep. Four books. Two heavy volumes – *The Poems of Ossian – In the original Gaelic with a Literal Translation into English and a Dissertation on the Authenticity of the Poems by the Rev. Archibald Clark, Minister of the Parish of Kilmallie, Together with the English Translation by Macpherson, in 2 Vols., 1870.* And two small books. *The 60th Canadian Field Artillery Battery Book, 1919.* And *The Clans and Tartans of Scotland.* In this last book she looks up in the Gaelic Glossary the word for black. It says *dubh, dhubh, dhuibh, duibhe, dubha,* but omits to say under what circumstances each of these should be used. Morag Dhu. Ambiguity is everywhere.

The morning of Christie Logan's funeral is fair and cloudless, the sky a light newly washed blue after the recent rains. At the church, there is no music, no oration, simply the bone-bare parts of the order of service, the old words. At the Manawaka cemetery, up on the hill, the wind blows hot and dusty, carry-ing the sickly over-sweet perfume of peonies but also the clean dry pungency of the tall low-boughed spruces that sentinel the place like dark angels of light. Far below, the shallow amber water of the Wachakwa River flows rattling over the stones.

"Forasmuch as it hath pleased Almighty God to take unto himself the soul of our brother here departed, we therefore commit his body to the ground —"

The words are murmured with a kindly awkwardness by the young unknown minister whose brother Christie Logan manifestly was not, although this by no means the minister's fault. Perhaps he even wonders who Christie was, and perhaps, if Morag could bring herself to express the years, he might even like to know. But it is not possible, not now, not here.

Then the minister and the pallbearers (all unknown, per-suaded by Hector to serve) depart. Only Morag and Hector Jonas remain, and one other.

Scotty Grant is not as old as Morag has imagined him. He is in fact a good-looking man in his early sixties, with the red-tanned neck and arms of someone who has spent most of his life as a farmer, battling the land which he has now sold, or, hopefully but not likely, turned over to his sons. He wears a blue open-necked workshirt and unpressed grey trousers. Just as well – kilts in this context would make it into a farce. Maybe it is going to be that, anyway. Would Christie have laughed?

"You sure you want me to do this?" Scotty asks, uncertainly.

Morag glares at him, angry because as yet unable to grieve. But she must not take it out on him.

"Yes. Mr. Grant – please."

He swings the pipes up, and there is the low mutter of the drones. Then he begins, pacing the hillside as he plays. And Morag sees, with the strength of conviction, that this is Christie's true burial.

And Piper Gunn, he was a great tall man, with the voice of drums and the heart of a child, and the gall of a thousand, and the strength of conviction.

The piper plays "The Flowers of the Forest," the long-ago pibroch, the lament for the dead, over Christie Logan's grave. And only now is Morag released into her mourning.

TEN

The willows along the river had been changed by alchemy of autumn from greensilver to greengold. The maples were turning to a million shades of russet, crimson, scarlet, pale red. The air was beginning to have a sharpness about it, the first suggestion of frost. In the evenings, Morag lighted the woodstove. Soon it would have to be the furnace.

She had been working through the day, the words not having to be dredged up out of the caves of the mind, but rushing out in a spate so that her hand could not keep up with them. Odd feeling. Someone else dictating the words. Untrue, of course, but that was how it felt, the characters speaking. Where was the character, and who? Never mind. Not Morag's concern. Possession or self-hypnosis – it made no difference. Just let it keep on coming.

By dusk, Morag had a cramp in her right hand. Writer's cramp – joke. But it happened. Must quit. Go outside and walk off the tension.

Walking down to the river across the meadow of unmown grass, Morag realized what it was that was different about this day. It had been at the back of her mind since early morning, but she had not really seen it until now. There were no swallows. Yesterday the air had been filled with their swiftness. Now there were none. How did they know when to leave and why did they migrate all at once, every one of them? No stragglers, no members of the clan who had an imperfect sense of time and season. Here yesterday, gone today. There might be a reason, but she would just as soon not know.

Back at the house, Morag leafed through several newly arrived books which she had ordered, books on weeds and wildflowers. One told all about the plants hereabouts, which could be used as sustenance, boiled or raw, if ever one were to find oneself lost in the bush. Or, if not actually lost, at least how you could cook certain plants in somewhat fancier fashion at home.

Wait. What about the *Poison* plants? Morag turned to the section hastily. Oh heavenly days. Never attempt wild mushrooms unless you really know what you are doing – this seemed the only policy. The Destroying Angel. Dramatic Old-Testament name. Wonderful name. Terrible mushroom. And how about Water Hemlock? No known antidote. It looked to Morag's unknowledgeable eyes much like Queen Anne's Lace. Same family – Wild Parsley. Well, no one would go around eating Queen Anne's Lace, would they? Nonetheless, suppose you mistook the Deadly Water Hemlock for some innocently edible plant? Symptoms very nasty. "Vomiting, colic, staggering and unconsciousness, and finally frightful convulsions which end in death." Ever so cheery.

Morag: (summoning ghost) Catharine, I'll bet the Water Hemlock wouldn't have alarmed you. You knew what was what. No way you were going to boil up a tasty mess of Hemlock under the impression it was Lamb's Quarters. But didn't you ever worry that one of your kids would come home chomping on some lethal plant? How could you stand the strain?

Catharine Parr Traill: Ignorance, my dear, breeds fear and anxiety. I took great care to inform and enlighten my little ones, at the youngest possible age, of the hazards to be avoided in our beautiful woods and forests. Even the tiniest child can soon be taught the identification of plants. Thus my mind was easy, and could be freed for the important matters at hand. You, if I may say so, oftentimes see imaginary dangers.

M. Gunn: You're darned right I see imaginary dangers, but do you know why? To focus the mind away from the real ones, is why. Leave me to worry peacefully over the Deadly Water Hemlock, sweet Catharine, because it probably doesn't even grow around here. Let me fret over ravening wolves and poison-fanged vipers, as there is a marked scarcity of these, hereabouts. They're my inner demons, that's what they are. One thing I'm going to stop doing, though, Catharine. I'm going to stop feeling guilty that I'll never be as hard-working or knowledgeable or all-round terrific as you were. And I'll never be as willing to let the sweat of hard labour gather on my brow as A-Okay and Maudie, either. Even Pique, ye gods, working as a cashier in the bloody supermarket all day, and then going home and feeding those squawking chickens and washing dishes and weeding the vegetable gardens, etcetera. I'm not built like you, Saint C., or these kids, either. I stand somewhere in between. And yet in my way I've worked damn hard, and I haven't done all I would've liked to do, but I haven't folded up like a paper fan, either. I'll never till those blasted fields, but this place is some kind of a garden, nonetheless, even though it may be only a wildflower garden. It's needed, and not only by me. I'm about to quit worrying about not being either an old or a new pioneer. So farewell, sweet saint – henceforth, I summon you not. At least, I hope that'll be so, for your sake as well as mine.

C. P. Traill: (voice distant now and fading rapidly) "In cases of emergency, it is folly to fold one's hand and sit down to bewail in abject terror: it is better to be up and doing."

M. Gunn: I'll remember.

When Pique, Dan and the Smiths came over that evening, Morag was still poring over the books, this time the weed and wildflower one.

"You look engrossed, Ma," Pique said. "What you got there? Hardcore porn? Hey, a *weed* book?"

"The same," Morag said. "You know something? According to a book I read not long ago, the Eskimos have twenty-five words for snow and only one for flower, and yet there are zillions of wildflowers that grow up there in the small amount of summer they get. Knowing the different varieties of snow is essential to survival, but knowing the different varieties of flowers isn't. With us, knowing the weeds isn't essential to survival, either, at least not any more and not yet. But there they are all the same. Amazing, isn't it?"

A-Okay smiled awkwardly, but Maudie responded kindly.

"I think it's marvellous, to find out all about them, Morag."

"Oh, she doesn't," Pique said, laughing. "I'll bet she couldn't identify more than half a dozen. She just likes the names. Isn't that so, Ma?"

This girl knows me.

"Yeh," Morag admitted. "I guess so. But listen to some of the names."

Tom was more interested than the others. He came and looked at the book while Morag read aloud. Dan and Pique got out their guitars and began tuning them. A-Okay sauntered outside to have a look at Morag's dock-ladder, which he had offered to mend. Maudie got out her eternal and admirable knitting, murmuring that she must finish Alf's sweater before the cold weather.

"Hey, listen to these, Tom –"

Curly Pondweed
Silver Hairgrass
Old Witch Grass
Prostrate Pigweed
Night-flowering Catchfly
Queen-of-the-Meadow
Spiked Loosestrife
Hounds Tongue
Creeping Charlie

Heal-all or Self-heal

Black Nightshade

Sneezeweed

Pussy-toes or Lady's Tobacco

Common Mugwort

Rough Daisy Fleabane

Povertyweed

Staggerwort

Devil's Paintbrush

"Gee," Tom said. "Wow."

He and Morag exchanged glances of glee and mutual appreciation. But this pleasant mood was not to last.

"We've bought our first horse, Morag," Dan said.

"Really? What is it?" Not that she would know.

"A palomino gelding. Stands fifteen hands. We got it for two hundred and seventy-five bucks."

"*You* paid for it," Pique said, not sounding too happy.

"What you mean is, it nearly cleaned me out," Dan said, scowling. "Why don't you say so, then?"

"All right. It nearly cleaned you out."

Morag, thinking of Pique behind the cash register, felt a surge of anger towards Dan. Must not. Not her concern.

"Well," she nonetheless found herself saying, "it sounds a fine horse, but not exactly what I'd imagine the *Horse-Breeders' Gazette* would recommend if you're going into the horse-breeding business."

"Oh Ma – shut up, can't you!" Pique cried furiously.

A-Okay came back into the house, and feeling the tension, responded instantly by becoming tangled up with the rocking chair, which overbalanced, the pointed rockers missing A-Okay's unspectacled eyes by a quarter-inch.

"Watch it, Dad," Tom said.

"When I want your advice, I'll ask for it," A-Okay said in an unusually ungentle voice.

A-Okay raised his voice to Tom so seldom that it came as a shock. Obviously, all was not milk and honey at the Maison Smith, just now.

Stay out. Tread warily, Morag.

Dan's dark eyes were obviously battling his own angry responses. Towards Morag, for opening her big mouth, towards A-Okay for interrupting, maybe even towards Pique for defending him when she wasn't all that pleased by his purchase.

"The brood mares will come later," he said in a low and dangerously quiet voice which reminded Morag of Jules. "We can do without a studhorse. We can rent the services. But I can give lessons with the palomino. He's quiet and he's been shown good manners. He'd be a bit big for kids under eleven or twelve, but okay for those over that."

"I think you just wanted him to ride yourself," Pique said.

Dan turned furiously to her.

"If I had my choice, don't you think I would've picked a bigger horse and one with more spirit?"

"I don't understand that kind of talk," Pique said. "I don't know about horses. I never learned."

"Well, here's your chance."

"I'm not interested, thanks."

Her father's people, the prairie horselords, once. She never learned. Well, so what? What was so essential about it? Nothing, except that it was the mythical beast. Signifying what? Many would say potency, male ego, but it seemed that a kind of freedom might be a better guess.

Both Maudie and A-Okay were peacemakers at heart, the difference between them being that scenes of expressed anger made Maudie physically ill, sometimes to the point of having to rush for the bathroom to throw up, and at the same time she professed to believe (and with her intellect, undoubtedly did believe) in the necessity of expressing anger overtly before it became a dangerous canker in the blood, whereas A-Okay believed that anger could be dealt with from the inside, by the angry person or persons, and yet he could bring himself to enter the fray when necessary, bearing, as it were, cold towels.

"As far as I'm concerned, the horse is a-okay," A-Okay said. "If Dan wants to ride it, Pique, there's nothing so peculiar about that. But Dan and I are going to be doing something else, too, Morag. It was all Royland's doing."

Neat deflection from danger area. Well done, Smith.

"What's that?" Morag asked.

"Well, I was talking to Royland a few days ago, and he gave me hell. He said if we thought of doing anything more with the farm than raising our own vegetables, which, as he said, any fool can do if they're prepared to work a bit, and if we were serious about the option to buy, then we'd better smarten up. First, raise some money in the ways we could, me by writing more of those everlasting science articles, which is not my favourite form of entertainment, but not so bad once you get into them, and Dan by working in town this winter. Second thing was, next spring Dan and me to get jobs with some local farmer, for the summer. Dan knows about horses but he doesn't know fuck-all about farming. Royland says Charlie Greenhouse can't get help – he's sixty-five and aims to retire and move into the Landing in a year or so, and would likely take us on. *He's a mean old bastard*, Royland said, *and you won't like him, but he's been farming all his life and he knows what it's all about.*"

However dour and bad-tempered, and Charlie Greenhouse was certainly that, he could undoubtedly teach them things they couldn't learn from books. True, they wouldn't find him easy to get on with. Charlie hated trees, which he regarded as the natural enemy of man. He also appeared to hate the earth, but at least he knew enough not to fight it in impossible ways. Charlie reminded Morag of various prairie farmers – he wrestled with the land like Jacob wrestling with the Angel of the Lord, until (if ever) it blessed him. A-Okay and Dan would not have Charlie's outlook. They were different – they had seen Carthage; they had walked the streets of Askelon; they had known something of Babylon, that mighty city which dealt in gold and silver and in the souls of men; they had walked in the lion's den and had seen visions such as the prophet Daniel had seen while Belshazzar feasted. They came to the land in ignorance, perhaps expecting miracles which would not occur, but at least with caring, seeing it as a gift and not an affliction.

Morag said nothing for a while, afraid to speak in case she should say too much, too soon.

"It'll be a-okay," she said finally, not knowing whether it would be or not, but praying.

What of Pique? She was not settled here. Maybe never would be. Committed to Dan, but how much? Having to move on, hit the road? For how long?

Pique picked up her guitar and began to sing. Around her, there was an area of silence, as though all of them, all in this room, here, now, wanted to touch and hold her, and could not, did not dare tamper with her aloneness. She began to sing one of Jules' songs, the song for Lazarus. Her voice never faltered, although she was crying.

In the morning, groggy from insomnia, Morag went outside to clear her head. The air was distinctly cold. Autumn nearly over. Winter soon to descend. Sitting on the dock, Morag became aware of an unmistakable sound overhead. Very far up, they flew in their V-formation, the few leaders out front, the flock sounding the deep long-drawn-out resonant raucous cry that no words could ever catch but which no one who ever heard it could ever forget. A sound and a sight with such a splendour in it that the only true response was silence. When these birds left, the winter was about to happen. When they returned, you would know it was spring.

The Canada geese were flying south.

Memorybank Movie: Beulah Land

"Aren't you even going to read the reviews?" Ella asks.

Walton and Pierce have forwarded a sheaf of the clippings on *Jonah*. Morag has glanced through them and laid them aside. They appear, on the whole, to be favourable. So what?

"I guess so, Ella. Later. I can't work up any enthusiasm."

"Well, what about the book club sale? Can't you work up a trace of enthusiasm over that?"

"Yeh."

But she can't. Milward Crispin, faithful agent, has phoned from New York. *Jonah* has been taken by a book club, *Spear of Innocence* and *Prospero's Child* are coming out in paperback, and a film option has been taken on *Spear*. Probably nothing will come of the latter, Crisp says, but at least there's the option money. Things are looking up. Morag, meanwhile, appears to be looking down. She and Pique have been staying with Ella and Mort in Toronto for one month now, ever since Christie's death. Ella has infant twins and is run off her feet. She keeps telling Morag what a lot of help it is to have her here, as Morag washes diapers or dishes, or holds one yelling ravenous kid while Ella feeds the other. In fact, Ella needs Morag here like she needs an attack of flu at the moment.

Two extra people underfoot, and Morag with all the verve of a collapsed balloon.

"Ella, I've got to get up off my ass and decide what to do. My God, it's been good of you to have us here, but –"

"Now, will you kindly shut up, please?" Ella says. "So who's complaining? Wait until Mort and I start glaring at you before you begin the guilt bit, eh?"

"Yeh. Okay. Sorry."

That's a christly bloody useless word, Sorry. C. Logan. Christie, tell the garbage – throw those decayed bones like dice or like sorcerer's symbols. You really could see, though. What about me? Do I only pretend to see, in writing? What did I ever see about you, Christie, until it was too late? I told my child tales about you, but never took her to see you. I made a legend out of you, while the living you was there alone in that mouldering house.

Morag goes through the days like a zombie or a sleepwalker. In fact, sleeping is all she really wants to do. She finds she can sleep far too easily, even in the days. Insomnia would be almost welcome, to prove she is alive. She wakens each morning with the thought of her own death. When she rises, she coughs until she retches. Mort expresses concern, telling her to stop smoking and offering to let her have a prescription for a mild tranquilizer. She promises (hypocritically) to cut down on cigarettes, but refuses the pills, considering herself a perfect subject for instant addiction. Soon it will be time for Pique to go back to school. Where? Morag's mind refused to grapple with the problem. The Black Celt evidently has her by the throat and has no intention of letting go. Morag Dhu.

The city depresses Morag further. She refuses to go downtown, certain she will find herself walking past the apartment block where she once lived with Brooke, or that she will meet Brooke on the street, even though he is probably not here any more. Only once does she go downtown. She walks past the roominghouse on Jarvis Street where Jules used to live. What has she expected? That she could conjure him up?

Save me O God, for the waters are come in unto my soul. Psalm 69.

It is, however, not God who finally provides a solution of sorts, but the Goldenrod Realty Company. Or perhaps fate really does travel in strange disguises.

Late morning, and the twins are momentarily sleeping. Morag and Ella are having coffee. Pique is drawing with coloured chalks on large sheets of paper. Morag is glancing at the Classified section of the newspaper.

> The Goldenrod Realty Co.
> For Sale – Near McConnell's Landing; 80-acre farm, river frontage, good well, four-bedroom log house structurally very sound, needs some interior decoration, half-basement, nearly new furnace, forced sale – Don't Miss This Rock-Bottom Offer For Relaxed Country Living! Phone Steve Harchuk –

This ad strikes Morag like the spirit of God between the eyes.

"Ella – I've decided what to do. I'm going to buy this farm, here, if I can afford it."

"You're *what*? Morag, you're out of your head."

"Let's see, Mum," Pique cries, leaping up. "Is it a real farm? Can I have a dog?"

"Listen, Morag," Ella goes on, "you should excuse my shrieks of caution, but wouldn't you be pretty isolated? Are you really going to learn to drive? And anyway, isn't one supposed to – well – kind of shop around, some, before buying a house, much less a farm? Let's have a look – needs some interior decoration. That means it's a mess inside. Oh heavens, Morag, I'm sorry. I have no right to discourage you. But –"

"It will be all right," Morag says calmly. "You will see."

On the way out to McConnell's Landing, Morag stares out the bus window, experiencing profound qualms. What if the place is already sold? What if it really is a mess? What could she possibly do with eighty acres?

When she returns to Toronto that evening, she has made an offer to purchase and has left a cheque as deposit and proof of her earnest intentions.

Land. A river. Log house nearly a century old, built by great pioneering couple, Simon and Sarah Cooper. History. Ancestors.

Innerfilm

Outside, the blizzard rages and the snow piles up against the house and along the window frames. It is Forty Below. (Forty Below is the magic winter temperature figure. Only to prairie people? It means something more than temperature – it denotes amazing endurance and people say it with pride, almost reverence. They never say Forty Below Zero. Does it go that far down in southern Ontario?) Inside the little house, all is warmth, all is cheer. Morag, having put in an excellent day's work on the nearly completed novel (which will in time prove to be her best thus far) is reading in her comfortable chair near the black woodstove which is crackling a merry tune (safely; new stovepipes). Pique is contentedly working on a piece of embroidery (who? *Pique?*). Well, then, Pique is contentedly – hm hm – making a miniature log house, the very model of this one, for a History project at school, this house being of such historical interest. In the half-basement, the nearly new furnace is chonking away – a charmer, this furnace, no problems, ever. Morag is filled with a sense of well-being. The shed contains enough split wood for the winter. The basement contains shelves and shelves of bottled preserved plums, applesauce, pears, blueberries, chili sauce, crabapple jelly, and so on, the work of Morag's hands, the produce of her garden. All is well. The bank balance is healthy. The friendly neighbourhood farmer is a bachelor (widower? yes). Although by no means an intellectual, he is a well-read man. Also handsome. And and

Memorybank Movie: McConnell's Landing

Morag and Pique move in at the beginning of October. Despite Morag's many forays for secondhand furniture, the house looks bare. The old linoleum is cracking, and the nearly new furnace turns out to have been nearly new twenty-odd years ago, and now exhibits odd traits of temperament, making Morag fear it will explode or else simply fail to operate. The bathroom has been installed upstairs, replacing one of the bedrooms, but the hot water heater has not yet been put in. Baths are icy. The walls many years ago were papered with hideous floral wallpapers, pink peonies and drooping lily-of-the-valley in what look to be funeral wreaths. The paper is shredding brownly off most of the walls. In the bedroom closets are piles of ancient newspapers and decaying articles of clothing thoughtfully left by the previous tenants. The half-basement is reachable only by a trapdoor and a hazardous ladder. Why did she not notice these things when she first saw the place?

The old grey pine barn, so beautiful from a distance, is now seen to be falling down. It also contains bats.

Four windows are cracked and have been patched with adhesive tape. The electric pump for the well gets frequent air-locks or otherwise loses its prime, making helpless asthmatic noises. Morag makes calmly hysterical phone calls to the plumber.

The meadow from the house to the river contains grass about three feet high. A power mower will be necessary in the spring. Who will work it? Morag?

Pique is scared at nights. So is Morag, although she doesn't let on. Pique announces that if a bat gets in her bedroom, she will die. Morag yells at her not to be so stupid; bats are harmless. Then feels self-reproachful, as she herself also feels that if a bat gets in anywhere, she too will die.

"Are there coyotes in those woods, Mum?" Pique asks.

"*We* say *kiy*-oot," Morag says, with ludicrous pride and snappishness. "Only John Wayne says coy-*oh*-tee. And no, there are none in our woods."

Are there?

A colony of mice is discovered in the small cupboard under the stairs. Pique, perversely, takes to these creatures and accuses Morag of murder when the colony, with great difficulty and squeamishness on Morag's part, is destroyed.

Winter will soon be upon the land. Pique and Morag will obviously freeze in this broken-down old wreck of a place. No wonder it was so relatively cheap.

What have I done?

"C'mon, honey, let's go and have a look at the river before it's dark."

They walk through the long grass. Pique, suddenly happy, begins to run, sweeping at the grasses with her out-stretched arms. Across the river, the maples are trees of flame. The river carries on its ripples the last of the daylight.

"Hey, Pique, you know what? It's going to be all right here."

"Sure it is," Pique says. "Who doesn't know that?"

Oh. Pardon me. I thought you didn't.

They look up to see an old man approaching. He has an exceedingly tidy grey beard. He is wearing crumpled brown corduroys and a blue plaid windbreaker.

"My name's Royland," he says. "From the place next door, downriver a little way. Didn't come over sooner because I thought you'd likely want to settle in a bit first. Then I started wondering if maybe you needed a hand with anything."

"Well, thanks. I'm —"

"I know your name, Morag Gunn. Stevie Harchuk told me."

"This is my daughter, Pique."

"Hi," Royland says. "I'm divining a well tomorrow, Pique. That's my job, finding wells. Want to come along, as it's Saturday?"

"Gee. Well, sure. What's it mean, divining?"

"You'll see."

A hoarse eerie sound from overhead, and they look. Very far up, the flock is flying in its V-formation, the few leaders out in front. Again the flock sounds its deep long-drawn-out resonant raucous cry that no words can ever catch but which no one who ever hears it will ever forget.

The Canada geese are flying south.

Memorybank Movie: *Shadow of Eden*

Three years, and the novel is finished, the last few final revisions completed one moment ago. It has been accepted, although no doubt it will be a full year until it is published. Three years of trying to get inside the thing quickly in the mornings after Pique has left for school, and of trying to get outside in the afternoons before Pique arrives home. Morag feels a massive relief at having it done, and at the same time the emptiness that always follows the ending of a book. She packages the sheaf of paper, ready to return to the publishers, paces a little, considers phoning Ella, and decides that a letter will be cheaper. Finances are getting low. Pray God they hurry with the advance on royalties.

Dear Ella –

Just now finished the final touches on *Shadow of Eden*. I haven't wanted to talk about it until now, but now I do. Maybe you and Mort could come up for a weekend? Bring the kids – Pique thinks they're great, and would prevent their falling in the river. Let me know, eh? Any time.

Odd – the tales Christie used to tell of Piper Gunn and the Sutherlanders, and now this book deals with the same period. The novel follows them on the sea journey to Hudson Bay, through that winter at Churchill and then on the long walk to York Factory in the spring. Christie always said they walked about a thousand miles – it was about a hundred and fifty, in fact, but you know, he was right; it must've felt like a thousand. The man who led them on that march, and on the trip by water to Red River, was young Archie Macdonald, but in my mind the piper who played them on will always be that giant of a man, Piper Gunn, who probably never lived in so-called real life but who lives forever. Christie knew things about inner truths that I am only just beginning to understand.

I kept thinking about the tales Jules once told me, a long long time ago, about Rider Tonnerre. Which brings to mind a curious thing – something that must've come from Old Jules. Rider was called Prince of the Braves, Skinner said, and his rifle was named La Petite. In factuality (if that isn't a word, it should be), those names pertained to Gabriel Dumont, Riel's lieutenant in Saskatchewan, much later on. That's okay – Skinner's grandad had a right to borrow them. I like the thought of history and fiction interweaving. The tale of how Rider got his horse, Roi du Lac, I've recently discovered, comes from a Cree legend – probably Old Jules didn't know that. You wonder how long that story had been passed on.

Enough of this. I feel I've neglected Pique, to some extent, recently, trying to get this thing finished. And I mustn't. Especially right now, because she's feeling badly. My God, I meant to tell you this first, and didn't, and now feel heartless even though I'm just as upset as Pique, or thought I was. Our beloved Flame (the Irish setter we got shortly after you and Mort were up here last, about a year ago) was run over last week. Royland, good neighbour that he is, buried the dog. I don't think I could have. Pique won't even consider another dog, and I guess I don't really want one, either. Pique's first real encounter with death, because Flame *was* a member of the family. Christie's death didn't really affect her, because she'd known him only through stories, and in that way, he's never died in her mind.

Please try to come up for a weekend. The land looks splendid, and the crops are beginning to ripen – not, however, on my land. Here at the Gunn ranch we have a lovely crop of unmown grass, which I am hoping to lend to a local farmer as pasturing for his cows in exchange for cream, a ploy which I consider to be fairly brilliant.

Love to you all,
Morag

Memorybank Movie: Gainsay Who Dare
"Hi, Ma," Pique says, slamming the screendoor.
"Hi, honey."

This *Ma* bit is new. It is as though Pique, at fifteen, has now decided that *Mum* sounds too childish and *Mother*, possibly, too formal. The word in some way is a proclamation of independence, a statement of the fact that the distance between them, in terms of equality, is diminishing, and the relationship must soon become that of two adults. On balance, Morag is glad. But it will take some inner adjustment.

Pique is tall now, nearly as tall as Morag, and has a fine slender figure and what Morag's generation would call good breasts. Melon breasts no longer being in fashion, however, Pique is constantly moaning that hers are too ample.

Pique and Morag have been at McConnell's Landing four years now. Vast changes. Pique nearly grown-up. The log house renovated in various ways as finances have permitted. A large window now enables Morag to look out at the river while writing at the long oak table in the kitchen. An electric stove. New furnace. The old linoleum removed, and the original pine floors sanded and restored.

Morag's land is now only a few acres, meadow and woods. She has sold the rest, partly because she needed the money and partly because she did not like to see the land unused and it took her a very short time to realize that she herself wasn't going to work it.

Pique, crunching into an apple, casually flicks through the pile of reviews on the table, *Shadow of Eden* having come out at last.

"These come today, Ma?"

"Yeh. Quite a few favourable ones, thank God. Some snarling ones."

"Do those ones bother you? Doesn't it make you mad when people say terrible things about you?"

"Well, they don't exactly make me feel like a million dollars. On the other hand, they don't knock me out, either, the way they once did."

The thing that will take some getting used to, in the reviews of *Shadow of Eden*, is that so many of them refer to Morag Gunn as an established and older writer. At forty-four – an older writer? She has thought of herself as a beginning writer for so long that it has come as a shock to realize she no longer fits into this category. There are now a large number of writers young enough to be her children, and some of them are very good indeed. Morag reads their work out of fascination, not duty, and in the past few years has got to know quite a few of them as friends. Yes, *older writer* is the right phrase. Takes some mental adjustment, though, Meditation. Assimilation.

Pique has laid aside the clippings and is looking out the window. She turns and Morag sees from her eyes that she is troubled.

"What is it, honey?"

"What's the legal age a person can quit high school?"

"What?"

"Do you know? I'm just asking you. If you don't want to tell me, I can find out easily enough."

"I don't know for sure what it is, Pique. But why?"

"Because I'm getting out of that school the moment I can do it without some truant officer hassling me about it, that's why."

Pique's comment on the reviews. *Doesn't it make you mad when people say terrible things about you?*

"What happened, Pique?"

The girl sits down and lowers her head, spreading her long black hair like a veil or a mask around her face.

"I just can't see much use in what they're teaching, that's all."

"I don't think that's all. Is it?"

Pique is silent for a moment. When her voice bursts out, it is tense with pain.

"What do you know of it? You've never been called a dirty halfbreed. You've never had somebody tell you your mother was crazy because she lived out here alone and wrote dirty books and had kooky people coming out from the city to visit. Have you? Have you?"

The old patterns, the ones from both Morag's and Jules' childhoods, the old patterns even in Pique's own life. The school in England, Morag sees in retrospect, was a more fortunate thing than she had recognized at the time – the primary school in Hampstead was full of Pakistani and African and West Indian kids, and also full of kids whose parents were writers; amongst that lot, Pique was normal and accepted, nothing unusual. McConnell's Landing was a different matter. When Pique first started school here, she'd been given a bad time. Gradually, as she stuck it out (with how much anguish Morag will never know) the taunts tapered off, only to rise again in adolescence.

"No, I never had exactly that, Pique. Your dad had a lot of comments passed about him and his family, when he was a kid, I remember, but at least he could beat up on nearly any boy who gave him that kind of talk. With me, it was comments about Christie being the Scavenger, the town garbage collector, and about me wearing – at least in grade school – long droopy dresses like floursacks. I always thought I was going to spare my child that kind of pain. I haven't, though. It's different, with you, but it's the same. What happened today?"

"Yeh. Well. It was just that this guy, a real smartass, came up and started making these passes at me, see? And when I more or less told him to get lost, he said *Aw come on, don't give me that shit – you know halfbreed girls can't wait to get fucked by any guy who comes along.*"

Oh jesus.

"Goddamn," Morag says furiously. "Who was he? I am going to go and see the principal."

"No, Ma, don't. The guy's dad is on the School Board. It wouldn't do any good to see the principal. He'd be sorry and all that, but he couldn't do anything. Yeh, maybe a person's got to put up a fight. But not that way."

"What way, then?"

"I don't know," Pique says. "At least, not yet."

How to spare one's children at least some kinds of pain? No way. Where in the Bible does it speak of a new heaven and a new earth? That's what we need all right, Lord, but it looks to be a long time in coming.

"Okay. I'll do whatever you want me to do about it, then, Pique."

"I guess I don't want you actually to do anything, right now, Ma."

Pique's voice, this moment, is very far away from being young.

They eat dinner in silence, but a related silence, not a distant one. About nine, Pique is watching TV in the small and seldom-used livingroom (the big kitchen, in the age-old manner of farmhouses, having developed into the natural meetingplace). Morag is writing letters. The truck draws up noisily at the back of the house. Morag looks out the back window, but in the darkness cannot recognize the figure who climbs out. She goes to the door, opens it and waits. Odd – in a city she would never open a door before she knew who the unexpected visitor was. Out here it never occurs to her that it might be a threatening presence.

The man comes around the corner of the house up to the front door. Runs his hand through his greying hair in a gesture of awkwardness or embarrassment.

"Hi, Morag," Jules says. "Can I come in?"

At first it seems likely that for no apparent reason she is hallucinating. But no. Jules steps inside and she smells the good sweat smell of him, as always. She cannot say anything. She puts her arms out to him, and he holds her.

"These damn glasses of yours," he says. "They always did get in the way."

He takes them off and sets them carefully on the table. Then kisses her. She responds at first as swiftly as always, and then relaxes a little, realizing that it is different now from ten years before. The sheer force and urgency of it are diminished. They are kissing each other like two people who have known one another for a long long time and have not seen one another for a long time.

"Skinner –"

The old nickname comes out without Morag's having intended it. Jules laughs.

"The only other damn person who ever uses that name for me now is my brother Jacques. Even Billy Joe never has."

"Are you still singing with Billy Joe, then?"

"Yeh. We split up the team for a few years, and Billy went north to his people, there, but we got together again a year or so ago."

"How did you know I was here, Jules?"

"It's not so hard to find you. I phoned your publishers. They gave me your address."

He wouldn't have done that, years ago.

"How did you find the place, then? Rural Route One isn't very helpful."

Jules hugs her briefly, as though amused.

"Hell, nearly everybody in McConnell's Landing knows you, Morag. They think you're crazy as a bedbug."

He looks, of course, older. He *is* older. He must be forty-seven now. He looks more like Lazarus than he did ten years ago, and he was looking a lot like Lazarus then. His hair is longer and the grey in it is extensive. His old brass-buckled belt is now slung under an increased belly, and his eyes are the tough tired eyes of a man who still has to battle but no longer finds much joy in doing so. He is wearing purple corduroys and a wide-sleeved Russian-style mauve shirt, and this form of dress somehow seems less confident than the plain coarse Levi's and blue workshirt of a decade ago. In Toronto fifteen years ago, he had worn sequinned satin shirts, but only for his performances, and he had been scornful about that fancy-dress outfit. *Fifteen* years? That long? Pique is fifteen now, so in fact it was nearly sixteen years ago.

Morag becomes aware of the fact that it is not only herself who is doing the scrutinizing. What is Jules thinking? *Ten years have changed this woman.*

"We're both older," Jules says in the quiet voice which has always denoted either anger or hurt or both.

"Why did you come here, now?"

"Do I have to have a reason, Morag?"

"No."

"Maybe I wanted to see you. Maybe I thought it was time I saw her – Pique – again."

"Will you be staying awhile, then?"

Is she enquiring or pleading? It doesn't matter.

"No," Jules says. "I gotta drive back tomorrow."

And he will be sleeping tonight, she senses, alone in the spare bedroom, by his own wish. And yet, oddly, she realizes she is not taking this as a personal affront to herself. It is he who reaches out his hand first, now. Their hands tighten together. No explanations; merely a consolation against time.

"What do you hear of Christie, Morag?"

"He died a few years back."

"I'm sorry. He was okay, Christie."

"Yes. He was."

Morag realizes now that the TV voices from the livingroom have abruptly ceased. Pique stands in the kitchen doorway. Tall, strong, lovely, and incredibly vulnerable. Her dark eyes sizing things up.

"I know you," she says to Jules.

Just that. In a neutral voice, neither accusing nor demanding. Jules, who had been able to play it so cool when Pique was five, is now uncertain. There is nothing Morag can say or dare say.

"You've sure changed, Pique," he says finally. "Funny thing – I want to call you by your real name, but like your mother, I can't."

"Because of your sister," Pique says.

"Yeh. Would you have a beer handy, Morag?"

Morag goes to get it for him. There is no way he is ever going to apologize to Pique for his absence, and to defend himself would be to knock Morag, as it was her wish originally to have Pique. Still, Pique is his, and he will never in his life deny her. Does she see all these things? Why should she?

"Are you still singing?" Pique asks.

"Yeh. I'm still singing. That's how I live. I should've been born later. Lotsa new places now, and they don't think

you're some kind of nut if you sing your own songs sometimes, but most of those places, they're for the kids, and they
want young singers. Me, I'm gettin' older."

"You're not getting old." The young voice, crying out
against time, against the evidence of her eyes.

Jules laughs. Then goes briefly out to the truck, returning with his guitar.

"You want to hear, Pique?"

She nods, silently. Morag suspects that Pique would
like to tell him she is trying to learn guitar, that she sings
as well, that she plays the records of Baez and Dylan and
Cohen and Joni Mitchell and Buffy Sainte-Marie and James
Taylor and Bruce Cockburn and a dozen others whose
names Morag frequently misplaces, over and over and over,
trying to learn from them. Pique listens to groups, too,
but it is the solitary singers, singing their own songs, who
really absorb her. Pique cannot tell Jules any of this now.
Maybe later. If only he would stay longer. But probably
he can't.

"You don't remember, I guess," Jules says, "when you
were a little kid, there, in Vancouver, and I sang the song to
you about my grandfather Jules Tonnerre, your great-
grandfather? He fought with Riel, there, at Batoche, the last
flight, in 1885. You remember the song?"

Pique frowns. It was a long time ago. There is no resem-
blance between five and fifteen.

"I kind of remember," she says, "but not that much."

"Well, here it is," Jules says.

He tunes his guitar, and sings.

The Métis, they met from the whole prairie
To keep their lands, to keep them free,

They gathered there in the valley Qu'Appelle
Alongside their leader, Louis Riel.

They took their rifles into their hands,
They fought to keep their fathers' lands,
And one of them who gathered there
Was a Métis boy called Jules Tonnerre. . . .

He goes through the fifteen verses, but the song does not seem long. His voice is rougher than it was ten years ago, but it is still strong. One foot beats time. Pique, sitting on the floor beside the woodstove, keeps her head lowered. Her eyes cannot be seen. Jules finishes and reaches for another beer which Morag has placed beside him. Then he and Pique look at one another. Pique again nods silently. Apparently nothing needs to be spoken. The tension in Jules' shoulders eases visibly. It is all right, then.

How unlike me. I would have had to say what I thought about it, analyze the words, probably, yakkity yak. She doesn't have to, and neither does Jules. They do it in a different way, a way I can see, although it's not mine.

Jules turns to Morag.

"You remember, in Vancouver, there, I wanted to get a song about Lazarus, only I couldn't get it just then?"

"Yes. I remember."

"Well, after a while I did get it. Did you ever tell Pique about Lazarus?"

"Some."

Jules laughs.

"Yeh. Some. Well, here's some more."

And he sings. Pique again lowers her head, her hair spreading out like a veil, a mask, around her face.

Lazarus, he was the king of Nothing
Lazarus, he never had a dime.
He was sometimes on Relief, he was permanent
    on grief.
And Nowhere was the place he spent his time.

Lazarus, he lived down in the Valley;
Lazarus, he never lived in Town.
Now that damn town, still, see, it sits up on the hill,
But Lazarus, oh he belonged way down.

Lazarus was what they called a halfbreed;
Half a man was what the Town would say.
What made him walk so slow, well, they didn't care
    to know –
It was easier by far to look away.

Lazarus was nothing to the Mounties;
They knew he never had a cent for bail.
When his life got more than rough, and he drank
    more than enough,
They just threw him in the Manawaka jail.

Lazarus was not afraid of fighting;
It was the only way he knew to win.
But when the fight was o'er, he'd be in the clink
    once more;
Those breeds must learn that anger is a sin.

Lazarus, he went and lost his woman;
She left him when she found he wasn't king.

Then he had no woman there, nothing left,
    no kind of prayer,
And Nothing was his always Everything.

Lazarus, he had a bunch of children;
He raised them in the Valley down below.
So that they could eat, he shot rabbits there for meat,
Where his ancestors had shot the buffalo.

Lazarus, he lost some of those children,
Some to fire, some to the City's heart of stone.
Maybe when they went, was the worst time that
    was sent.
For then he really knew he was alone.

Lazarus, he never slit his throat, there.
Lazarus, he never met his knife.
If you think that isn't news, just try walking in his shoes.
Oh Lazarus, he kept his life, for life.

Lazarus, rise up out of the Valley;
Tell them what it really means to try.
Go tell them in the Town, though they always put you
    down,
Lazarus, oh man, you didn't die.
    Lazarus, oh man, you didn't die.

Morag has stopped thinking about Pique and what she
may be thinking and feeling. It is again the valley, inside
her own head, and the last time she ever spoke to Lazarus,
after that first time with Jules when Lazarus held the bottle

up and said *This here, it's my woman now*, and Jules was angry, angry. Lazarus.

Pique raises her head.

"I didn't know it was like that."

"There's a lot you don't know," Jules says harshly. "Your mother probably didn't tell you that when my sister died in that fire, with her kids, she was stoned out of her head with home-brew, on account of she didn't give a fuck whether she lived or died, and she had her reasons."

"No. I just heard about the fire. I know about that. Do you have to tell me again? I don't want to hear it."

Jules reaches for another beer. To Morag, he looks much older than forty-seven now, and much younger. His purple costume seems to fall away from him, leaving only the bones of his being, and his implacable eyes.

"Yeh, I guess I have to tell you it, again."

My sister's eyes
Fire and snow –
What they'd be saying
You couldn't know.

My sister's body
Fire and snow –
It wasn't hers
Since long ago.

My sister's man
Fire and snow –
He ate her heart
Then he made her go.

My sister's children
Fire and snow –
She prayed they'd live
But it wasn't so.

My sister's death
Fire and snow –
Burned out her sorrow
In the valley below.

My sister's eyes
Fire and snow –
What they were telling
You'll never know.

Pique keeps her head down. Morag, too, can say nothing. What thoughts may be going on in Pique's head, she can only guess. And Pique has no notion of the thoughts in Morag's head. The fire, and Lazarus standing alone in the snow. Jules, years later, saying *Tell me, just tell me*.

"It's a good song," Pique says finally, out of the need for distance, but possibly also out of something else.

"Yeh," Jules says.

He puts his guitar away in its case.

"I never got around, yet," he goes on, "to doing songs for any of the other ones. I never managed to do one for myself, neither. Crazy, eh? I guess you didn't know what happened after that time, Pique. It was after Lazarus died. My brother Paul, he was twenty-five, and he was a guide up north, and they say he drowned. Well, he handled a canoe better than most, so I doubt he drowned. It *could* be, I know; it's happened. But he was taking a coupla tourists, eh, and they came back, all right, and reported to the nearest RCMP that he'd drowned. They had a lotta guns with them, those guys, I'd guess, and a lotta booze. I don't think he drowned. Jacques never got to first base with an investigation. After that, my sister Val finally died. She'd been trying hard for years, and she finally made it."

"How did she die?" Pique's voice is ageless.

"She was thirty-seven years old," Jules says viciously. "I used to think she'd likely die in some brawl, but she never. After Paul, she fell apart. She'd looked after him, mostly, as a kid. She died of booze and speed, on the streets of Vancouver. As a whore."

Pique looks at him, her eyes hurt and bewildered and angry.

"Why did you have to tell me? Why did you have to?"

Jules brings down one clenched fist upon the table.

"Too many have died," he says. "Too many, before it was time. I don't aim to be one of them. And I don't aim for you to be, neither."

Pique begins crying, then, silently, and he puts an arm lightly around her shoulder.

"My brother, Jacques, he lives away up at Galloping Mountain. I guess you'd like the mountain. If you ever go west, go and see him, eh? He talks better than me."

Pique lifts her head and smiles at him, and there is such a desolation in Jules' eyes that Morag longs to put her arms around him. But cannot move or speak.

"I'll show you something," Jules says, to lighten the atmosphere. "The only thing I got now that belonged to Lazarus, and it's not a thing which was even really his. Funny, eh?"

He reaches into his wallet and brings out a silver brooch, now blackened with lack of cleaning.

"Jules – that's a plaid pin," Morag says. "How in hell did Lazarus come to have that?"

"Is that what you call it? Well, when my dad was just a kid, he used to horse around, sometimes, with this other kid called John Shipley, and Lazarus traded his knife for this brooch, thinking it'd be worth a lot of money, I guess, but then he was scared to try to sell it – people would've thought he'd stolen it, see? When I came back from the war, there, Lazarus gave it to me. I would've liked to get that Shipley guy to trade back again, but he'd been killed a few years before the war, Lazarus said, when his truck piled into an oncoming freight train."

Morag stares in disbelief. These things do not happen. Oh yes, they do, though. Everything is improbable. Nothing is more improbable than anything else.

"Jules –"

"Yeh?" Then, as he sees her face, "What in hell's the matter, Morag?"

"Even if he hadn't been killed," Morag says, her own voice sounding detached from herself, "he wouldn't have had the knife. He'd sold it for a package of cigarettes. To Christie Logan. Christie never mentioned the guy's name, but he told me the story. Christie never knew whose the knife had been, or he'd have given it back to Lazarus. He gave the knife to me, years ago. That, and a few books, that's all I have of Christie's."

"You're crazy," Jules says. "You're kidding."

"She's not kidding," Pique said. "Where do you keep it, Ma?"

"Top drawer of my dresser."

Pique goes upstairs and returns. She is about to hand the knife to Jules. Then she hesitates and finally hands it to Morag. Jules hunches in his chair, motionless, eyes concealed.

It is an ordinary hunting knife, dulled and slightly rusty with age and lack of use. On the handle there is a sign: ⤙

"I always wondered," Morag says, "what the sign on the hilt meant. I see now it's a 'T.'"

He takes it without a word and turns it over and over in his hands, running his fingers over the blade.

"Jesus!" he says at last. "How about that? It could even be cleaned and sharpened, you know that? It's still a good knife."

Pique looks as though she were about to say something, then changes her mind and remains quiet, as though recognizing that all this is only between Morag and Jules.

"Here," he says, shoving the plaid pin across the table to Morag. "Fair trade."

She takes it and examines it. Neither of them has thanked the other. No need. A fair trade. Morag goes to her bookshelves and gets out Christie's *The Clans and Tartans of Scotland*. Leafs through it, trying to find an illustration of this particular plaid pin. Pique watches, curiously, but Jules is still looking at the knife.

"Here it is," Morag says. "It's the Clanranald Macdonalds. Where could he have got it from, John Shipley? We'll never know, of course. The crest, it says here, is *On a castle triple-towered, an arm in armour, embowed, holding a sword, proper.* Their motto was *My Hope Is Constant In Thee* – those are the words on the pin. Their war cry was *Gainsay Who Dare.*"

Clan Gunn, according to this book, as she recalls from years back, did not have a crest or a coat-of-arms. But adoption, as who should know better than Morag, is possible.

My Hope Is Constant In Thee. It sounds like a voice from the past. Whose voice, though? Does it matter? It does not matter. What matters is that the voice is there, and that she has heard these words which have been given to her. And will not deny what has been given. *Gainsay Who Dare.*

PART FIVE

THE DIVINERS

ELEVEN

The Canada geese had been gone for a week now, and wind was fringed with cold. The leaves were beginning to fall and the grass was splattered with them, red maple, yellow elm, brown oak.

Pique had quit her job at the supermarket and was having coffee with Morag.

"I never told you, Ma," Pique said, "about when I went to Manawaka, did I? I guess I should. I thought – I dunno – I guess I thought it might upset you, or something. I went down in the valley to see the Tonnerre shack, the one my dad rebuilt after the fire. There wasn't much left of it – it had sort of fallen in, and the boards were rotting. I was glad I'd gone, though. It seemed I really knew then that all of them had lived there, once. The grass was thick and high all around, and there were these thin prairie maples and the wolf willow. I liked it there. There wasn't any sign that there'd ever been a fire, not now. I stayed all night, not sleeping much, just sort of thinking, you know. It was very quiet. I could hear the river – it's really more a creek, isn't it? It sounded kind of like voices. In the morning –"

She hesitated.

"Go on," Morag said.

"Well, in the morning, I went up to the Manawaka cemetery, and looked up Christie and Prin Logan's grave. Zinnias had been planted, and somebody was there, weeding. It was this plain little middle-aged woman with kind of stringy hair, looking sort of exhausted, you know? But she sounded quite cheerful. I liked her. I told her who my mother and dad were, and she looked surprised, but all she said was *Well, now, think of that; I'm glad Morag did have a child after all.* She said you wouldn't recall her married name, but you would know her single name. It was –"

"I know," Morag said. "Eva Winkler."

"That's right. How did you know?"

"It couldn't have been anyone else."

"Ma – I did upset you, didn't I? I'm sorry. You're crying."

"It's okay. Honestly. It's just – well, I guess I can't explain."

Too many years. No brief summary possible. Accept it and let it go.

"I've decided what I'm going to do, Ma," Pique said. "I *will* be going west again."

"Where to, Pique?"

"Just as far as Manitoba. I'm going to my uncle Jacques' place at Galloping Mountain."

"You are? Does he know?"

"Sure. I've been writing to him."

"You have? What sort of place is it, Pique? Do you know?"

Would that sound suspicious? Shouldn't have said it. Still and all, a farm or whatever at Galloping Mountain. Forty Below all winter. Probably an outdoor john.

"I've been there," Pique said. "I went up there after I'd been to Manawaka. My dad said I should go, sometime, remember? When he was here that time about three years ago, he said that. So I went. He's got this small farm, Jacques, and he sets traplines in the winter, he and the boys. They're not well-off, but Jacques is some guy. He doesn't come on strong – I don't mean that, not at all. It's just that he's sure of what he's doing, and nobody is going to put him down, if he can help it. He and Mary – that's his wife – they've got four of their own kids, as well as the others."

"The others?"

"Valentine's three kids," Pique said slowly. "Mary and Jacques have been raising them."

"I see. I didn't know Val had –"

"Yeh. Well. They've been up at the mountain all their lives, just about. Also, there's Paul's son – he'd be about fourteen, I guess."

"Jules never said there was – did Paul's wife die?"

"No. She's got TB. There's some younger kids as well."

"Whose?"

Children of Jules? If so, Pique would not say. What did it matter, anyway?

"Jacques goes to Winnipeg sometimes, for Métis meetings and that. He usually comes back with some kid or other, kids whose parents have died or vanished. You know. They've had pretty rough lives, so some of them aren't that easy to get on with. That's what I'll be doing – helping Mary out with the work and with the kids who aren't at school yet."

"It sounds – well, like kind of a madhouse."

"Oh it is," Pique said, laughing. "You'd hate it, Ma. It's a messy house, with all those kids. It doesn't bother me. Yeh, sometimes it does, I guess, but not too much."

"Where in hell does any money come from? The farm wouldn't make enough."

"Well, there isn't much. Some of them work out — Valentine's two eldest boys, and Jacques' daughter, Val, who's about a year older than I am."

"What about Dan, Pique?"

Pique looked troubled.

"He wants to stay here, and I want to go. He doesn't see that it's necessary for me. Maybe I'll be back, or else he'll decide to come out for a while. Or maybe I won't and he won't. I haven't got the gift of second sight."

In a way, she almost did, though. But whatever Pique felt was likely to happen, she was not about to say.

"Pique, I hope —"

What? That Pique wasn't taking on more than she could cope with? That she wasn't making an error of judgement in going at all? Nonsense. Who could ever enter anything with a guarantee? Let her go. This time, it had to be possible and was.

"I hope everything goes well for you, Pique."

Pique smiled faintly.

"Thanks. It will and it won't, I guess. I wish I was better at explanations, Ma. I'm not going out there because they need me, particularly. All I can do is contribute my share, if I can. For me, it's more, really, that I need them, right now. For a while, anyway. I don't know how long they'll want me to stay. I don't know how long I'll want to stay. But my reasons for going — well, it's like when I went off before. I couldn't *say*, exactly, and yet I knew. Could I sing you this song I did? I haven't sung it yet for Dan and the Smiths, but I'm going to. At least, I hope so. Maybe Dan will see then — I don't know."

Morag had wondered why Pique had toted her guitar over here today. She must have had this in mind, not having quite decided whether to sing it or not, hesitating to make herself that vulnerable. It was easier, in some way, to make yourself vulnerable in front of strangers.

Pique sang. Morag had listened to Pique singing many times before, but never before her own song.

There's a valley holds my name, now I know
In the tales they used to tell it seemed so low
There's a valley way down there
I used to dream it like a prayer
And my fathers, they lived there long ago.

There's a mountain holds my name, close to the sky
And those stories made that mountain seem so high
There's a mountain way up there
I used to dream I'd breathe its air
And hear the voices that in me would never die.

I came to taste the dust out on a prairie road
My childhood thoughts were heavy on me like a load
But I left behind my fear
When I found those ghosts were near
Leadin' me back to that home I never knowed.

Ah, my valley and my mountain, they're the same
My living places, and they never will be tame
When I think how I was born
I can't help but being torn
But the valley and the mountain hold my name

The valley and the mountain hold my name

Then silence. Pique could not speak until Morag did, and Morag could not speak for a while. The hurts unwittingly inflicted upon Pique by her mother, by circumstances – Morag had agonized over these often enough, almost as though, if she imagined them sufficiently, they would prove to have been unreal after all. But they were not unreal. Yet Pique was not assigning any blame – that was not what it was all about. And Pique's journey, although at this point it might feel to her unique, was not unique. Morag reached out and took Pique's hand, holding it lightly.

"Could I have a copy of the words, Pique?"

This was apparently all she could say. Pique's fingers tightened around Morag's, then let go.

"Sure. I'll write them out for you now."

*

That evening, when Morag was having dinner alone, the phone rang. Morag, wanting only to be left to herself to think, answered reluctantly.

"Hello."

"Morag? Billy Joe. I thought I oughta phone you, maybe. Jules, he's not so good."

"What's the matter?"

"Well, I don't know that I oughta say, like. He's sick."

"What is it? Is he in hospital?"

"No. He won't go."

"What *is* it?"

Then Billy Joe's voice, uncertain, telling her.

"Billy. In his throat?"

"Yeh."

"Where is he?"

Billy gave the address.

"Do you think he'll see me, Billy?"

"Yeh. I think so."

"He didn't say he wanted to see me?"

"Well, no. But —"

"Never mind. He wouldn't. It doesn't matter. I'll get the seven o'clock bus. I'll be there about ten. Is he — is there a woman with him?"

"Not now," Billy Joe said. "Not after he got real sick."

Royland drove Morag to the bus station in McConnell's Landing. She told him what had happened.

"Look, Royland, phone over to A-Okay's, will you, and just tell Pique I decided to go in and spend a few days with Ella and Mort, and I'll be back before she goes."

"Okay. But are you sure she shouldn't know?"

"No, I'm not sure of a damn thing. But I think it's better to wait and see how he is, and also what he wants me to tell her."

"Yeh. Okay. You gonna be all right, now, Morag? You seem pretty shaky. Want me to come along with you?"

"No. But thanks anyway."

The bus crawled along the highway. Morag shut her mind, as she was sometimes able to do in time of need. If she began thinking about Jules now, about his whole life, about the way he looked when he was young, she could not face whatever it was that she would have to face.

The place was on Spadina, a three-storey house which seemed to be slumped in upon itself with the years and lack of repairs. Billy Joe answered the door. He had been waiting for her. Morag had not seen him for — how long? Nearly nineteen years. Was that possible? Indeed. Billy Joe looked shorter than she had remembered. His hair was still black as crows' feathers, but his face was seamed and wrinkled, even though he could not be more than in his early fifties. He evaded her eyes.

"I dunno if I done the right thing, Morag, phoning you. I never told him I done it, yet. You can't do nothing. We got two rooms, top floor. C'mon."

Outside the door to Jules' room, Billy Joe stopped. He looked oddly determined, as though Jules might not approve of what he had done, but also as though he knew that this was necessary and what Jules wanted even though in an un-admitted way.

"You go in," he said.

Then he left her, and went into his own room. Now Morag was afraid. Not afraid, any longer, that Jules might mock her or tell her to get out. Not that, not now. Simply afraid of what she might see, of how he might look. Afraid that she might have to look at something she could not bear to look at. She opened the door. One ceiling light, not more than forty-watt, was burning, and the small room was shadowed. The usual one-room setup. Discoloured linoleum on the floor. A table, a couple of straight chairs, a hotplate, a cupboard. Tatty lace curtains on the window. And in one corner, a double bed with a grey blanket.

Jules was lying outstretched on the bed, his arms bent upwards and his hands clasped behind his head. He was wearing an old pair of blue jeans and a plaid flannel shirt, the kind you buy at the cut-rate clothing stores for $3.33 or there-abouts. He looked more like himself than the last time she had seen him. His leather belt, though, wasn't his old one – this was wider, new, with a clasp buckle in brass braid. Then Morag remembered he'd given his old belt to Pique. His hair was now nearly as long and as grey as her own. He was much thinner, but not with the hard leanness of his young manhood – this was a different thing, the erosion of the flesh. His face looked bonier, but the same, the face of Skinner Tonnerre, and behind and within that face, the face of Lazarus. There were no outward signs of the sickness. What had she expected?

His eyes were open and he was looking fixedly at the dull light on the ceiling. He heard the door open and turned his head.

"Billy –"

Then he saw who it was, and raised himself on one elbow.

"For God's sake – what're *you* doing here?"

His speaking voice had always had that gravel quality. Was it increased so much now, or did Morag only imagine it? She closed the door behind her.

"Billy Joe phoned me. Maybe you don't want me to be here, Skinner. But I'm here. I won't stay long."

Jules sank back. And, strangely, laughed. A grating sound which made him cough in spasms. He turned away and spat into a basin beside the bed.

"Do you want some water?" she asked, helpless.

"Rye would be better," he managed at last. "There's a bottle in the cupboard. Mind getting it? Bathroom's on the floor below. Get some water, eh?"

She did, and poured stiff drinks for them both. Jules did not get up from the bed. He propped himself on an elbow, again, and gulped the drink quickly.

"I don't see why you came, Morag."

No way of talking to him any differently, now, than she ever had. No way of saying everything she would like to say, either. Maybe none of it really needed saying, after all.

"You crazy bugger, I wanted to see you, that's all. Billy told me. Don't blame him."

"No. It's okay."

This Jules was different. Perhaps he, too, had found that although you needed to do battle, you didn't always need to, every minute. Or was she interpreting him, as usual, only through her own eyes? How else could you interpret anyone? The thing now was not to interfere, not to enter fear. She would, of course. It was her nature.

"Jules – maybe you should go into hospital? What did the doctor say? Maybe they could –"

She sat down beside him on the bed. He put one of his hands on her wrist, not the angry gesture of years ago. Now, a still-strong but almost neutral touch.

"They couldn't," Jules said. "You know, Morag, I was always pretty mad, there, about Lazarus not being taken to the hospital. And I tried, you remember, to get Val to go, but she wouldn't stay, and I thought she was a crazy woman. I see now it wasn't like that. By the time they got around to needing a hospital, it was already too late. Except that for them, there, it wasn't the same as with me. With them, it was somebody's fault or everybody's fault, and it started a long way back, but with me, it's just bad luck. I had some luck in my time. It's run out, that's all."

Morag's mind fought this concept.

"If you'd been president of the Royal Bank of Canada, they'd have every specialist on the continent in, and –"

Jules laughed again.

"And in the end, it would've made no damn difference. You think I want all that? People punching you here and there, tubes down your nose, parts of you cut out like you were beef being butchered? The president of the Royal Bank can keep it. It's all shit to me."

"Yeh. Okay. I won't say any more."

He motioned to her to pour another drink. It was only

when she saw the sweat on his forehead and around his mouth that Morag realized he was dwelling within the kind of physical pain which she had never experienced and could not imagine.

"Jules – did he give you anything for – I mean –"

"Yeh. Second shelf of the cupboard."

She got the bottle of tablets, and he swallowed three. Lay back for a while. Then raised himself again, and drank.

"I haven't sung for some time, here," he said. "It was gonna stop soon, anyhow. Lotsa good young singers around now. Jesus, the shitty gigs Billy and me have had these past coupla years. Well, never mind. I didn't do so bad. I've done what I wanted to do, mostly."

What would he be recalling, now? What memories of uncaring audiences, in fourth-rate dives? She would never know. He contained his own pain.

"Pique's going west again, Skinner."

He half sat up and looked at her.

"Yeh? Where?"

"To Jacques' place. She went there, before, after she saw you in Toronto that last time. She went to Manawaka and then up to Galloping Mountain. She only just told me. She's been writing to him. He's not like you – you never wrote letters, remember? She'll be going soon. Maybe she'll be back, and maybe she won't."

Jules reached out to the floor for his drink. When he faced her again, it was with some residue of the ancient anger, the ancient grief.

"You let her be, see? You just let her be."

Even now, he felt he had to speak like that, did he? And perhaps he did, perhaps he did.

"She sang me one of her songs," Morag said. "I brought the words. That's all. Just the words. No music. I don't know about all that. So you can't hear it. Unless she comes here."

"No," Jules said. "I don't want her to come here. Not with me like this. Don't tell her, either, you hear? If you do, she'll be here. Yeh, it would be good to hear it. But there's no way. Let's see."

He reached out for the paper, and read the words. Handed the page back to Morag, then changed his mind and took it again.

"Yeh. Well. I'll keep this. You can get another copy. You can tell her – oh, the hell with it, you don't need to tell her anything. Nobody does."

They drank some more rye, not speaking much. Jules' voice seemed to have run out and he spat more frequently into the basin beside the bed. He was getting fairly drunk now, and his pain was lessened by the pills and the rye. The pain in his throat, anyway. The night was wearing on. Finally Morag got up and turned out the light. Kicked off her shoes and lay down beside him, both of them clad, lying silently, connected only by their hands.

Then Jules turned to her and put his arms around her, and she put her arms around him. The brief sound in the darkness was the sound of a man crying the knowledge of his death.

In the morning, Morag left before he wakened.

Morag, unable to write, sat at the table looking out at the river. She had been back for four days now. Had pretended all was fine. Pique was preparing to leave within the next week or so, as usual vague about the time of her departure.

How can I not tell her about Jules? How can I tell her? He doesn't want me to tell her. He doesn't want to see her. He wants to see her, but not for her to see him.

The aeons ago memory. The child saying *I'll just go up and see my mother and father, now, for a minute.* And Mrs. Pearl, holding tightly to the child's wrist, saying *No you don't; they're too sick to see you; they don't want to.* They had wanted to see her; they had not wanted her to see them. The gaps in understanding, the long-ago child wondering what was being kept from her, wondering why they did not want to see her. Morag had been five. Pique was not a child. Nevertheless, she would want to see him and would not likely understand why she must not.

The truck drew into the driveway that evening. Jules' old pickup truck. For an instant Morag thought he might somehow have had a reprieve, the doctor having diagnosed wrongly.

Billy Joe got out of the truck and came inside. His face wore its usual masked expression, but only just.

"Billy. He's dead, isn't he?"

"Yeh. He's dead."

Morag poured them both a drink, and Billy Joe drank without saying anything.

"It happened very quickly, didn't it?" Morag said, numbed. "I guess that's lucky for him, although it's hard to think of it that way. It's not usually that fast. Is it?"

"He didn't wait for it," Billy Joe said.

Just that. He didn't wait.

"I see." Her voice had an unreal calm. "Billy – how did he –"

Billy Joe turned to her. Jules had been his partner, his songbrother. How could she know anything about that, about what Jules and Billy Joe had been to one another, over more than twenty years?

"It don't matter, how he done it," he said with finality.

No use asking. Billy Joe would never say.

He fished in his pocket and drew out something. Jules' knife, the knife of his father Lazarus. Morag looked at it.

"Billy –"

"He wanted Pique to have his knife, that's all," Billy Joe said, very quietly.

Morag picked up the knife. The blade had been sharpened since Jules first got it, three years ago. The steel was, of course, perfectly clean.

"Where – where is he, Billy?"

"I wired Jacques. He said to send the body to Galloping Mountain. So I done that. Jacques would've sent the money for that, but there was no need. Some of us here, we done that."

The Métis graveyard up at the mountain, where the grey wooden crosses stood above the graves of the Tonnerres. Nearby, Jacques Tonnerre had his livingplace, his living place.

"Morag," Billy Joe said. "I'm gonna go now."

"Yes. All right."

Morag wanted to hold onto him, and cry. But could not. Nor could he. And yet, at the doorway, they held to one another after all, momentarily. Then Billy Joe left without speaking again.

Morag phoned to A-Okay's and told Maudie to ask Pique to come over. Morag had not cried. When Pique arrived, she saw the knife on the table.

"Ma – something's happened to him, hasn't it?"

"Yes. He's dead. Of throat cancer."

Abruptly, like that. Unable to speak it otherwise. Pique said nothing. Then crumpled, knelt, put her head on Morag's lap and cried. But later, when she rose and saw her mother's face, it was she who comforted Morag.

After a while, they could manage to talk once more.

"He didn't know I was going to Jacques' place, Ma. I wish he'd known that."

"He did know."

"How?"

"I told him," Morag said. "I – went in to see him. That's where I went, a few days ago. Billy phoned me."

"Why didn't you tell me?" Pique's voice was sharp with hurt.

"He didn't want me to. He didn't want you to see him, the way he was. He was in a lot of pain. I showed him the words of the song."

"He didn't hear the music," Pique said. "I wish he could have heard that."

"I know. It's always too late for something. But he kept the words."

Pique picked up the knife.

"Did he – is this for me?"

"Yes."

"What was it used for, Ma?"

"*What?* Oh – that. Lazarus used it on his traplines, when he was young."

Would Pique create a fiction out of Jules, something both more and less true than himself, when she finally made a song for him, as she would one day, the song he had never brought himself to make for himself?

Pique was going by train this time, thank God, not hitching. The day she left, Morag decided not to go to the station after all. She preferred to say goodbye to Pique here. Why put yourself through more harrowing scenes than necessary? A sign of advancing years, this, no doubt, but what the hell.

Pique came over in the boat alone.

"Hi, Ma."

Morag wondered when next she would hear Pique saying that. But did not express this thought.

"Hi, honey."

"Listen, I'm not gonna stay long here," Pique said nervously. "I can't stand these long farewells. They destroy me."

"Yeh. Me, too."

"Ma – maybe this is kind of presumptuous of me, but – you wouldn't consider letting me have that plaid pin, I suppose?"

Morag thought about this for a while. Finally she shook her head.

"Not right now, Pique. It's some kind of talisman to me. You can have it, though, when I'm through with it."

"Meaning what?"

"When I'm gathered to my ancestors."

Pique grinned.

"That's a new one in euphemism."

"It's not euphemism," Morag said, "and it's not new, either."

"Well, I didn't really think you'd want to part with it," Pique said, "but I thought I'd ask. It's okay. I hope I don't get it for a long time, then."

She shivered slightly, and her eyes darkened.

"Ma –" she added, "you'll take care, eh? You'll be okay?"

"Of course. I *am* okay."

And in a profound sense, this was true.

Pique put one thin brown arm around Morag's shoulders.

"So long, then."

"So long. Go with God, Pique."

"Ma, you have some pretty funny expressions."

"Now, then, don't I just?"

She watched while Pique walked across the meadow to the river and the boat. Then she walked back inside the house.

Late that afternoon, Morag heard the train whistle from McConnell's Landing. The train was moving west.

Finally able to get back to work, after only several days, Morag did not welcome interruption. But it was Royland at the door. He rarely came in during what he knew were her working hours.

"It's not a good time to come over," Royland said. "But maybe you won't mind, this once."

"Royland — what's the matter?"

To superficial glance, Royland looked the same as always. The same old bushjacket and beat-up trousers, the same greybeard as neatly trimmed as ever. The usual smile. But something different.

Please, Lord, no more anything for a while, eh? I've had enough for just now.

"I went over to Tim Mackie's place today," Royland said. "His old well had seepage."

"And?"

"And nothing. I knew the moment I started that nothing would happen, and that is just what happened. Nothing. It's not so strange. People often lose it, I mean the divining, when they get older. It's a fact. It's gone on with me for a long time."

"Royland — anybody can have a temporary setback, for heaven's sake."

"No," Royland said clearly. "I had it for a long while, and now I don't have it. It's as simple as that."

The Old Man of the River, his powers gone. What happened to an ex-*shaman*? Was he honoured as an elder of the tribe, or was he driven forth? In Royland's case, the former. But would that help how he himself felt about it?

"Royland – I'm so damn sorry."

"Well, not that much need to be, really, I guess. I'm not actually going to starve. I've got a little put by, and I own my place, so with the old-age pension I can manage. It's not that, though."

"I know."

Royland sat down and accepted a cup of coffee, but didn't drink it.

"It's not so easy to take," he said. "But you know, Morag, there's something I never told you."

"What's that?"

"It's something I don't understand, the divining," Royland said slowly, "and it's not something that everybody can do, but the thing I don't usually let on about is that quite a few people can learn to do it. You don't have to have the mark of God between your eyebrows. Or if you do, quite a few people have it. You didn't know that, did you?"

"No. No, I didn't."

Royland laughed.

"A-Okay tried," he said. "He was that nervous and suspicious. But he could learn, if he has a mind to. That was plain. I think he was kind of upset by it. But he could learn."

"Really? Will he?"

"If he can just get over wanting to explain it," Royland said, "maybe he will. That's up to him."

The inheritors. Was this, finally and at last, what Morag had always sensed she had to learn from the old man? She had known it all along, but not really known. The gift, or portion of grace, or whatever it was, was finally withdrawn, to be given to someone else.

"This that's happened to me —" Royland said, "it's not a matter for mourning."

"I see that now," Morag said.

When Royland had gone, Morag sat in her armchair looking out the wide window. Contemplating. Could this be termed an activity? It was to be hoped so. She certainly spent enough time doing it.

At least Royland knew he had been a true diviner. There were the wells, proof positive. Water. Real wet water. There to be felt and tasted. Morag's magic tricks were of a different order. She would never know whether they actually worked or not, or to what extent. That wasn't given to her to know. In a sense, it did not matter. The necessary doing of the thing — that mattered.

Morag walked out across the grass and looked at the river. The sun, now low, was catching the waves, sending out once more the flotilla of little lights skimming along the green-bronze surface. The waters flowed from north to south, and the current was visible, but now a south wind was blowing, ruffling the water in the opposite direction, so that the river, as so often here, seemed to be flowing both ways.

Look ahead into the past, and back into the future, until the silence.

How far could anyone see into the river? Not far. Near shore, in the shallows, the water was clear, and there were the clean and broken clamshells of creatures now dead, and the wavering of the underwater weed-forests, and the flicker of small live fishes, and the undulating lines of gold as the sand ripples received the sun. Only slightly farther out, the water deepened and kept its life from sight.

Morag returned to the house, to write the remaining private and fictional words, and to set down her title.

ALBUM

THE BALLAD OF JULES TONNERRE

The Mé-tis they met from the whole prai-rie To keep their lands, to keep them free, They ga-thered there in the valley Qu'Ap-pelle A-long-side their lea-der, Lou-is Ri-el.

THE BALLAD OF JULES TONNERRE
(Written by Jules "Skinner" Tonnerre, for his grandfather who fought with Riel in 1885)

The Métis they met from the whole prairie
To keep their lands, to keep them free,
They gathered there in the valley Qu'Appelle
Alongside their leader, Louis Riel.

They took their rifles into their hands,
They fought to keep their fathers' lands
And one of them who gathered there
Was a Métis boy called Jules Tonnerre.

He is not more than eighteen years;
He will not listen to his fears.
His heart is true, his heart is strong;
He knows the land where his people belong.

Macdonald, he sits in Ottawa,
Drinking down his whiskey raw,
Sends out west ten thousand men,
Swears the Métis will not rise again.

The young *Anglais* from Ontario,
Out to the west they swiftly go;
They don't know what they're fighting for,
But they've got the cannon, so it must be war.

It was near Batoche, in Saskatchewan,
The Métis bullets were nearly gone;
"If I was a wolf, I'd seek my lair,
But a man must try," said Jules Tonnerre.

Riel, he walks with the Cross held high,
To bless his men so they may not die;
"God bless Riel," says Tonnerre,
"But the cannon *Anglais* won't listen to prayer."

Dumont, he rides out to ambush the foe,
To hunt as he's hunted the buffalo;
He's the bravest heart on the whole prairie,
But he cannot save his hunted Métis.

Jules Tonnerre and his brothers, then,
They fought like animals, fought like men.
"Before the earth will take our bones,
We'll load our muskets with nails and stones."

They loaded their muskets with nails and stones;
They fought together and they fought alone;
And Jules, he fell with steel in his thigh,
And he prayed his God that he might not die.

He woke and found no soul around,
The deadmen hanging onto the ground;
The birds sang in the prairie air.
"Now, it's over, then," said Jules Tonnerre.

Riel, he was hanged in Regina one day;
Dumont, he crossed to the U.S.A.
"Of sorrow's bread I've eaten my share,
But I won't choke yet," said Jules Tonnerre.

He took his Cross and he took his gun,
Went back to the place where he'd begun.
He lived on drink and he lived on prayer,
But the heart was gone from Jules Tonnerre.

Still, he lived his years and he raised his son,
Shouldered his life till it was done;
His voice is one the wind will tell
In the prairie valley that's called Qu'Appelle.

They say the dead don't always die;
They say the truth outlives the lie –
The night wind calls their voices there,
The Métis men, like Jules Tonnerre.

LAZARUS

La-za-rus, he was the king of Noth-ing;

La-za-rus, he ne-ver had a dime.

He was some-times on Re- lief, he was

per-ma-nent on grief, And No-where was the

place he spent his time.

La-za-rus, he lived down in the val-

-ley, La- za- rus, he ne-ver lived in

Town. Now that damn town,

still, see, it sits up on the hill, Oh but
La‑za‑rus, oh he be‑longed way down.

LAZARUS

(Written by Skinner Tonnerre,
for his father, Lazarus Tonnerre)

Lazarus, he was the king of Nothing;
Lazarus, he never had a dime.
He was sometimes on relief, he was permanent
  on grief,
And Nowhere was the place he spent his time.

Lazarus, he lived down in the Valley;
Lazarus, he never lived in Town.
Now that damn town, still, see, it sits up on the hill,
Oh but Lazarus, oh he belonged way down.

Lazarus was what they called a halfbreed;
Half a man was what the Town would say.
What made him walk so slow, well, they didn't care
  to know –
It was easier by far to look away.

Lazarus was nothing to the Mounties;
They knew he never had a cent for bail.
When his life got more than rough, and he drank
  more than enough,
They just threw him in the Manawaka jail.

Lazarus was not afraid of fighting;
It was the only way he knew to win.
But when the fight was o'er, he'd be in the clink
    once more;
Those breeds must learn that anger is a sin.

Lazarus, he went and lost his woman;
She left him when she found he wasn't king.
Then he had no woman there, nothing left,
    no kind of prayer,
And Nothing was his always Everything.

Lazarus, he had a bunch of children;
He raised them in the Valley down below.
So that they could eat, he shot rabbits there for meat,
Where his ancestors had shot the buffalo.

Lazarus, he lost some of those children,
Some to fire, some to the City's heart of stone.
Maybe when they went, was the worst time that
    was sent,
For then he really knew he was alone.

Lazarus, he never slit his throat, there.
Lazarus, he never met his knife.
If you think that isn't news, just try walking in his shoes.
Oh Lazarus, he kept his life, for life.

Lazarus, rise up out of the Valley;
Tell them what it really means to try.
Go tell them in the Town, though they always
    put you down,
Lazarus, oh man, you didn't die.
            Lazarus, oh man, you didn't die.

PIQUETTE'S SONG

My sis—ter's eyes   Fire and   snow—

What they'd be   say—ing   You could—n't know.

My sis—ter's   bo—dy   Fire and

snow—   It was—n't   hers   Since long a—

go.

PIQUETTE'S SONG
(Written by Skinner Tonnerre, for his sister)

My sister's eyes
Fire and snow –
What they'd be saying
You couldn't know.

My sister's body
Fire and snow –
It wasn't hers
Since long ago.

My sister's man
Fire and snow –
He ate her heart
Then he made her go.

My sister's children
Fire and snow –
She prayed they'd live
But it wasn't so.

My sister's death
Fire and snow –
Burned out her sorrow
In the valley below.

My sister's eyes
Fire and snow –
What they were telling
You'll never know.

PIQUE'S SONG

There's a val–ley holds my name, now I know In the tales they used to tell it seemed so low There's a val–ley way down there I used to dream it like a prayer And my fa–thers, they lived there long a– go.

PIQUE'S SONG
(Written by Pique Gunn Tonnerre)

There's a valley holds my name, now I know
In the tales they used to tell it seemed so low
There's a valley way down there
I used to dream it like a prayer
And my fathers, they lived there long ago.

There's a mountain holds my name, close to the sky
And those stories made that mountain seem so high

There's a mountain way up there
I used to dream I'd breathe its air
And hear the voices that in me would never die.

I came to taste the dust out on a prairie road
My childhood thoughts were heavy on me like a load
But I left behind my fear
When I found those ghosts were near
Leadin' me back to that home I never knowed.

Ah, my valley and my mountain, they're the same
My living places, and they never will be tame
When I think how I was born
I can't help but being torn
But the valley and the mountain hold my name.

The valley and the mountain hold my name.

AFTERWORD

BY TIMOTHY FINDLEY

Maybe it would be best not to read this until *The Diviners* has had a chance to sigh and to settle; until you, yourself, have had a chance to sigh and to settle.

My friend and I have a rule when we go to plays and movies: neither of us is allowed to talk when the play or the movie is over if we perceive the other has been upset or moved by what we've just seen. Surely there's nothing worse than somebody breaking in on your own reflections with: "Wow! What a piece of garbage!" Or even with: "Wasn't that terrific!" It doesn't really matter whether the voice breaking in agrees with you or disagrees. The point is, the only voice that matters when an experience is over is the voice of the experience itself.

A psychologist once remarked that what we experience in dreams can be just as affecting – whether for ill or for good – as what we experience in what we call "reality." Books can hit us hard – or leave us cold. We can set the book aside and say: "I forget." Or we can close the covers and know we will always remember what is between them. Books, like dreams, are essentially private realms. Nothing should be allowed to detract from each person's right to read a book privately and to interpret it freely in the light of what each person has experienced and knows of life. This is why what we receive from critics can be so dangerous. Not that critics are inevitably wrong; only that critics forget, too often, to remind us they speak only for themselves.

The Diviners, since its publication in 1974, has suffered from a plethora of critics – many of them negative, some of them positive – all of them loud. It has been the eye of a storm that has raged off and on from the moment Margaret Laurence wrote its final sentences up to the moment of her death in 1987 and beyond. To be brief: it has been plagued by the dread fear of honesty.

The sources of this fear have been as influential – and crazy – as school boards and pulpits. "Crazy" because it would seem to be self-evident that school boards and pulpits should have a vested interest in honesty. And yet, they have mounted attacks against *The Diviners*, charging both it and its author with everything from malicious propaganda against the sanctity of the family to undermining the morals of the young; from pornography to blasphemy. Nothing, of course, could be further from the truth. At its worst, the campaign against *The Diviners* took on the colours of riotous comedy, as when its author was accused of being "personally responsible for the current increase in teenage pregnancies."

As a consequence of the attacks against *The Diviners*, few of its readers since 1974 have been able to retire into a quiet place to read it alone. Now, it is achieving the status of a classic and, while there is an obvious rightness in this, it would be a pity if its classification as "literature" were to prove to be intimidating. Nothing we can read should be less daunting than this book.

Yes, it is difficult – but only difficult because it pulls no punches. Difficult isn't daunting, anyway. Difficult is exhilarating.

The only kind of book that daunts – if such a word exists – is a book that lies: a book that clouds or obscures the truth with sentimental claptrap or mind-easing platitudes. Earth and air and fire and water and all that these imply of reality abound in *The Diviners*. The flesh, too – and all it implies of being alive. The people here are whole and imperfect – rampant, afraid, and terrifying – and they ask of life and one another nothing more and nothing less than we would ask if we were written on these pages. Such things cannot be said of every book. In fact, they can rarely be said of any book. We know such books when we find them in our hands because they breathe. Books as seemingly different as *One Hundred Years of Solitude* and *Madame Bovary*, as *Lady with a Lapdog* and *The Moons of Jupiter* all speak of one condition: of being alive, and of the subtle horror we all experience of being trapped in human flesh when what we want – and long for – is something only the spirit can attain. I know this – and you know this. We all know this, at heart. But it takes a Marquez, a Flaubert, a Chekhov, a Munro, a Laurence to articulate it. Why?

Don't ask.

Be glad.

Late one summer afternoon – in August of 1973, to be exact – Margaret Laurence walked out onto the lawn behind her cottage on the banks of the Otonabee River in Ontario. She wore an oversized cotton *mumu* and a pair of untied running shoes, and she carried a pack of cigarettes and a glass of wine. Under her arm there were a few loose pages of her inimitable typing – criss-crossed with penciled notes and amendments.

Inside the cottage, a pot of chili was simmering and a large wooden salad bowl stood ready on the kitchen table. The smell of the food was tantalizing and comforting. One of Margaret Laurence's guests came up out of the water, flopped onto the dock, and grabbed a towel.

"It may look warm," he said, referring to the river, "but it's really cold. And I wasn't alone in there . . ."

Margaret Laurence laughed.

"That's the snapping turtles," she said. "You better count your toes, kid!"

The sun began its long descent beyond the trees on the opposite bank and the swimmer put on his sweater.

Three other guests were sitting down on steps and on the grass.

Two people passed in a rowboat, drifting on the current – one of them fishing, both of them absolutely silent.

Margaret Laurence slipped her pages into her lap and adjusted her glasses. One of the guests lay back and watched the swallows swooping overhead.

Someone lighted a cigarette.

The swimmer poured himself a glass of wine.

Margaret Laurence began to read. It was just as if they had all been having a conversation – and now it was Margaret Laurence's turn to speak.

"Morag," she said, "is nine, and it is winter. The snow is a good four feet thick outside and you have to walk to school on the roads, where the snowplough has been . . ."

She read for some time.

She ended with the piece about *Christie's First Tale of Piper Gunn* and the bit about *Morag's First Tale of Piper Gunn's Woman*.

This is how books are made. By trial and error; speaking entirely from the heart – letting the mind cope later with the writing of the words.

Five people out on the lawn beside a river: chairs and grass and water and one of them reading as the dark comes on:

". . . and Morag was never afraid of anything in this whole wide world. Never. If they came to a forest, would this Morag there be scared? Not on your christly life. She would only laugh and say, *Forests cannot hurt me because I have the power and the second sight and the good eye and the strength of conviction.*

"What means *The Strength of Conviction*?"

"Morag sleeps."

Not Margaret Laurence.

What means *the strength of conviction*?

Perhaps, when you have let *The Diviners* sigh and let it settle, you will know.

BY MARGARET LAURENCE

AUTOBIOGRAPHY
The Prophet's Camel Bell (1963)
Dance on the Earth (1989)

ESSAYS
Long Drums and Cannons: Nigerian Dramatists
and Novelists 1952–1966 (1968)
Heart of a Stranger (1976)

FICTION
This Side Jordan (1960)
The Tomorrow-Tamer (1963)
The Stone Angel (1964)
A Jest of God (1966)
The Fire-Dwellers (1979)
A Bird in the House (1970)
The Diviners (1974)

FICTION FOR YOUNG ADULTS
Jason's Quest (1970)
Six Darn Cows (1979)
The Olden Days Coat (1979)
The Christmas Birthday Story (1980)

LETTERS
Margaret Laurence – Al Purdy: A Friendship in Letters
[ed. John Lennox] (1993)

Selected Letters of Margaret Laurence and Adele Wiseman
[ed. John Lennox and Ruth Panofsky] (1997)

HISTORY

A Tree for Poverty: Somali Poetry and Prose (1954)

The
SAFE
HOUSE

Published by Kensington Publishing Corp.

The
SAFE
HOUSE

KIKI
SWINSON

Kensington Publishing Corp.
www.kensingtonbooks.com

DAFINA BOOKS are published by

Kensington Publishing Corp.
119 West 40th St.
New York, NY 10018

All Kensington Titles, Imprints, and Distributed Lines are available at special quantity discounts for bulk purchases for sales promotions, premiums, fund-raising, and educational or institutional use. Special book excerpts or customized printings can also be created to fit specific needs. For details, write or phone the office of the Kensington special sales manager: Kensington Publishing Corp., 119 West 40th St., New York, NY 10018, attn: Special Sales Department, Phone: 1-800-221-2647.

Library of Congress Card Catalogue Number: 2019932230

Dafina and the Dafina logo Reg. U.S. Pat. & TM Off.

First Kensington Hardcover Edition: July 2019

ISBN-13: 978-1-4967-2003-0
ISBN-10: 1-4967-2003-2
First Kensington Trade Paperback Printing: January 2020

ISBN-13: 978-1-4967-2005-4 (ebook)
ISBN-10: 1-4967-2005-9 (ebook)
First Kensington Electronic Edition: July 2019

10 9 8 7 6 5 4 3 2 1

Printed in the United States of America

The
SAFE
HOUSE

1

MY AFTERLIFE

I felt my consciousness slipping into a quiet place. It almost seemed weird because there was no noise around me. It felt soothing to finally be in a peaceful place. There was no one in this dark place but me. Why hadn't I done this before? Why was I afraid to leave that other world? Here I have no worries and I'm pain free. I was told all my life that it was wrong to do what I did. They said that you'd be condemned. But then I realized, it was my way out. In fact, it was a win-win for me. I would get the chance to see my grandmother and my cousin again and they were all that mattered to me, since my life had gone to complete hell. Who would've thought that I would screw my life up? I went from being a college graduate in the field of pharmaceutical science, and working as a pharmaceutical tech, to being a fucking murderer and informant.

I'd been wanting to work in the medical field for as long as I could remember, but I ruined my life by stealing prescription drugs for my drug addict–ass cousin, which led to a robbery gone bad. Not only that, I fucked around and murdered my ex-boyfriend—but in self-defense. But who's gonna believe that? Especially since I paid someone to discard his body. What has happened to me? Why have I allowed these things to corrupt my life? I was doing good for myself. But look at me now. I'm a fucking idiot with a target on my back. What are the odds of me getting out of this? Slim . . .

"Got an A-24! In the bedroom. Need some help!" I heard faintly, and then everything went silent.

Wow! This place is nice. Everything is so white and clean. It kind of has the feel of a hospital, but with no one around.

"Hello," I said, but no one answered. I traveled down what seemed like a hallway, but there was no floor. It felt like I was floating around on thin air. Now, how was this possible? I didn't have superpowers. Nor was I immortal. So, what was going on?

"I can tell you what's going on," said a voice behind me.

I turned around and, to my surprise, my grandmother was standing behind me. Oh my God! Seeing her standing there before me dressed in all white took my breath away. "Grandma, is that you?"

She smiled. "Yes, it is, sweetheart!"

When she confirmed to me that it was, in fact, her, I leaned in and embraced her. "I thought I lost you," I told her while I held on to her as tight as I could.

"No, baby, you will never lose me," she assured me.

"But I thought you were dead? The agent said that you and Jillian were both murdered."

"Yes, that's true—" she started, but I cut her off.

"What do you mean 'that's true'? And where is Jillian?" I wanted to know. Things she was saying were not adding up.

"I have passed on, darling. And as far as Jillian is concerned, I don't know where she is. But I'm sure she's around here somewhere."

"So I'm dead too?"

"Not quite. You're in a realm that is called the After Life."

"I don't understand."

"Listen, baby, I'm just a messenger that was sent to tell you that your work on earth is not yet done," my grandmother told me, and then she smiled.

"What do you mean that my 'work on earth' isn't done? What am I supposed to do?"

"Misty, God has a calling on your life, so He will not allow you to die. You can't get into heaven by committing suicide. He said that He's going to give you another chance to do it right."

"Do what right, Grandma? You're scaring me."

"There's no need to be scared, darling. You're gonna be okay."

"What am I supposed to do?"

"You're gonna have to help those agents bring those mafia guys to justice. Those guys have killed over a dozen people. They're into human trafficking amongst some other things. They are some very dangerous people. And then you're gonna have to make it right with Terrell's family. You're gonna have to tell his mother that you killed him and show them where his body is."

"I can't do that. I would go to prison for life if they found out what I did."

"I'm sorry, Misty, but you're gonna have to make it right. You won't be able to see me again if you don't."

I covered my ears with both hands and tried to block out every word she uttered. I mean, what kind of demands were these? I couldn't go back, testify against those guys, and then turn my own self in. Who would do that? I refused to snitch on myself. The end result of that would mean that my life would be over.

"Misty, I know that you don't wanna hear what I am saying, but there's no other way around it."

"Please let me stay here with you." I began to sob. Tears started running down my face uncontrollably. I leaned into my grandmother again and embraced her. But this time, I held on to her tighter. In my mind, I wasn't going to let her go.

Somehow she managed to push me away from her. "I'm sorry, baby, it's out of my hands. I can't help you right now. You gotta do the right thing," she said, and then she started stepping backward.

"Grandmom, where are you going? I'm not done talking to you."

"I have to leave now, darling. Do as I instructed you, and you will be fine. Also tell your mother that despite how she felt, I always loved her," she told me, and before I could utter another word, she disappeared into thin air.

I stood there with a troubled mind and broken heart. Here I was standing in the After Life with my grandmother, hoping to join her, but was told that now wasn't my time. And then to be told that I had to help the agents take down Ahmad and his family, and reveal to the cops that I murdered Terrell. I'd really be committing suicide then. The whole thing was unfathomable.

While I tried to piece together my next course of action, I started hearing voices around me. I heard a woman say: "We just updated her vitals. She's stable and breathing on her own now."

"So, when will I be able to talk to her?" I heard a male's voice ask.

"It's all just a waiting game now," the woman continued.

"Will she remember what happened?"

"Yes, she will."

"Okay. Great. Thank you for your time."

"You're welcome, sir," the woman replied, and then I heard two sets of footsteps. It lasted for a few moments and then I didn't hear it anymore, so I opened my eyes slowly to prevent any light from blinding me. Halfway into full focus, it became apparent that I was in a room, but it wasn't the same room I talked to my grandmother in. This room was different. This room looked like a hospital room. In fact, it was a hospital room and I was hooked to every machine placed around my bed. "Oh no, I'm here. Back here alive," I whispered after I opened my eyes completely. Instantly anxiety consumed my entire body. I didn't want to be here. I wanted to be where my grandmother was. This godforsaken place was nothing short of hell. Bad people lived here and they made sure everyone knew exactly who they were.

"What am I gonna do? I can't be here," I continued to whisper. My heart became very heavy.

"Who are you talking to?" a female's voice asked me.

I looked in the direction in which the voice came from and realized that a nurse had walked into my hospital room. The woman smiled as she walked toward me dressed in her scrubs.

"I was talking to myself," I told her, feeling very saddened that I was lying in my bed alive.

"How are you feeling?" she asked me while she stood alongside my bed. She checked my IV to make sure that it was intact.

"I don't wanna be here," I got up the nerve to say.

"You mean here in the hospital?" she questioned me again. I figured this was a test question, a suicidal test question.

"No, I mean *here*. On this freaking earth," I boldly replied.

"Why don't you wanna be here?" Her questions kept coming.

"Because there's nothing left on this earth that I want to live for. My grandmother is gone and so is my cousin. I wanna be in heaven with them."

"So you are aware that you tried to commit suicide?"

"I wasn't trying to commit suicide. I was only trying to exchange my life with my mother's."

"Well, I'm sorry to hear that."

"Don't feel sorry for me. Just disconnect me from all of these freaking needles and tubes so I can get out of here," I said quietly, but in an aggressive manner.

"I'm sorry, but I can't do that. You're gonna have to speak with your doctor. He's the one that would be authorized to discharge you."

"Tell him I need to speak to him right now."

"I'm afraid he's in surgery right now, but I will let him know when he's done."

"Yeah, whatever," I said, and turned my focus to the window in my room.

"Is there anything else I can help you with?"

"No, you can't. Just leave me alone."

"There are a couple of federal agents outside the door, and one of them instructed me to let him know when you wake up. So I'm going to go outside and let them know."

"No, don't tell them anything. I just want to be left alone. Tell him I'm still asleep."

The nurse took a deep breath and then she exhaled. "As you wish," she said, and then she opened the door to my room. While she tried to leave, Agent Sims met her at the door because he was trying to come in the room himself. "Excuse me," he said to the nurse.

"No 'excuse me,'" she replied while she scooted by him.

Agent Sims smiled as he approached me. "I'm glad to see you up and alert," he commented.

"I'm not."

"Come on, Misty, it cannot be that bad," Agent Sims responded.

"You wouldn't have the slightest clue," I replied sarcastically, because he didn't. I had a bunch of mess going on in my life. Shit, that would make me look like a heartless bitch. But more important, I would have been in jail for the rest of my life.

"Want to talk about it?"

"No, I don't. But I do want to get out of here."

"I'm sorry, but it's not going to be that simple."

"Explain that to me."

"Do you realize that you tried to commit suicide? If I hadn't come in that bedroom, when I did, you'd be dead right now."

"What'cha want me to say, thank you for saving my life?"

"We can start from there."

"News flash, I wanted to die. And I'm glad I did it too, because I saw my grandmother and we had a nice time talking. She held me in her arms and told me how much she loved me."

"So you're telling me that you went to heaven and came back?"

"Why are you smiling? You think I'm a freaking joke?"

"No, I don't think you're a joke. I just never talked to someone that went to heaven and came back. You know, I see people on TV claiming that they've done it."

"Well, I have, and I'm going back."

"If you went there, and you liked it so much, then why did you come back?"

"Because my grandma said that my work here on the earth wasn't complete."

"She's talking about this case, huh?"

"Oh, shut up! And get out of my face."

"Is your life that screwed up, that you want to die?"

"Give me another chance and I will prove it to you."

"Your doctor has you under suicide watch so you won't try that stunt again."

"Are you done? Because let's keep it real, you only want me to be alive so I can help you put those guys away in prison."

"You're a very smart girl."

"So this is funny to you? You're holding me hostage so I can testify against Ahmad and the rest of his family?"

"This isn't just about putting Ahmad and his family behind bars. Remember, you're getting a get-out-of-jail-free card."

"Are you kidding me right now? You think you're doing me a favor by testifying against those people? Do you know that I lost my grandmother and cousin behind this bullshit?" I spat, the volume of my voice got louder.

"If you would've kept your hands clean and never taken any prescription drugs from the pharmacy, then we wouldn't be having this conversation."

"You know what, fuck you! Fuck you and the boat you got off of."

Agent Sims chuckled. "Don't get upset. It's not healthy. And besides, I don't want to be the reason that you try to commit suicide again. I wouldn't be able to look at myself in the mirror anymore."

"You're so fucking phony."

"What gave you that idea?"

"Will I be free to go on with my life after this case is over?"

"That depends on if you go into witness protection."

"Well, let me be the first to tell you that I won't need you guys' protection. I'm gonna move so far away it would take one of those drones in space to find me."

"Are you sure you wanna do that? Those guys have ties to contract killers all over the world," Agent Sims warned me.

"I'm gonna be fine. Thank you," I assured him. "Has the doctor said when I would be released?" I changed the subject.

"No, he hasn't. I believe he wants you to speak with a psychiatrist before he can make a medical prognosis."

"Fuck a prognosis! I'm fine and I'm ready to get out of here."

"I'm sure you are, Misty. But we have protocol here."

"So you say," I commented, and then I turned my focus back toward the window in my room. Looking outside at all the birds flying back and forth was more entertaining than Agent Sims. All he wanted to do was talk about my testimony for his case. He couldn't care less about anything. But whether he knew it or not, I had a trick up my sleeve, and he and no one else was going to hinder me from doing it.

"Listen, I'm gonna let you get some rest. There are two agents outside of your door, so if you need anything, you let them know."

"Yeah, right," I said nonchalantly as I continued to look in the opposite direction.

2

NEWS FLASH

I lay in my hospital bed and tried to come up with a plan on how I was going to get out of here without the agents knowing. Let's not forget the hospital staff too, especially since they're the ones that had me on suicide watch. *Ugh! I hate when I can't do what I want to do.*

A couple hours passed and I was still trying to mull over ways that I could make a successful escape. But that all went down the drain when I got a knock on the door. "Coming in," I heard a woman's voice say. I immediately turned my attention toward the door and in came my mother. She rushed over to my bedside and gave me a big hug and a kiss on my forehead.

"Ah, baby, look at you. Are you all right?" she asked as she looked at me while combing my hair with her hand.

"Mom, I am so glad to see you," I told her.

"I'm glad to see you too, baby girl. How are these people treating you in here?"

"All right, I guess. I like that pink fingernail polish on your nails."

"Thank you," she replied, and then she switched the

subject. "So, what is going on with you that would make you attempt to commit suicide?"

"I just got a lot on my plate, Mom, and I was tired of dealing with it."

"You know I was hurt when I got a call from that agent telling me what you tried to do."

"I know you were. And I'm sorry, Mama, but I'm tired. I just want to live in peace. Look at what happened to Jillian and Grandma. They didn't have to get killed like that."

"You're right. But there's other ways to work through obstacles that come into our lives."

"So, what'cha want me to drink my problems away like you do?" I replied sarcastically, because who is she to try and give me advice? Her life was more fucked up than mine. She can keep her advice to herself.

"Really, Misty, did you have to go there?!" my mom said. I could hear the hurt in her voice.

"Ma, I'm sorry for saying that."

"It's okay, darling. I know you didn't mean it," she said, trying to cut through the tension I had just created. "Carl says hello and that he hopes you get well soon."

"Where is he?"

"He's downstairs in the waiting room on the first floor. Seeing all the cops standing outside your door made him feel uneasy."

"You are staying with his family, right?"

"We haven't officially moved in with them yet. But don't worry, most of our things are in his car, so as soon as we leave here, that's where we're heading."

"Mom, please do. If I lose another person I am going to lose my mind."

"Don't worry about me. Carl and I can take care of ourselves. You're the one that needs to be looked after."

"Have you thought about who's going to help bury

Grandma and Jillian?" I asked her, forcing her to talk about my grandmother, since she hadn't mentioned her from the time she walked into my room up until this very moment.

"Misty, I can't deal with that right now. You're asking too much of me. I've already agreed to leave my house because of something you did. And now you want me to take on the task of handling my mother's burial arrangements. Now, how selfish is that?"

"Mom, do you hear yourself?"

"You damn right, I hear myself. I will not take on that responsibility. That woman didn't love me. She only loved my brother and his damn daughter."

"Mom, will you please give it up? It's not about you anymore. Your mother was killed by the people that are looking for me, so have some freaking compassion."

"Didn't you just say that she was killed by people that were looking for you?"

"Yeah," I said, trying to hold back my tears.

"Then you take care of their funeral arrangements because I'm out of here," she replied, and then she kissed me on my forehead and exited the room.

After the door closed, I couldn't hold back my tears any longer. The hurtful words she uttered from her mouth stabbed me like a dagger in my heart. I mean, how heartless could she have been? She acted as if my grandmother hadn't given birth to her. Despite what my mother had said all her life, my grandmother was a good woman. And she was selfless. So to see my mother carry on like she just did sent me into a deeper depression than I was already in.

"Are you okay?" a black guy asked me. I suspect that he was one of the agents Agent Sims had sitting in on my watch. He was dressed in casual clothing from head to toe and was a clean-cut–looking guy.

"Who are you?" I asked him while I wiped the tears away from my eyes.

"I'm Agent Taylor. I'm assigned to protect you during your stay here at the hospital."

"Where is Agent Montclair?" I wanted to know, trying to figure out how many agents were standing outside my room.

"Agent Montclair is downstairs in the cafeteria getting us something to eat."

"How long are y'all supposed to watch me?"

"I'm not sure. Our details change every minute, it seems like," he said.

But I didn't believe him. He was full of shit. I knew he knew what his schedule was for my detail. He just didn't want to tell me, for fear that I'd try to hang myself again. "Did you hear my mother get upset before she left?"

"Yes, I did. But that's family business. That's where I draw the line."

"Do you know when I am getting out of here?" I asked him, testing whether or not he was going to spill the beans.

Once again, he kept tight-lipped. "No, I'm afraid not."

"What the hell do you know?" I snapped, because I knew he was lying to me.

"All I know is that I was told to keep an eye on you, that's it," he replied.

"Yeah, right. You're a bullshitter, just like Agent Sims."

Agent Taylor smiled. "I'm sorry that you feel like that, ma'am."

"Please, you could care less," I told him. "I'm done talking. You can leave now." I continued while I grabbed for the TV remote to change the channel.

Thankfully, he listened to my instructions and exited my room. If he would've given me a hard time, then I would've done something extreme, like yelling out to hospital staff, accusing him of screaming at me and causing me mental anguish. Believe me, it would've been classic, to say the least.

Immediately after he left my room, I stopped sifting through the television channels after seeing a very familiar face plastered around the TV screen. I turned up the volume to listen: "My son Terrell would not get up and leave town without telling me or his family. We all have a good relationship. People tell me all the time that he was a mama's boy, so if he hadn't said anything to anyone else, he would've at least called and told me. But I do have a strong suspicion that his ex-girlfriend named Misty Heiress had something to do with his disappearance. The police tracked his phone and the last pinging alert was a cell phone tower only a mile from her apartment. Now I've talked to her a few times and she's done nothing but lie. So I'm standing here and pleading to anyone that knows his whereabouts, please call the police. You don't have to leave your name. Just call us if you heard or seen anything," she said as the tears from her eyes flooded the cheeks of her face.

I instantly saw the pain in Mrs. Mason's eyes. She was doing everything in her power to find her son, and if that included throwing me under the bus, then so be it, I'm sure she thought. After the news break ended, I got sick to my stomach. All I could think about was what were the chances of them getting a search warrant to search my apartment? And what if they gained access to my apartment and found traces of blood on the living-room floor or my bathroom left by Terrell's body? The thought of that happening consumed me. Fear stricken, I closed my eyes and started praying silently. At this point, that was all I could do. No one could save me now but God. He was the only one.

Of course, God knew that I had killed Terrell, but He also knew that He had forgiven me for the act. But getting arrested for it right now isn't in the plan. My grandmother told me that I had several jobs to do and confessing the murder wasn't the first thing on my list. What I needed to do now was concentrate on helping these loser-ass agents so they can convict Ahmad and his family. After I'm done with that, then I'll wait on God to tell me what I needed to do next. But in that order.

3

ON PINS & NEEDLES

I swear shit can't get no worse than it already has. I hate not being in control. This mess is running me crazy. Why can't I just snap my finger and disappear from this place? I would go off to a far land, where no one would be able to find me. Ever!

A few hours had gone by and I had a total of six visits inside my room, all of them where hospital staff checked my vitals and monitored my blood pressure. I even got a visit from the resident psychiatrist. She introduced herself as Dr. Mary Gleason. She was an older white woman that looked to be in her late fifties. She had a small frame, but she looked like she had a lot of fire in her. She came in my room, asked me a few questions, like "Have you ever tried to commit suicide before this last time?" Then she asked, "Do you have plans to do it again?" I told her no. I was done with it. She also asked me if I had a family that would come here and talk to her. I told her no. And she asked me why. So I told her that I had just lost my grand-mother and my favorite cousin, and the only person left in my family was my mother and we weren't on good terms as of this moment. "Is there something you want to talk about?" she asked me.

"No, not really," I told her after she sat down in a chair near my bed.

"Well, can we talk about the incident that happened last night?"

"What? About me hanging myself?"

"Yes."

"There's nothing to really talk about. I did it and now I'm here because of it."

"Are you having thoughts of doing it again?" she asked, pressing me.

"No, I'm not."

"Would you tell me how you felt when you regained consciousness?"

"I didn't feel anything," I lied. I was not trying to open up a can of worms so she could dig around in it. I really wanted her to get lost because she was wasting my time.

"Well, I was told by Agent Sims that when you were away from us for those two to three minutes, that you saw and spoke with your grandmother. Was that true?" She kept on, pressing me.

"Yes, I told him that."

"Was it true?"

"Yes, I saw my grandmother, and I spoke with her too."

"Do you mind telling me what you two talked about?"

"She told me she loved me, and that it wasn't my time to come where she was, and that I had to come back."

"Were you disappointed?"

"Of course, I was. I didn't want to come back to this godforsaken place."

"Did she tell you why it wasn't your time to stay where she was? And I'm presuming she was talking about heaven."

"No, she really didn't." I lied to her once more. I wasn't

going to divulge my conversation between my grand-mother and me. Was she insane or what?

"Did you talk about anything other than you not being able to stay with her in heaven?"

"If you want to know if she and I sat down, had a cup of hot tea, and talked about how great the weather was, then that's what it was. I mean, come on, I wasn't with her that long."

"I'm sorry if I'm upsetting you, but I have to ask you these questions so I can get a sense of where your state of mind is," she tried to explain.

"But I didn't ask you to do that. I told you that I was fine."

Dr. Gleason paused for a moment and then she said, "Will you please help me so that I can help you?"

"What part of 'I don't need your help,' don't you under-stand? I am fine!" She was wrecking my nerves. I swear, I wanted to wrap my hands around her neck and choke the shit out of her.

"Listen, Misty, all I'm here to do is help you overcome any issues that you may have. I want to see you well or at least heading in that direction." Dr. Gleason wouldn't let up.

"Will someone come in here and get this fucking lady out of my face! She's getting on my nerves!" I yelled at the top of my voice.

She immediately stood up. "Misty, there's no need for that. I'll leave, but if you change your mind and want to talk, then have the nurse page me," she said as she was walking toward the door.

When she opened the door, Agent Taylor bumped into her. "Is everything all right in here?" he asked, looking at me and then at Dr. Gleason.

"She was harassing me, so I told her to get out, but she wouldn't listen. So that's why I yelled for help."

"Don't worry. I'm leaving," she told Agent Taylor as she stepped by him.

"She's leaving, okay," Agent Taylor said as if he was trying to defuse the situation. But he didn't do anything but tell me what I had already witnessed.

"Will you close my door?" I instructed him, and then I turned my attention back toward the television.

Approximately thirty minutes after the psychiatrist left, Agent Sims came storming through the door, looking like he was mad at the world. "Have you seen the news?" He didn't hesitate to ask me.

"Yes, I did. Why?" I asked him. But I knew where he was going with this.

"What's this I hear about your ex-boyfriend being missing?" he continued after he stood next to my bed.

"What about it?" I replied nonchalantly. I knew I had to control my actions around him. Didn't want to let on that I had something to do with Terrell being missing.

"Misty, don't play games with me. Your ex-boyfriend's mother was just on TV asking if anyone knows anything about her missing son. So, if you know something, I suggest you tell me right now."

"I don't know anything," I told him, trying to hold on to the same facial expression.

"You better not be bullshitting me! Because if I find out otherwise, I'm going to personally give local authorities permission to bury your ass in a maximum-security prison for the rest of your life!" he roared, looking like he was about to lose his mind.

"I told you I don't know anything, so leave me alone about it."

"When was the last time you saw him? Because if my memory serves me, he was visiting you when Agent Montclair and I stopped by there."

"That day you stopped by was the last time I saw him," I lied. "And when he stopped by that day, he came without an invite," I continued, talking with the utmost sincerity.

"Well, tell me why I found footage of Terrell from the cameras inside the pharmacy?"

"Once again, he came by uninvited. And if you saw the whole thing, you'd see that he and Ahmad were having words with one another. Terrell was being really disrespectful to Ahmad, so Ahmad told him to leave."

"Is that during the time Ahmad grabbed for his handgun?"

"You saw that on camera?"

"We kind of knew what it was, when Ahmad took a step toward Terrell."

Hearing Agent Sims say that he saw Ahmad reach for his gun, while confronting Terrell, gave me an idea. "Think he may have had something to do with Terrell's disappearance? I mean, Terrell did say a lot of slick shit out of his mouth toward Ahmad." I threw that out there, hoping Agent Sims would take the bait.

He stood there a moment and then he said, "That's a good possibility."

"Do you remember the last thing Ahmad said to Terrell?"

"I remember Ahmad telling him to leave the pharmacy."

"And what did Terrell say to him?"

"Terrell tried to act tough, but after he saw that Ahmad was packing a gun, he told Ahmad that he wasn't trying to make any trouble and left."

"Was that all the dialogue they had? Because they were talking for at least two minutes, so I believe that you're not telling me everything. You're leaving something out, so I want you to think long and hard—and not to leave anything out this time."

"What do you mean? That was everything."

"Tell me what Terrell said to Ahmad, after Ahmad walked into the pharmacy?" Agent Sims asked me. He gave me this stern look. Somewhere inside his mind told him that I could be bullshitting him. "Think long and hard."

"But I told you everything." I tried to reason with him, but he wasn't falling for the whole banana in the tailpipe.

"Misty, think long and hard." He wouldn't let up.

It felt like I was carrying a lot of weight on my shoulders and I wanted it off. And the only way I'd be able to do it was to tell Agent Sims everything. I took a long sigh and then I said, "When Ahmad walked in the pharmacy and noticed how Terrell was harassing me, he asked him to leave, but Terrell told him in so many words to mind his business because I was his girlfriend. So I interjected and told Ahmad that I wasn't Terrell's girlfriend and that I wanted him to leave. Ahmad turned toward Terrell and told him to leave, and Terrell asked him, 'Who are you?' Ahmad told him that he was the owner of the pharmacy. Immediately after Ahmad said that he was the owner, Terrell said, 'Oh, so you're the one selling prescription drugs out of here?'"

"What did Ahmad say?"

"I'm not sure Ahmad understood what Terrell said, because he asked Terrell to repeat himself. But I prevented Terrell from saying anything else by grabbing him and escorted him to the front door of the pharmacy."

"Do you really believe that Ahmad didn't hear or understand what Terrell said?"

"There's a possibility that he could have."

"Why had you not told me this before?"

"Because I didn't think it was important."

"Every word of dialogue is important when it's coming out of the mouths of those mafia guys."

"Well, you should've mentioned it."

"Misty, we've been telling you this from day one."

"Yes, you have, but you didn't spell it out to me this way."

Agent Sims turned his attention to the birds flying outside

of the window. After they disappeared around the building, he turned his attention back toward me. "Are you prepared to tell the detectives the same thing you just told me?"

"No, I won't. They'll try to trick me into saying something they want me to say and I can't let that happen. And especially without a lawyer present."

"I will be there with you, if they decide that they want to talk to you," he assured me. But I wasn't giving in to that lame-ass alternative. What did he think—I was stupid or born yesterday? It may not look like I have a bit of sense, but trust me, I do.

"No, if I don't have a lawyer, then there's nothing else to talk about," I said, making it plain and clear.

"As you wish," he replied, and changed the subject. "How was your visit with your mother? The agent outside your room told me that she visited you."

"What do you want me to say? She came in, she said hello, and then she asked me, how was I doing?"

"What did you tell her?"

"There wasn't much for me to say. Seeing me lying in this bed speaks for itself."

"Were you able to talk her into going into witness protection?"

"We didn't talk about it. She was more concerned about why I tried to kill myself than anything else."

"Is she still planning to go to her boyfriend's family's house?"

"Yes, she assured me that she would."

"I hope she does. If she doesn't, then she could be signing her own death certificate."

"Is that all you can think about? I'm so sick of hearing about people dying," I stressed to him.

"I'm sorry, but that's the world we live in."

"Look, can we talk about something else, please?"

"Well, what do you want to talk about?"

"Anything but that."

"Okay, well, let me be the one to tell you that immediately after you arrived here at the hospital, we had the doctor discharge him so we could transfer him to the federal holding facility."

"Is that supposed to make me feel good? Or am I supposed to say thank you?" I replied sarcastically.

"Listen, I'm only trying to keep you informed as we proceed with this investigation."

"Why don't you do me a favor and bring my grandmother back!? Bring my cousin Jillian back too, while you're at it."

"Oh, don't try to put that blood on my hands. You're responsible for the death of your cousin. Remember, she and two other guys came to your place of employment to rob it. Now she'd still be alive if things hadn't gone down the way it did."

"I told you I had nothing to do with it!" I roared. The fact that he was trying to get me to confess that I had something to do with the botched robbery made my blood boil. I'm sure he knew I had something to do with the robbery. Any blind man could see it. But as long as I could hold on to my freedom, the more time I'd have to take care of what I needed to take care of.

4

PLEAD THE FIFTH

A gent Sims could not have left any sooner than he had. The sight of him was making me become nauseated. While I lay in the bed, I tried to watch TV, but I couldn't focus. Instead, I continued to sift through all the channels. I finally settled on watching a TV movie about a woman recently diagnosed with HIV and hospitalized while she was pregnant and in her last trimester. The night-shift nurse and the woman became very close. Knowing that the nurse couldn't have babies, the woman started the adoption process so she could gift her baby to the nurse. The movie was great and it invoked a lot of feeling inside of me. I cried at the end after the woman with HIV died. The nurse was brokenhearted when the woman died, but she was totally grateful that the woman had gifted her that beautiful little girl.

All and all, the movie was great. It was also an eye opener for me: the fact that that woman died, but still had love and compassion in her heart. People like her come a dime a dozen. My takeaway from that movie was not to take things for granted.

After the movie had gone off, I found myself a little restless, so I turned the volume of the television down a little and closed my eyes. While I was lying there with my eyes closed, I heard two voices outside of my room door. One of those voices I knew belonged to Agent Taylor. The other voice came from a woman. Before I could decipher what they were saying, the door to my room opened and in came two plainclothes detectives wearing their badges strapped to their belts. I was not happy to see them. "I already told Agent Sims that I didn't want to talk to y'all. So please tell me why you are here?" I asked sarcastically.

"Ms. Heiress, my name is Detective Belle, and this is my partner, Detective Caesar," she said, extending her hand as she approached my bed, while her male partner smiled.

"I don't shake hands," I told her while I gritted my teeth at her and him.

They were both cops that looked like they weren't a day over thirty years old. "Will you give us just a couple of minutes to ask you a few questions?" he spoke up, pleading.

"I don't have anything to say," I replied.

"Can we at least tell you why we're here?" Detective Belle pressed the issue.

"Look, I saw you on the news standing next to Mrs. Mason."

"Yes, we were there. And that's why we're here. Hoping you could shed some light on where Mr. Mason could be," the female detective said.

"I told Agent Sims that I haven't seen Terrell since the other day."

"And what day would that have been?"

"Ask Agent Sims."

"Where is this Agent Sims?"

"Ask the agent sitting outside my room, he'll tell you."

"Could you think of anywhere Mr. Mason could be? His family would greatly appreciate it if you could help us find him."

"That's bullshit and you know it. His mother was talking shit about me on live TV. She basically said that I knew where he was, because the last time she spoke to him, he said that he was on his way to my house."

"So you didn't see him the night that he disappeared?" she asked me.

"I don't know what night that was."

"We're guessing it was the night of the last time his cell phone pinged at the cell phone tower near your apartment building," she explained.

"Once again, I don't know what night that was. I told Agent Sims the thing I'm telling you now. The last time I saw him was the day the agents came by my apartment to talk to me. Now, I don't know exactly what day that was, but that was the last day I saw him," I lied. As much as I tried to prevent myself from giving these detectives any information about the last time I saw Terrell, they managed to get it out of me anyway.

"Does he have any enemies?" the female cop asked me.

"Who doesn't have enemies?" I said nonchalantly.

"I don't have any," she said.

"Neither do I," Detective Caesar interjected.

"Oh yes, you do, you just don't know it." I made them painfully aware of that.

"Has Terrell ever been abusive to you?" Detective Belle asked.

"What do you mean, when you say 'abusive'?" I wondered out loud.

"Has he ever beaten or attacked you?" she clarified.

"No, he never put his hands on me," I told her. I saw where she was going with this question. If I told her that Terrell and I had fought before, then she would suspect that if something happened to him, I could be behind it.

"That's not what his mother said," Detective Caesar said.

"Look, I don't care what Mrs. Mason said. He and I have argued over a dozen times, but we never had a physical fight!" I roared, because by this time, they had pushed me to the limit.

"Misty, I'm sorry. Detective Caesar and I didn't come all the way here to upset you. We came here today so you could clear up some things for us. That's it. So, if there's anything else you could think of, we'd really appreciate it," she said, changing her tone to a meek and calm woman. She knew that she had to change the tone of her voice so that she could continue to get me to answer her questions. She had no idea that I saw right through her bullshit-ass antics.

"I told you all I can tell you," I told them. I figured if I kept talking to them, they'd get more information out of me that I didn't want them to have. And who knows? I could possibly put my foot in my mouth and incriminate myself. They'd put handcuffs on me faster than I could blink my eyes.

"Can you tell us why you and Terrell broke up?"

"It was because he couldn't keep his dick in his pants."

"How many times had he cheated on you?"

"Let's just say that it was a lot."

"Do you know any of the girls that he cheated on you with?" Detective Caesar wanted to know.

"What do you think, I walked around with a pen and clipboard?"

"Most women I know would know these things," Detective Belle said.

"I stopped counting after he cheated on me for a third time, causing me to have a miscarriage."

"I'm sorry to hear that."

"Don't feel sorry for me. Not having a baby with him was the best thing that could've happened to me," I told them. Finally acknowledging verbally that I had a major loss sank deep into the pit of my stomach. No one knew this but Jillian and me. Terrell hadn't even known this. If he had, I knew he'd have tried to kill me sooner than he tried the night I took his life.

"How did he take it when he found out that you had a miscarriage?"

Becoming frustrated, I said, "Look, I've answered enough of your questions. I'm done. So, will you please leave?"

"Sure, we can do that. But would you take a polygraph test for us?" Detective Caesar asked me.

"Hell nah, I'm not taking a polygraph test. Are you motherfuckers crazy?" I roared. Now they had really crossed the line. "Agent Taylor, would you please remove these cops from my room?!" I yelled loud as I could.

"Well, tell us what you're involved in that would have US Marshals babysitting you?" Detective Caesar asked. He was acting really petty.

"What I'm doing for them doesn't have shit to do wit you," I spat.

"It would give us an idea of what kind of person we're dealing with," Detective Belle chimed in. By this time, Agent Taylor had opened the door to my room. "What's going on?" he asked as he stood in the entryway of the door.

"Get these rookie-ass cops out of my room. We've talked enough."

"Don't mind us, Agent Taylor, my partner and I are leaving now," Detective Belle said as they both began to walk toward the door of my room.

"You should've left when I told you the first time!" I yelled.

Before Detective Belle walked completely out of the room, she looked at Agent Taylor and handed him her card. "If she decides that she wants to talk to us further, please call me."

"Agent Taylor, you might as well throw that card away, because I don't have anything else to say to them. I don't know where Terrell is, so leave me alone."

Agent Taylor took the card and shoved it down into his pocket.

After both detectives left my room, Agent Taylor stood at the doorway and said, "What happened?"

"If you were in here, then you'd know," I replied sarcastically, and then I turned my attention right back toward the television. Instead of commenting, Agent Taylor closed the door.

5

AN UNEXPECTED GIFT

After those detectives left my room, everything from there calmed down, just like I wanted it. I was surprised that Agent Sims hadn't come back to the hospital to check on me. But what he did do was swap Agent Taylor out for another agent. He walked into my room and introduced himself as Agent Fuller. He was an older black agent, and in my eyes, he was an Uncle Tom. A kiss-ass, if you will. Immediately after he made the introduction, he asked me if I needed something and I told him no, and that's when he exited my room.

The following morning I woke up very early. It was six o'clock, to be exact, and I felt rejuvenated from the day before. The nurse that was assigned to me, along with the medical tech, came and went at least five times. Thank God for His angels, because He sent one in here with my breakfast in tow. When it's time to eat my food, the ladies always gave me my space.

I powered on the television while I ate my food. First I watched *The Price is Right* and then I tuned into the reality show *Shahs of Sunset*. I swear that is one of my favorite reality shows on Bravo. As soon as that show ended, I flipped the channel again to watch *The Wendy Williams Show.* That show is another one of my favorite reality shows. While I was caught up in the drama that those women also found themselves in, the local news station interrupted the show for an emergency broadcast.

"Just over an hour ago, the remains of a decapitated male were found inside of a heavy-duty satchel in the crematory area of Webbers' Funeral Home during a routine inspection by the Virginia Beach Fire Marshal Department. From what the marshal told us, the remains were badly decomposed, which means that the body had to have been there for more than a few days. When we spoke to the owner of this family-owned business, he said that he'd been out of town for a week on business and that he left a trusted staff member to run things while he was away. He also expressed that nothing like this has ever happened before and that he would cooperate fully to help Virginia Beach Police solve this gruesome mystery. No one knows the identity of the male, but Virginia Beach Police said that they will work tirelessly to find out. My name is Tonya Spaulden and you're watching *Ten on Your Side.*"

Anxiety paralyzed me instantly. It felt like I couldn't breathe and that all the walls around me were collapsing. "Oh my God! That's where Tedo and that girl took Terrell's body to." I whispered so that only I could hear me speak. Lying in the bed made me feel helpless. If only they would've done what they were supposed to do. *Now I'm fucked!*

"Come on, Misty, you got to think of a master plan and pray that that body doesn't belong to Terrell," I spoke in a whisper-like manner.

After mulling over every word that the news reporter had uttered, I completely lost my appetite. I mean, who would want to eat after seeing their life flash right in front of them? There was no way in the world that I was going to get out of this situation. With Tedo dead, all I had to worry about was homegirl April. Because if the cops found out that she had something to do with Terrell's body being there, then I knew that she was going to throw my ass underneath the bus.

The lady that had brought my breakfast came back to pick up the tray. "You hardly touched your food," she commented.

"I know. I just lost my appetite."

"Would you like for me to get you a cup of ice?"

"No, I'm good. Thanks," I told her, and then I watched her as she walked out of my room. "Misty, what the hell are you going to do?" I started whispering to myself again while I searched my mind for a flawless plan so I wouldn't get sucked into that murder case. I just hoped that even if April got caught, she wouldn't remember who I was and would take the fall herself. I knew that was wishful thinking, but anything other than getting charged with murder sounded good to me.

I finally got my anxiety under control and was ready to think clearly, until Agent Sims showed his face. As soon as he knocked on the door and I gave him the green light to open the door to walk in, I zoomed in on his facial expression and body language and immediately knew why he was here.

"Are you coming in here to tell me that I'm leaving this place?" I asked him, knowing that wasn't what he had come here for.

"Did you see the news?" He got straight to the point.

"No, I haven't. What has happened now?" I replied, disinterested.

"Local authorities found a decapitated male body inside of a funeral home."

"Where are you going with this?" I asked him, trying to play it cool. Didn't want to come across as afraid or nervous. Sims was a great judge of character, so if I showed him anything other than me being unfazed by what he had to say to me, he'd know on the spot that I had something to hide from him.

"I just want to know how you'd feel if that body is, in fact, Mr. Mason."

"I really wouldn't have any feelings about it either way you put it."

"So you wouldn't be upset about it?"

"Of course, I'll be hurt by it, but with everything I've got going on, I can't think about him. And speaking of which, why did you allow those Virginia Beach detectives to come here to talk to me, after I told you that I didn't want to talk to them?"

"Sorry about that. I never got a chance to inform the agent on duty yesterday that that interview shouldn't have happened."

"Yeah, tell me anything," I commented.

"So, how did it go?" he questioned me.

"Well, it was two detectives. One of 'em was a lady, and the other one was a man. The woman did the most talking."

"So, what did she say?"

"She basically wanted to know when was the last time I saw or spoke to Terrell. So I told her the last time I saw him was when you and Montclair stopped by my house."

"But that's not accurate. Remember, we've got footage of him stopping by the pharmacy right after we saw him at your apartment," he corrected me.

"Okay, well, my bad. I forgot."

"Well, you know that I'm gonna have to give them the correct information, huh?"

I became frustrated. "But what difference does it make? I was only a day off."

"I understand that, but I'm an officer of the courts, so I can't withhold that information from them, especially since there's an open investigation going on."

"See, I knew I shouldn't have talked to them. You were supposed to keep them from confronting me. I'm in your care. Not the other way around!" I snapped. I was pissed off.

"Let's not get emotional."

"There's no other way to be but to get emotional. You left me amongst a pack of wolves."

"Look, did they put you in handcuffs and read you your rights?"

"No."

"Well, lighten up. It's not the end of the world."

"You're such an asshole!"

He smiled at me. "You know what? I've heard that twice today already."

"Then it should mean something."

"Not really," he replied nonchalantly.

"When am I getting out of here?" I changed the subject. "I'm so tired of being confined inside this room. I wanna go outside and get some fresh air."

"I'm getting ready to speak with the doctor on duty in a few minutes. I'm sure he's going to release you today, because you've been here for two days, and by law a suicidal patient has to be in the hospital and under watch for forty-eight hours."

"I've told everybody that has come in here that I won't ever try to commit suicide again."

"I'm sure you won't. But a lot of people say the same thing you're saying right now, which is why medical professionals are placed in situations like yours, just in case circumstances change."

"Look, do what you have to do so I can get out of here."

"Will do," he said, and then he exited the room.

While Agent Sims went to go and talk to the doctor on call, I sat there with all kinds of emotions ricocheting inside of me. One minute it felt like I was having an anxiety attack, then feeling optimistic. But then my feelings changed again. I knew it would be hard, but I wanted to be at peace. Be at peace with everything going on around me, regardless of my outcome. I guess in time, I might get just that.

It didn't take Sims long to come back to my room. "Got some good news," he said, giving me the phoniest smile he could muster up.

"So I'm being released today?"

"Yes, you are. The doctor said that he'll fill out the discharge papers by lunch and then you can leave." I looked at the clock and it read: 9:50. That meant that I was going to be in this hellhole for another two hours. "I've gotta be here for two more hours?" I complained.

"He gave a window of two hours, just to be on the safe side. I'm sure he's gonna let you out of here within an hour. So let me run back to the office and get a few things so we can take you to a safe house."

"Please don't take long, because I am ready to get out of here."

"I will be right back. But if you need anything, Agent Montclair is standing right outside your door," he assured me, and then he left.

Once again, I found myself sitting alone, trying to figure out my next step, especially since there's only an amount of time before the cops reveal that they have Terrell's remains. And when this happened, there'd be a strong possibility that they're gonna want to come back and talk to me. Now I can't allow those rookies to play me like they did the first time. I'm gonna have to be on my A game. At this point, I can't afford to take any losses.

I started preparing myself mentally, since I was leaving this godforsaken place. It didn't feel like I was in a freaking institution versus a hospital. I figured it probably felt that way because I couldn't leave and go as I pleased. In addition, the fact that I was monitored closely swayed me to feel that way too.

It had been almost an hour since Agent Sims left my

room. He said he had to run to his office to get some paper-work and then he was going to head back my way, so I watched the clock on the wall like the staff was watching me. While doing this, I decided to get dressed. I grabbed my purse too. I wanted to be ready when I was officially escorted out of this place.

Moments passed and I heard someone standing outside my door talking. A couple of seconds later, the door to my room opened, and in came the nurse that took care of me. She was smiling from ear to ear, carrying a beautifully wrapped gift box. "Got some chocolate-covered sweets for you," she announced as she walked toward me.

I smiled and zoomed in on the box and noticed that it was from a locally owned gourmet chocolate shop. They were known for their chocolate-covered strawberries, ba-nanas, and pineapples. "Where did it come from?" I asked as she placed the gift box on the wheel table in front of me.

"A young lady dropped it off to the nurses' station and asked me if I could bring this gift to you."

"Really?!" I said, wondering who could've bought me this edible arrangement. Curious as to what chocolate-covered fruits were inside, I pulled the box closer to me so I could open it.

"Enjoy!" the nurse said as she exited my room.

With anticipation, I took the bow off the box and lifted the top up slowly. Instantly I screamed. *"Ahhhhhhhhhh!"* I pushed the box onto the floor.

Alarmed by my yell for help, Agent Montclair burst into my room with his gun drawn. "My mama's hand is in that box. Oh my God! They got my mama." I began to sob hysterically. I jumped up from the bed and rushed toward the door. By this time, the nurse had turned around and come back to my room. "What's going on?" she asked.

Meanwhile, Agent Montclair was picking up the box and my mother's hand with a surgical glove he got from the box near my bed. "My mama's hand was in there.

They got my mama! We gotta help her before they kill her!" I started crying uncontrollably as I pointed toward the floor.

"Did you say your mother's hand?" the nurse asked me while she stood in the entryway of the door.

"Agent Sims, you need to get back here ASAP." I watched Agent Montclair speak through his cell phone. "Grab her things and get her out of here!" Agent Montclair instructed the nurse.

"Where do you want me to take her?" the nurse wanted to know.

"Put her in another room!" he yelled at her.

"Wait! Who's gonna get my mama back? They gon' kill her if we don't hurry up and get her back!" I yelled. I wanted everyone in the freaking hospital to hear me.

"Come on, let's go," the nurse said after she grabbed my purse from the chair near the bed. "I'm gonna put her in the medical suite," she informed Agent Montclair, and then she grabbed my hand and pulled me into the hallway.

Scared and panic stricken, I followed the nurse down the hallway. "What's going on, Pamela?" another nurse asked.

"Get on the radio and call security," the nurse with me said.

"What should I tell them?" the other nurse asked.

"Tell them we have a Code 33. And tell security to locate a young, small-framed white female wearing a blue T-shirt and white jeans. Don't let her leave the hospital."

"Okay, I'm on it," the other nurse said as she raced in the opposite direction. It was apparent that she was on her way toward the nurses' station.

Meanwhile, the nurse with me continued on our walk toward the other end of the hallway. The moment after we arrived at the room I was supposed to stay in, the nurse unlocked it and pushed the door open. "This is where you'll stay until we are told otherwise."

"Okay," I said, still sobbing from the images I had in my head about my mother's hand. I took a couple of steps toward the bed in the middle of the room and then I took a seat on the edge of it. I watched the nurse close the door and lock it while I scooted around, trying to find a soft spot on the bed.

As I sat there, all I could do was cry and wondered why my mother's hand was chopped off and sent to me in a fucking chocolate box. It wasn't a secret about who did it. The answer I needed was why? Why cut off my mother's hand and send it to me? I also wondered what kind of message they were sending. And what state was my mother in? Was she dead? Or was she alive? I needed these questions answered? And I needed them now.

Trying to juggle every thought in my mind, I wondered how those motherfuckers found her. And if they also had her boyfriend, Carl, too? If they did, why take him? He had absolutely nothing to do with what I had going on. Nor had my mom. Now I've got to figure some things out.

I continued to cry my eyes out when I heard the lock on the door click and then it opened. When I looked up, Agent Sims walked in. I sat there and bawled my eyes out.

"How are you feeling right now?"

"I just opened a box and found my mother's hand inside of it, and you want to know how I'm feeling? What kind of question is that?" By this time, my tears had saturated my face. Moments later, I got up from the bed and started pacing the floor in that room.

"How do you know it's your mother's hand?"

"Because when she came to see me yesterday, I complimented her on the color of her fingernail polish." I cried even harder.

"We took the hand down to our office so we can get a forensic professional to examine it."

"What is there to examine? I told you, that's my mother's hand. So what you need to be doing now is getting a team together and going to look for my mother," I snapped. Agent Sims was surely testing my patience.

"Listen, Misty, I know you're upset, but I'm gonna need you to calm down so I can get your full cooperation," he said.

"Is it about my mother? Because I don't want to hear anything unless we're talking about how we're gonna get my mother back. Getting her back is all I care about."

"Don't worry about your mother right now. I've got another team of agents searching for her at this very moment."

"Do they know where to go? Or where she is?"

"We got some very good leads, so let us handle it. Right now, we need to concentrate on getting you out of the hospital and into a safe house, at least until all of this is done and over with."

"Are we leaving now?"

"Yes, we are. So let's go."

6

MOVE INTO ACTION

Still sobbing my eyes out, I stood up and proceeded to the door. Sims snatched a couple of tissue papers from a napkin box near the door. After he handed them to me, I wiped my eyes and my cheeks. By the time Agent Sims and I walked into the hallway, two other agents were waiting for us there. The only one I recognized was Agent Taylor. The other one I hadn't seen before. "We're gonna take her down to the basement and exit the left wing of the hospital adjacent to the coroner's office," Sims said.

"Let's move it," Sims continued, and then he led the way to the stairwell. It was me with a total of three agents escorting me down to the basement. I had a mixture of emotions while the agents and I raced toward the nearest exit. My tears wouldn't stop. They started coming with every step I took. And all I could think about was where my mom was and if she was still alive.

We finally made it to the basement garage of the hospital and Sims started giving the other two agents instructions. "Taylor, you stay here with me while Kennedy goes and gets the car," he said.

"I'm on it," the very tall, medium-build Caucasian man said, and then he walked off.

While Agent Kennedy went to fetch the car, Agent Sims and Agent Taylor started a dialogue. I stood there and wallowed in my own state of emotions and misery.

"Do you have a location yet?" Agent Taylor asked Sims.

"Yes, it was just confirmed about five minutes ago," Sims told him.

"When we find my mama, will she be able to come where we're going?" I threw out there. I wanted to know if they were hatching out a plan for her.

"Misty, I can't confirm that right now. Let's focus on getting you safely out of here and then discuss getting your mother next," Sims said.

"That's not good enough. You guys pulled me into some bullshit-ass drug investigation, when I wanted no part of it. And when I was forced to be your eyes and ears, I realized that I didn't have a choice. On top of that, I lost my grandmother, my cousin, and only God knows that I could have lost my mother too. But do y'all care?"

"Yes, we do."

"That's bullshit! All you care about is arresting those drug dealing–ass killers and putting them in prison. Outside of that, it doesn't mean shit to you!" I shouted while I sobbed even more.

"Will you shut the fuck up with all that crying! You've been running your mouth since I met you. And it's getting old!" Agent Taylor shouted, and then he pulled his government-issued handgun. Shocked by his sudden outburst, Agent Sims and I looked at him like he had just lost his damn mind. We both looked at Agent Taylor's gun and then we looked him in the face.

"What are you doing?" Agent Sims asked him.

"Yeah, why the fuck you got a gun pointed at us?" I asked, trying to see through my glassy eyes.

"Didn't I tell you to shut up?!" Taylor roared. I could see the veins protruding through his forehead.

"Taylor, what's going on?" Agent Sims wanted to know. Sims even took a couple of steps toward him with his hands half up, like he was trying to play it easy and not cause any trouble.

"Stop right there. Don't move another fucking inch or I'm gonna have to take you out," Taylor warned Sims.

"I knew there was a reason why I didn't like you. You're a fucking traitor!" I spat as I gritted my teeth.

"Call me what you want, you fucking informant. I'm gonna get one million dollars to deliver you to the Malek family. And do you know what I am going to do with that money? I'm gonna get on a one-way flight out of here and never look back," Taylor explained.

"What about your wife and kids?" Sims asked him.

"What about her? She a low-down, dirty bitch!"

"Come on, Taylor, don't say that."

"Don't tell me what to say. Do you know that those two kids aren't really mine? Now, could you imagine how I felt when I found that out?"

"No, buddy, I can't. But I promise you, if you put your gun away, I will make sure that you get the best therapist so they could help you cope with what's going on at home." Sims was trying to reason with him.

"I don't need you to help with shit. Just take your gun from your waist, put it on the ground, and slide it over to me," Taylor told him.

"Please, Taylor, don't do this," Sims said carefully, still trying to play it easy.

"Look, I'm gonna only say this one more time. Take your gun from your waist and slide it on the ground toward me." Taylor was repeating himself, and I could tell that he was getting agitated by Agent Sims.

"All right, all right," Sims said, and slowly removed his

pistol from the waist area of his pants. I watched him as he kneeled down to place his gun on the ground, and immediately after he slid the gun across the concrete floor, we heard the car that Agent Kennedy was driving. It was coming in our direction. Agent Sims and Agent Taylor and I looked back at the car to see how far it was from us. This took the focus off Agent Sims's gun, so when they realized how close Agent Kennedy was, they turned back around simultaneously. Agent Sims rushed toward Agent Taylor and they started wrestling each other for the gun Taylor had in his hands. Seeing this gave me my way out. Before Agent Kennedy got any closer, I took off running back toward the door that led to the stairwell. As the door closed behind, I heard two gunshots. *Pop! Pop!* Alarmed by the sounds, I raced back up the stairs and only traveled up one flight of steps. Panting and breathing erratically, I knew that I had to calm down and act normal when I opened the door to the first floor and walked through the lobby. So that's what I did.

I wiped my eyes as the door closed behind me. I was fortunate that only four people were sitting around near the front entrance of the hospital. I could tell that the three people sitting down near the help desk were family. The older woman had to be the grandmother, the second person was the mother, and the last person was the daughter. Three generations of love. I would do anything to have that right now. The other person was an old black man that looked like he was waiting for his wife to come back from the bathroom or something. He was reading a newspaper and was the least interested in what was going on around him.

I continued toward the front door, and luckily by the time I had walked to the curb, I saw a taxicab dropping two people off. I took a couple of steps and leaned into the passenger-side window. "Could you please give me a ride?"

I asked him, hoping he'd say yes, considering he could've taken another call before he dropped these two people off now.

"Where are you heading?" the white man asked me.

"Anywhere but here," I told him without giving it much thought. My only mission was to leave this place before the agents came looking for me. Knowing that Agent Taylor had agreed to bring me to the Malek family for $1,000,000 was horrifying to think about. I mean, who could I trust now? If the Maleks managed to get Agent Taylor to work for them, then who else had they put on the payroll? *Damn! My life is worth that kind of money?*

I jumped in the taxi and instructed the cabdriver to head toward I-64. "Copy that," he said.

I sat in the back seat and found myself looking out the back window at least over a dozen times. The cabdriver noticed and asked me if everything was all right. I let out a long sigh. "Yes, it is. I'm just making sure that my boyfriend wasn't following us," I managed to say. That answer was the only thing I could come up with.

"Listen, lady, I don't want any problems. Men can be really crazy and dangerous. I see it all the time when guys beat up on their wives and girlfriends."

"Sir, I promise you don't have to worry about that."

"That's what they all say."

"I'll tell you what, after you get on the highway, take me straight to the IHOP restaurant on Military Highway."

"Okay, we're on our way," he said, and then he pressed down on the accelerator a little harder. While en route to IHOP, I couldn't help but tear up again. I was an emotional wreck right now. My mind was going in circles and my anxiety level shot through the roof. How could a young woman like me manage all this stuff that I was going through? Coping with the murders, now I sat in this back seat and wondered if Agent Sims had been shot. I do know for sure that someone had to have taken that bullet. I'd find out later who it was, I guess.

The cabdriver finally dropped me off at the IHOP, and before he pulled away, I paid him and included a tip. He was pleased and told me to take care of myself. I told him I would, and then I headed into the restaurant. I waited inside the IHOP in the sitting area and watched the cabdriver as he drove out of the parking area. As soon as he was completely out of sight, I headed back outside and flagged another taxi driving by. When he saw me waving, he slowed and came to a complete stop alongside Military Highway and Raby Road.

"Where to?" the cabby asked.

"Take me downtown," I said.

"Where exactly?"

"Down on Cleveland Street."

"North or south?"

"South," I told him, and then we were off.

I sat there with my head resting against the headrest of the back seat. I racked my brain trying to piece all my thoughts together, but I couldn't. *Here I am sitting in the back seat of the taxi, trying to figure out where to go or where to hide, because there is a gang of mercenaries and dirty cops looking for me. How has my life come to this?*

I knew I'd done some bad things in my life, but I'd never done anything that would warrant me to be in this situation. My heart ached because I didn't know what kind of state my mother was in. For all I knew, she could be dead, just like my grandmother and my cousin. Not only that, but I had blood on my own hands. So when the authorities figured out that they had Terrell's body, I was going to have to figure out how I was going to deal with that.

My whole life was screwed up because I stole a couple of muscle relaxers, which I gave to my cousin. How stupid could I have been? My only hope right now was to find a way to get through all of this bullshit before the cops found out that I had killed Terrell.

"We're here, ladybug," the cabdriver announced.

I lifted my head and noticed that we were in the downtown area, traveling down Cleveland Street. I looked around at the different people walking around on this busy street. Cleveland Street had a multitude of restaurants, retail shops, and grocery stores. ALDI was a grocery store located two miles from my apartment. I frequented this place when I wanted fresh seafood. My purpose for driving by was to check out the scenario before I had the cabdriver circle around the outskirts, near my place. I would not have asked the cabdriver to drive down my street, no way. That would've been a dummy move! But I did have him cruise the area so I could see what was going on. I figured that there could be a possibility that the DEA could have a couple of agents posted up around here, waiting to see if I pop up out of nowhere—or so they thought.

"Will you slow down?" I asked the cabdriver after he zoomed up on an older lady walking out of the grocery store. I looked at her twice and realized that I was looking at my neighbor Mrs. Mabel. My heart stopped. I wasn't sure if I wanted the driver to stop and let me out or have him continue driving. After I thought about it, my gut told me to get out of the car. "You can let me out here," I instructed him.

When I stopped the cab, I paid him and then I exited the car. I walked with my head down as I pursued her. I had no idea what I was going to say to her, which was scary because what if she screamed for help and grabbed the attention of the people in the immediate area. "Misty, just remain calm. She's not going to give you any problems," I whispered quietly to myself.

By now, I was within a few yards of her, and she was stuffing grocery bags into the trunk of her car, so I began to rehearse what I was going to say to her. Everything in my head said that if I stay calm, then she'll cooperate with me. But it seemed like the closer I came to her, all that confidence went out of the window.

Within a matter of minutes, she had put her grocery bags into her car and had made her way into the driver's seat. I had no other option but to call her name. "Mrs. Mabel," I said, loud enough for only her to hear me.

And even though she heard her name being called, she had no idea where it came from.

She turned around and looked to the right side of her car and then she looked behind herself, failing to look to the left. "Mrs. Mabel, I'm right here!" This time she heard me and sat there like she was paralyzed. Thankfully, she didn't drive off. "What are you doing around here? Do you know that police detectives have been all around the apartment complex? They've been asking all the neighbors questions about you," she told me as I stood before her.

"Mrs. Mabel, whatever the cops are saying about me is a lie. They're trying to make me look like a bad person, but I'm not," I began to explain to her.

"Why don't you get in my car before someone recognizes you," she insisted as she removed her purse from the passenger-side seat. After I climbed into the seat, I leaned the seat back a little, just in case I had to duck down.

"Mrs. Mabel, you have no idea what I have been through these last few days, so I really appreciate you talking and letting me into your car."

"It's okay. I know you do," she said to me, and then she drove out of the grocery store parking lot. "So tell me what's going on, because cops have been on high alert these last couple of days."

I knew I had to choose my words carefully before I uttered anything. Mrs. Mabel was an elderly woman, and she had to be at least sixty-five years old. If I told her that I was involved in a drug heist gone bad, and I'd also managed to kill my ex-boyfriend on top of that, this lady would probably call the cops on me in a heartbeat. And looking at it from her perspective, I wouldn't blame her. After thinking about what would be more appropriate to say, I told her that the cops were looking for me because they thought I had something to do with my ex-boyfriend going missing.

"You know what? That's exactly what the police said when they came by my place," she acknowledged.

See, I knew it. I knew that if I had said anything about the DEA drug bust, how my grandmother and my cousin were murdered as a result of it, this lady wouldn't have let me into her space. In her mind, the cops can't convince her that I had something to do with Terrell's disappearance because that's not the person she sees me as. She sees me as this very polite young lady that lives alone and aspires to be a pharmacist. That's it.

"When did they come and speak with you?" I asked her.

"They stopped by yesterday. It was very early in the morning. It was about eight. I had just prayed and read my Bible. It was a white woman and man. They were both nice. I asked him if they wanted to come in, so I let them in. The woman did the most talking."

"What did she say?"

"She wanted to know how long you been living in the building. Then she showed me a picture of your male friend and asked me when was the last time I saw him with you—"

"And what did you say?" I cut her off.

"I told them that I didn't remember. But I did tell them how disrespectful he was toward you. I even told them how I've seen him push you around outside your car a few months ago."

"You saw that?" I asked her.

"Yes, I saw it. I've seen and heard some other things too, but I knew what to say and what I shouldn't. See, I was a victim of abuse at the hands of my first husband forty years ago. One day I woke up and said that I wasn't going to let him put his hands on me anymore. And he didn't."

"What did you do?" I wanted to know.

"I tried to take his head off his shoulders with our son's baseball bat. After he fell down on the floor, I called the cops and told them what I did and where he was."

"What happened when the police got there?"

"They didn't do anything to me because a week earlier I filed a restraining order, so by him coming into our house, he violated the order, so I had just cause to defend myself."

"Where is he now?"

"He died a few years ago due to colon cancer."

"Oh, I'm sorry to hear that."

"Don't feel sorry for me. I'm living my best years right now."

"So where is your son?"

"He lives in California with his wife and kids. And they are doing wonderful."

"You mentioned that that guy was your first husband. Where's your second husband?"

"He died in a car accident ten years ago."

"Wow! You've been through a lot," I commented. I mean, she'd been through more drama than I had. She was definitely a strong woman. While she gave me some back-story on her life, I realized that we were driving around in a circle, and I pointed that out. "Are you sure that we should be doing this?"

"What's wrong with me doing this?"

"I don't wanna bring any attention to your car, just in case the cops are hanging out around here."

"Would you feel better if I pull over?"

"Yes, please," I replied.

"Will it be all right if I park in the shopping center across the street?"

"Yes, Mrs. Mabel, that would be great," I told her.

Having her take instructions from me, I felt even more comfortable being in her presence.

Right after she found a parking spot in front of Carlo's Bakery, she powered off her car. "So, what are you going to do? Go back to your apartment?" she questioned me.

I thought for a second, and it was only because I needed to come up with a plausible answer. After hearing stories from her past, I now knew that she was a very smart lady, and she wouldn't take shit from anyone. So, after mulling things over, I said, "I figured that if I go home, the cops are only going to harass me, and I can't have that kind of drama in my life. I just want to be left alone."

"I can understand that," she agreed. "Why don't you go to your grandmother's place?"

"She's in the hospital. I literally just came from seeing her," I lied, trying to sound as sincere as possible.

"What is going on with her? Will she be all right?"

"Yes, she's going to be fine." I lied once more. What I really wanted to do was get off this subject concerning my grandmother. I was really hurting inside just thinking about the fact that she was dead.

"So, what about your mother? Why don't you stay over there for a while?" Mrs. Mabel suggested.

"My mother is out of town and she left her boyfriend at the house, and see, he and I don't get along, so I'd rather just stay away from over there. At least while she's gone." My lies continued. I swear, I had no idea how I was so able to come up with these stories so quickly. My only hope was that I would remember these same lies if I was confronted with them later.

"I'll tell you what, why don't you stay at my place for a while. At least until your mother comes back," she offered. I couldn't believe that she uttered those words from her mouth. As much as I wanted to take her up on her offer, how was I going to sneak into her house without anyone seeing me?

After thinking about it for several minutes, I said, "Okay, I will stay with you, but I cannot let anyone see me."

"So, how are we going to do that?"

"Okay, I'll tell you what, since we don't have parking garages and only carports, I want you to drive back home and act normal, just in case the cops are watching our building. Park in your designated spot, get your things from the trunk, and go into your house like everything is cool. And while you're doing that, I'm gonna stay inside your car and wait until nightfall before I get out. After I get out, I'm gonna duckwalk the entire time, until I get to your front door. So make sure you keep watching out for me. As a matter of fact, when you see me coming toward your apartment, shut off the light so no one will see you opening your front door," I instructed her.

"All right, I can do that."

"Well, then, that's our plan," I said.

"But wait, do you really think you can stay in my car all those hours. It's just after two o'clock now."

"Don't worry about me. It gets dark around five thirty or six, so I will be fine," I assured her.

Mrs. Mabel let out a long sigh. "Okay, I guess you know what you're doing," she commented, and then we put our plan in motion.

7

SCARED SHITLESS

Ms. Mabel and I did a little small talk until we got in front of our apartment building. We stopped talking immediately after she put her gearshift in Park. "Well, we're here," she said without a lot of movement from her mouth. A lot of people can read lips, so this was why she used that tactic to communicate with me. And before she got out of the car, she told me to be careful not to let anyone see me. I promised her that I would do just that. I also thanked her for helping me out. After she told me "you're welcome," she closed the driver's-side door and walked away from the car. From there, the time started ticking.

I knew I had at least four hours to hide out in this car before I would be able to exit. I thanked God for the cool weather outside, because if it had been a typical summer day, I'd be in a world of trouble.

While I hung out in Mrs. Mabel's car, I heard several comments from one of my neighbors as she walked by Mrs. Mabel's car or stood thirty feet from it. The voice sounded familiar, and as I continued to hear it, I realized that it was my neighbor Candace. Candace lived in the building next to Mrs. Mabel and me. She was a small-framed black woman. She and I never talked really, but we did do the introduction thing, which was why I knew her name. I also found out that she was married with three kids, and that she was middle-aged, with a bum for a husband. All of her children were in middle school, so I knew that they were young. Unlike her, her husband was very social. I saw him canvassing the neighborhood many times to see who he could flirt with while Candace was at work. He never tried to flirt with me, because if he had, I would've hurt his feelings.

Candace was talking on her cell phone. I couldn't hear the other person, but Candace sure made up for it with the juicy details of a fight she had with her husband. Judging from her conversation, I figured the fight with her husband started because he called her a ho! "I told him that he better not ever call me a ho again. Or I was going to put him out of the house for good," I heard her say.

She fell silent for about eight seconds and then she said, "The only reason why I am still with him is because of the kids. If we didn't have the kids, I would've divorced him long ago." Once again, she fell silent. But after a few more seconds, she said, "I told him he needed to go and live with his mother because I am so tired of coming home every day and seeing him sit on the sofa playing video games. This is not the life I signed up for after I married him," she continued. The rest of her conversation started fading away because she had started walking toward her apartment building.

After sitting on the passenger-side floor for some time, my back started hurting, so I climbed into the back seat of Mrs. Mabel's floor. This freed my legs up, so I was able to stretch them out.

An hour and a half later I heard voices again. This time it was two guys walking by. Thankfully, they didn't walk directly by Mrs. Mabel's car, because if they had, I wasn't sure if they'd see me or not. I was able to eavesdrop on their conversation. Well, at least seven seconds of it. "Yo, dude, what was the last time you seen that chick that lives in that apartment building?" one guy asked.

"I don't know. Maybe a few days," the other guy answered.

"Did you hear that she probably had something to do with her boyfriend going missing?" the first guy said, but I still wasn't able to recognize either one of their voices. I peeped between the two front seats and was able to get a look at them both. To my surprise, they were my neighbors Sid and Lloyd. They were roommates and college students at one of our local universities. Both of them tried to flirt with me, on more than one occasion, but after I assured them that I would never date either one of them, they stepped back and gave me some space. But according to another neighbor, those two said that I tried to flirt with them and they told me that I wasn't their type. Fortunately for them, I decided not to confront them. Because if I had, I would hurt their poor little feelings.

"I can't picture her doing that. But you never know," Lloyd said as they walked on toward the apartment building.

After I analyzed the conversation between the two, the one thing I could take away from it was that when people heard that I might have had something to do with Terrell going missing, they didn't believe it. That, of course, was a good thing in my eyes. I just hoped the detectives saw it that way too.

No one else walked into the area of Mrs. Mabel's car, so I was forced to lie back on the floor and reflect on my life. I remembered growing up with both my mother and my father in the same home. A lot of my friends didn't have that, so I was fortunate from that aspect. The unfortunate thing about it was that I found my mother and me fighting for my father's attention. My mother has always thanked my dad for coming into her life when he did. She would tell him all the bad things my grandmother did to her as a child after my grandfather had passed away. My grandfather was a savior in my mother's eyes. So she felt like she had to fight my grandmother for my grandfather's attention. And because of it, that behavior trickled down to my mother. She found herself fighting me for my dad's attention. It was one bad cycle. I just wished that my mother would've had a healthy relationship with my grandmother. If she had, my relationship with her wouldn't be strained. And to know that she could be somewhere dead, that caused me so much pain that I couldn't live with right now. "God, please help me," I said aloud. "God, if You help me to get out of this situation and find my mother, I will be in total debt to You." I started praying aloud. "And, Lord God, I know it seems like I only come to You in prayer when I need something. But I really don't feel that way. I just know that You can handle my situation better than I can. So I beg You right now, to help my mother and Carl. Because they shouldn't be punished for something I did wrong. They don't deserve it. They need You, Lord God. In Jesus' name, I pray. Amen."

After my prayer to God, I closed my eyes and thought about how I cannot be spotted getting out of Mrs. Mabel's car. I was gonna have to stay as long as I could on the ground while traveling up to her front door. But what was most important was not allowing my neighbors to see me too. Not all of them like me, or know me, for that matter. So, if they saw me and watched me go into Mrs. Mabel's apartment, they could report me to the cops. And the last thing I wanted to do was get picked up by the cops. After seeing Agent Taylor turn on Agent Sims for a million-dollar payoff, I cannot trust anyone with a uniform or badge. For all I know, all the cops and agents are crooked. So falling into their hands would end dangerously. And I couldn't have that. Not today or tomorrow.

I looked up at the sky and saw how the sun was beginning

to set. And, boy, was I happy, because I had to pee like a little kid that had just consumed a gallon of Kool-Aid. It was that bad.

Fortunately for me, though, Mrs. Mabel decided to walk back out to her car. She got in the driver's seat, placed her purse on the passenger-side seat, and then started up the ignition. "I want you to keep still and stay where you are," she instructed me.

"What's wrong? Is everything all right?" I questioned her from the back seat.

"Those same detectives are camped out on the other side of the street so they can see if anybody comes close to your apartment."

"You're kidding, right?" I asked her, even though I believed her already. I just needed her to confirm what I had just heard.

"No, I am not kidding. I have to drive by them, so stay calm."

"Will they be able to see me in the back seat?"

"No, but we can't take any chances."

"So, where are we going?"

"I'm taking you on a ten-minute ride so we can get you a wig and another set of clothing. That way, when we come back, you won't have to stay in the car. You'll be able to walk in my house with me," she explained.

I was partly relieved that Mrs. Mabel cared for my well-being more than I thought, but the other part of me was scared that her plan for me might not work. What would be the chances if the cops saw me walking into her apartment? Boy, that would be devastating.

"Do you know how long they've been out here?"

"It's been a little over an hour. I saw another car drive by our building too. But they didn't stay. They did stop alongside the other detectives' car for a few minutes and then they sped off."

"Did you see which direction the other cop car went?"

"They headed in the opposite direction of where you and I are going," Mrs. Mabel said, and then she fell silent. I, on the other hand, became a nervous wreck. Every thought in my head began to spin around in circles. I couldn't think straight at all. I almost told Mrs. Mabel to drop me off at the nearest police station. But when I thought about the possibility that my mother could still be alive, I decided against it. I figured I would be of more help if I stayed out on the street, instead of in jail. I was my mother's only savior, so I knew I had to remain strong and figure this thing out.

While I was still lying on the backseat floor, I heard Mrs. Mabel pulling into a shopping center parking lot. She told me that she would be right back. I lay on the floor of her car for about ten minutes, if that. As soon as she got back into the car, I heard her scrambling items around inside of a plastic bag. Couple of seconds later, she handed me a wig and a jacket. "Put both of them on. Now, I know it ain't fashionable like the wigs that you young girls wear, but it'll do what it is supposed to do," she instructed me. A few minutes later, she pulled her car up to the side of the road and told me to get in the front seat. And I did just that. After I closed the passenger-side door, she sped off.

I turned around and faced her. "How does it look?" I wondered aloud.

"It looks perfect," she replied, and then she smiled.

"Now, when we get back to the apartment building, I want you to walk directly beside me and pretend like we're having a conversation. Don't look at anyone but me. Got it?"

"Got it," I assured her.

As planned, Mrs. Mabel drove back to the apartment building. Immediately after she parked the car underneath our carport, she and I got out of the car and headed toward her apartment. Thankfully, we didn't see those detectives sitting in their parked car across from our building. And even though they weren't around when we came back, something in my gut told me that they were somewhere near. "Come on, we only got twenty yards left before we get to my apartment," she coached me.

It seemed like with each step I took, the closer we were out of the woods. I couldn't help but look at my front door as I approached the building. From the outside, everything looked intact. The kind of look like no one lived there. And what's crazy about it is, the apartment belonged to me. I lived there. Everything I owned was inside and I couldn't get to it. Now, how messed up is that?

"Here we are," Mrs. Mabel said as we walked up to her front door. I stood beside her while she unlocked the door. "Come on in," she continued after she walked through the entryway. I followed her inside. And when I stepped to the side, she closed the door behind me and locked it. I let out a sigh of relief. I couldn't believe that I had made it inside of my neighbor's apartment without being detected. It felt like a whole bunch of weight was lifted from my shoulders.

"Can I use the bathroom?" I asked her immediately after she locked the door.

"Sure, honey, it's right there to your left," she pointed out, and then she walked into another room in her apartment.

It didn't take me long to use the bathroom. After I washed my hands, I headed into the front area of Mrs. Mabel's apartment. She was in the kitchen pouring a cup of hot water. She didn't hesitate to ask me, "Want a cup of hot tea?"

"No, I'm fine. Please let me thank you again, Mrs. Mabel. You are a lifesaver. I really appreciate everything you did for me today. You went over and beyond for me.

And I can't thank you enough," I expressed, getting a little teary-eyed.

"Why are you about to cry? Is everything all right?" she asked me while she added a tea bag to her coffee mug.

"I'm not about to cry," I lied while I wiped my glassy eyes with the back of my hand.

"It sure looks like you're about to cry, to me." She handed me a paper napkin from the paper towel holder near the kitchen sink.

"I'm just tired. Tired of everything I've got going on with my family. I wish I could go on a vacation and just forget about all the drama I have in my life," I told her after I took the paper napkin from her.

"Whatever you got going on, baby, you can always count on God to make everything right."

"I talk to God every now and again."

"What you need to do is talk to him every day. Three times a day if you have to."

"I know. I'll get better at it," I assured her.

"Come on into the living room so we can sit down and watch some TV together. What kind of TV shows you like? And don't be talking about the reality shows. I don't watch that mess. Those people be airing all their business on TV. I know their parents are ashamed of them. I know I would be if my child was up there. I will cut their butts off and change my number."

Mrs. Mabel was an old soul—a woman with years of experience and wisdom. So to hear her talk about how the new generation of children is today gave me a warm feeling, because she spoke from the heart. Looking at her made me think about my grandmother. Lord knows what I would do if I could have her with me right now. Life with her would be really good.

"I know this may shock you, but I like this show called *Shark Tank*. A person can learn so much by watching that show," I said.

"I watched it a couple of times. The episodes I saw were good. But I don't know if it's on right now."

"I'll watch anything you wanna watch. Just as long as it is not the news. I've been watching the news channel for two days straight and I am so tired of seeing or hearing one bad thing after the next."

"If you don't watch the news, then how are you going to keep up with what's going on around the world? It's important to stay informed, especially since I live alone," she said.

"That's understandable," I said. But on the flip side, I wasn't interested in watching anything being broadcast from a news station. If Mrs. Mabel saw my face plastered across her television screen, along with the journalists reporting that I escaped federal custody and was a person of interest involved with Terrell's disappearance, I knew she would change her mind about me. And how could I come back from that? And who could blame her? I would probably act the same way. So, to prevent any of this from happening, I just prayed that my name didn't get mentioned while we were watching TV.

She and I agreed to watch the movie *The Green Mile*. When the movie started, she didn't like it at all. But I talked her into giving the movie another ten minutes. She did and eventually began to like it. Unfortunately for her, she fell asleep on the couch before the movie ended. I started to wake her up, but she looked so peaceful that I left her alone.

While she was asleep, I tried watching another movie, but I couldn't give it my full attention. Every time I heard noise, loud or small, I found myself peeping through Mrs. Mabel's window blinds. Nothing significant was going on outside. A few neighbors from the other building walked by to either go to their cars or take their trash to the nearby Dumpster.

During my peep shows, I found myself watching my apartment too. I couldn't see my entire apartment from the window I was looking through, but I was able to see my kitchen and living-room window. All the lights were off, of course, but somehow I was still able to make out a few things I had propped up near my windows.

Sitting here and being able to watch my apartment made me homesick. I was also sick because I wasn't aware of my mother's state. I could only hope that she was still alive, despite my seeing her hand cut off and placed in a fucking treat box. I swear, if I found out who did that to her, I was going to fuck them up. And that's my word.

8

BLINDSIDED

Mrs. Mabel woke me up the next morning with the smell of bacon and eggs. I had fallen asleep on the couch so I could be close to the front door. I figured if I stayed on the sofa, I'd be able to hear all the movement coming from the other side of the front door.

"Hungry?" she asked me after she noticed that my eyes were open.

"Kind of," I told her as I sat up on the couch.

"Well, go on in the bathroom and freshen up. I've got clean wash towels on the vanity next to the bathroom sink. There's a bottle of mouthwash underneath the sink," she replied while she continued shuffling plates and forks around near the stove.

"Okay, thank you," I said, and then I headed in the bathroom. I peed, washed my face, and gargled a mouthful of mouthwash. As soon as I was done, I headed back into the kitchen with Mrs. Mabel. She had two plates of food on the table when I walked into the kitchen. "This food looks so good," I commented as I approached the table.

"Well, come and have a seat. We can't let the food get cold," she instructed me as she was taking a seat at the table herself. I took a seat next to hers. "Come on, bow your head so we can pray."

Upon Mrs. Mabel's request, I bowed my head, closed my eyes, and then I let her take it away. Her prayer consisted of thanking God that she woke up this morning. She even thanked Him for keeping her with a sound mind. I said a quiet prayer. And my prayer was that God would allow me to look for my mother without getting hurt. I even asked God to cover me from the dirty cops, the dirty DEA agents, and the Malek family. Those guys didn't play fair, so I would need to stay on my A game and try to stay alive as long as possible. The slightest slip and fall would definitely cause my demise. And I couldn't have that.

My prayer was simple and quick. Mrs. Mabel's prayer was a few minutes longer than that. She ended it by thanking God for having me as company and she told Him to guide my steps. Her words were touching. I got filled up with emotions. And immediately after she said the word *Amen,* I thanked her.

"Oh, sweetheart, you don't have to thank me. Thank our Lord and Savior. I'm just His vessel," she explained as she picked up her fork.

I picked up my fork too and started eating. After I put the first forkful of eggs in my mouth, it melted on my tongue. "Hmmm, Mrs. Mabel, your eggs are so good."

"Thank you, darling, but you haven't tasted my bacon yet."

"I'm about to do so right now," I assured her while I broke the bacon in half and stuffed the first half of it into my mouth. Just like the eggs, it also melted in my mouth. "I haven't had eggs like this in a long time."

"I'm glad you're enjoying them," she said while she continued to eat. "Did you get a good night's rest?"

"Yes, ma'am, I did."

"I heard you talking in your sleep a few times last night."

"I was told that I do that from time to time."

"You better stop it. Because one day, you might say something and the wrong person could be around to hear it."

"I know," I agreed.

But before she uttered another word, we heard a knock on the door. I went straight into panic mode. My heart fell into the pit of my stomach. I placed my fork down on my plate of food and stopped chewing, thinking that it could be heard from the other side of the front door. "Are you expecting any company?" I whispered.

"No," she whispered back, and then she stood on her feet.

"Please don't let anyone know that I'm here," I begged her, pressing my hands together like I was beginning to pray.

"Don't worry. I won't," she assured me, and walked away from the table.

Instead of staying at the kitchen table, I hid myself in a small room in the kitchen that she used for storing her food. It was just big enough for me to fit in there.

"Who is it?" I heard her yell to the person outside her front door.

"I'm Agent Sims, and I'm with Detective Belle. We were wondering if we could ask you a few questions," I heard Sims say.

I also heard when Mrs. Mabel opened her front door. That move scared the crap out of me. I felt that in any moment, Agent Sims and that local cop could walk into the house without giving Mrs. Mabel consent and find me hiding in this closet. Boy, would my life be over.

"How you doing, ma'am?" I heard Sims say.

"I'm doing well. Now, what can I help you with?" Mrs. Mabel got straight to the point.

"Detective Belle and I are looking for the young lady that lives in this apartment next door to you. So we were wondering if you've seen her."

"No, I haven't. And what are you guys doing in her apartment?" I heard Mrs. Mabel ask. She seemed alarmed by it.

"Ma'am, it's official police business," Agent Sims said.

"Police business, my foot. You just can't go into her apartment like that," Mrs. Mabel protested. I heard the anger and frustration in her voice and she was upset.

"Listen, ma'am, it's really important that we find her, because she may be in serious danger," I heard Detective Belle say.

"Wait a minute, why are you guys taking fingerprints and stuff? Who's gonna clean up all that black dust on her door and in her apartment?"

"Ma'am, wiping away fingerprint dust is the least of our worries. We need to find Misty before someone else does," Agent Sims chimed in. "Here, take my card, and if you hear anything, please call me," he continued.

"I sure will. And when I talk to her, I will definitely let her know how you're messing up her apartment," Mrs. Mabel warned them.

"Thank you for your time," Detective Belle said.

"Yes, thank you," Agent Sims spoke up.

After I heard her close her front door, I walked out of the food pantry and took a seat back at the kitchen table. She walked back into the kitchen and placed the business card down on the kitchen. "Did you hear what they said?" she wondered aloud after she sat back down in her chair.

"Yes, I did."

"They said that your life may be in danger."

"They're lying, Mrs. Mabel. They're just saying that as a tactic to get you, and whoever else, to help them find me. And look at me! I'm here with you. So, how could I be in danger? They are full of lies." I was trying to convince her.

"You know, they're messing up your apartment with all the black fingerprint powder?"

"I heard."

"You know that stuff is really hard getting off."

"I'm sure I'll find a way," I said nonchalantly, even though I was on pins and needles. I began to rack my brain, trying to figure out why they're dusting my apartment for fingerprints. And then it hit me that they can't be looking for anything else but Terrell's fingerprints. This realization shot my blood pressure through the roof of Mrs. Mabel's apartment. The thought of them using forensics gave me a ton of mixed emotions. I knew that before they left my place, they were going to find every piece of DNA they could find. And before I knew it, I was going to be on the FBI's Most Wanted poster. *Fuck! Fuck! Fuck!*

Mrs. Mabel dug back into her food, but to save my life, I couldn't lift the fork from my plate. I had literally lost my appetite. "You're not gonna eat the rest of your food?" she wanted to know.

"Yes, I'm gonna eat it," I told her, but in reality, I wasn't. My mind was too fixated on them motherfuckers that were looking for me. *Why won't everybody just leave me alone?* I'm speaking of, Sanjay's family, the homicide detectives, the DEA agents, and the people who have been ordered to kill me. And in the mix of things, I now found myself trying to cope with the death of my grandmother, my cousin, and maybe my mother. *How much longer am I gonna have to go through this?* I was a strong woman, but I still have weaknesses. So, if I'm given enough strength to go forward, then I will do that and see where it takes me.

"Will you excuse me?" I asked her.

"Sure, honey," she replied.

I stood up from my chair. "Is it all right if I look out of your living-room window?" I asked.

"Sure. You go right ahead," she insisted, and then she stood up behind me. "When you look out the window, look through the blinds this way," she instructed me as she pointed at the side she wanted me to touch.

"Mind if I sit on the arm of the sofa?"

"Sure, honey."

Taking directions from Mrs. Mabel, I sat on the arm of her sofa, giving it just a small amount of pressure; then I pulled back the blinds on the right side of the window. Once again, I couldn't see the front door of my apartment, but I got an eyeful of traffic patrolling the sidewalk and grass that led to my apartment. I didn't see Agent Sims or the other detective, but I saw a team of forensic investigators and two uniformed policemen. I saw them looking around their surroundings. I saw one of them look at the window I was looking out of. I pulled the blinds closed a little to prevent either one of them from seeing me. You can never be too careful.

Mrs. Mabel sat on the couch and began watching TV. She asked me a few questions while I peered out of her window. "Have you wondered what they could be looking for? They're over there going all over your personal things. I know if they were going through my stuff, I would go over there and put a stop to it."

"See, that's what they want me to do. But I won't give them the satisfaction," I reasoned. I had no other choice but to come up with that lame-ass rebuttal. I just hoped that Mrs. Mabel bought it.

"The police officer that said her name was Belle was the one that stopped by here before, asking me when was the last time I seen my ex-boyfriend?"

"Oh, so that was who you were talking about?"

"Yep, that was her," she confirmed.

Hearing Mrs. Mabel confirm that Detective Belle was one of the cops that talked to her about Terrell put a big perspective on what was going on at my apartment. I now knew the reason why they were in my place. They just found out that they did have the remains of Terrell's body, so now they needed to trace his DNA to something or someone. But guess what? If they did, I could argue the fact that he and I used to date. And even after we broke up, he still came around. The only way they'd be able to link him to me was if Tedo's homegirl April stepped up to the plate. Otherwise, I was good.

I sat at that window for at least two hours and watched the cops and the forensic team sift inside and around my building. I even saw local cops talking to a few of my neighbors. I noticed a couple of them creating dialogues with them, but the rest of my neighbors weren't that interested. That made me feel safe and secure.

After fishing around my apartment for almost three hours, those cops finally left. It was a weight lifted when I saw them leave, but it also gave me a feeling of anxiety. Being in the dark about things concerning you can be torture. The only thing good that came from the knock at Mrs. Mabel's door was that I finally found out that Agent Sims was not shot when we were in the underground garage of the hospital. I was now left to wonder what happened to Agent Taylor. I mean, I was not concerned for that traitor. But I am curious to hear if he was shot or killed. I was sure that information would come in due time.

9

TAKING NO PRISONERS

I sat around on the couch and watched a few TV shows, but I wouldn't be able to tell you anything about them. Mrs. Mabel hopped in the shower and changed clothes. When she reappeared in the living room, she asked me if I wanted to take a shower too. "I need a change of clothes," I told her.

"Well, I'm too big for you to wear my clothes."

"I see that."

"Why don't you go over to your place," she suggested.

"I was just thinking that. But what if one of those detectives is watching my apartment?"

"What's the worst thing that could happen?"

I wanted to tell her that if I was caught, I'd be locked up on sight. I also wanted to tell her the reason why they would lock my ass up was because I'm a person of interest concerning Terrell's murder, and I was a government informant for the DEA. But let's not forget that I'm also supposed to testify against several members of a mafia family. But I knew she would freak out if I had, so I left well enough alone. Instead, I said, "I just don't like them harassing me is all. But what I will do is when it gets dark, I'll sneak over there and get some things then."

"Okay, well, I got a doctor's appointment, so I'm gonna head on out. If you need something, call me."

"You don't mind leaving me here in your place by myself?" I asked her. It was shocking to see how trusting she was of me.

"What are you going to do? Rob me of my millions of dollars?" she joked.

"Oh, stop it, Mrs. Mabel. You're being funny now."

"No, you're being funny!" She smiled. "Remember, if you need anything, give me a call," she continued.

"I will," I assured her.

I watched Mrs. Mabel as she headed out her front door. I even watched her as she headed down the walkway toward her car. After she got into her car, she sped away. Seeing her go made me begin to miss her, even though she had only been gone for a second. It felt good to have her stick by my side. This time yesterday, I left the hospital and had no idea where I was going. Now I'm here in the comfort of my neighbor's house, with access to views of my apartment that I would not have had if she hadn't opened her doors for me.

I sat there at the window and gazed out into the neighborhood and watched everybody come and go as they pleased. It's funny how we take the small things for granted. I would love to leave here and take a stroll down the road and take in some of this fresh air. But since I can't, staring out this window will have to do.

Unexpectedly, an unmarked car pulled up and the driver parked it alongside the street directly across from this apartment complex. My heart began to race uncontrollably. Not knowing who was in the driver's seat concerned me, especially since all the windows were up and tinted. Being that I couldn't get a look into the car, I stepped back a few inches from the window, just in case whoever was in the car had binoculars and was able to see me from that distance. While anxiety filled my entire body, I wondered how long those people in that car planned to be there. *Damn! It sure sucks being a wanted woman.* Just think, a month ago, I was happy to go to work, enjoyed talking to the customers, and relished the fact that one day I was going to be a pharmacist. The head pharmacist, at best.

But no, I ruined those chances by getting caught up in the illegal prescription-drug ring. How stupid was that? Now I sit here taking the repercussions like a boxer would take a jab to the face. Unfortunately for me, I didn't know how to fight back. And that's why I was in this situation.

While I sat there and watched the car, I noticed the similarities of this car and Agent Sims's car, and that's when I realized that this was the same car. Agent Sims had to be somewhere inside of it. Knowing this, I got an eerie feeling in my body. My stomach and my head were so screwed up, I needed some antidepressants to calm me down and put me to sleep. In the back of my head, I could hear Agent Sims saying, "Misty, you gotta be straight up with me. And if I find out that you're doing anything different, I'm gonna lock you up and you will never see daylight again."

He always found a way to threaten me, so I could service him with all his needs, which included being an informant. He didn't care about me. All he cared about was a victory in court and locking everyone up that I testified against. That's it. That's all he wanted. Which is why I believed he was sitting in that car. He was sitting there, and hoping that I would come back to the area, so he could take me back into his care. But I couldn't let him do that. Not today. Not tomorrow. I'm gonna need to be on my own so I could figure all of this stuff out.

*   *   *

After sitting there for over two hours, the unmarked car finally drove away. But I knew he was coming back. I couldn't say when, but I knew for a fact that he was. I was his meal ticket for a promotion, so he was going to pull out all the stops, so he could stuff me right back into his back pocket.

I stood up from the arm of the chair and headed into Mrs. Mabel's kitchen. I hadn't worked up an appetite from my surveillance duties, but I was thirsty. I poured myself a glass of juice and tried to enjoy every ounce of it. And when I was done, I rinsed the glass out and placed it in the dish rack. Right when I was leaving the kitchen, it hit me that right now would be the perfect time to sneak into my apartment. The agents had left and might not come back until later on. *Come on, Misty, you can do it.* I began to give myself a silent pep talk. *If you go there right now, it will only take you three minutes at the most to grab a few things to get out of there.* I continued to encourage myself.

While I began to mull over whether or not I was going to go into my apartment, I looked back out the window, just to make sure the car hadn't circled back around. When I noticed that it hadn't, I raced over to the sofa, grabbed my shoes, and placed them on my feet. Then I grabbed my house keys from my purse. Unsure as to whether or not I planned to go into my apartment, I raced back over to the window and gave it another look. Once again, the car hadn't circled back around, so I felt like I was good. *If I'm gonna do it, I need to do it now.*

Come on, Misty, you can do it. Is gonna only take you less than three minutes.

I raced for the front door and snatched it open. To my surprise, someone was already standing at the front door. "Hi, ma'am, would you like to buy a chocolate bar?" a little boy asked me while he held out a box of different kinds of candy bars.

Unsure as to how to answer this cute little boy, I paused

and then asked him how much it cost. His answer was one dollar. I hurried over to the couch, where my purse was, grabbed one dollar from my wallet, and then I raced back to the door and handed it to him.

"Which one do you want?" he asked me.

"It doesn't matter. Just give me one," I told him.

After he handed me the candy bar, he thanked me and then walked away. I watched him as he headed to my front door, so I stopped him. "No one is there," I told him.

"How you know that?" he asked me.

"Because I live there."

"If you live there, then what are you doing over here?"

"Because I'm visiting my neighbor."

"What is all that black stuff on the door?"

"Just some black dust. It can be wiped off," I assured him.

"Cool," he said, and then he walked away.

I watched the little guy as he headed to another neighbor's apartment. I smiled at him because he was learning the hustle at a young age. He couldn't be older than eleven years old. Seeing him get his hustle on put a huge smile on my face. Boy, what would I give to be his age right now? He had no worries. No bills. No girlfriend problems. Nothing. And here I was with the world on my shoulders while everyone died around me. How fucked up was that? Hopefully, one day I'd have that same measure of peace that little boy had. *Wishful thinking, huh?*

"Hey, you better watch out where you're going!" I heard someone yell. I couldn't see who said it, but it brought me back to reality.

My main focus was to get into my place, grab a few pieces of clothes, and get the hell out of there. Time was of the essence, and I had to make it count. "Let's get it," I said, and then I rushed over to my front door, grabbed the doorknob with the bottom of my shirt, and then I used my other hand to unlock the door. Within seconds I had opened my door. I pushed it open just a tad bit to scope out my living room. When I felt like the coast was clear, I looked back at the street, to make sure no one was watching. When that checked out, I pushed the front door in, even farther, and scrambled inside.

As I got farther and farther into my apartment, I saw how those fucking cops had ransacked it. *How dare they have all my stuff out of place like this? Are they freaking crazy? Just look at the pillow cushions from the sofa on the floor, black dust all over my doors and doorknobs. Who they think is going to clean this shit up? Ugh!*

As the anger built up inside of me, the more my blood started boiling inside my veins. And as bad as I wanted to clean up the mess they made, I knew that I couldn't. I only came in here to get a couple of outfits, so that's what I was about to do.

I made my way into my bedroom and grabbed one of my overnight bags from my walk-in closet. After I tossed it on my bed, I grabbed one of my perfume bottles from my vanity, my deodorant, a couple pairs of jeans, shirts, panties, bras, and socks. Whatever I could grab, that's what I did. Once my bag was filled to the rim, I picked it up from the bed, turned around, and headed toward my front door. Three steps in, I heard a voice coming from outside my apartment, so I stopped in my tracks. While my heart rate tripled in speed per minute, an overwhelming amount of anxiety consumed me. "Stay calm, Misty," I whispered to myself while I stood there, wondering what was going to happen next.

"I'm sure that I left it here," I heard a woman's voice say. And then I heard the sound of someone turning the doorknob from outside. That's when I knew that person was coming in here.

Oh my God! Whoever it is, they're coming into my apartment. Shit! What am I gonna do? I panicked. Without hesitation, I turned around and ran back into my bedroom. Afraid to hide in my walk-in closet, I got down on the floor of my bedroom and pushed my overnight bag underneath my bed. As quietly as I could, I slid underneath my bed as well.

"I think I left the warrant documents in the kitchen," I heard the woman say. And that's when it hit me that she was on a call with her cell phone.

I heard her walk into the kitchen and then she stopped moving. "It's not in here," she told the caller. "Let me check the bedroom. It might be in there," she continued while her footsteps alerted me that she was coming in my direction. Boy, I was a nervous wreck.

Immediately after she entered into my bedroom, I was able to get a look at her shoes and that's when I realized that the woman behind that voice was Detective Belle. She was right inside my bedroom. And the documents she was looking for had to be the search warrant and my arrest warrant. That had allowed the forensic team to go through my apartment and fuck it up. On a different day, I wouldn't be hiding underneath my bed. Instead, I would be cursing her ass out and showing her to the front door. But since I was a wanted lady, my desire to fuss her could only be a thought in my head, and that was as far as it would go.

"I got it," she told the caller. "It was lying on top of our suspect's dresser," she continued, and then she fell silent. A couple of seconds later, she said, "She was a person of interest, but now we have his remains, she's a suspect. Finding her before she tries to leave town takes precedence," she continued as she walked back out of my bedroom. She didn't utter another word until she got into the living area of my apartment. "If those stupid fucking agents hadn't let her get away, she would be in my custody right now. Speaking of which, we just learned that the mother was kidnapped forty-eight hours ago, so the DEA agents and my office assembled a team to try to locate her mother, since we just found out that she's still alive."

She made her way out of my apartment, and the next thing I heard was the front door closing. When I heard her locking the door from the outside of my apartment, I slid back from underneath my bed and then rushed over to my bedroom window. I peeped through my window blinds and watched Detective Belle as she walked back to her vehicle. "Lord, please let her get into the car and pull off. I can't afford to be arrested right now. I've got a lot of stuff I need to do, so please help me, God!" I prayed out loud.

I noticed that I always prayed to God when I fell into a trap. But it's not like I'm trying to use Him; it's just that I can't do these things on my own. And besides, if I get Him to handle it, things would end well.

After waiting for what seemed like forever, Detective Belle got back into her vehicle and drove away. Boy, was I happy to see that. Without any incident, I grabbed my bag and raced toward the front door of my apartment. On my way there, I passed by my lamp table and was sidetracked when my eyes glanced at two photos of my family in the picture frames. One of the pictures was of my mother and me when I was five years old. We were attending my preschool graduation. My mother really looked sober and proud of me. I swear, I would give anything to revisit that time in my life. It was a simple and drama-free life.

The next picture was of me, my mother, and my dad. This picture was taken while we were out together on one of our weekly family nights. We all looked happy too. I would pay anything to relive those days, but I can't. I will just be grateful that my mother was still alive, and maybe this situation would bring us closer, once we see each other again. Well, at least I hoped so.

Immediately after I realized that I couldn't go back in

time, I once again snapped back into reality. "Come on, Misty, it's time to go," I said underneath my breath, and before I took another, I grabbed both pictures, tucked them underneath my right arm, and then I made my way back out of my apartment.

10

MY TO-DO LIST

It took me less time to get out of my apartment and return to Mrs. Mabel's apartment than it did when I left Mrs. Mabel's apartment to get into mine. Talk about speed. The moment after I closed and locked Mrs. Mabel's front door, I walked over to her couch and collapsed down on it, and then turned on her TV. "Fuck! Fuck! Fuck! That bitch said I'm now a freaking suspect in Terrell's murder! What the hell am I going to do now?" I began to sob. "When they catch me, they're going to lock my ass up without bond. And what will I do then?

"Why couldn't Terrell just leave me the hell alone? I told him on many occasions to go on with his life, but he wouldn't do it. So now I'm gonna have to go to jail because of him? This shit is unfair." I continued complaining while I sobbed. I swear, I wished that I had enforced my restraining order against that guy by calling the cops every time he reached out to me, then I wouldn't be in this jam. *Fuck!*

While I lay back on the couch, a news bulletin started broadcasting: "This just in, the Virginia Beach Police have released the name of the person whose dismembered remains were found two days ago inside the Webbers' Funeral Home. We're told that the body belonged to twenty-seven-year-old Terrell Mason. We understand that he lived in Virginia Beach and was the owner of a janitor business, which was thriving."

"He didn't own shit! He was a fucking drug dealer!" I blurted out.

"We spoke to the family not too long ago and they're saddened by this news and ask that we give them their privacy so that they can mourn the loss of their loved one. We reached out to the lead detectives of this murder investigation, but so far, we haven't heard back from them. We will keep you informed as this investigation continues. My name is Tonya Spaulden and you're watching *Ten on Your Side*."

I can't tell you how many times my stomach did somersaults. I just wished that everyone would shut up about Terrell. *Who cares if he's dead?* He was a piece of shit. He was disrespectful, a cheater, and he was abusive. So, why won't they air that? Why won't they talk about him being a drug dealer? He wasn't an owner of a janitorial business. He was a fucking swindler. And he didn't give a damn about anyone but himself, so kill that noise.

After the news report for Terrell ended, I wasn't interested in watching anything else, especially after almost running into Detective Belle and now hearing that Terrell's body had been identified. *What am I going to do now?*

I cried about my situation for the majority of the time Mrs. Mabel was gone. When she returned, I had managed to pull myself together by taking a shower and changing clothes. "Good evening, sweetheart," she greeted me when she came in the house. I was sitting on her couch and watching television.

"Hi, Mrs. Mabel," I greeted her back, giving her a warm smile.

"I see you changed your clothes." She noticed this after she had closed the front door and locked it. She walked farther into the apartment.

"You won't believe what I've done."

"It looks like you went into your apartment and got some clothes."

I smiled bashfully. "Yeah, that's exactly what I did."

"How does it look over there?" Her questions continued as she walked by me. I didn't realize she was putting her purse in her bedroom until she came back into the living room empty-handed.

"It's a mess. I started to stay in there and do a major cleanup, but I didn't want to take the risk of the cops coming and seeing me."

"What exactly did they do over there?" she asked as she took a seat on the love seat across from me.

"There's black dust everywhere. Doors, doorknobs, window seals, tables, and chairs, you name it."

"Why would they do all of that?"

"Mrs. Mabel, I haven't the slightest idea. Cops will tell you one thing and do another. They do it to keep everybody in the blind."

"So I hear that they found your ex-boyfriend."

"How do you know?" I asked her. I wanted to pick her brain to see exactly what she knew.

"The news came on while I was in the waiting area of my doctor's office. They showed his picture."

"Really?" I said, trying to act surprised.

"Yes. The news reporter said that they found his body and they have a few leads."

"I hope they find the person that did it." I wanted to make it look like I was concerned about Terrell and his family getting justice.

"I hope they do too. Because regardless what that guy did, no one deserves to die, especially the way he did."

"You're right," I agreed.

"You might wanna call his folks and send them your condolences."

Shocked by Mrs. Mabel's suggestion, I agreed with her gesture, but I knew I was never going to call Terrell's family. They would send the cops on my ass quicker than I could blink my eyes. In addition to them calling the cops on me, they'd tell me to shove my condolences up my ass, and rightfully so. They didn't care about how Terrell used to treat me. All they cared about was that the person that killed their loved one got what she deserved. Point-blank!

"Remember when the cops said that your life was in danger?"

"Yes, ma'am."

"Do you think that the person that killed your ex-boyfriend could be looking for you too?" she asked me. She gave me an expression of concern.

I thought for a second, because first of all, I'm the one that killed him, so if I tell her that, I'd be sealing my fate in a court of law. On the flip side, it was important that I be careful with my words because I didn't want her to think that by having me staying here in her place, she would also be putting her life in danger. So, what should I tell her? "Terrell had a lot of women. When he and I first started dating, an ex-girlfriend of his started stalking us. She threatened him bodily harm if he continued to see me. And she threatened me as well. Thank God she never went through with it, because I don't know what I would've done if she had. Oh, but just recently, I was told that Terrell owed a lot of money to some very bad people. So the only thing I can think of is that they went to him for payment, and when they realized that he didn't have it, they killed him," I said. Telling her this made-up story didn't take much to conjure up. I just hoped that the words I chose didn't scare her to the point that she wanted to get me away from her as quickly as possible.

"And you're not afraid for your safety?"

"No."

"And why not?"

"Because I don't know them. The only people he introduced me to are the people in his family."

"People in this world are so mean and cruel," she commented.

"Yes, they are, Mrs. Mabel. That's why I try to stay by myself."

"That's the way you gotta be sometimes. Can't trust people nowadays. You better learn from this situation with your ex-boyfriend and watch the company you keep," she warned me, and then she got up from her sofa and headed into the kitchen. "Want something to drink while I'm in here?"

"No, I'm good. Thank you, though," I said, watching her as she walked into the kitchen. Mrs. Mabel was a small woman in size, but she was a strong woman in wisdom and heart. You can't pull the wool over her eyes and tell her that it's cotton. And knowing this, I knew that I had to stay two steps ahead of her. While she grilled me with one question after the next, I wasn't sure if she was trying to catch me in a lie or she was trying to gain the facts about the saga concerning Terrell and my safety. Thankfully, the story I gave her sounded plausible and to her satisfaction, because if it hadn't, she'd probably send me packing.

11

A FEW HOURS LATER

Four hours passed and all I found myself doing was flying around Mrs. Mabel's apartment and watching television. Mrs. Mabel cooked an early dinner for us. The oven-baked salmon and steamed veggie medley hit the spot, considering I really hadn't had anything good to eat in the last two days. The food was delicious.

Once I filled my tummy, I got Mrs. Mabel to watch a couple of movies instead of watching shows with commercials running every seven to eight minutes. I felt like the less commercials we saw, the better my chances were that she wouldn't see any news reports concerning Terrell's murder case or anything with my name attached to it.

While the television was playing, I started thinking about my mother. To hear Detective Belle say that she wasn't dead gave me the happiest feeling in the world, which was why I cried after coming back into Mrs. Mabel's apartment. And even though I saw a light at the end of that tunnel, I now had to find out where my mother was. I had no idea how I was going to do it, but I would find a way, even if it meant putting my own life on the line.

* * *

On her way to bed, Mrs. Mabel suggested that I sleep in the guest bedroom this evening. I thanked her, but insisted that I'd rather sleep on the sofa again. That way, I could hear what was going on outside. She told me she understood and went to bed. "Let me know if you need something," she said, and then she disappeared into her bedroom. I knew that it would be impossible for me to get a good night's rest because of everything I had going on. When I knew for sure that Mrs. Mabel had gone to sleep, I turned the TV station to the local news so I could stay informed of what was going on around the city. For the first couple of hours, there was no breaking news, so I grabbed a blanket from the hall closet and found a good spot on the sofa to snuggle into.

I hadn't realized it until I heard a noise that I had fallen asleep. At first, I thought it was Mrs. Mabel doing something in her bedroom, but when I muted the TV, I heard the shuffling sound again. After I listened for a minute or so, I realized that the sound was coming from outside, so I jumped into action. I powered off the television, and then I tiptoed to the window and peered through the blinds. I didn't see anything on the sidewalk or the grass that led up to this apartment building, so I crept to the front door and looked through the peephole. My heart sank into the pit of my stomach when I saw two men creeping into my apartment. I couldn't tell who it was because their backs were facing Mrs. Mabel's front door. One part of me wanted to open the door and let them know that I saw them, but then I realized that if I did say something, I could be putting myself in danger or at risk of being caught. So I stood there and watched as those two guys entered into my personal domain. I felt so helpless and defeated to have no say-so or be able to take action against something that concerned me. As I continued to look at my apartment door from Mrs. Mabel's apartment, my helplessness elevated to anger.

The feeling of hopelessness began to take over my entire body, and I felt like if I continued to stay there and did not do anything, then I might be allowing these guys to take things from my house that had sentimental value. And what they couldn't take, they could possibly destroy. I knocked on Mrs. Mabel's bedroom door and asked her if I could come in.

Swiftly she got up and opened her door in less than three seconds. She stood there with a puzzled expression on her face. "What's wrong? Is everything okay?" she asked me.

"No. I just saw two guys break into my apartment and now they're inside, probably stealing me blind."

"How do you know two guys are in your apartment?"

"Because I heard a booming sound while I was lying on the sofa. So I got up and looked out the window, and when I didn't see anything, I looked through your peephole, and that's when I saw them going into my apartment."

"Maybe it's the police," she suggested.

"The police are not going to break into my apartment. I heard them kicking my door, and then when I got up and looked at the peephole, they were going inside."

"Think we oughta call the police?"

"By the time they'd get here, those guys would probably be gone."

"So, what do you want to do?"

"If you could open the door and scare them, or let them know you see them, I'm sure they'll run away."

"I don't know, Misty. That sounds a bit dangerous. I mean, what if it's the men that killed your ex-boyfriend?" she asked me, her facial expression very grim-looking.

She went from this hard-ass lady that won't take anyone's shit to this meek and scared old woman. I guess that when I told her that Terrell probably was murdered at the hands of some men he owed money to, I must have terrified her. *Damn! I really put my foot in my mouth.* Now I had to think of another way to get her on board so I could find out who was in my apartment.

"Look, I'll tell you what, we'll do it together, okay?" I tried compromising with her.

She hesitated and then said, "I don't know. I think it would be best to call the police."

"Never mind," I said, and stormed off.

"So, what are you going to do?" she asked in a whisper-like tone.

I ignored her because I didn't even know what I was going to do. So having her ask me irritated me, because all I needed her to do was open up her front door, yell to let them know what she knew—that they were inside my apartment—and that she was going to call the cops. And I really didn't know if this tactic could possibly scare them away.

"Hey, what are you going to do?" she repeated, but I ignored her again. And before I knew it, she was down on my heels.

I stood there for a moment, trying to figure out what I was going to do, and that's when she said, "Why don't you do it?"

I thought for a second and that's when that same idea popped into my head. And without further thought, I opened her door, slightly ajar, and yelled, "I know you're in there. Now you better leave before I call the cops."

I stood there and nothing happened. I couldn't tell you if they heard me and they were laying low to see if I was going to close the door. Or if while I was in the back of Mrs. Mabel's apartment, trying to get her to do what I was doing now, they had already left.

I continued to stand there while Mrs. Mabel stood behind me. She and I both stood still to see or hear what was going to happen next. And then a minute had passed and we heard a little crackle sound coming from my apartment. It startled me because I knew that there was still someone inside my apartment.

"Did you hear that?" Mrs. Mabel whispered.

"I heard you in there. Now this is your last warning. If you don't leave right now, I'm gonna call the cops," I threatened, and then I stepped backward just in case the people in my apartment wanted to wave their guns at Mrs. Mabel's apartment door.

"You heard her. We're going to call the cops if you don't leave right now," Mrs. Mabel blurted out. I couldn't believe that she opened her mouth. Just a few minutes ago, she didn't like the idea of opening her front door and making her presence known. Now she's all over the top of me, damn near breaking her neck to be heard. I looked back over my shoulder with a *now you wanna open your mouth* expression.

"Look, there they are!" she yelled, and startled the hell out of me.

I turned my attention back toward my apartment, and by the time I did, I could only see the backs of both men. I couldn't tell if they were white or black or young or old. I did manage to see that they hadn't had anything in their hands, so I felt a little better. "Did you get a chance to see their faces?" I asked her.

"I did."

"What did they look like?"

"Two young guys with dark hair."

"White or black?"

"White, I think," she said.

I pushed the front door closed and ran to a nearby window. I opened the blind and peered out between them and didn't see anything or anyone. "Fuck!" I spat. The frustration inside of me began to boil over.

"Watch your mouth, young lady," Mrs. Mabel chastised me.

"I'm sorry, Mrs. Mabel, but two guys were just in my apartment," I explained, trying to reason with her.

"They were probably some young punks that live in the neighborhood. They see the cops walking around this neighborhood, asking questions about you, and then running in and out of your apartment sends the message that you're not home. And if you're not home, your place is a breeding ground for robberies," she pointed out. But I wasn't trying to hear a word Mrs. Mabel was saying. It was bad enough that I had to deal with the fucking cops ransacking my place. Now here come more petty thieves. *Why don't these people just let me live in peace?*

Seething on the inside and dealing with the many thoughts circulating in my head, I felt like I was about to have a nervous breakdown. *Tell me what's going to happen next? Ugh!*

Without saying anything, Mrs. Mabel opened her front door and then she walked out of the apartment. I was too distraught to find out what she was doing. I knew I needed to calm myself down so I wouldn't say or do anything that I might regret later.

"Those guys broke the lock on your door," she announced.

"They did what?" I asked her, even though I already heard what she said.

"I closed your door, but it wouldn't lock. The doorknob is slightly hanging off," she explained.

"You have got to be kidding me?!" I said, and then I removed myself from the arm of the couch, sat down on the cushion, and then buried my face into the palms of my hands.

"I'm gonna call the cops," she informed me, and reached for the cordless phone for her landline, which was on the end table beside her lamp.

I quickly looked up. "No, don't do that." I was totally

against the idea of her calling the cops. What was she trying to do, get me arrested?

"Why not?"

"What are they going to do? I mean, it's not like they're
gonna fix my door."

"I think they will."

"I don't," I said, and then I stood up on my feet. "When
you closed my door, did it open back up?"

"No, it didn't. It closes, but it doesn't lock," she replied,
giving me a strange look.

"Okay, well, it'll be all right. I'll just stay in the living
room and listen out for anyone else who tries to go into
my apartment."

"I don't think that would be wise. What if someone else
goes in there and comes back out and starts shooting at
you this time?"

"That's just a risk I'm gonna have to take," I told her.
And I was not backing down.

"I'm sorry, but I can't let you do that. You'll be putting
me at risk if someone fires their gun the next time."

"I understand, Mrs. Mabel," I said, because I really
wanted her to be quiet. Just a couple of days ago, she was
taking up for me when she saw the cops ransacking my
apartment. But now, her constant worrying was straining
my nerves. What I needed her to do was to be quiet until I
figured out what to do next.

"Are you still against me calling the cops?" She was
pressing this issue.

"Don't call 'em. I'll take care of it," I said with finality,
and then I fell silent. I didn't want to talk to her anymore.
I was done engaging with her.

"Well, if you don't need me anymore, then I'm gonna
head back into my bedroom. I got another doctor's appointment tomorrow morning," she announced, and then
she went back into her bedroom.

I wanted to say, "Good riddance, you old bitch!" but I had to remind myself that she did open her house to me. So I needed to be patient and play by her rules.

I really needed this lady and to lay low here in her house. My safe house for now. But I was beginning to wonder what her deal was. All of a sudden, she wanted to talk to the cops? She didn't want to talk to them when they questioned her on two occasions. I could really see how flaky she was getting. Before too long, she was gonna want me to leave. And to be ready for it, I was gonna have to get my exit plan together. I was gonna need a new place to lay low.

It had been a few hours since those guys broke into my apartment, so I hadn't had one wink of sleep. I'd walked from the window and back to the couch over one hundred times, to say the least. And in that time, I heard movement in front of the building, but when I looked out the window, I could tell that the noise came from cats and dogs running around the Dumpster near the street. I also saw a couple of cars drive by the building. Surprisingly, I hadn't seen any cops in plain clothes ride by. And this was strange too. I figured now that I was a suspect in Terrell's murder, why wasn't some cop patrolling my neighborhood tonight? Or maybe they were and I just couldn't see them . . . food for thought.

Sleep finally caught up with me. It didn't stick with me long. I dozed off around five o'clock, and when Mrs. Mabel woke me up around eight, I realized that I slept for three hours. "I'm heading out," she told me as she headed toward the front door. "Let me know if you need something before I come back."

"Okay, thank you," I replied, and then I got up from the couch and headed to the bathroom. After I peed, I washed my face and brushed my teeth. When I came out of the bathroom, I walked over to the front window and peered between the blinds. A lot of my neighbors with cars were gone. Most of them were military, so I knew they were on the military base ten miles from here. I also didn't see an unmarked car parked across the street either. Something was going on and I hated being in the dark about it.

While I was looking out of the window, I thought about my apartment. As bad as I wanted to leave here and sneak in there, so I could see how my place looked after those guys left late last night, I realized that I couldn't risk getting caught. So I left well enough alone. I'd have my chance to go back in there, but today was just not the day.

12

AMERICA'S MOST WANTED

As I thought about all the shit that happened last night, with the guys breaking into my apartment and Mrs. Mabel doing the switcheroo on me, it showed that it was only a matter of time before she was gonna get tired of me being in her apartment. I was gonna need to figure out something before it was too late.

I wasn't in the mood to eat anything, but I did, however, make myself a hot cup of tea. I added a little bit of honey to it and it was perfect. I found over the years that tea and two teaspoons of honey was a match made in heaven. It relaxed me too.

Once I had my hot cup of tea in hand, I headed back into the living room and powered on the television. I turned to the news on channel 10 to see if anything concerning Terrell's case was being reported, since Detective Belle mentioned to her caller that I was a suspect now. I needed specifics, so I waited thirty minutes, and nothing happened. Thirty minutes turned into an hour, and nothing happened. And one hour turned into two hours, but finally a reporter started her broadcast.

"Channel 10 has been following this story for a few

days now. We first reported that during a routine fire inspection, the city's fire chief found a dismembered body in the crematory area of Webbers' Funeral Home. The body was identified and the deceased victim is Terrell Mason. Late last night, the Virginia Beach Police arrested a woman who, they believe, played a key role in this murder investigation. We're told the woman's name is April Roberts, she's thirty-four years old, and a bartender at a local gentlemen's club. Right now, there's no word on what charges Ms. Roberts is facing. But we will keep you updated as this investigation continues. I'm Mitch Leman and I'm reporting live for *Ten on Your Side*."

"No fucking way. This can't be. How the hell they find April?" I started off saying as my heart started beating uncontrollably. "She is going to throw me underneath the bus! There's no way she's going to take an L for the team, especially since she never got paid for it."

See the plan was for Tedo to pay her after we walked away with the shipment of Percocet and Vicodin. But since the heist fell apart, and Tedo is dead, she lost all the way around the board. So, once again, I knew she was not going to take this fight lying down. She was going to implicate me as soon as the cops pulled her into the interrogation room.

When the news report ended, I sat back on the sofa and thought about how my whole world was falling apart around me. The only good thing I had left in this world was when I heard Detective Belle mention that my mother was still alive. Knowing this lit a fire underneath me. And before anything bad happened to me, I had to make things right for my mother. She was the last blood relative that I had left. So that was what I would do.

Paranoid that there was a huge chance that Detective Belle told Agent Sims that I murdered Terrell, I had a sick feeling in my stomach. This whole time, I had played the I-don't-know game; and for them to find out different was going to give them a huge amount of playing field, so they could use me all they wanted.

Out of nowhere, and while I was sitting on Mrs. Mabel's sofa, I heard loud knocking from outside her front door.

Boom! Boom! Boom!

"Open up the door, bitch! We know you're in there!" I heard a woman say. Alarmed by it, I jumped to my feet, tiptoed to the front door, and looked through the peephole. I saw four women standing outside of my apartment. "Open this door, bitch, and come out here and face us!"

Realizing that Terrell's mother, two sisters, and his female cousin were standing outside my front door, and banging on it like their minds were going bad, started a whole new anxiety attack inside of me.

Standing there with their backs facing Mrs. Mabel's apartment didn't allow me to look into their eyes. I knew that they were mourning the loss of Terrell, but they needed to do that shit somewhere else. I didn't need that attention on my place. I just thanked God that Mrs. Mabel wasn't here. If she was, then shit would've really hit the fan. I could see her now, telling me to go outside and confront Terrell's family. I could also see her confronting them herself, talking about what kind of good person I was. And then that's when Terrell's mother and sisters would argue the fact I wasn't a good person. This whole thing could get ugly quick.

I stood there for at least five minutes, listening to them berating me like I was some fucking mass killer on the run. I thanked God that they didn't try to open my front door, because if they had, they would've definitely had access to my apartment. Shit would go downhill from there, I was sure.

Getting sick of hearing their mouths and the noise that they were making, I called 911 and explained to the operator about how loud and intrusive those women were and that they needed to be escorted from the property. Calling the cops today versus last night was a whole different ball game. Last night Mrs. Mabel's reason wasn't concrete enough for me. I figured since the guys had gotten away, why waste time calling the cops? How were they going to help the situation? They weren't going to be able to make any arrests because the guys had already left. Now today was different. These annoying chicks were causing a scene in front of my apartment. What was the point of it all? Since they hated my guts, then why don't they go about this differently?

"Everybody, this bitch that lives in this apartment had something to do with my brother's death," I heard one of his sisters yell.

"She sure did, and we ain't gonna let her get away with it either!" Terrell's mother yelled.

"She better turn herself in to the cops, because if she doesn't, I'm gonna beat her ass!" Terrell's other sister yelled.

"Could y'all take that somewhere else?" I heard a voice say. By looking through the peephole, I couldn't see who the person was, so I raced over to the window to see if I could get a better look. And sure enough, I saw my neighbor that lived on the opposite side of my apartment. He was an older white guy. I can't tell you how old he was, but I do know that he was a UPS driver. He was also a quiet guy. Don't know if he has a wife or kids because I barely ever saw him.

"And if we don't, what's going to happen?" Terrell's cousin challenged him.

"Yeah, what are you going to do? Call the police," Terrell's mother interjected.

"Listen, lady, you guys are disturbing the peace," he replied.

"The chick that lives in this apartment disturbed our peace when she murdered my brother."

"Yeah, what do you have to say about that?" Terrell's mother chimed in.

"Look, I'm sorry to hear about your brother. But the cops have been all over this apartment complex. They've been asking everyone if they'd seen that lady. And none of us have, so what you need to do is get behind the cops that are investigating your brother's case and take that stuff up with them. Hanging out in front of her apartment door isn't going to bring your brother back," he said, trying to find a soft spot in this debate so he could defuse this situation.

"We understand what you're saying, but you can't tell a person how to mourn a deceased family member," I heard Terrell's cousin say.

"You're absolutely right. But as a resident, I felt like I had to tell you guys that you're going about all of this the wrong way. That's all." His tone turned sympathetic.

"We appreciate what you're saying," Mrs. Mason mentioned.

"Oh, no problem, ma'am! Now y'all have a nice day," he said, and then he walked off. I watched him walk to his truck, get in, and drive off.

A few minutes later, Terrell's mother, sisters, and his cousin all walked back toward the parking area of the apartment complex. I watched them until they climbed into a black Cadillac SUV and sped off.

I literally had to wipe the sweat trickling down from my forehead. *Damn! Who would've thought that Terrell's family would come to my apartment and create a scene like that? Fuck!* I was so glad that Mrs. Mabel wasn't here! If she was—oh my God—things would've blown right up in my face. That *I'm an innocent person* would've gone right over Mrs. Mabel's head. I'm sure she would've gone to the extent of making me face Terrell's family while they were outside of my apartment. I could see Terrell's mother calling the cops and telling them where I was, and while the cops were en route to my apartment, I would've been fighting one, if not all, of them. And three-girls-on-one wouldn't have been a fair fight, but they would not have cared. Getting revenge for Terrell was all they would've focused on.

13

PROOF OF LIFE

I settled my nerves after Terrell's family left. I thanked God for my neighbor. If he hadn't checked them, those silly-ass hos would've still been standing outside of my apartment making threats. I also thanked God for Mrs. Mabel not being in here too. Things would've definitely gotten out of hand.

As I sat in Mrs. Mabel's apartment, I did feel somewhat safe. But then again, I didn't. I couldn't say it enough about how I was going to get myself out of this situation. I was stuck between a rock and a hard place. I was beginning to feel stifled in this apartment. In addition to that, I felt like I had no say-so about anything concerning me. Everything was good in the beginning when Mrs. Mabel opened her door to me. Now I was having regrets and wanted a way out. But if I left, then where was I going? I couldn't go to my grandmother's house. I couldn't go to my mother's house either. I no longer have a job, so I couldn't hang out there. So, what the hell was I going to do?

Now that the cops had April in custody, it was only a matter of time before they came looking for me. There was not a doubt in my mind that they were going to plaster my face all over the TV and Internet. And once that happened, I probably wouldn't be able to walk anywhere in public. Talk about losing your freedom.

To get my mind off the stresses in my life, I hopped in the shower and thought that it would help me relax, but it didn't. Instead, I found myself bawling my eyes out. Tears soaked my face, and no matter how much I tried to wipe my eyes with my bath cloth, tears kept coming.

Thinking about my mother being in the hands of Ahmad's mafia was causing me to have a panic attack. I knew my mother has probably shitted on herself by now. My mother wasn't a ride-or-die chick like me. I knew how to survive a little. But she didn't know how to do that at all. *I gotta get her out of this situation, and I mean now.*

Immediately after I took my shower, I dried off and put on another change of clothes. Upon my arrival back into the living room, I looked outside to see if any new cars had parked in the area. When I didn't see anything new, I sat down on the couch and sifted through the channels on TV. It didn't matter what channel I turned to, I just could not get into it. I turned the channel back to the news station so I could stay current with the news. What had been bothering me was that my mother's name hadn't been mentioned in the news. What was the cops' angle? Was it not important to broadcast? Someone needed to say something to the public, just in case someone saw her and knew where she was.

So, what the fuck is going on?

I swear, I wanted to call Agent Sims and Detective Belle so badly and curse their asses out. What kind of game were they playing? My mother's life was on the line, so why hadn't anyone publicized it yet? Was it because she was my mother and her life wasn't important? Or were they waiting for me to turn myself in and make them do something in exchange for my role in Terrell's murder?

Better yet, they wanted me back to testify against Ahmad's family, and once I did that, they'd send out a team to rescue my mother?

Whatever was going on in Agent Sims's and Detective Belle's heads, it needed to stop. An innocent woman's life was on the line and she needed to be found. Point-blank. I knew one thing, if they didn't spring into action, then I would, and I was going to expose everyone in my path.

After traveling back and forth to the window and back to the sofa over five times, I saw Mrs. Mabel as she pulled up underneath her carport and got out of her car. While she was taking a couple of bags from the back seat of her car, I saw the little boy that came by the day before. He was approaching her with his box of chocolate candy bars. I watched him as he talked to her about the assortment of candy he had. She smiled at him the entire time as he talked about what he had. A few seconds later, she started walking toward this apartment, and the little boy was in tow. To prevent her from unlocking the front door on her own, I stood there and opened the door myself. "I see you're back," I commented as Mrs. Mabel approached the front door.

"Yes, I'm here. And I got a little salesman with me," she said as she walked into the apartment. After she walked by me, she looked back at the little boy and said, "Come on in here, baby. And I'm gonna get you that dollar after I put these groceries down."

The little boy walked into the apartment and looked up at me. "Did you eat your candy bar?" he asked me. And that's when it jogged my memory that I hadn't eaten my chocolate bar. It also dawned on me that I had no idea what I did with it after he handed it to me. But then it hit me that as soon as he gave it to me, I took it with me into my apartment during which time I packed up a couple of outfits and stuffed them into my overnight bag. Alarmed by the fact that it was still there, and that it wouldn't be a good idea if the cops came back to my apartment and found it, I asked the little boy to go and get it for me. "Sweetheart, if you go into my apartment and get my candy bar that I bought from you yesterday, I will buy one more from you," I said.

"Where is it?"

"When you go in there, go straight to a bedroom straight down the hallway and you should see it on my dresser, near the mirror, or on my bed," I instructed him.

"Okay," he said, and then he turned around and walked away from me.

"It's already unlocked, so just push it open," I told him. I watched the little boy as he pushed open my front door and stepped inside my apartment. "Leave the front door open and go down that hallway." I instructed him further while I continued to watch him.

"Where did he go?" Mrs. Mabel asked after she walked up behind me.

"I just sent him into my apartment to get something for me," I told her.

She handed me a dollar bill. "Give him this dollar when he comes back," she said.

"Sure," I replied.

In a flash, the little boy disappeared in my bedroom and came out two seconds later with my candy bar in his hand. I smiled because he didn't know how he had saved my life by doing what he had just done. I mean, if Detective Belle or Agent Sims would've gone back into my apartment and noticed that a candy bar was there now, but it wasn't there the first time they searched it, they would've known automatically that I had been there. Thank God for little boys like this cute thing walking back toward me.

When he walked up to me, he handed me the candy bar I bought from him yesterday, and then he handed me two more. Another bar for me, and one for Mrs. Mabel. "Two dollars, right?" I said, and then I handed him the money.

"Yep," he replied as he took the two single bills in his hand.

Immediately after he took the money, he thanked me and then he turned around to leave. I stopped him. "What is your name?" I asked him.

He looked back at me and said, "John."

I smiled. "Hi, John," I said.

"What's your name?"

"Suzie," I lied to him with the biggest smile I had. Once again, seeing this little boy getting his hustle on was so rewarding. I could see this young boy growing up to be a CEO of a Fortune 500 company. I hoped his parents saw the entrepreneurship in him because he had the potential to go straight to the top.

I closed and locked the front door after the little entrepreneur walked away from the apartment. I set all three candy bars on the counter as soon as I walked into the kitchen. "Have you eaten lunch?" Mrs. Mabel yelled from the back of the apartment.

"Are you gonna cook?" I yelled back.

"No, I bought a couple of tuna fish sandwiches from the deli down the street."

"Sounds good. I'll wait until you get in here so we can eat together," I insisted.

"I'm on my way now," she replied, and then she appeared around the corner. Armed with a smile, she walked into the kitchen, carrying a clear package with a new doorknob lock-and-key set. "I stopped by the hardware store and picked up this beauty," she said while she handed it to me.

"Cool. Thanks," I replied after I took it from her hands and looked it over. "How much did it cost?" I wanted to know. She was already allowing me to stay in her apartment, so buying me a new lock for my apartment was very thoughtful.

"It was a little over forty dollars," she told me. And before I could comment, her cell phone rang. "Where did I leave my phone?" she wondered aloud.

"It's in your bedroom. I'll get it," I told her, and then I headed to her bedroom. Midway to her bedroom, her doorbell rang. I stopped and turned toward her. She stood there in the entryway of the kitchen and looked back at me. "Are you expecting someone?" I whispered.

"No. I'm not," she whispered back. "Go to my bedroom and close my door. I will come get you when they're gone," she assured me.

"Okay," I said as my heart rate sped up.

Mrs. Mabel watched me until I walked into her bedroom and closed the door behind myself. I stood there on the other side of the door with my ear to it so I could hear whoever was at the front door. I was so freaking nervous; it sounded like I was breathing hard at one point, so I held my breath. When I couldn't hold my breath any longer, I started breathing as quietly as I could. "Who is it?" I heard her yell.

I couldn't hear the person on the other side of the door, but when Mrs. Mabel asked the person to repeat it, I heard a man's voice, but I couldn't decipher his words.

"How can I help you?" she continued, and that's when I cracked her bedroom door a little. It was slightly ajar so I could get a good look at who was at the front door, but at the same time, they wouldn't be able to see me.

"My name is Officer Kahn and this is Officer Pax, and we would like to ask you some questions," I heard the guy say to Mrs. Mabel.

I couldn't get a look at the guy talking at the front door. At this angle, all I could see was the police patch stitched to the arm of the uniform. "What kind of questions do you need answering?" Mrs. Mabel asked him.

Before the gentleman answered, he swayed his head to the right of Mrs. Mabel's shoulder so he could get a look inside of the apartment. "Are you looking for something?" Mrs. Mabel asked. It was apparent that she caught him looking over her shoulder.

"I'm just acting with precaution, ma'am," he replied.

"I should be the least of your worries," I replied sarcastically.

"Is there someone else in this apartment?" I heard the other person say. This alarmed me. And I felt that at any moment those cops could move Mrs. Mabel out of the way and rush back here with their quickness!

"No, I'm the only person here. And why do you ask?" she questioned them. The cop that looked over her shoulder the first time did it again. This time I saw his face. "Oh my God, it's Ahmad," I said, barely audible.

Fear and anxiety consumed my body all at once. I immediately closed the door to Mrs. Mabel's room and locked it. Then I ran to the window and opened it. I punched the screen out of the window and watched it fall down on the ground. "Where are you going? You can't come in here," I heard Mrs. Mabel say, and then I heard a loud thud.

Confused and scared to death, I ran into Mrs. Mabel's walk-in closet and closed the door. Only residents of the apartment complex knew that we have a small storage space in the ceiling of our closet, so I climbed to the top shelf and eased the hatch back quietly.

"The door is locked. She's gotta be in here," I heard an unfamiliar voice say.

"Open it," I heard Ahmad instruct the other guy.

"Fuck! Fuck! Fuck!" I whispered, trying to pull myself carefully up into the ceiling.

Boom! The sound of the bedroom door after it slammed the wall behind it terrified me. "Fuck! She climbed out of the window!" I heard Ahmad roar. His voice boomed. Anyone would be terrified to be around this guy. "Go get her before she gets away. Kill her. I want her dead," Ahmad continued.

The other guy's footsteps went from walking to running, while Ahmad stayed behind. I thought one part of him must have had doubts that I climbed out of the window, because I heard him pushing around the stuff stored underneath Mrs. Mabel's bed. He walked to the closet next. I couldn't see what he was doing, but I heard him open the closet door, move the clothes hangers around, and then I heard him shut the closet door back.

When I heard Ahmad open another door and close it, I knew he was looking in the hall closet directly across from Mrs. Mabel's bedroom. After he closed that door, I heard the shower curtain move, so I knew he was in the bathroom.

I heard Ahmad making his way back out of the bathroom and I also heard the other guy with him panting. "She got away," the other guy said.

"How the fuck did we let her get away?!" Ahmad's voice boomed again.

"I told you we should've gotten her after we sent the kid to sell her the candy bar the first time," the other guy said.

"You know we couldn't get her. The feds were all over this place yesterday. Leaving when we did was the best course of action," I heard Ahmad say.

"You may be right, but the boss isn't gonna be happy when he calls today and we tell him that she got away."

"We'll tell him that the cops have been all over this place, and as soon as we get the chance, we'll have her in our hands," Ahmad explained.

"What about her mother and her boyfriend? What are we going to do with them?"

"Kill the boyfriend. And the mother, we're gonna use her as bait."

"What do you mean?"

"If we don't pick her up by day's end of tomorrow, we'll get word out to her that we'll trade her life for her mother's."

"How are we going to do that?"

"Just sit back and watch. Now let's get out of here."

"What we going to do about the old lady?" the other guy wanted to know.

"What kind of question is that? We're going to leave her here," Ahmad replied sarcastically, and then I heard them both as they left the apartment.

14

MY FLESH & BLOOD

Trying to piece everything I just heard together was becoming overwhelming. I mean, how fucking stupid did he think I was? To find out that Ahmad had that little boy come here to set me up was pretty clever, but I was two steps ahead of him. On the downside, the fact that Mrs. Mabel got caught up in this setup was pretty fucked up. Once again, I got someone shot and killed because of their affiliation with me. Granted, Mrs. Mabel was starting to get on my freaking nerves, but she helped me by giving me a place to lay low so the DEA and the local cops couldn't touch me. She was a rider. So, how can I just let this shit go? Besides that, what would the cops say if they came here and saw this lady dead? My fingerprints would be all over this place. I'd be their main and only suspect. *Now, how am I getting myself out of this one?*

Afraid to move an inch, I sat there in the small space above the closet. Thinking about how I was going to maneuver around this situation, I buried my face into the palms of my hands. Filled up with a bunch of sorrow, I let out a floodgate of tears. Why was all this shit coming at me like this? I was just a fucking pharmacy tech at a pharmacy with an aspiration to become a pharmacist, but look at how I screwed that up. It seemed like every time I tried to remedy my situation and move forward, I got caught up in some bullshit. It never failed.

After sitting around in this little-ass ceiling space for every bit of ten minutes, I figured the coast was clear, so I very carefully slid the ceiling square cover from the opening off to the side; then I carefully stepped down onto the top shelf. Once my foot was firmly placed on the top shelf, I put my other foot down and then I made my way down to the closet floor. Immediately after I planted both of my feet on the floor, I opened the closet door as quietly as I could, to prevent anyone from hearing it if they were still lingering around the apartment. Things seemed quiet, so I stepped out of the closet, tiptoed to the bedroom door, and peered around the corner.

When I realized that I was still in the clear, I looked down the hallway toward the front door and noticed the door was closed shut. Taking direction from my gut, I tiptoed down the hallway toward the front door. When I got halfway down the hall, that's when I saw Mrs. Mabel's lifeless body lying on the floor four feet away from the front door. I rushed over toward her, and right when I was just about to drop down on my knees to see if she was breathing, my gut spoke again. It told me how that would be a bad idea, especially if I got her blood on my hands. But as I stood there and watched her lying in her own blood, I thought about the fact that if I hadn't come here in the first place, then Mrs. Mabel would still be alive. I even thought about the fact that my mother's boyfriend, Carl, was about to be murdered because of me. Now, why was that? Why was I always putting all these people in harm's way? I knew my grandmother said that I wasn't going to get into heaven by way of suicide, but what if I wasn't supposed to go to heaven? With all the mess I caused, I deserved a one-way trip to hell. I guess I would soon find out.

Knowing that I needed to leave this apartment ASAP, I grabbed my duffel bag from the guest bedroom and started piling all of my stuff inside of it. I went into the bathroom, grabbed my bath cloth, and toothbrush. Next, I ran into Mrs. Mabel's bedroom with my duffel bag in hand and grabbed her purse, took her car keys and $74 she had inside of it, and stuffed them both down inside of my front pants pocket. From there, I ran into the kitchen and grabbed both deli sandwiches, because I knew that I was going to be hungry at any given moment. But then something happened and my peripheral vision caught it. I turned my complete focus around and that's when I saw three cops running toward Mrs. Mabel's apartment.

"What the fuck!" I said as fear engulfed me, and then I sprinted back to Mrs. Mabel's bedroom, where my duffel bag was. "No! No! No! They're gonna pin her murder on me. And then I'm gonna be booked on two counts of murder. I can't let this happen. No! No! No!" I whispered while my heart rate far exceeded sixty miles per hour.

The moment I walked into Mrs. Mabel's bedroom, I locked the bedroom door, grabbed my duffel bag from her bed, and then looked at the window. Realizing once again that I probably wouldn't be able to squeeze my body through it, much less my bag, I raced to the closet and climbed back up the shelves. At the top shelf, I shoved my duffel bag into the space first, and while I was pulling myself into the ceiling space, the cops kicked in the front door. "Virginia Beach Police," I heard one of them shout.

"Oh shit!" I heard another cop say.

"Is she alive?" I heard a third voice say.

"No. I'm dispatching homicide right now."

"Check the other rooms. We may not be alone," the first officer said. By then, I had climbed back into the ceiling space and closed the square peg back into its place. Feelings of regret, fear, and trepidation overwhelmed me as I heard cops emerge.

"Clear," one said from another room.

The cop that entered Mrs. Mabel's had to kick the door in first. I couldn't see what he was doing, but I heard him meticulously covering himself with every step he took. When he opened the closet door, he pushed and pulled the clothes hanging from their hangers. Once he saw that it was empty, he yelled to the other officers that his area was clear. "Whoever was here had to have jumped out of the window. So I'm gonna go outside and check the perimeter," he continued.

"Johns, have you dispatched the coroners?" I heard one of the officers ask.

"Yeah, they're en route now," another officer replied. Although all three of the cops were in the front room of the apartment, I could hear every word they uttered.

"Who could do this to an old lady?" one of the cops said.

"We got a lot of heartless people in the world," another cop replied.

"I'm gonna go back to the car to get the yellow tape," the other cop said.

"Make sure you keep the neighbors back an extra sixty feet."

"Will do."

It didn't take the local cops long to dispatch homicide detectives and the city coroners. They were all in Mrs. Mabel's apartment five minutes after they were called. It didn't surprise me when Detective Belle and her partner, Detective Caesar, appeared on the scene. I realized they were here after they entered into Mrs. Mabel's bedroom and asked the forensic specialist that was at the window dusting for prints if he had found any visible prints. He told them he had two sets of prints and this made them happy. "Think her murder is connected to the Misty Heiress case?" I heard Detective Caesar ask.

"There's a huge possibility," I heard Detective Belle reply.

"If that's the case, what do you think happened?" he wanted to know.

"I don't know. But we will have an answer by the end of the day," Belle said.

"Hey, you guys, I found prints in the second bathroom. Whoever was here used the toilet, the sink maybe to brush their teeth, and they also took a shower, because they left a bath cloth, so there's gonna be DNA all over it."

"Sounds good," Belle said.

"Yeah, that's awesome," I heard the other detective agree.

"Hey, Caesar, Belle," another person shouted.

"Yeah," Belle and Caesar said in unison.

"Got a lady outside saying that the lady who lived here had a female visitor," I heard the person say.

"Where is she?" Belle asked.

"She's right outside of the yellow tape," the guy replied.

"Come on, Caesar, let's hear what she has to say," I heard Belle say to Detective Caesar.

Hearing Detective Belle instruct her partner to follow her outside to speak with an eyewitness made my heart nearly jump out of my freaking chest. *Who in the hell knows that I am here?* No one saw me when I initially walked into Mrs. Mabel's apartment, so where did they get their information from? Had Mrs. Mabel had a chance to tell someone that I was here? And if she did, who could it be? And why would she do it? She knew I was trying to lay low. Was I missing something here?

Knowing that Detective Belle and Detective Caesar were

on their way to speak with this so-called witness had me terrified. Not to mention, the fact that I left my bath cloth behind in the bathroom. And now that the cops had it, they would indeed pull my DNA from it. How in the hell did I forget to grab it?

For the duration of the evidence gathering, I heard different cop voices as the cops walked about Mrs. Mabel's apartment. I heard one guy say that whoever murdered Mrs. Mabel was a heartless person. I heard another guy say that it looked like a robbery. The same guy who had just spoken also said that he found a store receipt in the kitchen that indicated that Mrs. Mabel purchased two sandwiches, and from the time of the receipt, it was 12:05, which was less than thirty minutes ago. So, not only were the two sandwiches missing, they knew what time Mrs. Mabel was killed. I swear, all of this news was killing me on the inside. These cops weren't going to let up with this investigation. When they found out it was me, Detective Belle and Agent Sims were not going to sleep until they locked my ass up. I felt sick in the stomach and wanted to throw up all over this ceiling storage, but when I thought of them finding me and hauling me off to jail, I fought back the urge of regurgitating.

15

THE FIRST FORTY-EIGHT HOURS

It seemed like time was creeping by slowly. It felt like these guys had no intentions of leaving. Every time I heard one cop announce that they'd cleared one room, meaning they logged all the evidence, I'd hear another cop say that they found something else. It was like a fucking circus; everyone was juggling their own act with no intentions of leaving.

Detective Belle walked back into Mrs. Mabel's apartment with her partner, Caesar, in tow. She made an announcement and it sounded like she was making it in the living-room area. "I just spoke with one of the neighbors. Her name was Tina. She's an older woman. Looked to be in her late forties. She said that she knew Mrs. Mabel for a long time. She was like the neighborhood grandmother. She was a nice lady and everyone loved her, so it's hard to believe that someone would kill her. She also said that she spoke to Mrs. Mabel this morning and everything seemed fine. But when she saw two uniformed cops run away from this apartment, she felt something was wrong, because cops only run when they're in pursuit of someone. And you know what, guy?" Belle said.

"What?" a few cops said in unison.

"She's right. And you wanna know why?" Belle continued.

"Why?" the same cops said.

"Because within the last hour, there weren't any calls from dispatch for this area or any area within twenty miles. So tell me who were those two cops that the lady saw?"

"Was she sure that they were cops? I mean, they could've been security officers," I heard one of the guys say.

"We asked her that same question. And she said she knows what Virginia Beach Police uniforms look like. She also said that they were driving one of the city's police vehicles too," I heard Detective Caesar reply.

"Don't you think it's ironic that a murder was committed at the apartment next door and now we're investigating another one?" I heard someone ask. I couldn't make out the voice because there were over eight to ten people.

"There's a strong possibility. And also remember that we have the suspect April, who has agreed to testify in front of a grand jury and say Terrell Mason was already dead when she entered into the apartment next door. Now fast-forward to now, when Agent Sims and I tried to speak with this lady here, she wouldn't cooperate with us. It almost seemed like she had a bond with Misty Heiress, which was why she expressed her grievances with us for going through Misty's things in her apartment. So, what if someone from Terrell's family or a friend of his came by Misty's apartment to seek revenge and Mrs. Mabel got in their way?" Belle said.

"I can definitely see that," Detective Caesar commented.

"Me too," another voice said.

"Yeah, that's plausible," someone else said.

"Okay, so we may have a motive here. Now I'm gonna need you guys to comb through this place very thoroughly. Too many dead bodies are popping up. So let's get a handle on it and let's do it now," Belle demanded.

* * *

It took all those cops a total of five damn hours to collect all the evidence they needed. When they finally filed out of here, one by one, it felt like a ton of anxiety lifted from my shoulders. I let out a long sigh of relief and then I laid my head down on my duffel bag.

Thinking about everything I heard from the police got my mind racing. Okay, so they got one thing right, which was that the two guys that ran away from this apartment weren't real cops. But as far as who they think killed Mrs. Mabel, they were all wrong. Terrell's family or close friends had nothing to do with Mrs. Mabel's murder. But if they wanted to believe they did it, then so be it. My main priority was me. Not only was Ahmad, along with his henchman, looking for me, but Agent Sims and Detective Belle were too. So, as soon as they pulled my DNA from the towel and bath cloth I left behind, they're gonna think I murdered Mrs. Mabel and they'd have me on something like *America's Most Wanted*. Once that happened, I wouldn't be able to stay in this area. Finding somewhere to go was what I needed to concentrate on.

I had no idea where I was going to go. Nor did I know what I was going to do. I had no plans. All I had were the keys to Mrs. Mabel's car. So I figured that if I could use it to get away from here, I'd have a clearer mind to be able to come up with a good plan. "Okay, Misty, it's time to go. You gotta get out of here before someone else comes here," I whispered to myself.

After building up enough courage, I finally willed myself to climb back out of the ceiling space. On my way down, I made every step carefully. I wanted to be as quiet as a mouse. Getting caught was not an option for me. Once I had landed with my feet placed firmly on the floor, I slid the closet door back as quiet as I could. I stood still for a moment to see if I could hear any movement. After realizing that there was no more movement in the house, I stepped out of the closet and tiptoed over to the bedroom door. I peered around the corner of Mrs. Mabel's bedroom and into the hallway. I looked toward the front door, where her body had been, and it was gone. I was relieved to see that. I was even more relieved when I walked around the apartment and saw that I was alone. But the cops and forensic officers had left a lot of black dust and markers around the apartment to let someone know that they had been there. It was one of those crime scenes that you'd see in a movie. I stood there and looked down at the puddle of blood and felt so bad that Mrs. Mabel was murdered because of me. I mean, if she hadn't picked me up at the freaking grocery store and brought me into her home, she'd still be alive now. Probably watching her favorite shows. But no, the moment I stepped foot into this apartment, everything went downhill from there. I had a hand in creating this lady's demise. Now, how fucked up was that?

I knew that I wasn't going to be able to leave this apartment just like that. I also knew that in order for me to leave this place without being seen, I was gonna have to move strategically. That might entail leaving here with a wig on and sunglasses. I might also need to leave here when it got dark outside. More important, whenever I did decide to walk out of this apartment, no one, including the agents, cops, or Ahmad, could be able to see me. If they did, then I'd be fucked.

16

GETTING REVENGE

While I waited for the perfect time to leave, I kept my eyes fixed on the parking lot area of my neighborhood. It seemed like every time I saw a good chance for me to walk out of this place, I either saw one of my neighbors walking by or hanging out in the parking lot with someone else. I swear, I was about to pull my fucking hair out. It was becoming a little nerve-racking, to say the least.

After waiting in the living room for another hour or so, I finally saw my opportunity to leave. There were no cops around watching the apartment building, nor did I see any federal agents camped outside in their cars. This was my time, so I grabbed my duffel bag and raced toward the front door. Immediately after I opened the front door to leave, a Channel 10 news station van pulled up into the parking space next to Mrs. Mabel's car.

"Nooooooo! This can't be happening," I whined softly. One part of me wanted to rush toward Mrs. Mabel's car and get into it before this news crew set up. But then, the other part of me wanted to turn around and go back into Mrs. Mabel's apartment. "Shit! This can't be happening. Ugh!" I said once more, and then I sighed heavily.

The distance between Mrs. Mabel's car and the news station van from where I was standing was too close, and I knew that I wasn't going to make it in time before either the news reporter or the camera guy would see me.

"Damn! I just can't get a break!" I cursed, and then I turned back around. But instead of going back into Mrs. Mabel's apartment, I opened my front door and slid in there without anyone noticing it. I was pissed that I couldn't lock my front door after closing it. I did stick one of my kitchen table chairs underneath the doorknob, hoping to keep anyone from getting into my apartment. This was just a temporary fix, but it worked.

I dropped my duffel bag down on the floor and peered out the window of my living room. Trying to figure out what this reporter was about to say had me on edge. I mean, I knew it's her job, but damn, can't you just leave well enough alone? I was trying to get out of this place and they were keeping me hostage. I was not supposed to be in my apartment right now. What if the cops decided that they wanted to come back and reexamine some areas in my apartment? I'd be screwed up if that shit happened, because not only would they be able to sneak into my place from the back of the apartment building, they'd be able to come into my apartment without unlocking the door. Okay, so I pushed one of my kitchen chairs to hold the door back, but that wouldn't hold up against the pressure of a couple of cops. They'd be able to kick that door in on the first try. Hopefully, that wouldn't happen. I prayed to God that it wouldn't.

I stood there on pins and needles and my heart racing, trying to figure out what was going to be said. Would the news reporter mention what had happened in my apartment, or would she only cover the murder of Mrs. Mabel? Lord knows, all eyes would be on this place as soon as the camera started rolling.

A few of my neighbors started coming outside to see what was going on. They began to huddle around one another in a circle. A couple of them looked in the direction of my apartment, as well as Mrs. Mabel's apartment, since they were connected. I wondered what they were saying. The mere thought that I was a topic of their discussion caused me a serious amount of shame and embarrassment. This wasn't how my life was supposed to be. So, how can I stop it? How can I take things back to where they were? I swear, I don't know how much more of this that I can take. Hopefully, not much more.

The camera started rolling when I saw the light illuminating from it and that's when I knew this thing was for real. I couldn't make out what the black woman was saying, because not only was her back facing the building, she was too far away for me to hear anything. So I rushed over to my television and turned it on. After it came on, I turned to the news channel and there they were reporting live outside.

"I'm standing in front of building 210 of Kings Grant Apartments, where an elderly woman was murdered inside of her apartment. She was found dead from two fatal gunshot wounds to her abdomen a little before one o'clock today. I spoke with several neighbors, who say that she was a beautiful and kind lady, so to hear that she was murdered was both shocking and sad. The woman's identity will be released, once her family is notified. As of right now, investigators have no suspects or motive. Anyone with information is urged to call the crime line. I'm Christian Lundy, and I'm reporting for *Ten on Your Side*."

"Hey, I see a light in that apartment next door," someone a few feet away from the cameraman said.

This caught the eyes and ears of the reporter. "What are you talking about?" the reporter asked as she walked over toward the woman standing a couple feet away from her.

The cameraman turned his camera directly at a full-figured black woman dressed in an oversized blouse and blue pants.

I watched the woman as she pointed toward my apartment. Caught off guard by this sudden change of events, I raced over to the window to see if my neighbor was actually pointing at my apartment. When I opened my blinds, just enough to see, I gasped for air at what happened next.

"What do you mean someone is in the apartment?" the news reporter questioned my neighbor as she damn near shoved her microphone in her face.

"That other apartment next to the one with the yellow crime tape. It belongs to the lady the police are looking for. That apartment has been dark for days, because no one has been there. But now it looks like someone is there. Yeah, see someone is looking out of the window." My neighbor continued as if she was a private investigator, solving a damn problem; that's when I let the blinds go and stepped back from the window.

"Did you get that, Jim?" I heard the news reporter say while the live report was airing.

"Yep, I'm still rolling," I heard him acknowledge.

"It has been alleged that a woman wanted by the local police may, in fact, be hiding in her apartment. I have her neighbor here who just noticed movement in that apartment. My cameraman, Jim, and I are on our way up to this apartment to check things out." The news reporter continued to report, all while making her way up to my apartment. But I couldn't let her come up here and see me. If I did, then I'd be sealing my own fate. I was either gonna be captured by the DEA or by Ahmad and his crew. So the best thing for me to do was to get the hell out of here.

Without hesitation I powered off my television, grabbed my duffel bag, and ran over toward the front door. I removed the kitchen chair that secured the doorknob, snatched the front door open, and then made a run for it.

Instead of running toward the front entrance of the complex, I made a run for the back of the apartment complex.

"Hey, wait. Stop!" I heard the news reporter yelling for me to stop. I ignored her and kept running. I was not about to let this lady put me on camera. But then I stumbled over a glass bottle and slipped and fell down on the ground. Pain shot through my ankle. "Fuck!" I said, gritting my teeth. And before I could stand back up, the news reporter had managed to catch up with me. The high voltage of light coming from the camera nearly blinded me. The news reporter leaned down toward me, almost shoving her microphone down my throat. "Hey, are you the woman that the police are looking for? Did you know anything about your neighbor's murder? And were you hiding inside of that apartment?" Her questions continued.

"Get that damn camera out of my face. I am innocent of all that shit the cops are trying to plant on me. And I saw who killed Mrs. Mabel!" I said after I finally stood up on my feet.

"Who was it?" the reporter asked me, keeping the microphone in my face.

"It was the mafia that kidnapped my mother and her boyfriend. Now tell the cops to go and do their jobs and try to find out where they are and leave me alone," I spat out, and then I ran off again with my duffel bag in hand.

"Well, there you have it, folks. The young woman from that apartment just sent Virginia Beach their first clue. Now let's see if they take it and use it. I'm Christian Lundy reporting for *Ten on Your Side*."

After running three blocks, I felt like I was finally out of the woods. More important, I felt a little liberated. Not to the point that I just cleared my name, but to allow the world to see and hear me say who really killed Mrs. Mabel, and that Ahmad and his family had my mother, and the cops needed to do something about it.

I thought about finding a back way to enter into my

mother's house, but I knew the cops and Agent Sims would come there looking for me, since I went back into my apartment after I felt that it would be safe to do so. If I went back into my place, there was a huge possibility that they'd come looking for me at my mom's house too. So I left well enough alone and decided to figure out another place to go. But before I did that, I hid behind the nearest tree and changed my shirt, since the entire viewing audience saw what I was wearing on TV. I even put on the wig I took from Mrs. Mabel's apartment. I didn't have a mirror on hand, but I knew that I had a good disguise. I just hoped that it kept me undetected until I could find another safe haven.

17

KISS MY ASS

Trying to figure out where I was going to hide out had become harder than I expected. I'd been walking for an hour and a half now. I was pissed off that I didn't get a chance to take Mrs. Mabel's car. The freaking news reporter snatched that option from me when she started running down behind me. *What am I going to do now?*

Luckily, it was dark out, because if it wasn't, the cops would probably have me in handcuffs right now. Speaking of cops, a total of three cops had already passed me. I can't tell you why they *weren't* looking out for me, but I can tell you that I was fortunate that they weren't.

I walked up Virginia Beach Boulevard and approached the traffic light at the corner of Newtown Road. At this intersection, I saw a truck that looked like my mother's boyfriend's son's truck. His name was Carl Jr. I wasn't sure how old he was, but I knew he was over the age of twenty-five.

I raced toward the truck before the light turned green. And by the time I approached the passenger side of the truck, I was disappointed to find out that the driver wasn't him. "Ugh!" I said, and let out a long sigh.

While I turned around to get back to the sidewalk, that's when it hit me that I should reach out to Carl Jr. If I could get him to help me get my mother back, everything I was doing would be worth it. But I figured that it would only work if he believed that his father was alive but in harm's way. So, as of right now, that's what it was going to be.

After walking a block and a half, I was able to flag down a taxicab. The driver was a black older woman. She was in her own world listening to her gospel music. The only words she uttered when I got in her car were "Good evening. And where are you going?"

I spoke back to her and requested to be taken to Norfolk. I told her that I didn't know the exact address, but I knew the name of the street. With that, she said okay and then we headed uptown.

The entire drive to Norfolk, I bounced words back and forth in my head, trying to figure out how I was going to approach him when I asked him for his help. I knew I had to be convincing, because this guy really didn't know me. He'd only seen me maybe twice, if not three times. And all of them were at Thanksgiving and Christmas get-togethers. I just hoped that he didn't turn me away or call the cops on me. If he did, then I was going to be screwed.

Approximately fifteen minutes later, the cabdriver had gotten me to my destination. "We're on Thirty-fourth Street," she announced.

I sat up in the back seat, trying to eyeball the block. This street was a one-way street, so for all I knew, the cops could be watching his house. So I needed to be extra careful. "Could you drive all the way down and circle the block?" I asked her.

"Sure," she said.

Halfway down the block, I recognized Carl Jr.'s town house. It was located to the left side of the street. I also recognized his truck parked in the driveway. Only one light was on in his house, and that light was coming from his bedroom. That gave me hope that he was, in fact, inside the house.

When the taxi driver made a left turn to circle back around to get back on Thirty-fourth Street, I stopped her. "You know what? Just pull the car over. I'm gonna get out right here," I instructed the woman.

She pulled her cab over to the side of the road. Immediately after I paid her from the money I took from Mrs. Mabel's purse, I got out of the car and walked onto the sidewalk. I saw an entryway alongside an old house, which would give me a way to hop the fence to get to Carl Jr.'s house. Thankfully, there were no dogs in sight, barking and alarming neighbors that something or someone was coming.

I climbed an old, raggedy metal fence that separated Carl Jr.'s backyard from the other land owned by the homeowners that lived around him. The backyard of his home was completely black. This was good for me, being in the dark and everything. I climbed onto the back porch and knocked on his door, as lightly as I could. I just hoped that I was doing it loud enough for him to hear.

The first four tries hadn't worked, so I was forced to knock harder. After doing it another four times, I finally got Carl Jr.'s attention. As soon as he walked to the back door, I heard him shouting, asking who was at his door. I told him who I was, and almost at that instant, he opened the door. He stood on the other side of the screen door, with his cell phone against his ear, and just looked at me. "Can I come in?" I asked him.

"Hey, Mom, let me call you back," he said, and then I watched him as he disconnected his call. A couple of seconds later, he unlocked the screen door and pushed it open. "Hey, you're Misty, right?" he said after he opened the door.

"Yes."

"Come in," he insisted, and quickly moved out of the way.

I stood to the side of him after I crossed the threshold. "Would you please close your door?" I asked. He saw the alarmed look I had on my face.

"Yeah, sure," he said, and immediately closed the door. "I just saw you on TV. But your hair wasn't like that."

Hearing him tell me that he saw me on TV instantly caused me to have an anxiety attack. I placed my right hand over my heart while I leaned against the nearby wall.

"Are you okay?" he asked as he placed his hand across my right shoulder.

"I need to take a seat."

"Let's go into the living room," he said, and then he led me toward the front area of his house.

I took a seat on the couch only a few feet away from the entrance of the kitchen and then I took Mrs. Mabel's wig from my head. "Thank you for letting me in. 'Cause I really had nowhere else to go."

"Don't worry about it. It's cool," he replied.

"I take it you and your mother were talking about me being on the news?" I questioned him, even though I already had the answer to my question. As he explained how he was shocked to see me lying on the ground and telling the news reporter what I said, I began to size him up. He wasn't that tall. Maybe five-eight and 150 pounds. He had the body frame of Floyd Mayweather, but was average-looking in the face. So far, he seemed like a good guy, but time would tell.

"You know, the cops came by here two days ago. They were asking me when I last talked to my father. And I told them that he and I talked on the same day he was supposed to come by here and stay for a while. But he never showed up."

"Did they tell you what happened to your dad and my mother?" I asked him.

"They didn't tell me that they were kidnapped. I heard

that come out of your mouth when you were on the news. But they told me that they were missing."

"Who told you that? The cops or the federal agents?"

"Federal agents are on this?"

I let out a long sigh. "It's complicated."

"So, is it true? The mafia has them?"

"Yes," I said regretfully.

"But why?"

"Is there someone else in here?" I asked him. I wanted to make sure that if someone is here, then I needed to choose my words carefully.

"No, my girlfriend is at work."

"Do you guys have kids?" I pressed the issue.

"No. It's just me and her."

I hesitated for a moment and then I said, "The guy I was working for at a local pharmacy was dealing illegal prescription drugs right underneath my nose. According to the DEA, my boss had been dealing since before I got there. After two months of working there, I kind of figured that he was dealing. I needed a job, so I turned my head and continued to mind my own business. Unfortunately, someone robbed the pharmacy, so the cops had to get in on it. One thing led to another, and before I knew it, the DEA agents wanted me to wear a wire, but I declined. So, one day, my boss saw me talking to the cops outside the pharmacy and thought that I was snitching on him. And it didn't help clear my name, because a few days later he got arrested.

"Word got back to his family and everything went downhill from there. I guess when it got hard for them to find me, they started looking for anyone close to my family. I'm sorry that they got my mother and your father. But, just so you know, we can get them back. But I'm gonna need your help to do it," I explained to him.

"As much as I want to help you, I'm not into that life. I

got locked up shooting a nigga that stole a grand from me when I was nineteen years old. Did ten years upstate. Had to fight niggas almost every day to prove my manhood. I'm thirty-two years old now, so I'm not interested in anything that would put me back in that situation. But I do have someone that would love to help you out," Carl Jr. said.

"Who?"

"My baby brother, Rich. When I called him and told him what you said on TV, he became angry and started threatening to do something to the mafia guys that took our father."

"Can you get him to come here so I can talk to him?"

"Yeah, I'll get him on the phone now," he told me, and then he started pressing buttons on his iPhone. A couple seconds later, I could hear the other line ringing from where I was sitting. That's how loud his cell phone volume was. "Junior, what's up?" I heard the other guy say.

"Yo, come to my crib now. Got something I want you to see."

"A'ight, I'm on my way," I heard the other guy say, and then Carl Jr. disconnected their call.

"He's on his way."

"Yeah, I heard him. How long do you think it'll take him?"

"You in a rush?" Carl Jr. asked sarcastically.

"No. I was just asking."

"He's not too far from here. Give him about thirty minutes and he'll be here," Carl Jr. said, and then he started walking toward the kitchen. "Thirsty?"

"I'll take a bottle of water, if you got it."

"Bottle of water coming right up," he said as he opened the refrigerator door. After he grabbed a bottle of water and a bottle of Heineken from the side door, he walked back into the living room. He handed the bottle of water to me, but kept the bottle of beer for himself.

"Thank you," I said after I took the water from his hand.

"You're welcome," he said, and then he sat in the chair directly across from me. "Tell me why you were running from the news reporter?" he asked after taking a sip from his bottle.

"Because I didn't want to be on TV."

"How did you fall?"

"I tripped over a bottle."

"Is it true that you killed your ex-boyfriend?"

"What made you ask me that?" That question came out of thin air. Was it a trick question?

"The guy's family went on TV and said that you killed him."

"That's a lie. I didn't do shit. They need to talk to all of his side bitches!" I spat. I was getting frustrated by his implication, even though I was lying. *I'm the real victim here, not that piece of shit–ass nigga, Terrell. He fucked up my life. Not the other way around!*

"I'm sorry if I offended you," he apologized.

"It's okay. It's just I went through a lot of shit behind that guy. I regret the day I met his ass. He didn't give a fuck about anyone but himself. And people like him don't get far in life. To be honest with you, I'm glad somebody got rid of his ass!" I roared. Just the mere thought of that bastard got me in an uproar. Not only that, but the fact that April had ratted me out and would testify against me when the cops finally caught me had me on edge too.

"I'm sorry if I made you upset."

"Don't apologize. I'm good," I tried to assure him, and then I took another sip of my bottled water. "Tell me about your brother," I said, changing the subject.

"What do you wanna know about him?"

"How old is he? How close are you two? Is he a street cat? Or is he a hothead? You know general questions."

"Well, he's twenty-four years old. He did a three-year

bid upstate for selling dope. Now he's out and right back in the streets selling drugs. And as far as him being hot-headed, he would definitely snap out and put a bullet in somebody's ass if he feels like someone's disrespecting him."

"Think he'll help me get our parents back?"

"Oh, most definitely."

"Does he drive?"

"He has his driver's license, but he doesn't have a car. He drives his girlfriend's around, most of the time, especially when she's at work."

"Are you gonna talk to him first? I mean, I would rather for you to break the ice when he gets here."

"Sure. I can do that," he said. "But can I ask you something?"

I braced myself for this question; I swear, I didn't know what he was going to ask me.

"How well did you know my dad?"

"Well, I didn't see him much when I stopped by my mother's place. He'd either be at work or in the bedroom, watching TV."

"Did you like him?"

"Yes, I thought he was a cool guy. He didn't talk much, but I knew he loved my mother."

"Good, I'm glad," he replied, and then he said, "Did you know that your mother was turning into an alcoholic?"

"Where did you hear that from?" I asked sarcastically. I wasn't liking where this conversation was going.

"My dad would stop by and tell me how much he loved your mother, but her drinking was kinda pushing him into leaving her."

"Okay, and what does my mother's drinking have to do with them both getting kidnapped?"

"It has nothing to do with it. I was just sharing a concern that my father had concerning your mother, being as though my father used to be an alcoholic. He's concerned that he may relapse."

I sat there and thought for a moment. I didn't want to continue down this road that Carl Jr. and I were going. I mean, I understood his concern for his father, but him relapsing wouldn't be a problem if he was dead. Too bad he didn't know. "Look, I understand how you feel. And I'm sorry for snapping at you. It's just that I wanna get my mama back safe and sound. She doesn't need this shit in her life."

"What about my father? He's there with her and he had nothing to do with none of it," Carl Jr. interjected.

"Well, that's what I meant. Both of them need to come home," I recanted, even though I didn't mean a word of it.

"Do you think that they're going to be all right? Are those guys really bad people?"

"I don't know. It's really hard to tell." I lied once again, knowing full well that his father could be dead.

"What do you mean?"

"Those guys don't want your dad and my mother. They want me. So I believe that they're willing to exchange their lives for mine," I said. I swear, those words literally tumbled from my mouth like a leaky faucet.

"And how do you know that?"

"Because I know. Remember I used to work for those guys."

"Don't you think that it would be better if you let the cops handle it? I mean, you talking about exchanging your life for their lives, like it's that easy. Don't you care about living too?"

"Of course, I do. But when I think about what my mother could be going through right now, it puts me in the mind frame to think more about her than myself."

"You're talking about my father too, right? I mean, because every time you bring your mother up, you never add my father to the equation. Do you know something that I don't?"

"I'm sorry if I keep doing that. It's just that I got a lot of stuff on my mind," I told him after I took another sip from my bottle of water.

Carl Jr. kept our conversation going with one question after the next. At one point, it felt like I was going through an interrogation. But I knew he just needed the questions concerning his father answered. So I did my best to answer his questions as delicately as I could.

18

IN KILLING MODE

Carl Jr. was right. It took his baby brother, Rich, less than thirty minutes. I must admit that this guy was a character. He walked through the front door with another guy in tow. As soon as he saw me, he smiled. "So, is she that something you needed to show me?" he asked after looking at me from head to toe.

"Yes, this is Misty, and, Misty, this is my brother, Rich."

Rich walked over to where I was sitting and extended his left hand. "Nice to meet you," he said as we shook hands. The guy that was with him stood by the front door.

"Same here," I told him when he let my hand loose.

I stared at Rich for a brief moment while he stood before me. I had to admit that this little fellow was kind of cute. He looked like the actor Larenz Tate. In fact, he had the look and the height. It was crazy weird. But I went with it.

"Are you the lady from the news?" he asked.

"I was about to ask her the same question," the big guy by the front door said.

"Yeah, and that's why I'm here," I began to say.

"Yeah, she said she knows where her mom and our dad is," Carl Jr. spoke up.

"Ain't that what she said on the news?" Rich said as he looked at Carl Jr.

"Yes, I did, but it's more complicated than that," I began to explain.

"Hey, wait, what's your name again?" Rich asked me.

"Misty."

"Oh shit! You're the girl that supposed to killed that nigga Terrell," Rich added.

Instantly my insides were engulfed with a ball of nerves mixed with anxiety and fear. Hearing Rich say that I was the girl that killed Terrell paralyzed me. How am I supposed to act after hearing this? Stay here and defend myself? Or run out of here and never look back? I needed some help trying to figure this thing out. Finally, a thought popped in my head. "Look, I don't know where you got that information from, but I didn't have shit to do with that nigga getting killed."

"That ain't what April said." Rich pressed this issue as he stood a few feet away from me. For a minute, he looked like he was about to interrogate me. My heart rate sped up at an increasing amount. I wasn't sure how I was supposed to react to his statement, so I just sat and looked at Carl Jr., hoping he'd step in and help me.

"You worked at the pharmacy down on Church Street, right?"

"I used to."

"Yeah, your cousin Jillian got with my homeboy Tedo and tried to rob that spot, but got shot up and killed by the cops," Rich added.

"That's not how that happened."

"Explain it to me," he insisted.

"When my cousin and Tedo came down there to rob it, the

owner of the store's family had come there, and so they had a shoot-out with Tedo and the other guy that was with him."

"You didn't tell me that a robbery took place," Carl Jr. interjected.

"That's because you didn't ask me."

"That was because I didn't know."

"Look, we can sit here all day and go back and forth about who robbed who, and who got shot. I lost my cousin Jillian and my grandmother behind those guys. And now they got my mother and y'all father, so are you going to help me get them back, or what?" I replied sarcastically. I needed these fucking idiots to realize that it's not about what happened; it was about where we were now and how did we start from there.

"Answer this one question," Rich said.

"What is it?" I asked him, but at the same time, I dreaded what he was about to say. *You never know where stuff is going to go with this fucking guy.*

"Are you working with the cops or federal agents? Because that's what's going around on the streets."

"No, I am not. I mean, if I were working with them, do you think I'd be running from the fucking cameraman and that dumb bitch of a news reporter? Do you think I'd be here asking for y'all help? If anyone is snitching, it's that April chick. She's the one telling the police that I murdered Terrell, and her and Tedo chopped his body up," I said further.

Rich stood there and looked at me like he could see through me. He did this for the next sixty seconds, and then he finally said something. "If I find out that you're lying to me, I'm gonna kill you dead. Now do we have an understanding? Because I don't fuck with snitches. Snitches are rats. And I don't like rats. They are nasty and filthy!"

"I get your point," I told him, but deep inside of me, I became fearful and petrified of this guy. He might have been a small guy in stature, but his heart was cold and vicious. I wanted no part of it.

"I'm gonna only do this because my father got caught up in this shit. So tell me who we're dealing with?"

"I really don't know how many there are, because most of the family lives in DC, but I do know they have an Indian restaurant near the JANAF Shopping Yard. They open at eleven o'clock in the morning and close at ten o'clock at night. I figure if you follow one of them home, you'll find out where our mom and dad are."

"Think we could rob those motherfuckers?" Rich wanted to know.

"I don't think that would be a good idea. The first time my cousin and Tedo tried to do it, the whole thing fell apart."

"That's because they didn't know what the fuck they were doing. If me and my crew run up on them, we're gonna come out on top."

"I'm sure y'all are good at what you do, but all I'm interested in doing is getting my mother back," I expressed.

"Well, I'm interested in getting compensated for my work. So, if you want to get your mama back, then you're gonna have to do it my way," he said. I watched his body language while he was looking at me, and from there, I knew that he meant what he just said.

I sat there for a moment and mulled over the pros and the cons of his proposition. On one hand, I wanted no part of his robbery scheme. Getting involved with another robbery would take me on a slippery slope. On the other hand, this was the only way I was going to get my mother back. And I couldn't leave her like this. I got her into this mess, and now I had to figure out how I was going to get her out. "I'm willing to do it your way," I finally told him.

"I knew you would see it my way," he said confidently.

"So, when are you trying to make a move?" I asked him.

"It's too late to do it tonight, so if everything goes right tomorrow, we can do it then."

"So, what am I going to do until then?" I asked both him and Carl Jr.

"What do you mean?" Rich asked.

"I don't have anywhere to stay. Remember, I was running from my apartment when the news reporter was following me."

"If it was up to me, then I would let you stay. But my girlfriend isn't gonna have it," Carl Jr. spoke first. So I looked at Rich next.

"Look, I be at the trap all night long. So, if you don't mind watching a nigga hustling, then you can come with me," Rich offered.

Before I opened my mouth to give him an answer, everyone in the living room heard someone on the other side of the front door trying to come in. Rich and I both looked at Carl Jr. He stood up from the chair and told Rich's homeboy to move to the side so his girlfriend could come walk into the house without the guy blocking her way.

As soon as she unlocked the front door and pushed it open, I zoomed in on her at first sight. She was pretty, like La La Anthony, and petite, like Jada Pinkett Smith. She was definitely an eye catcher. "Hi." I smiled and spoke to her first.

"Hi," she spoke back as she took off her jacket and hung it up on a coatrack next to the front door. She hung the straps of her purse there too.

"Why you home so early? I thought you had to work late tonight," Carl Jr. asked her.

"I got Tammy to come in and take over my shift," she replied, looking at him. And then she looked around the entire room.

"What's good, Sabrina?" Rich smiled at her.

"Everything is good. What's going on in here?" she wanted to know as she closed the door and locked it.

"We're just in here reminiscing about old times," Carl Jr. lied.

I don't know how he came up with that lie that quick. I did know that if she believed it, then he was bad, man.

"And who is she?" She continued to hurl her questions in the air.

"I'm Misty," I said, making the introduction.

"Wait, isn't she your father's girlfriend's daughter?"

"Yes, I am," I answered before anyone in the room could.

"You were on the news tonight too, right?"

I hesitated for a second and then I said, "Yeah, I was."

"So, what brings you here?" She wasn't letting up. She was going to ask me as many questions as she wanted to, and if I decided that I didn't want to answer them, then I could definitely see her throwing me out of her house.

"She came here to let us know where our daddy is," Carl Jr. spoke up.

"Well, where is he?" she asked Carl Jr.

"Some mafia guys," he replied.

"And how do you guys know that?" she asked, this time looking directly at me.

"The same guys got her mama," Carl Jr. answered.

"I'm not talking to you. I'm talking to her. So let her answer," the girlfriend replied impatiently. The way she looked at me, I knew she wasn't liking me at all.

"Because I used to work for those guys and I heard things," I told her in a nice and respectful manner. As badly as I wanted to curse her ass out, I didn't. I knew that it wouldn't be the greatest idea, considering that I was at everyone's mercy. I needed shelter. And I needed a team of street dudes to help me rescue my mother, even if it meant that I would have to trade my life for hers. Doing it alone wasn't an option.

Sabrina took a seat on the couch next to me. But she was on the far left side of me. "Do you know why those guys got your mother and their father?" She directed more questions to me.

"If I get into that, we'll be here for the rest of the night," I responded, because I really was not interested in repeating everything, I had just told the guys.

"I got all night," she told me.

"Come on, Sabrina, we don't have time for that," Carl Jr. interjected.

"Why not? I wanna know if she's bringing drama to my household. Now, am I wrong for that?"

I stood up to my feet. "I'm sorry. I swear, bringing drama to this house was the last thing on my mind. I just came here to tell the guys I know where their father was. That's it."

"You could've called them and told them that," she continued.

"I didn't have their number," I said, and started making my way toward the front door. "Are you ready?" I asked Rich.

"Yep, let's go," he said, and then he pointed to his homeboy and told him to open the door.

"Me and you are going to have a heart-to-heart," I heard her warn Carl Jr. while we were walking out of the house.

"Look, I'm not going to be arguing with you tonight. I'm not in the mood."

"I don't wanna argue either. But you're gonna tell me why she was in our house. Remember, you just got out of jail not too long ago." She didn't back down.

I didn't hear Carl Jr.'s rebuttal; Rich had closed the front door behind us. But after we got into the car, I made mention of it. "Is she always like that?" I asked Rich.

"Yeah, she's got a lot of mouth. I couldn't deal with her shit. I would've kicked her ass out of my house a long time ago," Rich commented after he climbed into the passenger-side seat, while his homeboy climbed into the driver's seat. After he put the key into the ignition, he put the gear in Drive and sped off down the one-way street.

"So that's his house?" I asked after him while I looked at my surroundings. It had just hit me that we left using the front door. I looked over my shoulders and through the back window to see if we were being followed.

"It's my dad's house. But he let me and my brother stay there after he started dating and moved into your mom's crib. The house is paid for. All we gotta pay are the taxes, utilities, and the cable bill."

"If your dad left the house to you and Carl Jr., then why aren't you there?"

"Because I hustle and sell drugs. And I can't disrespect my pops by bringing that shit to his crib. He worked hard for that spot, so I'm gonna treat it like he does. You understand?"

"I sure do," I replied, still looking over my shoulders with every left and right turn the big guy made.

"So let me ask you something," Rich said.

"What's up?"

"What were you going to do if me or my brother would not have helped you?"

"That's a good question. But I don't know what I would've done."

"So, is it true that your cousin and Tedo would've struck gold if they would've gotten away free and clear?"

"What do you mean?" I asked him.

"How much would they have made if they got away with all those pills?"

"I don't know. Maybe a couple of hundred grand," I lied. I figured if I told him that the street value of that robbery would've been over a million dollars, he'd probably go into this thing thinking he could get something close to that. I didn't need that headache. I mean, he already told me that if I didn't help him with this robbery, then he wasn't going to help me get my mother back. He was a fucking moron, and I hoped he didn't bite off more than he could chew. Whether he knew it or not, I was going to devise my own plan for my mother after he got me inside. After that, he and his crew would be on their own.

Rich got excited and turned around in the seat and faced me. "You gotta be shittin' me! Two hundred grand? And Tedo and that other nigga fucked that up? Shit! If it was me, I would've come out of that spot with every pill they had, and I wouldn't have left any witnesses. Everybody in that joint would've gotten spread."

"Yeah, right," I mumbled. Listening to this fool hype himself up like he's Scarface was a joke.

"Where did you say that restaurant was?" Rich changed the direction of the conversation.

"It's right around the corner from JANAF," I told him.

"Come on, Mike, let's head down there," Rich instructed his big friend.

"I'm on it, boss," Rich's flunky said.

Mike made his way onto Princess Anne Road and then he took it all the way up to the intersection of Military Highway. After he made a right turn, he drove another two miles and there we parked fifty feet away from the Indian restaurant. "Pull into that parking lot over there," Rich instructed Mike as he pointed to a parking lot in front of the restaurant.

While Mike headed into the parking lot, I looked at the parking lot of the restaurant and noticed that there were only a few cars parked in front of it. It was close to closing time, so I knew that a couple of those cars were patrons.

"Do any of those cars look familiar?" Rich asked me.

"Those cars that are parked in front of the restaurant belong to customers. The family that owns the restaurant park their cars on the side of the building," I told him, and then I turned my focus on every angle around the vicinity. I knew the DEA agents were watching this place, so I had to make sure they weren't tucked somewhere in the background, watching the car I was in.

I think I looked over my shoulders at least twenty times just to make sure. I knew one thing, for sure, if the agents were watching this car too, they were doing a helluva job. I couldn't find their cars nowhere in sight.

"Do they have a lot of traffic going in there?"

"Yeah, every time I went there to eat, they were always packed with customers."

"Do you know how many family members work there?"

"It varies. Sometimes seven. Other times ten."

"Think they sell the pills there too?"

"I don't know."

"What'cha think, Mike? Think they sell their pills wholesale out of there?" Rich asked him.

"I know I would, especially if I had a legit restaurant."

"Yeah, me too. Having that restaurant is a nice cover-up," Rich added.

"I think so too," Mike agreed.

"A'ight, so this is what we're going to do. We're gonna sit out here and wait for those motherfuckers to come out of there so we can see how many of them work the late shift. Then we're gonna follow them to their crib so we can find out where they live. After we accomplish that, we'll put our plan together," he said with finality.

At this point, there was really nothing else to say to Rich. Listening to his plan made me believe that he was more concerned about robbing those guys than trying to rescue our parents. In his conversation, he said absolutely nothing about how he planned to save his father. All Rich saw right now was how he was going to make off with a bunch of money so he could go and fuck it up to buy weed, bottles of champagne, and stripper bitches. That was it. This further gave me the drive to come up with my own plan. My mother was all I had left, and I would do anything to make sure she didn't suffer for my mistakes.

19

MY LIFE FOR YOURS

Rich made Mike and me sit out in the parking lot for over an hour while we waited for those people to come out of the restaurant and get into their cars. Five people, in all, came outside. Rich seemed excited about it. "I thought you said about seven to ten people work there?" Rich asked me.

"They do."

"Well, it looks like five people just came out of there."

"Maybe someone left right before we got here," I tried to rationalize.

"If I'm gonna rob this place, I'm gonna need the right numbers," he said, sounding like he was getting agitated.

"Things change all the time. So, why don't you plan to run into seven guys instead of five. I mean, it's better to plan for more than the other way around?" I responded sarcastically.

"Look, I don't need you telling me how to do my shit! So sit back and only speak when I ask you a question," he shot back.

I could tell that this guy wasn't woman-friendly at all.

He was a fucking bully. And the longer I was around this nigga, I knew things were going to get a little heated. It was time for me to make an exit plan. This Rich guy was worse than I had expected.

"Come on, let's go," Rich instructed Mike.

Mike backed out of the parking spot and followed two cars to Highway 264, which was only one mile away. As soon as they approached the ramp, one car took the ramp, while the other one decided to take the far left to travel north of the ramp. Mike looked at Rich for direction. "Which one do you want me to follow?" he wanted to know.

"Follow the guy who's traveling alone."

"Why not follow the other car? There are four people in there, so you know that they're going home," I wondered aloud.

"Because that car had a woman in it, and no mafia-type family is going to have their women around anything illegal. They need her to cook, clean, and take care of the kids. That guy who's alone is going somewhere he didn't want that woman to see."

"If you say so," I said, and let out a long sigh.

Mike followed the guy who was in the car alone. He managed to tail the guy for three miles down South Military Highway without being detected. While he kept his eye on the guy in the car in front of us, I kept my eyes on everything around me. For all I knew, the agents could be following the guy in front of us too. Or even worse, they could be following us because we're following him. Well, after looking over my shoulders at least two dozen times, it looked as though no one was following us or the guy in front of us either. I felt relieved.

The guy driving ahead of us finally ended up taking us to a house in the Greenbrier, off Volvo Parkway. A lot of doctors, lawyers, and hedge fund executives lived in this waterfront community. The homes in this area ran you from $750,000 to $1,250,000. A golf club and boat lifts were all inclusive.

Rich and I watched the guy drive his vehicle into the garage. A few seconds later, the garage door closed. Mike parked the car at the corner of the guy's block, so his home was in full view. "That's a big-ass house he lives in, huh?" Rich said.

"Damn right. That shit is huge. I know it's gotta be worth one million," Mike commented.

"If he lives in a house like that, they gotta be worth double that," Rich pointed out.

"Think they may have drugs in there?" Mike said aloud, giving me or Rich a chance to answer him.

"They might. You can never tell with people like that. I mean, they ain't street people like us. You know that we'll hide drugs anywhere," Rich spoke up.

"You damn right. It's called survival of the fittest," Mike commented.

"Think we should go and check the layout? Maybe walk around the back of the house. See if there is another way to get in when we start making our plans?" I suggested.

"No. That's too risky. We know where the guy lives, so we'll come back," Rich replied.

"But what if it's too late? What if this is the last night that our family will take their last breath? What if they are trying to get in touch with us now so we can pay their ransom?" I asked, tossing out every scenario.

"Look, homegirl, I know you miss your mama, because I miss my pops, but we can't go into those people's house like we run shit. We gotta come up with a plan. Because when I go in there, I'm coming out with everything I want, because I'm not going back."

"But what about my mother and your father? It seems like all you care about is robbing these people. When you talk about these people, the first thing that comes out of your mouth is that you want to rob them. Saving our parents from them is the furthest thing from your mind." This guy was truly annoying me. And from his facial expression, I was sure he was about to let me have it. So I braced myself and listened to what he had to say.

He turned around in his seat and gritted on me really hard. I wouldn't be surprised if his blood was boiling. "First of all, you don't know me. All you know was that Carl Sr. is my daddy. So, homegirl, when you step to me, come at me with some facts and some respect. Because if you don't, I'll show you a side of me that you'll never want to see again. Got it?"

"Yeah, got it," I replied nonchalantly. Because in reality, I couldn't care less about what he was talking about. Okay, he might be a street thug, and I was sure he had beaten up a lot of people and maybe even shot someone, but I couldn't focus on that right now. My main focus was to get my mother back. But since he made it clear that we were not doing any surveillance work tonight, I could do nothing but roll with it and pray that my mother would be all right until I could rescue her.

"Let's get out of here," Rich instructed.

"I'm on it," Mike said, and sped off.

En route to Rich's trap house, we stopped at the 7-Eleven located at the corner of Military Highway and Indian River Road. After Mike pulled into a parking space, he and Rich went into the store. Mind you, neither one of them asked me if I wanted something while they were in there, so I was really pissed off about that. But nothing prepared me for when I looked around to the left side of the car and noticed a government agent's car parked three cars over from the car I was in. The car was a dark gray Ford sedan with tinted windows. I couldn't see into the car, but I saw a silhouette of a man sitting in the driver's seat of the vehicle. With my heart racing at an uncontrollable speed, I turned my head slowly to the left. Every few seconds, I'd look through the front windshield of the car, hoping that these dudes would hurry up and get in the car so we could leave.

"Please come on," I said, even though I knew they couldn't hear me.

After a few more minutes, Mike came and got into the car first. Rich came and got into the car one minute later, carrying a pack of Oreo cookies, a six-pack of Bud Light, and four lottery tickets.

"I gonna win tonight, nigga!" Rich said cheerfully.

"You say that shit every time you buy tickets," Mike joked.

"Nigga, laugh all you want. When I do win, don't come smiling in my face, talking about 'Man, what's up? You gon' look out for me.' 'Cause I'm gon' tell you to haul ass!" Rich joked back.

While all of this was going on, I noticed the agent looking over at this car. Mike noticed it too when he backed out of his parking space. "See narcos watching us?" he asked Rich.

Rich turned around slowly and got a glimpse of the agent looking at us. Luckily for me, I couldn't be seen in the back seat. So my only hope was that these guys weren't carrying a gun or drugs, because if they were, they'd get arrested and I'd be hauled into the DEA office with a set of shiny handcuffs.

"Can you see how many in the car?" Rich asked both Mike and myself.

"It only looks like one," I said, and as soon as I said it, another agent emerged from the 7-Eleven. I didn't recognize the face. And as bad as I wanted to let out a sigh of relief, I knew I couldn't. I wasn't out of the woods yet.

"See that one coming out of the store?" Rich mentioned.

"Yeah, I see 'em," Mike replied while he backed the car in reverse.

"Have you ever seen him before?"

"Nah, I don't know who he is," Mike told him.

"Think he know us?" Rich sounded worried.

"I don't know, dude. But let's get out of here before they start fucking with us," Mike insisted, and then he continued to make his way out of the 7-Eleven parking lot.

While he drove away with caution, I watched the car with the agents inside while they were in view. The farther Mike drove away from them, the more relieved I became knowing that they weren't following us. Rich seemed more relieved than I was. "Thought I was gonna have to blast those niggas!" Rich announced.

"Me too," Mike agreed.

"Damn right! I won't let them niggas take me down, especially after Hitler just hit me off with that pill package."

"You got that shit on you now?" Mike wanted to know.

"Yeah, where else is it gon' be? The nigga stopped by the spot and gave it to me right before you got there."

"What he want back from that joint he gave you?"

"A grand."

"Damn! That's it?"

"You damn right! That nigga knows what time it is. He knows I be putting in that work. And I ain't never been short when I gave him his dough," Rich bragged.

"Remember he gave you that bad shit two weeks ago. Yo, Rich, you acted like you was about to kill that nigga!" Mike joked.

"Yeah, I almost gave that nigga the business when he did that shit. But when he kept telling me he was sorry that he didn't know and took the price down, I couldn't do nothing but let 'em slide. I did tell 'em not to play with me like that again, because having that bad dope can fuck up your clientele. The worst thing that could happen to you in the hood is to be known for having bad dope. And you know that I ain't trying to have that shit lingering over my head. And that's why he made shit right between us. He knows I'm that nigga!" Rich boasted proudly.

"He didn't want you to pull that strap out either," Mike continued to joke.

"Nah! He sure didn't." Rich chuckled.

I sat in the background and listened to these idiots talk about how much respect they got in the hood and how ruthless they were. And that cats in the streets know they be hustling hard. Those two even talked about how many hos they were fucking. Rich acted like he had the most women chasing him to give him the pussy, and Mike complained about how much his girlfriend was getting on his nerves. The way this borderline fat boy looked, he had no room to talk about how his girlfriend stressed him out. In my opinion, he needed to constantly remind her about how good he had it. Because if I was the only chick left in the world, I still wouldn't fuck him. No way!

Rich was also boasting about how well a chick named Precious sucked his dick. I mean, he was really rooting for this woman, telling Mike that hands down Precious sucked his dick better than any of the chicks he ever had. The downside to her working her magic on him was that she worked all the time. "Man, a couple nights I called her and told her that I wanted to see her. But she told me that she was at work. So I told her to tell her boss that she had a family emergency and that she had to leave, and she told me that the only way she'd do it is if I pay her for the hours she's gonna lose. So I told her ass, hell nah! I don't pay for pussy. Then she said, 'Okay, I gotta get back to work,' and then she hung up."

"She hung up on you?"

"Yeah, that ho hung up on me."

"And what'cha do?"

"I didn't do shit! After she hung up, I called the next bitch!" Rich bragged. "And guess what?"

"What?"

"When I told the ho I wanted to see her, she said a'ight and brought her big-booty ass over to the spot. And I fucked the shit out of her ass too. I took my frustrations of that first chick out on the one that came through and let a nigga like me bust two nuts. I punished her ass!"

Listening to Rich tell his story about how he treated the women he slept with immediately made me think about how Terrell used to treat me. And the more Rich bragged about how disrespectful he was to the women in his life, it brought back bad memories of the horrible things Terrell did to me.

I remembered the first signs that he was cheating on me. He went from laying his cell phone around wherever he felt like it, and would answer all his calls in front of me, to either turning his cell phone off completely or he'd leave it in his car while we were chilling in my apartment. I didn't say anything about it at first. I didn't want to be that jealous girlfriend all guys run from. But then he started being blatant about it, by going outside to talk on his phone and not answering his phone at long hours of the day when I called him. And from there, it got messier. One night he and I had just come from the movies. On our way to my apartment, he decided to stop at the BP to get gas. When he got out of the car to go inside the store to pay for it, he forgot that he had his cell phone on his lap, so it fell down on the floor. I started to tell him that he dropped his cell phone, but then I thought, how would I find out who he's cheating with, if I didn't have the evidence? It was now or never.

As soon as he stepped foot into the store, I snatched his phone from the floor. When I pressed the Home button, the screen lit up and I was freaking devastated to see that this nigga had activated the thumbprint function so I couldn't get into his phone. There was no doubt in my mind that this nigga was cheating on me. I was so upset that I couldn't log in to his phone.

But let me tell you how God works.

While I was sitting there with his phone in my hand, the

damn thing started to ring. My heart did a nosedive into the pit of my stomach when the name Simone was displayed on the screen of his phone. I didn't hesitate to answer the call. Simone and I had a very quick conversation about Terrell, because when he realized that he didn't have his cell phone on him, I saw him race out of the store and start running toward his car. Before he was able to open the car door and snatch his phone from my ear, Simone told me that they had been screwing around with each other for a couple of months. She told me where they met, how often they saw each other, and she even told me that they were talking about getting married. I swear, my whole world was turned upside down when she told me that. I remember Terrell yelling at me, asking me why I answered his phone. And how fucked up I was for doing it. I mean, he really turned that thing around on me like I was the one who had cheated. He was a piece of work.

From there, my insecurity level plummeted and I began to question if I was pretty enough to be with him. At the end of those thoughts, my answer was always no. To prevent myself from wallowing in the unhappy life I had with Terrell, I decided that it was time to take myself from that toxic relationship some months later. What was unfortunate was that when he noticed that I had officially left him, he started stalking and became physically aggressive toward me. I wished that things hadn't gone the way they did, because if he would've just left me alone, he'd be alive today.

20

TRAP HOUSE

Mike finally pulled into the neighborhood where he and Rich sold drugs. "Home, sweet home!" Rich commented after pulling up on the block where his trap house was located. We were on Bland Street in the Norview area of Norfolk. Like on all the blocks in the hood, you had to have a few cats on the corner watching out for the narcos when drugs are being sold that street. They were called the lookouts. When we passed them, I knew the drug spot was only yards away from the corner.

"Time to make the donuts," Rich commented after Mike brought the car to a complete stop. After Rich closed the passenger-side door, Mike got out of the car next and I followed suit. I gave this old-ass brick duplex a look and was instantly grossed out with how it looked. Trash cluttered the small parking area. The smell of urine dominated the amount of trash we had to walk through to get to the front door.

Rich walked ahead of Mike and me, so he entered into the house first. I walked into the house second and Mike followed me. "Make sure you lock that door," Rich told him.

"I'm on it," Mike assured him.

"You can sit right here." Rich pointed toward a love seat that looked really dingy and grimy. I'm talking juice stains, pizza sauce stains, other food stains; you know it, it was there. I started to protest because how filthy the sofa looked, but I knew I wasn't in any position to win this fight. He didn't need me; I needed him. So I zipped my mouth and kept my thoughts to myself. The television had already been turned on, when we walked through the door, so I just sat there and started watching it.

"Want some juice or something?" Rich asked me while he walked toward the kitchen.

"No, I'm good," I told him. But in reality, I was kind of thirsty. I just didn't want anything from his house. It looked like a hoarder was living here. Shit was all over the place.

"You sure? We got Patrón," Mike said as he walked behind Rich.

"Yeah, I'm sure."

"You hungry? 'Cause we can put a frozen pizza in the oven." Mike was pressing the issue.

"Yo, nigga, leave her alone. She'll let us know if she wants something," Rich interjected before I could even open my mouth to answer Mike's question.

"Yeah, a'ight," Mike replied, brushing Rich off by shaking his head.

I watched Rich and Mike both as they were in the kitchen. Rich took a small aluminum foil–wrapped item from his front pants pocket. The package item was about the size of the palm of his hand. After he had it in his hand, he placed it on the table and took a seat down on one of the kitchen chairs. "Mike, hand me that scale from the drawer," Rich instructed Mike.

Mike grabbed a digital scale from the drawer next to the stove and handed it to Rich. After Rich took the scale, he placed it down on the table in front of him. There was a plate, clear sandwich bags, and razor blades already on the table. When Rich dumped out the contents inside the aluminum onto the plate, I instantly recognized it. This negro was selling crack cocaine.

"That shit looks like a missile," Mike commented after he took a seat across from Rich.

"Yeah, I'm only gonna cut up twenty blocks," Rich told Mike as his razor cut the first rock.

Mike chuckled. "That shit looks like ten block."

"I bet'cha I get twenty for it."

"What'cha wanna bet?" Mike challenged Rich.

"Nigga, I'm not betting you for real! Look, if they don't wanna give me twenty, then I'm gonna tell 'em to get out of my damn face and haul ass!"

Mike continued to chuckle. "Man, you're a funny-ass dude!"

We hadn't been in Rich's trap house a good ten minutes before people started knocking on the door. Mike got up from the kitchen chair to answer the front door. "Who is it?" he asked.

"It's Ray-Ray. I gotta sixty sell," I heard the guy say from the other side of the front door.

"A'ight, hold up," Mike said, and then he walked back to the kitchen. The guy Ray-Ray stood at the front door and waited for Mike to come back. The moment Mike approached Rich, he dropped the money down on the table.

"Who that at the door?" Rich asked.

"Ray-Ray. Somebody out there wanna spend that whole sixty dollars."

While Mike was conducting the exchange with Rich, this Ray-Ray character stood at the front door and started eyeing me up and down. I couldn't get a good look at him because it was night out. But I heard him as he began to flirt with me. "How you doing?" he asked.

"I'm fine," I replied nonchalantly.

"Got a man?" he asked me.

"Yes, I do," I lied.

"Well, can we at least be friends?"

Before I got a chance to answer him, Mike interrupted the conversation. "Ray-Ray, cut it out. She doesn't want your crackhead ass."

Ray-Ray chuckled. "Come on, man, why you cock-blocking? I was about to ask her if I could take her out."

Mike handed him the drugs. "Take this shit and get out of here."

"Mike, I thought you were my boy?" Ray-Ray laughed and then he ran off.

After Mike closed the front door, he looked at me and said, "The day in the life of a crackhead."

I didn't respond. I just shook my head with disgust.

Mike headed back into the kitchen. He sat back down at the table and started having small talk with Rich. They talked about how much money Rich was going to make once he sold all the crack cocaine. They also talked about how they could change the way they distributed their drugs too—only allowing one drug runner to come to the house. This way, they could eliminate a lot of foot traffic. Mike agreed.

Once all the dope was cut up and packaged, Mike rolled up a blunt filled with some strong-smelling weed. Immediately after he rolled it up, he lit it, took the first drag from it, and then passed it to Rich. Ten seconds later, Mike released the smoke from his nose. "Now that's some good shit right here," Mike commented.

"Yeah, this shit is a missile," Rich agreed after he blew the smoke from his mouth.

As Rich passed the blunt back to Mike, someone knocked on the front door again. Mike stood up from the kitchen chair and walked back to the front door. "Who is it?" he asked.

"It's Monty and Jason," I heard a guy say.

Mike opened the front door and in came two thug-looking cats. They were both dressed in blue jeans, Michael Jordan sneakers, and hoodies. They spoke to me as they walked by me. I spoke back and turned my attention toward the television.

They didn't notice it, but I started watching them both from the corner of my eye. And when they entered into the kitchen, I was able to get a full view of them. Both were fairly decent-looking guys. They were around the same height, so one didn't stand out more than the other, expect that one wore a Caesar haircut and the other one red-colored dreadlocks. They even possessed that bad-boy exterior. Rich called out the guys' names and they appeared before him in the kitchen. "What's good, Monty?" Rich asked the guy with the Caesar haircut as he shook his hand. The guy with the red dreadlocks walked into the kitchen behind his friend. Rich shook his hand second. "Jason, when you gon' take that bright-ass color out'cha head? You know your ass is hot. Every policeman in Norfolk know who your ass is," Rich joked.

"That's why I wear my hoodie all the time," Jason told him.

"It's too late now," Rich replied.

"Nigga, never mind about my hair, pass me that damn blunt," Jason continued, and reached for the blunt. Rich handed it to him.

Mike, Rich, and Monty made small talk as they watched Jason take a long puff from the blunt. As soon as he took the blunt away from his mouth, he passed it to Monty. And then Monty passed it to Mike. They started a rotation while they joked with one another. They started talking about the drought of cocaine they were experiencing and how it was important not to run out of product. Then the conversation's topic changed, and I was the topic.

"Yo, who that chick in there with?" Jason asked Rich and Mike.

"Ask him," I heard Mike say.

"That's your girl, Rich?" Jason pressed the issue.

"Nah, nigga, she's my meal ticket to some Arab cats with a lot of fucking money," Rich told him after he took another puff from the blunt and passed it on to Mike.

"What'cha gonna do, rob 'em?" Monty asked.

"You damn right! I'm tired of these out-of-town cats coming to my city and taking money out my pockets. It's time that they start paying restitution," Rich expressed.

"Yeah, bro, I'm wit'cha on that," Jason agreed.

"Yeah, me too," Monty agreed.

"Need any help? Because you know me and Monty got yo back," Jason offered.

"Say no more," Rich told him after he blew more marijuana smoke from his mouth.

"So, when you trying to do this?" Monty asked.

"I gotta check out a few things first. I'll know by tomorrow night," I heard Rich say.

"What's her name?" Jason repeated his earlier question.

"Misty," Rich told him.

"She got a man?" Jason wouldn't let up.

"Ask her," Rich insisted.

Seconds later, Jason came walking toward me. "Hi, Misty," he said.

I dreaded looking in his direction, but I did it anyway. "Hello," I replied.

"Hey, wait, did that nigga just say her name was Misty?" Monty interjected. When he did that, I knew he knew something about either the pharmacy robbery gone bad, or he knew what I did to Terrell, which was something I would continue to deny doing.

"Yeah," I heard Rich say.

"Yo, is that the chick that supposed to have killed that nigga Terrell?" Monty wouldn't let up.

"What'cha watching?" he asked as he took a seat on the chair next to me.

There was a commercial running, so I gave him a pass. *"Family Feud,"* I replied quickly, because I wanted to hear what the guys were talking about in the kitchen, especially since they were talking about me.

"Yeah, that's her," Rich confirmed Monty's question.

"Got a man?" Jason asked.

"Yes," I lied. I said it as quietly as I could, so I could hear the dialogue between Rich and the new guy Monty.

"Well, the next time you see him, tell him his services are no longer needed because I'm gonna take you from him?" he commented.

"I know a couple of niggas looking for her," I heard Monty say to them. And instantly I became panicked. All I could think about was how that guy Monty was going to put the word out that he knew where I was and collect on the bounty, once he delivered on the goods, which was me. "That bitch April told the police that that chick in there murdered that nigga, and that April and Tedo cut up his body and then they got rid of it. The same niggas got two chicks in jail that's gonna murk that bitch April. And they said that if Tedo hadn't gotten shot in that shoot-out, he would've gotten dealt with too."

"Did you hear me?" Jason asked me. He knew I wasn't listening to him, but he had no idea why.

"No, I'm sorry. My mind just drifted off for a minute," I told him. But inside my head, I did more than that. The words that had come out of Monty's mouth not only affected me emotionally, but they affected me mentally. It was hard sitting here, trying to answer this guy's questions. Whether he knew it or not, my life was on the line, and for the moment, his friend Monty had my life in his hands.

While Jason continued to badger me about where I lived, if I had kids, and what high school I went to, I continued to eavesdrop on the conversation Rich and Monty had about me. Before their talk ended, Rich began to whisper his plans to Monty. But I still managed to hear him tell Monty, in so many words, that he would agree to hand me over to the guys, but only after he used me for bait to rob those Arab cats and get his father back. I was floored when I heard Rich whisper that shit to him. He acted like I was nothing, a disposable piece of trash. To hear it come out of his mouth really put things into perspective for me. I knew that I was in here alone, and Rich had no intention of helping me to get my mother back, and he was going to throw me away to the pack of wolves, once this whole thing was over.

"What's up my dude? You got homegirl handcuffed in here," Monty said jokingly as he walked into the front room where Jason and I were.

Jason looked up at Monty. "Come on now, Monty, you know how I do," Jason said confidently.

"You better leave her alone. I heard she be murking niggas!" Monty commented.

"I be doing what?" I asked him, giving him a hard stare. As bad as I wanted to let sleeping dogs lie, I knew that he was trying to ruffle my feathers. If I didn't stand my ground, then he was going to tumble all over me.

"We know what you did to that nigga Terrell," he replied as he stood with his back against the wall by the entryway of the kitchen.

At this very moment, I was sitting on the couch, and Jason sat a few inches away, but my attention was directed toward Monty. I wasn't feeling this asshole at all. The fact that he was trying to throw me underneath the bus was an uncomfortable space to be in. I wanted to curse him out and storm out the front door, but then where would I go? I had nobody. The last person that had my back was Mrs. Mabel, but now she was dead. *So, what do I do? Sit here and take these dudes' mess?* "Listen, dude, you don't know shit about me," I told him.

"So you're denying that you murked that nigga Terrell?" He continued to stand there.

"Who wants to know?" I asked him defiantly.

"I wanna know. All these niggas wanna know too." Monty pointed to Rich, Mike, and Jason.

"Wanna know what?" Jason interjected.

"She's the one that murdered that nigga Terrell," Monty told Jason.

Jason looked at me. "Yo, word!" Jason said, as if he needed me to confirm what Monty had just said.

"Look, I haven't done anything. So I wish you would leave me alone," I told him, and then I looked at Rich, who was sitting in the chair by now.

"Come on, Monty. Leave her alone, dude!" Mike stood up and defended me.

It felt good to have someone in this freaking house take up for me. I saw Rich wasn't going to do it, so to hell with him. And whether he knew it or not, I was brewing up a plan for his grimy ass. And what was going to be so satisfying to me was that he wasn't going to see it coming. *Fucking asshole!*

"Nah, fuck that, Mike! That nigga Terrell was good people."

"I didn't know him like that," Mike spoke up.

"It don't matter. I know him. Him and his cousins lived on my block. His cousins helped me when these dudes tried to rob me at this New Year's Eve party last year," Monty explained.

"So, what'cha gon' do? Rat me out to them? Tell them where I am?" I spat out. This guy was starting to rub me the wrong way. I had tried to keep my mouth closed this whole time, but this dude Monty had plucked my last nerve.

"If it was up to me, I'd call 'em now. But Rich told me not to. So you better tell him thank you," Monty continued, gritting his teeth at me. This guy had never seen me before, but he acted like he hated my guts. He was having some serious issues.

"Is this the moment when I tell Rich thanks?" I gritted back at him. I wasn't backing down. I was tired of being Ms. Nice Girl. I figured if I kept my mouth closed, I wouldn't start up any drama. But this guy made that very hard to do. So, where do I go from this point now?

"Nah, bitch, this is the moment when you tell me to take out my dick so you can give me a blow job," Monty snapped. He took a couple of steps toward me too. Jason stood up and told him to chill out.

"Stop, man. Just chill out." Jason tried to reason with him.

"Yeah, dude, leave it alone," Mike agreed.

"Oh, I see what you niggas trying to do. Y'all trying to fuck her, that's why you're being nice to her. Making her feel like you gon' save her," Monty suggested. He was getting more agitated by the second. He even turned around to face Rich while he was still sitting at the kitchen table. "Rich, you hear these niggas taking her side?" Monty said to him.

Rich started chuckling. "Monty, you bugging out, dude. Just chill out, like Jason said. Everything is going to be a'ight," Rich said in hopes of calming Monty down.

Monty hesitated for a moment and then said, "Yeah, a'ight. I'm gonna leave it alone for now." But then he turned around toward me and said, "You're a lucky bitch! But I guarantee that that luck is gonna run out really quick."

"Yeah, whatever!" I told him. Because at this point, I knew he wasn't going to do a thing to me. And as of right now, Rich wasn't going to let anything happen to me because I was his meal ticket. But that's all going down the drain, and I couldn't wait to see Rich's face when it did.

21

I'M A MAD WOMAN

Monty and Jason left about twenty minutes after all that shit hit the fan. I swear, no one has talked to me like that since I was with Terrell. See what happened to him? I tell you what, things would eventually turn around in my favor. Just wait and see.

Rich ended up going outside to sell the drugs he'd just packaged up. Mike stayed in the front room with me and watched television. During a commercial, he sparked up a conversation with me. His icebreaker was asking me if I needed something, since I hadn't said much after Jason and Monty left. "I need to use the bathroom," I told him.

"It's upstairs on the left side," he told me as he pointed toward the staircase.

"Thanks," I replied, and stood up from the couch. I had to walk by Mike to go upstairs, so I stepped by him and headed up the flight of steps. I was up at the top of the staircase within eight seconds. When I entered into the bathroom, I was repulsed when I saw drips of piss on the toilet bowl seat. I wasn't going to sit down on that thing. It was fucking disgusting. So, how was I going to relieve myself? I looked around the bathroom, thinking about how this small-ass box looked worse than a restroom at a gas station. After realizing that the only safe place I could empty out my bladder would be the sink, that's what I did. I figured, why not? The motherfuckers in this house didn't like me anyway, so pissing in their bathroom sink was a great start to plans I had stored away for them.

After I urinated in the bathroom sink, I threw the toilet tissue into the toilet and didn't flush it. I washed my hands, but didn't rinse the sink out, so you could clearly see yellow drops of my pee around the sink bowl. I wanted those bastards to see what I did, even though I planned to deny it. The reward for me was knowing that I had one up on those assholes. Fucking idiots.

I walked back downstairs and sat in the same spot I was before I went upstairs. It seemed like as soon as I sat down and got comfy, fate reared its ugly face. An emergency broadcast from *Ten on Your Side* flashed across the television, with my image: "This just in, authorities are looking for Misty Heiress."

"Oh shit! That's you!" Mike blurted out after seeing my face on the news.

"She is a murder suspect in the killings of Terrell Mason and Mrs. Mabel Davis. She is a Virginia Beach resident and a former employee at Rx-Pharmacy Depot. She is believed to be armed and dangerous. If you've seen this woman or know where she is, please contact your local Virginia Beach Police at once," the newswoman reported.

"I'm not armed and dangerous!" I spat. I was about to spaz out. *Really, I'm armed and dangerous? And I didn't kill Mrs. Mabel. Ahmad and his accomplice killed her.*

"Her last sighting was earlier today when my colleague Christian Lundy witnessed her running away from her apartment. No one has seen her since then, so again, if you have any information on her whereabouts, please contact Virginia Beach Police. Remember, she is armed and dangerous. I'm Belinda Givens, reporting for *Ten on Your Side.*"

"Damn, girl, you're gangsta-ass shit!" Mike sat there in awe.

"I didn't kill that lady. Those Arab guys did it. And I'm not armed and dangerous. I don't have a fucking gun on me. Ugh!" I protested.

"It's bad when the police put your picture up on TV," Mike expressed.

"No shit! I can't believe that they're trying to pin that murder on me. And then to say that I'm armed and dangerous! That's some bullshit right there," I said with frustration.

"You know you can't be out on the streets now. If somebody sees you, they gon' call the police," Mike assured me.

"I think I'll take my chances with the cops than with those guys that know Terrell. Monty made it perfectly clear that those guys want to seek revenge on me," I mentioned.

"Don't worry about Monty right now. Rich told him that he couldn't fuck with you," he replied.

"Don't leave out the part where Rich told him that he couldn't mess with me until *after* he robs those Arab dudes and gets his father back."

"Nah, he didn't say that," Mike said, trying to lie.

"Listen, Mike, I know Rich is your boy and all. And I know you aren't trying to rat him out, but I heard him. I mean, he didn't even add my mother to the equation. So, why shouldn't I be worried about that? Rich don't give a damn about me. His main agenda is to rob those Arab guys, walk away with as much money and drugs as he can, and get his father back before the heist is over," I explained.

"Look, I'm not trying to get into all the politics with you about what Rich said, but I will tell you that Monty isn't the type of dude that would let stuff go. He's a hothead. And he has no conscience. When he say he's going to do something, take his word for it," Mike warned me.

"What kind of guy talks to a woman like that? He acted like I did something to him," I pointed out.

"It doesn't matter with Monty. He's one of those guys that would die for something he believes in. So just watch your back and what you say from now on."

"Yeah, all right," I said, and turned my focus back to the television.

A few seconds later, I looked back at Mike and said, "Please don't tell anyone that I was just on the news."

"Sure, no problem," he said, and then we both turned our focus back on the television.

Seconds turned into minutes, and minutes turned into hours. About three hours into my stay at this nasty-ass house, I found myself becoming drowsy. Before I even realized it, I had fallen asleep. Startled by the front door slamming, I jumped out of my sleep. When I opened my eyes, Monty started walking toward me. "I'm back," he announced, with a bottle of liquor in his right hand.

I looked around the room and noticed that Mike was nowhere in sight. I looked back at Monty and sat straight up in the chair. "Please leave me alone," I begged him, dreading what was about to happen.

Monty stood in front of me and took another swig from the liquor bottle. "You know that you are one lucky-ass bitch!" he commented after he swallowed the alcohol in his mouth.

"Look, I don't wanna start up another argument with you," I told him.

He laughed. "You think I wanna argue with you? I'm standing right here because you owe me."

Puzzled, I said, "Owe you for what?"

"For not telling Terrell's cousins where you at. I saw those niggas about an hour ago and I could've told them where you were hiding, but I didn't. So you owe me. And I'm ready to collect," he continued, and took another swig

from the bottle. After he swallowed the alcohol, he un-
zipped his jeans with his left hand, then pulled out his
dick. "Suck it," he continued, looking down at me like I
was his slave.

"You better get your little-ass dick out of my face," I
said calmly. In my mind, I had decided that if this dumb-
ass motherfucker didn't get his penis out of my face, I was
going to show him where to put it.

"What'cha gon' do if I don't?" Monty tested me while
taking another swig from the bottle.

"I'm telling you right now, you better get that thing out
of my face," I warned him again. I was two seconds from
ripping the head of his penis from the shaft. I pictured
blood gushing out of him like a waterfall while he squirmed
around like a little bitch.

"Why the fuck you taking so long? Lick it," he instructed me, and started gyrating his penis in my face.

Without giving it a second thought, I grabbed his dick
in my hand and tried to rip it from his groin. Monty
screamed like a little bitch and dropped the liquor bottle
on the floor in front of us. Vodka splattered everywhere
after the bottle shattered. Some of it got into my eyes, but
that didn't stop me from unleashing the beast on this disrespectful bastard. "I told you to get this shit out of my
face, but you didn't. Now you wanna scream like a lil
bitch! Man up, you stupid piece of shit!" I mocked him
while I gritted my teeth.

Rich and Mike heard all the commotion in the house
and ran in from outside. Rich came in the front door first
and Mike followed. When I saw them rushing toward us, I
let Monty's dick go and stood up from the couch. I figured
whatever was going to happen next, I was going to be
ready for it. I was tired of these losers treating me like shit.

While Monty rocked back and forth on the floor, with
his hand covering his dick, Rich rushed to him, towering

over Monty, asking what just happened. Mike stood a few feet away from the whole thing and watched as an on-looker.

"That bitch tried to rip my dick off me!" Monty shouted as he continued to rock back and forth. He was holding on to his penis for dear life.

"What the fuck is wrong with you?" Rich yelled at me.

"That nasty motherfucker took his dick out and told me to suck it. And I told him to get out of my face, and he wouldn't listen. So I did what I had to do!" I roared. I was ready to go head-to-head with Rich for even taking this asshole's side. He was the one out of line. *Now I'm the bad one?*

Rich got in my face. "Do you know what that nigga would do to your stupid ass?" He continued to yell and curse.

"What about what I just did to him?" I snapped.

"What, you think this is a joke!" Rich screamed at me.

"Why the fuck are you screaming at me? I was sitting in here, minding my own business, and then he comes in here and demands that I suck his dick! Was that not fucked up?" I continued to scream at him while I stood my ground.

With no warning, Rich lunged at me and smacked me with the back of his hand. The force from the sudden blow knocked me back and I collapsed on the couch. After I landed on my back, I held my face with my hand. "Are you out of your fucking mind?!" I screamed at Rich.

"Shut the fuck up, bitch!" Rich roared while holding his arm up in the air like he was ready to strike me again.

One part of me wanted to stand up and charge him with all the strength and force I had inside of me, but then I thought about how badly things could go if I did. But at the same time, I didn't deserve any of this treatment I was getting. What was I supposed to do? So I sat up on the couch, holding the palm of my hand against my face.

Meanwhile, Monty had gotten a grip on himself and was finally able to deal with the pain I inflicted on him. He climbed onto the couch near me. Immediately after that, he gave me the stare of death. "You feeling better, man?" Rich went to his aid after hitting me in the face.

I sat there and watched both of these assholes as Mike stood away from us, but at the same time, I surveyed what had just happened. I really wanted him to be the adult in the room and tell those two bastards that what they did to me was wrong. But he didn't open his mouth—not one time.

"Yo, I swear, I wanna kill that bitch right now," Monty said through clenched teeth. I could see the veins bulging through the skin near his temple.

"Don't worry about her right now. She'll get dealt with," Rich assured him.

"What the fuck you mean, I'm gonna 'get dealt with'?" I spat out at him, even though I already knew what that comment meant.

"Bitch, just know that you're on borrowed time," Rich replied menacingly.

"Be a man and say what you gotta say!" I yelled at him.

Within a flash, Rich made a dash toward me; Mike must've known what was about to happen because he slid between us before Rich got within a couple of inches of me. "Move, Mike!" Rich roared at him. Mike's back was facing me while he shielded me from Rich.

"Come on, Rich, we got things to do, so let's keep this ship moving." Mike was trying to calm the situation.

"Nah, fuck that! She keeps running her mouth, and I need to make her close it for good." Rich kept ranting while trying to push his way by Mike. Thankfully, Mike wasn't allowing that to happen. Not only was he bigger than all the guys there, but for some reason, he acted like he wanted to protect me. He didn't say it out of his mouth, but his actions showed it.

"Rich, man, come on, dawg. You're better than that," Mike continued, trying to hold Rich back.

"Move out the way, Mike," Rich warned him.

"Nah, fuck that bitch!" I heard Monty say, and then he lunged at me with full force. *Bam! Bam! Bop! Bop! Bam!* Monty's blows hit my face, one after the other. I tried to shield my face with my arms, but it didn't work. "You fucking bitch! I told you I was going to fuck you up!" He continued to hit me with one fist after the other. I tried desperately to cover my face, but it wasn't working out. At one point, I tried to get up from the couch, but I couldn't. Monty was hitting me so fast and so hard. "Bitch! I'm gon' kill your ass today!" He gritted his teeth.

Realizing that I was getting my ass wiped, Mike turned away from Rich. "Come on now, Monty!" Then he bear-hugged Monty and lifted him up in the air. This gave me only half of a second to hop off the couch and make a run for the front door. Unfortunately for me, Rich caught up with me before I could make it to the front door. He grabbed me by my hair and snatched me backward. "Bitch, you ain't going nowhere!" he growled at me.

I lost my balance and collapsed onto the floor. I started kicking Rich and screaming like my mind was going bad. "Get the fuck away from me! Leave me alone!"

"Damn, Rich, man . . . ," I heard Mike say, and then I heard a gunshot. *Pop!*

Next came a loud thud. *Boom!* It seemed like everything from that point went in slow motion. Rich stood up and turned around to face Mike and Monty. I stopped kicking and screaming and looked in the same direction as Rich. I blinked my eyes so I could be clear about what had just happened. Then I looked and saw that Mike had collapsed on the floor, while Monty was standing over him with a revolver in his hand. My heart rate went from twenty miles per hour to 150; fear had engulfed my entire body. All I could do was sit there on the floor. My body felt paralyzed, while Rich rushed over to Mike's side. "Yo, Monty, look what the fuck you just did!" Rich snapped.

Monty continued to stand there with the gun in his hand. "I told him to get off me," Monty said, trying to justify his actions.

"Man, give me that fucking gun!" Rich said, and took Monty's pistol from his hand.

I watched Mike in disbelief as he covered his stomach, where Monty had shot him. "He's gonna die if y'all don't take him to the hospital," I pleaded to them as Mike tried to speak. No one could understand him.

"Shut the fuck up, bitch! This was all your fault!" Monty roared.

"That shit wasn't my fault!" I roared back at him.

"Look, both of y'all shut the fuck up! We gotta get him to the emergency room before he dies! Help me get him off the floor," Rich said.

"Who's taking him to the hospital?" Monty wanted to know.

"Nigga, you're taking him. You the one shot him," Rich replied pointedly.

"But I'm driving my girl's car and she's gonna know something happened if he leaves a lot of blood in her car," Monty expressed.

"Man, I ain't trying to hear that shit! You're taking him to the hospital. Let's hurry up and get him out of the house and put him into the car," Rich told Monty.

Monty let out a long sigh; then he helped Rich pick Mike up from the floor. Mike whimpered like he was in a lot of pain. I felt so sorry for him. To see him in this situation made me feel so bad for him, especially since he was taking up for me. He tried to do everything in his power to prevent Monty and Rich from attacking me. And even though he couldn't hold them back like he intended, I still appreciated his gesture, because he didn't have to do it.

I watched Monty and Rich as they carried Mike out of the house. As they struggled with his body, I noticed Mike's cell phone had fallen out—I assumed from the back pocket of his pants. Getting my hands on that phone would give me an edge on them.

22

DANGER IS NEAR

As soon as they walked outside, I scrambled over to where Mike's cell phone was and snatched it up from the floor. I shoved it down into my pants pocket. It only took Rich and Monty a few minutes to put Mike into Monty's girlfriend's car, because Rich was back in the house with me less than a minute later.

"Get yo ass up and clean that blood off the floor!" Rich demanded.

"Why I gotta get it up?" I protested.

"Because you started this shit!" Rich argued.

On any other occasion, I would've cursed Rich out and told him to kiss my ass. But I couldn't do it now. I mean, he and Monty just beat my ass for running my mouth a few minutes ago, while Mike tried to defend me. So, do you think that I am going to run my mouth while I am alone in this fucking house? Hell no!

"What the fuck are you waiting for? Get up and wipe that blood up from the floor before I jump on your ass this time. Unlike Monty, I'll make you suck my dick, with the barrel of my gun to your fucking head. I dare you to do anything other than put it in your mouth, because if you don't, I'll splatter your brains all over this motherfucker!" he roared while giving me the look of death. It was an expression of evilness and I wanted no part of it. Hearing this guy say out loud that he'd shoot me in my head sent a lightning bolt of horror through me. I was in a complete state of fear. The amount of torment I would endure could be unimaginable. What should I do?

I stood up slowly while Rich changed out of his jacket and shirt. He grabbed a white T-shirt from a package of T-shirts he had in the closet by the front door and changed into it. After he pulled it down on himself, he looked at me and said, "Why the fuck you just standing there?"

"I need some cleaning stuff and a rag or something," I told him.

"Go in the kitchen. There's some dishwashing liquid in there. Use the dishrag hanging from the faucet," he instructed.

Taking Rich's instructions, I headed into the kitchen and grabbed the dishwashing liquid from the counter and the cloth rag tied around the faucet nozzle. I also grabbed a gallon-sized pot from the stove and filled it halfway up with water. Thankfully, Mike bled out on the ceramic floor. If it had been a rug or carpet, then there's no way I would've been able to clean it up.

"You know, I thought you were a nice guy," I said to Rich after I got down on my knees to clean up Mike's blood.

By this time, Rich had taken a seat on the couch across from me and had started counting money he had taken out of his pocket. "What makes you think I'm not one?" he replied without taking his eyes off his money.

"You and Monty beat me up like I was wrong for what I did," I began to explain. "Do you know how much my face hurts right now? And as bad as I want to look in a mirror, I know I'm going to cry, once I see all the bruises," I continued talking while dampening the floor with the water from the pot.

"You should've kept your mouth closed when I told you to."

"Rich, he pulled his dick out in my face and told me to suck it. And I was supposed to sit back and not say anything? Was I supposed to let him disrespect me like that?" I pressed the issue.

"I'm gonna need you to shut up."

"Why won't you just answer my question? I mean, don't you think I deserve an answer? Do it for your dad and my mom, because we're technically brother and sister," I reminded him, hoping he would catch the bait.

"You mentioning my father isn't going to work with me. I'm gonna let you in on a secret," he started off, looking straight at me. "I don't like my father. He was a piece of shit when he was married to my mother. He cheated on her. When he was an alcoholic, he beat on her. He even beat up my brother. My brother forgave him, but I didn't. So to hear you say do it for my father makes me wanna jump on you right now and beat the daylights out of you. So you'll know how my dad used to do me when I was a kid. That motherfucker was a mean-ass dude. I remember when I was a child, I used to hope that he would get in a car accident and die so he wouldn't come home and put his hands on me and my mama. He was a fucked-up nigga. So I hope that those Arab dudes kill him slow when they start chipping away at his life. See, I can't say too much about your mama because I really don't know her. But if she's anything like my dad, I wish death on her ass too."

"So you don't care if they kill my mother?" I questioned him.

"Why should I? She ain't my mama! My mama is dead! So stop with the questions before I spaz out on your ass again," Rich said with finality. And to oblige his wishes, I closed my mouth and continued to clean up Mike's blood.

Who would've known that Rich felt this way about his father? I swear, I wished that I had known this before his brother introduced me. I wouldn't have left the house with Rich, much less gotten into the car with him and Mike and come to this freaking trap house. I sure fucked up this time.

Thankfully, it only took me a few minutes to clean up Mike's blood; the sight of it gave me a queasy feeling in my stomach. Not to mention, there was a lot of it. I only hoped that Monty's dumb ass got Mike to the hospital in time so an emergency physician could operate on Mike. Mike was a good guy and didn't deserve getting shot. As much as Rich wanted to blame this whole incident on me, it wasn't my fault that Monty shot Mike. Mike made the judgment call to come to my rescue because he saw how these barbaric-ass niggas tried to hurt me. My only hope for him was that he came out of this all right. It would break my heart if he died.

After I cleaned up the rest of the blood, I took the pot and the rag back into the kitchen. I emptied the bloody water into the sink and then I set the pot on the stove with the nasty dishrag inside of it. I dreaded going back into the front room where Rich was, but I had no other choice, so I headed back in there and took a seat on the sofa.

While I sat there and watched the television, another breaking-news segment popped on TV. There was no doubt in my mind that it would be about me. It was all bad timing. If they were going to broadcast my face up there again, then Rich would see it, and I didn't want that to happen.

"This just in, authorities were called to the Ghent area of Norfolk by a resident walking their dog. It has been told by homicide detectives that a man's body was dumped alongside the curb on Twenty-first Street. It appears that he was shot in the head twice, execution style. No word if this was a mob hit. The identity of this victim will remain anonymous until the family has been notified. There has been speculation that this murder could be linked to the other murders we've been reporting on these last couple of days. Police said that if anyone knows what happened to this man or who murdered him, please contact your local Virginia Beach Police at once. My name is Tonya Spaulden, reporting for *Ten on Your Side*."

Before the camera was taken off the news reporter, Rich's cell phone started ringing. I watched Rich as he answered the call. "Yo, what's up?" he said to the caller. I couldn't hear what the caller was saying, so I waited for Rich to speak again, giving me some indication as to who was talking to him.

"I just saw it on TV," he spoke again, and then fell silent. "Nah, I ain't going. You go," he continued. And when he uttered the words "I ain't going. You go," I knew he was talking to his brother. Surprisingly, he didn't say anything else. He disconnected the call and then placed his cell phone alongside him, so he could continue to count his money.

"Was that your brother?" I asked him.

"Yeah," he replied.

"So that was your father that they found?"

"Yep."

"Did he say anything about my mother?"

"Nope."

"So, how do you feel?"

"What's with the fucking questions? You're my therapist now?" he snapped, giving me the evil eye.

"No, I'm not."

"Well, so you know, since my dad is dead, I'm no longer doing a rescue mission. I'm just running up in the spot and robbing those cats."

Rich telling me that he was no longer doing a rescue mission was old news. I heard him mention it to Mike. So, why try to break the news to me now? Fucking loser!

"So my mother is shit out of luck, huh?" I boldly asked.

"Unless you go in there and rescue her yourself."

"You know what? That's some bullshit! How am I gonna walk in the Arab's spot and take my mama without a gun? Do you know what they'll do to me and my mother?"

"That's not my concern."

"You're a grimy-ass nigga! I don't know why I let you and your brother talk me into coming here with you. Not only have I gotten my ass wiped by two niggas, now I gotta deal with the fact that you aren't going to help me get my mama back."

"Call me *grimy* again and see what happens!" he dared me.

"Yeah, whatever," I said. I could tell that he was getting agitated really quickly, so I left him alone and turned my attention back toward the television.

For the next hour or so, Rich and I didn't say a word to each other. When the crackheads knocked on the front door to buy drugs from him, he served them, they gave him the money, and then the deal was done. He did this for the next ten times without incident. One of the crackheads gave him a hard time about the size of the drugs, so he cursed them out and told them to leave before he whipped their asses. Instead of leaving, they took the micro-sized drug, paid him the money, and then left. Rich couldn't care less if they bought the drug or not. He knew he would sell it because the product was good. And that's all he kept telling them.

While he took care of his business, I told him I had to use the bathroom. When he gave me the green light to go, I went upstairs. When I got into the bathroom, I closed the door and locked it. Rich didn't know that I had Mike's cell phone. And I wasn't going to tell him either. This cell phone was going to be my ticket out of here if I came up with a strategic plan to get out of here and rescue my mother in the process.

Immediately after I entered the bathroom, I turned the bathroom sink water on so Rich wouldn't hear me when I started talking on the phone. Before I got on the phone, I looked at my face in the mirror. When I saw the bruises on my face, I got filled up with tears. The purple and blue bruises around my eyes and around my mouth made me very sad. I didn't deserve this beating. I didn't do anything to warrant this treatment. So, why did they do this to me? To scare me into a submissive state of mind? If that's what their intentions were, then they were sadly mistaken, because it would *not* happen. Whether they knew it or not, I was a very strong woman and I would show them just that when all of this shit was over.

Standing there with the phone in my hand, I knew I had to call people that would help me execute my plan to help me get my mother. And I knew that I would only have one opportunity to do it. There can't be any fuckups, because people's lives were hanging in the balance. The most important life would be my mother's, so timing was key and I planned on using it wisely.

The first person I knew I had to call was Agent Sims. I knew his cell phone number by heart, so I knew I wanted to call him first. Whatever I needed to tell him could only be in a one-minute phone call. I figured calling him and telling him that I had nothing to do with Ms. Mabel's death would be a good place to start. I could also tell him that I was with Rich, who was Carl Sr.'s son, and that he planned to rob and kill the Arabs to avenge his father's murder. Most important, tell him that I'd call him back when I had more information.

After taking a deep breath and then exhaling, I dialed Agent Sims's number and pressed the Send button. "Agent Sims," he said.

"This is Misty and I only have thirty seconds to talk, so be quiet and listen to what I gotta say."

"Where are you? We thought that you were dead," he said.

"Well, I'm not, and just so you know, I'm calling from a burner phone, so you won't be able to track it."

"Can you tell me where you are so I can come and get you?"

"Shut up before I hang up the phone," I threatened him.

"Okay, I'm listening."

"Look, I had nothing to do with Mrs. Mabel's death. Ahmad and another guy did it. I saw them when they shot her."

"We know that, and that's why we want to bring you in."

"I am not gonna tell you where I am, so please shut the fuck up," I hissed, letting him know that I meant business. "Now, I know that you guys found Carl's body, and one of his sons wants to seek revenge. He's preparing to go after them by robbing them and avenging his father's death. So stay on guard and I will call you back with more information when I get it." I then hurried and disconnected the call. My heart rate raced at an uncontrollable speed. I tried to calm my nerves, but my heart wouldn't let me. So I just went with the flow and kept the train moving.

My next call was to Ahmad. I just hoped that he hadn't changed his cell phone number, because if he had, then I was fucked. And my plan would only be a half-sided one, meaning I got Agent Sims on board, but Ahmad wouldn't be. I crossed my fingers after I dialed the number and pressed the Send button.

"Hello," I heard Ahmad say. But I was too afraid to respond. Hearing his voice struck me like lightning. I could open my mouth, but no words would come out. "Hello," he said again. I knew he was wondering who was calling him, and I wanted him to know that it was me, but I could not speak. What was wrong with me? I had it all planned in my head, what I was going to say to him, but nothing happened. "Who's there?" he asked.

"I saw what you did," I finally said. But I kept my volume at a whisper.

"Who is this?" he wondered aloud.

"I saw you when you killed that lady, you fucking jerkoff! You're a fucking coward," I ranted, but I kept it in a whisper.

"Where did you go?" he asked me. His voice sounded menacing. I could tell that if I had been in front of him, he'd probably break my neck with his bare hands.

"Don't worry about where I went. Just know that the man you killed, and left his body on the side of the road, his sons want to kill you. They want to make you pay for what you did to their father. And they say they're going to rob you of every dime you have. And if you have drugs, they are going to take that too."

"Send them over."

"Oh, don't worry, they're coming for you. They will find you too," I warned him.

"You do know I still have your mother?" he told me.

"Yes, I do."

"You do want to see her again, right?"

"Of course, I do. What kind of question is that?"

"Well, you're gonna have to make a trade."

"What kind of trade?"

"Your life for hers."

"Let's do it," I said without hesitation.

"You do know I'm gonna kill you slow, right?"

"Okay what you do to me, to let my mother go, so we can even the score."

"When?"

"I'll call you back with that information. But before I call you back, I need proof of life. Where is she? I need to hear her voice," I told him.

"Hold on a minute," he said, and then I heard complete silence. No movement. No talking. Nothing. But then a couple of seconds later, I heard someone fidgeting with the phone. "Hello," I heard a tiny voice say.

Just like that, it felt like fireworks exploded inside of me. For the moment, I began to feel excited, because I knew my mother was on the other end of the line. "Mom, is that you?" I said anxiously.

"Yes, baby, it's me. Where are you?" she wanted to know. But before I could answer that question, Ahmad took the phone away from her. "That's enough. You know she's alive. Let's make the trade now," he said with finality.

"I will call you back with that information."

"Don't take too long, because as you know, the DEA is closely watching my family. And if they decide to intervene in this thing between you and me, then I'm going to kill her, and no one will ever find me. Understood?"

"Yeah, I understand. But you better keep your word, or I'm gonna have my mother's boyfriend's son and his friends kill some of the innocent people in your family. Now, do you understand where I am coming from?"

"I don't like threats, Ms. Misty."

"I don't like them either. So stay by the phone and I'll call you back by noon tomorrow."

"I'll be waiting," he assured me.

Knock! Knock! Knock! Startled, I fumbled with the cell phone in my hand and almost dropped it. "Yo, what'cha doing in there?" I heard Rich ask from the other side of the bathroom door.

"I'm using the bathroom," I replied as I powered the phone off and shoved it down into the back pocket of my pants.

"Hurry up. I gotta pee," he told me.

"Okay, I'm coming," I told him, and then I flushed the toilet like I had just used it. I turned on the faucet water too, to pretend like I was washing my hands. I turned the faucet off and then I opened the door. Rich was front and center when I laid eyes on him.

"Can you get the fuck out of my way?" he said impatiently.

"Sure. No problem," I replied, and moved out of his way.

While he handled his business in the bathroom, I headed back downstairs. When I stepped foot back in the front room, I looked at the front door. Something inside of me wanted to leave this place and not look back. But then I figured that if I left, I wouldn't have the backup I needed to help me get my mother back. Ahmad would kill both my mother and myself if I came for her alone, and I couldn't have that. Not now. Not ever.

23

WALKING TWO STEPS AHEAD

Iwas shocked when Monty brought his dumb ass back to the house. Rich was standing at the front door serving one of his crackhead customers when Monty pulled up in his girlfriend's car. "What's going on with Mike? Is he going to be all right?" Rich didn't hesitate to ask Monty after he stepped foot in the house.

"I don't know. When I got to the emergency room, I helped him out of the car and walked him inside. When the nurse saw him bleeding, she got him a wheelchair and wheeled him back behind the double doors," Monty explained.

"Was he still breathing?"

"Yeah, he was breathing. He was talking too. So I told him to hold on and that he was going to be all right," Monty continued.

"As soon as the cops find out he's been shot, you know they will show up and start asking him a whole bunch of questions."

"You think he's gonna snitch on me?" Monty sounded worried.

"Hell nah! What kind of nigga you think Mike is? That

nigga is legit! I trust him with my life. Because he's that type of dude!" Rich told Monty.

"Well, he sure didn't act that way when he was takin' up for that bitch right there." Monty pointed at me.

"There you go with that bullshit again," I commented. This guy had only been in the house for two minutes and he was talking about me already.

"Shut the fuck up! Ain't nobody talking to you." He gritted his teeth at me. His horns were flaring up again. Now, how would I handle this nigga if he decided he wanted to fight on me again? I couldn't take too many beatings.

"Calm down, Monty. Let it go, man. We got other shit to do," Rich spoke up. "You know they found my pops." He changed the subject.

"Who found him?" Monty changed his tone.

"The police. The cats that got her mom killed my pops and dumped his body on the side of the road on Twenty-first Street."

"You talked to the police?"

"Nah! But it was on the news. My brother called me and told me that the cops stopped by his place and told him."

"Yo, dawg, that's messed up. That shit makes me so mad that I want to go out there and kill those motherfuckers on sight," Monty expressed.

"Me too. But we'll get them, so don't even worry."

"Have you thought about when you're trying to go to their spot?"

"I want to do it tomorrow night."

"Since we ain't got Mike, want me to bring in two more dudes? I could get Jason and my homeboy Paul to come with us."

"I only need you and one more person, but hit 'em both up. Let 'em know what we're trying to do and tell 'em we gonna do it tomorrow night."

"A'ight. I'ma call 'em now," Monty said, and then he

pulled out his cell phone. He took a walk outside of the house and returned less than one minute later. Immediately after he closed the front door, he looked at Rich and said, "They're in."

"Good," Rich said as he walked back into the kitchen. I watched him open the refrigerator and pull out a bottle of beer. "Want one?" he asked Monty.

"Nah, I'm good. I wanna talk about this job we getting ready to do," Monty said as he walked into the kitchen behind Rich. He stood at the entryway of the kitchen and gave Rich his undivided attention.

"I want to rob the restaurant first. And before we leave, I wanna kill everybody in there except for one person, because that person will take us to their big house not too far from the restaurant."

"Which house was that?"

"It's a big-ass house down on Military Highway. That shit is big as hell. I know that gotta have a ton of money and drugs in that spot."

"Well, you know I'm down. But what'cha gon' do with her?" Monty asked Rich after he looked back at me.

"She's going too."

"What, we gon' leave her in the car? 'Cause she might be a distraction when we go up in the restaurant," Monty pointed out.

"Nah, she ain't gonna be a distraction. She wanna get her mama out of there, so I'ma let her do it."

"So you mean to tell me that you're gonna help that bitch get her mama back?" Monty questioned Rich, sounding and looking like he had a bad taste in his mouth.

"I'm not helping her do shit. When she goes inside their spot, she's on her own, 'cause I'm not giving her a burner and I'm not gonna watch her back. Like I said, when she goes in there, she's on her own."

"Sounds good to me," Monty said, and then he started

rubbing his hands together like he was about to eat a delicious piece of cake.

I swear, it took everything within me not to curse both of these niggas out. These two dudes were the most grimy and selfish niggas I knew. All they cared about was themselves.

I don't know how I made it through the night. When I woke up the next morning, I noticed that I had fallen asleep on the couch and that I was all alone. That was until I heard the toilet flush inside the bathroom upstairs. Not too long after, I got up and headed upstairs so I could use the bathroom myself. It only took me a matter of minutes to unload all the pee I had inside my bladder. As I exited the bathroom, it shocked me to run into a female companion of Rich's. Surprisingly, she was a very pretty girl. She was about my height, but a tad bit smaller in weight. She kind of resembled the singer Keri Hilson. She smiled and said good morning; I said good morning too. And before we could exchange any more dialogue, Rich walked into the hallway, where we were standing. "She seems nice," Kim said.

"Don't let her fool you. She's a real bitch when she wants to be," Rich replied.

"I'm sure everybody can be that way," I responded defiantly, and then I headed back downstairs.

He chuckled. "I told you," he told her, and then I heard him walking down the staircase behind me.

I immediately started saying a quiet prayer, hoping he wasn't following me to start up drama. All I needed was to stick around just a little bit longer so that I could get the details of Rich's plans to rob Ahmad and the rest of his family. With his plans, I could come up with my own so I could rescue my mother in the process. That was it.

As soon as I made my way back downstairs, I sat on the

couch, where I had slept just a few minutes ago. Rich, on the other hand, went into the kitchen, grabbed a container of orange juice, and started drinking out of it. When he was done, he put the container back into the refrigerator and headed back upstairs.

A few minutes later, I heard him and the girl arguing from one of the bedrooms. "I'm not leaving here until you give me my money!" I heard her shout.

"I told you, I'm not giving you no more money."

"Yes, the fuck you are. You promised me," she added.

"Well, I lied," I heard him say.

"You know what, you ain't shit! You just like all the rest of them niggas!" she spat out at him.

"Yeah, I heard that before."

"Oh, so you think this shit is funny? I'ma call my cousin Reggie and he gon' fuck you up," she threatened him.

"Look, I ain't trying to hear all that bullshit! Get your shoes and your bag and get the hell out," I heard Rich snap. Seconds later, I heard a tad bit of scuffling.

"Get off of me."

"I'ma get off of you when you get out of my house."

"You think this is a house? This is a dump. A fucking trap house!" she shouted. I could tell that she was very angry with the way Rich was treating her. But how did she think he was going to treat her? He didn't hide the fact that he was a disrespectful-ass loser. The whole world knew this. So why was she getting upset? He played her. Now she needed to get over it and keep it moving.

Rich and the girl argued for the next three minutes, if not more, and when he got tired of going back and forth with her, he ended up escorting her downstairs. When they entered into the front room, she looked at me and said, "Oh, I get it now. You're trying to get rid of me so you can fuck her."

"Oh no, ma'am. Trust me, it's not that type of party," I told her.

But she didn't believe me. She continued to rant about how she knew that I was going to suck his dick, and how she knew that I was going to let him fuck me in my ass. But the kicker was when she said that while I was sucking his dick, he would be tasting my pussy. All I could do was shake my head. She was one delusional chick. Whether she knew it or not, I wouldn't fuck or suck Rich's dick for all the money in the world. Too bad, she wouldn't believe it.

"She seemed really nice," I said sarcastically after he closed the front door and locked it.

"Yep, just the marrying type," he shot back, giving me just a tad more sarcasm as he walked right by me.

"Don't forget to send me the invite," I managed to say while he headed back upstairs. I thought he would have a rebuttal, but he didn't.

While he was upstairs, doing God knows what, my stomach started growling like there was no tomorrow. I had a few dollars in my pocket, but going to the store wasn't an option. I either would need Rich to make a trip for me, or he needed to get someone to bring food to me. Or if he had something in the refrigerator for me to eat, that would be better. And the only way I would know that would be to ask Rich. "Rich, do you have anything in here that I could eat?" I yelled from the front room.

"There's some Frosted Flakes and milk in the refrigerator," he yelled back.

"Can I get some?"

"I don't give a fuck!" he shouted.

Instead of continuing the dialogue with this guy, I stood up from the couch and went into the kitchen. As I entered, I got an eyeful of dirty dishes in the sink, with mildew and old food stuck to the dishes. I saw a couple of roaches skittering around on the countertop, and when I opened the refrigerator and saw old and expired food inside of it, I immediately lost my appetite. There was no way in the world I was going to eat anything coming out of this kitchen. This place was a hazard to eat from, so I backed myself out of the kitchen and headed back into the front room. I figured I had been hungry for a few hours, so waiting another couple of hours wouldn't hurt me.

After I sat down on the couch, I powered the TV back on. I sifted through the channels to see if I could find something good to watch, but it seemed like every program I ran across, I had already seen it. So I settled for *48 Hours* on the ID channel. The show was about a missing twelve-year-old girl that went to school one morning and never came home. As the show was coming to an end, the investigators found out that the little girl's uncle on her mother's side had something to do with her disappearance. In fact, he had picked her up from school, took her out for ice cream, and then raped her in a hotel room. And to prevent her from telling what he had done, he strangled her until the last breath in her body. What a sick individual, that man was. She was such a beautiful and innocent little girl. And while I sat there, I wondered why people could kill other people so easily? Especially little innocent children that only wanted to do little kid things. If that guy had left her alone, she wouldn't be dead. The same thing goes for my grandmother, my cousin, Mrs. Mabel, and Carl Sr. We live in a cruel world, and there was nothing we can do about it.

Five minutes into another TV show on the ID Channel, someone knocked on the front door. Rich rushed down the staircase and answered the door. When he realized that Monty was on the other side of the door, he opened it and let him in. "What's good, dawg?" Monty said as they both did the handshake to the body dap.

"Trying to figure out how we gon' do that job tonight," Rich replied after he closed the front door shut.

"Trust me, it can't be that hard. Remember, we've done a whole lot of robberies, so it can't be any different from all the other ones."

"Yeah, you're right," Rich agreed.

Monty sat down on the sofa across from me, while Rich stood up and leaned against the wall next to the entryway of the kitchen. "Have you figured out what time we going?" Monty wanted to know.

"Yeah. We gonna go to the restaurant they own first. They close at ten o'clock tonight. So I want to run in there, right before they close. This way, we can wait until all the customers leave and then we got 'em."

"Think they gonna have a lot of money in that joint?" Monty wanted clarity.

"They got to. It's the weekend."

"What if they don't?"

"Don't worry, they will. After we hit their restaurant, we gon' kidnap one of the family members and make them take us to their house. They're bound to have a lot of money there. Cats from outta the country don't put all their money in the bank. They stash that shit in their houses. But what's even better about the situation is that these motherfuckers sell drugs. So they gotta have a lot of dough stashed away in their crib. What drug dealers you know put that money in the bank?" Rich asked.

"Nobody I know."

"My answer exactly."

"Sounds like we gon' be rolling in some serious cash later on tonight."

"You damn right!" Rich commented while he rubbed his hands together.

I tried to pretend that I wasn't listening to their conversation by not taking my eyes away from the television. Monty brought my name up in their discussion. "Misty, your face looks like shit!" he said like he was mocking me.

"If women-beating niggas like you would keep their hands to themselves, we wouldn't be having this conversation."

"Oh, so now I'm a woman beater?"

"I'm a woman, and you're a beater, and when you put those two things together, you come up with a woman beater," I stated, and then I turned my focus back toward the TV.

"See, this is why I need to get her in a room by myself. I would straighten her ass out. She'd be a model citizen, when I got through with her."

"Come on, Monty, let's chill out. We got bigger shit going on. So let's stay focused," Rich instructed. And thank God Monty listened, because I wouldn't be able to handle another attack, especially the way they beat me the other night. All I could do right now was pray that God would be with me as I went through this journey tonight and then have my mother back in a safe place. That was all I cared about at this point. Nothing else.

24

STRAIGHT BULLSHIT

I don't know where the time went. It went from sunlight to sundown in a matter of minutes, it seemed like. I was both nervous and anxious at the same time. While Rich and Monty relished the idea of robbing the Arabs for their drugs and money from their stash, I was thinking about how I was going to get my mother back and into a safe place. She was my main priority while I still had breath in my body.

An hour before we left the house, Rich and Monty and the two guys that Monty had recruited were all sitting at the kitchen table. They were suiting up and filling up the clips for their handguns for tonight's robbery. I also listened to Rich give them last-minute instructions and plan B directions, just in case things went south. The two guys Monty brought into the fold were Jason and Paul. I knew Jason from the first night at the trap house, but this Paul fellow, he seemed like a hothead with no limits as to how far he would go. His entire conversation consisted of him bragging about how he was going to kill everyone in sight. And that included kids. He even boasted about how many bodies he laid to rest in the past two years. He talked so much that it was becoming unbearable to listen to him. Rich interrupted him, thank God, by announcing what the overall goal was. And how much time they had to do it. His plan seemed solid. But with any heist, something always seemed to go wrong. I just hoped they were ready for it, because it would happen.

When it was time to leave, everybody, including myself, grabbed our things and headed out the front door. I climbed in the back seat with Paul and Jason while Monty and Rich climbed into the front seat. Monty was the driver and Rich rode shotgun. "Y'all niggas ready to get this money?" Rich said with excitement.

"You damn right!" Monty said.

"Sure 'nuff," I heard Jason say.

"Been ready," Paul said.

Pretty much everybody in the car was ready to rob Ahmad and his family for every dime they could find. I could hear the greed in their voices. These guys meant business. And there were no ifs, ands, or buts about it.

"Think we might run into some pretty women while we're there?" Monty asked Rich.

"What'cha trying to get married?" Rich joked.

"Nah, dawg, I just wanna fuck one of them chicks while their husband watches," Monty replied.

"Damn, nigga, that's some cold shit right there," Jason commented.

"Call it what you want. I just wanna show 'em how Americans fuck their bitches," Monty explained.

Everybody in the car laughed, like Monty had told the funniest joke in the world. Jason and Paul thought it was really funny. "Yo, dude, you say some crazy shit out of your mouth," Jason told him.

"Yeah, man, you's a funny nigga!" Paul commented.

"It ain't like I try to be funny. I just be saying some real shit," Monty explained to them.

"Look, ain't nobody fucking nobody's wife. We're going in there for two reasons. One is to rob them of all their drugs and their money. And two, to leave no witnesses. Understood?" Rich said.

"Yeah," Paul said.

"You got it, boss," Jason said.

"You always gotta take the fun out of stuff," Monty replied jokingly.

"Look, Monty, I ain't got time for all that crazy shit. I just want to go in there, do what we got to do, and get out."

"A'ight, say no more," Monty said, and then he changed the subject. "I wonder how Mike is doing."

"I talked to his girl last night."

"What she say?"

"She said he was doing good. So I asked her if the police had been by there to talk to him yet and she told me no. So I told her, when they do come, to get Mike to tell them that some dude in a black hoodie tried to rob him and shot him," Rich explained.

"What did she say?"

"She said okay."

"Did she say when he was getting out?" Monty asked.

"She said she doesn't know yet."

Monty paused for a moment and then he said, "I feel so bad I shot that nigga."

"You should," Rich said candidly.

"I'ma look out for him after we do this job," Monty suggested.

"I think it would only be right," Rich agreed.

"Say no more," Monty concluded, giving Rich the sign that he was going to look out for Mike when he was paid for his part in the upcoming robbery.

For the rest of the ride, the guys talked about what chicks they fucked, what local dudes were snitching, and how much time the cats they knew were doing in prison. Their conversation topics were dumb and meaningless.

The fact that they seemed entertained by it was completely absurd. I swear, if we didn't hurry up and get to this restaurant, I was going to go fucking crazy in this car.

"Why are you always quiet?" Jason sparked up a conversation with me.

"Because there's really nothing to talk about," I answered.

"There's a lot of stuff we could talk about," he insisted.

"Well, I guess it may be that way for you, but for me, I can only ask to trade for one thing."

"She's blowing you off, dude," Monty interjected.

"Nigga, mind your business," Jason replied.

"I think you better listen to Monty," Paul spoke up.

"Nigga, you need to mind your business too," Jason told Paul.

Paul and Monty both started chuckling. "Remember, chicks that help you rob the next man ain't to be trusted," Monty announced to everyone in the car.

"Yeah, and remember that these are the same people that kidnapped my mama and Rich's daddy too. They don't mean shit to me."

"She got a point there," Jason commented.

"Nigga, you just agreeing with her because you want to fuck her," Monty pointed out.

"Why can't he be agreeing with me because I'm telling the truth and I'm stating facts?"

"Bitch, don't talk to me. I don't fuck wit you like that," Monty hissed at me.

"Damn, dude, you really don't like her, huh?" Paul chimed in.

"She talks too much," Monty told him.

"I only talk when I need to," I interjected. Monty was really starting to get on my damn nerves again. I was trying to hold back, but he was trying my patience.

"Sound like you might have to leave her alone, dude," Paul chimed in once more.

"Yo, dawg, why don't you just chill out. I've got too much shit going on in my head to be listening to y'all going back and forth with each other. Try to figure out how we gon' walk away with all this money we about to get," Rich spoke up.

I was happy that he did speak up, but I was more shocked than anything. I was even more shocked that Monty didn't say anything back to Rich. I guess he figured that he didn't want to get on Rich's bad side. At least while we were on our way to the restaurant. Whatever his reasoning was, it worked out for all parties involved.

We pulled up to the Indian restaurant a little after nine o'clock. It was Rich's idea to send Monty, Paul, and Jason into the restaurant to get a table and also to check out the scenery. Rich and I sat in the car and waited for the place to close.

Rich didn't know this, but I was also watching the scenery out here. Knowing that the DEA are actively investigating Ahmad and his family, I knew I had to look over my shoulders just to make sure that the DEA agents weren't watching Rich and me on this very night. So far, everything looked cool; I just didn't know how long it would stay this way.

"I wonder how many people are in there?" Rich blurted out.

"Well, I see four cars, so it can't be any more than ten to fifteen people in there, and that's including the staff."

"I hope you're right," he said, and then he fell silent.

I let out a long sigh and said, "I sure hope I get to see my mother tonight. I swear, I miss her so much. I can't believe that I've been able to hold myself together this long."

I thought Rich would comment about my desire to see my mother, but he didn't. Once again, he made me painfully aware that he couldn't care less about whether or not I rescued my mother. This was a reminder that I was on my own.

One by one, the customers started leaving the restaurant. During the departure of the last white couple, Rich and I entered the restaurant and were greeted by an Arab woman dressed in hijab, covering her entire hair and her neck. "Sorry, but we are closed," she told me. I could tell that she was a woman, in her mid- to late forties.

"Can we get takeout?" Rich chimed in.

"No, I'm sorry it's too late. Our cook has already started cleaning the kitchen."

"Do you have anything that's already cooked? I would take that," I asked her.

"No, I'm sorry. You're gonna have to come back tomorrow when we open at eleven." She stood firm.

Without any warning, Rich pulled out his gun and pointed it directly at the woman. She gasped. "If you scream, I'm gonna kill you," he threatened her.

"You can have anything you want," she told him.

"Where's everybody?" Rich asked her.

"They're all in the kitchen," she replied nervously, her voice was cracking.

While Rich had the woman in front of us cornered, Paul, Jason, and Monty went into the kitchen, where all the other staff members were. I heard a lot of commotion coming from the kitchen. Loud screaming, someone dropping pots and pans, and I even heard two gunshots sound off. *Pop! Pop!*

I rushed into the kitchen area to see if my mother was back there or hidden in a back office. When I entered into the kitchen, Monty had one Arab dude lying on the floor in front of him, but I could tell that he was dead. The puddle of blood around the area of his chest painted that picture very clear.

Paul and Jason had another older lady and two middle-aged guys facing the wall near the freezer. Monty had Jason grilling them about where they were hiding the money. The woman spoke up and told them that the money they made today was in the back office. She even volunteered to take him back there and give it to him if he promised not to kill anyone else and leave. Monty wasn't going for it and started cursing the lady out.

"You don't call no shots, lady! We do!" Monty's voice boomed.

"What about the drugs? We want them too," Rich said from behind me. I had no idea he was behind me until he opened his mouth and spoke. The woman that he held his gun on had come into the kitchen with him. She looked scared shitless.

"We have no drugs here. My cousin owned the pharmacy until it was closed down a few days ago," the woman that Monty had his gun pointed at said.

"How much money do you have here?" Rich asked the same woman.

"Whatever we made today. Every time we close out the register at night, we make our drops to the bank the very next morning," the woman continued.

"Monty, take her back to that office and get all the dough they got. Jason, take everybody else to the buffet room. Paul, you follow me." Rich was laying out the instructions.

"Wait!" I shouted to get everyone's attention. "What about my mother? Ahmad kidnapped my mother and her boyfriend a couple days ago. And I am looking for her. Now, can anyone tell me where she is? Where has Ahmad put her? Where does he have her hiding?" I continued. I desperately needed at least one of them to have the answer to my question.

Everyone looked back and forth at each other. "No, we don't know where," one of the guys facing the wall said.

"We don't know anything about that," the woman standing next to Rich chimed in.

I stood there, hopeless. "Are you sure? Please tell me," I begged them all. "I promise I won't tell the cops on you. I just want my mother. That's it."

"No, I'm sorry. We don't know anything," the woman standing by Monty replied.

"Tell me, where is Ahmad? Where does he live?" I pressed the issue. I couldn't let up. Someone was going to answer my questions.

"We don't know," the chef said.

"You're lying. You do know where he is!" I yelled at him. I was losing my patience with these fucking people.

"Look, fuck all that! They said that they don't know where your mama is. So let it go," Rich interjected.

"That's really fucked up. I bet'cha if your mama had been kidnapped by one of these motherfuckers, I bet you'd kill these people on sight," I argued.

"You damn right I would. But you ain't me. They said they don't know where homeboy is or your mama, so let's move on," Rich stated, and then he turned his focus back toward the staff of the restaurant. "I gave everybody instructions, now let's get to it," Rich concluded, and then he headed out of the kitchen.

Instead of following Rich to the buffet area, I followed Monty and that woman to the back office. When we got back there, she walked straight to a desk in the corner. She walked around it and pulled the top left drawer and grabbed a stack of bills. After she handed the bills to Monty, he noticed that there was a safe in the far left corner of the office. "Why the fuck didn't you tell me that there was a safe in here?" he wanted to know. He was not a happy camper.

"No money in there," the Arab woman told him.

"Don't fucking lie to me. Open it up!" he roared. While the woman crawled down onto the floor to open the safe, I started searching through important documents that would list any and all real estate properties owned by

Ahmad's family. I figured by doing so, I would find a possible location of where they could be hiding my mother.

"I told you there was no money in here," I heard the woman say.

"What's all that paperwork in there?" Monty asked her.

My back was facing them both at this point. I was more focused on trying to find something that would help me find out where my mother was.

I heard the woman rattling pieces of paper. "It's just our stock accounts," she said.

By this time, I had turned around and was now facing them both. Monty had snatched the documents out of the woman's hand and had started looking them over. "Are those bank statements?" I asked him, hoping he'd say yes. This way, I'd find out that there was a house address on the statement, and that would be where my mother was.

"Nah, it says Fisher Investments. Looks like they got stocks and bonds," Monty told me.

"What does the home address say on it?" I asked him, and began to walk in his direction.

"It says 7113 Wisconsin Avenue, Bethesda, Maryland," he read.

"That's probably where the head mafia family lives," I replied.

"Might be. But it ain't got no money attached to it, so it does me no good," he said, and then he flung the papers across the desk. "I know y'all got more money somewhere else. Now tell me where it is, or I'm going to kill everyone in here," Monty threatened her.

"My husband has money at our house."

"How much?"

"Maybe thirty-five to forty thousand dollars."

"Well, let's go," he continued, and then he grabbed her by the arm and escorted her to the buffet area, which was where everyone else was. I followed.

"What'cha find?" Rich asked as soon as Monty, myself, and the woman reappeared.

"Looks like a grand, if that. But after she gave it to me, she said that she and her husband got money at their crib," Monty stated.

"How much?" Rich wanted to know.

"She said that they got about forty thousand."

"What we waiting for? Let's get out of this place," Rich instructed us.

"What are we going to do about these people?" Monty asked.

"Kill everybody but the chick that's riding with us to her house," Rich said, and he said it like he had no respect for humanity.

Before I could digest what Rich had just said, every one of the restaurant workers started whining and crying. "No, please don't kill us," one woman begged.

"Sir, please don't kill us. We promise that we won't call the police. Just let us go." I watched the chef plead for his life.

"Yes, we promise not to call the police. We have children. Please . . ." Another one of the workers started sobbing.

"All y'all just shut the fuck up!" Rich shouted.

The woman that we were taking with us started crying too. "I told you that I will give you all the money at our home if you don't kill my family. I won't do it if you kill them," she challenged Monty.

Monty smacked her hard. *Pop!* The woman stumbled, almost losing her balance. "Don't you ever tell me what you're going to do. Me and that man over there, we're in charge, and we get the last word around here," Monty explained to the woman while pointing at Rich.

"You keep your hands off my wife!" a man roared from the floor. Rich had everyone lying flat on the floor with their faces turned to the right side. At this angle, the guy was able to see his wife getting smacked by Monty.

Monty walked over to the man and kicked him in his leg. "What'cha just say to me?" Monty tested him. Everybody in the room had heard the man; Monty heard him too. I think he wanted the man to repeat himself, to prove a point.

"Don't touch my wife anymore," the same guy said.

After he made it clear to Monty that he wanted him to keep his hands off his wife, Monty felt disrespected by the guy and made an example of him. Without saying another word, Monty drew his pistol and shot the guy in his head, execution style. *Boom!* Blood spewed from the man's head like a running faucet. Both of the Arab women cried out. "Noooo!" the guy's wife screamed, and ran to her husband's side. "Wake up, Faheem! Wake up!" She wept as she tried to lift his head up from the floor.

"Get that bitch under control!" Rich roared.

Monty snatched her up from the floor. "Shut that crying shit up!" Monty lashed out at her.

"Get your hands off her," the other guy yelled from the floor. He attempted to get up, but Paul aimed his gun at him and shot him twice. Blood started oozing from his head.

The only person left alive on the floor was the other Arab woman. She cried the entire time while members of her family were being killed right before her. Rich instructed everyone to exit the restaurant and that we would head over to the house where the money was. But before anyone could leave the room, Paul asked what they were going to do with the lady that was still alive on the floor. Rich looked at Paul and told him to kill her. So that's what Paul did. He shot her in her head at point-blank range. *Boom!*

25

LIVE BY THE GUN

I can't believe that I was one step closer to finally seeing my mother. I didn't care that I would only get to spend a few minutes with her before I traded my life for hers. All I wanted to do was see her one last time. Look into her eyes and tell her how much I loved her and how I appreciated everything she has done for me, even if I hadn't projected it that way. She was still my mother, and I loved her.

"Make sure we ain't being followed," Rich said.

"I don't see anybody following us," Monty assured him after turning his body around and looking out the back window. He even looked into the passenger-side window.

"Please don't kill me," the woman begged.

"Nobody is gonna kill you, just as long as you do what we tell you to do," Monty told her.

"You promise?" the woman asked. She needed some assurance. And I didn't blame her. She was riding in a car with a bunch of misfits—the same misfits that beat me for no reason; the same misfits that just murdered her husband and their son. So, why should she believe them?

"Look, I said we weren't going to kill you. Now shut the fuck up before we change our minds," Monty told her.

But it was all a lie. Before we went into the restaurant, Monty and Rich had already planned to kill everybody in there. "Leave no witnesses," they said. So, what had changed from then to now? *Nothing*. They were heartless criminals and there were no changes in that.

"How much do we walk away with?" Rich wanted to know.

"So far, I'm close to a grand," Monty said happily.

"That's it?" Rich commented.

"Yeah."

"I thought we had about two to three grand," Rich said.

"I thought so too. But what can I say? There were more ones and fives than anything else," Monty explained.

"So we killed four people for one grand?" Rich questioned Monty. I could tell that he was getting extremely aggravated. The tone in his voice went from excitement to anger.

"You're saying it like that's a bad thing."

"Because it is. I don't kill people for that kind of money, unless they stole something from me or disrespected me. And in this case, neither one of them has happened," Rich said.

"You acting like we're done. We got one more spot to rob and then we're good. You are with the lady, and she said that the house we're going to has most of their money in it."

"What if she's lying?" Rich questioned Monty again.

"She knows that if she's lying, we're going to kill her, so I believe her."

"You better be right," Rich warned Monty as he drove in the direction of the house we went to the night before.

It seemed like the closer we got to the house, the more fearful I became. I knew I was with four street niggas with guns, but for some reason, I didn't feel protected. I didn't think that they were ready to go head-to-head with these men from the Middle East. I just really thought that they were out of their league. But we would see because there was no turning back. Not for me anyway.

"How much longer do we have to get there?" Monty's friend Paul asked.

"What, you gotta be somewhere?" Rich asked sarcastically.

"Nah, it's just that this lady keeps farting back here. I keep telling her to stop, but she won't," Paul told Rich.

"I'm sorry. I'm just so nervous," she spoke up.

"Look, I don't care how nervous you are, just stop doing it before I get mad with you and do something mean to you," Paul cautioned her.

"Okay, I will stop," she promised him, and then she fell silent.

As much as I wanted to feel sorry for this lady, I couldn't. I couldn't, because her family had kidnapped my mother and held her hostage. They even cut off her hand and sent it inside of a package and had it delivered to the hospital where I was. *How gross and heartless is that? You don't cut off a person's loved one's body part and send it to them. That's not cool. No matter how you look at it.*

"Yo, dawg, we got one thousand and sixteen dollars," Monty told Rich after he completed the money count.

Rich shook his head in a manner to express how frustrated he was becoming. After doing it for about five seconds, he said, "I'm telling you right now, we better come out of the house with at least the forty grand she promised to give us, because if I don't, I might be the only nigga walking out of there when it's time to leave." Rich expressed his anger to everyone in the car.

The entire car went silent. *I would pay a million dollars to read the minds of Jason, Paul, and Monty.* There was no doubt in my mind that these dudes were thinking shit about Rich. It wouldn't surprise me if they were saying to themselves that they'd kill Rich before he'd have a chance to kill them. That was what I would be thinking.

During the drive, I noticed that Monty had been getting a lot of text messages. It had become so annoying that Rich had to say something about it. "Yo, dawg, who the fuck is texting you like that?" he asked.

"Some niggas I know from around the way."

"Well, tell them niggas you working."

"They already know. They just wanna see where we gon' be done so they can come back and pick up home-girl," Monty explained.

I knew that the homegirl he was talking about was me. So I felt that I needed to address the situation. I mean, damn, he just killed three fucking people and I knew he was plotting my demise. How heartless could he be? "I know you're talking about me," I got the gumption to say.

"You fucking right I was talking about you," he didn't hesitate to say.

"You're one grimy-ass nigga! All you fucking care about is seeing people die. What kind of life is that? And how do you sleep at night?"

"I sleep very well, thank you. And I'm gon' sleep even better after Terrell's cousin do your ass in after I hand you over to them."

"You think it's gonna be that easy, huh?" I was really getting tired of this guy running his fucking mouth. He talked more than a freaking woman, more than a nagging-ass chick during her menstrual cycle. I just wished that someone would help me put this asshole out of his misery.

"Bitch, I'll end your fucking life now. Keep running your fucking mouth!"

"Do you think Rich is going to let you do something to me? I'm his cash cow right now," I defended my position. I knew the reason I was still alive was because Rich needed me to help him score money and the drugs that Ahmad's family had. So, whether he knew it or not, I had a little more time to burn. That time would be used to find my mother, and not for him to call Terrell's family and have them come and drag me to hell.

"I wish both of y'all shut the fuck up. I'm tired of hearing your mouths. I just wanna hear myself think for a minute," Rich interjected.

"She came at me," Monty tried to explain.

"Monty, just leave it alone. Let's take care of this business. After we get what we came for, then I don't give a damn what y'all do," Rich told him.

Hearing Rich tell Monty that he didn't care what he did after they robbed the house gave me an instant headache. Anxiety in my stomach started rumbling like a volcano. Just for that moment, I couldn't think straight. I wanted to think of a way that I'd be able to escape Monty's grasp after leaving that house, but I couldn't put two and two together. I couldn't even think about when my birthday was. I was a complete mess. *God, please help me.*

26

DIE BY THE GUN

When we arrived at the house, Rich pressed the garage opener that was clipped onto the sun visor. After the garage opened, Rich drove the truck inside of it and then closed the garage door behind us. "How many people are here?" was Rich's first question.

"Just my mother-in-law and my two children," the woman answered.

"Where will they be in the house?" Rich threw another question at her.

"My children should be in their bedroom asleep. And my mother-in-law should be in her bedroom as well," she said carefully.

"You said that the money was in a safe, so where is the safe?"

"It's in my husband's and my bedroom closet."

"Okay, now are you sure no other adults are in this house?"

"No, only my mother-in-law," she assured him.

"All right. Now, when we go in there, don't start yelling and screaming, because I will blow your fucking head off your shoulders if you do. Now, do you understand?" Rich threatened her.

"Yes, I understand," she told him.

"Okay, now I want you to stay close to me, because I'm gonna be walking behind you, so don't try no funny shit."

"I won't."

"Strap up and let's get this dough," Rich instructed the guys, and one by one, everyone filed out of the SUV and followed him and the woman into the house through the garage entrance.

We entered into the kitchen of the house, and no one was in sight. "Walk slow," Rich coached her.

"Okay," she whispered as she guided Rich, myself, Monty, and the other two guys through the kitchen.

"Where is your bedroom?" Rich started acting anxious.

"It's upstairs," she replied in a whimpering fashion.

"I don't wanna hear that whining shit, so cut it out before I get angry," Rich told her.

"Okay," she said, trying to suppress her sobbing as she continued to lead the way.

Upon approaching the staircase, Rich instructed the guys to go in different areas of the house. "Jason, I want you to go and check around the rooms down here, just to make sure no one else is here," Rich told him.

"A'ight," Jason said, and then he walked away.

"Paul, I need you to stay by the front door and make sure no one comes in here without any of us knowing," Rich told him.

"Got it," Paul replied, and walked off toward the front room.

"Monty, you come with me so we can get this money," Rich told him.

"Let's do it," Monty said eagerly.

"What about me?" I asked.

"Your job is done. We're here, so I don't give a damn what you do. Go kill yourself if you want to," Rich commented, and then he headed upstairs with Monty and the woman in tow.

"Oh, so my job is done, huh? We shall see about that," I mumbled to myself.

After Monty and Rich disappeared around the corner, when they reached the top step, I found a corner in the kitchen and started texting Ahmad. I needed to let him know that he had a nemesis here. **Come to the house near Military Hwy. Bring my mama with you. If you don't these guys said they will kill everyone in this house.**

OK, he replied.

As I looked at his text message, it gave me an uneasy feeling, even though he had only typed the word *OK*. I knew what kind of man Ahmad was. He was a calculating and dangerous man. I was sure that when he came, he was going to have an entourage consisting of his family with him. Rich and Monty had no idea what they were going to be up against. I just hoped that they were ready.

"Bingo," I heard Rich say from the kitchen. I also heard Monty laughing, giving off a sound like he was the Joker. It sounded evil and frightening.

"How much do you think it is?" I heard Monty ask.

"These straps are ten thousand each, so it looks like we got forty grand."

"You shitting me! I've never seen that much money in my life," Monty commented.

"Well, here it is. *Forty grand,*" Rich emphasized.

"How much is my cut?" Monty wanted to know.

"Take this ten grand and do whatever you want to do with it," Rich insisted.

"What about Jason and Paul?"

"What about 'em?"

"What? Wait. I gotta share my money with them?"

"I thought you knew that."

"Nah, I didn't."

"Well, now you do."

"Come on now, Rich, you know that's not fair. Me and Jason put in a lot of work. We killed those people back at that restaurant. You didn't have to do a thing."

"Nah, I didn't. But remember, this was my job. I put y'all niggas onto this. If it wasn't for me, you wouldn't have that ten grand in your hand right now."

"Yeah, I know, but let's be fair about it. I mean, you can at least give up another ten grand and let Jason and Paul split it."

"That's not gonna happen. I'm keeping this thirty grand because I set up this sting and I gotta share it with Mike when he gets out of the hospital."

"Rich, you know that's a bullshit-ass excuse, right?" Monty protested.

"Look, dawg, I'm not gonna stand here and go back and forth with you about this money. I'm keeping this thirty grand and that's the end of it. Now, if you don't like it, then do something about it. And if you ain't gonna do shit about it, then just shut the fuck up because you're beginning to sound like a bitch!" Rich scolded him.

"Yeah, a'ight," I heard Monty say, and then I didn't hear him utter another word. But I did hear someone else.

"Sania, is that you?" I heard an older, Middle Eastern woman's voice say. I rushed to the staircase because I knew this was not going to end well.

"Yes, Mama, now go to bed," Sania instructed her.

"What do you mean, 'go to bed'? Are you okay? You sound upset." The woman pressed the issue as she slowly made her way into the bedroom where Monty and Rich were.

Oh my God, lady, please go back in your room like the woman told you, I thought as anxiety ricocheted throughout my body.

"I'm not going back into my room until you tell me what's wrong with you."

The next thing I heard was Rich telling the woman to

back up. "Who are you? What are you doing in this house?" I heard the woman ask boldly. I was shocked to hear her stand up against Rich and Monty.

"Mama, stop it. I will handle it. Please go back into your room," Sania pleaded with her.

"Put that gun away before I call the cops," the woman threatened Rich.

"Mama, please go back in your room," Sania asked once again. They all were in the hallway upstairs, so I could see everything they were doing.

"No, she's not going anywhere. Monty, grab her and take her downstairs," Rich hissed.

When Monty reached for her, he grabbed her hard and tried to pull her close to him, but when she jerked her body backward, she used all her weight and that caused her to fall backward down the stairs. "Mama!" Sania yelled as she ran down the staircase behind her mother.

I stood there and watched in horror as the woman tumbled down the steps toward me. I immediately got out of the way.

The woman finally landed at the bottom of the staircase, and when I looked down at her, I noticed how she wasn't breathing. I looked up the staircase at Rich and told them both that this lady was dead.

Immediately after I announced it, I saw Sania rushing toward us. "Oh my God! You broke her neck." Sania started crying hysterically.

Taking another look at this lady, I realized that Sania was right; her mother-in-law's neck was broken. I could see a huge bone sticking out the side of her neck.

Rich and Monty ran downstairs and looked at her themselves. But when they bent down toward her, Sania snapped on them. "Get away from her, you fucking killers! You killed my husband, my uncle, my cousin, and now my mother-in-law. You're fucking monsters!" She was going crazy, swinging at them and trying to fight them.

After she took the second swing at Monty, Monty lunged back and threw a punch so hard at Sania that when it connected to her face, she flew backward and landed on her back about three feet from where her mother-in-law was lying. Monty hit her really hard. "You know you gotta off her, right?" Rich said.

"Yeah," Monty replied, and pulled his gun from the waist of his pants and let off two shots. One hit her stomach and the other one hit her in the chest. I stood there and watched these innocent women get the lives sucked out of them, and it was all for nothing. Okay, their family had something to do with the killing of my cousin, my grandmother, and Mrs. Mabel, but it wasn't them that pulled the trigger. It was the men. So, why punish them?

"Mommy. Nanny. Where are you?" I heard a little voice come from upstairs.

My heart dropped into the pit of my stomach after I heard the voice. I immediately looked at Rich and Monty and said, "Please don't kill those little girls."

"If they stay out of the way, then it won't happen. But if they see our faces, then they gotta go," Monty spoke up.

I gave him the nastiest facial expression that I could muster up. He was a low-down, dirty-ass dog. He was the worst nigga that I ever met. Instead of commenting on what he just said, I walked up the staircase and headed in the direction where I heard the little girl talking.

After I pushed open the door that was slightly ajar, I saw a little three- or four-year-old girl standing in the doorway. She was so freaking adorable. And it hurt my heart when I thought about the fact that she wouldn't have a mother or grandmother anymore. My heart went out to her more after I thought about the fact that if she and her sibling saw Rich's and Monty's faces, then they would kill her. I couldn't let that happen, so I leaned over toward her and said, "What's your name?" I asked her.

"Hamina," she replied.

"Well, Hamina, I'm letting you know that your mommy and grandmommy have gone to the store. And they left me here to watch you, okay?" I said nicely.

She hesitated for a moment and then said, "Okay."

"Come on, let's watch TV in your room until they get back, okay?" I suggested after I grabbed her hand and walked her back to her bed. I saw the television on the TV stand next to the dresser, so I turned it on and then sat on the edge of the bed next to her and waited to see what was coming on. "What kind of television shows you like?" I asked her.

"I like *iCarly, PAW Patrol,* and *Phineas and Ferb.*"

"Well, that's what we're watching," I replied, giving her the biggest smile that I could muster up. Besides, she didn't need to know what was really going on downstairs. If she saw her mother and grandmother in the state they were in, she'd probably be traumatized for the rest of her life. I couldn't allow that if I could help her.

27

WE GOT COMPANY

I heard a car pull up in the driveway of the house, so I stood up from the little girl's bed and looked out of the window. I noticed that it was a dark-colored car. But I couldn't tell the make and model of it. "Is that my daddy?" The little girl looked back at me and asked.

"I don't know, sweetheart," I told her, and then I stood back away from the curtain. I figured that it had to be Ahmad because I texted him to meet me here. When he texted me and told me that he was in the car parked outside in the driveway, I was tempted to let the guys downstairs know that he was here. But then I figured that it wouldn't be in my best interest to do so. Rich had instructed Paul to be the lookout person at the front door, so I let him do his job.

We're in the house, I texted him back.

I saw him slowly emerge from the back seat of the driver's side. And while he was doing that, I noticed that there were two other people in the car. The person in the passenger-side seat looked like a woman. From what I could see, the body of the woman was full-figured, like my mother was. I couldn't see her face, so I prayed to God that it was her.

The person sitting in the driver's-side seat was probably one of the mafia hit men that Agent Sims was investigating. "I see somebody coming to the front door," I heard Paul say.

From there, all I heard were footsteps scurrying around downstairs. "How many is it?" I heard Rich ask.

"I just see one, dude," Paul told him.

"Does he have anything in his hands?" Rich kept the questions coming.

"Nah. He just walking with his hands on his sides. So, do you want me to answer the door if he knocks on it?"

"Fuck nah! We don't live in here, so we ain't answering nobody's door."

"But what if he doesn't go away?" Paul sounded worried.

"Nigga, are you all right? Because you sure are acting like a bitch right now!" Rich roared. Paul was irritating the heck out of Rich, and I enjoyed every minute of it. Before Paul could say another word, Ahmad rang the doorbell.

"What are we going to do, stand here and listen to that dude ring the doorbell?" Monty interjected.

"We ain't gonna open the door and let him in."

"We don't even know who it is. It could be a family member, so if we don't answer the door, he may call the cops," Monty suggested.

"And that's why we're going out the back door and leaving this motherfucker," I heard Rich say, and then I heard footsteps. I assumed that they were heading toward the back door of the house. I knew that it would be a bad idea to get caught in the house alone if Rich and the rest of them were able to get away, and especially without any fighting power. So I grabbed Hamina's hand and told her that we were going to take a walk.

Without giving me any problems, she allowed me to hold on to her hand and walk her downstairs. While we were walking down the staircase, the doorbell chimer continued to ring. "That's probably my daddy," Hamina said with excitement. And as soon as we made it down to the last step, she tried to run toward the front door. I held on to her tightly and pulled her back. "No, we're not going that way, we're going this way." I showed her by pointing in the direction of the kitchen, and when she looked in that direction, she saw her mother's and her grandmother's lifeless bodies on the floor. She took off running.

"Mommy . . . Nana." Hamina started whining. I looked into her pretty little eyes and saw how they were quickly filling up with tears. Damn, I couldn't believe that I fucked up and allowed this little girl to see her dead mama and grandmother. *Ugh!*

"Come on, baby girl, everything is going to be all right." I tried to console her, but it wasn't working. I could tell that she really wanted her daddy now.

"My daddy is at the front door and he wants to come in the house," she told me. She knew in her heart that something wasn't right and she made me aware of it. "I want my daddy!" she started screaming, walking midway through the kitchen.

As she began to resist me, I started hearing gunshots. *Pop! Pop! Pop! Boom! Pop! Pop!* This startled Hamina and we scrambled down to the floor. We hid underneath the kitchen table. With the tablecloth in place, no one would be able to see us, but we were able to see them. Truthfully speaking, we could only see their legs and their feet. Nothing more.

After hearing the popping sounds from the gunfire, Hamina and I saw two sets of feet scramble back to the kitchen. "Be quiet, okay," I whispered in her ear.

"Okay," Hamina whispered back in my ear as the tears continued to fall from her eyes. My heart went out to her. She was a sweet little butterfly and it bothered me that I couldn't stop her from crying. She wasn't supposed to see the lifeless bodies of her mother and her grand-mother lying on the floor. Rich had already warned me that if she got a look at him, he was going to murder her in an instant. So I hoped and prayed that I could keep her alive, at least while I was here.

"Yo, what the fuck just happened?" I heard Monty panting.

"Did you see those two dudes shooting at us?" Rich asked him. He sounded out of breath, along with Monty. "I think they got Jason and Paul," he continued as he huffed and puffed. "Did you get a chance to bust a shot at him?"

"I think I did," Monty replied, but I could tell that it was a lie. And I knew Rich could tell too.

"Turn the kitchen light off," Rich told Monty.

"A'ight," he said, and flipped off the light switch that was near the sliding door to the patio, which was how they had run back into the house.

They stood there quietly. And so did the little girl and I. But that didn't last long, because a few seconds later, we heard movement coming from upstairs. I knew it had to be the other little girl that was in her bed asleep after the other little girl and I walked out of that bedroom. "Nana, where are you?" I heard the little voice call out.

The one that was with me couldn't hold her tongue. She shot out from underneath the kitchen table and sprinted toward the staircase to see her sister. "Bella, I'm coming," she said.

My heart went out to her when she ran away from me; I knew her life was about to be over. Rich and Monty both ran in her direction. "Get her, and I'll get the little girl up-stairs," Rich instructed Monty.

"What are we gonna do with them?" Monty wanted to know.

"We're gonna use them to get out of the house," Rich told him, and then I heard footsteps running up the stair-case.

"Who are you? And where is Nana?" I heard the little girl from upstairs ask.

"Get off me! Don't touch me!" the little girl down here demanded.

"Get off of her!" Bella, the little girl upstairs, said.

"Shut up before I kill you!" Monty's voice boomed. And then I heard a gurgling sound. I knew then that Monty was choking Hamina.

Thank God Rich heard it and demanded that he stop it. "What the fuck is wrong with you? We gotta keep her alive until we get out of here!" Rich roared.

"She wouldn't shut the fuck up!" Monty tried defending his actions.

"Touch her again and I'm gonna kill you myself," Rich warned him.

I couldn't see Monty's facial expression, but I knew he wasn't too happy about Rich's threat. I thought he would have a rebuttal for Rich, but, surprisingly, he didn't. I knew the relationship between these two was gonna fall apart, and I didn't want to be around when it happened.

Meanwhile, they had to figure out a way to get out of this home without being shot. Their ace in the hole was keeping those two little girls alive. I just hoped neither one of them got killed in the process.

"Come on, let's go," I heard Rich say to the little girl named Bella.

"I know we got them, but how are we going to let the guy outside know that we have them?" Monty wanted to know.

"We're going to yell outside the window. Trust me, they'll hear me," Rich assured Monty.

As soon as they both had the girls in hand, they escorted them toward the front door. Rich cracked the door open just enough so that the guy outside could hear what he had to say. The lights in the house were still out, but the light from the street slightly lit the foyer area around the front door. This allowed me to see their every move.

"Hey, whoever you are, I just want to let you know that I have your wife and kids. So, if you try to shoot us again, we will kill the rest of your family!" Rich yelled outside.

No one returned any dialogue, so Rich repeated himself again. "Whoever you are, I just want you to know that I have your wife and your kids. So if you try to shoot us again, I will personally kill the rest of your family *slowly*. Don't try anything now, because I am a man of my word," Rich continued, and then he closed the door.

"Think they're gonna go forward?" Monty asked him.

"For the sake of these little girls, they better," Rich said with finality.

"So, what are we gonna do now? How are we going to get out of here?" Monty's questions kept coming one after another.

"We're going to leave out of here with that truck in the garage," Rich told Monty, and then he turned around and led the way to the door that opened to the garage. Monty followed him with Bella in tow. "Monty, I want you to drive, and I'll sit in the back seat with the girls," Rich said.

"What if they don't see the kids and shoot me while I'm trying to get away?"

"Don't worry. They won't try to shoot the truck. Get inside the driver's seat now, or I'm gonna do it, and when I do, I'm gonna leave you here," Rich warned him once again, and then he stormed off into the garage.

Monty heeded Rich's demand and followed him into the garage. Knowing that Monty and Rich were about to bail out of here and use the truck in the garage to do it, I knew that if I didn't leave with them, my chances of rescuing my mother wouldn't happen. That is, unless I got in the truck with them and derailed their escape before they could get off the block. This way, I could possibly get them to hand over my mother in exchange for the little girls. Who knows? I might not be able to trade my life at all.

While they were getting into the truck, I climbed from underneath the table and ran toward the doorway that led to the garage. "Don't leave me," I said loud enough for them to hear.

"Where the fuck was you?" Rich asked me before he closed the back door of the truck.

"I was looking around all the rooms for my mama," I lied.

"Get in the front seat," Rich told me.

"Nah, let that bitch stay here. She was ghost the whole time we was popping these pistols at them cats around the back of the house."

"Nigga, fuck you!" I said, gritting my teeth at Monty. I was fuming on the inside of my body. This guy had no knowledge of how bad I wanted him dead. He would find out tonight after I turned his ass over to these cats.

"I ought to smack you in your face, you dumb bitch!" Monty hissed. I could tell that he was seconds away from hitting me. Thankfully, Rich wasn't in the mood to watch Monty beat me up. He was more focused on getting out of this house and he wasn't going to let Monty interfere with it.

"Monty, shut the fuck up and close the damn door. I'm ready to get out of here!" Rich's voice boomed.

Seeing the urgency, I jumped into the front passenger-side seat and shut the door behind me. I watched Monty as he started up the truck and revved the engine. "Hit the gas and back out of here!" Rich shouted.

"Do you want me to open the garage?" he asked Rich.

"Just let it up a little bit and then flood the gas, just in case they start shooting."

"What about the car that's parked in the driveway? I'm gon' run into that when I back up," Monty expressed.

"I don't give a fuck about that car! Back into it!" Rich roared.

"I want my mommy," Hamina said.

"Yes, I want my mommy too," Bella whined.

"Shut up! I don't wanna hear shit else out of y'all!" Rich snapped.

Both little girls started crying. "Can you get them to shut up?" Monty shouted at the girls. He thought that he was going to shut them up by yelling at them, but it only made things worse. Both girls started sobbing uncontrollably. And Rich couldn't handle it, so he slapped both girls down on the floor.

One of the girls screamed at the top of her voice, scaring me and Monty both. Shocked that he could be so violent to a child, I stood up and screamed, "Stop it!"

I guess he was surprised by my audacity; Rich immediately let go of the girl. "God help me," I said quietly, sitting back in my seat. I couldn't wait to get away from these assholes.

Instead of opening the garage door first, Monty put the truck in reverse and sped backward through the door.

Boom!

The garage door burst open. We sped backward until we hit the car that was parked behind us.

Boom!

That was the sound that I heard when Monty slammed the truck back into the car. I quickly got a moment to see if my mother was still in the car, but when I looked a second time and saw that it was a man in the car instead of a woman, I knew that Ahmad was playing games with me. He wasn't really trying to get me to trade my life for my mother's. He tried to pull the wool over my eyes so I could hand him *me* on a silver platter. I thought of the intuition that I had to get in the truck when I had the chance. If I had stayed in the house, Ahmad would've found me and killed me right on the spot.

Immediately after I realized that my mother wasn't in the car, I got back down on the floor while Monty pushed that car back with the force from the truck. I couldn't believe it, Monty was really able to get the car out of the way.

I guess Ahmad and the other guys that were with him realized that the only way they were going to prevent the truck from leaving the house was by shooting out the tires. That was exactly what they did.

Boom! Boom! Boom!

One by one, the guys successfully shot both of the back tires. But that didn't stop Monty from putting the truck into Drive and attempting to barrel down the street. The drive was rocky and I could smell the rubber burning as the air from the tires oozed out of them.

But out of nowhere, I heard shots coming from behind us. *Pop! Pop! Pop!* The driver's-side window glass shattered. "I'm hit," I heard Monty say as shards of glass rained down on me. And before I knew it, I heard another shot, and that's when the truck started swerving. And when I looked up and saw Monty's lifeless body slumped over on the steering wheel, I knew that it was going to be a matter of seconds before this truck slammed into something. So I got up and grabbed the wheel and tried to steer it as best as I could. Meanwhile, Rich barked orders at me from the back seat.

"Move him out of the way and drive this motherfucker before we crash!" he shouted. We had gotten at least a half of a mile down the road, giving us at least a three-minute head start to escape from their grasp, but the timing of preventing the truck from hitting the telephone pole had run out. The collision rattled me a little, but I shook it off. I knew I had to think quick; in a matter of seconds, I was going to be staring down the barrel of a gun. I needed to get out of here. But before I ran off, I wanted to get my hands on that ten thousand dollars. And I knew it would be in my best interest to get it from Monty. If I didn't, Ahmad would take it back.

While I was taking the money out of Monty's jacket pocket, Rich climbed over the girls and exited the truck on the side where I was. I thought he was going to close the door behind himself, but he didn't. He took the little girls with him and ran as fast as he could. Before I exited the truck, I took Monty's gun too. I knew I was gonna need it more than anything else. The money portion was good, but it wasn't going to save my life. So I held the gun as careful as I could and then I exited the truck, making sure that Ahmad and the other guys didn't see me.

I thought that I was going to run into Rich the farther I ran from the crash, but he disappeared into thin air. I didn't even hear the little girls crying while I made my way out of the neighborhood. I saw two police cars and a paramedic vehicle coming my way, so I ducked down behind a massive tree alongside the road. I knew that they were going to that house we just left, so I made sure they didn't see me.

After they drove by, I put some pep in my step and got the hell out of that neighborhood. I came here with plans to get my mother back, but it didn't work. So now I had to come up with a plan B. It was now or never.

28

RUNNING OUT OF TIME

People will only do things that you allow them to do. In this case, I allowed Rich and Monty to treat me terribly within hours of meeting them. I swear, I can't keep dealing with guys like this. Rich didn't like me. Monty didn't like me. Terrell didn't like me, and Ahmad didn't like me. *What is it about me and this weird dynamic that I have with men? Am I allergic to them?* Whatever it was, it hadn't been conducive to me, because I'd been having some bad reactions because of it. Hopefully, I would get it right one day. But until then, I was gonna take the bitter with the sweet.

I was afraid to take this taxi ride back to Rich's spot, but I didn't have anywhere else to go, so that was where I headed. I got in a taxicab with an older Hispanic gentleman, who, I believed, wouldn't put me in any danger by being around him. For one, I knew that he wouldn't recognize me, and two, if he did, I was sure that he wouldn't rat me out. People from other countries tend to stay out of other people's business, especially since there was a language barrier. All and all, I knew that I wasn't in any risk of this guy contacting the cops, but to be sure, I paid him in advance and added a nice tip to it, and then we headed into that direction.

I had no idea if I was going to see Rich when I got there. At this point, it didn't matter. All I wanted to do was get into that neighborhood so I could hide amongst the street hustlers and blend in with the girls that hung around in that area.

I couldn't give the cabdriver the exact address to Rich's trap house, but when we arrived within a mile of it, I pointed him to the exact location. It only took us a minute or so to get me to drive up to the building. After I got out of the car, I walked up to the door and knocked on it. Surprisingly, Rich opened the door. When he saw me, he acted like he saw a ghost.

"I thought they got you," he commented as he stood in the doorway of the front door.

"I thought they got you too," I replied in a nonchalant manner.

"Hell nah! I wasn't going to let them get me. I got that money and got out of there."

"Can I come in?" I asked him.

"Yeah," he replied, and then he stepped to the side so I could walk by him. "How did you get here?" he asked after I got out of the way so he could close the front door.

"I caught a cab," I told him immediately after I sat down on the sofa.

"I caught a cab too," he stated as he stood in the middle of the floor.

"Where are the little girls?"

"Oh, they're gone. I left them on somebody's front porch."

"What do you mean you 'left them' on someone's porch? Are they dead or alive? What?"

"They're alive."

"You're pulling my leg, right?"

"Nah, I'm serious." He tried to assure me, and I pretty much believed him. He wasn't the type of guy that would lie about something like that. He was a heartless asshole, but when it was time to lay the truth out there, he'd do it. And he wouldn't care if you liked it or not.

"I see you hurried up and changed clothes," I pointed out.

"Why not? Who wants to walk around with bloody clothes?"

"Interesting" was the only response I could come up with. This guy was insane. But I'd seen men who were crazier than he was, so I gave him a pass.

Before Rich and I could engage further, there was another knock on the front door. He walked over and said, "Who is it?"

"Choppa!" I heard the guy say.

I watched Rich as he opened the front door. Choppa was a very short young guy with a headful of dreadlocks. The locks were unkempt and so was he, from where I was sitting. His body reeked of marijuana and his actions demonstrated exactly how high he was. "Yo, dawg, I got two hos out here trying to spend a hundred dollars. So show a nigga some love so I can make a few dollars off the sell."

"Here, take these five twenties and do what you want with 'em," Rich told him, and dropped the packaged drugs into Choppa's hand.

"Come on, Rich man, these joints are small as hell. Give me one more," Choppa begged.

"Take it or leave it." Rich stood firm.

Choppa stood there for a minute as he looked closely at the drugs. After looking down at them for a moment or two, he said, "A'ight, fuck it!" And he handed Rich a one-hundred-dollar bill. Afterward, he stood there, opened every plastic wrapped Baggie of the drug, poured them in his hand, and then he took two away from that pile and stuffed them down into his pocket.

"You're only giving 'em three of those joints?" Rich laughed.

"Yep, that's it," Choppa said, and then he walked away.

Rich laughed at Choppa once again after he closed the front door and locked it. When he sat back down on the couch, his cell phone started ringing. He answered it. "Hello."

I could hear the caller just a tad bit to know that it was a woman. But when she started talking at full speed, I couldn't keep up with what she was saying, until Rich said, "I'm glad he's doing good. But did the police come up there and talk to him yet?" Right then and there, I knew he was talking to a woman that had information on Mike's situation.

"Well, if they come up there, just tell Mike to tell them that the guy wearing a dark-colored hoodie tried to rob him. And when they found out that Mike didn't have any money on him, they got mad, shot him, and ran off."

The woman Rich was talking to said a few more words, and right before Rich ended the call, he told her to keep him posted, and if Mike needed anything, she should call him back.

Right after he disconnected the call, I acted like I was watching television, but that was far from the truth. I was watching him from my peripheral vision. Judging from his mannerisms, I could tell he couldn't care less about how Mike was doing. All he cared about was if the cops visited Mike or not. And if they had, what was their conversation about? Rich was a heartless piece of shit. So the quicker someone put him out of his misery, the better things would be for all parties involved.

"It's good to know that my boy Mike is okay," he blurted out.

"That's good to hear. I was really worried about him."

"Well, worry no more," Rich said cheerfully, and then he started chuckling loudly.

"I see you're in good spirits. What are you so happy for?"

"Because I'm thirty thousand dollars richer than I was about two hours ago."

"Oh yeah, I heard about that."

"What did you hear?"

"I heard you and Monty going back and forth about the forty thousand y'all got from that house, and how you weren't giving up more than the ten thousand that you gave him. And that he had to share that same ten grand with the other two guys he brought along with y'all."

"Yep, I said every word, and I meant it too. Because him and his homeboys came in on the tail end of that job. That job was supposed to be for me, Mike, and one other person. I didn't ask for Monty to bring that dude Paul and Jason back to the spot. But since it happened that way, then it's his job to hit 'em off with his share."

"Where's my part?" I asked sarcastically. "Remember, I set the whole thing up."

"The deal was for you to help me and I would help you get your mama back."

"Yeah, it was. But did I get my mother back?"

"Was it my fault that she wasn't there?"

"Come on, Rich, let's keep it funky. Your intentions were never to help me get my mother back. All you wanted was the stash, that's it. Not to mention, every guy that went into that house with us didn't make it out."

"That's on them. I did my part."

"Are you really gonna share that money with Mike?"

"Yeah, I'm gonna look out for him."

"How much?"

"None of your fucking business!"

"Sorry! My bad!"

"Yeah, it is," he commented while gritting his teeth at me. And then he changed the subject. "So you say that you didn't murder that nigga Terrell, huh?"

"No, I didn't."

"Well, I don't believe you. I think you did. And I think you did it because he cheated on you and you couldn't handle it."

"Sorry to disappoint you. But that did not happen. I don't know who killed Terrell, and I don't care. He was a fucking asshole, so in my book, he got what he deserved."

"You're sticking to the script, huh?"

"It's the truth."

"Yeah, tell me anything," he said, and then he stood up from the couch and started walking slowly toward me. I was getting a little nervous, because I had no idea what he was about to do to me.

"Look, I don't want no more beef with you," I told him, and I held up both of my hands. "If you want me to leave right now, I will do it."

"Don't worry, I'm not bringing no beef to you. And you ain't gotta leave either," he assured me as he continued to walk toward me.

Even though Rich just said that he had no beef with me, my intuition told me something totally different. So I braced myself for the inevitable. "I hit you pretty hard earlier, huh?" he asked me as he laid his hand against the side of my face. The bruises around my right eye and the cheek area were still purple and blue, so he could see them very well.

"Yes, you did," I replied, and pulled my face away from his hand.

"I wanna make it up to you," he insisted.

"No, I'm good," I assured him.

"Come on now, don't act like that," he said, and tried to lean toward me so he could give me a kiss on the lips. I yanked my head back.

"I told you that I'm good," I reminded him.

"Stop playing hard to get." He grabbed the bottom of my chin and tried to pull my face toward him.

I yanked my head back again. "I told you I was good.

So, can you please stop? I don't look at you like that." I was becoming aggravated.

He stood straight up and gritted at me. "Bitch! Don't be acting like you're better than me. Do you know how many hos be throwing themselves at me? I can have the whole damn city of Norfolk, if I wanted," he boasted.

"Good. I'm glad," I said, and slid a couple of inches away from where he was standing. Having him standing before me gave me an uneasy feeling. I hoped my actions indicated it.

"Ho, you ain't all that!" he snapped, and took two steps toward me.

"I didn't say I was," I corrected him. In no way was I trying to cause another disturbance between him and me. I needed somewhere to stay for the night so I wouldn't be in the street. But he was really making it hard for me to be here.

"You ain't gotta say it. You're showing me right now."

"Look, Rich, I'm really not trying to fuss with you. I'm tired and I'm frustrated that I couldn't get my mother tonight. So, will you just cut me some slack so I can re-group?" I asked.

"If you ain't trying to give me some pussy, then you might as well get out."

"Are you serious right now?"

"Fucking right I am. No pussy, no overnight stay. So, what is it going to be?" From the looks of things, he wasn't going to move until he had gotten an answer.

"Rich, please tell me that you're joking." I searched his face for a twinkle in his eye.

"Fuck nah! I ain't joking. Now I'm gonna say this one more time, if you ain't trying to give me some pussy, then you gotta go. And I'm talking about leaving *right now.*"

"Damn, Rich, that's fucked up, especially since I'm the reason why you got that thirty grand," I pointed out.

"Come on, let's go," he said, grabbing me by my arm

and pulling me up from the sofa. Immediately after he helped me up on my feet, he looked down at the breast area of the jacket and wondered what was bulging out. But before I could answer him, he reached over and patted my left breast. "Wait a minute, is that the dough I gave to Monty?"

I pushed his hands away from my jacket. "It's my diary," I lied.

"Yo, you can't even lie right. I can see that dough sticking out of your jacket clear as day. Now hand it over to me," he demanded. But I wasn't going for it. I wasn't about to allow this guy to take away this money that I helped him get. And besides, he gave the money to Monty, and now that Monty was gone, it now belonged to me.

"If you don't give me that money right now, I'm gonna put a slug in your head," he threatened me.

"Look, I don't have time for this," I said to him, and then I reached down into my inside jacket pocket and slowly pulled out the ten grand I took from Monty after he got shot. Before I could get it out of my jacket pocket free and clear, Rich snatched it from my hands.

"You thought you was going to keep this dough for yourself, huh?" He cracked another smile.

"Yeah, I did," I told him, and watched him as he shoved the money down into his front pocket; then he turned his back toward me and started walking toward the kitchen. Before he took one step, I took the gun from my other pants pocket and aimed it at him. "I'm gonna ask you really nicely to give me that money back," I warned him.

He turned around slowly, and when he noticed that I had a gun in my hand, he chuckled. "I see you took Monty's pistol too," he said.

"Yes, I did. Now I am gonna only tell you one more time to give me that money back."

"What's gonna happen if I don't?" He tested me.

"I'm gonna lay you out on the fucking floor and then

I'm gonna make you clean up your own blood." I needed to let this bastard know that I wasn't playing any games with him.

"I don't believe you got the heart to pull the trigger," he challenged me.

"Act like you aren't gonna give me that ten grand back and see what happens." I made it very clear.

"Do you even know how to use that gun?" he asked me, and took a tiny step toward me.

"Rich, I told you that if you move, I'm gonna lay your ass out. Now call my bluff," I threatened him.

Refusing to believe what I said, Rich took a bold step toward me and smiled. "See, I knew you didn't have the guts to pull that trigger. So hand me the gun and I'll forget about all of this," he said.

Without saying a word, I pulled the trigger of Monty's .38 handgun. *Pop!* After the bullet went through his left leg, he fell down on the floor. "*Awoooo,* you stupid bitch! You shot me in my fucking leg," he growled in a fetal-like position. He began to rock his body back and forth.

"I told you not to move. Now if you don't give me that money, I'm gonna shoot you again," I warned him once more.

"Here, take it!" he yelled, and snatched the money from his pants pocket. After he threw the stack of one-hundred-dollar bills at me, he continued to rock his body back and forth. "You need to take me to the emergency room before I lose a lot of blood." He was still in the fetal position.

"I'm not taking your grimy ass anywhere. You're gonna stay right here and take that pain like a real man."

While Rich whined like a fucking toddler, I got on Mike's cell phone and called Ahmad. He answered after the first ring. "I'm gonna kill you very slow when I get my hands on you," he hissed through the phone. I could hear the hate riding the wave signals as they vibrated through the phone.

"I'm not the one that killed your father. Three of the men responsible for killing your family were already killed by you and your men. But I have the ringleader here with me. So I am willing to trade him for my mother right now," I told him.

"No deal. I want you too," he replied.

"Where is my mother now?" I wanted to know. It had been a while since I heard her voice over the phone. I needed to know that she was still alive, or there was going to be no way I was going to make the trade.

"Don't worry, she's still alive."

"How long will it take for you to get her and meet me in downtown Norfolk?"

"I can meet you within the hour."

"Do that. And call me when you get close by. Don't try no funny shit!"

Instead of responding to my comment, he disconnected our call. I shoved Mike's cell phone back down in my pocket after our call ended. And when I turned around and looked at Rich, he gave me this weird facial expression. "When did you get a phone?" he wondered aloud.

"I picked it up from the floor after you and Monty's dumb ass picked Mike up from the floor and carried him outta the house."

"So you had that phone all this time?"

"I sure did." I smirked at him.

"Wait a minute, so you know that Arab dude's phone number?" Rich seemed confused.

"Yep, I sure do. And I set you and those dumb-ass niggas up too. Ahmad knew how many of you were in that house. He knew exactly where everyone was at too. The only bad thing was that he didn't keep up his end of the bargain. He didn't bring my mama with him, like he promised. So I'm giving him another chance to make it right. And as a bonus, I'm offering you up, since it was all your idea to rob and have his family killed."

"You sneaky bitch! Do you know that he's going to kill you too?" Rich snapped. He punched the side of the couch and hurt his fist.

"I know he is. But at this point in my life, my life is meaningless to me. See, unlike you, I love my mother. So, if I have to exchange my life for hers, then so be it." I tried to explain this to him, but it went right over his head.

"You got to be the stupidest bitch I know! None of that shit you just said made any sense to me," Rich continued, still applying pressure to his bloody leg.

He and I kept going back and forth about how ignorant I was for selling him and myself out to the guys that were coming our way. From the position I was sitting in, our argument wasn't going anywhere. So I ended the conversation by telling him to just let things fall where they might, because our lives would be put in someone else's hands. And there was nothing he could do about it.

29

MAKING THE TRADE

It took Ahmad approximately forty-five minutes to call me back. My heart started beating rapidly after I answered the call and he told me that he was ten minutes away. I gave him the address to the house and warned him about the guys that were posted on the corner of the block. "If any of them ask you where you're going, just tell 'em that Rich knows that you're coming and they'll let you pass," I told him.

"Is there anything else I need to know?"

"Let me speak to my mother, because you didn't keep your end of the bargain back at your family's house," I insisted.

He paused for a second and then I heard a woman's voice in the background. "Is that my daughter on the phone?" I heard her say. It was faint, but I knew it was her.

I heard some crackling sounds and then I heard, "Misty baby, is this you?" I could hear the fear and pain in my mother's voice. I swear, I wanted to lose it and flood our talk with cries and tears. But I held it together. She was already upset from what she had endured while she was with those bastards, so I felt it was best to stay calm. Still,

I wanted to make sure she knew that I was doing everything within my power to get her back safe.

"Yes, Mama, it's me. Are you okay?" I asked her.

"They cut off some of my fingers." She started sobbing.

"I know, Mama, I know. Don't worry. I'm gonna get you to the nearest hospital as soon as I get you back," I lied to her. She had no idea that I was trading my life for hers.

"Baby, I can't wait to see you."

"And I can't wait to see you too. But for right now, I'm gonna need you to do what they tell you, until we see each other, okay?"

"Okay," she replied.

"Give that guy the phone," I instructed her.

When Ahmad got the phone back in his hand, he said, "I will see you in a few minutes, so don't fuck me over. It's you and that guy for your mama. Got it?"

"Got it," I assured him. Once again, he ended the phone call.

Anxiety stricken, I tried to collect my thoughts. How was I going to proceed with my plan of getting my mother safely out of harm's way? While I was going over my plans in my head, Rich said, "You think my boys outside are going to let that cat walk out of here with me?"

"We shall see," I commented, and then I started stuffing the money I took from Rich into my pocketbook. When I finally saw my mother, I was going to hand her my bag with the money inside. She didn't know this, but she would find out later that she was gonna need this money to live on after I was gone. I mean, this was the least I could do for her, knowing that none of her family was going to be around to help her go on with her life. I just hoped that she did the right thing and went into hiding. She could be a stubborn lady at times and she didn't like change. Hopefully, after realizing that I was gone, she would move on with her life.

"So you just gon' drag me into your shit?" Rich asked.

"I didn't drag you into anything. You volunteered for this job. And now you don't wanna get caught in the middle of it? I mean, you was talking all that tough-guy shit since yesterday. And now today, you wanna sing a different tune. You're a weak-ass, wannabe gangsta!"

"Oh, so you think you're tough shit because you shot me in the leg? Bitch, I'd murder your ass right now if I could get my hands on a gun."

"You had a gun on you when I walked into the house, but you didn't know how to hold on to it," I replied sarcastically.

"Give it back to me and I'll show you how I'll use it," he insisted, giving me the look of death.

"Nah, I'll pass. You look better on the floor with a bullet wound in your leg. I figured it would be better to injure you enough so that you wouldn't resist what was about to come," I warned him.

"You fucking ho! I knew I should've let Monty rape your ass! But nah, I caught myself looking out for your stinky ass! If I hadn't stopped Monty, he would've made you his bitch! And he would've beat the hell out of you!" Rich roared. He tried to get up from the floor, but the pain from his leg wouldn't let him. He even looked around to see if he could find something to throw at me, but nothing was in reach. He was becoming more and more angry by the minute.

I don't know why, but I started laughing at him. I was chuckling like I was looking at a comedy on TV. I swear, I don't know where it came from, but everything he was doing had cracked me up. "Oh, so you think this shit is funny, huh?" He gritted his teeth.

"Yeah, it is," I replied nonchalantly.

"How the fuck can you laugh when you got a motherfucker coming over here to kill us?"

"Because I've already accepted the fact that I'm going to

die. And where I'm going, I'm gonna be very happy," I replied, and smiled while I was doing it.

"You're sick, bitch! And—" he tried to say.

"Hold that thought," I said, cutting him off in midsentence. I pulled Mike's cell phone back out of my pocket and made another call. "Agent Sims, this is Misty," I said, and then I put the call on speakerphone. I wanted Rich to hear my entire conversation.

"Misty, where are you?"

"I'm in Norfolk, on Bland Street. Not sure if you know a drug dealer named Rich. But he's the son of my mother's deceased boyfriend, Carl. Well, I'm hiding inside of his trap house. He and his street soldiers killed family members of Sanjay and Amir tonight inside their Indian restaurant."

"She's fucking lying!" Rich yelled, hoping Agent Sims would hear him.

"And then they took a woman named Sania hostage and made her take them back to her house. When we got there, he and the rest of his boys killed the grandmother and Sania. He didn't kill the little girls. They're running somewhere around her neighborhood, crying and afraid. So please send someone out there to find them."

"Is there someone else there with you guys?" Agent Sims wanted to know.

"No, it's just Rich and me."

"She shot me in my fucking leg and I'm losing a lot of blood!" Rich yelled out.

"He's shot?" Sims continued with the questions.

"Yeah, but he's okay. Enough about him. I hope you're on your way here, because I just got off the phone with Ahmad and he's bringing my mother here to this house. So I'm gonna need you and your agents to make sure everything goes off without any hiccups. Getting my mother back is my main priority. And if that doesn't happen, then there will be hell to pay."

"Do you know what kind of car Ahmad is driving?"

"No, he didn't say. But whatever it is, he will have a gang of guys with him, because he knows that Rich had something to do with killing his family and he knows that Rich is here."

"Are there any guns in the house where you are?"

"Yes, but I have them both. So, are you on your way?"

"Yes, Misty, but I'm gonna need you to do me a favor," he pointed out.

"What is it?" I wanted to know.

"I'm gonna need you to call me as soon as you talk to Ahmad again. I need to know what kind of car he's driving and how many people he's bringing with him. But more important, I'm gonna need to know how you two plan to make the switch."

"I can do that. But where will you guys be?" I asked him.

"Don't worry about that. Just know that we'll be watching. And when all of this is over, I'm gonna have to bring you in for Terrell's murder," he mentioned.

I let out a long sigh and then I said, "I know." And then I ended the call.

The second after I ended my phone call with Agent Sims, Rich said, "Oh, so you did kill that nigga, huh?"

"I gave him everything he had coming to him," I replied, and then I walked over to the window and peeped through the mini blinds. I didn't see anyone but the cats that hustled on the block. I saw a handful of crackheads and dope fiends running around like their heads had been dismembered from their bodies. I couldn't believe where I was, speaking about this house and in this neighborhood. My mother and grandmother made it their missions to keep me and my cousin Jillian away from places like this. But look at me, caught up in a mess of organized crime that killed all my family except for my mother, which was why I got to make this thing right.

"You think because you called the feds that they're gonna help you? They couldn't care less about your ass! All they care about is locking our asses up!" Rich shouted at me.

"I wish you would just shut the fuck up! You lost your privilege to talk when I took the gun from your dumb ass!"

Rich punched the couch again, this time bringing a greater pain to his hand. "Fuck! Fuck! Fuck!" He was yelling like a little bitch.

I chuckled. "Go ahead and bruise your hand up."

"What? Like your face? You smart-ass bitch!" he yelled at me.

"Exactly." I smiled at him.

Before he could say another word, Mike's cell phone started ringing again. I knew this time it had to be Ahmad calling me back. I took a deep breath, exhaled, and then I answered the call. "Hello," I said.

"I'm outside in the dark blue Cadillac SUV," he said.

I rushed over to the window and instantly saw the truck. I couldn't see inside the truck because all the windows were tinted. From where I was standing, the windshield even looked tinted. "Where is my mother?" I asked him.

"She's here in the back seat," he replied.

"I need to see her. Show me something. Like maybe let her stick her head out of the window?" I suggested.

"Roll down the back window and let her poke her head outside of it," I heard Ahmad instruct someone who was in the SUV with him.

A few seconds later, my mother stuck her head out of the window. I swear, it felt really good to see her face again. It also felt good to see that she was still alive. "Tell her to wave at me."

"Wave your hand," I heard Ahmad say.

Once again, Ahmad had my mother show me proof that she was, in fact, where he said she was. This brought joy to my heart, even though I knew my joy would be short-lived after I turned myself over to Ahmad. I just hoped my mother would find a way to live with my decision to do this.

"Now let's make this exchange," Ahmad instructed me.

"Okay, I'm gonna send Rich out first," I told him.

"I'm not going anywhere. You're gonna have to drag me!" Rich roared, and then he started scooting himself away from me, in the direction of the kitchen.

"No, fuck that! You ain't going nowhere." I gritted my teeth and threw the phone down on the couch next to me. I ran over to where Rich was and tried pulling him back in the direction of the front door. I grabbed his shirt, but he was strong and ended up coming out of the shirt he was wearing. Because of this, I lost my balance and fell backward on the floor. I hit the back of my head against the edge of the TV stand. *"Owww!"* I screamed, and immediately grabbed the back of my head. It felt like a sharp pain shot through the back of my head and exploded. I got up from the floor and walked around in a circle while I grabbed both sides of my head. *Boy, is my head throbbing!* "Fuck! Fuck! Fuck!" I yelled, trying to get my pain under control.

When I looked around to see where Rich was, he had made it to the back door of the house. This negro had managed that quickly to get the back door open. I raced to the couch and grabbed the cell phone. "He's trying to get away. Send one of your guys to the back of the house!" I shouted through the phone.

"Go around back," I heard Ahmad say.

I ran back to the window and peeped through the blinds again. In a flash, one of Ahmad's men hopped out of the front seat of the SUV and fled on foot, going in the direction of the back of the trap house. He had his gun already drawn. I knew that in a matter of minutes, Rich was going to be staring down the barrel of a gun and would wish that he hadn't fucked with me. It felt like a weight was about to be lifted from my shoulders, and that was the relief and satisfaction that I needed.

"Ahmad, you can go ahead and send my mother out of the truck. I'm gonna open the front door so you can see me," I told him.

Feeling a knot in the pit of my stomach, I hesitated for a second or two, and then I walked over to the front door. And when I grabbed the doorknob, I heard three gunshots. *Pop! Pop! Pop!* It startled the hell out of me. My heart did a somersault underneath my rib cage, because I knew that Rich was dead.

"Come on, Misty, I know you're scared, but the hard part is almost over," I mumbled underneath my breath. I needed this pep talk.

The back door opened, but then nothing else happened. The anticipation of my mother walking out of the truck was taking too long. "What are you doing? Send her out!" I was getting nervous.

"She's coming now," he said calmly over the cell phone, and then I saw a foot appear from the back door. I swear, it felt like everything was going in slow motion. I'm talking about some *Matrix*-type shit.

"Tell her to step down onto the ground," I instructed him.

Without saying a word to my mother, he stepped completely out of the back of the SUV. Then a second later, she appeared from behind the back seat's door. I was finally able to see her face and, I swear, it was a relief. But then I had to realize that we were not out of the woods as of yet. "Now, why don't you open the front door and come outside, because she's not moving another inch until you do," Ahmad stated. I knew he wasn't bluffing because I heard the finality in his voice.

I dreaded this moment, but I knew that it was either now or never, so I grabbed my purse that contained the money Rich and Monty had taken from Ahmad's family's house; then I slowly opened the door. "I'm gonna hang up with you now, since you can see me fully," I told him.

He didn't know it, but immediately after I disconnected our call, I called Agent Sims back without looking at the key panel or saying hello after I heard the phone ringing. What Ahmad didn't know was that I had just gotten off the phone with Agent Sims, so all I had to do was press the Send button because he was the last person I had called. That's what I did. I held the phone down by my waist area of my pants; this would give Sims a clear and detailed account of the movements that Ahmad and I were having.

What Ahmad also didn't know was that I had Rich's gun underneath the front waist area of my pants. I had to do this because he wasn't a trustworthy guy. He lied to me the first time about bringing my mother to his family's house, but that bogus-ass ploy of his went south. I couldn't let that happen this time.

"Come from behind the door, Mama," I yelled from where I was standing.

"Okay, I'm coming," she yelled in a whining tone, and then she took two steps around the back door.

When I saw her entire body, a calm wind brushed over my face. My plans to get my mother away from Ahmad were finally becoming a reality. "I see you, Mama!" I yelled back at her, but she wouldn't move.

"She's not going anywhere until I see you walk away from that door!" Ahmad yelled.

With a ton of apprehension consuming me, I tried to move a few steps away from the front door, but my legs wouldn't move. I felt paralyzed. "What is taking you so long?" I heard Ahmad yell from the truck.

"I'm coming," I managed to yell back. And right when I took that first step, I felt a strong force pulling me backward. I stumbled a bit. "Move, you dumb bitch!" I heard a male's voice say. And when it hit me that that voice was coming from Rich, I froze. I tried to turn around toward him, but he fought that from happening by pushing a pistol into my back really hard. I was able to turn my head to the side, and that was when I realized that he was using his one good leg to position himself to stand up to me from the waist down.

"Move now or I'm going to shoot you in your fucking back," Rich hissed. I knew he was livid. I couldn't see his face, but I knew he wanted nothing else but to see this guy Ahmad finish me off, once and for all. "Now give me that fucking money back," he instructed me.

"You want me to give it to you now?"

"Fucking right! Slide your purse strap from over your head and give it to me."

"What are you doing? I said to walk away from the front door!" Ahmad yelled from the truck. He was losing patience with me.

"I am going to do this," I said underneath my breath, trying to come up with a foolproof way to escape the clutch of Rich's hands.

Without giving it much thought, I shook Rich off me and made a dash for the truck. "Mom, run the other way!" I yelled while stooping down.

I raced toward the front grille of the truck and ducked down low the entire run. And from there, everything went in slow motion. I heard gunshots fire from both directions, all while taking the purse strap away from my neck.

"Here, Mom, take this!" I managed to yell at her despite all the firepower coming from Rich's and Ahmad's guns.

My mother turned around and looked at me, but when I threw the purse at her so she could catch it, it missed her by one inch. "Get it, Mama! Get it!" I yelled at her.

Thankfully, after failing to catch the purse the first time, she was able to get the purse off the ground and continue to run away from the war I had created between Rich and Ahmad.

Instead of moving from the front right tire of the truck, I hunched down behind until I felt like the coast was clear. I didn't care if I died, but I didn't want my mother to see me die. I'm sure Ahmad had her boyfriend killed in front of her, so having another tragedy happen in her face, I knew that it wouldn't have been a good idea. Planning this whole thing out this way took the proper calculations and, magically, I made it happen.

The gunfire stopped completely. But I hadn't known that it was over until I saw a set of shoes coming from the driver's side of the truck. I pulled Rich's gun from my front pants pocket and aimed it right at the feet. But I was shaking so badly that all my shots missed. Before I could decide what to do next, he was right in front of me, and I knew my life was over.

My heart was beating uncontrollably. My hands even started sweating profusely. I tried to slow my breathing down, but it just wouldn't happen. Resigned to my fate, I felt my gaze roll up from the feet, to the pants, and to the shirt. When I looked up to the neck, my heart took a nose-dive into the pit of my stomach. I couldn't believe that by looking at this guy, my life had come around in a circle. I wasn't about to meet the end I'd thought was near.

With his gun aimed directly at me, he said, "Misty Heiress, 'you have the right to be silent. Anything you say can and will be used against you in a court of law. You have the right to an attorney. If you cannot afford an attorney, one will be provided for you.' Now, do you understand the rights I have just provided for you?"

Hearing Agent Sims's voice reading me my rights gave me a relieved feeling that I just could not describe. I'd never been so happy to know that I was on my way to jail. The whole time, I had been waiting to be killed by Ahmad, but instead of a murderer standing before me, I was now being recaptured by the law.

After Sims helped me up from the ground, I looked at him and said, "How were you able to get in this truck? I was talking to Ahmad the entire time. And where is he anyway?"

Agent Sims moved out of the way and pointed to Ahmad, who was sitting in the back seat of the truck.

"Remember when you walked away from the window so you could get Rich to come out the front door?" he asked me while he was putting me in handcuffs.

"Yeah."

"Well, that's when it all happened. My men and I were able to sneak up on them without them even noticing. And thanks to you, we came at the right time. So I wanna thank you," Sims said. "This was more work than I expected, but we'll finally be able to wrap up this case."

30

WHAT NOW?

I couldn't believe that I was sitting in the back seat of a fucking unmarked FBI agent's vehicle. To add insult to injury, I was handcuffed and heading down to the county jail.

Two minutes into the drive, Agent Sims tried to spark up a conversation. "You have gotten yourself into a whole lot of trouble since I last saw you."

"Is that a question? Or a statement?" I asked.

"It's a little bit of both. I mean, you did manage to kill your ex-boyfriend, get in the middle of a shoot-out, and become a suspect in the murder of your next-door neighbor . . . ," he said, letting those statements hang in the air for me to either confess or debate. Instead, I gave him a bland comeback: "Trouble always seems to find me."

"You know we're gonna have to turn you over to the local homicide detectives, once we are done with you?"

"Is there a way that you could work out a deal with them, considering that I'm gonna help you guys with the federal case?"

"They're gonna charge you with murder, so there's no

way that they will cut a deal with us. That's not our juris-
diction."

"Come on now, Sims. I know you can do something," I
pressed him. I needed some help, and he was the only person I had access to who had any leverage.

"Do you realize that you killed a guy?" he asked again,
trying to get me on the charge.

I was tired of pretending, so I finally responded, "Do
you realize that I was only trying to defend myself? Terrell
was abusive to me. I had a restraining order against him
and he violated it on numerous occasions. It was either kill
him or be killed."

"I'm sure that if you tell the detectives what you just
told me, they'll probably be lenient with you."

"*'Lenient,' my ass!* Those crackers downtown are gonna
try to put me behind bars for the rest of my life. That's why
I'm gonna need you to put in a good word for me. If you
don't, then I'm gonna be up shit's creek."

"I can't make you any promises, but I will see what I
can do."

For the rest of the drive, silence filled the air. Agent Sims
saved the rest of his lip service until after we entered the
holding tank of the jail.

"I've got a female that needs to be processed," Agent
Sims told the female officer sitting behind a counter.

"Put her in cell three," the officer instructed him.

"Will do. Thank you," he replied, and escorted me to
the nearby cell.

While we were walking toward the cell, he said, "See, if
you would've done what I told you to do, you wouldn't be
in this situation. All you needed to do was testify in the
drug case and you would've been scot-free."

"Look, I know all of that. Can we move past that and
help me make my current situation better?"

"I told you, I can't make any promises."

"Well, would you at least try?"

"I'll see," he assured me.

He and I stood in front of the cell he'd been directed to take me to. I didn't want to go in, so I kept giving him an expectant stare, like I was waiting for a better answer. Instead, he insisted, "Here we are," and tried to wave me into the cell.

"So I guess this is it, huh?"

"Another agent and I will be picking you up in the morning, so try to get a good night's rest."

"Tell me, who gets rest while they're behind bars?"

"I wish I had the answer to that question," he replied as he took the handcuffs off me.

Immediately after he put the cuffs in the leather pouch next to his gun, he instructed me to step back so that he could close the door of the cell. "See you in the morning," he said.

I sucked my teeth and said, "Yeah, whatever!" Then I took a seat on the metal bench.

There was one other person in the cell with me, a woman who looked like she was around my age. But she looked like she'd had a hard life. And she looked like she hadn't had a decent amount of sleep in a long time. It was plain to see that she was a drug addict.

"What they got you in here for?" she asked.

"Murder."

"Damn, girl, you're hard-core. You don't look like you could harm a fly."

"It was done in self-defense."

The woman chuckled. "That's what we all say."

"Who did you kill?"

"My ex-boyfriend."

How was she in here for the same thing as me? This was crazy. "Well, you ain't gotta worry about him cheating on you while you're in here," I joked.

"You got family in the streets that gonna help you while you're in here?"

"My mother. I'm hoping that I get bond so she can bail me out." I didn't think it was possible with my extra charges, but she didn't need to know that.

"Oh naw, sweetheart, there's no magistrate in this place that's gonna give you bond."

"If I tell 'em that I did what I did in self-defense, then I'm sure they'll give me one."

"Good luck wit that! Because the people in here are racist as fuck! After they process you, you belong to them. They ain't gonna do shit for you. If you're sick, then you might as well deal with it on your own. Their food is nasty. The CO's got a bad attitude. The women in here love fighting. They will steal from you and the whole bit. So keep your eyes open at all times," she warned me.

The whole idea of possibly looking over my shoulders the entire time I was locked up alarmed me. I didn't want to live like that. I couldn't believe that I recently was about to start a new job in another pharmacy, but ended up dragged into this. *Damn! I just can't catch a break.*

After finally getting processed, I had to change into an orange jumpsuit and shower shoes. I was led up to the area in the jail where I was going to remain until all of my court cases were resolved. I felt defeated. This wasn't where I was supposed to be.

EPILOGUE

While I was in federal custody, I had to testify against Sanjay's brother and a couple of others I had witnessed coming into the pharmacy when I worked there. In exchange for my cooperation, Agent Sims offered my mother witness protection, but she refused to go. I ended up with nothing.

When the trial ended, everyone connected to the drug ring received sentences from forty years to life in federal prison. The two little girls that got caught up in the mix were returned to family members that weren't a part of the ring. And even though they were in the custody of family, I knew they'd always remember what happened to their mother and grandmother that terrifying night.

And as soon as the government used me up, they turned me over to the local homicide cops and I was transferred to a local county jail. My mother hired a lawyer to help with my defense, but that didn't help any. I was sentenced to twenty years in prison for the murder of my ex-boyfriend, Terrell Mason.

I had a few choice words for the judge after she threw the book at me. "How the hell can you sentence me to twenty years when I was defending myself? He was abusive to me and he violated all of my protective orders."

And she responded, "I'm not giving you twenty years for murder. I'm giving you twenty years for having his body chopped up and his remains discarded like he was an animal."

"No disrespect, Your Honor, but he was an animal. And he got what he deserved." When I uttered those words, all his family and friends screamed and shouted obscenities at me, so the court deputies hurried up and ushered me out of the courtroom.

I was transferred to a state prison and I came to the realization that it wasn't all that bad. I figured that if I survived all of what I'd gone through prior to this, then doing a twenty-year bid should be a cakewalk. Thankfully, I was taken to a state prison that was only two hours from where my mother now resided. She ended up selling her house and moving. I was happy about that because I was concerned about her safety. Now she was able to see me every other month. Our relationship had gotten so much better. And I was finally in a place where I didn't have to look over my shoulders. I could concentrate on serving my time in peace. Who knows? I might get out of prison sooner than everyone thinks.

STAY TUNED FOR THE NEXT INSTALLMENT IN
THE BLACK MARKET SERIES

Prisoner of the State

DON'T MISS

The Black Market

Kiki Swinson's bestselling novels burn with extraordinary characters, triple-down twists—and a raw portrait of Southern life only she can deliver. Now she turns up the heat as a young woman cashes in on a sure thing—only to find some addictions are always killer . . .

Enjoy the following excerpt from *The Black Market* . . .

1

MISTY

I'd been in this world too long to just now be finding my way. But here I was, feeling grateful and shit about being healthy and having a roof over my head, thanks to the steady pay from my latest employer.

For the last five and a half months, I'd been collecting a check working as a pharmacy tech. The job was easy and my boss, Dr. Sanjay Malik, was a dream to work with. Not only was he a nice guy, he was very generous with the monthly bonuses he paid me and he would occasionally let me get off work early. The bonuses were for the extra work I did delivering prescriptions to senior citizens who weren't mobile or couldn't pick up their medication. Sanjay would have me deliver their meds to them, and after I completed the deliveries, he usually told me to take off work for the rest of the day, which I found awesome.

But three weeks ago, I noticed that Sanjay had me delivering meds to dark and questionable neighborhoods. I never said anything to him about it because who was I? And what was I going to get out of questioning him? He owned this place, which meant that he could fire my ass on the spot. So, I left well enough alone and minded my own damn business.

Sanjay wasn't aware of this, but I'd taken a few pills here and there for my cousin Jillian. Jillian got into a bad car accident over a year ago and hadn't fully recovered from it. Her doctor cut off her prescription meds six months ago, so I stepped in and threw a few pills at her when I was able to get my hands on some.

The first time, I stole two Percocet pills and two Vicodin pills. Each time I stole from the pharmacy, I took a few more pills. My nerves used to be on edge for about a day after each time I pocketed those pills, but since cops never showed up to cuff me, I knew Sanjay hadn't figured out I'd been stealing from him. I hoped he never would.

As soon as I walked into the pharmacy, I noticed that there were only three customers waiting for their prescriptions. I said good morning to everyone waiting as I walked behind the counter, clocked in, and went to work.

It didn't take long for Sanjay and I to ready those customers' prescriptions and get them on their way. After ringing up the last customer, I turned to Sanjay. "We got any deliveries?" I asked him while I searched through our online refill requests.

"I think we have six or maybe seven," he replied, before turning to answer the phone.

Sanjay was a handsome man. He resembled Janet Jackson's billionaire ex-husband. But unlike Janet Jackson's ex, Sanjay wasn't wealthy, at least to my knowledge. He owned this little pharmacy on the city limits of Virginia Beach, near Pembroke Mall. There was nothing fancy about the place, just your basic small business. But I often wondered why this doctor, who was doing well enough to own this place and have employees like me, wasn't married? From time to time I'd jokingly tell him that I was going to set him up with one of my friends. And his response would always be, "Oh, no. Believe me, I am fine. Women require too much."

Not too long after I started working here, he told me that his family was from Cairo, Egypt. From the way he talked about their homes and travel, I knew they were doing well for themselves. He also told me that education was a big deal in his country. And arranged marriages too.

"Think I could get me a man over in Cairo?" I'd teased. But his answer had no humor in it.

"You wouldn't want a husband from my country, because the men are very strict and the women they marry are disciplined. The things you say and do here in the US wouldn't be tolerated where I'm from."

Damn! "Yeah, whatever, Sanjay!" I'd chuckled.

Working at Sanjay's pharmacy was fairly easy. Time would go by fast. The first half of the day, it would be somewhat busy, and after two p.m. the traffic would die down. This was when I'd take my lunch break. If I didn't bring in my lunch from home, I'd leave the pharmacy and walk over to the food court in Pembroke Mall. This day was one of those days.

"I'm going to lunch, Sanjay. Want anything from Pembroke Mall?" I asked him.

"No, I'm fine. But thank you," he replied.

I walked over to the computer, clocked out, and then I left the building. On my way out, I ran into Sanjay's brother, Amir. As usual, he said nothing to me.

I'd always found it odd that Amir would stop by to see Sanjay during my lunch break. And if I was there when Amir walked into the pharmacy, Sanjay would send me on my lunch break or even send me home for the rest of the day. Now, I wasn't complaining because I loved when he let me leave work early, but at the same time, there aren't any coincidences. Something wasn't right with that guy and I knew it.

Sanjay had spoken to me about his brother, but I didn't

know much. He lived close by and was married with three children. And just like Sanjay, Amir was also very handsome. But Amir never said a word to me. If I hadn't heard Amir greet Sanjay, I'd wonder if he could speak at all. He'd wave at me when he'd come and go, but that was it. I never asked Sanjay how old his brother was because you could clearly see that Amir was younger. He was never flashy. He always wore a pair of casual pants and a regular button-down shirt. He had the look of a car salesman.

I grabbed some Chinese food from the food court in the mall and then I took a seat at one of the tables near one of the mall's exits. While I was eating, I got a call from my cousin Jillian. Her father and my mother are siblings. My uncle committed suicide when we were kids, so she lived with her mother until she turned eighteen. From there she'd been back and forth from having her own apartment to sleeping under our grandmother's roof. Jillian was a pretty, twenty-six-year-old, full-figured woman. She wasn't the brightest when it came to picking the men in her life, but she had a good heart and that's all that mattered to me.

She'd barely said hello before she asked, "Think you can bring me a couple of Percocets on your way home?"

"Jillian, not today," I griped.

"You're acting like I'm asking you to bring me a pill bottle of 'em," Jillian protested. "And besides, you know I don't ask you unless I really need them."

I let out a long sigh and said, "I'm gonna bring you only two. And that's it."

"Thank you," Jillian said with excitement.

"Yeah, whatever. You're such a spoiled brat," I told her.

"So. What are you doing?"

"Sitting in the food court of Pembroke Mall, eating some Chinese food."

"What time do you get off today?"

"I think I'm gonna leave at about seven since it's Saturday."

"Has it been busy today?"

"Kinda . . . sorta," I replied between each chew.

"So, what are you doing after work?"

"Terrell has been harassing me, talking about he wants to see me," I told her. Terrell was my on-and-off-again boyfriend.

"That sounds so boring."

"What do you want me to do, sit around all day like you and get high off prescription drugs?" I said sarcastically.

"Oh, Misty, that was a low blow. You know I don't do this shit for fun. If I don't take those drugs I'm going to be in serious pain."

"Look, I know you need 'em, so I'm going to get off your back. But from time to time, you do ask me for more than you should have."

"That's because I be trying to make a few dollars here and there. Oh, and speaking of which, I got a business proposition for you."

"What is it now?"

"I got a homeboy that will pay top dollar for twenty to twenty-five Vicodin pills."

"Jillian, are you freaking crazy?! There's no way in hell that I'm going to be able to get that many pills at one time."

"He's paying four hundred dollars. But I'm gonna have to get my cut off the top, which would be a hundred."

I sighed. "Jillian, I'm not doing it."

"Come on, Misty, stop being paranoid. You can do it," Jillian whined.

"Do you want me to lose my job?"

"Of course not. But you're acting like you've never taken drugs from your job before."

"Look, I'm not doing it. Case closed."

"Just think about it." Jillian pressed the issue, but I ignored her.

I changed the subject. "Is Grandma home?"

"She's in the laundry room folding clothes."

"Did she say she was cooking dinner?"

"Yeah, she's got a pot roast in the oven."

"Save some for me," I told Jillian.

"You know I will."

I changed the subject again. "You still talking to Edmund?"

"I just got off the phone with his frugal ass!"

I chuckled. "What has he refused to pay for now?"

"I asked him to order me a pizza online and he told me that he ain't have any money."

"Doesn't he own and operate a janitorial business?"

"Yep."

"Then he shouldn't be broke," I said. "Look, just leave that fool alone. You give him too much pussy for him to not feed you."

"I know, right!" she agreed. But I read her like a book because as soon as we got off the phone with one another, I knew she'd call that selfish-ass nigga and act like her stomach wasn't growling.

She and I talked for another ten minutes or so about her finding another job instead of sitting on her ass all day, crying about how much pain she's in. It seemed like my grandmother let her ride with that lame-ass excuse, but I knew better. My grandmother knew exactly what was going on, but looked the other way because she enjoyed Jillian's company and she didn't want to be alone in that big house. Jillian had a free ride any way you looked at it.

"Don't forget to put some of that pot roast aside," I reminded her.

"I won't," she said, and right before I hung up, I heard her add, "Don't forget my meds either."

My only response to that was a head shake.

2

WHAT AN EYE OPENER

I headed back over to the pharmacy after I finished eating my lunch. When I walked through the front door there were two people waiting for their prescriptions, but Sanjay was nowhere around.

"Has anyone been helped?" I inquired as I circled around the customers to get behind the counter.

"No. We've been standing here for about five minutes," an elderly man said.

"He's right." Another white man spoke up. "I even peeped around the counter to see if anyone was there," he continued.

"Well, don't worry. I'll help you two gentlemen," I assured them as I walked around the counter.

I took both men's prescriptions and then I logged them into our system. Immediately after I did that, I searched the storage room where we kept our drugs and medical devices. I thought I might find Sanjay in there, but the room was empty. Alarmed, I walked to the bathroom and knocked on the door.

"Sanjay, are you in there?" I asked. But he didn't answer. So I knocked on the door again. "Sanjay, are you in there?" I repeated, and when I didn't get an answer, I grabbed ahold of the doorknob and twisted it lightly, opening the door calmly. It was plain to see that Sanjay wasn't in there.

The only other place I figured Sanjay could be was in the back of the building. So I closed the bathroom door and headed in that direction. The back door was slightly ajar, so I pushed it open.

"Sanjay, there you are," I said after I laid eyes on him shoving boxes in the trunk of his brother Amir's car. I could tell that he wasn't expecting to see me. He looked very nervous. While Amir continued to maneuver boxes that obviously came from the pharmacy, Sanjay walked toward me.

"Did you need something?" he asked me in a weird kind of way. The way he said it sounded like a mafia boss asking an innocent bystander who witnessed a murder, did he see something?

I was taken aback and I really didn't know what to say. But then it hit me. "We have two customers in the pharmacy who said they've been waiting for over ten minutes for someone to help them." I twisted the truth a little.

"Take care of them," Sanjay insisted.

"I already have," I lied.

"So, what's the problem?"

"There's no problem. I just wanted to make sure that you were still around."

"Well, I'm here," he said.

"Okay, well, I'll go back in and take care of everything while you're out here . . ." I said, and then I turned around and left him standing at the back door. I heard it close behind me as I headed back inside to the waiting customers.

"Sorry about that," I said. "The pharmacist is in the back of the building signing for some deliveries from the UPS driver." It seemed like a solid excuse.

"He may not want to do that the next time around, because instead of me and this other fella waiting around, it might be some young kids robbing you guys of all of your prescription drugs," the younger man said.

"I agree," the other man said.

Seriously? These two watched too much TV. "I will definitely make mention of that as soon as he gets back in here," I assured them.

Since Sanjay had basically given me the green light to process these gentlemen's prescriptions, I ran straight over to the cabinet where the Percocet pills were stored. I knew I had a small window of opportunity to get these pills for Jillian so we could make a few extra dollars. Immediately after I grabbed the pill bottle I heard Sanjay open and close the back door of the pharmacy. My heart started racing while I struggled to open the plastic bottle. But to no avail, it didn't open for some crazy-ass reason. I've never had a problem opening and closing a pill bottle.

"I'm so sorry, you guys," I heard Sanjay say. So I knew he was standing behind the counter near the cash register. Frozen like ice, I stood there not knowing whether to put the bottle of Percocet back in the supply cabinet or stick it in my pocket. I heard Sanjay walking in my direction, so I nearly panicked.

"Misty, who are you working on first?" he called out to me.

Feeling like I was about to have an anxiety attack, I shoved the bottle of Percocet into my pants pocket.

"Hey, there you go," he said as soon as he saw me. "What are they waiting on?" he continued as he stood in front of me.

"Mr. Lewis is refilling Trexall. And Mr. Williams is getting another refill of Metformin," I told him while I placed my right hand over my pants pocket to prevent Sanjay from seeing the bulge.

"Get the Metformin and I'll get the Trexall," he instructed me.

"I'm on it," I said and walked away from him. I swear, I couldn't tell you how scared I was when Sanjay walked up on me. I would've shit in my pants if he saw me with that bottle of Percocet in my hands. I couldn't lie and say that I had it because I was refilling one of those guys' prescriptions. No, that wouldn't have made any sense. I needed a cover, so I wasn't going to take any more pills unless I was filling a prescription for the same drug. Other than that, I was gonna chill.

A few hours later, Sanjay said, "You can leave now."

I looked at my watch. "Are you sure? I mean, we'll be closed in fifteen minutes." I needed to delay leaving cause I needed a chance to put the bottle of Percocet back.

"Don't worry. I've got everything covered. There's a storm coming our way, so get home safely," he insisted.

I sighed heavily. "Okay," I replied reluctantly. I mean, what other choice did I have? He was my boss, so I wouldn't dare tell him that I had just pocketed a brand-new bottle of Percocet from the storage cabinet and now I wanted to put the bottle back. If I did, I'd be asking this man to fire me on the spot.

"Don't forget to drive carefully," he reminded me.

"I will," I assured him as I grabbed my jacket and purse.

Sick to my stomach, I dreaded leaving the store. Why couldn't I be more careful? If I hadn't listened to Jillian, I wouldn't have this fucking big-ass pill bottle in my pocket. I could see it now: After Sanjay goes through the inventory in the morning, he's going to look me in the face and ask me where the missing Percocet bottle is. And I'm going to have to tell him the truth because who else could've moved it? I was the only employee there. Or, let's say that I did deny it, all he would have to do is look through his security camera. Now it wouldn't show me actually taking the meds because of the angle, but it might show the bulge of the bottle in my pants. Damn! I'd really fucked up now.